Secrets

Volumes 9 and 10

The Best in Women's Erotic Romance

Secrets

Volumes 9 and 10
The Best in Women's Erotic Romance

Red Sage Publishing, Inc.

SECRETS Volumes 9 and 10
The Best in Women's Erotic Romance

This is an original publication of Red Sage Publishing and each individual
story herein has never before appeared in print. These stories are a
collection of fiction and any similarity to actual persons or events is
purely coincidental.

Red Sage Publishing, Inc.
P.O. Box 4844
Seminole, FL 33775
727-391-3847
www.redsagepub.com

SECRETS Volume 9
A Red Sage Publishing Book
All Rights Reserved/December 2003
Copyright © 2003–2004 Red Sage Publishing, Inc.

Publishing by arrangement with the authors and copyright holders
of the individual works as follows:

WANTED Copyright © 2003 by Kimberly Dean
WILD FOR YOU Copyright © 2003 by Kathryn Anne Dubois
FLIGHTS OF FANTASY Copyright © 2003 by Bonnie Hamre
SECLUDED Copyright © 2003 by Lisa Marie Rice

SECRETS Volume 10
A Red Sage Publishing book
All Rights Reserved/July 2004
Copyright © 2004 Red Sage Publishing, Inc.

Published by arrangement with the authors and copyright holders
of the individual works as follows:

PRIVATE EYES Copyright © 2004 by Dominique Sinclair
THE RUINATION OF LADY JANE Copyright © 2004 by Bonnie Hamre
CODE NAME: KISS Copyright © 2004 by Jeanie Cesarini
THE SACRIFICE Copyright © 2004 by Kathryn Anne Dubois

ISBN: 0-7394-4769-6

Printed in the U.S.A.

Contents

Contents

Wild For You

by Kathryn Anne Dubois

To My Reader:
Ever fantasize about being kidnapped and held captive by a modern day Tarzan? I have. Which is why I had so much fun writing this story. An implausible premise some might say? You bet. Which only doubled the fantasy for me as I hope it does for you. Enjoy!

Chapter One

Georgie wasn't lost, technically speaking. At least not completely. According to her protractor or compass or whatever it was, she was three miles north and maybe a little west of their camp with just a few fifty foot cliffs, rapidly rushing creeks, and thundering waterfalls between her and civilization and ultimate safety. She gave a little snort.

Hardly either. No more did she want to return to that malaria infested scorching patch of dirt that the professor called a village than she wanted to be hiking circles in this steaming overgrowth of vegetation that sported banana leaves longer than her body. Course, she *could* use them for clothes should she be stranded into the next millennium.

She cursed the professor. If he hadn't tried to hunt her down she never would have slipped away. But she refused to haul another water jug up that steep hill just so the village women could cook gluey stew they'd all have to choke down. What else could she do but hide out?

And she doubled-cursed him for earlier insisting she wear this Salvation Army scrap of a sundress that the chief had presented to her with such pride—a threadbare cotton floral too short, even for her small frame, to keep her legs from getting scratched up as she hacked her way through brush and tangled vines. Its spaghetti straps bared her shoulders and much of her breasts to the unrelenting heat of the sun and overgrown jungle so that now she burned and itched all over her fair skin. She could only imagine the multitude of parasites that lived in the oozing bark and wet moss.

But she wasn't desperate. Not yet. She kicked aside a rotting log and watched a swarm of insects cloud the air. True desperation was twelve lousy credits away from graduating and parents who threatened to cut you off and take away your red metallic Miata until you do. *This* nightmare she could handle, if this little internship gained her the promised credits and freedom.

A college degree by her 21st birthday had meant access to her two million dollar trust find and independence from her fire-breathing parents. She was 26 now and still working on it. Her parents thought *they'd* lost patience? What about her? Imprisoned in academia during her prime was not exactly her dream either. She should have been honing her underdeveloped sailing skills and nurturing her love of nature—at least the nature that included a smooth Grenade on a hot sandy beach.

The darkness hovered lower, whether from the sun setting or from traveling deeper into the jungle, she couldn't be sure, but either way, it wasn't a good sign.

The hair on the back of her neck prickled. She glanced up at the canopy of trees above, aware that the tiny dots of light peeking through the ceiling of vegetation were growing dimmer. She wasn't frightened. Just concerned. She'd find a cave to sleep in, hopefully a nice studio whose lone tiger had taken off on a little jaunt.

She crawled through what looked like an opening to somewhere and ran smack into a pair of hairy feet with nails long overdue for a manicure. For one paralyzing moment she looked up into the small beady eyes of the largest Silverback gorilla she had ever seen. Only gorilla she had ever seen. But before she allowed terror to strike, she remembered the professor describing the species' lack of aggression and innate gentleness.

The huge-skulled beast reared up on two legs and let loose a roaring growl that rivaled King Kong's best. Then it beat its chest with a fury, its dagger-like teeth glinting in its ugly face. *So much for the esteemed professor.*

She did an about face without daring to look back to see if her furry friend followed and made a run for her life. After she had run for what seemed like the distance of three laps around Central Park and was sure he wasn't chasing her, she dropped herself down by a rubber tree in a thick part of the forest and applauded her skillful escape. But not for long, because the darkness was growing and the eerie silence of the day was slowly being replaced by the sound of creatures. And they seemed to be coming closer by the minute.

She gave a quick glance around. Nothing. She was starting to rethink the cave idea when she was yanked up from behind by her ponytail and dragged out into a small clearing.

Pain shot through her as she grabbed frantically at her scalp and twisted to see if her attacker was animal or human. But before she could catch her breath, she was whipped around to face her aggressor. A band of hunters, three native men with rifles in hand and ammunition and knives strapped to their chests, stood before her while the fourth one hauled her to her feet. He thrust her into the pack. They jostled her, clicking their tongues and laughing. She blanched at the feel of sweaty palms sliding down her bare arms.

When she pushed back at them, she was scooped up from behind around her waist, one thick arm trapping her. She dug her nails into hairy skin and kicked out her legs, but the man held her tight. The others surrounded her, chuckling and stroking her face, trying to flip her dress up, and terrifying her as she imagined what they would do next.

No doubt they were poachers, because a pile of satchels, filled with the scent of blood, rested nearby.

The professor had bemoaned the profitable illegal trade in gorilla meat and warned his adoring student groupies of bands of outlaws roaming the jungle. She wished she had paid more attention, like that kiss-up graduate student, Kristy, who hung on his every word.

The men's toothless grins widened when one poked a stubby finger at her nipple, raised against her sweat soaked dress. She thrashed and kicked, cringing at the feel of him.

But then abruptly they released her and stepped back when a small figure emerged from between the trees and stood before them. His wide safari hat did nothing to disguise his weak-jawed face and his white legs looked like bamboo shoots under his baggy shorts. A leer split across his face the instant he saw her.

"Well . . ." he murmured. "What's this?" His thick nasally voice made her skin crawl. Her heart pounded in her chest as her eyes darted around seeking an escape. But while she could probably take this little runt, the numbers were not in her favor. She took a cautious step back, but before she could get her bearings, he signaled to the men. Instantly, they surrounded her and dragged her to a large tree.

"Get off of me!" She scratched down at a face, drawing blood and an angry bellow from one attacker, but it didn't stop him and the rest of them from smashing her back against the tree and tying her arms around the trunk.

Then they fanned out as one, facing the perimeter of the clearing and stepping a few feet into the jungle, as though guarding against intruders.

Alone now with the white man, she watched as he took a few deliberate steps toward her, at the same time he reached slowly into a side strap of his shorts. He whipped out a long gleaming blade. Its shiny metal glinted even in the growing darkness. Her heart leaped in her throat. Did he plan to slice her like he did the animals he hunted? For what purpose? Unless he was plain crazy.

"My . . ." He lifted a blonde curl from her neck with the tip of his knife and smiled. "I haven't seen skin this creamy in a long time."

Her heart raced as he trailed the knife along her neck clear down to her collarbone and then took the cold metal tip and pricked at the peaks of her nipples through the worn fabric of her dress. A paralyzing fear gripped her unlike any she'd ever felt. Her mother's oft-recited complaint came back to haunt her. "The child has no fear. Just once she needs the living daylights scared out of her, then maybe she'll listen." As right as her mother probably was, Georgie was sure this was not what her mother had in mind.

"You're such a pretty little thing. I don't know where to look first, your lovely face or your luscious tits." She shuddered beneath his twisted smile.

In one swift movement, he grabbed the front of her dress and sliced down to her waist, popping every button. He drew aside the fabric and feasted his eyes on her, letting out a low chuckle. "You are too beautiful. I've surely died and gone to heaven." He lifted her skirt and tried to hook his fingers under the elastic of her panties.

With perfect aim, she kneed him in the groin and watched in relief as he doubled over. A hefty whoosh left his lungs as he struggled to stay on his feet.

"You little bitch," he growled, grabbing her skirt. He brandished the knife and made menacing slicing gestures with the blade into the space between them. He was furious now and out of control. He lunged for her.

A scream froze in her throat. With alarming dexterity, he slipped the knife under her panties and ripped through them, sending them to fall at her ankles. Then he unzipped his shorts. She writhed in confusion as he fumbled with his limp penis. What did he plan to do with that?

After her precision slam, he should be out of commission for some time, but the rage in his faded blue eyes and his shaking body told her he'd rape her with his knife if needed. She fixed her eyes on the polished blade, willing her brain to move fast and figure an escape.

He prodded her thigh with the sharp tip of steel. "Open up!" he spat. With his initial shock aside, the raw pain must have surfaced because he grabbed his balls now and moaned.

"My father is Minister of the Interior," she warned, hoping such a position existed. She yanked against the leather line at her wrists.

For a half second the man faltered and then grinned wickedly. "Minister of the Interior?" He gave a cynical laugh.

Behind him, a bush shook and then a dull thud sounded, but he was too intent on her to notice. She hoped against reason that this little band of thieves was being followed by the authorities and had just been tracked down. She listened for more sounds but only silence followed.

"What's he gonna say when I fuck his daughter?" He pushed up her skirt and gawked at the golden tuft of hair between her legs. Another tree shook, followed by a gentle whishing sound, metal slicing flesh. She dared to hope.

"You wouldn't be the first man to fuck me," she quipped, saying anything that would keep him distracted from what was going on behind him. She only prayed it was good. His sickly eyes clouded with lust.

"Open yourself for me," he rasped.

Oh, God. The thought of spreading herself for this creep made her want to vomit.

"Do it," he shouted.

Behind him, a half-naked male dropped out of the sky, landing with a grace that belied his muscled bulk. Without making a sound, he lassoed his forearm around the white man's neck. His eyes met hers and held as the hunter dropped his knife to claw at the thick arm suffocating him.

The poacher's skin turned a satisfying shade of blue and spittle formed at the corners of his mouth while he stared at her without seeing, bug-eyed. Her gaze flicked between her attacker and her rescuer. Her rescuer's gaze remained steady. A crack of bone signaled a crushed windpipe and then, with a flick of his elbow, the man snapped the hunter's pale white neck. He dropped the body at his feet.

She stared, open-mouthed, as the loin-clad barbarian dragged aside the crumpled figure and dumped him into the trees.

Her heart pounded.

She had never seen someone killed right before her eyes, or seen anyone die for that matter. Her eyes followed the movements of her rescuer, this disturbingly solid violent man she was now alone with as she contemplated what would happen next.

He towered well above six feet and with his long dark hair in a wild tumble to his shoulders, he looked like a throwback to a medieval warlord. All he lacked was a good set of chain mail to replace the primitive loincloth that draped his muscled thighs. He, too, brandished a long swordlike knife and with those boulder-like shoulders and biceps as thick as tree trunks, she knew one well-executed swipe could slice her in half.

Her eyes widened when he came to stand before her, legs braced apart and hands on hips, sweaty muscles flexing. He shoved his knife into a leather pouch strapped to his thigh watching her closely as he did, his gray eyes intense. This bronze-chested savage was obviously wild and dangerous, primitive, a terrifying specimen of masculine power and . . . gorgeous. She swallowed.

His eyes followed the movement of her throat, traveled over her hair and then settled on her face. He gave a little frown and then took a hesitant step forward and raised his hand.

She startled, causing him to drop his hand abruptly and step back. He grumbled something under his breath.

"I'm sorry," she said, finding her voice. "I . . . I should thank you." His eyes followed her lips as she spoke. "You saved my life."

His thick lashes blinked and the little creases in his forehead smoothed out. After a moment he cocked his head and then took a hesitant step forward before he stopped again, as though gauging her reaction. She would stay still for now, until she figured out what he intended to do with her. A glistening layer of moisture skimmed his chest and clung to a tight patch of dark hair. He smelled of rain and fresh male sweat.

He eased a fraction closer and hesitated. Then he tipped her chin up with one finger and studied her, turning her face to one side and then the other before he ran his fingertips over her cheek with the softest touch. He dipped his head to her throat and moved in closer. Warm fingers slid along the curve of her neck. Then he breathed deep against her skin. He was smelling her.

The thought drew a pull of sexual awareness from her that took her by surprise.

He straightened a bit and cupped her face.

Behind him the trees wobbled and then thrashed. She glimpsed a blur of fur and claws. "Oh my God," she screamed. "Untie me!"

King Kong had returned.

Her rescuer glanced at their intruder and grunted, gesturing abruptly with his hand. She held her breath.

But Kong just ambled forward and plopped himself down to lean against a nearby tree. Her rescuer nodded and then returned his gaze to her.

Then it occurred to her. He had to be the legendary wild man of the jungle. Local legends echoed through the mountains of a creature not of their race who sliced and diced poachers with a vengeance, the reward for his capture rivaling the price the underground market paid for the largest catch of primate heads. Even the government was eager to rid the country of him with tourist revenue already taking a plunge.

As she stared at Kong she felt the press of fingers along her neck again. Tarzan was sliding his fingers down her throat and murmuring something unintelligible. His fingers came to rest on her rapid pulse. After her horrible ordeal, his touch was warm and surprisingly soothing. He leaned his big body in closer and she wondered if he would try to smell her again, but he continued to stroke her skin as though fascinated with its feel, his eyes following the deliberate path of his caress. Her blood pumped hot as his fingers continued a slow travel down, over her collarbone and then along the top swell of her breasts. His fingertips lingered on the sensitive skin between her breasts.

She glanced down. In her struggle with her captor, her dress had partially covered her breasts again, the opening edges catching on each nipple.

His brows knit together in a puzzled crease as he studied the sweat-soaked fabric that clung to her skin. Her nipples grew instantly taut under the worn cotton.

He frowned and then cupped her breast.

She gave a startled cry, struggling against her restraints. His expression grew more bewildered as he blatantly continued to cradle her, despite her protests, with both palms. He gave a grunt and grumbled.

She tipped her chin. So, she had small breasts, big deal. At least they were real. But his insult to her feminine pride was soon softened when his persistent feeling and fondling drew a warm sexual heat from her. Still, she squirmed and pulled on her restraints.

"Are you going to release me?"

His eyes glinted with interest, but he finally dropped his hands. Up this close the rough shadow of his jaw smelled deliciously of shaving cologne. She gave herself a mental shake at the crazy thought.

He turned to Kong and mumbled something indiscernible. Then he began to pace, casting her sideways glances as he did.

King Kong watched, his clumsy head cocked in curiosity. "What are you looking at?" she snapped.

He bared his teeth and let out a roar.

Oh God. She held her breath. The angry beast pumped up his chest and leaned forward on his thick arms as though ready to jump her. His small dark eyes gleamed bright under his wide forehead. She didn't dare move or speak. From out of the corner of her eye, Tarzan stopped his pacing and lifted a lazy hand to the animal. Immediately, the ferocious monster relaxed.

She sighed with relief. But still, she had to get him to untie her.

"Please . . . Tarzan. Untie my hands." She motioned to her back and pulled.

But he wasn't paying any attention to what she said. He was sweeping his eyes over the corkscrew knot of her curls that fell to her shoulders. He reached up and pulled gently on the tips of her curls and watched with fascination how they bounced back. He drew in a soft breath.

The air grew thick between them.

He lifted pensive eyes to hers and brushed his thumb along her bottom lip, his expression a mixture of pleasure and confusion.

She dropped her gaze and one look at his groin settled any confusion on her part. The rough leather loincloth grew right before her eyes. And it looked like his size there matched the rest of his body.

He stepped back and looked over at King Kong. After a moment of what she'd swear was male commiseration, they *both* stared at her. She straightened her shoulders and stared back. *For Heaven's sake, you'd think they'd never seen a woman.*

Her eyes widened. She watched them, her heart hammering. *My God. They hadn't.* She would bet her Tarzan had never seen a woman. The shock of it was more than she could comprehend.

His hands flew to the top of her dress. "What are you doing?"

she gasped. With a quick hand, he drew aside the fabric, fully exposing her small white breasts. She struggled against her restraints, burning with embarrassment as his eyes eagerly traced over the small swell of her cleavage and settled on her nipples. The smoky gray of his eyes lightened and he seemed truly fascinated.

He mumbled something, his voice low, and then smoothed his palms along the soft curves. She drew in a shocked breath and was mortified by how quickly she warmed to his sensuous caress.

His subsiding erection reversed direction.

She squirmed against his hands. "You can't just do whatever you—oh . . ." She stifled a groan when he pinched her nipples between his fingers, sending fire to her groin. Her nipples tightened to hard points. His eyes lit with interest.

Then he mercifully stopped.

Noticing her panties lying at his feet, he bent to pick up the scrap of lace. He drew the silky fabric to his face and breathed deep. He liked her scent, because there was no mistaking the full erection that was forming under the skimpy leather draping him. He turned his hot gaze back to her and stuffed her panties in his waistband. Then he dropped to his knees and threw up her skirt.

She gasped.

His eyes widened and he stared for several long moments.

Then he quickly opened the last of her buttons and let her dress fall open.

He gave a small sigh, then moved his palms over the swell of her belly and ran his fingers through the springy golden coils. She silently moaned.

He brushed with the lightest touch, smoothing aside the soft tangle of hair with his thumbs to see what was hidden beneath. He leaned closer, studying her. She blushed scarlet when his nostrils flared, sending shivers up her spine.

"You've got to stop this—"

He brushed one thumb down between her lips. She bit back a groan and squirmed. He locked his hands onto her hips and looked up at her with those intense eyes and grumbled. A warning? Was he telling her that she had better stay still or he wouldn't release her?

He grumbled again and cocked his head as though expecting an answer.

"Okay, okay. But then you better untie me."

He seemed satisfied and returned to his inspection.

With gentle fingers, he smoothed both thumbs down her

swollen lips, separating her, slicking the pads through every pink layer. His eyes widened.

It was torture not to squirm, but no man had ever examined her this closely. She swelled full and hot, restless under his penetrating gaze. He slipped around her moist folds with the tips of his fingers, stimulating her in a way he couldn't have known. Despite that she tried to ignore his stroking, she grew wetter. And then he found her center. She watched his eyes light up as his finger slipped up into her, disappearing up to his first knuckle.

He looked up at her a moment and then pressed forward. She closed her eyes with the feel of him sinking into her, not wanting him to see how he pleasured her. But when she opened her eyes he was staring at her flushed face. He slowly withdrew his finger and then licked it.

He growled.

And then everything happened at once.

He licked her sex, one burning swipe with the tip of his tongue drawing a groan of pleasure from her that she couldn't stop.

She was horrified and automatically glanced around.

King Kong still languished against the tree trunk, one finger scratching his forehead.

A deep moan escaped her throat. He licked her again and again, curling his tongue around her swollen lips like a wet flame igniting her flesh. A moan tore from her throat.

But when he dipped his tongue in to taste her, she nearly expired.

"Tarzan, please," she choked.

He growled and slid his tongue up as far as he could, sliding his palms around to cup her bottom and holding her still. She groaned and ground against him, hardly recognizing the soft needy sounds coming from her. This was crazy.

When he stopped a moment, she drew in a stunned breath and throbbed with the sudden loss of his heat.

King Kong decided at that moment to rear his hideous head. His nostrils flared and then he twisted his neck and lifted his face to the breeze. A low growl rumbled deep in his throat. Another warning growl? It had better be, to interrupt this.

In the time it took to catch her breath, Tarzan leaped to his feet, untied her wrists, and lifted her like she was a sack of feathers and tossed her over his shoulder.

Chapter Two

"What are you doing?" Georgie screeched, giving a frantic tug of her hem over her bare bottom.

He ducked under some low lying banana trees and soon they were heading farther up into the mountains with no sign of stopping. King Kong took up the lead, pausing regularly to see if Tarzan followed. Did this wild man think he could just keep her? And what if he truly had never seen a woman? But she decided he must have some concept of mating, having lived so closely among the animals, so recognizing her as his mate would be an easy stretch.

If her stodgy professor knew how close she was to this legendary anomaly he would expire. No anthropologist had gotten close to the elusive and sought after subject believed to be one of three children lost in the wild at a very young age. He had rejected all human contact and was considered homicidal, predictably deranged due to his lack of civilizing contact, expected to have been reduced to a dangerous predator of his own species.

It was a staggering thought. Yet, she was completely unafraid. She sighed. She supposed her mother was right.

After what seemed like two or more miles of heavy hiking through twisted and tangled brush and rocks, her mountain man showed no sign of fatigue. Finally, they hit a sizeable clearing. While he paused along a wide granite cliff, she twisted to peer over his shoulder. Below her, far below, rested an emerald green valley and all around stood steep jagged cliffs.

Without warning, Tarzan dumped her on her feet and stalked over to a large tree. When he yanked on a thick vine, it uncoiled like a rope and pooled at his feet. He wrapped it around his waist and grunted at her, motioning her to come.

She looked on in puzzlement. Where was King Kong? He motioned again, this time with impatience. Down below, movement caught her eye. Her gaze lit on their furry friend making his way down the sharp cliff towards the valley. From the looks of things, he was already half way down the one-hundred foot drop.

Too late, it dawned on her what Tarzan had planned.

With purposeful strides, he came at her and plucked her up, this time settling her on his hip.

"Oh no you *don't.*" She pushed against his rock-hard chest. "No way you're dragging me down there, you . . . lunatic."

He frowned and hugged her to his chest. Before she could level another protest he leaped off the edge.

"Oh, my God!" She closed her eyes and prayed to all the gods to help her. He bounced and then leaped, repeating the motion several times with horrifying speed. She climbed up his chest and wrapped her arms around the thick trunk of his neck and screamed while he continued his plunging descent in graceful arcs, her wild thrashing not enough to even break his rhythm. It was long moments before she got the courage to open her eyes. A mistake.

They were free-falling into a lush green canopy of trees just below them. She clung tighter, half burying her face in his neck with one eye open. Through the tops of the trees they sailed and then landed with a thud along a thick moss covered bank.

When he released her abruptly, she landed on her bottom on a soft mound of grass. She blinked up at him as he uncoiled the ropey vine from around his waist. Then she took in the unbelievable sight that greeted her.

A huge circle of mist rose between a wide oval of cliffs and the scent of sweet foliage filled the air. Tiny purple and pink buttercup-like flowers trailed along overhanging vines and twisted around dangling tree branches that stretched over the pool's edge and kissed its bubbling surface.

The gentle chirp of birds hovered around the edges of the quickly gathering darkness. Upon closer look, she spotted tiny creatures hidden among the branches, the whites of their eyes gleaming through a split in the leafy trees.

She drew in an awed breath and forgot for one moment that she was the captive of a dangerous, unpredictable, primitive being. She looked up at her abductor to find him gazing down at her with alarming intensity. He dropped down in front of her and touched her cheek. With a small nod he motioned to the pool. Then he leaped up and tugged on his corded belt. A minute later his knife dropped, along with his loincloth.

He was fully erect . . . completely, unabashedly aroused and growing thicker with each passing second.

"Oh, my. . . ."

He crouched in front of her. She swallowed a gasp. She shouldn't look, but he was beautiful, the entire pulsing, veined length of him . . . *considerable* length of him. While she tried to tear her gaze away, he stroked his hand down his full girth as though presenting his treasure to her hungry eyes. He tipped her chin up and motioned for her to turn around.

"What?" she breathed, reluctant to take her eyes off him but realizing that perhaps he'd like some privacy. She turned on her knees in a slow daze. Not a moment later, he tossed up her skirt and anchored his hands onto her hips. "Oh my God, no," she choked. He caressed her bottom with his palm and then drew her backside against him. He let out a low moan. "Stop!"

He rubbed his penis between her bottom cheeks and groaned, exerting gentle pressure on her back to keep her bent over. The hot tip of his cock probed her swollen lips before she wrestled her bottom away from him and turned to face front. "My God, you're a menace," she gasped, with as much indignation as she could muster, but there was no mistaking the heavy pulse of arousal throbbing between her legs.

He tipped his head and frowned.

"You can't just grab me up when you want and . . . and do what you will. Even animals have some kind of mating ritual or something, don't they?"

He was studying her lips and intermittently letting his eyes rove over her face. At least he paid attention, which was more than she could say for most males. He touched a finger to her lips, running it gently along the bottom curve. With a small nod, he encouraged her to continue while he cupped her chin as though trying to decipher how she formed the words.

"Maybe I could teach you to talk?" she said, and then chided herself at the ridiculous notion. He stroked his thumb along her jaw, drawing her closer, so close the rich scent of his skin taunted her, a mingling of musk and leaves after a good rain. He was so large and starkly masculine. She dropped her eyes. And he was still erect.

She scrambled to her feet. He followed her and then snagged her waist, pressing her against him. His eyes closed with the contact, his heat throbbing thick between them. She stifled a low moan as a rush of pleasure slicked between her legs and up her spine to tighten her nipples. He slid against her, the pressure against her tiny nub unbearable. They groaned in unison. *This was madness.*

With a quick hand he unfastened her few intact buttons and pushed her dress off her shoulders.

"No." She clutched the dress closed and stepped back a pace.

He gave an impatient grunt and ran one hand down his face in a gesture so entirely male that she almost smiled. Then he settled his warm gaze on her again and threaded his fingers through the sides of her hair, sifting the strands with an unhurried touch. She encircled his wrist, feeling the heavy beat of his blood, wonderfully warm and alive. She could lose herself in this man. *Where did that come from?*

She gave him a gentle push. "We need to get some things straight," she said, clasping her dress closed and smoothing down the front. "I don't know what your plans are. But I'm not sticking around, so just keep your distance."

He might not understand her words but he understood her intent. He backed up and frowned and then began pacing, his arousal subsiding slowly with his frustration.

He could simply take her, like that horrible poacher intended to, she'd have no way of stopping him, yet he didn't and his restraint touched a tender chord in her and drew a bit of sympathy at the thought that he was probably a virgin. He had to be. He must be dying to finally experience what he'd seen every other species enjoy. Picturing his rough hands sliding all over her body and his weight pinning her under him was deeply arousing.

He gave her a disgruntled glare before motioning again to the bubbling surface of the water. The darkness grew thicker. Soon they'd be unable to see each other anyway, she reasoned, and the clean water was so inviting to her sticky body.

"You first," she motioned, still holding her dress closed while he stood before her stark naked.

To her surprise, he gave an annoyed shrug and slid over the bank. Her eyes followed his tight backside and thighs. Even his back was riveting, hard and muscled.

She gave a naïve look around, as though someone would actually see her, and then dropped her dress on the bank and followed him to a wide ledge of rock across the pool.

The soothing warmth hit her first, so different from the heat of the day. But it would be more wonderful if the darkness had not almost completely settled, for now she grew eerily wary with the quickly encroaching nighttime and the thought of animals lurking.

He emerged from the water and stood waist deep by the granite slab, not even glancing in her direction. She peeked around, aware of the creatures surrounding them and wondering where Kong was and all those like him. They might not be quite as friendly. Were there alligators in this water or snakes? Her notes from that environmental science class would come in handy at a time like this. Of course, she never actually *took* any notes.

When she reached him, she swam around to his back, staying neck deep in the water and moving close to him for protection. He was so close she could feel the heat of his body, but he paid no attention to her. A large array of scented soap and shampoo littered the rock, no doubt the spoils from his tirades on the poachers. A cold chill stole up her spine at the thought of all the people he must have killed. Still, she pressed closer to him as it grew too dark to even see her hands. The strange sounds of the creatures encircling them grew more distinct in the silence as the darkness descended.

He grabbed a bar of soap, sudsing his hands and running them down his ample chest and then along his biceps. He smelled delicious. She had wondered about the traces of his dark beard and decided the evidence that he shaved was a sure indication that he had some connection with civilization.

A splash sounded behind her. She turned abruptly, just in time to see the shadowy outline of two huge animals slide into the water a few feet away. She screamed and scurried around Tarzan to take a diving leap into his arms and crawled up his body in a fury. She wrapped her arms around his neck in a fierce lock and held on for dear life.

"Something's behind us," she screeched. "Get us out of here!"

He let out a low groan but didn't even turn, just held her close, encircling her in his huge arms and rubbing his nose along her neck, breathing in her scent. A low murmur rumbled in his throat. He nipped her tender skin with his teeth and moaned.

"Tarzan!" she squealed, peeking behind her at the sea monsters. He hitched her higher and wrapped her legs around his waist. *Oh God. He was erect again.* The hot feel of him between her legs sent her into a swoon, threatening to dispel her concerns over the beasts behind her. He reached between her legs and probed with the blunt tip of his cock, pressing between her sex lips, pushing for an entrance that she knew instinctively was too tight.

She stiffened and tried to scamper down but he held her tight, nipping her earlobe and pressing onward. The full feel of him stretching her was heaven, but when she looked behind her, her furry friends were standing on their hind legs watching them closely.

She startled. With the help of a full moon that appeared suddenly from behind the clouds, her eyes focused on King Kong and what looked like a girlfriend. She pounded on Tarzan to put her down, pushing with conviction against the granite feel of his chest until he finally lifted her off him and dropped her unceremoniously into the water where she landed with a splash.

She came up sputtering a curse, but he was too busy leveling a disgruntled glare at his friends to notice. Then he turned his back on all three of them and continued his washing with frustrated swipes, grumbling something inaudible.

"Go away," she snapped at her four-legged intruders. "We were here first."

The female cocked her head and scratched. Then with an audible grunt, she turned and trudged away. King Kong tramped behind her. She watched them until they reached the edge of the water, where they started to scramble up, but the sight of Kong's girlfriend turning her bottom to him must have proved too much. To Georgie's fascination, Kong dipped down between his mate's legs and sniffed her. Then he licked her, his long pink tongue teasing her with gentle swipes.

Georgie was riveted. Kong's girlfriend squirmed and moaned in obvious pleasure. Then Kong mounted her, biting her neck and shoulders as he did so, drawing high pitched cries from her that didn't sound like pain. He plunged into her, turning her cries to a shallow keening. Georgie felt her face flush at their pleasure.

From behind her Tarzan's massive arms encircled her. She sucked in a breath as his rough hands slid along her breast and then smoothed over her belly to slide between her legs. He separated her with slippery fingers that stroked between her folds, making her tingle, leaving a hot path of pleasure wherever he touched. And he was so adept, oddly gentle, under all that strength.

How did he know what to do? He teased, exploring between her legs and squeezing her nipples to hard points.

He moaned deep in his throat and pressed full against her bottom, his hard warmth engulfing her. She clutched at his wrist, intending to push him away but the ache between her legs made her press against his hand. He growled into her ear and slid one thick finger up through her hot folds, the sweet pleasure of it causing her to dissolve into a long shudder against his chest. His breath hitched and, encouraged, he continued to gently thrust with two fingers.

His breath came fast and heavy when he imitated the gesture by pumping his cock against her bottom in rhythm with his fingers, easing her further forward so she lay on her belly along the rock. He bit gently along her shoulders, murmuring and completely covering her while he pressed his weight to keep her still. He drew her one knee up, opening her further to him. She muffled a groan and grew unbelievably restless. How could she deny him, deny them both?

She struggled to clear her head. Of course she could deny him, she'd never had trouble fighting off bumbling frat boys who made a game of trying to get in her pants. She might be wild and incorrigible but she wasn't stupid. She'd decided long ago that she wouldn't jeopardize her vibrant health for a quick lay with a stranger. And he was a stranger by all accounts.

He licked her neck, running his tongue up along the curve of her throat and sliding his cock between the swell of her buttocks. He was so patient, and obviously delighted with what he'd found. And she had no doubt he knew what to do, regardless of his lack of experience. Yet he waited, for a signal from her. Was there no concept of rape in the jungle?

On instinct and pure lust, she raised her knees, tilting her bottom up in silent invitation. It was all he needed.

He slid his fingers out and replaced it with the blunt head of his cock, hot and throbbing with arousal. She waited, breathless, for the thick feel of him filling her. His fingers played with her lips, spreading them, and sliding her wetness and the soap everywhere as though he knew it would ease his passage. Then she felt the unbelievable pressure as he shoved his full length into her, slipping in easily because she was so wet, and releasing a deep grunt of satisfaction as he impaled her to the hilt.

Oh, God, he was buried up to her waist, completely filling her. He let loose a guttural moan and twisted inside her, throbbing thickly, his hands in a lock on her hips. Every nerve in her tight passage was lit to bursting. A few deep thrusts and she would surrender, but he was so aroused and this was so new to him that she feared he wouldn't last through even a few shallow thrusts. Still, she couldn't resist wriggling her fanny in encouragement. To her surprise he growled and tightened his hold on her hips, keeping her still. Didn't he know he was supposed to move?

"Tarzan," she cried. "Please, I'm burning up." She squirmed her bottom against him, encouraging him to thrust, but he growled louder and then slapped her bottom.

"What the?" she gasped. The shock of it got her immediate attention. She stopped squirming and stayed still, but rather than decrease her ardor, his little spank fueled her desire beyond rational proportions.

He began to move slowly, too slow for her. She bucked against him and in response he landed another firm spank on her fanny and growled and then another.

"Oh, my God!" Heat swelled her groin, hardening her clit to tortuous proportions. She thrust against him. He withdrew and smoothed his hands over her bottom, murmuring low, before plunging back into her. He cursed in words she didn't understand. When his thrusts grew more violent, her clit burned and then throbbed out a pleasuring rhythm that was so sweet she thought she would die. Her entire body contracted tight into itself and then finally let loose with warm bursts of pleasure that spread through her whole body as she came with a force beyond imagining.

Her every nerve stayed lit to extreme sensitivity. When he drove deep into her and held her tight, her arousal spiked once again with the tight stretching of her sex lips. She couldn't believe it. She slid an anxious finger over her clit and then he moved forcefully again, stretching and plundering her, his body tense and rock hard.

He growled and wrapped his arms around her, covering her with his full weight so she lay prostrate along the hard surface of the rock as he hitched as far as he could fit and then finally released his seed. She came again with the thrill of feeling him pump deep inside her.

A slow meltdown followed.

It was unbelievable. While she was hardly a virgin, her few experiences hadn't brought her anywhere close to this kind of bliss. After some time she felt his weight lift. Then he turned her over to lie flat on the rock. He stood between her legs, looking down into her face with an intensity that was terrifying.

She wondered what he must be thinking. He nudged her legs apart and ran one finger along her wet and swollen folds. He licked his lips. She drew him to her clitoris, still hard and sensitive, and guided him to circle the rough pad of his finger around the edges and then down it's length. She moaned and throbbed in response, shocked to feel herself grow aroused and ready for more. When she spread herself wider, he sucked in a harsh breath and swelled to thickness again. She didn't think that was possible but the telltale pearly drop of his readiness soon gleamed in the soft moonlight as he continued his exploration.

He moved to turn her over.

"No," she whispered, grasping his wrists and urging him forward. She lifted her knees and arched her hips.

He immediately understood and clasped his penis, guiding the tip between her sex lips and pushing. This time, as he slid in deep, he held her eyes with his as long as he could, the whites of his heavy lids gleaming in the darkness, his raw pleasure palpable. Then his lids closed on a soft murmur and he eased himself down along her body, pressing skin to skin, his lips buried in her neck.

He lay still for some time, as though savoring the sensation while she skimmed her nails down the broad expanse of his back. The moon shimmered above them, a glittering beacon in the hovering darkness.

Little pinpoints of light peaked out from the surrounding vegetation and, a little disconcerted, she remembered her audience. Small harmless creatures, what did it matter? Then, like with the sudden flick of a switch, a stream of light cut through the overhead cover and illuminated their little cocoon. A full moon sliced a brilliant path from the sky to the slick granite slab where they lay entwined.

She peeked behind her. He reared up on his elbows and looked where they joined, his eyes aflame. He thrust deep, impaling her to her full depths. "Oh, my God." She shuddered. "You feel wonderful . . ." He grunted and watched himself pull out almost entirely only to thrust once again, this time faster, his breathing accelerating and his thick muscled body shaking with his pleasure. That she could bring such a powerful man to his knees with pleasure awed her.

He ducked and bit her nipples and then licked along her

breasts. But soon he threw back his neck and let out a tortured moan. He thrust faster, his urgency building.

Her body thrummed with sensation, every pleasure point strung to bursting. Within minutes, she was spiraling once again over the edge. For a short moment, she lost consciousness, shuddering with the sweet hot pleasure swamping her and the wonderful strong feel of him pumping his need into her once more in hot thick spurts. She swore she could feel the warm living liquid squirt hot against her womb.

He lowered himself onto her and groaned, his skin slick with sweat and hot, his muscles twitching. She collapsed under him, limp with exhaustion and held him close.

The next thing she remembered, she was awakening under his crushing weight. They must have both slept, for how long she couldn't imagine, and would probably still be sleeping if his body hadn't hindered her breathing. His breathing was deep and smooth and his smell so male. It seemed his body was everywhere, powerfully containing her movements. But she felt no fear. Only a contented safety in his arms.

What in the world was she thinking?

She gave him a hard shove. "Wake up!"

He grunted and rolled over to lay prostrate on the smooth slate of rock, looking as breathless as she felt.

"No one would believe this," she muttered to herself before slipping off the rock to wash up. "*I* don't believe it."

Chapter Three

A gentle morning mist filtered through the quiet valley deep in the jungle. The curious family of gorillas gazed at the grassy shelter, high up in the trees and waited, curious as to their new visitor.

As the warm rays of the sun peeked through the forest's top canopy and played along Georgie's cheeks, she slid with a yawning stretch against the cool crisp sheets and breathed in the sweet smell of honeysuckle. She lingered on the scent, momentarily confused as to its source, but stubbornly refusing to fully awaken. She pushed any uncertainty to the back of her mind, so reluctant was she to start the day and have to face the relentless dry dust of the village. She burrowed back into the pillows and shut her eyes tight against an image of the professor's boring drone as he described tribal custom. This morning, for the first time in the weeks since her arrival, she actually felt refreshed, having finally gotten a full night's sleep. Even the hard lumps of the grass and plywood mattress seemed a distant nightmare.

Why was that?

Without opening her eyes, she patted the soft pillowed mound beneath her. *What the?* Her eyes popped wide. When she rolled over, her face slapped into muscled chest, covered with a light sheen of summer sweat, bringing visions of last night flooding back in sharp focus along with all the smells and sensations . . . the wonderful feel of him. She breathed in a tantalizing breath of his rich scent, remembering his taste. She groaned.

She gazed up at the hard line of his jaw, relaxed in sleepy repose. Last night she'd succumbed to him three times. No, four. He was insatiable and so eager . . . fascinated with her.

The honeysuckle soap that he'd slathered all over her body still clung to her skin and scented the sheets. She glanced at her surroundings. A sheer mosquito net walled the space where they slept, the fabric tenting into a high peak that nestled among a thick cluster of trees. No. She let out a startled gasp. She was *in* the trees. She scampered up on her knees. They were high up. A roped ladder dangled from a split in the netting and plunged a good forty feet to the ground. A roped walkway spanned between the trees to another mosquito tented shelter. A jungle suite in the trees. It had its charm.

The sheet fell away. She was naked. She glanced down at him. He was, too. Gloriously tanned and golden. It was so dark last night. She looked her fill now, letting her eyes travel along the acre of muscle that spanned his chest and taking in the dark mat of wiry hair sprinkled along the ridges. The hand that lay on his chest was large but finely boned, rough, yet with long tapered fingers. She remembered those hands last night, exploring and satisfying his bone deep curiosity. She flushed crimson at the knowledge he had of her.

She didn't even know his name. *He* didn't even know his name. A wave of sympathy mollified her. She ran a thick strand of his hair through her fingers, recalling how his wild mane draped her when he entered her, the waves framing a face dark with passion, his eyes liquid with ecstasy. With her fingertip, she traced the long chord of muscle running from beneath his jaw to his collarbone. The texture of his skin was rough with beard growth. Then her eyes involuntarily dropped to his groin.

Even in his relaxed state, he looked powerfully male. He had needed very little time between climaxes. And she knew after last night's initiation, he could never go back to his celibate life.

She put that thought aside and looked again at her surroundings. On top of a small wooden stand sat a basin and along the wall, pegs made from broken off tree branches held scraps of cloth, small cups, her panties, some—. Her panties?

She scurried off the bed, taking the sheet to wrap around her and snatched the torn lace off the hook. She sighed in frustration. They were useless now. Where was her dress? She spotted it draped over a small tree stump.

She dropped the sheet and hastily donned it, securing the front buttons on the bottom and clutching the top closed, looking about at the same time for something that would hold it, when she felt him watching her. She met his gaze with a stern look, intending to start this day off right. Regardless of last night, she was going back to the village. He couldn't keep her here, a prisoner, to do what he wanted with her. And she couldn't leave without his help or she'd be lost in the jungle forever.

But the warm glow in his eyes as he studied her with his head propped in his hand and stretched completely naked along the bed melted her. Her eyes flicked to his groin, swelling quickly under her blatant admiration.

"Oh no you don't." She lifted her palms and backed up. "You're taking me back today, now." Her eyes dropped again to his erection, full and thick and then back to his face. She had to be imagining the amused glint in his eyes. He held a hand out, beckoning her to the bed.

"No," she said. "I know you understand me, even if you don't understand the words."

His hand stroked down his aroused length.

"Stop that," she demanded as she watched him. A warm drum of arousal filled her, heating her skin with alarming speed. Her nipples tightened and ached. Maybe just once more before she left?

He inched back from the edge of the bed and patted with his beautiful and oh so clever hand the place beside him.

She sighed in frustration. "What am I going to do with you?" she murmured while she went to him as if in a trance.

In the seconds it took him to strip off her dress and ease her down beside him, his lips were everywhere, tasting and licking and teasing her beyond belief. His moans of pleasure as he savored every inch of her body had her shuddering in his arms. He was so adept.

He had learned quickly the magic of her small pearly bud that heated and swelled her sex lips, opening her to him and making her burn, beg him. He was so focused on her pleasure.

His lips brushed down over her belly to lick at the tops of her legs. He spread her, running his tongue along the smooth skin of her inner thighs, first one and then skimming over her burning center as he moved to the other. She arched her hips with the gentle touch.

"Please," she breathed.

She felt the tip of his tongue sweep over her in a light caress, probing gently, separating her layers, teasing her. She dug her fingers into his hair and urged him further, but he held her at bay, murmuring something inaudible as he drew back and looked at her.

She was starkly aware of the morning light baring all her treasures to his hungry eyes, but she was too aroused to care. He touched her clitoris lightly with the tip of his tongue and then withdrew and watched as it contracted and throbbed.

"Stop it," she wailed, popping him on the head. He licked her, one quick thick swipe up through her lips and over her clitoris and then withdrew again. She groaned and thrashed. "You're just doing this to torture me." He slipped his thumb into her, but withdrew on her sigh of pleasure. She pounded on his shoulders. She couldn't believe it when he released a low warm chuckle. The brute knew exactly what he was doing.

Before she could beat him again, he crawled up her body and laid on top of her, nudging her legs wider, his expression no longer playful. She loved the hard, heavy feel of him, his muscled weight pinning her, and the scent of his skin, masculine and clean, the feel of him warm under her fingers. She clutched his shoulders as he reared up on his elbows and gazed down at her. The seriousness of his expression took her by surprise as well as the tenderness in his eyes.

She skimmed her fingers along the strong set of his jaw. He closed his eyes at her touch and then thrust deep, bringing a cry of surprise from her that turned into a moan of pure pleasure. He bit back a groan and shuddered, his strong face dissolving into an agony of bliss. He collapsed on top of her and buried his lips in her neck, holding her still, but spreading her wide with his knees and hitching deeper. She was burning up. She bucked against him, urging him to move.

"I need to feel you," she whispered. "Please."

He withdrew and thrust but then held her still again, his breathing labored, his lips still buried in her neck. When she squirmed, he moved, but this time with a slow sensuous, rhythmic thrusting that drove her crazy. The heat and thick feel of him filling her was heaven, the friction of his thrusting lighting every nerve. She clutched at him, digging her nails deep into his flesh and whimpered, begging for more.

He growled and thrust faster until the frenzied heat of it was too much for her. Every nerve cried out for release. "I can't, I . . ." she sobbed, not understanding what was happening to her. She would die if this lasted much longer.

He held her close and plundered her until she surrendered to his strength and warmth and exploded in his arms. His release followed right behind.

It was a long time before he lifted his face and with gentle fingers, smoothed the wet curls from her forehead. He murmured sounds but no words formed and the warm timbre of his voice stirred her in an entirely feminine way. She wanted to know what he felt, what he was thinking. It frustrated her that he couldn't tell her. She touched a finger to his lips. He closed his eyes and sighed and then rolled off her and lay on his back, looking up at the leafed canopy above. Deep furrows creased his brow.

On impulse, she ran her fingers along the lines, smoothing away the wrinkles with a comforting hand. He turned and looked at her, circling her wrist, his eyes filled with a longing that overwhelmed her and an intensity that she could too easily drown in. She drew away gingerly and began searching for her dress. Spying it on the floor beside her, she tipped on her side and reached for it. A warm palm settled on her bare bottom.

She groaned. "No," she said, snatching at his hand. He drew her against him, cradling her bottom against his rising erection.

"I have to go," she cried, giving his hand a firm yank. She jumped off the bed and shoved her arms through the straps of her dress and buttoned it quickly. Clutching the front closed, she eyed him with a sternness that she didn't feel. "You've got to get me back," she told him and motioned off in the distance, pointing down the ladder and beyond the trees. "Take me now," she said with little conviction. His eyes shone with a devilish gleam. "It'll take us all day and I don't want to be trapped in the jungle at dark."

He watched her speak, easing off the bed as she did.

"Good." She sighed, her eyes traveling involuntarily down his body when he stood. She told herself to look away, but she knew she wasn't likely to be rewarded with a look at such a virile specimen in the near future, probably in her lifetime. He pulled the leather loincloth off the hook and wrapped it around his ample bulge. Her eyes lingered on his bronze chest and followed the dark shadow of hair that ran up his neck. His beard was heavy this morning and his hair lay in an awry tumble to his shoulders. He looked fierce, but she knew better. His gentleness with her tugged viciously at her heart.

She stifled a small whimper and glanced away.

He smiled and took her hand, guiding her to the small table that held a large water bottle and a basin. Toothbrushes and hairbrushes hung neatly on hooks, surrounding it. Even mint toothpaste lay alongside the basin. He poured water from the bottle into the galvanized bowl and splashed his face. Then he drew her over to stand in front of him to do the same.

Although she still felt wonderfully clean from the hot tub last night, the heat of the jungle was already rising and the cool water refreshed her. She pulled back her curls and dabbed apricot scrub along her cheeks. She could feel him leave her side. When she glanced around, he had moved to a shelf along the wall.

He was shaving, using a small mirror that was anchored along a tree trunk. He skimmed down over his jaw and along his neck, his biceps rippling as he shook off the soap and rinsed the razor.

She had no brothers, no siblings at all, and the little experience she'd had with men didn't include this intimacy. Watching such a personal male ritual was oddly arousing. He glanced over when he dried off with a towel. His hair was tied back with leather into a thick ponytail and as he came toward her, she could smell the fresh scent of mint on his breath. He touched her cheek, smoothing along the soft skin and then took her fingers and laid them along his hard jaw. Then he smiled. A warm, drawing smile that melted her insides and told her that he, too, enjoyed their differences. For such a primitive man, one who had little contact with humans and none with females, he was marvelously perceptive.

He fingered the front of her dress, but she quickly stepped back further and clutched it closed. His smile widened. He released a small chuckle as he grabbed a leather cord off a branch hook and picked up a small pocketknife from the table and flicked it open.

"Stay back, Tarzan. I'm warning you." *Or what?* She'd deck him?

With a casual hand, he laced the leather through one button hole and then cut tiny holes along the other side of the dress so he could lace the cord through. He crisscrossed it over her bodice, pulling it snug, and then twisted the laces at the top into a small knot.

"Thank you," she said, giving him a warm smile.

He cupped her chin and drew his thumb along her jaw line, drawing her closer as though to kiss her. But of course he wouldn't know what a kiss was, would he? Even after all they'd done, they'd never kissed. It was tempting to show him, so tempting, but that would only lead to much more and she needed to leave here, not linger. He brushed his lips along her cheek, then his nose, breathing deeply. All she needed was to turn her lips to his and press.

Before she could give in to temptation, she ducked her head and walked around him to the top of the roped stairs.

He shook his head and gestured to their mouths and then their stomachs. She reluctantly agreed. She *was* hungry and had been since she'd come to these ends of the earth. But she longed for penne pasta with sun dried tomatoes and *Ben & Jerry's* New York Chocolate Chunk Fudge, not the gluing stew she feared he would feed her.

He took her hand and guided her through the roped bridge that connected to the other trees. The small room he brought her to had grass mats and a low table. After he settled her on a mat, he produced a small lime-looking fruit that he sliced in two, pressing half to his lips. He drank in the juice. Then he offered her the other half. The sweet juice had a delicious tang and she sucked eagerly, suddenly aware of her thirst and hunger.

Before long, he had enticed her with more. Some fruits she recognized, like the bananas and mangos, but others were unknown—all were delicious. When she approved each new taste with a smile, he smiled back in satisfaction. He watched her mouth as he fed her, running his fingertips along her bottom lip more than once and then licking the sweet nectar from his fingertip. How he would enjoy a kiss! When she licked her lips, his eyes grew stormy and he watched every move.

She shook off the tempting thought of a kiss and waved away his offer of what looked like fried banana slices with guava dip. "I'm full," she said, patting her tummy and wiping her lips with a cloth napkin made out of rough cotton.

Were his civilized ways traces of his life before his disappearance or were they due to his observing poachers and others who had wandered into his territory? Since he'd only seen men, she doubted the latter. If she were smart, she'd stay a while and study him, take notes to share with the professor, really impress him. It didn't appear that she'd starve here. He certainly wasn't.

Her eyes lit on a sizeable wooden box. His treasures? Silver items stolen from camps? Or maybe just extra supplies. Everything necessary for survival seemed to be hanging all around them.

Seeing her studying the box, he walked over and crouched before it but then hesitated. When he looked at her, his eyes were troubled, as though he questioned whether he could trust her. He lifted it a crack and peered in. Then he opened it wide and stepped back. With a nod and a small motion of his hand, he offered her a look.

She dropped to her knees and searched its contents. A leather wallet lay on top. She flipped through it. Credit cards, a few dollars, a drivers license from Boston—a Professor Stanton. She wondered if he was still alive. She wanted to believe he only killed poachers, those who harmed innocent creatures. Several gold chains and a watch lay across a few pieces of folded cloth, heavy denim and some leather. A small red shiny object in the bottom caught her eye. When she picked it up, she realized it was a *Lego*. Or rather, several *Lego* pieces fit together to make a car. All the wheels were intact and a little *Lego* man sat atop. Even the steering wheel remained.

She drew in a breath. A remnant of his past? If he was a small child when he was lost, perhaps this was in his pocket when he had wandered off? Her heart picked up beats. She riffled through the box in earnest. Rings, belts, lots of precious metals, no doubt scavenged from the poachers, a few more wallets with identifying information that meant nothing to her. Then she picked up coveralls that might fit a three-year-old. Blue denim shorts with the label carrying the unmistakable name of *OshKosh B'Gosh*. This had to be what he was wearing when lost! It startled her to see this ghost from his past. She fingered the cloth and looked back at him, trying to see the boy in his rough masculine features. He watched her closely with obvious apprehension. She poked in the pockets—nothing. A few more unimportant items and then her fingers brushed paper.

Sitting at the bottom was a small child's book, old and weathered, its bright colors dulled to whiteness. It looked so fragile, she feared picking it up. With great care she lifted it and then sat back on her heels.

He looked over her shoulder and peered down at the book on her lap.

"Richard Scarry," she breathed, stunned. "It's *The Please and Thank You* Book." She smoothed her fingertips along its surface and then carefully turned to her favorite part—"Pig Will and Pig Won't." She smiled in recognition at the familiar words she'd ceaselessly begged her mother to read and that she had listened to with such pleasure. As young as she was, probably two, she had memorized parts and would fill in as her mother recited the lines.

Now, she read the words aloud that told the story of Mother pig who was trying to teach her little pigs to be helpful. Tarzan was sprawled behind her and had settled his chin on her shoulder.

"Mother Pig had two little pigs—Pig Will and Pig Won't.

Whenever she asked them to do something, Pig Will said, 'I will.' But Pig Won't said—"

"I won't."

Tarzan's voice startled her. Not the rich timbre of it, because he had grumbled what sounded like curses to her several times and then later murmured soft endearments that she didn't understand. But this time his words had perfect diction.

"What did you say?" she asked, although she had heard him perfectly. She turned fully to him. He looked as perplexed as she felt, as though he hadn't understood himself why he'd said it.

She was anxious to read on. The pigs were asked by Daddy to play more quietly and of course that kiss-up, Pig Will, chanted again "I will." She read on with a smirk, relishing Pig Won't's part. "But Pig Won't said—"

"I won't."

She drew in a soft breath. There it was again, clear and unmistakable.

She set the book down with care and turned to kneel before him, searching his face for some recognition that he understood. But he was frowning. Cupping his face with her hands she said, "You were a Pig Won't too, weren't you?"

He blinked his long lashes and reached up to encircle her wrists, listening to her closely. "That's why you wandered away from your parents. You never listened either."

He ran his thumbs along the smooth skin of her inside wrists and stroked, never taking his eyes off her. A small part of her understood him. She pictured a small hellion of a boy, defying his parents at every turn and then lost, hopelessly separated from those same parents, never to see them again.

This was no savage beast. This was an intelligent strong-willed boy that had grown into a strong man who had somehow survived, separated from his world for far too long.

Well, no more. She would bring him back! But first she'd teach him what he already knew and of which he just needed to be reminded. His English was perfect, she was sure, but buried deep in the recesses of his mind.

She'd start her introduction back to civilization with a kiss.

Chapter Four

"Would you like to kiss me?" she asked.

He frowned.

"Kiss," she said clearly, slowly, exaggerating the *s* sound and showing how her lips formed the word. She touched his lips with her fingertips and then touched hers. "Kiss," she repeated. His eyes lit with interest.

She ran her finger along her bottom lip as she said the word again. "Kiss." Then she touched his, nodding her head, urging him to imitate her.

After a moment's hesitation, his voice came on a whisper. "Kiss," he said.

She smiled in approval.

"Kiss," he said a little louder.

"Okay," she said. Leaning forward, she pressed her mouth to his.

His eyes widened as he watched their lips meet. Then she drew back. "Kiss," she explained.

He swallowed. "Kiss," he repeated, his voice rough. He framed her face with his hands and drew her toward him. *He caught on quick!*

When their lips met this time, his softened and his eyes closed. She pressed and brushed along his, taking the lead, allowing their breath to mingle. She settled her palms on his chest and felt the pounding of his heart. But other than his lips softening under hers, he was still, content to learn what she was doing.

She licked his bottom lip and he groaned, instinctively parting his mouth and holding her face more firmly. She touched his tongue with the tip of hers and then withdrew a fraction, teasing, getting him to lean forward, searching for more. His tongue chased hers, playing and exploring until he would no longer be teased.

He delved deep, exploding with urgency, his mouth restless, moving over hers and drawing her closer, demanding more. He picked her up and settled her on his lap, stroking his tongue with hers. He tasted of mint and warmth and the forest, and he was wet, wonderfully wet and slick, then rough and smooth at the same time.

She soon lost herself in his plunging thrusts and the feel of him growing bone hard beneath her as he enveloped her in arms that felt like bands of steel. But rather than panic, she melted into his heat, turning soft and yielding. Her loins felt liquid and marvelously loose.

He licked along her lips and then plunged again. Who was teaching whom? She supposed some things were pure instinct.

Their tongues tangled together in a heated dance so sensual her body ignited and burned. He nipped her lips, pulling with his teeth and sucking her bottom lip gently. For only a kiss, it was unbearably erotic. Then his hands were under her skirt, cupping her bare bottom and lifting her. His finger slid into her slippery wet heat. He lifted her easily and slid her down onto him so that he impaled her completely. She thrilled at the full feel of him and breathed a deep sigh of satisfaction.

Her eyes flew open. He was doing it again. Capturing her, mesmerizing her, so she couldn't think straight. Before she could protest, he lifted her and thrust hard several times before he exploded inside her. The power of his climax shook her, and the fierce tension lines in his face that suddenly gave way to an expression of extreme pleasure only served to increase her fright. She had to get away from him.

But when she pushed against him, he reached between her legs with his thumb and stroked the hard knot of her pleasure to excruciating tautness until she was blind with it and begging for release.

He pinched her clitoris, and she exploded with primal moans that had her shaking in his arms. She lay limp against his chest where he cradled her, sifting his long fingers through her hair.

She wanted to cry. She'd never make it out of here.

She settled into the safety of his arms, still impaled by him, and let him soothe her, soothe away all the conflicts facing her. She loved the timbre of his voice. Even if she couldn't understand the words he murmured, she felt his calm wrap around her like a warm blanket. How was she to leave him now?

He would just have to come with her. After she taught him the words he had forgotten and brought back memories of his past life. But what if he wouldn't come?

They read the book several more times, each time with him repeating the "I won't" parts and learning a few more words as she pointed out the boat, TV, and car, and even the ice cream in the story.

How he would love ice cream!

A group of little animals ate chocolate ice cream with Pig Will. She had frowned as the rest of the story came back to her. Pig Will got to have ice cream with all the other "hard workers" but since Pig Won't had stubbornly refused to help, he'd been left home, missing out on both the work *and* the treat. She smiled despite herself, wondering how many such treats her stubborn Tarzan, like her, had missed out on.

Suddenly, it occurred to her to look inside the book jacket for a name. When she found the shaded square with *My name is* and looked at the line beneath it, she sighed with disappointment. The letters where his name would have been had long since faded. She held the book up to the light, hoping for a miracle. She got it.

Although the other letters were too faded, the first one was clearly an M. "Michael," she murmured. "Matthew, Mark." She held it closer, then farther. "Maybe Martin or Mitch—"

"Mark," he said, clear as a bell.

She held her breath and turned to him. "Mark?" she repeated.

He frowned and kneaded his temples with his forefingers and then gave a shrug and looked away, thoughtful. She wanted to shake him, but instead she forced herself to be patient. When his gaze finally returned, his eyes shone with conviction and then he placed his palm against his chest. He patted it. "Mark."

To her horror, she let out a small sob and leaped into his arms. "Mark," she called him, raining kisses over his face. He smiled with pleasure.

"Mark," he repeated and she kissed him all over again and yet again when he repeated it. Soon, she wasn't sure if his name really was Mark or he just wanted kisses for saying it. But she felt deliriously happy just knowing his name.

She patted her own chest. "Georgie," she said.

His eyes fixed on her breasts. "Georgie," he said and fondled her breast.

She slapped his hand away. "No, *I'm* Georgie," she scolded, "and you're Mark," she said, pointing to him. She repeated the gesture.

He studied her quietly for so long that she wasn't sure he understood. Then he slid his fingers along her jaw. "Georgie," he said, his voice low and with a reverence that moved her. He kissed her chastely on the lips, tenderly, and she filled with an emotion she didn't recognize. But at that moment, she felt a bond grow between them that she feared could not be broken.

❧✦(ﬁﬁ)✦☙

The next month was filled with lessons. But not all were for him. While he caught on to the language with a speed that astounded her, she was less quick to learn and adapt to the wilds of the jungle.

Cooking was a luxury because finding dry timber of any kind was near impossible. Since she had refused to eat anything raw that moved—although *he* felt no such aversion and feasted on a variety of food sources that made her gag just watching him—this left her with only fruits, vegetables, and nuts. The fruit slid down easily but the vegetables were a chore. She relished the crunch and chew of a multitude of seeds and nuts, however, for she missed sinking her teeth into a nice chicken breast or tender fish fillet, and she found she craved the oil taste in the nuts. But with such a small variety of food available to her, she worried that she'd lose the few pounds of fat she had and then she'd *really* look like a boy.

She had frowned a bit at her pique over the food. She knew she was spoiled—a little—having never wanted for anything in her life, other than more of everything that she already had. She wasn't greedy, her father had often said in her defense, just spirited. But she ruefully admitted now that even her father had lost patience with her these last couple of years. With that thought in mind, she determined to appreciate what food they had and not think about what they didn't.

Less easy to adapt to were the thousands—millions—of insects and other creepy crawlers. Flies, beetles, and stinging insects, and ants and spiders of every variety buzzed around the multitude of hanging herbs and flowers, eating and pollinating with a fury. She knew they were hungry, too, and just doing their job, but she found them almost impossible to ignore. It was weeks before she learned to casually flick a spider off her arm rather than screech with revulsion and leap off the forest floor.

Mark was always bemused by her outbursts. Everything she did seemed to bemuse and fascinate him. Just for entertainment he'd sometimes plant little bugs on her shoulders to tease her. But the game he enjoyed best was planting spiders on her thigh so he could rescue her by playfully slipping his hand up her skirt and saving her from the creature. Even more he enjoyed how quickly her skin heated and the way in which she eagerly rewarded him for his bravery.

And if she'd had any lingering doubt about his potential for violence it dissipated under his gentle protectiveness toward her.

❦

Georgie and Mark had been hiking for some time and he was patiently pointing out all the creatures of the rain forest. She supplied him with the names she knew, or at least the most likely family of species they belonged to, but she was far from an expert, despite that several units in her earth science class had covered the rainforest. She mentally calculated the number of those classes she had missed and could have kicked herself. But that class met on Mondays. What was she to do after a long weekend on the ski slopes? Certainly not show up for a class at the ungodly hour of 10:00 am.

He had already hesitatingly introduced her to his gorilla friends. And she didn't know who was more scared of whom. They stayed safely at a distance that first week. When Mark would swim across the hot spring or go over to their marked territory to meet with them, he always communicated exclusively with the large Silverback that she'd encountered that first day and who was the obvious leader of the clan. The two spoke in grunts and gestures. It saddened Georgie to think that perhaps they understood each other better than Mark understood her.

She grew grim. If it was the last thing she did, she would change that.

By the end of the fourth week, she knew which snakes to avoid and what a deadly scorpion looked like, and that, although the various conglomerates of lizards might be ugly, they were harmless—at least to everything but the insects. She even learned to sense when a jaguar was prowling the area. The forest would grow deadly quiet as all the smaller animals burrowed underground or deep into trees. She and Mark had stayed high up in his treehouse those few times and waited silently, he with his knife poised in one hand and a hatchet in the other, and she shaking like a leaf.

He understood her terror afterwards and gathered her into his strong arms until she calmed. And when he held her, she truly believed he was stronger, far superior to the jaguar, and could protect her from anything.

As they moved along now, with the steamy heat of the forest rising around her ankles and the sunlight like glass crystals shimmering through the canopy above, she thought she had never seen anything so beautiful. Soft blushes of pastels and purples smudged the emerald green leaves and vines that dangled all around. The rich clean scent of rainwater that sparkled and dripped from the ends of every leaf smelled so fresh and gently rinsed away the day's dust and pollen.

She breathed in the sweet fragrance, content to follow Mark deeper into the jungle, watching the flexing muscles of his backside and corded thighs as he stepped over logs and branches.

He stopped suddenly and put out his arm in a silencing gesture. "Stop," he ordered. "Listen." He grew very still.

Had he not sounded so urgent, she would have enjoyed the ease with which he used his new language skills but he tensed, his jaw rigid as he lifted his face to listen.

Then she heard it. Could almost smell them. Humans.

Her heart stopped. Male voices. One English speaking. Mark swung into action. In one swift movement, he scooped her up and hitched her onto his hip, darting around tree trunks and limbs until he found a thick oak. Before she realized what was happening, he climbed the trunk with a few strong strides and settled in the crook of a high branch, settling her onto his lap. He pressed a finger to her lips and held her close.

Not a moment later, two men passed below them, one clumsily swiping aside the twisting branches of the understory vegetation as he followed behind his native guide.

"Are you sure you're not lost?" the white man grumbled. "My mission is to find the girl, not get lost myself."

Georgie's breath stopped. The accent was New York. She must be the girl he was looking for.

"Her parents will pay me a small fortune to find her but will pay nothing if I don't—"

"Maybe in valley," the native grunted, pointing ahead.

"But what about that wild man who supposedly lives in the valley? What if we meet up with him?"

The native man scowled. "Kill wild man. Get big money from government. We both rich."

Georgie gasped and snuggled in closer to Mark. How could she have forgotten about her parents? Of course they'd be looking for her and must be worried sick. But one of these men wouldn't hesitate to kill Mark in the process of finding her.

The white man wiped his forehead and neck with a madras scarf. "Jesus, this is like a sauna. How much farther?"

"Few miles." The native man swung a leather pouch to his mouth and gulped.

Georgie wanted to leap from the tree as her brain filled with visions of home and her little red Miata, Thai food, her CDs. What she would give to listen to her *Diskman* while running along the Long Island shore.

The white man tipped up his canteen and drank greedily before saying. "If she's with the wild man, I hope she's still alive."

They moved on, with the native man moving gracefully through the thick foliage and the white man stumbling after him, their pace slow enough that she knew Mark could easily get them back to the valley before the two reached it. But then what?

Chapter Five

"What?" she breathed.

Mark's face darkened. "No," he roared, his body vibrating with fury. He advanced on her with powerful strides and swept her into his arms.

"Put me down," she demanded, pounding against him with little effect until he dropped her onto the bed.

If the investigator her parents had hired had made it to the valley with his guide, they'd yet to see them, and Georgie and Mark had returned hours ago. But the valley was huge, and most likely the pair was rooting around deep at the other end. It could take hours to cross the valley on foot if you didn't know the terrain and dark was falling quickly. Hopefully, the investigator wouldn't give up and would resume his search tomorrow.

She had been trying to explain to Mark about her parent's worry over her and that she had to talk with the investigator, that she couldn't stay. She didn't know how much he understood, but *she* understood that he didn't like what he heard. But she didn't know why.

"Mark," she tried to patiently explain while she lay sprawled out on the bed, watching his agitated pacing. "There are only two of them, and you have guns." She pointed to the abundant supply hanging off the walls. "They have more to fear than you do. They'll take me without harming you or the animals."

"No," he said, coming toward her. He dropped to sit beside her on the bed and leaned over her, trapping her between his arms and pinning her to the mattress. "You are mine now!" he growled, his eyes fierce.

Her eyes grew huge. She didn't know which stunned her more. The fact that it was the first time he had communicated with more than one word, having strung several words together to form a complete sentence, or the fact that he thought he owned her.

"You . . . you can't keep me," she stuttered.

He leaned in nose to nose. "Yes," he hissed, his eyes smoldering. "You are mine!"

She strangled a gasp of panic. His eyes blazed with vehemence and his fortitude terrified her. He *could* keep her here. She'd have no way of escaping him. And he could easily kill anyone who tried to take her. She was sure that he *would* kill anyone who tried.

His pupils dilated and his eyes blackened with restrained rage. She held her breath. She would *not* be a prisoner. *But now didn't seem the right time to tell him.*

She smoothed her palms over the muscles of his chest, tense and rigid now with the effort to control himself. The hard muscles flexed and then relaxed under her tentative touch. She flicked her nail over his nipple and he let out a soft moan. She licked the tiny flat nub, amazed again that he would be so sensitive. He tasted salty with sweat and smelled like the forest and him, tangy and fresh and male.

She spoke to him soothingly, knowing he wouldn't understand more than half of it. "You can come with me. We'll find your parents. I'll introduce you to all the delights of civilization." He eased down beside her, gathering her into his arms and trailing his lips along her forehead as she continued to lick his chest and neck. He was so warm and solid. They were meant to be together.

He unlaced her bodice and played with her nipples, his large palms completely covering her breasts. "Will you come with me, Mark?" she purred.

"No," he said, his voice low and sure.

Her lips stilled and she sat up. "Mark?" She tried to look him in the eye, but he had locked onto her breasts while attempting to slip his hand under her skirt. He palmed her thighs. "Look at me, Mark." She pushed at his shoulders. "We're going back where we *both* belong. You are *human*. You're coming with me."

He eased his finger up through her hot folds where, already, she ached for him, yet he had barely touched her. A tingling shiver snaked through her. She grabbed onto his wrist. "Mark, you—"

He shoved in deep and then looked at her, impaling her with

his gaze. His thumb, wet from his probing, grazed her clitoris. Pure pleasure stripped through her. *"You* stay with *me!"* he breathed.

She strangled on a protest as he pressed with his thumb, taking away her strength and reducing her to liquid. Her eyes rolled up into her head, and he stroked with greater pressure and thrust deep within her. She moaned and struggled against the urge to let him take her. He'd take her surrender as acquiescence. But as she sat crossed legged on the bed, fully exposed, as he relentlessly plunged her, she felt helpless to resist him. The front buttons of her dress were splayed open and she was spread wide for him, wider by his searching fingers. The juices of her arousal coated his fingers as he skillfully stroked her. He bit gently on her nipples and she exploded, in long shuddering groans that held her captive in his arms. The same way he planned to hold her captive in his treehouse.

He stripped off his loincloth and laid her across the bed. Taking his engorged cock in hand, he positioned himself between her legs. But while her body still wanted him, she would not let him win. Would not let him think she had succumbed to him and would stay.

She pushed hard against his chest and bucked her hips.

He frowned and held her hips, but as he drew back to guide himself, she kicked up with her knee, just missing her target. She scratched at his face. For one shocked moment he stilled, but then he grabbed her wrists with a vengeance.

"No," she screamed at him. "You can't force me. You can't keep me. Let me go!" She tried to bite his neck.

He growled deep in his throat and then clamped her wrists together above her head. The next moment she felt a leather cord tight around them, binding her hands together. He leaped off the bed and pulled on the cord. Her back arched as she was pulled upward. "What are you doing?" she shrieked. "You can't tie me up." But he did, pulling hard on the cord and yanking it around the tree at the head of the bed. She kicked wildly, her body bouncing off the bed. "Let me go, you beast." She pulled on her restraints.

He came around to the front of the bed. He was still fully aroused. She kicked at him, wishing she could make contact. His eyes smoldered and heated. Taking his eyes off her for just a moment, he grabbed up one of his knives and came at her. With one swift movement he sliced the straps off her sundress and ripped it out from under her.

He dropped her cut sundress onto the floor, leaving her naked as he feasted his eyes on her.

He stroked down his thick length. The small pearly drop of his seed glistened on the angry head of his penis. When her eyes dropped to the smooth wet skin, his cock pulsed and throbbed under her gaze. He was beautiful and so powerful but at this moment she despised his strength.

"I hate you," she choked, furious at her own helplessness.

He blinked and then went stone still.

She kicked again, a useless gesture that would accomplish nothing if he was intent on taking her, dominating her, showing her that she was his. It was blatantly apparent that that was exactly what he planned on doing.

He made the mistake of coming slowly around to the side of the bed, the tension lines in his forehead softening, telling her that he had let his guard down. As he went to ease down beside her, she kneed sideways and got him right in the groin.

A bellow ripped from his throat and he grabbed himself as he buckled over. His breath came in deep gasps. She had gotten him good.

While he crouched on the floor, she yanked and struggled against her bonds, hoping against the odds of him being careless in his knot tying this time. But her wrists held firm. She panicked now. What would he do when he recovered?

She glanced down beside her and watched him struggle to his feet. He stumbled over to the washbasin and splashed water along his face and neck and then dried himself, his back to her. The tight muscles on his bare buttocks flexed and tensed. His shoulders heaved in a long-suffering sigh.

Maybe he'd think twice about keeping her here now.

He dropped the towel onto the stool and turned slowly to face her. It wasn't surprising that he wasn't erect anymore, but he didn't look permanently damaged either, she decided with relief. His face relaxed as he studied her. She didn't dare utter a word as his eyes grazed down her body and then up again. She struggled defiantly with her bonds, but all that did was thrust her breasts up even farther. She felt boldly exposed and burned at her vulnerable position.

She could tell by his softened expression as he continued to study her that he would untie her. Relief filled her. She would be free and then she'd convince him to go with her. She hadn't meant to hurt or upset him. He just needed to know that she was in charge. If he would just listen to her, he'd soon see that everything would be all right.

He snapped another leather chord off a branch. She blinked in confusion as he approached her with slow deliberate steps.

"What . . . what are you going to do now?" she breathed. He slapped the chord against his thigh. "Mark?" She looked up into his black eyes, glittering now like polished marble. She swallowed. "You're not . . . you're not going to . . ." her voice trailed off as her eyes dropped to his hand, flexing against his thigh. His penis was throbbing to life.

When he pounced on her, it took her a moment to realize that he was tying her legs. After he clamped her ankles together, he then looped each ankle separately until she was bound to the bed, spread-eagled before him. "You're despicable," she railed at him. "A barbarian!"

He smiled in satisfaction as he looked down at her from where he stood at the foot of the bed, his gaze fixated between her legs. His erection rose to full glory.

She gasped. "Only a brute would take advantage of a helpless female."

He gave a snort.

With slow deliberate movements, he eased down onto the foot of the bed, hot eyes glittering and raking over every inch of her body as he kneeled between her legs. She burned, feeling so starkly exposed, helpless against his barefaced dominance of her.

But not complete dominance! She had her spirit.

She'd be damned if she'd allow herself to respond to him, no matter how clever his hands—

"Oh!" She let out a soft breath.

With the lightest touch, he scraped his nails down her breasts and over her nipples, causing them to pucker traitorously.

A knowing smile curved his conceited mouth.

She bit back an angry retort, determined not to give him the satisfaction of any response at all. She turned her face aside and closed her eyes, her mouth set in a determined line and forcing her thoughts elsewhere.

His warm palms settled on her thighs.

She wanted to go home. She'd think of that and all that she'd lost. Thoughts rose up and overwhelmed her with a terrible longing. It wasn't horrible here, with him, it was just that she didn't belong. She missed her life, her car, her apartment.

She choked back a sob. She missed her mother. Her mother

had promised to look after her flowers and collect her mail, to pay overdue credit cards so Georgie could start new when she returned after her successful internship.

More like aborted internship. Not halfway into her time and she had been lost, rescued, and now kidnapped.

She would not stay here!

The powerful feel of him settling between her legs drew her head up. His teeth nipped her chin and tugged the delicate skin. She kept still, even when his warm tongue laved where he had bitten her. He cupped her bottom, drawing her hips up to meet him. She went rigid under his touch. He probed, but got no answering moan from her.

Not until he slid a finger between her bottom cheeks and stroked. Instantly, she heated and squirmed. He growled in his throat and slid his thick shaft between her legs and then thrust deep, taking her breath away.

One long finger probed her backside and sunk, completely impaling her tight entrance. The low moan she struggled to suppress came tumbling out.

A few deep thrusts at both ends and she was shuddering and convulsing uncontrollably in his arms. He held her close and pumped greedily into her.

When it was over, she burst into tears.

Given her complete abandon with him, now he would never let her leave.

He turned her face to look at him. "Georgie?" he murmured, catching a tear with his thumb.

"Leave me alone! I hate you." She glared at him.

His face stilled and then tightened with rage. The next moment, he bounded off the bed.

"Untie me."

"No!" He whipped around, his eyes blazing with fury. "You will run. I won't let you."

"I won't."

"You will." His fists clenched. "You will stay. You will listen. You are mine!"

"*You* are a brute, a savage brute, a barbarian, a . . . a monster. I hate you. I *will* run. And you'll *not* catch—"

He all but leaped over the edge of the treehouse and slid down the roped ladder.

"Where are you going?" she shouted. "You can't leave me here. Mark!" She thrashed against the ropes, frightfully aware of how quickly the darkness was descending. A faint rustle of leaves in the breeze was the only answering sound.

"Mark," she sobbed. "I'm sorry." Though his eyes had been dark with anger she had seen the hurt, too. She didn't hate him. She shouldn't have said it. A heavy weight crushed down onto her heart. *She just wanted to go home.*

When next she awoke, it was morning. He hadn't come back and she had cried herself into an exhausted sleep and now her chest ached and her wrists and ankles stung from her struggles.

But when she opened her eyes, he was with her, sitting beside her, his brow creased with tension.

She sat up, startled to find herself tucked safely into crisp sheets, her bonds no longer holding her down and him offering her a cup from his large hands.

"Drink," he said.

She covered his hands and drank greedily, spilling the sweet cold nectar down her chin and over her breasts. She couldn't get enough.

When she was finished, he licked the drops off her lips and chin and then tried to clean her breasts but she pushed him away, remembering his vow not to let her leave.

His eyes filled with regret and he sighed.

"Food?" he suggested.

"Take me home."

He ran a hand down his face and rose wearily. When he came back, he handed her a damp cloth. She ran the refreshing coolness of it along her face and throat.

He offered up her tattered dress, the straps neatly repaired now with needle and thread.

He touched her jaw, a tentative touch that nearly broke her heart. "Stay." His voice was rough with suppressed emotion, his jaw tense, but it was the gentle plea in his eyes, raw with feeling, that almost drove her to answer that she would.

She loved him. The knowledge of it shocked her to the core. She didn't think she could ever love anyone, not like this, with this soul wrenching torture. This overpowering, all consuming, crazy love that she'd read about and that drove lovers to sacrifice everyth—

She stopped on that thought. What sacrifice? She wasn't willing to do it. She wasn't going to sacrifice anything for him. She wanted it all—*her* life, *her* home, and she wanted him with *her*.

Even in love she was selfish.

It shouldn't have surprised her.

For the first time, she fully accepted her nature. She was self-centered, immature. A Pig Won't who always got what she wanted and gave up nothing in return.

Why didn't he realize that in the long run he was much better off in civilization, with his own kind? He was young, intelligent, and strong.

And she loved him. Or did she? Not enough if her plan was to wear him down until he agreed to come with her regardless that she truly believed he was better off. And what if he did come with her simply because she selfishly insisted? She supposed he wouldn't then *be* the fierce, independent, strong-willed King of the Jungle with whom she'd fallen in love.

They were hopelessly doomed. She couldn't stay and she couldn't make him come.

She closed her eyes, fighting back tears. When she opened them she spoke with deliberate slowness, making sure he understood every word. "I can't stay," she told him. "I want you to come with me, but I know this is *your* home." She made a gesture that took in the contents of the room and the jungle beyond. "I won't make you come. But please, take me home." While she meant every word, she also couldn't imagine being without him.

His hand dropped and he looked away.

When he returned his gaze, his eyes were sad. "We go. I take you back," he said and then rose from the bed.

"We?"

"First eat." He yanked the mosquito net aside and strode down the roped bridge.

"Mark, do you mean that you're going, too?"

He didn't answer and she was too afraid to press him, fearful that if she badgered him he might change his mind.

On shaky legs, she stood and followed him, hopeful for the first time that he might be considering going with her.

Chapter Six

As he swung through the branches, she clawed up his chest and hung on with a tenacity of someone who feared for her life. She knew it had to be a quicker way out of the valley as they soared from cliff to cliff, but she wouldn't have minded the slow route either.

She tried to convince him, but he said little and apparently ignored her pleas. The same way he ignored her explanations about what he could expect if he came with her. But he never once said that he wasn't coming with her.

When they cleared the valley and were heading steadily downhill to the edge of the rainforest, she outlined once again her plans for them, explaining more than she knew he could understand but wanting to tell him everything.

Dr. Cahill would want to claim him, interview him endlessly and examine him, but the professor was harmless, she assured him, annoying but harmless. No doubt the villagers would fear him and be in awe of his size and reputation. He was a legend, she explained, and had been for some time. But while the authorities no doubt had their own plans for him, the professor, here at the invitation of the highest government officials in concert with New York University, one of the most prestigious universities in the world, would see that he remained in his custody.

Georgie could tell by Mark's responses that, while he might have missed some words, he understood the main gist of what she was telling him. Like any person learning a language, he understood far more than he could yet speak.

When they reached a clearing high up the hill and could see

the small cluster of grass huts as dots below, they stopped to rest.
A feeling of relief consumed her. If someone had told her a month
ago that she'd be weak with joy to see those twig shacks teetering
on a clump of dirt, she'd have thought them crazy. But that was
when she'd had more than two miserable months to go. Now,
she'd be going home. Surely she wouldn't be expected to finish
out her internship after her horrific experience. They'd hand her a
college diploma on a silver platter.

Strong warm hands encircled her from behind and slid up over
her breasts. Within moments she was wet for him and he knew it.
His searching fingers spread her sex lips and probed, his voice
groaning at the feel of her arousal.

"Mark," she breathed. He nuzzled her neck and pinched her
nipples while his finger still played between her legs. He was rut-
ting behind her and soon she felt the smooth tip of his cock, hot
against her thighs. He slid into her quickly, easily, filling her, and
the pleasure she felt with him, the desire, was like the first time.
She would never get enough of him.

The wet friction of their mating and his clever hands burning a
path wherever he touched had her crying out for him.

He clutched her hips and pounded into her. Just when she
thought she couldn't stand anymore, he stopped and pushed his
thumb into her tight bottom hole, filling her completely.

She burst apart, giving herself over to the flood of ecstasy en-
wrapping her, and then she felt him empty his seed in long pulsing
throbs. The guttural groan that tore from his lips sounded like a
cry of pain.

He held her tight for long moments afterwards, her bottom
snug against his groin and his lips buried in her hair. Perched on
all fours as she was with him covering her, she felt oddly at one
with nature as though their act of love blended with the beauty
surrounding them.

Too soon he lifted her to standing and turned her to face him.

His expression was somber as he bent slowly, reverently, and
pressed his lips to hers. He lingered, his breath warm on her skin,
his scent of leather and rain filling her pores as he brushed gently
along her lips. He drew back, his eyes clouded with sorrow.

In that instant, she knew what he had planned.

"No." She grabbed onto the corded rope circling his waist.
"You're coming *with* me."

He unwrapped her fingers and dropped her hands roughly, stepping away. "Go," he growled and leaped up onto a boulder at his back. She scurried forward, trying to reach him, her arms flailing. "No," she choked, tears stinging her eyes.

"Go," he hissed. "Go home!"

Then he was gone. She watched as his dark mane and the bronze glow of his skin peeked through the trees while he traveled up and away from her, making his way so fast that he seemed a fleeting aberration until he finally disappeared.

She was too stunned to move.

The air left her lungs and all feeling drained from her body. She stood like a stone, looking in the direction he had gone, unable to believe that he'd left her.

But while he hadn't contradicted her when she explained how it would be, he also had never agreed with her and a small part of her knew this could happen.

Was she never to see him again? The thought seemed impossible. She could never go back to the way things were, not after what they'd shared. Once she was safely home, she'd find a way for them to be together.

But then she thought about how easily he had just left her. It broke her heart to think she'd meant so little to him that he could leave her without saying goodbye.

꧁༺✧༻꧂

"What do you mean, you can't take us to him?" Professor Cahill balked incredulously, taking off his gold-rimmed glasses and pinching his nose for the umpteenth time. "Okay." He shoved his glasses back on and dug one hand into his scalp. "You were with him for one month. He must have formed some connection with you. Right?"

Her face burned at how connected they had been.

"I see." He ducked his head and began pacing. "Maybe he'll come for you."

"He won't," she said forlornly. "I tried to get him to come with me, begged him."

"Yes, well." The professor cleared his throat and dragged his glasses off again. He wiped an arm across his forehead. "I guess it depends on how . . . connected you were, doesn't it?" He plopped down onto the rock next to her. "I mean, a man like that, isolated for so long happens upon a young woman . . . and one that looks like you, well . . ."

"Looks like *me*?" She stared at him. "I'm hardly a double for Marilyn Monroe."

"So?" He frowned and slapped his knees as he stood. "That's it. We wait. He won't be able to stay away from you for long. And when he comes for you, the trap will be set."

"Trap?" She jumped up.

"Metaphorically speaking of course." He looked uncomfortable. "We know he doesn't want to re-enter society, yet we know that's what he needs. So, in a sense it is a trap, but a humane one." He took her hand and gave it a fatherly pat. "He'll thank us one day, believe me, no matter what his initial reaction."

⁂

Georgie had tried to warn Mark of the professor's trap, but had failed miserably and now Mark, or Marcus Richard Steadman as he was believed to be, was literally in chains in a tent, by order of the Tribal Chief.

From the time Georgie had returned, the local agents had lied, the top government officials hedged, and the University apologized while Georgie's parents, locked out of the country, threatened to sue everyone. Upon Mark's capture, his parents had been found and they, too, were kept from him. Now Georgie was under house arrest—in this case, grass hut arrest—until everything was sorted out.

For two tortuous weeks she had worried that he would come to her at the same time that she yearned for him to. Then when he didn't, she cursed him bitterly, bemoaning how callously he had left her while her heart had ached for him every minute. Meanwhile, her parents petitioned the government, the embassy, and the University for her release, but no one was sending her anywhere, not while she purportedly knew the whereabouts of the legendary beast and was telling them nothing.

In order to pressure her to give up information, the University had vowed to protect him and the government promised to turn him over to his mother country after they questioned him, but Georgie trusted no one. Not even her esteemed professor.

While he waited to trap Mark, he had hounded her relentlessly for details of Mark's life and how he had responded when they first met, but Georgie feared the professor wasn't interested in

Mark as a human being as much as for his potential to make the professor famous. He was not happy that Georgie refused to tell him anymore than the government which amounted to zero.

And then Mark *had* come for her, just as the professor had predicted.

She had managed to slip away again to one of her many hiding places, as she had done all week, hoping to warn Mark should he come for her. What she didn't know was that she was being closely followed the entire time. On that day, Mark had been lying in wait and caught her.

"Mark!" She hadn't know whether to warn him about a possible trap now that he had finally come or to hug him tight to her and never let him go.

He swung her into his arms and carried her over to a soft bed of moss. "Make love," he growled, slipping a hand under her skirt.

"No," she gasped, tugging at his warm palm as he cupped her mound. "Oh," she strangled a moan. "I don't mean no exactly, but we can't do this now. Mark, listen to me."

Instead he knelt back on his heels and lifted a leather pack from off his back. He opened it to reveal its contents. Included among one gun and other valuables were the little blue coveralls and the Pig Will book.

He cupped her chin. "I go home with you." His eyes filled with warmth.

At first she was too stunned to respond, hoping it was really true that he was leaving the only home he knew to be with her. That he could leave his animal friends whom he trusted and amongst whom he had grown into the strong man that he was and enter a life of which he remembered nothing hardly seemed possible. But why else would he have brought the small treasures that linked him to his past if not to come back to civilization with her, to his human family that awaited?

At that moment she realized how much he must love her and how unworthy she was of his sacrifice.

She choked back a sob.

And then all hell broke loose.

Mark was lassoed and chained, his leather pack swooped up by the guards, while she was muzzled behind him and dragged away before he could see what was happening. While they kept her tied and gagged to a tree in the bushes, she watched him fight and claw against the band of men who struggled to shackle his arms and legs, while his eyes searched for her, but she had disappeared.

He had sensed betrayal, his eyes shone with it, and the raw emotion in his face haunted her then as it continued to torture her now.

But Georgie couldn't have known, as she did now, that the villagers, eager for the reward money, were laying in wait for him to come to her.

Now, he must think she had abandoned him, maybe even tricked him and was responsible for turning him over to the villagers before fleeing.

She had to get to him now and tell him that she hadn't betrayed him, that she loved him, and that she'd never hurt him.

Although in some ways, she had, by not staying with him but instead forcing him to come to her. She hadn't been willing to sacrifice her life to stay with him as he had been willing to do for her.

She kicked at the wooden tray of food and sent it flying across the hut. The guard peeked in, poking his rifle through the low arch that served as the front entrance. He lifted the curtain aside with the barrel and grunted when he saw the mess she'd made. "You eat. You too skinny, anyhow. Legs look like chicken."

"Shut up, you stubby little weasel."

He grinned wide, the gold on what teeth he had left glistening in the sun. He stepped into the hut, hitched his jean shorts higher, and then patted his protruding gut. "No stubby. Big and strong."

She snorted. He was five feet two if he was lucky. But she was getting nowhere with him. If she planned on getting to Mark, she had better try a new strategy. Nearly three full days had passed since he'd been captured.

While the tribal elders fought with the local officials, guarding their catch until they saw the money, the rest of the villagers regarded their prize with eager curiosity and gave Mark no privacy, but at least they weren't hurting him. A few times a day they took him out to walk and stretch, albeit in his chains and other roped restraints. Mark looked so big next to this small tribe of people, truly fierce. She understood their fascination with him and their fear. But so far, he had not been alone.

At night when the tent was illumined with a lantern, she could see that he was fed, although still tied. An older woman performed this duty, the same woman who washed his face with care and readied his bed at night. Still, Mark was never alone.

The professor was no better than the villagers.

He hounded Mark, bombarding him with questions and then mystified when Mark wouldn't answer him. When the professor complained to Georgie, he was then furious with her because she wouldn't help him either and leveled veiled threats at her about needing his internship to graduate.

Georgie wanted to scream with frustration. If she openly attempted to go to him they would banish her to the other end of the village, and she might never have a chance to get to him. So she waited for him to be alone at night, so she could slip out while the guards slept and talk to him. But now she watched as another group of young girls passed by, giggling and whispering, heading toward Mark's tent.

This had been going on since yesterday. And they grew bolder today. They flirted and cajoled the guards, distracting them at their posts while each girl took her turn slipping into Mark's tent. Georgie burned to know what they did in there. Her only consolation was that the taboo against losing your virginity before marriage was very strong in this tribe to the point where a girl could ruin her chances of ever marrying. She took comfort in the knowledge that they were innocents and probably just curious about the legendary Wild Man.

She watched the young girls now. One dangled across the lap of a young guard near the tent entrance. He was slipping his hand up her thigh and she was swatting him playfully, but ineffectually. It seemed his hand slipped up farther each time. Georgie frowned. Perhaps not so innocent after all.

Another girl leaned against a thick oak tree while another guard pressed her against the trunk with his hand . . . digging in her neckline? He was squeezing one breast and grinning stupidly. The girl hardly looked shocked.

Georgie wanted to scream out, sure now that they were experimenting with Mark, too, but if she did, they'd move her farther from his tent.

She gritted her teeth. Would no one let Mark alone? She needed to call to him. Let him know that she was captive, too, and that she loved him, and that somehow they needed to make it out of here together. *Especially since he was being regularly entertained by the girls of the village.*

⁂

"Let's make a deal, Professor." Georgie leaned forward slyly. "For every question I answer about Mark, you answer one for me."

His eyes lit up. "Deal. What do you want to know?"

"Okay," she said. "For starters, I want to know what the parade of girls are doing in his tent?"

When darkness had descended last night, the train of young girls blessedly stopped, but then grown women, *married* women, took up the slack, each one slipping the guards some bribe to get in Mark's tent. Just when the two guarding his entrance would nod off in sleep, and there was a lull in traffic, another woman would show up.

They couldn't be doing what she thought, could they? If the guards outside had not been talking and laughing the whole time, she might have been able to hear.

Professor Cahill cleared his throat. "I think it's pretty obvious what the girls are visiting him for. Of course, I can't be sure, but I don't think it's hard to figure out."

"What about your stupid lecture on the power of taboos in a small village?" Georgie snapped. "They're virgins, remember?"

"Well, yes, but there are *virgins* and then there are *virgins.*"

"What in the world does that mean?"

The professor puffed up. "That's the best I can do—"

"Well it's pitiful. And you'll get the same from me unless you find out."

Georgie almost wished she hadn't given the professor hope that she would cooperate if he helped her, because the result was two sizeable mirrors rigged up in a tree in back of her hut, one that angled toward Mark's side window, with the other at a right angle to it so it reflected what the first mirror caught. And it caught plenty.

At first she was just so happy to see his face. Although his hair was unrestrained, giving him that Wildman look that the villagers must have loved, he was clean and seemed comfortable resting against a large cushioned mat. His restraints were not pulled so tight that he didn't have some freedom of movement. And the older woman who tended him even smiled as she fed and cared for him.

Now and then the professor or the chief would come in and talk to him, but Mark's face always turned to stone during these times, and he refused to even acknowledge them. While the tribal chief railed at him to tell him how many people he had killed, the professor spoke to him in the simplest English and very slowly as one would to a child.

Mark ignored them both, although Georgie could tell that he understood most of what was said.

It was only when the young girls came for their little visits that Mark perked up.

It broke her heart to see the eagerness with which he responded to them. But she had no one to blame but herself.

Mark had loved her enough to let her leave, and she was too self-centered to realize just how hard that must have been for him. Instead she had screamed that she hated him.

And now he thought she had betrayed him.

Why wouldn't he turn to these lovely young girls for comfort?

For the first time Georgie realized just how much she had lost. And it terrified her that she might have lost him for good.

Chapter Seven

Mark's latest young guest dropped down before him, all shyness and innocence, her long black lashes fluttering and her pert breasts thrust high. She gazed at him with adoring eyes. No wonder in all these days he hadn't once attempted an escape.

Georgie gritted her teeth as she watched the girl coyly toy with her dress strap, letting it slip off her shoulder until her bodice trim hung enticingly off her nipple.

Mark's eyes, level with her breasts, lit up.

Georgie's heart sank.

When the girl nudged closer, Mark stripped her to the waist and cradled her dark golden breasts. Why didn't his stupid captors shorten the chains of his restraints? He suckled her greedily, going from one breast to the next, as though he couldn't get enough of her, causing her to moan and writhe. Within minutes his hands were exploring under her skirt. The girl's gasps of pleasure infuriated Georgie, but not as much as when he tossed up her skirt and licked between her legs. The girl collapsed onto her back, her legs spread before Mark while he anchored his hands onto her hips and continued to torture her.

Georgie forgot her fury for a minute, fascinated with the rosy flush to the girl's breasts and the way her nipples tightened to sharp points until she came with a shuddering groan. Georgie was breathless.

Mark lifted his face and stroked soothingly along her inner thighs. He slipped his finger between her wet folds and then drew it out and licked it.

Georgie's jaw clenched so hard she thought her teeth would

snap. Tonight, come hell or high water, she'd get a message to him. He had to know she was here and that . . . she loved him and *they* were meant to be together, before it was too late.

She sank down onto the dirt floor of her hut and sighed in frustration.

How could she blame him for taking what pleasures were offered? She had abandoned him, or so he thought, forgotten him.

She choked back tears. Nothing was working out as it should. Where were the officials who would return him to his country? Georgie bent her head between her knees and ran her fingers through her scalp, clear down to the tips of her tangled curls. She couldn't blame Mark for being human . . . for being a man.

She rose gingerly and looked out her window again to see him reflected in the mirrors, eyes closed and neck thrown back, the corded muscles pulled tight. His friend's face was buried in his lap now and for a virgin she was doing pretty well.

He was thrusting his hips up and holding the girl's head, his fingers buried in her tight curls and groaning.

Georgie groaned herself at the look of the girls wet lips running the length of him, her tongue circling playfully along balls pulled up tight in arousal.

A thunderous roar broke their concentration and made them look toward the hut entrance. Georgie wondered what they saw.

The girl scurried around behind Mark, clutching him, her head peering above his shoulder as Mark sat there fully erect and wet from her mouth. The girl's eyes widened in fright. Mark blinked nervously.

A man loomed before them, shouting words that Georgie didn't understand. Behind Mark, the girl was arighting her dress. The man came around and grabbed her by the arm, dragging her to him. She looked as though she were pleading for mercy. Her father? Older brother? Georgie heard her call him the tribal word for Uncle.

The next moment Georgie watched in shock as the uncle dropped to a seat and draped the girl over his knee. He tossed up her skirt, yanked down her panties, and spanked her in full view of Mark and now Georgie.

Mark's eyes blinked wide and his subsiding erection returned full force. Georgie groaned at her own arousal at the wicked sight. What was wrong with her that she found it so stimulating?

She felt her sex grow heavy and full. Her skin flushed with warmth.

Apparently, she and Mark weren't the only ones who found it arousing. The girl's cries turned suspiciously to moans the redder her rounded bottom grew. The uncle paused to smooth his palm over the delicate curves before spanking her again with zeal.

Georgie shouldn't look, but she couldn't take her eyes off the licentious scene. And what about Mark? He was riveted.

The uncle interrupted his spanking to slide his hand between her mounds. He dipped one finger between her lips and then slid the finger up to play with her bottom hole. The girl wriggled beneath him, no longer even trying to escape. Georgie watched with curiosity. Mark leaned forward. The uncle slid the wet finger around the tiny opening, probing gently, and then sunk deep. Georgie sucked in a breath. The uncle thrust with his long finger, slowly at first and then faster. Georgie thought she would expire. She didn't know this was done. Mark looked as surprised as she and he was fully erect.

But it was what happened next that sent her beyond shock.

The uncle lifted her up and placed her on all fours, tilting her bottom up to him and then he shoved his pants down and stroked her backside with his erect penis. He slipped between her globes and probed. Georgie's breath stopped. He plunged between her bottom and the girl groaned deep and shuddered. It was obvious she was no virgin to this practice.

A few pumps and the uncle was growling out his release.

Mark fell back against the propped pillows and swallowed. His own release followed. Georgie watched, mesmerized, as he closed his eyes and then exploded into the air in powerful jets, his strong body shuddering with each pump. Her own body went liquid with desire.

Georgie dissolved onto the grass mat beside her and sobbed.

※※(♡♡)※※

On the fifth day, Georgie didn't have to wonder what that little suck-up, Kristy, was doing heading towards Mark's tent.

When the professor stomped out of her hut earlier today for the umpteenth time this week, Georgie figured he had given up, which was smart since Georgie had no intention of telling him a thing. She'd gotten her information and wanted to know nothing more. She'd already regretted knowing what she knew. Not even the professor's guarantee that she'd fail her internship and not graduate if she didn't cooperate got her attention.

So, it looked now that he'd found another route to Mark. Tall, lithe Kristy, with breasts the size of overgrown cantaloupes. Georgie wanted to rip every last red hair out of her head, with tweezers, one by one.

Even the guards at the entrance went bug eyed when she showed up at midnight, sheer dress clinging to every curve, her nipples tight and clearly outlined against the silky cloth. Her braless breasts swayed and bounced as she sauntered up to them. She didn't have to offer a bribe. Just bending low and asking politely to enter Mark's tent got her what she wanted and got the guards a full view of her cleavage. She hugged herself, feigning chill, puckering the fabric so they could look down her dress and ogle her nipples.

Georgie sneered in disgust. What some people wouldn't do to get ahead. Professor Cahill's star student was no doubt expecting a nice fellowship to result from her . . . cooperation.

Georgie groaned in dismay as Kristy ducked into his tent. Please Mark, don't play into her game. Pay no attention to her or her obscene breasts. Georgie knew Kristy intended on exploiting Mark for her own gain. She couldn't love him like Georgie did.

Georgie went to the back of her hut and studied the mirror. She could only see Mark. He scowled mildly. Maybe he knew Kristy was connected with Professor Cahill. Good, he wouldn't give her a thing.

Before long Kristy dropped to her knees and joined him on the cushions. He still eyed her warily, so different from the way he treated the village girls, as though he knew the girls were innocently experimenting, whereas with Kristy he sensed something different. Georgie should have realized he'd trust his instincts on this one. Kristy twirled a lazy finger through his hair and was talking to him softly, too low for Georgie to hear, but the look on her face told Georgie the message was seductive. Georgie was relieved to see that Mark kept silent.

More than a little piqued, Kristy frowned and then rose to her knees. She knelt before him and in one quick sweep slipped her dress to her waist. Her melon-shaped breasts came bouncing out.

Mark's mouth dropped. Kristy giggled at his response while he sat there stupefied, his eyes locked onto her monstrous boobs. Don't fall for it, Mark, Georgie soundlessly pleaded.

He buried his face in her cleavage.

She groaned in frustration. Men! They were so weak.

Chapter Eight

Georgie laid on her bed and stared up at the ceiling in her room, exhausted, the newspaper dropped onto the carpet beside her, and sure that she had no more tears left to shed.

A light knock sounded on her bedroom door.

"Honey, are you all right?" Her mother's soft voice threatened another eruption of tears. "Can I come in?"

Georgie wiped her eyes with the back of her hands and propped herself on her elbows. "Come in, Mom."

Her mother slipped through the door and set a silver tray of cocoa and sugar cookies on her bedside table.

"I thought these might make you feel better," her mother said.

Georgie knew her mother was only trying to help, but the only thing that would make Georgie feel better was being wrapped in Mark's powerful arms. But her mother had been wonderful since her return, so Georgie simply thanked her.

Spotting the abandoned newspaper, her mother picked it up. "So, this is him," her mother murmured. "He's certainly a handsome young man."

Georgie shrugged. "Maybe. But more important, look how gullible he is. I can't believe he would make such a spectacle of himself, trapezing around with that . . . slut, Kristy."

"But you said he's been kept in hiding. No one is allowed near him, including reporters."

"Well, apparently, *she's* allowed near him. The professor's pet. From the looks of her draping her arm through his, they've been around each other plenty."

"Says here, he's recently emerged from his seclusion—"

"But with *her*, Mom. Don't you get it?" Georgie accepted the cocoa her mother offered and took a comforting sip. "I just don't understand how he can't see through her. Why, even the university can't be trusted to consider his best interests. They just see him as a means to more grants." Georgie sighed in frustration. "Why aren't his parents *protecting* him?"

"I'm sure they are, honey."

"Protecting him from *me*, you mean."

It had been eight months, eight long torturous months, and not one word from him. The authorities had spirited him out of the village during the night, drugging the guards while the rest of the village slept, and whisking him safely to the embassy where he was flown immediately to Chicago, his home. He had never even known Georgie was in a hut close by. The next day, they came for her.

Her first month back home she had tried every way conceivable to see him, talk to him. She had no way of knowing if he knew. The team responsible for his re-entry into society chanted the same refrain each time she tried. "His parents have given strict orders that he is to have no contact with anyone until they deem him ready. They'll call when that happens."

But it had been eight months now, and then she saw that awful picture in the newspaper. He was dressed in a tux, his hair still long but stylishly restrained, making him look primitively male in his crisp white shirt. And Kristy's dress was tighter than ever. They were attending a fundraiser for the University of Chicago. Georgie bet Kristy wheedled a fellowship out of them in exchange for bringing Mark.

Her mother smoothed a tangle of hair from off Georgie's cheek. "That reporter called again. The one from the Enquirer."

Georgie growled and swung her legs over the side of the bed. "Don't those guys ever give up?" She grabbed her jeans off the bedpost and shoved her legs in. When she zipped them, she was relieved to feel them finally fit. Most of the bony angles of her body had smoothed back into curves under the watchful eye of the family cook.

"They've upped their offer," Georgie's mother said, eyeing her closely. "They're up to two million."

"I don't care if it's two billion, Mom, they're not getting a word out of me. I would never exploit him like that."

Her mother turned to the serving tray. "Well, I just thought you might have reconsidered," she murmured, as she poured herself chocolate from the carafe, "since the University rejected your final appeal and sided with Professor Cahill about not graduating you this semester."

"I can pick up the final 12 credits in the next semester . . . or two."

"Of course you can, honey." Her mother gave her a small smile and blew gently on her cocoa.

Georgie slumped down onto the bed.

Her mother laid a gentle hand on Georgie's shoulder. "What is it, honey?"

Georgie fought back tears. "The truth is, Mom, I love him. But it's time I face the fact that he doesn't love me."

"You don't know that until you talk to him—"

"He doesn't want to see me. And he's had plenty of opportunity. Sometimes I think I love him so much that I would do anything to get him back. But then I see how happy he looks in that photo, and I remind myself that he's made no attempt to contact me despite all my efforts and I realize . . . that whatever our time together meant to me, that it didn't mean the same to him."

Georgie pulled herself to her feet and walked over to her dresser mirror. Her mother came up behind her and placed her hands on her shoulders. She covered her mother's hands with hers. "It's possible, Mom, that he wants to put his past behind him so he can successfully adapt to his new life. If I really love him, I'll let him do that. Even if it means losing him forever."

Her mother turned Georgie into her arms. "Maybe he just needs some time, honey, to realize what he really wants." Her mother stroked a gentle hand down her back.

"I don't know, Mom. But I've got to stop this incessant crying over him. It's time that I grew up."

Chapter Nine

Mark wiped his brow. *Jesus, he was nervous.*

The long winding drive off the main road to Georgie's parents' shore house was interminable and yet not long enough. He ached to see her, but still hadn't figured out what to say, despite having gone over and over it in his head.

He had learned she was raised in wealth, been educated in the best schools, and that her family occupied a place within the highest social strata of New York Society and had for generations.

Mark ran a finger under his neck collar and tugged. He had nothing to offer her. While his parents, both college professors, promised to do everything to catch him up after a lifetime of isolation, it would still be years before he finished his formal education. In any career he'd be pathetically behind his peers and as far as social graces went, hell, he didn't think he'd ever fit into high society.

He should tell the driver to turn right around. What made him think she even wanted him? While his parents and the team they'd hired had been bombarded with calls and letters when he first emerged from the jungle, all requests were dismissed and no records kept. They had no way of knowing at the time how important Georgie was to him. He made himself believe that she had tried and failed to contact him from the moment they were separated. But now he wasn't so sure.

Then he remembered her total abandon with him in the jungle. He was behind in his experience with women, too, but he'd still bet Georgie had never given herself to anyone the way she had with him.

His jaw tightened. For the first time he thought of the possibility that she could be with another man. He ground his teeth. If that were the case . . . they'd just see how long *that* lasted.

The limo driver hit a small rut in the sandy road. Up ahead a large weathered cedar house with white shutters perched high, overlooking the ocean. Its large wraparound porch faced the side lawn and drive.

He reached instinctively and touched the driver's shoulder and asked him to stop.

Georgie was rocking in a large wicker chair, one leg draped over its arm, a sandal dangling from her foot. He watched as she ran an idle hand through her honey colored curls. He wanted to feel those curls sift through his fingers.

"Shall I leave you here, Sir? Maybe you'd like to walk the rest of the way?"

Mark glanced at the driver. If he was seventy, he was young. Mark wondered if he'd been with the family since Georgie was little.

It had surprised Mark when he had called Georgie's house and her mother had been so accommodating. While the entire world knew *of* him, Georgie's mother would have grilled her daughter about what happened between them during that long month in the jungle. He just hoped Georgie hadn't told her *everything*.

He was surprised when she offered to send a car to Kennedy Airport to pick him up and take him to Georgie. He shrugged. Apparently, Georgie *hadn't* told her everything.

He looked at the chauffeur. "What do you think I should do, Denton?"

The man turned to look at him fully and smiled. "No one ever knows what to do where Georgie is concerned." He gave a chuckle. "But why don't you go on up by yourself from here."

Mark sighed and then nodded. "Well, here goes."

"Good luck, lad."

Mark closed the door of the limo and brushed down the crease in his khakis. He undid his white button-down shirt to the second opening to give himself some air and rolled the sleeves up his forearms. Then he laughed. Preparing to wrestle a tiger was easier than this.

Then he envisioned wrestling his fierce tigress to the grass and he found himself smiling.

He hiked around the corner and then advanced up the hill. Before he reached the top, he heard the car engine start and then saw it head back down the hill. Georgie heard it too, because she had risen, and with her hand shielding her eyes from the sun, watched the family chauffer back down the drive.

He was no more than 50 feet away when she turned and spotted him. He stopped in his tracks. Her eyes clouded in confusion and then she sprang off the porch, kicking off her shoes, and dashed toward him. Her long hair blew out behind her and her sundress clung to her as she ran.

His heart turned over at her happiness at seeing him. "Mark," she cried, half-laughing and half-crying, and running like the wind. Then she jumped into his arms. The sweet scent of her skin washed over him, so familiar and comforting.

He held her so close he thought he'd snap her slender frame.

She buried her lips in his neck. "Oh my God. I can't believe it's you. I've missed you so much." She sobbed hard, clutching him to her. "I can't believe you're really here."

He was speechless, so filled with love for her and desire that he could barely breathe.

She pulled back and cupped his face in her palms and rained kisses all over him. "They wouldn't let me see you or talk to you." She stroked along his jaw. "Did they hurt you?" She stepped back and took in his full length. "God, you are so beautiful." She flew back into his arms. "I was terrified that I'd never see you again," she moaned, wrapping her arms around his neck.

She thinks I'm beautiful.

"I was so afraid you didn't want to see me ever again. That you'd left your old life behind and me with it." She hugged him close and brushed her mouth along his jaw.

How could she think he'd never want to see her again?

"Mark?" She stopped abruptly and looked into his face. "Say something."

He swallowed. He hadn't expected this. He should just cut to the chase and tell her that he loved her.

"What have they done to you?"

Done to me? He blinked.

Her eyes narrowed. "It was that slut, Kristy, who did this to you, wasn't it?"

Kristy? He raised both brows. *This could get interesting.*

"You were speaking in sentences in the jungle, maybe not complex sentences, but you could communicate." She grabbed both his hands and clutched them to her heart, her eyes filled with sympathy. The next instant she was pounding his chest. "How could you be so stupid to not have seen past those watermelon breasts."

He smothered a laugh.

She pushed at him. "Oh, I could scream." She whirled away and ran a frustrated hand through the crown of her soft curls. The sundress she wore billowed in the breeze around her shapely legs. *He didn't feel like talking anyway.*

Then she drew up close and wrapped her arms around his neck. "I'm sorry, Mark." She stroked his cheek. "I don't know what's happened, but none of it matters now." She choked on a sob. "We'll go back to the jungle and start all over again. And we won't leave until you're ready, no matter how long it takes." Her eyes filled with tears.

She was willing to live in the jungle for him? Indefinitely?

"We were doing so well together, Mark. We were both learning things everyday, together. We can do that again. I promise. And I'll never leave you, no matter what."

He was dumfounded and so filled with emotion he was paralyzed to respond. She had to be in love with him. There was no explanation for what she promised, other than that she loved him.

"Just give me a nod." She traced her finger along his lips. "To show me you understand even just a little."

He nodded. And then before he could form a sentence, she pressed herself against him.

He filled with arousal and grabbed her waist. A deep growl rose up from his throat.

She gave him a sultry smile. "I'll make you forget Kristy."

Why would she think he'd be interested in Kristy? Then he thought of the photo Kristy had grabbed with him before he could shrug out of her grasp while he was on the steps of the university.

Georgie stood on tip-toes and pressed her lips to his. He groaned and exploded with an urgency suppressed too long and just waiting to be released when he saw her again. He delved into the soft recesses of her mouth and plundered her, tasting her with a hunger that bordered on painful.

They collapsed together onto the soft bed of grass and he covered her, laying himself along her length. She yielded to him, offering herself with little groans and whimpers. "Oh God. I've waited so long for you to hold me again. I love you, Mark. I love you so much."

He stilled, now too *stunned* to speak.

She drew his face up. "I know you don't understand me, yet,

but soon you will." She kissed him with agonizing sweetness. "I want you inside me, now."

He plucked her buttons open and bared her to his eyes. He swelled full and hard. He'd never be able to get enough of her. She was so smooth against his rough hands as he lifted her breasts to his lips. He licked hungrily along the soft swells, taking special care to taste her swollen nipples, so large and ripe looking against the smallness of her breasts, the contrast so powerfully erotic. He had dreamed about these nipples for long months.

"I wish you could talk to me," she sighed, arching to his lips. "Anything. Even just my name."

She was going to kill him when she discovered he could talk. He'd keep her delirious. He suckled her with enthusiasm, feeling his own groin throb in response to her soft contented moans. He forced himself to slow down despite his driving need to take her, hard and fast and completely.

"I shouldn't have worried about Kristy," she purred, yielding to his lips and giving him greater access to her breasts. He slid his hand up her thigh and slipped his fingers under the elastic of her panties. "Oh . . ." Her breath came out in a whoosh. He met with delicious wet warmth when he slid two fingers up through her. She moaned in his ear and raised her knees up, sighing with pleasure. "It's obvious you couldn't have liked those huge D-cup breasts bouncing around, anyway."

He bit her nipples. "Actually," he murmured, "they were more like double-D's."

She gasped. "What?" She slapped his back.

"I said they were more like—"

"I heard you . . . you, you—" She gave him a furious push, struggling mightily against his heavy bulk. He accommodated her temper tantrum by tumbling off her and onto his back. He suppressed a chuckle. Life would never be dull with Georgie.

She kneeled beside him and railed at him. "How could you let me go on like that?" She punched his chest. "Oh, I could just—"

He plucked her up and brought her down on top of him. "I've missed you," he whispered. He slid his hand up her skirt and over her bottom, stroking the warm smooth curves, rewarded by her soft moans. "And I love you."

Her breath caught. "You love me?" She propped her hands on his chest and her eyes widened in wonder.

"Yes," he said, his voice husky. "I love you, Georgie."

"Oh, Mark." She collapsed against his chest. "I was so worried. But I kept hoping, so sure that we were meant to be together."

"Georgie, look at me." He lifted her up to face him. "You have to understand something. I have nothing to offer you."

"What do you mean? You said you loved me?"

"I do. And I always will. But look at me. My life has only just begun. It'll be years before I catch up. If I ever do."

She cradled his face. "None of that matters, Mark. We have a whole lifetime to catch up. We can do it together." She looked sheepish. "Besides,"—she gave him a small grin—"you don't really know how behind *I* am, and that you're the one who helped me to grow up. If it weren't for you I wouldn't have realized what's really important. I would still be the spoiled little rich girl that you met."

"Georgie . . ." He stroked along her cheek.

"So you see, Mark, we need each other."

He nodded. "I see." He kissed her tenderly. "I love you, Georgie."

"And I love you."

"I need you now," he breathed. He unzipped his pants and shoved them down over his hips. His penis came springing out as she straddled him.

With one good yank, he ripped the delicate lace between her legs in half.

"Oh my God, Mark."

His penis slipped around her wet swollen folds, torturing him, until he found heaven and slipped in deep.

She shuddered on a long moan. "My God, how could I have forgotten what a wild man you are," she groaned and rode him thrust for thrust. "This is one thing you have to promise will never change."

He thrust up hard and held her hips. Then he gave her a teasing smile. "If you don't stop talking, I'll have to tie you up."

"You wouldn't!"

"Strip off that dress."

Her eyes shone as she lifted her dress over her head and tossed it onto the grass. She sat astride him, fully impaled and naked and beautiful. He fought back the punishing release that threatened to overtake him.

"It's a good thing you've decided to listen to me, because if you don't, I'll have to spa—"

"Mark!" She slapped at him.

He chuckled and then thrust up hard several more times until she tightened around him and then cried out his name. He felt her explode all around him. He followed moments later with his own thunderous release.

Then he held her in a tender embrace he intended never to end.

About the Author:

Kathryn Anne Dubois lives the demanding life of a mother of five, wife of 30+ years, and a public school art teacher. What better reason to escape into the delicious fantasy world of writing erotic romance.

Visit Kathryn's website at www.KathrynAnneDubois.com.

Wanted

✿❀✿

by Kimberly Dean

To My Reader:
The thrill of the chase awaits. Enjoy!

Chapter One

The blue sedan was still there.

Danielle glanced nervously at the lights in her rearview mirror. It was two car lengths back, seemingly inconspicuous, but still . . .

"Damn it, Reno," she whispered. Her hunger disappeared, and she stuffed her Twix bar into its wrapper. Without looking, she tossed the chocolate bar onto the passenger seat.

Taking a deep breath, she tried to settle her nerves. If he wanted to get caught up in a high-speed chase, she'd be happy to oblige him. Of course, the rattletrap she was driving couldn't do more than sixty. No doubt, he had a high-powered engine concealed under the modest exterior of that car. Still, she wouldn't give up easily. He should know that by now.

Her gaze flicked again towards the mirror. The car had moved over one lane.

"Clever," she muttered. "You're trying to confuse me, make me doubt myself. Well, it's not working, Bub."

She knew that most of the world would consider her paranoid, but it wasn't paranoia if somebody really was chasing you. Over the past months, she'd learned to trust her instincts. And right now, they were screaming that it was no coincidence that the blue sedan had kept pace with her for the past ten miles.

"You're smart, Reno. I'll give you that."

He'd kept her on her toes for months now. He was always out there, somewhere, watching in the shadows, waiting to make his move.

The blue car suddenly signaled and took the off-ramp. Danielle was so surprised, she blinked twice to make sure she wasn't seeing things. Finally, she gave a sigh of relief.

"You are paranoid, you twit." Shaking her head, she reached for her candy bar. She bit off a piece of chocolate and tried to slow her racing heart. "You're paranoid, and you're tired."

She eased up on the accelerator and glanced down at the dash.

"Oh, good heavens. Some high-speed chase that would have been." She was nearly out of gas. With luck, she might have barely enough fumes to get to the next town.

"Dani, Dani, Dani. You know better than that. Always keep your tank full of gas. Always." Tiredly, she rubbed a hand across her forehead. A stupid mistake like that could cost her everything.

Shaking her head, she began to watch the passing highway signs. It was getting late, and it was time to find someplace to hole up for the night. Suddenly overwhelmed by exhaustion, she leaned her head back against the headrest.

"Well, you've made it through another day on the FBI Most Wanted list without getting caught," she congratulated herself.

A grim smile pulled at her lips. So far, she'd managed to elude Special Agent Jeff Reno. For half a year, he'd been on her trail and, for half a year, she'd been able to slip out of his reach just when he thought he had her.

That had to piss him off to no end.

"Serves him right," she said.

Sometimes, she'd escaped by mere inches. She remembered the time that she'd been washing dishes at that rundown diner in Tuscaloosa. She'd been talking to the cook when he'd strode into the place looking all tall, dark, and delicious. For a solid minute, she'd been caught frozen as she'd stared at him. She'd only snapped out of it when Old Mabeline had stepped up to the counter to wait on him. The woman's wide form had allowed her to make a break for the door without him seeing.

Sometimes she wondered what he'd do if he caught her . . .

"Stop it," she told herself, even though she knew better.

These dangerous little fantasies about him were sneaking up on her more and more. She didn't know why out of all the agents in the Federal Bureau of Investigation, she'd had to get the one who could make her toes curl. It had been a sick twist of fate, but she had to deal with it. It was just getting harder every day. She found herself thinking of him at the most inopportune times. His dark eyes, his sleek brown hair, his yummy tight ass . . .

"I said 'Stop it!' "

She shoved another bite of chocolate into her mouth and began to gnaw on it. Jeff Reno might look like something that just stepped out of *GQ Magazine*, but he suspected her of committing a horrible crime.

Treason.

"I'm not a traitor! How many times do I have to tell you that?" she said out loud. The words echoed throughout the small car.

The mere thought that she might sell government secrets was ludicrous. Why would she jeopardize all her hard work like that?

Half a year ago, she'd had a great life. She'd had an awesome job as a computer programmer for a defense contractor. The project she'd been working on was top-secret, and she'd loved the challenge. She knew she didn't fit the usual computer nerd stereotype, but she'd been extremely good at what she did. Sometimes she thought that she understood computer code better than she understood English. After all the blood and sweat she'd put into that project, there was no way that she could have sold it for her own gain.

It would have been like selling her soul.

But somebody had sold out—and Reno suspected her.

Damn his cute, tight ass! Because of him, she no longer had her awesome job. Because of him, she was on the run to avoid treason charges. She no longer had a home, and she hadn't seen her family and friends for months. Sometimes, she didn't even know where she was going to get her next meal.

She took another harsh bite out of the candy bar and noticed her fingernails. They were totally unrecognizable as the perfectly manicured set she'd had before she'd gone on the lam. Her gaze dropped from her fingers to the steering wheel and she remembered her Corvette. She'd been forced to sell it at a used car dealership for cash.

"That's something I'll never forgive you for," she said with an edge to her voice. "I don't care how tight your ass is."

The exit came upon her suddenly, and she had to pull hard on the wheel of the little two-door to make the off-ramp. The sign read Conrad, Population 16,201. It would have to do.

Driving slowly down Main Street, Dani considered her options. Her mind went to the meager supply of money in her purse. She had enough for a motel, but it was time to get another job. Not only was her cash supply low, she also needed a new car. She'd been driving this junker for too long.

"By now, he probably knows not only the make, model, and license plate number, but also the fact that it pulls to the left." She didn't know where he got his information, but it was uncanny what that man knew.

A flashing, pink neon sign caught her eye, and she turned into the parking lot of the Waterbury Inn. The place looked cheap, but clean.

Would it be too much to hope for hot water?

She reached into the back seat and grabbed a brown wig and a pair of plain, metal-rimmed glasses before she headed to the registration desk. Twenty-three dollars later, she found herself in Room One with a nice view of the busy street.

Sighing, Danielle carefully set her laptop down on the table next to the window before tossing her bag onto the bed. Just once, she'd like to treat herself to a nice hotel. Just once. Muttering under her breath, she grabbed her toiletry bag and headed for the shower.

Special Agent Jeff Reno sat on the bed in his hotel room with his back propped up against the pillows. His hair was still wet from his shower, and he'd only bothered to put on his jeans. Taking another swig from his bottle of beer, he glared at his laptop.

"Come on, Dani," he growled. He was tired and ready to catch a few Z's.

She'd spotted him; he was sure of it. He'd kept his distance from her when they'd been on the road, but somehow, she'd noticed him. She was getting eerily good at knowing when he was near.

He could have caught her this time, but he hadn't wanted her to get hurt. She would have run and too many car chases ended in crashes.

He didn't want their little hide-and-seek game to end like that.

"Not after this long," he said as he wiped a droplet of water off the beer bottle. After all she'd put him through, it was going to have to be something special when he caught her—something very special indeed.

He trailed his thumb down the gentle curve of the dark bottle, but his thoughts were on softer, more rounded curves.

"Damn," he said as he ran a hand through his wet hair.

There were much better things to do with that body of hers than to wrap it around a tree. That was why he'd taken the exit into

Gilroy. It had killed him to let her out of his sight, but she'd taught him a modicum of patience over the past few months. Tomorrow would be soon enough to catch up with her. He could wait one more night.

"One long, never-ending night from the looks of it."

The bulge behind the zipper of his jeans was going to make sure of that. Hell, his dick was like a divining rod when it came to her. It acted like this whenever she was within a ten-mile radius.

"Damn it, where are you?" he barked. He inspected his instant messages again. It was past time that she checked in.

With a curse, he flopped back against the headboard and stared at the ceiling. He'd been trained on how to avoid personal involvement in cases, but he'd gotten into the habit of chatting with her at the end of every day. Now, he couldn't sleep if he didn't know she was safe for the night.

It was still strange how their cyber relationship had evolved. The first time she'd emailed him, he'd nearly fallen off his chair. It had been soon after her escape. He didn't know how she'd gotten his email address, but she'd sent a scathing message protesting her innocence. He'd had his technicians try to trace the connection, but she'd woven such a tangled, knotted web they hadn't been able to unravel it before she'd signed off.

Now, he knew better than to even try. She knew computers better than his entire staff combined. Instead, he'd started talking with her. One conversation had turned into two and then ten. Now they chatted daily. Although he told himself that he looked forward to their talks for professional reasons, inside he knew better.

"Come on, babe." He glanced at the clock on the bedside stand. She wasn't still driving, was she? God, he didn't want to get back on the road to follow her. Was she planning on driving through the night? If she were, that would put a lot of distance between them.

"No, she'll be stopping soon," he said, trying to convince himself. Dropping the tail had been an inspiration on his part. The action had gone against the grain. She'd never believe that he'd just give up and let her go. By now, the blue sedan was a distant memory.

"Her guard will be down. Tomorrow will be the day." He glanced down at his crotch. "It's got to be the day."

Tilting his head back, he gave another pull on the longneck. Hell. He was going to have to drink the rest of the six-pack to get rid of the hard-on he was nursing. Reaching down, he carefully adjusted himself into a more comfortable position inside his jeans.

This sucked. He was edgy, irritable, and horny as hell. For too long now, she'd been leading him around by the nose—or more aptly, by the dick. The problem was that although his brain knew that she was a fugitive from justice and it was his job to bring her in, his libido tended to forget. From the first moment he'd set eyes on her, he'd wanted the lady in his bed.

He could still remember that day. He and his partner, Charley Squires, had intercepted disturbing information that Quadrangle Computing's top-secret code was up for grabs on the black market. They'd had little time to act. Plans had rapidly been set into motion and, without giving notice, they'd walked in and closed the company down.

Phone service had been stopped, doors had been blockaded, and records had been seized. Combining their intelligence with the information they gathered on-site, they'd narrowed the trail down to one suspect—a Ms. Danielle Carver.

From that point, things had moved quickly. Reno closed his eyes and, suddenly, he was back in that moment.

"Bring this Carver woman in," he told her boss. "I want to question her."

The manager threw him a nervous look, but picked up the phone. When a blonde head popped up over the cubicle wall, Reno didn't pay much attention. As the woman started moving in the direction of the office, though, he began to watch more closely. When she finally came into full view, his entire body went on red alert.

"You've got to be kidding me," he said. He'd been suspecting somebody . . . geekier.

The short, balding man smiled knowingly. "Her IQ is probably twice yours," he replied smugly.

Reno's eyes narrowed. "*That* should be illegal."

Just watching the way she walked made his mouth water. She had a smooth, effortless gait that swiveled her hips in a manner that wasn't overtly sexual, but packed a punch nonetheless. When she entered the room, her understated perfume traveled across the air, and he broke out in a cold sweat.

He didn't like his reaction. He didn't like it one bit. The crimes he suspected her of committing were serious. The code she was writing was for the Air Force's newest fighter planes. If she planned to sell it, she was willing to jeopardize American lives.

He didn't care how hot she was—the entire idea left him cold. "Ms. Carver," he said icily. "Please take a seat." "What's this about?" she asked.

She settled into the chair in front of the desk and looked at him uneasily. Caught in the stare of those clear, startlingly blue eyes, he forgot what he'd been about to say.

All he could do was look at her.

She was wearing close-fitting jeans that showed off her shapely ass. The way they cupped her buttocks made the palms of his hands itch. Her hair was pulled up into one of those plastic clips. Some of the ends had slipped loose, and the mussed look made him ache.

He wanted to see her hair down. He wanted to touch it. He wanted to feel it brushing against his hips as she lowered her mouth to his dick.

"Damn," Reno breathed. He shifted restlessly on the bed as the vivid memory overtook him. Thinking of her like this wasn't helping his uncomfortable condition at all. Still, he couldn't stop himself from remembering the most important part of that picture.

The sweater.

She'd been wearing one of those little, cropped sweaters that were so popular these days. The material had been stretched across her full breasts, and a good two inches of her midriff had been exposed. He'd gotten so hard looking at her tight, smooth skin that he'd quickly had to make sure that his suit jacket hid the bulge in his pants.

"The birth of the divining rod," he noted.

The memory of her tight stomach still made his jaw clench. Back then, he'd had to fight the urge to drop to his knees and kiss and lick every single exposed inch of skin. He'd wanted to drop his tongue into her sexy, little belly button and feel her quiver against his face.

With a curse, Reno sprang off the bed and began to pace around the room. "If you hadn't let yourself be so affected that day, you wouldn't be in this situation right now!"

He still blamed himself for her escape. He'd gone soft on her. There was no other excuse for it.

Once his frazzled brain had finally kicked into gear, he'd begun to ask her questions. *Pointed, delving questions.* Her skin had taken on an unmistakable green tinge as she'd slowly comprehended what was happening. When she'd clapped a hand over her mouth and rushed to the restroom, he'd let her go.

"I had to," he told himself for the millionth time. "She was sick."

Damn it, he'd followed procedure. He'd sent a female agent to accompany her, but apparently the woman also had a weak stomach. When Dani had gotten sick, the agent had gone into the next stall and puked right along with her. When the agent had recovered, their suspect had been gone.

That had been six months ago, and he was still trying to catch up with her.

Reno stalked around the room. Frustration had his nerves stretched tight. He was tired of this cat-and-mouse game. It had gone on for way too long. Something was bound to snap soon.

The way things were going, that something might be him.

He swiveled on the ball of his foot and glared at the computer. "Damn it, Dani. Come on!"

Back in her hotel room, Dani stared at her laptop as she damp-dried her hair with a towel. Shivering, she pulled the belt of her robe more tightly around her. The water in the shower had been tepid at best. She knew the robe was too thick and bulky to tote around with her, but she doggedly kept it nonetheless. It was her one comfort, her one indulgence.

She tossed the towel over the back of a wooden chair and sat down crossed-legged on another. She tucked the flaps of the robe around her legs until they began to feel warmer and, at last, felt like she could concentrate. She hit the power button on her computer and waited for the machine to boot up.

Was he still awake? She hoped so. She couldn't relax without talking to him. If he was online, he couldn't be out there tracking her. Besides, that blue car still had her worried.

Quickly, she began typing. By now, the process was old hat. She waited as the connection was routed through various servers across the country. She wasn't stupid. Every time she chatted with Reno, she hooked up differently, always making sure she put in enough twists and turns to discourage a trace. The first time she'd done it, she must have sent the call across three different countries.

She still wasn't quite sure why she'd taken that risk. The shock of being accused of something so horrendous had surely had something to do with it. She'd just been so angry, she'd had to yell at somebody. The Fed had been the obvious choice. Of course, he hadn't believed her, but gradually, their chats had become more and more frequent.

In a weird, philosophical sort of way, their cyber relationship made sense. Over the past six months, she'd lost contact with everybody she knew. She'd made acquaintances along her travels, but she could never tell anybody what was truly happening in her life. She never stayed in one place long, so she hadn't been able to make friends. Who knew what she was going through better than her hunter?

He knew the struggles she fought. He knew how much she missed her life. So, even though she knew that he was her enemy, she relied on the connection they had. Their relationship kept her sane.

A message was waiting for her when she entered the system.

"You're late," it said.

"You're grouchy," she responded.

She waited for him to notice that she was there.

"You've kept me up past my bedtime," he typed more quickly than she expected.

He *was* grouchy.

Something about the response made her inner alarm start to sound. Was his mood due to the fact she was late or because he'd been driving a pesky blue car?

"Were you chasing me tonight?" she asked carefully. He might not be able to trace her computer connection, but he was very good at tracking her down the old-fashioned way. If it had been him and she said anything about cars or the interstate, he'd know he was on the right trail and be back on the road in ten seconds flat.

"I'm always chasing you, sweetheart. You know I'm coming for you."

Dani shivered involuntarily. Her body, so relaxed after its recent shower, immediately tensed.

Was he that close?

Cautiously, she peeked out the window. Blinking lights from the strip club across the street greeted her. Was he out there, hiding in the shadows?

An unexpected gust of wind shook the tree outside the window, and she let out a startled shriek. The curtain dropped back into place, and she pulled her robe more tightly around her waist. "You don't scare me," she typed stubbornly.

"Liar."

The hairs on the back of her neck stood up. He did scare her—but in more ways than he could possibly know. She shifted uneasily in her seat. For the longest time she'd tried to deny her feelings, telling herself it was a Stockholm Syndrome of sorts, but her attraction to him refused to go away. It only seemed to grow, and that was more frightening than anything. "Is that a threat?" she asked.

"No, it's a fact. I'm not going away, baby. One day soon, you're going to have to deal with me."

"I've been dealing with your stupid treason charge for six months."

He didn't reply, and she began to wonder if she'd lost the connection.

"That's not what I'm talking about," he finally typed. "You're going to have to deal with me. With us."

"I don't understand."

"I think you do."

She swallowed hard. "There is no *us*. You're the predator, and I'm the prey. That doesn't make this a relationship."

"No? Then why are we both starting to wonder what will happen when I lay my hands on you?"

Dani froze with her fingers poised over the keyboard. He couldn't mean—. She had to be misinterpreting him. Still . . . "You'd get fired for something like that, Reno," she typed experimentally.

"At this point, do you think I really care?"

There was no misinterpreting that declaration.

Dani stared at the screen and shivered at the promise—because that's what it was. He couldn't have been more blatant.

She'd always felt the sexual danger that he presented, but neither of them had ever dared to mention it before. She'd certainly never thought he'd follow through on it. After all, he was Mr. Fed, and she was an embarrassing blotch on his record. He was supposed to be chasing her because she was wanted—not because he wanted her.

Suddenly, her blood began to pulse hotly through her veins. "Leave me alone, Reno," she ordered.

"Are you sure that's what you want?"

Her stomach flipped. He couldn't know. She pulled her hands away from the keyboard as if they'd been burned.

She'd thought that she'd hidden her feelings well. If he knew . . . Oh God, this made him a thousand times more dangerous. She held no misconceptions when it came to him. He was out there to do a job, and he wouldn't hesitate to use her feelings against her if he thought it would help him accomplish his goals. "What I *want* is my freedom," she typed with clumsy fingers.

"Turn yourself in, Dani. You know you can't keep running forever."

"I can try."

"You won't succeed. Run and I'll chase. Eventually, I'll catch you."

Her gaze flicked once again to the window, and she couldn't help but scoot her chair further away. She didn't know what made her more nervous, the "chasing" or the "catching".

"Why won't you believe me? Haven't we gotten to know each other? You should know by now that I'm innocent."

"Baby, we've been over this. The evidence says otherwise."

"The evidence is wrong."

"Then show me what's right."

Dani slumped back against the wooden chair, and her heart tumbled. They'd had this discussion a million times. She was innocent until proven guilty, but the evidence wasn't helping her cause. She'd wracked her brain for months now trying to find a way to refute it.

"I can't."

Reno stared at the simple admission on the computer screen. Tiredly, he leaned back against the headboard. He'd like nothing more than to believe her, but the evidence against her was overwhelming. "We might be able to come up with something if we worked together," he typed. "Just meet with me."

The answer came back almost instantaneously. "Nice try, GQ, but I'm not falling for it."

He cursed. Just when he thought they'd been getting somewhere . . . Irritated by his warring emotions, he reached over and grabbed his beer from the bedside table. He drained the bottle and slammed it back down. "Did you eat today?"

When he got no response, he tossed the empty bottle into the trashcan and sat upright. "Danielle, you've got to eat."

"I did."

"What, exactly?"

This was yet another argument they had on a regular basis. Due to her lifestyle, she'd fallen into the bad habit of grabbing food wherever she could get it. He knew her constant motion had kicked her metabolism into high gear, but it wasn't healthy. Nothing about the lifestyle they led was healthy.

"I had an apple for breakfast and a turkey sandwich for lunch," she wrote.

"Dinner?"

"A candy bar. Okay?"

"No, damn it, that's not okay. You've got to eat better."

"I was in a hurry."

That was right. She'd been hurrying away from a blue car on the interstate. "Slow down next time and get a good meal," he typed grouchily.

"If I slow down, you might catch up with me."

He gritted his teeth. "Would that be such a bad thing?"

There was a long pause before she answered. "What's gotten into you?" she finally asked.

You have. Reno rubbed his gritty eyes. She'd gotten into his blood.

Suddenly, he'd had enough. He was tired of talking to her through a machine. He wanted to hear her voice. He wanted to see her in person. He wanted to touch her.

And damn it, he was going to have her. There had to be a way.

He ran a hand through his hair and tried to get his tired brain to function. Maybe there was a deal they could strike—one that would keep her out of prison. For all he knew, there could be mitigating circumstances. Maybe she'd been coerced into selling the software, or maybe she'd been an unwitting accomplice. That could be the reason she was running; she'd fallen into something bad and didn't know how else to get out of it.

She wasn't a hardcore criminal; he knew that.

His hands dropped limply to his sides. If only she'd confide in him . . . If she'd meet him halfway, they could stop this insanity.

"I'm tired, Dani. It's been six months. For half of a year, I haven't had much more of a life than you have. I spend all my time thinking about you, chasing you, and having these stupid email conversations. It's gone on long enough."

"Then let me go."

"No way, baby. You're mine."

Knowing she was so close was driving him mad. If he made it through the night with his sanity intact, it would be a miracle. Six months was a long time, but the game was nearing its end. He could feel it. Soon. Soon, he'd have her just where he wanted her.

"This is ridiculous," she said. "I'm going to sign off now."

"Running again?"

"Goodnight, Reno!"

A muscle in his jaw worked, but he knew that he'd pushed the issue hard enough for tonight. She just needed to get used to the fact that when he caught her, he wasn't going to immediately turn her over for prosecution.

No, that wasn't how this was going to play out. He had questions. Lots of questions . . . Like why did all the evidence point to her? Why had she run? And how were they going to get her out of this mess? He was willing to put in a lot of hot, dark hours with her until he got his answers.

His fingertips caressed the keyboard. "Sweet dreams, baby," he typed.

Danielle unplugged her computer from the phone jack and hopped out of the chair as if it were a hot seat. Her heart pounded in her veins, and she felt little, electric sparks shoot deep into her belly. Quickly, she checked the lock on the motel room door.

The sudden move caused her robe to gape open, and she snatched the lapels back together. She was naked underneath the soft terrycloth. She glanced around the room nervously.

He was coming for her.

She'd always known that he was hunting her. She'd even known that one day he might catch her. She just hadn't known what he intended to do if that ever happened.

Now she knew.

She pulled the robe together at her throat, but her nipples poked up like twin tent poles beneath the fabric.

Now she knew.

Chapter Two

In the end, it took Reno three days to find her. Three, indescribably long days. By the time the call came in, he was in a near panic fearing that he'd made a huge mistake in letting her go.

"Damn local boys," he muttered as he drove down the interstate.

He'd expected them to track her down more quickly. Strangers couldn't hide very easily in small towns and an unfamiliar car would ordinarily attract attention. Somehow, though, the Conrad Police Department hadn't been able to spot her for almost half a week.

Conrad!

He still couldn't believe it. For three days, he'd been cooling his heels in Gilroy, and she'd been hiding in the next town down the road.

He took the exit and drove slowly down Main Street. Her car had been spotted behind a cheap motel called the Waterbury Inn. The neon sign wasn't hard to find; the pink was almost blinding. It forced him to squint as he scanned the parking lot, but he didn't see her car. Turning at the stoplight, he drove along slowly until he found the dark alley that ran behind the place.

There it was.

He pulled into the alley and parallel parked behind her car, effectively blocking her exit. He made a tsking sound as he quietly got out of his sedan. She'd made a mistake pulling in so close to that tree.

"Come out, come out, baby," he whispered. "I'm ready to play."

The gravel crunched loudly beneath his feet, so he moved onto the soft grass. He didn't want to spook her now. Carefully, he rounded the building and looked into the window of Room 1. The lights were off, but the pink neon let him see through the slit between the window shades.

She wasn't there.

But her bag was. It sat, ready to go, on the edge of the bed. She couldn't be far.

Most likely, she was making some cash. He turned around and looked over the area. If she hadn't taken her car, she must have walked. Right across the street was another neon sign, this one blue and screaming "Grinders." A strip club. His eyebrows lowered.

"Maybe."

Down the street was an all night diner.

"More likely," he said. He started down the street.

Ten minutes later, he was back at the strip club.

He looked over the place with a practiced eye. Damn it. What the hell had she gotten herself into this time? This was no "gentlemen's club." It was a sleazy, down low, hump and pump. His blood pressure went up ten points just imagining her working inside.

Putting his palm firmly on the wooden door, he pushed his way into the nightclub—and froze where he stood. A blonde bombshell stood on stage with her back turned to the audience.

It was her.

Lust hit Reno in the gut like a two-by-four. It was Danielle, all right, and all she was wearing was an impossibly high pair of stiletto heels and a tight, little G-string. His gaze was pulled to the spot where the thong disappeared into the crevice between her buttocks, and he forgot to breathe.

Somebody bumped against him as they made their way out the door, and he stepped to the side. Air rushed into his lungs, but he couldn't take his eyes off of her. She was absolutely mesmerizing. He watched in fascination as her sleek hips rocked to and fro, muscles clenching and releasing to the beat of the music.

Her long, blonde hair swung from side to side, brushing suggestively across her back. The need to have her turn around so he could see the rest of her was so strong, he almost called her name. The only thing that stopped him was his clenched throat.

"Good God," he choked.

The music faded away too soon, and he took an unconscious step forward when she looked over her shoulder and threw the audience a wink. Wolf whistles permeated the air, and the noise broke him from his trance. Still, he watched as she strutted off the stage and disappeared behind the curtain.

"The case," he muttered to himself. He had to keep in mind why he was here.

A hard smile pressed at his lips when he remembered their discussion from a few nights ago. Tonight. Tonight, he had her.

With purpose, he made his way to the bar. After a moment, he got the bartender's attention. He waved the guy over and slapped a hundred dollar bill onto the counter. "I'd like to make a special request."

Fifteen minutes later, Dani stood outside the door leading to the private back room. A three hundred-pound bouncer stood quietly nearby, waiting for her to gather her nerve. She looked at him and pressed a hand against her stomach to try to stop the butterflies.

"Don't worry," he said. "I'll be right here if you need me."

She smiled at him weakly.

She really didn't know if she could do this. Dancing on stage was one thing, but did she have the guts to put on a private show?

She still couldn't believe that she was stripping for a living! It had all happened so fast. She'd started out waitressing. That decision alone had been a big one. Going topless had been intimidating, but simple economics had taken the decision out of her hands. She'd known that she'd make better tips at the strip club than at the diner down the street.

Still, her waitressing job had only lasted for about three hours. She'd been ready to quit when the manager had pulled her aside and asked her if she'd consider filling in for a dancer who'd called in sick. At the time, she'd wanted so badly to get away from the bar floor that she'd said "yes" without really thinking about it. Her butt had already been pinched more times than she could count and her "titties," as the boys liked to call them, were sore from being grabbed by mauling hands.

The thought of getting up on stage had been daunting, but it had to be better than waiting on tables. Dancers made more money and were further away from wandering hands. She was already topless, so what difference did it make?

"This is just one more step," she told herself quietly. "You managed to do that. You can do this."

It hadn't been easy, though. She'd only received a few bits of advice from the other girls before she'd been thrust upon the stage. Once there, she'd frozen like a deer in the headlights. Every eye in the room had been on her, and the hoots and whistles had been deafening. Pure fear had made her turn to run, but something inside her had made her stop.

She still didn't know why, but suddenly, she'd been tempted.

Experimentally, she'd started moving her hips to the beat of the music. The roar inside the club had gotten louder and the sound had filled her with a sense of power unlike any she'd ever known. Slowly, she'd begun to take off her clothes. With every stitch of material that hit the floor, her crowd's appreciation had increased.

It had been such a freeing experience. For months, she'd felt trapped. The FBI had been tracking her down, running her life, and making her hide. On stage, she'd been out in the open, but she was the one in control. She was the boss. Innately, she'd known that she held the attention of a roomful of men in the palm of her hand. With a twitch of her hips, she could have had them all begging.

When she'd bared her breasts, a groan of masculine approval had swept through the crowd, and she'd been hooked. The power she'd yielded with her body had made her head swim. The men wanted her, but they couldn't have her.

It was like the game she was playing with Reno. He could chase her all he wanted, but he couldn't catch her. Like him, they could look, but they couldn't touch.

"Neither can this guy. You can drive him crazy, but he can't do anything about it."

The teasing was the best part. And wasn't that exactly what she'd be doing if she went into that room? Her belly clenched, and she looked at the closed door.

Her mother would die of mortification if she ever found out what she was doing, and her dad would probably try to kill every man who looked at her. Still, Dani couldn't help it. Deep inside, a naughty part of her loved to strip.

But this? Could she do this?

Apparently, her last dance had inspired some guy from the audience to request a one-on-one show—a lap dance, to be precise. She'd had to ask what that was. When she'd found out, she'd turned white as a sheet, but inside, she'd been more than a little excited about the prospect. She knew that as long as he wasn't allowed to touch her, she could let herself enjoy it.

"And it will put even more money into your pocket," she said out loud to bolster her nerve. That, really, was the deciding factor.

With a deep breath, she nodded to the bouncer. He opened the door for her, and she walked into the room. The lights were off, and she stopped in the doorway to let her eyes adjust to the poor lighting. She reached for the switch, but the bouncer stopped her.

"He paid extra for you to keep it dark."

One of her eyebrows rose as she considered the request. Hesitantly, she turned around to look across the room. The man was already sitting in the chair. She could see his boots and his jeans in the dim light cast by the moon. A sliver of light slanted across the room from the window above his shoulder, but she couldn't see his face. That suited her just fine.

Quietly, she shut the door and waited until she could see enough so that she wouldn't make a fool of herself. As her eyes adjusted, she realized that the moonlight was enough. The shadowy haze was cool and seductive. The undistinguishable figure remained silent and a little thrill shot down her spine.

With his face hidden in darkness, he could be anybody.

A powerful surge of wanting hit her when she realized she could pretend it was Reno.

"Hey there, big boy," she said in her sexiest voice. "I'm Candy."

Her stiletto heels clipped across the floor as she made her way to the stereo. She'd been told that the music had already been chosen, so she hit the play button. A sultry melody started floating across the room, and she let herself be drawn into its captivating tone. Slowly, she closed the glass case.

She turned on her spiked heel and walked across the room so she could stand in the lone sliver of light. Stopping mid-floor, she spread her legs into a wide stance and simply looked at the shadowy figure. Dark pleasure unfurled in her stomach when she saw the toe of his boot twitch unintentionally.

The motion told her a lot. It told her that she was the one in control.

"Tell me what you like," she said. "I'm here to please you."

With deliberate movements, she began to gradually sway with the rhythm of the song until her hips began to bump and grind suggestively.

"Only you," she crooned as she let her hands skim her hips.

Reno's Adam's apple lodged in his throat as he watched her. He'd meant to lure her into the room and then surprise her. Now, he couldn't have moved if he'd tried.

Oh God, she was good.

Too good. He shifted his weight in the chair. What the hell did she think she was doing, flaunting herself in front of a stranger like this?

His teeth clenched as her hands skimmed temptingly over her body, teasing him because he knew he wasn't allowed the same liberties. When her hands stopped at her waist and balled up the material of her blouse, his job, treason charges, and the rest of the world were forgotten.

"What should I take off first?" she asked.

Reno knew he shouldn't talk. She might recognize his voice. "The top," he said hoarsely.

Would she do it?

She slowly lifted the hem out of the waistband of her short skirt, and his fingers bit into the arms of the padded chair when he saw her smooth flesh. She took her time toying with the material, pulling it and twisting it until he thought he'd go mad. She finally lifted it over her head. She tossed the garment carelessly aside, and his gaze lasered in on her flat belly.

Her body was tight, and her skin was smooth. She rolled her hips, and a distressed sound left his throat. "The skirt."

She hesitated when she heard him, but then her hips started grinding again. Her hands moved down. She fought with the zipper, and eventually the material plopped onto the floor.

For a moment, Reno forgot to breathe. He'd never thought she'd actually follow through.

"Get over here," he whispered hoarsely. He wanted her in his lap. Or under him. Or on all fours.

Her movements stilled, and she stood frozen in the middle of the room.

Good, he thought. So it wasn't so easy after all. "I paid for a lap dance, baby," he said, testing her.

His fingers nearly ripped holes in the upholstery when she took timid steps towards him. She stopped only a foot away, and his knuckles turned white as he forced himself to stay put. It was either destroy the furniture or grab her.

He couldn't touch her, so he let his gaze wander where it wished. It wished for everything. In the pale moonlight, she had to be the sexiest thing he'd ever seen. The stilettos lifted her heels high off the ground, making her legs look incredible. Sheer, black hose covered those long legs up to her thighs, where a skimpy garter belt met them. Under that garter belt, she was wearing an even tinier black G-string. It was so tiny, it would hardly have been worth mentioning if it hadn't barred his gaze from the most private part of her. He couldn't help it; his gaze zeroed in on that spot between her legs.

Somehow she sensed his attention. Her hands moved and, suddenly, the tiny triangle was hidden from his sight. The self-conscious gesture made him feel better, but she made no move to stop things.

Just how far was she willing to go? His hungry gaze settled on her breasts as they nearly spilt out of the lace bra. Uncontrollably, his hips shifted on the chair. "Take it off," he said, the words escaping before he could catch them.

Dani took a step backwards when she felt the man's lust buffet her. Somehow the balance of power had shifted. She didn't like it. "Take what off?" she asked nervously.

"The bra."

A moment of fear gripped her when she realized what she was about to do. *Think of Reno*, she told herself. She'd love to get him in a situation like this. She'd love to make him sweat, knowing that he couldn't do anything to her.

The man wasn't allowed to touch. If he got off by ordering her around, she could do that for him. He still couldn't touch.

The thought comforted her, and a slight smile crossed her lips. She stepped back up to him, so close that her knees brushed against the denim of his jeans. Again, the reins of control were in her hands.

Reaching behind herself, she found the clasp of her bra. With a slight tug, it came undone. The material loosened around her, and she wiggled her shoulders. She bent forwards slightly so that the bra slipped off her body and down her arms.

She heard his sharp intake of breath and immediately felt proud of her body. When the lace confection reached her hand, she twirled it about her finger and boldly dropped it in his lap. He snatched up the material as if it burned, but she could tell that his eyes were centered solely on her.

The attention was flattering.

It was also a turn on.

Dani couldn't help it; she was becoming aroused. She didn't know if that was supposed to happen, but all her muscles had gone warm and loose. Her breasts felt heavy, and she could feel the moisture gathering between her legs.

"Now what?" she asked silkily.

Reno's eyes narrowed. There was something about the throaty

tone of her voice. He let his gaze drop slowly. It immediately got stuck on her tits. They were full, more than a handful, but still so ripe. They lifted proudly off her chest, with the nipples charging perkily into the air. He swallowed hard and let the visual journey continue. There was an even rise and fall to her stomach with every breath she took, but her thighs were pressed together almost rigidly. As he watched, she rubbed them against each other.

She was aroused. The knowledge hit him in the gut like a sledgehammer.

Godammit, she was getting into this!

He stared at her hard through the pale moonlight, and the air between them practically crackled. There was no doubt about it. Her nipples were tightening as she stood there. She was reacting, all right, but what was she reacting to—the act or him?

He had to find out.

"Get rid of the stockings," he said roughly. "*Now.*"

She wavered for a split second. Then her eyes closed and she took a deep breath. Her breasts lifted and the reckless half of him nearly went crazy.

When she opened her eyes again, they were filled with determination. He groaned when her stiletto heel landed on the arm of the chair next to his clenched fist. *God, he wanted to touch her.*

"Slow," he ordered. "Keep it slow."

Her long, nylon-clad leg was propped right up at eye level. He watched in fascination as her fingers fumbled with the strap of her garter until the black hose loosened. His fingers itched to help her when she reached for the back catch, but it soon gave way with a silent pop. He started breathing harder when she began to roll the silk down her leg, past her knee, and towards her toes. When she pointed the heel of the shoe at him, he grabbed it and threw it across the room. She flinched, but the thin hose soon followed, and he fought to stay in the chair.

Dani's heart pounded as she moved to the other leg. She couldn't believe she was doing this. A man she couldn't even see was sitting in front of her, hidden in the shadows, watching her do something extremely intimate. She was baring her body to a total stranger.

Her nipples tightened almost painfully at the thought, and a shiver ran down her spine. She'd never been so sexually excited in her life.

Finally, she pushed the garter belt down over her hips and stood in front of him wearing nothing but the G-string. She tried

to look through the shadows, but she couldn't see him. She preferred it that way.

If she couldn't see him, she could stay lost in her fantasy.

She could pretend she was teasing Reno mercilessly, punishing him for all he'd put her through over the past half-year. And
she *was* tormenting this man . . . She could tell by the way he
shifted uncomfortably in the cushioned leather chair.

She swallowed hard and tried to gather her nerve. It was time
to make him suffer even more. She was supposed to get up on that
chair with him. As he'd said, this was a *lap* dance.

"Is there room on that chair for me?"

She took a cautious step towards him. He drew his knees together so she had room to straddle him, and her heart leapt into
her throat. Warily, she put one knee onto the cushion beside his
hip. She could feel his heat. His desire lashed at her like hot
flames. It intimidated the hell out of her, but she lifted herself
fully onto the chair and settled across his lap. His thighs bunched
up beneath her, and her pussy clenched.

Reno watched her come at him, totally stunned. There was a
far away look in her eyes as she climbed onto the chair with him,
but she knew exactly what she was doing. And she wanted to do it!

He made himself stay glued to the seat. Her breasts bounced
lightly as she settled into position, and he clenched his teeth together hard. Her shyness was gone, and in its place was thick
arousal. It melted over him like warm syrup. He was no longer
some hazy, hidden figure to her. He was flesh and blood.

She was reacting to *him*.

His cock surged against the zipper of his jeans. He didn't
know what was going on in that complicated head of hers, but by
God, he deserved this. She'd put him through hell over the past six
months, but now she was sitting all but naked in his lap. He deserved a little slice of heaven.

"Start moving," he growled.

She flinched, but slowly began to sway to the music. His fingers pulled the leather to its ripping point as he watched her body
undulate. Good Lord, she was incredible. Her breasts were inches
away from his face, and he was dying to kiss them.

He forced his gaze to move up to her face. Her gaze flickered
around the room as if she didn't know where to focus. She looked
as if she was either scared or uncertain as to how to proceed.

He wanted to believe it was a little of both. She'd only been
working here three days. She sure as hell better not have danced

like this for anybody else. The mere thought of her sitting on somebody else's lap made him see red.

What was she doing here anyway? She was better than this. Why had she lowered herself to using her body to make money? Didn't she know what kind of lowlifes frequented places like this?

"Look at me," he whispered harshly when her eyes closed. "You're dancing for me."

The sudden order surprised Dani, and she jerked back from the voice that was so close to her. The motion made her breasts jiggle, and she was suddenly embarrassed of her nudity. The widespread position of her legs made her feel vulnerable, and she bit her lower lip as she fought back the uneasiness.

She kept moving, but the fantasy she'd clung to disappeared. This was her job; she had to remember that. She was getting paid to help this guy get off.

"Like this?" she asked shakily.

Reno. *Think of Reno*, she told herself.

Her eyelids became heavy as the rhythm of the music floated through her veins. She began to rock her hips in time with the beat and lifted her hands over her head. Sensuously, she brought them down and covered her breasts. She'd learned that men liked it when she did that on stage. They liked it when she touched herself. Intentionally, she lifted the twin globes and flicked her thumbs over the already-taut nipples. Her eyes popped open when she felt him move.

"You can't touch me," she said, stopping mid-motion.

"I'm not," he whispered as his hand reached for the butterfly clip in her hair. "This doesn't count."

With a quick pinch, the clamp on her hair was loosened. Dani felt her hair drop down across her shoulders, and she shivered. That was supposed to have been her move. Instead of enticing him, though, she felt her own muscles go weak.

She froze as the man softly began to comb her hair with the teeth of the hair clip. She didn't know what to do. Technically, he wasn't touching her; the plastic was. He dragged the clip softly across her scalp, massaging it lightly, and she closed her eyes.

"Oooh," she sighed. Some of the tenseness in her muscles relaxed as shivers of delight ran down her spine. He combed her hair diligently, but carefully avoided any contact between their bodies.

He was following the rules. She didn't need to call the bouncer.

"Keep dancing," he whispered.

The sensual haze drifted over her again, and she obeyed. She began to rock softly, and she gasped when he mirrored the movements with his own hips. The motion was blatantly sexual. The moonlight cast enough glow that she could see his huge erection as he pushed it towards her.

"God, baby. Yeah, just like that," he said.

"Yes," she agreed. "Just like this."

Every muscle in Reno's body was taut. She was killing him with this little teaser dance. It was all he could do not to rip that G-string off of her and thrust up into her. He knew she'd be hot and wet. He could tell from the way she was breathing that she was as excited as he was. The pulse at the base of her throat was pounding wildly.

He wanted to see her get even wilder. Watching her reactions closely, he settled the teeth of the hair clip against her shoulder. She looked down hastily, but didn't stop the gyrations of her body. Carefully, he dragged the clip over her chest down to her quivering breast. Thin white lines scored her flesh, but he made sure that the pressure was light and arousing, not painful. When he finally made it down to the pretty red tip, he heard her whimper in anticipation.

"Easy," he crooned. He flicked the delicate nub with the plastic teeth of the comb, and she nearly came out of his lap.

He almost reached out to pull her back down, but she stayed of her own accord. His hand lifted again, and she reached out to grab the arms of the chair. She stared at the moonlight coming through the window as he brushed the plastic back and forth. At last, she cried out in pleasure. He moved to her other breast, and she bit down hard on her lower lip. He watched it turn white as he tortured her responsive flesh.

"More?" he asked.

She gasped when she saw him pinch the clamp, opening it like jaws.

"No!" she breathed.

He ignored her and directed the teeth towards her nipple. Her eyes widened as the clamp approached her quivering breast. She was shaking, but she didn't move away. Carefully, he let the butterfly clip close. It caught the rosy nub in its teeth, and she let out a short scream.

She cut it off quickly and looked worriedly towards the door.

Satisfaction settled deep in Reno's chest. She didn't want to call the bouncer any more than he did.

When she looked at him again, her eyes were cautious. He

opened the clamp and let it close in a soft bite. She turned her head to the side as her body bucked.

"Oh God!" she moaned. "It's too much."

A muscle worked in Reno's jaw. "Looks like it's just right to me."

Her hips were rocking wildly against him. He doubted if she knew it, but she was rubbing hard against his erection, nearly causing him to explode. He nipped her breast playfully, drawing out her torment until he couldn't take any more himself. Finally, he pulled the butterfly clip away from her nipple and aimed it lower.

"You didn't finish undressing," he said in a low voice. "This has got to go."

She squirmed as the plastic slid down her stomach and over to her hip. When he slipped the teeth around the strap of her G-string and began to pull it downwards, she froze.

"I want it off," he said firmly.

Slowly, she shifted her hips to help him. He pulled the G-string down as far as he could with her legs spread so widely. The straps pulled tightly, digging into her thighs, but he'd uncovered what he wanted to see. He let out a curse, and her breath hitched when the air from his words touched her abraded nipples. With a sound of desperation, she grabbed hold of the chair behind his head.

"A true blonde," he said. He hadn't expected anything less.

Suddenly, looking at her wasn't enough; he had to touch. He wanted her to take her pleasure from him, not some toy. He tossed the hair clip aside and reached his hand between her legs.

Dani reared back when the man's fingers began prodding against her most sensitive flesh. "You're not supposed to—! Oooooo . . ."

She couldn't stop him. *She didn't want to stop him.* One of his thick fingers had found her opening and was burrowing into her. He pushed it deep, and with a groan, she let her head drop back.

She couldn't fight him when he leaned forward and took one of her nipples into his mouth. Somewhere, somehow, the balance of power had shifted. He had her irrevocably under his control, but she didn't care. She reveled in her submission.

He flicked his tongue across the rosy tip, and she quaked against him. He'd worked her so hard, his mouth felt like fire when he latched on. He began to suckle intently, pushing the nub hard against the roof of his mouth.

Her neck arched and stars danced behind her eyes. He wasn't being gentle. He wasn't even trying.

She moaned in delight and finally let herself touch him. She wove one hand through his silky hair and held his head against her as he sucked greedily. She gripped his shoulder as the hand between her legs became more insistent.

"Please," she begged. It had been so long.

He shoved another thick finger into her and found her clit with his thumb. She flinched at the intimate touch, but he wouldn't let her get away. His fingers plunged into her and his calloused thumb rubbed relentlessly. He worked her until she was trembling wildly in his arms.

She was close, so close. She rocked hard against his hand and pushed herself against his teasing thumb.

"Dani," he groaned.

Danielle froze. The glimmering haze left her with a lurch and sent her crashing back to earth. Her name. He knew her name!

"No!" she cried.

Her muscles clenched, but then exploded into motion. Frantically, she began pulling away from him. "No! Not you!"

It was a trap! *It was Reno!*

Her fists pounded against his shoulders, but he stopped her by simply wrapping one arm around her waist and pulling her flush against his chest.

"You want it," he bit out as he wormed his fingers inside of her.

She gasped at the way his fingers rasped against her sensitive flesh, but reached down and pushed at his forearm. "Let me go!"

"Never."

Suddenly, she remembered the bouncer.

"Help!" she screamed at the top of her lungs. "Get him off of me!"

The door to the hallway sprang open and slammed against the wall. The guard who'd been standing outside rushed in and flicked on the light, illuminating the lewd picture they made. His face darkened when he saw her naked in the arms of the man who wasn't supposed to touch her. "Get your hands off of her," he growled.

Reno looked at the three hundred pound behemoth and then back to Dani. Her face was flushed and accusations of betrayal flashed in her eyes. His expression tightened, but there was nothing he could do with the bouncer headed his way.

Quickly, he removed his hand from between her legs and

pulled up her G-string. He didn't want anybody else seeing her that way. As soon as he let her go, she hopped off his lap and began scrambling for her clothes. Out of the corner of her eye, he saw her grab her skirt, but then it was time to defend himself. He ducked just as a right cross whizzed past his ear.

⁕٭(૭ૐ)٭⁕

Dani knew she didn't have much time. Her blood pounded in her ears as she leaned down to pick up her blouse. How could he do this to her? How could she not have known it was him?

Because she was wishing it was him?

Her hands shook as she pulled the shirt over her head. She was about to look for her shoes when she heard the scuffle break out behind her.

She could do without the shoes.

She ignored the astonished looks of the patrons as she ran barefoot to the bar. The manager looked at her in surprise, but she didn't give him time to ask questions. "Give me my money!"

He didn't move.

"Now!" she yelled.

He opened the cash register, and she grabbed the wad of bills he held out to her. She headed out the door at full speed.

"Damn you! *Damn you!*" she cried.

Her hands shook as she reached for the keys in the pocket of her skirt. She couldn't believe that she'd been fantasizing about him the entire time he'd been touching, squeezing, and suckling at her. A low sound left the back of her throat. He'd certainly been true to his word. Not only had he laid his hands on her, he'd left her wanting and aching, with her body craving completion.

"You rotten bastard," she said through clenched teeth.

Rocks bit into her feet as she ran across the street to the Waterbury Inn, but she didn't even feel the pain. She hurried to her room and cursed when her hands shook so badly, she couldn't get the key into the lock.

"Come on!" she cried. Finally, the key slid home, and she pushed her way inside. As always, her bag was packed and ready to go. She grabbed it and her purse before tossing the room key onto the table by the window. Skidding to a stop, she reached for her laptop before making a mad dash to her car.

It was parked behind the motel, hidden in a dark alleyway. She'd moved it every day to try to make sure the police wouldn't notice it. Apparently, her little trick hadn't worked. She rounded the corner, but came up straight when she saw a familiar blue sedan parked behind her.

"I knew it," she hissed. It had been him on the interstate.

She glared at the car. He'd used it to block her in! He'd pulled right up on her butt, barely leaving her any room to maneuver. But barely wasn't the same as none.

Determinedly, she hopped into her car and tossed her belongings into the back seat. She jammed her key into the ignition, and the little car roared faithfully to life. Looking in the mirror, she threw the transmission into reverse and hit the gas.

Bam!

The crunch of fenders wasn't nearly loud enough. She shifted into drive and cranked hard on the steering wheel. She pulled forward until she was inches from the old tree. Then, it was back into reverse and *Wham!* The crunch of a headlight made her smile.

"There," she said without humor. "That's better."

It took valuable minutes to complete the twelve-point turn, but by the time she cleared the tree, his front end was sufficiently mangled to satisfy her. She inched by the old oak, and gravel flew when she hit the gas. He'd come too close this time. She'd made a mistake in not trusting her gut, but she was listening to it now. It was time to run.

She took the turn onto the street almost on two wheels and gunned the accelerator as she headed for the interstate. She needed to get out of Conrad and out of the state. Maybe it was even time she left the country.

❧⟨ᴄᴊ⟩❧

By the time Reno emerged from the fight in the back room, Dani was long gone.

"Shit!" he said as he looked down the hall. He slapped the doorjamb and immediately reached for his aching side.

He'd received a black eye and some bruised ribs, but he'd left the bouncer moaning on the floor. He knew that the cavalry would soon be coming to the man's rescue so he turned to the back door. Gingerly, he made his way around the bar and across the street.

She couldn't have gotten far. He'd made sure of that. His footsteps quickened when he saw the light in her motel room was on.

"Dani," he called as he knocked on the door. "Let me in. We have to talk."

He looked in the window when she didn't answer, but he didn't see her. His eyebrows lowered; he doubted she was in the bathroom. He held his side as he turned around. She must be on foot.

Which way would she have gone?

It was impossible to tell, but he knew he'd make better time on her if he drove. He reached into his pocket for his keys and headed to the alley. His footsteps skidded to a stop, though, when he saw his battered car. "Fuck!"

Her car was nowhere to be seen.

"Son of a bitch!" he roared as he hurried to his car.

The front end looked like a crushed aluminum can. Worse, glass covered the ground. She'd made sure to smash both his headlights. Impulsively, he kicked the crushed bumper, but had to step back quickly when it fell off completely.

"Ah, hell," he said as he reached for his ribs. That had been a smooth move.

He let out another curse as he planted his hands on the hood of the car and hung his head. She was gone, and he was hurting. Not only were his ribs sore, he still had a steel-hard erection.

"Idiot," he said as he slapped the hood.

Could he have been any more stupid? She'd done it again. She'd slipped out of his reach just when he'd been certain he'd had her. Only, this time, he'd helped her escape.

"What the hell kind of agent are you? Just when did it become more important to screw her than to arrest her?"

His professionalism had flown right out the window the moment she'd walked into that dark room. He hadn't thought once about her supposed crimes or his job to apprehend her. All he'd been able to think about was getting between her legs. He'd just wanted to grab her and screw her until she was too tired to run from him anymore.

Yeah, that had worked.

Shaking his head, he reached into his pocket for his cell phone. The car was probably still drivable, but without headlights, he couldn't chance it. He needed to find a repair shop quick, or better yet, a rental agency. He'd have to let the Conrad boys follow her and catch up to them.

"Ah, Dani," he sighed. He lowered the phone. He couldn't send anyone after her. She wasn't safe to be driving right now as it was. He wasn't going to put some overeager highway patrolman on her tail.

He ran a hand through his hair. Hell, he'd really done it tonight.

Only he wasn't fully to blame. She was the one who'd crawled right onto his lap.

He pushed himself away from the car and started pacing. What had she been thinking, anyway? He thought he understood the reason why she'd begun stripping. It was a good way to make fast money. He just didn't like how much she obviously enjoyed her new occupation. She'd been squirming around on his lap like a cat in heat. For all she'd known, he could have been any neighborhood pervert, yet she'd let him touch her and masturbate her almost to the point of orgasm.

A garbage can suddenly stood in his way. He let his foot fly and it clattered down the alleyway. "Only it wasn't a stranger, it was me."

Cautiously, he rubbed his sore chest. She'd responded to him. Nobody and nothing would ever make him believe otherwise. She might not have known who was touching her, but she'd definitely been attracted to the man in that chair.

"We're good together," he said in wonder. Real good. So good, he hadn't cared about his job or his reputation. All he'd cared about was her.

He stopped pacing and leaned against the back wall of the motel. Damn. He'd been close for months, but he'd just officially gone over the edge. To hell with the rules; he was emotionally involved.

And she was still out there running for her life.

With a heavy sigh, he tipped his head back and looked at the stars. It had taken only minutes for them to return to where they'd started; he was chasing and she was running. Only now, things were different.

Things had suddenly gotten very personal.

Chapter Three

Dani drove until nearly four o'clock in the morning. She would have kept going, but her eyelids finally got so heavy, she had to pull over to avoid falling asleep at the wheel. The rest stop was filled with semis, but she found a spot near a streetlight. Making sure all the doors were locked, she closed her eyes and fell into a disturbed sleep.

The early morning movements of the truck drivers woke her a few hours later. Sleepily, she made her way to the women's restroom, where she splashed cold water on her face, changed her clothes, and brushed the knots out of her hair. On the way back to her car, she grabbed a cup of coffee from a vending machine and tried to wake up.

For the next two days all she did was drive, drive, drive—and then drive some more. The road became a blur as the miles passed, but she only stopped when it was absolutely necessary. By the third day, she ran out of fuel. Her car tank was full, but she was just too exhausted to run anymore.

Giving in to her fatigue, she found another cheap motel room in another no-name town. Her body was on autopilot as she walked into the room, but she was torn between the bed and the shower. Two days of sponge baths in gas station restrooms tipped the scales. Her clothes hit the floor as she made her way to the bathroom.

"It's warm," she said in tired surprise when she ran her hand experimentally under the shower nozzle.

Her head dipped as she stepped under the spray of water. It eased the stiffness in her muscles and soothed out the kinks in her shoulders. For the first time in days, her body relaxed—but so did her mind. She'd been running on adrenaline for so long, she hadn't allowed herself to slow down to stop or think. With the warm water sliding down her curves, she couldn't stay numb anymore.

Her body still ached for him.

"Damn you, Reno," she said. Turning, she leaned back against the shower wall.

The water caressed her breasts and followed the lines of her body down to that sensitive area between her legs. Her hands clenched into fists and her eyes closed. He'd done this to her.

Pictures and sensations flew through her brain. She couldn't believe she'd reacted so strongly to what she'd believed was a complete stranger. For God's sake, she'd been so aroused, she'd thrown caution to the wind and slinked right onto his lap. She hadn't even given a thought as to the danger. All she'd cared about was that it felt good.

Why? Why had she done that? It was so unlike her.

Unless, of course, she was thinking of Reno. She took a deep breath. Did it matter what had tripped her trigger? The man in her fantasies and the man in the chair were one and the same.

With a shaky hand, she pushed her wet hair out of her face.

He'd told her he wanted to lay his hands on her, but he'd done a lot more than that. He'd stroked her, prodded at her, squeezed her . . . She bit her lower lip and turned her face away from the spray.

He'd been as into it as she had.

She'd heard it in his sighs and groans. She'd felt the urgency in his touch, and there was no way he could have faked that bulge in his jeans.

"Oh, God," she said softly.

He'd told her that she'd have to deal with what was between them. She'd just never dreamed it could be something so powerful. It had rocked them both. She'd been right in his grasp, but he hadn't made a move to arrest her. He'd been intent on screwing her brains out. The realization made her knees go a little weak. She knew how important his job was to him. For him to ignore it to satisfy his own wants and needs was staggering.

But he'd also promised he'd bring her in.

Her eyelids snapped open and the erotic memories fizzled. When had he ever let anything stand in the way of his job?

"Never," she whispered.

She knew him better than anyone, and his commitment to his

job was something that was ingrained in his very DNA. He believed in truth and justice and would do almost anything to uphold them.

Almost anything.

"It was a trap," she said numbly. Her hands fell to her sides. "It just got out of hand."

She turned and grabbed the soap. She rolled it between her hands and began scrubbing her body fiercely. "I knew he'd use it against me," she said past the lump in her throat.

Her hands worked her hair into a lather. This new power he held over her was unnerving. Now that he'd found her Achilles heel, he was going to keep poking at it until it gave way.

Even realizing his intentions, she didn't know how long she'd be able to resist. The pull she felt for him was strong, and she was so very tired. It would be so easy to give up and let him have her. At least she'd find some pleasure and happiness before he locked the door and threw away the key.

"No!" she cried out. She turned off the water abruptly and whipped back the shower curtain. "I'm not going to make it that easy for you."

Her skin turned red as she rubbed it briskly with a towel. She wrapped herself in her robe and went to find her laptop. He'd changed his tactics, so would she. "You need a strategy," she said as she massaged her aching temples.

She couldn't keep running blindly. He was too close. She had to find a new set of wheels and put some direction behind her moves. She wouldn't feel safe until she'd put more distance between them.

With determination steeling her spine, she logged onto the Internet and pulled up a map of the state. Looking at her options, she realized that Longmont was within an hour's drive. It was a town of over seventy thousand people. She could easily sell her car there. An idea came to mind, and she called up another web site. "Aha," she said when she found what she needed. "Go Greyhound!"

He'd be expecting her to get another car. If she hopped on a bus instead, she might be able to lose him—at least for a while. She hadn't used a bus before.

"It's a plan, at least." A weak plan, probably, but her brain was still fuzzy. It would have to do.

She started to shut down her computer, but the temptation to check her email account was too strong. She hadn't spoken to anyone in over two days, and Reno wasn't the only person who sent her messages. Her parents also knew they could get in touch with her there. Convincing herself that she needed to keep in contact, she began the rigmarole of logging onto her account.

When she plugged in her password, though, she immediately saw that there weren't any messages from her family. Her in-box, however, was filled with messages from Reno.

Her hand jerked back from the mouse. "You snake!"

He had balls.

She squirmed uncomfortably on the chair. It was best if she didn't go there.

Curiosity got the best of her, though. She couldn't help but reach for the mouse and begin paging through each and every message. The more she read, the more upset she got. Apparently, Mr. Fed wanted to know where she was and if she was okay.

He was acting like he cared.

Her chair tumbled over when she abruptly stood. "Don't you dare do this to me," she hissed.

She couldn't take mind games. His messages sounded so honest, so concerned.

"No," she whispered. Before she could do something she'd regret, she reached out and closed the connection. With shaking hands, she shut down the system and yanked the power cord out of the wall.

She needed to get moving. Now. She'd planned to stay the night here, but she couldn't waste that much time. He was closing in from every angle. Hurrying, she dried her hair, got dressed, and packed up her belongings. She looked longingly at the bed, but she couldn't risk it. She'd have to sleep on the bus.

꧁꧂

Reno unlocked the motel room door and stepped inside. He knew within seconds that Dani had been there. He could sense her. Slowly, he wandered around the room. According to the manager, a woman matching her description had checked in yesterday afternoon—only to leave less than an hour later.

"Why didn't you stay, baby?" he asked quietly. "Why waste good money like that?"

She was behaving erratically, and it made him uneasy. He'd pushed her too hard. Now, she was scrambling around acting on impulse. It wasn't like her.

If only he'd been able to keep his hands off her.

"Yeah, right," he muttered under his breath. He'd come to terms with what had happened between them.

It was clear that she hadn't.

He put his hand flat on the bathroom door, and it swung open with a creak. His gaze went immediately to the sink. The salesman at the used car lot had described her as a brunette. He leaned his shoulder against the doorframe. She'd be just as sultry with dark hair, but he was kind of attached to her soft, blonde tresses. He'd never forget the way they had spilled over her shoulders when he'd taken her hair clip.

"Come on, now," he told himself as he pushed away from the door. "Get it together."

The car. It was what had brought him here. He'd just about thought he'd lost her when the VIN number popped up on a trace. She'd sold it at a used lot in Longmont, and he'd backtracked her movements to this motel through the license plate. He'd thought he might find a clue as to her whereabouts here, but looking around the room, he could see that was hopeless.

Where was she, and how was she moving? It was like she'd vanished into thin air. The used car salesman said she'd just sold him her car and walked away.

"Smart," he muttered. "Mix things up."

Wearily, he sat down on the bed and tried to think. She'd checked in here, changed her appearance, and left to sell her car. Where would she go from there? He had no doubt that she was still on the move. Mobility had been the key to her survival.

"Godammit, you'd better not be hitching, Danielle."

The thought curdled his stomach. She was desperate, but she wouldn't put herself in danger like that. Would she?

"A bus," he said, the answer popping on in his head like a spotlight. It was so obvious. He should have figured it out before, but his brain was fried. He hadn't slept much at all since he'd limped out of that strip bar.

The idea brought a bit of energy with it, and he pushed himself off the bed and headed to his car. He retrieved his laptop and brought it back inside. Sure enough, Longmont was a stop on the Greyhound line. A quick scan of the available destinations, though, made his shoulders droop. She could be anywhere by now.

"Ah, crap," he sighed. He got up to pace the room. Which way would she have gone?

He'd only made it halfway across the room when he heard a beep. Every nerve in his body jumped at the sound, and he swiveled on his heel to look at the computer.

"What the hell?" He hadn't received any messages for days.

It was probably a note from Charley, but he hurried across the room and pounced on the laptop just the same. Relief flooded his system when he saw Dani's email address. His eyes quickly scanned her message, but the light feeling in his chest soon became a dead weight.

"I hate you."

A knife turned in his stomach. He'd been out of his mind with worry for days, and she had the nerve to send him a message like that? "It didn't feel like hate when you were shoving your nipple into my mouth," he typed quickly.

Danielle's jaw dropped at the sudden, unexpected response. She hadn't thought he'd still be watching his email. She hopped out of her chair and took three good-sized steps backward. He wasn't supposed to have been watching.

She stared across the room, but the cursor blinked at her relentlessly. She'd just gotten sick of cleaning out her in-box. He'd overloaded it, and she couldn't stand to read another heartfelt message from him. Her defenses weren't that strong.

And now he was sending her a note like that? Impulse carried her back across the room. Leaning over the table, she typed, "I was just doing my job. You're the one who crossed the line."

The accusation made Reno even angrier. "I thought your job was to dance, not to let men paw you."

"I thought it was your job to arrest me, not to rape me."

He almost sent the laptop flying through the window. "That wasn't even close to rape, and you know it! You were getting off, letting a strange man touch you."

"It wasn't a stranger. It was you!"

"But you didn't know that," he fired back.

The computer blinked at him, and he waited for her response. It was a long time in coming, and he felt some of his anger begin to fade. "You didn't know it was me, did you, Danielle?" he asked.

"No."

Something about her closed-mouth response made him stop. She hadn't known who was sitting in the shadows; she couldn't have. If she'd known he was in that room, she would have run in the other direction.

He was onto something, though; he could feel it. He took a

deep breath and tried to remember the situation detachedly. She'd been timid when she'd first entered the room, but she'd gradually grown bolder the closer she'd gotten to him. And she hadn't been shy at all when she'd climbed onto the chair, closed her eyes, and begun rocking her hips against him.

A jolt caught him unexpectedly. She'd *closed her eyes.*

His heart started thudding in his chest. It was like she'd been lost in some kind of fantasy.

"Were you pretending you were dancing for me?" He stared at the question for a long time before hitting the send key.

The cursor didn't move.

Bingo! Reno slapped his palm onto the table. A smile settled on his face, and he couldn't stop grinning. *She'd been dancing for him.* Satisfaction took root deep in his chest. "Where are you, babe?" he typed quickly. "Tell me, and I'll come find you. We can finish what we started."

"You're not getting within a hundred miles of me ever again," she wrote in capital letters.

His mood wasn't about to be dampened. "Come on, sweetheart. Give me a chance."

"Don't 'sweetheart' me. Why should I ever trust you after that little stunt you pulled?"

"You're the one who decided to take off all your clothes in front of me. I can't help it that I'm a red-blooded, American male."

"You'll understand, then, why I don't trust you."

Touché, Reno thought. A grin still lit his face as he settled down into the chair, turning it backwards so he could straddle it. Things were suddenly getting very, very interesting. "Did you take care of yourself?"

"I always take care of myself," she snapped. "Nobody else is looking out for me."

Reno laughed out loud. "I'm asking if you let yourself have an orgasm."

"You have no right to ask that!"

He'd never seen her send so many typos. Obviously, he'd hit a nerve. He decided to push it a little further. "I have every right since I'm the guy who took you ninety percent of the way there before he was forced to stop."

"Shut up!"

"Hell, I'll admit I did it. I jacked off in the shower that night. Baby, you were so hot, not even the cold water could cool me off.

I had to resort to some soap and my own hand, but I was thinking of you the entire time."

Just the visual image of Reno in the shower was enough to make Dani's insides melt. She remembered the size of his erection, and she almost crumbled to the floor. "Don't tell me things like that!"

"Why not? Because they excite you?"

"Just stop."

"Do it, Danielle. I would have gone mad days ago if I hadn't done something. Stop torturing yourself. Let yourself go."

She ran a hand through her disheveled hair. The conversation alone was making her hot.

"Call me, and I'll talk you through it," he typed.

Her jaw dropped. "No!"

"No, what? No, you won't finger yourself, or no, you won't call?"

"You'd trace it."

"Ah."

Dani dropped her head into her hands. He'd tricked her. She could practically hear him chuckling in her ear.

"I promise it will just be you and me, babe."

"No," she typed again. She'd never call him. She'd have to be an idiot to do that, but still . . .

She pulled back and wrapped her arms around her stomach. She'd given in to the temptation of emailing him. It would take so little to get her to pick up the phone. The way he talked to her was as sexy as anything. And she was still so uncomfortable. Just one stray thought, and she was right back in that chair. She glanced at the phone next to the bed, and pressed her legs together hard. Would it be so wrong to try to find some relief?

Yes! her brain screamed. Forget call tracing, what about Caller ID? The name of her new motel might be displayed before he even picked up the phone. Even if it wasn't, she couldn't make herself that vulnerable to him. There was no telling what she might say in the throes of passion. He was smooth enough that she might betray herself even as her hand was moving between her legs.

"All right, then," he wrote. "Don't call. Just lay back on that big, soft bed and pretend I'm there with you."

Her hands dropped to her sides, and she stared at the words. There was nothing she could say.

"Close your eyes and put your hands on those gorgeous breasts of yours," he typed. "Rub them in circles until the nipples press hard against your palms. When they're ready, pinch them a little, pretending it's me with the hair clip—or my fingers, you decide which."

Danielle bit her lower lip when she felt her body respond to the memory.

"Remember how my fingers felt inside of you? You can do that yourself, sweetheart. You might have to use three instead of two, because my hands are a lot bigger than yours."

Her eyelids grew heavy, and she gripped the tail ends of her robe belt tightly.

"Play with yourself, baby. Do whatever feels good. Let yourself experience what you should have felt with me."

She couldn't take any more. He was trying to lure her in, and she could feel herself drifting. With shaking fingers, she quickly logged off the system and shut down the computer.

She couldn't turn off her feelings, though.

Her body was positively humming. Her muscles felt as hot and tight as they'd been the other night when she'd been on his lap. She tried pacing about the room, but nothing seemed to help. She just couldn't get his suggestive words out of her head.

"You shouldn't," she said.

But she had to.

Finally, she gave up and took a hesitant step towards the bed. Nobody would ever know. Nobody was here to see her.

He'd know, though. He'd know what she'd done.

Instead of worrying her, instead of making her fear she'd given him the edge, the thought made the blood rush even more swiftly through her veins. She reached for the tie of her robe. The terrycloth fell onto the floor as she climbed onto the bed. She closed her eyes, and Reno's face was emblazoned on the back of her eyelids.

She could remember vividly how he'd looked when the bouncer had turned on the lights. His face had been fierce with passion. He'd been ravenous for her. He'd wanted her.

Slowly, she lay back and reached for her breasts.

※⟨♡⟩※

Reno finally headed back to the home office. He'd lost track of Danielle completely and was just wasting his time driving down miles of open road. He didn't feel good about chasing her anymore, anyway. Now that she felt vulnerable to him, she'd only run harder and that would put her in even more danger. The idea put him in a bad mood, and it only got worse when he walked in the door and found Charley waiting for him.

Although the case had been frustrating, his partner seemed to take delight in hearing how she managed to foil him at nearly every turn. This time, Reno didn't feel much like talking.

"A strip club, huh?" Charley asked. He shifted his weight in his specially designed, ergonomic chair. "Did you get to see her dance?"

"Some," Reno said shortly.

Charley's eyebrows rose, making his chubby face look even rounder. "That good?"

"She was all right."

He laughed out loud. "Looks like she knocked you right off your rocker. How did you say she escaped again?"

"The bouncer got in the way," Reno growled. He turned towards the coffee machine and poured himself a cup. "She ran out while the guy busted my ribs and gave me this black eye."

"I heard that you did worse to him."

Reno threw a glare over his shoulder. "He was aiding and abetting a fugitive."

Charley chuckled at the flimsy excuse and rubbed his hands over his expansive belly. "And the fact that he cut her dance short had nothing to do with it."

"You think this is funny?" Reno asked harshly. Coffee spilled out of his cup as he turned sharply. He could think of a lot of words to describe the hell this case had put him through, but "funny" wasn't one of them.

"No, I think it's humbling," Charley said seriously. "The FBI has put significant resources into catching this woman, but she's managed to thwart our efforts using only ingenuity and sheer guts. You've got to admit she's one of the smartest and slipperiest suspects we've ever come up against."

"What did you expect? She's got an IQ like Einstein."

"True."

Reno sipped some of the strong brew. "The stubbornness of a mule," he added.

"Mm hm."

"And the tenacity of a Komodo dragon."

"I'd say." Charley tipped his head to the side. "Looks like she's got something else, too."

Reno looked over the rim of the Styrofoam cup. "What's that?"

"You. By the balls."

Reno's jaw tensed. "Watch it."

Charley rocked forward and caught his partner's arm when he tried to walk past him. He voice dropped low, but it carried a sense of urgency. "I have watched, Jeff, and until now I've kept quiet. But no more. You've been chasing that hot piece of ass until you can't see straight, and now she's using it to her advantage."

Reno jerked his arm away.

"Hey, don't give me that. My sixteen-year-old looked at me the same way when I took away the keys to the car." Charley leaned forward in his chair. "He had the hots for a blonde, too, if I remember correctly."

Reno concentrated on taking slow, deep breaths. "This is none of your business," he said.

"Uh, yeah. I think it is. I need to know my partner's head is in the game—the one that sits on the top of his shoulders, that is."

Reno's muscles hardened, and his temper flared. "If you've got issues with the way I'm doing my job, just say so."

Charley slapped his hands on the armrests of his chair. "I am saying so, and I'm not the only one. People are starting to talk—like about how maybe you don't want to catch her. It's never taken you this long to bring in a fugitive before."

"Yeah, well, she's different."

"How? She's still a criminal, for God's sake."

"Who says?"

Charley's mouth dropped open. "Uh, I thought we did," he said sarcastically.

"Well, what if we've been wrong?"

Charley leaned back slowly in his chair and gave his partner a good once over. "Man, you've got it bad."

Reno started to deny it, but found that the words wouldn't come out. Warily, he looked over his shoulder to see if anybody else was listening to their conversation. "Yeah, I do," he admitted, "But it's not getting in the way of our investigation."

"Bullshit."

Reno's teeth ground together. They never should have gotten on this subject, but now that they had, he might as well lay it all on the line. "Think about it, Charley. She doesn't fit the profile. Why would she sell the software? She didn't need the money. Hell, she drove a Corvette. We've gone over her background with a fine-toothed comb, but we haven't been able to find any political affiliations. So why? Why would she do it? Where's the motive?"

Charley's face turned red. "Don't do this. Don't start dreaming up holes in our evidence. It's solid. Hell, you were instrumental in building the case against her."

"Yeah, well maybe that case is built on quicksand."

Charley's eyes rounded. "Okay, now you're freaking me out."

Reno ran a hand through his hair. The pressure inside his chest was almost ready to explode, but he couldn't describe it to his partner. Something about this whole mess was off. Way off.

"Maybe it's time you took a break from the case," Charley finally said. "You've been going non-stop for too long. Go get some rest. Let someone else take over."

"I can't."

"Why not?"

"Because she didn't do it." The words came out of Reno's mouth so easily, they stunned even him.

She didn't do it, he realized. And it wasn't wishful thinking on his part; it was the truth. That was why she'd kept in touch with him even as she was running. She could have gone underground before now and stayed there, but she hadn't. She was scared, but she was still fighting to clear her name. He'd just been too bull-headed to listen to her.

He reached up and ran a hand over the lax muscles in his face. How could he not have seen it? He'd fought his attraction to her for so long, it had made him blind to something right in front of his nose.

"I have to help her," he whispered under his breath.

"Oh, God," Charley said, flinging his arms into the air.

Reno quickly pulled up another chair. He sat down next to his partner and looked him in the eye. "We've missed something, Charley. Something big."

Squires gave him a hard look—one that had broken down many a suspect in the interrogation room. "You're my partner," he finally said, "But I need something more than that. Just wanting it to be true won't make it so."

"It's not a wish. I know it in my gut."

"In your gut or in your cock?"

"My gut."

Charley rubbed his chin. He knew what the evidence indicated, but he was also an old-timer. You didn't ignore an agent's instincts.

Reno saw him wavering and pressed on. "Everything seems a little too set and dried to me."

His partner nodded slowly. "I've noticed that, too. It's like somebody placed a line of bread crumbs right to her door."

"Why didn't you say something sooner? It's been six months."

Charley's hands came up defensively. "Hey, evidence is evidence. I can't help it if it's all just a little too clean."

Reno rubbed his forehead. He needed to slow down and think. Dani needed him. He had to do this right. "Okay, so we agree that maybe we haven't got all the facts. We need to go through everything again, piece by piece."

Charley smiled, knowing how against the grain that was for his partner. He was the detail man of the team, but Reno preferred action. "You're serious? You're going to sit at a desk while she's out there waiting for you?"

Reno's fingers bit into the Styrofoam. She wasn't waiting for him. She was running from him. "She's gone underground. I'm hoping that if we do our homework now, I might have some good news to tell her when she comes up for air."

"She must really be something," Charley said, shaking his head. He pressed his toe against the floor and spun back to his computer. "All right, I'll pull up the files again."

The knots in Reno's stomach eased. "Thanks, buddy. You won't regret it."

"I'd better not."

Reno pushed himself to his feet. He wasn't going back out on the road, but he couldn't sit behind his desk all day. Waiting for the phone to ring would drive him crazy. Kind of like waiting for an email . . .

"I'm going to take one of the tech guys over to Quadrangle." He tossed his empty cup into the garbage and headed to the door. "We're going to take that place apart piece by piece."

It turned out that Mr. Hanson, Dani's former boss, was more than willing to work with the FBI to find additional evidence on the case. The man still believed in her innocence, and to prove so, he gave them his best man to help in the investigation. For the next week, Reno and his computer guru consulted with Arnold Pfizer, the man who'd taken over Dani's job.

The geeky little man was more what Reno had expected in the

position. He was short and thin with horned-rimmed glasses, a pocket protector, and allergies. Plenty of allergies. The guy spent more time reaching for the box of tissues next to the monitor than the keyboard. Somehow, though, he just didn't look right sitting at Danielle's desk.

He was competent, though. Whenever the tech or Reno had questions about the password protection system, the back-up system, or the security procedures, Pfizer was there to answer them. As a team, they looked for any weakness in Quad's system. Painstakingly, they searched for anything that would have allowed somebody other than Dani access to the code that had been intercepted.

Unfortunately, although they looked in every nook and cranny, their investigation turned up nothing new. The person who had tried to sell the code had definitely used Danielle's account to access the information. The FBI tech was certain.

Reno was dejected when he returned to headquarters a week later. He'd put everything he had into looking at the finer points. Things just hadn't panned out like he'd wanted. When he walked into the office, Charley shook his head. He hadn't found anything either.

Reno slumped into a chair. "Shit," he sighed.

"This is getting us nowhere," Charley agreed. "We need to find her and bring her in."

The fax machine started to whine, and Reno looked at it tiredly. Leaning onto the back legs of his chair, he reached over and grabbed the paper the machine spat out. The front legs came down hard when he got a good look at the information. "We've got her," he said. "She's working as a maid at a hotel in Vailport."

"How did you find her?" Charley asked, even as he snatched the piece of paper out of his partner's hand.

Reno was already reaching for his things. "Before I left Longmont, I checked the Greyhound stops north to the border. I figured it wouldn't hurt to send her wanted poster to all the motels and hotels along the route. That's one thing about her M.O. that hasn't changed. Dani's all about comfort."

"Yeah, yeah. What hotel?" Charley asked as he scanned the fax.

"The Roquefort," Reno said with a hard smile. "The manager's been watching her closely. Apparently, she's making herself at home in the empty rooms. He's not too happy about that."

"She's made a mistake," Charley said, his eyes rounding.

"Give me that address," Reno said grimly. He grabbed the info and his partner didn't try to stop him as he headed to the door.

This time was it. There was a certainty in Reno's gut that hadn't been there before. This time he was going to catch her; and this time, he wasn't letting go.

Chapter Four

It had been a long day. Danielle tiredly let herself into her hotel room, peeled away the tape she'd put over the lock, and shut the door. She turned the deadbolt and, drained of energy, leaned back against it.

She looked at the expansive room. She'd wanted to stay in luxurious surroundings like this for the past six months. After endless nights of lumpy pillows and cold showers, she'd craved some of the finer comforts. She just hadn't thought she'd have to work so hard to get them.

Be careful what you wish, she thought.

She pushed herself away from the door and headed towards the bathroom, removing her maid's uniform as she walked. She'd made enough hospital corners today to please even her grandmother. She hadn't realized what slobs some people were until she'd taken this job. How could they make such a mess when they stayed for such a short time?

"Pigs," she muttered.

A hot shower sounded so inviting. She turned the water on full blast and ran her hand through the mist. It almost made all the work worthwhile. Almost. She stepped into the tub, pulled the shower curtain closed, and bent her head under the pelting spray.

"Ahhh," she sighed.

This latest job of hers paid next to nothing, but she knew opportunity when she saw it. The hotel paid cash, and their hiring practices were questionable because she hadn't had to fill out a W-4 form or show any type of identification for employment. That suited her fine. So did the free room and board she received—

although the hotel wasn't exactly aware of the arrangement. She'd been using her master key to let herself into empty rooms at night.

She rolled her shoulders to loosen up the knots and reached for the soap. She could remember the good old days when she could tell people that her name was Danielle Carver. She remembered when she could pay for a nice hotel room like this with a credit card.

"I remember having a life," she said miserably.

She slicked back her hair from her face and felt tears press at her eyes. This was so unfair. Not long ago, she'd been a happy, productive member of the community. How had she been reduced to cleaning toilets and sneaking into empty rooms for shelter?

The doldrums settled upon her, and she couldn't shake them. She turned off the water and dried off with one of the hotel's big, fluffy towels. Not even laundry softener managed to cheer her up. She wrapped herself in her robe and dried her hair, but the lonely feeling remained.

She desperately wanted somebody to talk to.

She shuffled out of the steaming bathroom and looked longingly at her laptop. She'd had no contact with Reno since their last, heated email conversation. Things were too edgy and complicated now. Getting physical at the strip club had changed everything. She wished they could go back to the way they were—not the running and chasing part, but the camaraderie. She'd never been so lonesome in her life. She'd even be happy to hear him criticize her eating habits.

She ran her finger along the edge of the sleek, black screen. Could he still be waiting to hear from her? The rules of their relationship had changed, but was he still there?

The pang in her stomach was hard to ignore. Without him, she felt stranded. He'd been her one true constant. This total isolation was beginning to make her desperate—desperate enough to consider his offer to work with her. What if he'd meant it? Her instincts screamed at her that it was a trick, but that lonely, aching part deep inside of her reminded her that he'd never lied to her.

He'd had his chance to arrest her, but he hadn't.

Ignoring everything that was telling her not to, she began to set up the system. The procedure was so habitual, she disconnected the phone and plugged her modem into the wall without even noticing. She pulled out a chair and settled down onto the plump cushions.

"Looking for me?"

She jolted at the sound of a voice right behind her. In one fluid motion, she shot out of the chair and spun around.

"Reno!" He was standing just inside the door connecting to the next room. Her heart stopped for a split second and then took off at triple speed.

No, this couldn't be happening! She'd been so careful.

With morbid fascination, she watched as he closed the door behind him and locked it with a decisive click. The sound set her into action, and she poised herself on the balls of her feet, ready to take flight. "How did you find me?" she asked.

"I have my ways." He took a quick, nonchalant look around the room. "Moving up in the world, aren't you, Danielle?"

Sweat broke out on her palms. She'd been in tight jams before, but this was different. She hadn't seen this coming. She was so unprepared. Nervously, she clutched her robe together and looked for an escape route. "I'll scream," she warned.

He gave a soft chuckle and began to walk slowly towards her. "That won't work this time, sweetheart. Your manager is the person who turned you in, and you're the one who chose a room on a nearly empty floor."

He was bigger than she remembered and more intimidating. She took a cautious step backwards, but bumped into the table behind her.

He ran a hand across the cream colored wall at his side. "That's the thing about these expensive hotels. The walls are a lot thicker than the places you've been living in lately."

Dani's breath shortened, and she looked frantically towards the phone. It was unplugged. A desperate laugh left her lips. Who was she going to call anyway? He was the law.

He moved again, and her head snapped back towards him. His dark gaze settled on her, full of determination. She tried to back up, but the table pressed solidly against the back of her thighs, telling her she had nowhere to go.

"Time's up, baby," he said softly.

Without warning, she charged for the bed. If she could get past it, she had a slim chance.

"Hey," he called.

She managed to get one foot up on the mattress before his hand wrapped around her ankle and gave a solid tug. She fell hard, but the plush mattress cushioned her fall.

"Let me go," she cried as she flipped onto her back. She kicked outwards and he took a cautious step backwards. She lashed out again and squirmed towards the far edge of the bed. She still had a shot.

Reno had seen the way she'd eyed the door, but he wasn't about to let her get to it. He was trained in hand-to-hand combat, but he didn't want to hurt her. He blocked another kick and lunged at her before she could get in position to throw another blow.

"Stop it, Dani," he said, breathing hard. "The game's over."

He leveraged himself over her, using his body weight to pin her torso to the bed. It only infuriated her. A flurry of punches came at him, and one managed to clip him across the chin. It didn't have much force to it, but it irritated the hell out of him. There'd already been enough violence between them. His black eye was still fading.

He grabbed her wrists and pressed them solidly to the bed. "Assaulting an officer? Honey, you're better than that."

Her next attack plan shown clearly in her eyes, and he quickly wrapped his legs around hers. "That's it," he growled.

He pulled her hands over her head and caught them in one of his as he reached behind him for his cuffs. She heard the jingle of metal just before he waved the shiny links over her face.

Her eyes went round, and her body heaved beneath him. "No!" she pleaded.

He was in no mood to compromise. The way her body was working beneath him, he had no doubt she'd send her claws at his face if he let her go. He looped the restraint over one delicate wrist, and clicked the handcuff into place.

"I'm innocent!" she cried out. "This isn't right. You can't do this."

"Watch me."

She began to struggle more violently, but he caught her under the armpits. Her eyes flashed towards the headboard when she saw his intent. "Don't you dare!"

"It's for your own good," he growled. "You need to settle down or one of us is going to get hurt—but I'll be damned if it's going to be you."

He tugged her resisting body into position and looped the handcuffs around a slat in the headboard. She fought him as he pulled her other wrist upwards, but he easily locked the metal bracelet into place.

"No!" she screamed when she heard the click of metal against metal.

That one, little sound signaled the end of her freedom.

She went a little wild underneath him, and Reno couldn't help his reaction. He felt for her, but his body had other ideas. Letting go of her wrists, he pushed himself up onto his haunches and looked down at her. "Take it easy."

He cupped her cheek gently, and her fiery blue gaze seared him.

Lord, she was magnificent. Her blonde hair spilled across the dark bedspread, making the strands seem like sunshine. Her curves were swamped in an over-sized, white robe, but he knew what the terrycloth was hiding. She was the embodiment of pure, hot adrenaline.

She fought like a tigress, and a growl left her lips. She bucked her body, trying to dislodge him, but barely lifted him an inch. A hard smile crossed his face. Leaning down close to her, he whispered, "Gotcha."

Dani closed her eyes as she felt the bitter taste of defeat. It settled in her chest, blocking out any hopes for her future. She wouldn't be slipping out of his clutches this time. No, she'd just drawn a "Go Directly to Jail" card.

She almost cried out from the frustration. She was trapped. It didn't matter how she twisted her wrists or pulled against the metal. He had her.

She opened her eyes and found him looking down at her. His dark brown eyes were deep and fathomless, but she detected a hint of some emotion . . . sympathy? Did he feel sorry for her? "Please take them off."

He let out a low laugh. "Not on your life."

Watching her closely, he shifted his weight. All of a sudden, she became vividly aware of the bulge behind the zipper of his jeans. It nudged purposefully against her mound until it settled in the niche at the top of her legs.

Danielle sucked in a harsh breath.

The position was full of intent.

Slowly, he reached for the tie of her robe.

She watched, her muscles tense, as he methodically undid the knot at her waist. There was nothing she could do when his fingers sank into the soft material and parted the robe. Her body was bared to his gaze, and she'd never felt so exposed—not even at the club.

"Bastard," she hissed.

She watched anxiously as a muscle ticked in his jaw. Her nipples tingled, and she bit her lip in embarrassment. Slowly, deliberately, he reached out and settled his hands firmly over her uplifted breasts. The intimate contact made her back arch and the air catch in her lungs.

"Were you going to try to email me?" he asked in a hoarse voice.

Dani hardly heard the question. He'd begun to mold and shape her with his big, strong hands, and her pulse was pounding in her ears. She felt so helpless. Here, all the lights were on, and she knew exactly who was touching her.

She squirmed under his fondling, but it was impossible to move more than a centimeter with her hands chained above her head and his heavy weight pinning her hips. She'd never been more vulnerable in her life, and her most feared enemy had her body at his mercy.

She flinched when he leaned down close. He ran his tongue softly over her earlobe. "I've missed you, Danielle," he whispered.

The words rumbled into her ear, and she felt her pussy clench. He began to roll her nipples between his forefingers and thumbs, and the combined pleasure and pain was intense. Too intense. She pulled hard against the handcuffs and tried to roll away from him.

He didn't ease up. "I think you missed me, too."

She looked up at her persecutor through hazy eyes. He knew exactly what he was doing to her—and he knew that it was working. "Like a rash," she said defiantly. A lie.

"Liar," he said with a chuckle. "Your body missed me."

To prove his point he let his hands wander. He sat back again and began to stroke her. His hands left her breasts to massage her shoulders. His fingers caressed her underarms, tickled her nipples, and swept down her stomach. Playfully, he tugged at the triangle of hair between her legs, and she couldn't stop herself from crying out.

He combed the hair covering her mound. "I'm glad you're still blonde. I had reports that you'd gone brunette."

His hand pushed more firmly at the crevice between her legs, and Dani's toes curled. She couldn't escape his touch. He could do anything he wanted to her. And God help her, she wanted to let him.

"Oh," she groaned.

He leaned down towards her chest, and she waited in breathless anticipation. After all his attention with his hands, her nipples were swollen and craving his hot mouth. She whimpered when his teeth grazed her sensitive flesh.

"You're so responsive," he said. He licked her and teased her before finally opening his mouth and suckling her.

Dani closed her eyes and gave in to the hot waves of pleasure that coursed through her belly.

"That's better. Just like the night at the strip club," he crooned. He moved to the other breast and laved the nipple with his rough tongue. "Did you touch yourself after we talked, sweetheart?"

Crimson color flooded her face as she remembered what she'd done at his encouragement. She turned her head and pressed her face against her arm.

"I knew you did. I was with you. Could you feel me?"

She had. In her mind, it had been him touching and caressing her. Her skin had burned under his attentions, but it had been nothing like this. "You can't do this," she panted. "If you do, I'll tell your superiors and you'll be fired before you can say 'sexual harassment'."

Reno lifted his head and shot her a hard look. Inside, his guts were churning. Her smooth skin was driving him crazy, but she was still fighting the combustible attraction between them.

Fine, he thought. He'd just turn up the heat a little higher and see if she could still ignore it.

Slowly, he lifted his weight off of her and onto his elbows. He slid further down her body but kept his gaze locked with hers. "My superiors are very thorough in their questioning. You'll have to be very specific when you tell them what I did."

Her head lifted sharply off the pillow.

"For instance, you'll have to tell them that I did this."

She gasped in surprise when he experimentally let his lips rub across her skin. Her belly quivered, and he let out a groan as he gave in to his own private fantasy. Opening his mouth, he began to kiss and nibble his way across her abdomen. Little choked sounds erupted from her throat, and she began to squirm with arousal. When he licked her skin and softly bit her flat stomach, she let out a sharp cry.

"And they'll want to know about this," he growled.

Reno felt himself getting light-headed. She tasted as good as she looked. He wrapped his arms around her writhing body and held her still for his mouth. Giving into temptation, he dipped his tongue into her belly button. She shuddered, giving him the reaction that he'd wanted for so long, and he felt his own control slipping.

"And you'll definitely have to tell them about this," he rumbled.

Frantically, she tried to kick him, but she had no angle or leverage. He caught her legs and opened them. She cried out when his hands slipped under her buttocks and lifted her hips off of the mattress.

"I'll have your job," she said between short, hitched breaths.

"You'll have me."

Within seconds, he had her immobilized with her hands chained above her head and her thighs draped across his shoulders. His fingers bit into her waist as his head nudged deeper between her spread legs.

Why was she still fighting him? Why wouldn't she surrender to what they both wanted the most? "Stop running, Dani," he said.

She wriggled in his hands, but he held her still for his mouth. He let his tongue rake across her swollen, pink lips, and she jerked. He heard her panting cries and zeroed in for an intimate kiss.

"Let yourself enjoy it," he said. "You know you want to."

He licked, stroked, and sucked until her body was rocking with sensation. He could feel her heated muscles contracting. Still, she fought the orgasm—fought the inevitable. He refused to let her deny herself pleasure. His tongue prodded at her, and she sobbed when it pushed inside.

"Reno," she gasped.

"Do you want me, Dani?" he said against her skin.

He could feel her beginning to come undone. Deliberately, he moved his attentions up to her apex and firmly licked the tight bud of nerves.

Her back arched, and her muscles went tight.

"Dani?" His tongue prodded her clit, and the caress seemed to push her over the edge.

"Yes!" she said in a strangled voice.

He pushed his face hard against her bucking hips and gave her what she needed. Her body heaved, and the climax held her in its grip for a long, long time before letting her go. When it did, she went limp in his arms. His own body was surging, but he lowered her hips gently to the mattress before reaching for his zipper.

Danielle was vaguely aware of Reno leaving the bed. She heard something hit the floor and, groggily, looked over towards him. Her eyes widened with surprise. He was stripping uninhibitedly in the harsh light of the room, and her gaze was drawn to the obvious.

He was hung like a horse.

She'd felt his erection against her, but she'd underestimated his length and thickness. She looked at him unabashedly. For such a big man, he was all muscle. Dark hair covered his chest in an inverted V, and her nipples tingled in anticipation. The same dark hair circled the base of his prick.

She felt a flutter of feminine fear when she saw that his balls were drawn up tight. He was aroused to near the bursting point and she knew that within seconds, she'd be taking that big cock deep inside of her. He walked towards the bed, and her fingers wrapped around the headboard tightly.

"Reno, please." She drew her knees together instinctively and rolled away from him. "It's been a long time for me."

"Me, too," he rasped. He crawled onto the bed and grabbed her thighs. He rolled her onto her back and pushed her knees towards her chest before she could try any more evasive maneuvers. "Stop running from me, damn it. Surrender."

"I can't," she breathed.

The muscles in his jaw tensed. He positioned himself, and her heart thudded against her ribs when she felt the broad head of his cock find her slick opening. Without giving her any time to prepare, he thrust hard and true, driving himself deeply into her.

Dani cried out at the sudden penetration. He felt huge inside her. The pressure was enormous, spreading her, opening her. His weight pressed her knees back against her chest, forcing her to take him deeply. She felt every thick inch of him as he took advantage of her vulnerable position.

"Ah, ah," she panted.

She bit her lip and waited for the pain, but felt nothing but pleasure when he began to move.

"There you go, babe," Reno crooned. He rocked gently back and forth, trying to give her time to adjust. His hands moved on her ass until he held her at just the right angle for his thrusts. Leaning forward, he spread the vee of her legs wider and let the rough hairs on his chest scratch at her sensitive nipples. A feeling of triumph surged through him when she groaned.

She turned her head away in defeat, but accepted his slow, deliberate, deep thrusts. Soon, his needs had him plunging harder and faster. Beads of sweat popped up on his forehead, and her fingers turned white around the headboard. Out of the corner of his eye, he saw her toes point like a ballet dancer's.

"God, you're tight," he said on a rough breath.

She was gripping him in a hot, snug vice. It felt so good, he was worried he wouldn't last.

He didn't want it to end so soon. He'd waited for so long. He wanted to tie her to him, bind her in a way that would make her never want to run again.

"Fuck!" he said. He lowered his head and let his hips ram against her.

"Ah, Reno," she cried. "Oh, oh, oh!"

He tried to kiss her. She turned her head away, so he dropped his head into the gentle slope of her neck. His grunts and groans echoed in her ear as he screwed her into the mattress.

The bed rocked with their motions, and the headboard banged against the wall with every thrust. The handcuffs jingled and her cries blended with his curses, until suddenly, he crested.

Mindless with pleasure, Reno clenched her to him. His fingers bit into her slick buttocks, and somewhere in the back of his mind, he felt her fly over the edge with him.

After an eternity, he collapsed upon her in exhaustion. Their skin clung to each other, and they both struggled to catch their breath. Reno waited for his heart to slow. When his faculties returned, he lifted his head out of the crook of her shoulder. He smoothed her hair out of her face and looked down at her. "Okay?"

Dani nodded because her throat was clenched too tightly for her to speak. Why did it have to be this way with him? Why did it have to be Reno? She saw his lips begin to move towards hers, and she managed to choke out, "Don't."

If he kissed her, she'd fall totally, irrevocably, in love with him—and then it would be over for her.

His jaw tightened when she resisted, but he kissed her forehead instead. Suddenly, he seemed to remember her bindings. He leveraged himself up, and she felt his softened cock twitch inside her. His hands settled on her shoulders, and he began to massage her tight muscles.

"I think we can take these off now," he said as he ran his hands up to her wrists.

She flinched when he started to pull out of her. She gave him up with as much difficulty as she'd taken him, and he seemed to realize that. He moved slowly, watching her face every second. She felt empty when he was gone.

He bent down to retrieve his jeans. Her eyes lit up when she saw the keys in his hand, but he shook his head slowly. "Don't get too excited. You're not going anywhere."

Her heart sank as he took one of her wrists in his hands and unlocked the handcuff. She pulled her hand down from over her head, but he caught it. His thumb ran softly over the bruise that was already forming and a frown lowered his brow. He lifted her sore wrist to his lips and gave it a soft kiss. He quickly removed the other cuff and gave that wrist the same attention.

Danielle watched anxiously as he strode naked towards the door to the room. She couldn't read what was going on inside his head. He'd done what he'd promised to do to her, but what were his plans now? Was he going to call his partner? Was he going to drive her down to the local police station?

Her heart began to pound again, but this time from fear, not arousal. When the light went out, she became even more skittish. He moved to the bathroom next, and soon, all that was left on was the bedside lamp. Was he getting ready to leave? "Please don't turn me in, Reno," she blurted.

He looked at her sharply. "Oh, babe," he sighed. "Don't worry about that. We'll work it out tomorrow."

Dani's chest tightened. But how? How did he plan to work things out?

"Let's just enjoy tonight," he said gruffly. "Come on, stand up."

Her insides tangled. She wanted desperately to believe him. It was just too much to hope for. He might be feeling magnanimous now, but she knew how sex could cloud issues. When his brain cleared, he'd remember his job and his duty. Her legs shook as she got off the bed and drew the robe around her.

"Don't you think it's a little late to play shy?" he said.

She rubbed her sore wrists. "What are you going to do with me?" she asked quietly.

"Fuck you," he answered simply as he pulled down the covers.

"But we already . . ."

His smile turned wolfish. "It's been six months for me, too, baby."

Her face flushed. "But the . . . arrest."

"All that can wait." He began pushing the robe off her shoulders. She tried to stop him, but he simply brushed her hands aside. Soon she was naked like he wanted. "I can't."

Her arrest could wait. His intentions hadn't changed at all.

"What if I told you I don't want you?" she snapped.

His smile broadened. "Then I'd say you're damn good at faking it."

Dani gasped when he caught her about the waist. He pulled her to him and lifted her like a feather. Her legs wrapped around his waist as if it was the most natural thing in the world, and her arms went around his neck. Without ceremony, he pushed his thick cock into her. The fullness made her back arch.

"Damn good," he growled as he licked her turgid nipple.

Her fingers bit into the muscles of his shoulders.

"Relax, baby," he said. "Let me take care of you. Let me make everything all right."

He began to pump in and out of her, and her resistance melted. God, she wanted to let herself sink into that fantasy. She wanted to trust him. She wanted to believe he'd protect her.

She wanted to believe that he loved her as much as she loved him.

Her eyes closed in surrender. She knew she shouldn't let this happen. He was her hunter. He'd been chasing her forever—but she reveled in finally being caught.

"Reno," she sighed as her fingernails raked down his back.

Tonight, she'd give in to all the wants and needs that had been building inside her for months. Tonight, she'd love him like she wanted to, but tomorrow . . .

Tomorrow, she was going to go down fighting.

Chapter Five

Sunlight streaming through the window woke Reno the next morning. He didn't know what time it was, but he could have slept for another four to five hours *easy*. With a groan, he pressed his face into the pillow.

God, what a night. He and Dani had gone at it until almost dawn. He hadn't been able to get enough of her, and once she'd let go . . . Man, he'd had a wildcat on his hands. Hard and fast. Slow and easy. It hadn't mattered how, as long as he'd been inside her.

He reached out to pull her warm body closer, but his head jerked up when his hand touched cool sheets. She wasn't there.

He surged upright. The move nearly separated his shoulder. His head snapped towards the headboard, and a flurry of curses flew from his lips.

She'd handcuffed him to the bed.

"Shit!"

He twisted his wrist and tried to pull his hand through the cuff, but it held tight.

"Damn it!" She'd turned the tables on him *again*.

His temper snapped. Had last night meant nothing to her? He'd thought they'd made a connection.

He tugged hard on the headboard. It held solid. He wrapped his fist around the spindle he was chained to and yanked it so hard, the bed bucked. As he'd been so quick to tell her, though, The Roquefort was a nice hotel. That meant good furniture.

Twisting about, he tried to push with his feet for more leverage, but that didn't work either. Kicking was useless. He didn't have the flexibility.

"Ah, hell." Finally, out of breath, he gave up.

His breath pumped in and out of his lungs. She'd gotten away again. This time, though, it hurt like hell.

He sank back against the pillows and stared hard at the ceiling. She was still running—running from him. Only now, he felt like his heart had been ripped out of his chest.

Opening his eyes, he looked around the room. A bitter laugh left his lips when he saw the mirror. How sweet of her to leave him a note. The word "key" was written in lipstick with an arrow pointing downwards to the dresser.

He laughed again and, suddenly, the humor of the situation got to him. "You are going to pay for this, baby. Big time."

There was nothing he could do but make himself comfortable, but it was an hour before he heard somebody in the hallway. Embarrassing as it was, he called out for help. A little maid responded, and her dark eyes got huge when she discovered his predicament. Reno didn't know who was more embarrassed when she picked up the key and timidly approached him.

He didn't have time to explain, though. As soon as she turned him loose, he grabbed the sheet from off the bed and made a beeline to the bathroom. He heard her giggling behind him and his face, along with most of the rest of his body, turned red with embarrassment.

If that wasn't bad enough, it took another half-hour to explain the situation to the irate hotel manager. He'd had to lie through his teeth. Reno was so frustrated and embarrassed; by the time he got out of there he had a pounding headache. He walked out to the parking lot, but his mind was on other things—like his pride, his reputation, and his weakness for a hot-blooded, but cold-hearted blonde. He reached into the pocket of his jeans for his keys and stopped in his tracks.

"Fuck!" She'd taken them, too.

His head snapped up and he looked for his car. He couldn't have been more surprised to find it still parked in the space where he'd left it.

Even more shocking, Danielle sat on the hood.

A band of steel circled Reno's chest, and suddenly, he found it hard to breathe. She was huddled into a ball with her feet propped up on the bumper. Her elbows were settled upon her knees, and her face was buried in her hands. She looked so sad and alone his heart squeezed.

He didn't say a word as he approached her. She heard his footsteps, though, and glanced up quickly. When she saw that it was him, she hurriedly wiped the tears from her face. She swallowed hard and watched him with wary eyes.

The tears were what did it. He walked straight up to her, reached out, cupped the back of her head, and kissed her.

They'd done a lot of things last night, but this was the one intimacy she'd denied him.

Her lips trembled under his. He changed the angle of his mouth and the contact deepened. With a groan, she leaned her head back. Her fingers dug into the leather of his bomber jacket, and he wrapped his arms tightly around her.

At last, she surrendered.

The band around his chest loosened, and he swept her off the hood of the car and into his arms. Her fingers dove into his hair, and their tongues rasped as they learned each other's taste.

When they finally broke apart, they were both breathless. "Baby," he said hoarsely. "You've got to stop running."

Dani found she couldn't look at him. Nerves had her stomach churning. She was putting a lot on the line. No, not a lot. *Everything.* "Were you telling the truth when you offered to work with me to prove my innocence?"

"Yes," he said without hesitation. "I should have made that clear last night."

Her heart lodged in her throat, and her voice went tight. "I didn't do it. I swear. I wouldn't do something like that."

A muscle in his jaw worked, and he cupped her face with both hands. "I know."

"Really?" Dani asked, tears pressing at her eyes.

"Really."

She jumped so hard against him, she almost knocked him over. She buried her face against his neck and hugged him tightly. Her air worked in her lungs, but she tried not to get too excited. Her name hadn't been cleared yet.

But he'd said he believed her, and that was worth almost as much.

"Okay, now. Stop that," he muttered. His hands swept up and down her back. "I'm not good with tears."

She let out a long breath. His hand ran over the top of her head, and she sagged against him.

He kissed her temple. "How long have you been sitting here? Have you eaten yet?"

She shook her head.

He sighed and looked at her sternly, but gave her a quick hug. "That's the first thing we need to do. Come on, we'll find someplace that serves a big breakfast. Then we'll talk."

She pulled back and wiped the moisture from her cheeks. She gestured towards the hotel. "The restaurant here is pretty good."

"No way."

She looked up at him, and her eyes rounded. Special Agent Jeff Reno's face had gone bright red.

He rolled his shoulders self-consciously. "After what you did to me, I can't ever show my face in that hotel again."

Dani couldn't help it. A smile pulled at her lips, and for the first time in months, she broke out into laughter. "Was your face really the problem?"

He looked sheepish. "One of your maid friends got the surprise of her life."

She covered her mouth with her hand to hide her smile, but her eyes lit up with laughter. "There's another restaurant down the street."

He reached out and caught her by the hair. "You know I'm going to make you pay."

It didn't sound like much of a threat. "Promise?"

"Promise." He leaned down and kissed her again. "Let's go. I'm starving. We burned off a lot of calories last night."

She gave him back the keys to his car and they walked down the street together. When his hand slipped around hers, she looked down quickly. He gave her fingers a squeeze, and the last bit of tension in her shoulders eased.

He had no idea how hard it had been for her to turn herself in. She'd been so nervous when she'd slipped out of bed and retrieved the handcuffs. She'd been sure that he was going to wake up and grab her. Her entire body had been shaking with nerves when she'd found his car keys in his pocket. She'd hurried out to the parking lot and used the remote to locate his car. She could have escaped. It would have been easy—if only she could have turned the key.

She just hadn't been able to do it. She was too tired. Tired of running. Tired of hiding. Tired of being alone.

Last night . . . What they'd done . . . It had been shockingly intimate. All the emotions and desires they'd suppressed for months had come to the surface. Reno had taken control of her body, but once she'd given herself to him, he'd taken incredible care with her. She'd let herself go with him, and it all came down to one thing.

Trust.

She'd put her body in his hands. Now, she'd put her future.

She hoped he wouldn't let her down.

⁂

Reno made Dani eat every bite of her of her bacon and eggs before he let her talk. When she put down her fork, he pointed to the blueberry muffin sitting on a side plate.

"Oh, I can't. I'm about to burst," she complained. She sank back against the back of the booth and wrapped her arms around her stomach.

"Fine, we'll save it for you to eat later." With a wave of his hand, he sent a waitress scurrying for a doggy bag.

Danielle rolled her eyes. "What is it with you and my diet?"

He shrugged. "You've always brought out the protective side of me."

"Always?"

"From day one." He took a sip of his coffee. "You should have seen my reaction when I walked into that strip joint and saw all those men panting over you."

She looked at him through the veil of her eyelashes, and a trace of a blush graced her cheekbones. "You saw me on stage?"

"You're kind of hard to miss—especially when all you're wearing is butt floss and fuck me pumps."

Her blush reddened, and she looked out the window. "I liked that job."

"You *liked* it?"

She shifted in her seat.

"You got off on it," he said slowly.

She didn't answer.

"What was it, the attention?" He looked at her closely and shook his head. "No, it was the power. You liked being in control."

"Can you blame me?" Her gaze leveled with his, and her chin came up. "I haven't had control over my life for half a year."

"But you kind of liked that, too. You liked being under my thumb." His gaze heated. "In fact, you'll take my thumb any way you can get it."

"Reno," she hissed. "Keep your voice down."

He chuckled. "It's the truth."

She ran a hand through her tussled hair. "All I know is that working at Grinders sure beat cleaning kennels. I certainly made a lot more money. Do you know that I made as much stripping as I did writing computer code?"

He set down his coffee cup slowly. "I thought that Quad paid good money."

She shrugged. "They do, but a computer programmer doesn't make tips."

"No bills in your G-string for a good line of C++?"

She chuckled. "Not in that manner of speaking."

Reno sat back in his seat. It was time to get into it. He couldn't let this liaison go on for long. He needed to clear her name before anyone at HQ found out that he'd made love to her. "So money could have been a strong motivation for whoever accessed that code," he said.

She went still. "Are you sure we can talk about it here?"

"Here's as good of a place as any."

"I've thought a lot about it," she finally said. "Whoever took that code did it for either money or political reasons. There are countries out there that would pay a lot for that application."

She wasn't telling him anything he didn't already know, but he listened carefully to see if she recalled anything he might have missed. "Explain it to me again," he said. "Tell me exactly what the code is intended to do."

He could see she was tense. Her restless hands picked up a paper napkin and began smoothing it on the tabletop.

"Fighter planes are governed by a system called fly-by-wire," she said. "That means that the controls such as the ailerons, the elevator, and the rudder are governed electronically—not with the old-fashioned hydraulic and cable systems."

He nodded his head in understanding, and she looked quickly around the restaurant to make sure that nobody else was listening to their conversation. With that one, unconscious gesture, Reno knew she was innocent.

He'd believed it before, but now, he knew it with a certainty. Relief filled his chest. Suddenly, his interest was upped a hundredfold. Now he *had* to prove her innocence—for himself as much as for her. His job was to jail the criminals, not the victims.

Her voice lowered. "The code that Quadrangle Computing is writing will double the speed with which the commands are relayed to the control surfaces. I mean, it's already fast. It's imperceptible to humans, but there is room for improvement. Once that code is installed on our fighter planes, they'll be some of the most maneuverable birds in the air."

"They'll be able to respond to the pilots' commands that much faster."

"Exactly. That split second could be the difference between life and death."

Reno sat back in his seat and looked at her closely. "There are armies out there who would kill for that advantage."

"I know." She tossed her napkin on her plate and looked him square in the eye. "That's why the project was top-secret. That's why I've never talked about it with anybody outside the company. Until you, of course."

He leaned forward and set his elbows on the table. "Dani, the section of code that Charley and I intercepted was one that you had written."

"I know."

His eyebrows rose. "What do you mean, 'you know'?"

"Why else would the FBI send their bloodhounds after me?"

"A bloodhound? Do I look like a bloodhound to you?"

"I've always thought of you more as a wolf."

He leered at her. "Don't distract me," he warned.

He ran a hand over his chin. "Whoever slipped that code outside of the company intended for you to take the blame. It had to have been somebody who had the opportunity and the motive. Who don't you trust at Quad?"

She sighed heavily. "I hate even thinking about this."

He nodded. "I know you considered your co-workers friends, but try to take a step back and look at it. Had anyone been acting strangely? Was there anything unusual that caught your attention?"

"Don't you think I would have told you long ago if I had?"

"Think back," he said patiently. "This person couldn't sell their own work because they knew that the trail would lead straight back to them. They needed to put the focus on someone else—namely you. Why?"

She ran a hand through her hair. "I don't know. I can't think of anyone who would want to hurt me like that."

"Do you have any enemies?"

"No. Everybody at Quadrangle gets along really well. We have our occasional arguments, but the hard feelings never last. Everybody knows how stressful the job is."

"Is anybody jealous of you?"

She gave him a blank look. "Well, I couldn't answer that. I can't read minds."

"I can." He reached out and caught her hand. "Danielle, have you ever looked at the people you work with? Really looked at them? You're like a square peg in a round hole."

Her forehead furrowed as she looked at him in confusion.

He pressed his palm against hers and intertwined their fingers. "Sweetheart, to be blunt, you work with a bunch of geeks."

At that, she laughed. "Maybe, but they're very talented geeks."

"I won't deny that, but those talented, high paid geeks were probably unpopular losers in school." He let his gaze run over her body. "A sexpot like you would turn their world upside-down. Hell, Arnold Pfizer probably gets a boner every time you talk to him."

"He has asked me out a couple of times."

"Did you go?"

She let out a very unladylike snort.

"I hope you didn't respond like that."

She looked at him and finally realized how serious he was. "I was nice about it. He didn't say anything."

"He wouldn't. It would be too embarrassing." Reno ran his thumb up and down the side of hers. "That doesn't mean he wants you any less. Baby, I don't think you understand the effect you have on men. A never-ending hard-on can really piss a guy off."

"I'm not a tease."

"Of course, you are."

"I—"

"It's not intentional," he said, interrupting her, "But with that blonde hair, those amazing tits, that tart little ass . . . It would be pure hell for a guy like Arnold to sit next to you every day. You might have been working hard, but I guarantee you that he was trying to figure out a way to get into your pants."

Her gaze dropped. "But if he liked me, why would he want to hurt me?"

"Because he couldn't get past your chastity belt."

She shook her head. "This is all supposition."

"Could he have gotten into your account? I've seen the security system, but he's the one who showed it to me."

She shook her head quickly. "Absolutely not. He'd have to have my . . . *password*."

Reno leaned forward. "What?"

She pushed her hair back and licked her lips uncertainly. "His account went down one day, and he had a deadline to meet. I let him use mine."

"So he did have your password."

"He had it for one day, several months before you and Charley showed up at our door. I changed it as soon as I got back into the system." Her words slowed.

Reno looked at her closely. He could practically see the gears turning in her head. "Dani?"

Her face was solemn when she finally looked at him. "He might have put in a temporary back door. That way, he could have gone back later, gotten what he needed, and erased his tracks."

Reno stood and held out his hand to help her out of the booth. "Let's get out of here. We've got a lot of work to do."

Chapter Six

Reno pulled his cell phone out as soon as he'd paid the bill. He had an idea, but he needed help. He dialed Charley's number as they walked down the street and waited impatiently for his partner to pick up the line. "Charley? It's Reno."

"Hey, partner. It's about time you called. What happened? Did she get away again?"

"No, she turned herself in."

There was the sound of a chair squeaking. "You're kidding me."

Reno glanced at Dani. Tension radiated from her like a nuclear bomb. "She claims she's innocent, and I believe her. Listen, Charley, we need you to do something for us."

"Us?"

"Us." Reno refused to elaborate. "You know that fence that we picked up on this case? I need you to ask him a few more questions."

Charley gave an uncharacteristic grumble. "Like what? We questioned him to death before we locked him away. He doesn't know anything that he hasn't already told us."

"We might not have been asking the right questions. I want to know more about the voice at the other end of the line."

Charley's grumble got a little louder. "He couldn't tell if it was male or female. The person whispered. Remember?"

The fence who'd sold the code to the FBI hadn't been very helpful when it came to identifying the source inside Quadrangle Computing. He'd never seen the person. He claimed that all their interactions had been conducted over the phone and through a post office box.

"I remember. I'm the one who questioned him," Reno said. Charley was patient as a saint when dealing with information and data. His fuse just tended to get short when the human element was involved. "We need to ask him one more thing."

"All right, all right. What do you want to know?"

"I want to know if the source had allergies. Was there ever a sneeze? Was he or she hacking all the time? Did he have to stop to blow his nose?"

"I'm not following you."

"Arnold Pfizer," Reno said. Just the guy's name was enough to make his stomach sour. "Dani said that he hit on her a couple of times, and she blew him off. It might be the motive we've been looking for."

"Pfizer? Isn't that the guy you worked with last week?"

"The one and only."

"Holy cow." Charley paused for a second. "I see where you're going with this. Don't worry. I'm on it."

Reno hung up and stuffed the phone into his back pocket. He looked at Danielle, who was waiting anxiously. "He's going to work on it and get back to us," he told her.

Dani put a hand on her stomach. The butterflies inside felt like they were riding a roller coaster. She couldn't ever remember being so nervous in her entire life. There was just too much riding on this wild assumption. Arnold had never been anything but nice to her. Were they grasping at straws, trying to pin this crime on him?

"Relax," Reno said. He put his arm around her shoulders. "Making yourself sick isn't going to help. Believe me."

"I just don't want to accuse him of something he didn't do," she said.

"I understand. How do you think I feel about what I've done to you?"

She relaxed against him. "I don't know if I can take this."

He softly kissed her temple. "It will be over soon."

It was going to take more than words to make her feel better. She knew more than anyone how quickly things could go wrong. She turned so she could see his face. "What if we're jumping the gun? If your partner doesn't find anything, we'll be right back where we started."

"No, we won't." They'd reached his car and he opened the passenger side door for her. "For one thing, I won't have to chase you anymore."

Dani paled and took a step back. "I thought you believed me."

He caught her by the arm. "Easy, baby. Have a little faith. I meant that I'm not going to let you go. I didn't say I was going to let you take the fall for this."

His dark gaze leveled with hers. "If this thing with Pfizer doesn't pan out, we'll just start over. Together. No more running. Got it?"

The knot in her chest eased when she saw the emotion in his eyes. He didn't even try to hide his feelings from her. "Got it," she said past the lump in her throat.

She blinked back the tears that threatened to fall. He was going to protect her. She'd taken a huge risk this morning, but he was making good on her trust. She could rely on him, lean on him if she needed to. A lightness that she hadn't felt for a very long time suddenly filled her chest. It was relief—with more than a tinge of hope.

His hands slipped down to her rear, and he pulled her flush against him. Her eyes widened when she felt a familiar ridge press against her abdomen. "What do you say we go work off some of this nervous energy?" he said.

His head swooped down, and the kiss he gave her was potent. It had her knees buckling and her hands clutching at his jacket for support. At last, she had to come up for air. "How long do you think it will be before Charley calls back?"

His eyes lit up, and he started bundling her into the car. "Hours."

⁂

Soon, they were checked into another hotel. Danielle followed Reno into the room and found herself quickly caught in his strong arms. He pushed her up against the door as he shut it.

Her eyes drifted closed as he pushed her jacket off her shoulders and began tugging on her shirt. His wicked tongue danced along the side of her neck, and goosebumps made her shiver.

"I want you so bad," he growled against her neck. "I was ready for you this morning, but you weren't there."

His hips rubbed against her, and she let her hands trail down his back. "Reno," she sighed.

His hands spanned her waist, and his fingers set up an insistent massage. "The bed. Now."

Dani looked over his shoulder. She hadn't even taken a look at the room. She saw the bed, but a flame lit inside her belly when she saw an easy chair in the corner. "Wait," she said.

He drew back to look at her.

She took his hand and stepped around him. He looked at her in confusion, but comprehension hit when he saw where she was leading. "This time, we're going to do things my way," she whispered.

His eyes burned with fire. "I'm all yours, sweetheart."

Her belly clenched in delicious anticipation. He was going to let her take control.

Determinedly, she tugged him to the easy chair. He turned, but caught her by the waist again. He started to pull her down with him as he sat, but she stopped him with her hands on his chest. "My way," she repeated.

She let her hands drift down to the front of his Levis, and he jerked under her touch. "Whoa, be careful there, babe."

She smiled and slowly rubbed her hand over his fly. "Don't worry, big boy. You're in good hands."

He cursed under his breath, and the sound emboldened her. She gave him a firm squeeze and he went right up on his toes. When she thought he could take no more, she dropped down to his feet to remove his socks and shoes. Slowly, she rose back up and looked into his deep brown eyes. "Had it really been six months?" she asked.

He nodded towards the bulge that was trying to get out of his pants. "In case you haven't noticed, baby. I've got a thing for you."

Without breaking his gaze, she reached for his belt buckle. She pulled the belt out of its loops, but her hands began to shake when she reached for the fastening of his jeans.

"Want some help?" he asked.

"Take off your shirt."

"Anything I can do," he said. He grabbed the t-shirt, pulled it over his head, and sent it flying.

Dani swallowed hard. God, she loved his body. Her nerves settled, and she let herself lean into him. She kissed his chest close to his heart and felt it pound under her lips.

He was excited.

So was she.

She let her fingers explore the hard muscles of his abdomen, and the beat of his heart took off under her tongue.

"Baby," he growled. His fingers dove into her hair and pulled her head up for a harsh kiss.

His teeth scraped against her lips when she tugged at his zipper. She nipped him right back as she caught his jeans and pushed them downwards. His briefs went along with them, and every muscle in his body went rigid.

Including the muscles of his cock.

It bumped insistently against her belly, and Dani felt her body grow warm. She reached for him blindly and wrapped her fingers around his hardness. He shuddered against her and exhaled sharply into her mouth.

"Into the chair," she said.

"Danielle," he warned.

He wasn't in the mood for teasing.

Neither was she.

He fell back when she pushed lightly against his chest. When he reached for her, she caught his hands and pressed them against the arms of the chair.

"Oh, God. No. You can't expect me not to—"

"I thought you wanted me to pay."

With a groan, he dropped his head back against the chair. "Lord help me."

His cock stood upright like a fat flagpole. Dani touched him again, and his hips bucked. Her eyes widened. His size was impressive, and she remembered how completely he'd filled her. How had she managed to take him at all?

Inquisitively, she dipped her fingers lower and cradled one of the puckered sacs at the base of his cock. She ran her thumb lightly over him and a guttural sound broke through his lips.

"Get down there," Reno said in a rough voice. "You're supposed to be paying—not me."

Reno thought he was going to have a coronary for sure. His heart was pounding faster than it had ever pounded in his life, and sweat had broken out on his brow. Even the balls of his feet were sensitive. He rubbed them against the carpeting, trying to find some relief.

He watched as Dani dropped to her knees in front of him. He spread his legs for her, and she crawled closer. Her gaze was on his pulsing cock. She slowly bent her head, and his hand left the arm of the chair of its own volition. His fingers sank into her blonde tresses and pushed her head gently downwards.

"Suck me, baby."

She dipped her head low and placed a kiss near the base of his prick. Her hair draped across his lap, and his hips shifted.

"Oh yeah. That's it," he said. It was even better than in his dreams.

She let her tongue glide up his cock until she found its head. She licked him, and his hand clamped down harder on her skull. She opened her mouth and began sucking lightly.

"Holy mother of . . . Shit!"

Both of Reno's hands dug into her hair, and his hips came off the chair. She whimpered when he pressed himself deep into her throat. Harsh, wild words passed his lips, but he held her against him, not letting her go.

She sucked harder, and his vision started to blacken. His hips began to pump, and her head began to bob. It was good, but he liked her hot, tight pussy even better. With a growl, he slipped his hands under her armpits and pulled her upright.

"Reno!" Dani gasped.

She missed the taste of him, but when he started to rip at her clothes, she knew he was out of control. She groaned when he pushed her t-shirt upwards and began to wildly kiss and lick her stomach. Her knees buckled, and she grasped his shoulders for support. His teeth raked across her skin, and she bit back a cry. Suddenly, she, too, was at a fever pitch.

"Do you want me, Danielle?" he asked.

"Yes," she groaned.

"How?"

"Inside me. Deep inside me."

He clapped his hand over her mound and squeezed. "Here?"

She ground herself against his palm. "Yes!"

Together, they tore at her clothes. He pulled at her jeans and pushed them down her hips. She kicked them off and felt his hands go to her panties. Her trembling hands tried to free herself of her t-shirt and bra. As soon as she felt the cups loosen around her breasts, he was there, ready to take her offering.

"Tell me you never danced for another man like that," he growled. "Tell me!"

"You were my first," she panted.

His mouth fastened on her nipple, and his hands closed around her waist. Naked, he pulled her onto the chair with him. She spread her legs wide to straddle his hips. He thrust, but she rocked away from him.

"Let me," she whispered. She caught his cock in her hand and felt him pulsing under her fingertips. Her pussy almost cried in wanting. She swiveled her hips and guided him to her.

The head of his cock slipped inside, and Dani felt as if she might melt from pure pleasure. She pushed down and slowly took him, inch by inch. Her breath hitched, and he quickly looked at her face.

"You're swollen," he whispered.

"Last night . . ." she said weakly.

He'd used her well last night, and he was big. It hurt a little, but the hurt was good.

He understood. Bending his head, he licked at her nipple.

Danielle felt her juices start to coat him. She bit her lip, and let the muscles in her thighs relax. Gravity impaled her on his cock.

It was hot, so hot. The pressure inside her was nearly overwhelming. Wanting to feel more of it, she raised her hips and began a mindless, pounding rhythm.

"Dani!"

"Ohhhhh," she moaned.

His pelvic bone bumped against hers with every thrust. She caught the chair behind his head and began to ride him more roughly.

"Fuck!"

Reno was sure the top of his head was about to come right off. He wrapped his arms around her shuddering body and pulled her close. Their lips tangled in a hot, breathless kiss, and they strained to reach completion.

He knew the sounds of their lovemaking; the sighs, the moans, and the cries had to be reaching the hallway, but he didn't give a damn. He'd finally caught her. He'd caught Danielle Carver, and she was *his*.

With a powerful surge, he thrust upwards. Both their hips lifted into the air, and he felt her squirm helplessly. Two more pushes, and she went taut as a bow. Her pussy squeezed him tightly, and he called out her name as he came inside of her.

With an expulsion of air, they collapsed onto the chair. She melted over him like warm butter, and he held her with limp arms. Exhausted, he leaned his head back against the cushion of the chair and gave a final groan. Closing his eyes, he waited for the room to stop spinning.

"Dani?" he said, not bothering to open his eyes.

"Hm?"

"Were you about to email me yesterday when I found you?" His proprietary instincts were skyrocketing. He'd just placed his stamp on her, but he wanted more. He wanted the whole package.

"Yes," she murmured as she burrowed closer to his neck.

He wanted to see her face. He gently pulled her head back. "Why?"

She licked her lips and cautiously looked into his eyes. "Because you're all I've got, Reno. I was so lonely without you."

His heart skipped a beat and then began to thud. His gaze ran over the delicate features of her face. He felt her curves pressed solidly against him and the part of him that was still inside of her began to stir. "You've got me, babe. I almost went out of my mind this morning when I woke up, and you were gone. Don't ever do that again."

"Oh, Reno. I didn't know."

"Well, now you do," he said gruffly.

Standing abruptly, he carried her towards the bed. "And I'm going to make sure you never forget it."

Hours later, they were awakened from a sound sleep by the ringing of his cell phone. Before the second ring, Reno was alert and moving. He rolled out of bed and dove for his jeans. "Yeah?" he answered.

"Reno, it's Charley."

"Charley! Give me some good news, partner. Did you find anything?"

Dani sat up on the bed and pulled the sheet up to her chest.

"We hit the motherload, my friend."

A jolt of excitement hit Reno square in the chest. "Tell me everything."

"Your hunch paid off big time," Charley said happily. "When we asked the fence about the allergy thing, he said that the source had been a regular sneezing machine. We took his statement along with some other evidence to a judge and got a search warrant for Pfizer's home."

"What happened?" Dani asked.

Reno nodded at her. Her eyes rounded with shock, and he quickly climbed back onto the bed with her.

"What did you find?" he said into the phone as he nibbled on her neck.

"What didn't we find?" Charley said. "Somehow, that little weasel found a way around the security checks at Quad. He'd brought home disks, documents—even hardware."

Reno's head came up quickly as a thought hit him. "Have you got him in custody?"

"That's the best part. When we showed up at his office and slipped the stuff under his nose, he fainted. Honest to God, he fell right out of the chair. When he came to, he starting singing like a bird."

"He confessed?"

"Oh yeah."

Dani's fingers bit into his arms.

Reno put his hand over the mouthpiece. "They got him."

Her face drained of color. She covered her face with her hands, and her body began to shake. He wrapped his arm around her, but tried to concentrate. "Did he say why he did it?"

Charley cleared his throat. "Well, I don't know if you want to tell your lady this or not. Ah hell, Jeff. When we searched his house, we found all kinds of pictures of Danielle. This guy was obsessed. My guess is that she rejected him somehow, and he snapped."

Reno's teeth ground together. "He's never going to get near her again. You hear me, Charley? *Never.*"

"I don't think he'll have a chance. With the evidence we've got against him, he's going to be put away for a long, long time."

"Good. Otherwise, I'd have to go after him myself."

"I didn't hear that," Charley said tactfully.

Reno took a deep breath. "Right. You're right. Thanks, partner. I owe you."

"You don't owe me anything. Just treat her right. She deserves it."

Reno looked down at Dani, but her face was buried against his chest. He kissed the top of her shiny head. "Yes, she does."

He hung up the phone and tossed it on the floor. He hooked his finger under her chin and lifted it. Her face was still white, but the shaking had stopped.

Dani was dying for answers, but all Reno seemed to want to do was look at her. She caught his shoulders and shook him. "Well? What did he have to say?"

"Pfizer confessed. They found all kinds of proprietary information from Quadrangle Computing in his own home."

Her eyes went wide. "In his home? But how did he get it out of the building? And why did he frame *me?*"

"He was a nut, sweetheart."

"But . . ."

"No 'buts'," Reno said sharply. "He's crazy, and that's all there is to it."

Dani couldn't believe it. The Arnold she knew was so unlike the man he was describing. How could she not have seen it?

"We've got him, and the case is closed. It's over, baby. It's finally over."

Danielle froze when she realized what that meant. Everything inside her went still, but she didn't want to hope too much. Her hopes had been crushed too many times. "Does this mean that I'm a free woman again?" she asked hesitantly.

"Free as a bird," he said with a smile.

Her breaths went short. "No more cheap motels? No more rundown diners?"

"And no more strip joints," he said sternly.

Danielle lct out of whoop of joy. She threw her arms around him. She'd never thought this would ever happen. She'd thought that she'd be running for the rest of her life. To have everything fall into place so perfectly stunned her.

She had her life back.

Only her life wasn't there for her to go back to anymore.

"What's wrong, sweetheart?" Reno asked. He gently pushed back a strand of her hair and hooked it behind her ear.

"What am I supposed to do now?" she asked. Her fingers dug into the muscles of his back. She'd never thought about what would happen if she ever did manage to clear her name.

"What do you mean?"

"I don't have a place to live. I don't have a job. I don't even have a car," she said in a near panic.

He pulled her down with him so they were lying face-to-face. "First of all, I happen to know of a company who just lost a computer programmer. Quad would certainly be glad to have you back. Your manager believed in your innocence the entire time, and now, he probably feels pretty guilty about trusting Pfizer. He'll hire you back so fast, it will make your head spin."

She wasn't so sure.

"Secondly, you might not have a car, but I do," he said. "There's a red Corvette that's been sitting in my garage for about four months."

Dani blinked and pushed herself up onto an elbow so she could look down at him. "My car? *You bought my car?*"

His smile was devilish. "I was only about a day behind you

when you sold it at that used car lot. The guy gave me a sweet deal that I couldn't pass up. It's a hot car and, besides, it had something that no other car in the world has."

"What was that?" she asked as she poked him in the shoulder.

"It smelled like you," he said with a growl. She shrieked when he zeroed in on her neck. He pulled her back down next to him and kissed his way up to her ear. "I could smell your perfume when I took the test drive."

Dani moaned softly when she felt his tongue delve into the soft recesses of her ear. "That still leaves me without a place to live. I'm sure that the lease on my apartment expired months ago without me paying rent."

"I know a place," he said.

"Where?"

"With me."

Her heart flipped. She felt his hands tighten against her waist and, for a moment, she was uncertain. When she saw the vulnerable look in his eyes, though, everything made sense. "Okay," she breathed.

"Okay?"

A smile suddenly lit up her face. "It's time you paid for all the hell you put me through, Agent Reno."

His eyebrows rose. "That's *Special* Agent Reno."

Dani screeched when she found herself suddenly thrown off balance. She gripped his body tightly as he rolled on top of her.

"And I always get my man," he growled. "Or in this case, woman."

His head lowered, and she lifted her lips for his kiss. As his weight settled more heavily upon her, she knew that she was trapped. She'd been caught by the long arm of the law, but for the first time in ages, the thought didn't send her into a total panic.

She trailed her fingernails down his back to his hips. "I guess that means I'm off your wanted list."

"You're joking, right?" He thrust heavily into her and groaned. "Baby, you're the most wanted woman I know."

About the Author:

Kimberly Dean is very excited to be joining Red Sage. When not slaving over a keyboard, she enjoys reading, sports, movies, and loud rock-n-roll.

Secluded

❦

by Lisa Marie Rice

To My Reader:

Nicholas Lee walks on the dark side and always walks alone. By choice and by necessity. Anyone Nicholas loves would be destroyed by his enemies. Luckily he's never loved anyone—until now. When Nicholas loses his heart to beautiful, gentle Isabelle Summersby, he will allow himself only a week with her. One week of bliss and then they must part. Any longer and Isabelle will die. But what if Isabelle wants more?

Dear Reader, impossible loves have always tugged at my heartstrings. I hope the story of Nicholas and Isabelle will tug at yours.

Chapter One

"I want your daughter."

Nicholas Lee kept his voice low but the man sitting across from him heard and turned pale.

Thunder rumbled in the distance. Four heartbeats later, a blinding bolt of lightning lit the darkened study with a violent phosphorescent glare. Richard Summerby IV started. "I—I beg your pardon?" he stammered.

Ah, Nicholas thought. The perfect manners of the upper crust. Good thing he himself didn't have any manners at all.

Summerby had the pale refined looks only generations of wealth and privilege could bestow, and the dissipated features of the soft and the weak. For all that he'd been born rich, he'd managed to whore and gamble it all away. He was a whisper from total ruin and Nicholas would have been happy to push him over the edge if it weren't for the fact that Summerby had something he wanted very, very badly.

Nicholas studied the storm raging outside the big beveled window panes then brought his gaze back to Summerby. He smiled and the man paled further. Good. Nicholas needed for him to be afraid.

"I said I want your daughter," Nicholas repeated, his voice hard. "For a few weeks. And you will make sure I get her."

"This is—this is crazy." Summerby gave a half laugh. It strangled when Nicholas remained silent. "You can't have my daughter. Why, you're nothing more than a—a gangster."

"No, I'm not." Nicholas lifted his eyebrows. "Not any more, anyway."

He let his eyes roam thoughtfully around Summerby's elegant study. Original Chubb watercolors, Georgian furniture, an Aubusson carpet. And the paler spots on the dirty off-white walls where paintings had been taken down and sold, the Chippendale desk which needed restoring, the empty shelves where first editions had been auctioned off. The house itself would be the next to go. "Though I do keep my hand in some . . . ventures. For example, I just bought Morris Caneman's business."

Nicholas smiled as Summerby jerked in shock and made a choking sound in his throat. Now the man was beginning to understand just what kind of trouble he was in. "Caneman's creditors are mine now, Summerby. You owe Caneman three million dollars you don't have. Owing Caneman three million dollars is bad. Owing me three million dollars is much, *much* worse."

Summerby had broken out in a sweat. Lightning flashed again, followed a second later by a clap of thunder so loud its echo boomed in the room. Outside the study windows, the branches of the massive oak on the front lawn dipped and swayed, whipped into a frenzy by the rising wind.

"I'll be very clear." Nicholas speared Summerby with his gaze. "I might be persuaded to forgive the debt and save you from ruin. You might even get to keep the house. I understand it's been in your family for four generations. But you have to do something for me."

"What—" Summerby's voice came out as a croak. He wet his lips and tried again. "What would it take for you to do that? And what do you want with my daughter?"

"Sex," Nicholas said. "For a few weeks. After which you get your life back again." Summerby's eyes rounded and he made a strangled sound. Nicholas watched him coldly. "This is the way it's going to be, Summerby. Your daughter, Isabelle, should be here in a few minutes. She always visits you on Thursday afternoon. You will introduce me to Isabelle as an old family friend and as a man you've done business with for years. You will be perfectly natural and at ease. For all she knows, I am an old friend of her father's. And then for the next few weeks, you will cease all contact with her. If Isabelle contacts you, you'll avoid her. You will, above all, say nothing about me, my past, my . . . business dealings. Otherwise I call in my debt and you lose everything you have. This magnificent house, your Yacht Club membership, the mistress in Fairview Heights. The lot. I will strip you of every possession you own and I will leave you a broken man. Is that clear?"

Summerby's head nodded jerkily.

"Oh, something else," Nicholas said smoothly. "You will never ask your daughter for money again. I know all about you, Summerby." Nicholas didn't even try to hide his contempt. "You dumped your first wife and let her and your daughter go hungry while you lived it up with your second wife, who's now about to take you to the cleaners because you cheated on her. When your first wife became ill, you cut off all contact. Isabelle nearly killed herself putting herself through college while paying her mother's medical bills. And now that she's earning decent money with the TV show, you crop up with the daddy act and start asking for 'loans', which you never pay back. It's despicable and it's going to stop right now, is that clear?"

Summerby made a strangling noise in the back of his throat.

"Pops?"

Both men turned their heads at the soft voice. Nicholas's muscles tightened as Isabelle Summerby walked into the room, carrying the essence of springtime into the dark winter afternoon.

Nicholas rose from his chair, out of deference to a lady, and because he knew from experience that if he stood up to his full height while she was close to him, he might make her feel overpowered. If he stood while she walked towards him, he would give her time to adjust.

His size and obvious strength intimidated a lot of people and he used that fact often. There were plenty of people in this world he wanted to intimidate, to frighten, but not Isabelle. Never Isabelle.

Nicholas eyed her hungrily as she crossed the room, grace in every line of her slender body. This was the closest he'd ever been to her and every step she took seemed to echo in every beat of his heart.

He never missed her show on TV. He'd watched the recordings over and over again until he knew the programs by heart. She'd given a talk two weeks ago on new mysteries and he'd stood at the back of the packed hall and watched her. Watched her charming the crowd with her gentle humor, touching their hearts with her understanding of human nature. Making him yearn for what couldn't be.

He couldn't count the nights he'd sat in his car outside her bedroom window, waiting for the odd glimpse before she shuttered her windows for the night.

But this was the first time he'd been within touching distance. His heart thundered.

He'd seen her first on TV. One dark, rainy night when he'd let the despair seep into his soul, nursing it together with half a bottle of Glenfiddich. Reading had helped for a while, staving off the loneliness and heartsickness, but the book had ended, as did everything. *Deep in the Beast*. He could have sworn the author had had a direct line into his soul. He'd turned the book over and studied the author's picture. Lamont Serrin. A young black man with dreadlocks and small, scholar's glasses perched on his nose. Dark, piercing, all-seeing eyes and a poet's mouth.

It was as if Serrin had spoken for Nicholas, had lived Nicholas's childhood and written about it. The shock of reading his deepest thoughts had still echoed when Nicholas turned on his TV and stopped, frozen. It was Lamont Serrin, talking. But what had him springing to his feet to come closer to the wide screen was the woman Serrin was talking to.

Beautiful, yes, but then most women on TV were good-looking. It went with the territory. But this woman had an old-fashioned beauty, a romantic beauty, tinged with sadness. The expression on her heart-shaped face was intent as she spoke with the young black man, speaking somehow to Nicholas, too. She was reading his mind, his heart. All his life Nicholas had felt alone. He was used to it, used to feeling on his own. And in one night, two strangers reached out to him, one a beautiful woman. Isabelle Summerby.

He watched her program religiously after that and made it his business to find out everything about her. Finding things out about people, legally, illegally, was just one of his many money-making talents.

The more he found out about Isabelle, the more obsessed he became. Through his sources he discovered her history, her likes, her dislikes. Her courage, her steadfastness, her loyalty. Her intelligence, her gentleness.

Isabelle was standing in front of her father's desk, ash-blonde eyebrows drawn together in a frown. Her eyes were a pale, silvery blue, flashing like lightning as she looked uncertainly from her father to him.

"Pops? Are you all right?" Summerby started, a bead of sweat trailing down his cheek. Nicholas watched coldly as Summerby battled with himself. But Summerby had a great incentive to play the part. Three million of them. Summerby straightened. He passed a hand over his pale blond hair.

"Isabelle . . ." His voice became smooth, unctuous. "How nice to see you, my dear."

Isabelle looked at him, then at Nicholas. "Am I interrupting anything?"

"Not at all, not at all." Summerby managed to sound jovial. "We've finished our business anyway. My dear, I'd like to introduce you to a very good friend and old business partner of mine, Nicholas Lee."

Isabelle smiled gently, extending her hand. "Mr. Lee. Pleased to meet you."

"The pleasure is mine." Nicholas smiled back, though smiles had never come easily to him. He folded her hand in his. Her hand was slender and long-fingered, bare of rings. Her skin was amazingly soft and he felt an electric shock run through his body at her touch. He had become semi-aroused just watching her walk across the room and now his entire body was signaling acute pleasure. Her perfume, a subtle cloud of meadow flowers, enveloped him.

She looked at him curiously. He was mesmerized by the silvery sheen of her eyes. Her look was feminine curiosity mingled with a desire he suspected she wasn't aware of. He was. He was used to that look of sexual speculation in a woman's eyes, as if the woman could tell that he was a man who liked his sex long and hard and often.

Isabelle's pupils expanded and her nostrils flared. The female animal in her smelled the scent of a dominant male. She stood stock still for a moment, and Nicholas could feel panic and excitement war in her. Her hand trembled. Her soft lips were slightly open and the sound of her sharp intake of breath was loud in the silent room.

His eyes narrowed as he honed in on her mouth, open and moist, the mouth that would receive his tongue, his cock. He wanted that mouth violently. Now.

He wanted to sink to his knees with her in his arms. He wanted to lay her out on his bed, naked and wet and shaking with desire, and take her with his mouth, his hands . . . He wanted to penetrate her, body and soul, over and over again until she lay limp in his arms, completely his. He wanted to tug at her breast like a child while his fingers stretched her sex before he mounted her. He was big and he didn't want to hurt her. He would always make sure she was ready for him.

Through the silk, he could make out the shape of her breast and it was perfect, for his mouth and for his hands. Perfect.

She would fit him perfectly in every way.

Almost shaking with the effort it took him, he released her hand, subtly pulling his long dark jacket to disguise the full erection touching her had given him.

She was outlined against the darkness of the window, grace and light and woman in pale peach silk. She stared for a moment longer than was polite, then turned to her father. "I'll be at the Southside center tonight."

Southside. Nicholas froze. Southside was the most dangerous part of town.

"Bye, Pops." Isabelle leaned over gracefully and kissed her father on the forehead. She turned her head. "Goodbye, Mr. Lee. It was nice meeting you."

Nicholas bent his head solemnly and watched her walk across the room. Her hair fell like a sheaf of wheat between narrow shoulder blades. He could just imagine burying his face in the soft, fragrant mass. She was slender but womanly, hips flaring from a small waist, begging for his touch. The second time he took her would be from behind, plunging into her warm sheath, hearing her moans as he used his knowing fingers on her.

Mine, he thought. *You're going to be mine, Isabelle.*

Chapter Two

Nicholas Lee. Her father knew Nicholas Lee.

At the Southside Center after her lecture, Isabelle started stuffing her briefcase with the books and slides she'd used in the adult literacy lecture. A book fell off the edge of her desk and the sound echoed eerily in the empty hall.

Nicholas Lee. The man was as mysterious as he was notorious. His name was never in the newspapers. He never attended parties and was never seen around town. And yet everyone knew about him. Though immensely rich, no one really knew where the money came from.

Gun-running, Isabelle suspected. Smuggling, maybe. Not drugs. The one indisputable fact about Nicholas Lee everyone knew was that he hated drugs with a passion.

He was a man who was beyond the bounds of society, essentially an outlaw. How on earth could her father know such a man? Be friends with him? There were a lot of things she didn't know about her father. She'd only recently re-established relations with him after her mother's death.

Nicholas Lee had a reputation as a very dangerous man to know. Not a man to cross, not a man you'd want as your enemy. Dark rumors swirled about his name.

But maybe he wasn't so dangerous, after all, if he was her father's friend.

Very dangerous to women, though, she imagined. Certainly dangerous to *her* peace of mind. She hadn't been able to shake him from her thoughts. She could still see him, in her mind's eye. Long black hair, black eyes, dark blade-like features, black linen jacket, black silk shirt, black fine wool trousers. He was immense—powerful and dark with an almost palpable aura of menace around him. He also had seemed superbly fit. For all his bulk, he had moved with the grace of a panther.

A small sound at the back of the hall made her lift her head suspiciously.

The Southside Center was in a rough part of town. Of course, she took precautions. She had pepper spray in her purse, on top of the various items there, within easy grabbing distance. She always walked close to the walls, away from the street side of the sidewalk. Her car was parked only two blocks away. Five minutes after leaving the center, she'd be inside her locked car, on her way home.

Still, it would have been nice to have someone waiting for her, to walk her safely back to her car. Someone who cared, someone to watch over her.

In the large, dark auditorium, something shifted in her heart.

Isabelle's hands stilled. This was totally unlike her. She'd had a lover or two and dated. Not much, but enough to know that she wasn't missing much by not having a man in her life. She was used to solitude. After her father had abandoned them, she'd watched her mother descend into a frightening depression and then into illness. She'd learned early on the price you paid for love and trust and it had never seemed worthwhile up . . . up until now. What was changing? Why was she even thinking of a man to protect her? She'd been on her own for as long as she could remember and had learned the hard way to look after herself. Not to count on anyone else. Men were weak, anyway.

Most men.

A sudden vision of Nicholas Lee, standing silently in her father's study, flashed before her eyes. He hadn't seemed weak at all. He had looked exactly like the kind of man who would protect to the death what was his.

Stop that, Isabelle told herself. She knew nothing about Nicholas Lee, except that he had a reputation as a dangerous man. In the rare moments when she had fantasized about falling in love, she'd imagined someone gentle and tender. Certainly not someone like Nicholas Lee, a man who walked in darkness.

She was the last person in the large auditorium. As always, the janitor, an elderly black man, showed up at a side door. He motioned to her and she waved back. For a moment, Isabelle thought she saw a large, dark figure behind him and her heart leapt. But a second later, no one was there.

For a moment, she thought she'd seen Nicholas Lee. It seemed that she was having trouble dismissing the mysterious and oh-so-attractive Mr. Lee from her mind. She shook herself and tried to concentrate on her surroundings. Maybe once she got home safely and sat in her favorite chair with a cup of tea, she could let herself go and wonder about the man who'd made such a strong impact on her senses. But not now. Walking out on the streets of Southside while woolgathering was as good a way to commit suicide as any she knew.

Two women had been carjacked in Southside last month. She kept her cellphone in her jacket pocket, switched on, with 911 on speed dial.

Isabelle walked across the dark auditorium, the sound of her high heels echoing sharply in the large space. She frowned. She should have worn lower heels, but she had had so little time to change, she'd forgotten.

She opened the heavy steel doors of the auditorium and gave a gasp, shrinking back instinctively as a bright bolt of lightning cut through the bruised-looking sky, followed immediately by a clap of thunder so loud she felt as if her eardrums would burst. The rain was coming down so hard it looked more like a waterfall than a shower, pellets of water bouncing waist-high off the cracked sidewalks. She sighed and set off, holding her briefcase over her head.

If she'd spent less time in the center mooning over Nicholas Lee, she'd be halfway home by now. She skittered in her high heels down the street, trying to avoid the major puddles, but was soaked within a minute. The roar of the rain sounded in her ears and she could barely see. At least the weather should keep the low lifes away. She hoped.

She ducked her head down lower and tried to pick up speed. Another minute and she'd reach her car . . .

Isabelle staggered at the sharp blow to her head. It took her completely by surprise and almost knocked her off her feet. She thudded into the brick wall she'd been following by touch more than by sight. A heavy body slammed into her.

She couldn't seem to catch her breath, her bearings. Her ears rang and she couldn't focus her eyes. It was all so sudden, she didn't have a chance to react. Suddenly she was surrounded by men with sharp, angry faces. She blinked blood out of her eyes as one of the men tore her purse out of her hands. He opened it. With a laugh, he tossed out the pepper spray. Instinctively, Isabelle reached for the spray bouncing away and received another hard slap which made her head bounce off the wall and her ears ring.

Fumbling, her fingers numb, she tried to get to the cellphone in the jacket pocket, but her fingers tangled with his and he pulled it out and threw it to the ground.

Dazed, Isabelle stared at the little plastic rectangle in its bright blue holster in a puddle of muddy water. Whimpering, she stretched her hand down towards the phone and received a powerful punch to the stomach.

She sagged weakly. The man's body tightly pressed against hers was the only thing holding her upright. She tried to pull away, but there was only the hard brick wall against her back.

"Who ya thinkin'a callin', huh?" he breathed into her ear. His breath was horrid—hot and fetid with the smell of liquor and cigarettes. "The cops?" He snickered. "No cops down here, lady."

A chorus of coarse male voices echoed him. "Yeah man, tell her!"

It was all happening so fast. Isabelle had no time to catch her breath, to fight back. Hard hands grabbed her and threw her to the ground. The rough concrete of the sidewalk scraped her legs and hands. Her head bounced hard and she gritted her teeth not to lose consciousness.

The man curled his hand around her necklace and tugged hard. Again, harder. It was a thick gold chain. If he ripped it off her, he'd break her neck.

Isabelle tried to scream but, like in nightmares, only a strangled cry came out. Vomit tickled the back of her throat. She tried to kick the man in the groin, but missed. He slapped her, hard.

"Bitch!" he hissed. "You'll pay for—"

He stopped, an almost comical look on his face. Isabelle was so battered it took her several seconds to notice the gaping hole in his forehead, like a monstrous third eye. The man started toppling forward, the heavy rain washing away the blood as fast as it could spurt from his head.

Horrified, she rolled away before he could fall on top of her. Sobbing, she turned to see another body lying on the pavement, the rain turning bright red next to it, gradually fading into pink as the water sluiced away from the body.

One of her assailants lifted a gun, but never got a chance to shoot it. It was kicked out of his hand by a tall, dark, powerful figure, who then whirled and, almost faster than Isabelle's eye could follow, felled him with another kick, so powerful the sound of the booted foot meeting flesh carried over the din of the rain.

Her rescuer looked up, powerful chest lifting in a deep breath. She recognized him with a surge of emotion. Nicholas Lee. Their gazes met and held as he moved towards her.

"Look out!" Isabelle's voice didn't carry above the roar of the rain, but something in her face must have warned him. Another powerful whirl, a sickening thud, and the last of her assailants went down like a bull in the slaughter-house.

He didn't even look to see where the man had fallen. A second later, he was at her side, kneeling in the rain.

"Isabelle," he said. His voice was so deep it seemed to reverberate through her. That single word released her from her frozen terror. With a choked cry, she leaned forward into his open arms.

She barely knew him, but the violence of the attack had blown away her usual caution. At the deepest level of her being, she sensed that there was safety and shelter in this man's arms.

"Shh, it's okay. You're safe now. No one's going to hurt you. You're safe, I've got you." Murmuring comforting words over and over in that deep compelling voice, he slid his arms under her legs and back and stood up in a smooth, fluid motion.

Isabelle's head ached and the terror of the past few minutes still rushed through her. Her arms clasped his neck and she shivered, edging closer to him in her terror.

She turned her head into his neck and inhaled, and somehow the smell of him—intensely male, yes, but worlds away from the raw feral smell of her attackers—calmed her on some deep, primitive level.

He walked swiftly, carrying her as if she weighed nothing. Her ears rang, every muscle in her body hurt and her heart was still racing with the horror of the attack. But being in his arms soothed her.

His even strides, the power she sensed in his arms, the strong planes of his face—all reassured her. She didn't know him, not really, but in some unknown way she sensed she'd been waiting for him.

"You came for me," she murmured, barely aware of what she was saying.

"Yes, Isabelle," he said, his deep voice tender. "I came for you."

Chapter Three

Nicholas placed Isabelle gently in the passenger seat of his car and reached behind to the back seat where he kept a blanket. Spreading it over her, he tucked the edges around her shaking body, then hurried to the driver's side of the car.

He was drenched. It didn't matter for himself but Isabelle was injured and in shock. The cold and wet weren't doing her any good and she risked pneumonia.

He turned on the engine and revved it up, then turned the heat on, full blast. Isabelle needed medical care as soon as possible, but she also needed to get warm. Her teeth were clacking and he could almost feel the air around her vibrate with her intense shivers.

With one last look at her, Nicholas put the car in gear and sped off. He was a good driver and rarely exceeded the speed limit, but now he rocketed through town, taking the curves dangerously fast, blessing his reflexes and the makers of the Lexus.

He knew these streets well. He should. He'd grown up on Southside, until he'd been able to claw his way up and out.

Paying careful attention to where he drove, to changing the gears and keeping the powerful car fast and steady in the high winds and driving rain, he tried not to dwell for even a second on the rage that pulsed inside him or he'd be lost. He couldn't lose control. Not now. Isabelle needed him.

That thought alone kept his rage from overpowering him. Just thinking about those thugs attacking her almost sent him out of control.

He hadn't even intended for her to see him. He'd hung out in the back of the auditorium and had followed at a distance, just to see she got home safely. In those few minutes, she'd been attacked.

His hands tightened on the steering wheel until the dark skin of his knuckles turned white. Until he took his last, dying breath, he'd never forget the sight of Isabelle being beaten.

Taking another sharp corner, Nicholas exited Southside onto Herbert Boulevard.

"Where—where are we going?" Isabelle asked.

He looked sharply at her. Her tremors had abated somewhat, but her face was colorless, even her lips. She clutched the blanket tightly around her, the pale hand emerging from the soft folds of the blanket trembling.

"I'm taking you to St. Luke's. It's the closest hospital."

"No!" Isabelle's voice was anguished and her eyes widened in panic. "Please." She reached out with her pale, slender hand and touched him. "Please, *please* don't take me to St. Luke's. I'd rather die!"

Nicholas took one hand off the steering wheel and enfolded her hand in his. It was icy cold. "I have to." Surely she was in shock. "You need medical attention, Isabelle. You're probably concussed. You were beaten. What if you're bleeding internally? A doctor's got to see you. If there's nothing wrong, you'll just check out tomorrow."

She shook her head. "No." Her voice was low and stark. "Please, Nicholas, *please* don't take me to St. Luke's."

At any other moment, he would have been pleased to hear her say his name so naturally, as if they'd known each other for a long time, but he was too puzzled by her behavior to linger over the thought.

Isabelle took in a deep breath, as if to steady herself. "St. Luke's is where my mother died. I spent the better part of two years there. Please don't make me go to St. Luke's," she said quietly.

"Okay." He gently disengaged her hand to turn the steering wheel to the right. "Then I'll take you to Wallington Memorial. It's only a few miles further than St. Luke's would be."

"No." Isabelle whispered the word. As if exhausted by her pleas, she leaned her head back against the headrest and closed her eyes. "No hospitals. I've had enough of hospitals to last me a lifetime. No doctors, no needles, no prodding. I beg of you. Please. I couldn't stand it." A tear slipped out, falling down an alabaster cheek. *"Please."*

"Isabelle . . ." He didn't know how to resist her. It would have been easier if she'd ranted and railed. But that forlorn whisper and that single tear did him in. It simply wasn't in him to deny her anything. "You might be concussed."

"If I'm concussed, there's nothing anyone can do."

"Or wounded."

"No." She drew in a deep breath. "I'm scared and shocked and I have cuts and scrapes but nothing serious. I want to go home. God, I want to go home. Can't you just drive me home? The address is 1165 Rosewell Avenue." She turned her head against the headrest towards him and opened her eyes. They glowed silver in the pale light of the dashboard. "Please take me home." Her voice had sunk to a whisper.

She bit her bottom lip and closed her eyes again, as if she couldn't bear to watch him make his decision to hospitalize her.

He was helpless. "Okay. I'll take you home." His voice came out harsh and low. "But here's the deal. You do exactly as I say. I'll stay the night and at the first sign of something wrong, I'm bundling you up and taking you to the nearest medical center. Is that understood?"

"Yes." Her voice held a world of relief, as if his words hadn't been harsh, as if he'd given her a reprieve. When she closed her eyes again, he pulled out his cellphone and called his assistant, Kevin. He spoke quietly.

The rainstorm didn't abate in the twenty minutes it took him to drive to her house. He drove straight there, but Isabelle was too shocked to notice that he knew the way without direction. Pulling into the driveway, he threw the car into park and slanted a glance at Isabelle.

The worst of her trembling was over but there was such a look of desolation on her face his heart clenched. "Get your keys out and ready," he said quietly.

"Keys." She blinked and stared at him blankly. Her eyes widened suddenly. "My purse!" she exclaimed. "They—"

"Here. Your cellphone's in there, too. I picked it up." He handed her the purse. It was muddy and scratched, but he was fairly sure everything was still in there. The bastards hadn't had time to rifle through it.

"Oh." She bent her platinum head over the purse and pulled her hand out, holding a set of keys with a silver key chain in the shape of a dolphin. She placed it in his outstretched hand. "I seem to have a lot of things to thank you for."

Taking the keys, he kept his eyes on hers while lifting her hand to his mouth. "My pleasure."

Though wind howled outside and rain beat a tattoo on the roof and hood, utter silence reigned in the car. She stared at him, eyes wide, gentle mouth slightly opened.

Slowly, he ran his thumb over her soft knuckles and heard her trembling sigh.

He let her hand slip away and exited the car. Opening the passenger door, he wrapped her in the blanket and lifted her out.

In a few moments, he had her in the building and at her door on the second floor. He let her slide down gently next to the overstuffed soft green couch in the living room, and held her hand as she gingerly sat down.

"Where's the bathroom?" he asked.

"Second door to the right."

He went into the bathroom and ran hot water into the tub.

Nicholas was used to taking in a situation quickly, to focusing on two, even three things at once. Keen senses had helped him rise out of Southside quickly and make a million dollars before he was twenty, though he didn't want to remember how. While depositing Isabelle gently on the couch, he was observing her living quarters.

The apartment building was carefully calibrated to appeal to people whose tastes were elegant and genteel, but whose pocketbook didn't stretch to luxury.

The stairwell had been spacious, with low risers on the stairs and a graceful mahogany balustrade, but there was no elevator. The rooms were high-ceilinged and good material had gone into their construction, but they were small. The kitchen and bathroom were standard issue—no fancy additions such as ice makers and jacuzzis.

He knew that Isabelle had finished college with student loans pending and massive debts due to her mother's medical expenses. Her grandmother had died then and left Isabelle a house which she'd sold to help pay off her debts. The few good pieces in Isabelle's apartment were clearly heirlooms, the others cheap department store knock-offs which Isabelle brightened with throw rugs and pillows.

She had started to earn decent money from the TV show, but there still wasn't much to spare after the medical payments.

Nicholas vowed that when their affair ended, as it had to end, he would leave Isabelle financially set for life.

She would never have money problems again.

And he would never see her again.

Isabelle watched warily as Nicholas Lee walked back to where she huddled on the sofa. Nervously, she clutched the blanket more tightly about her shoulders.

She'd just survived an encounter with four terrifying men and here was another one, right in her living room, coming closer. His powerful body moved fluidly, gracefully. She'd seen for herself how dangerous he was. If she lived to be a hundred, she'd never forget how quickly and violently he'd overwhelmed four street punks. He was a violent man.

A violent man who'd also saved her life, she reminded herself.

Nicholas stopped in front of her and hunkered down until he could look her in the eyes. He lifted her chin with a long finger. "How are you feeling?"

Isabelle pulled in a breath. "Better," she said softly.

He watched her so intently it was as if he were walking inside her head.

"Your pupils are the same size." He reached out and put two fingers on her pulse. "Your pulse is a little fast—90 to a minute—but that's only to be expected after what you've been through. You don't have a temperature." He tilted her head and carefully touched the abraded skin on her cheekbones. Gently, Nicholas pulled her hands and then her arms from the blanket to examine them. "Nothing needs stitches. Let me feel your head." Probing gently, he felt through her scalp, stopping when she winced. "You've got two small lumps, but the skin isn't broken. All in all, you're lucky the damage wasn't worse."

"I'm lucky you arrived when you did," she said.

He shrugged. "Come on," he said softly, and pulled her to her feet. Once she was up, he lifted her in his arms.

"Where are you taking me?" she asked, startled.

"You need a hot bath and something hot to eat, in that order."

He carried her into the bathroom, all steamed up from her bath water. Isabelle realized that he'd deliberately left the door closed so the steam would cloud the air and had dumped half a bottle of bath foam into the tub. The steam and the bubbles would afford her some privacy in the tub.

"Take your clothes off and get in." The words were stark, impersonal, but a muscle was jumping in his jaw.

Isabelle froze. She didn't know this man, not in any real sense of the term. How could she strip with him in the room? The idea of being naked in his presence made her shiver.

"Go ahead." He turned and spoke with his back to her. "I put some shampoo on the rim. Can you wash your hair yourself?"

Isabelle hesitated. "Yes."

"Then get in while it's still warm."

She looked at that immensely broad back. She'd seen him in action. She'd felt his strength as he carried her. He could do anything he wanted with her. She looked with longing at the frothy tub, steam rising in wispy tendrils, then back to him. Shivering with nerves, she clutched her torn and tattered clothes.

He seemed to understand. "Go ahead, Isabelle." His voice was low and steady. "I'll wait until you get in. I just want to make sure the hot water doesn't make you feel faint." His head bowed. "Go on. I won't hurt you. I could never hurt you."

Something about his deep low voice, the bent head, the stillness of his wide shoulders reassured her. Stripping quickly, she eased into the hot water of the tub and sighed. The unease she felt at being naked with him was overridden by the relief of the warm water seeping into her sore muscles.

"Can I turn around?"

The silvery foam covered everything below her neck. "Okay."

Their gazes met. He didn't drop his eyes, didn't try to catch a glimpse of her body beneath the foam and water, but she was acutely aware of her nakedness. Her breasts ached, the warm water seemed to burn between her thighs. There was complete silence, except for the silvery sound of the bath water as she shifted.

He broke the silence. "You'll need something to put on."

"My bedroom is the first door on the left. There's a chest of drawers. My nightgowns are in the second drawer."

Without a word, he disappeared soundlessly through the door. Isabelle would have liked to have breathed a sigh of relief now that he'd gone. But while he'd been in the room she'd felt . . . safe. Scared, anxious and even—now that he was gone she could admit it to herself—aroused; but also safe from the outside world. Safe and cared for.

Isabelle slipped further down in the warm, fragrant water. When was the last time she'd had someone to take care of her? When was the last time she could actually just . . . let go? She couldn't even remember. She'd spent most of her life caring for her depressed mother, particularly in the last years of illness. Even her father seemed so childish and needy. Certainly not someone she could count on.

She was being ridiculous. Nicholas Lee was a stranger. He was a man shrouded in mystery, a man whose name was whispered. An underworld kingpin. Why should she imagine that Nicholas Lee would be a man she could count on? Because her father knew him? Because he'd been able to dispatch a bunch of street punks with ridiculous ease? Because his dark eyes seemed to penetrate her mind? Because his shoulders were so broad, his hands so strong, his touch so gentle?

Because he was so impossibly attractive and her body reacted with pulse-pounding desire?

There were no answers.

Her head tilted back, resting on the rim of the bathtub. Her eyes drifted shut.

Nicholas answered the doorbell.

"Here you go, boss." Tall, as blond as Nicholas was dark, Kevin Morris stood outside Isabelle's door with a large insulated case. He hadn't had much time since Nicholas had called him on the cellphone, but Nicholas knew that Kevin would come through for him. He always did.

Nicholas had caught Kevin trying to lift his wallet twelve years before. He'd been about to break the kid's wrist and toss him to the police when Kevin had fainted on him. From hunger.

Turned out what he thought was a hardened street punk was a fifteen year old boy who'd run away from a brutal foster home and had been living on the streets for two months. Turned out he'd been suffering from malnutrition. Turned out he still had raw wounds from the beatings he'd taken. He had burn marks all along his arms from where cigarettes had been put out on his skin.

Nicholas had been there, knew what that kind of abuse was like.

He'd taken the boy home, fed him and straightened him out. He'd hired tutors so Kevin could get his high school equivalency and had offered Kevin a room, clean clothes and daily meals in exchange for household chores.

Like most of his instincts, this one had been rock solid. Kevin had taken to education like a cactus soaks up water in the desert. And like a cactus, Kevin had blossomed. The tutors could barely keep up with him.

He'd shown an unusual affinity for computers and numbers and was finishing an advanced degree in accounting while working as Nicholas's right hand man.

Kevin was the one man in the world Nicholas trusted. And Kevin had shown over and over again that he was worthy of that trust.

Nicholas took the heavy, warm case. "Thanks, Kevin. Be on standby for the next few days."

"Right, boss." Kevin nodded and left.

Nicholas put the case in the kitchen. In Isabelle's bedroom, he pulled open the second drawer and rummaged. The nightgown he found was made of thick, soft white cotton and buttoned up to the neck. A nightgown more suited to a grandmother than to a desirable young woman.

He was going to buy Isabelle negligées in pale rose silk and in every other color of the rainbow that did justice to her delicate beauty, but for the moment he knew she'd feel better in a nightgown designed for comfort, not seduction.

He walked back into the bathroom and stopped to look at her. Isabelle was dozing, her head tilted back over the rim of the bathtub, her long slender neck exposed. He could see delicate collarbones, the slight swell of her breasts, and one narrow knee rising out of the foam.

"Isabelle." He shook her shoulder gently. Her skin felt like satin and he gritted his teeth. "Don't fall asleep." He still wasn't entirely certain she wasn't concussed.

Her eyes opened slowly and he saw the exact moment when the memories returned. He didn't want her dwelling on them a moment more than necessary.

"Here," he said, and opened a large bath towel. She hesitated, and with one last quicksilver glance at him, she rose and stepped out of the tub and into the towel.

A silken lock of pale blonde hair had fallen down from her topknot. It spilled over her shoulder and down her breast. The last pale soft curl fell over her soft full breast to circle her nipple, like a frame offering him her succulent breast. Both nipples were full and pink. Her nipples were erect because she'd gone from the hot bath to the relative coolness of the air in the bathroom. But he'd also seen her shudder at his look. She wasn't aware of it, but she was aroused.

Not as much as he was.

He stifled a groan as he held the large bath towel open and enveloped her in it. Her breasts brushed his chest and he had to work to keep his hands gentle.

He was painfully aroused. Nicholas marveled at that bitch-goddess, fate. Six hours after meeting Isabelle in person, she was in his arms—and he couldn't act on what his entire body was clamoring for.

He was as far from making love to her as if she were on the dark side of the moon.

Every muscle was rigid with the desire to bear her to the floor and mount her immediately, slide into her warm, welcoming sheath, feeling those long, pale, slim legs hugging his waist, full breasts crushed against his chest . . .

He stepped back, grateful that he'd kept his jacket on. "Can you make it to the kitchen?" he asked, his voice low.

At her murmured yes, he made his escape.

By the time she entered the kitchen in her granny nightgown, he'd found her dishes and cutlery and was filling a bowl with soup.

She stood framed in the doorway, pale hair drying in tendrils about her face, eyes wide and shadowed.

His body clenched with desire to take her and wipe the sadness from her face. He wanted her to think only of the pleasure he could give her, feel only his body in hers.

Not now, he vowed to himself. But soon. Soon.

"Sit down and eat. You'll feel better." He pulled out a chair.

Isabelle stood for a moment, looking at him. She studied his face so intently he swore she would have seen into his soul, if he'd had one. "You're being very . . . nice to me. Why is that? I hardly know you."

"Don't worry about that now. Eat something."

Isabelle continued scrutinizing his face. Finally, she moved forward slowly and sat down. After a long moment, she picked up the spoon and dipped it into the rich-smelling brew. He'd asked Kevin to have the cook send whatever he'd been cooking for dinner and he had—a thick cream of tomato soup.

Nicholas uncorked the bottle Kevin had taken from his cellar and poured a glass for Isabelle and one for himself. He glanced at the label and smiled at Kevin's excellent taste.

There was total silence, broken only by Isabelle's spoon lightly glancing off the rim of the bowl and the soft sounds as they sipped the wine.

By the time she'd finished the soup and the glass of wine, a little color had come back into her face. She was far from over the shock of the attack but the healing, however long it would take, had begun.

She hung her head, a few strands of drying blonde hair falling forward over her breast. She still held the spoon in her hand. It clanged tinnily against the china bowl as her hand started trembling.

Nicholas picked her up and carried her into the living room. He sat down on the lone armchair with her in his arms. Threading his hands through her hair, careful of her injuries, he held her tightly as she turned her face into his neck and burst into tears.

They were the tears of a strong woman who didn't cry easily. At first, she resisted, holding herself stiffly, shaking with the effort to keep the tears at bay.

Nicholas brushed pale strands away from her face and leaned down. He kissed her ear, then whispered into it. "Let go." He shifted her in his arms to hold her more closely. "I'll be here to catch you."

Isabelle shook once, a deep tremor and then the tears started coming, quickly, silently. Nicholas cupped the back of her head and gave her his warmth and his strength. They were hers for the asking.

He remembered Isabelle in the bathtub. The delicacy of her, the satin softness of her alabaster skin. And the bruises on her arms, the finger marks on the side of her face and neck. Nicholas clenched his fists, wishing he could kill the bastards all over again.

If he hadn't been there . . . but he had. He expelled his breath in a long, controlled stream to rid his body of tension. If there was one thing life had taught him, it was to look forward, not back. 'What if' didn't exist. Only the here and now existed.

And here and now was Isabelle who needed tending.

Gradually, Isabelle's breathing slowed. He glanced down to see the tears drying on her cheeks, long lashes lowered, so thick they cast shadows over the delicate cheekbones. She was slumped bonelessly against him, half-lying in his arms. She felt delicate and soft and . . . right. Long after she'd fallen into a deep sleep, Nicholas sat and held her, one hand cradling her head, the other around her back, holding her tightly.

He sat with her in his arms while the sky outside her living room window turned pewter, then slate, then black. The rain stopped and stars shone coldly down as the wind pushed the clouds away and still he held her. She was deep in the sleep of exhaustion. At the most primitive level, she knew he would keep her safe and her mind had just shut down completely to give the body rest.

Around ten, the rain started again, drumming against the windowpanes. Somewhere in the house the thermostat kicked in.

Nicholas rose easily from the armchair with Isabelle in his arms. He carried her into the bedroom, gritting his teeth as she turned instinctively towards him in her sleep. She felt so soft and light and right in his arms. The temptation to simply sink to the floor with her, pull up her nightgown, spread her legs and thrust into her was almost overwhelming. He shook with a tangle of lust and love. He would be taking care of his lust very soon. The love was something he couldn't allow to happen.

He placed one knee on the mattress and lowered Isabelle to the bed. She sighed and moved her legs restlessly. She was frowning. Was she reliving the attack in her dreams?

Nicholas sank down on the bed behind her and put his arms around her. He put his nose in her soft hair and inhaled deeply. She smelled of shampoo and bubble bath, of woman and the lavender sachet he'd found in her dresser drawer.

This was exactly where he'd planned to be this evening—in bed with Isabelle in his arms. Her house or his—it wouldn't have mattered. He'd intended to 'bump' into her after her father's introduction and invite her out to dinner. He was used to the dance of seduction; they'd have ended up in bed together, he knew how to make sure of that. Nicholas lifted the corner of his mouth in a half-smile. Of course, the plan was for Isabelle to be awake and participating.

She stirred, her breast fitting perfectly in his hand, her soft bottom rubbing up against him. Nicholas bit his lip and resisted the urge to slide her nightgown up, lift her leg over his hip and slide into her. Instead, he held still as blood rushed to his cock. He couldn't remember the last time he'd been this full, this hard. He was hard as stone. Nicholas tortured himself again by pressing his cock against her and clenched his teeth to stop from groaning aloud.

He wasn't a masochist but this was the best way he knew to torment himself. Isabelle settled back against him.

He shouldn't be this needy. He certainly wasn't deprived. He had sex as often as he wanted. Just the other night he'd fucked an attractive woman five times and in the time it took to leave her apartment and go down in the elevator, he'd forgotten her name. He'd felt cold and dry and empty, the fleeting pleasure of orgasm already forgotten. This was happening more and more often lately. He could fuck for hours and feel nothing.

It was in the elevator that he finally decided he needed Isabelle. For just a while. She'd been his far off star, the woman who inhabited his dreams, the last thing he thought of before drifting off to sleep, the first thought in the morning. She was his obsession and he realized that he needed to live his obsession just once before dying.

He cupped her breast gently and moved his groin against her and grew, impossibly, even harder.

It was hell.

It was heaven.

Chapter Four

Isabelle awoke slowly, grudgingly from the depths of a deep sleep. Dimly, she was aware of a dull, far-away noise and it took her a few moments to realize that it was the patter of rain outside the window. A steady rain, not like—suddenly she stiffened as yesterday came back to her in a rush. The thunderstorm, the wild men attacking her, Nicholas Lee's rescue.

In a way, he was still rescuing her.

As if he knew that waking up alone after the terrors of yesterday would frighten her all over again, she had slept clasped in his arms. He was behind her, his big body enveloping her, wide shoulders bracketing hers. She was lying on one of his brawny arms, the other was around her waist.

She was warm and felt utterly enclosed and protected. She realized that she'd come awake slowly, as if her subconscious didn't want to face the coming day, and that at each stage of her awakening, she'd been subconsciously aware of his protection.

She also remembered that he'd shaken her awake a number of times during the night, to see if she was concussed.

Yesterday had been shocking and horrible, but it had only lasted a minute or two before Nicholas had rescued her. Since then she had been tenderly handled, even pampered.

Isabelle had faced many hard things in her life, including a mother dying slowly and horribly of cancer, and she had faced them completely alone. She possessed a core of strength deep inside her, which would allow her to recover from this ordeal, too.

Being with Nicholas had helped. She couldn't ever remember not being alone to face a problem.

She had wept her heart out on Nicholas Lee's shoulder last night while he had held her tightly, one big hand covering the back of her head, his other arm around her waist in an embrace of total protection. While she'd cried, a hard knot of tension and fear, not only from the attack but from other, older sorrows, had begun to dissipate.

She stretched slightly . . . and froze at the feel of the enormous erection against her backside.

"Don't panic." The deep voice was wry. Those huge arms tightened briefly, then he slid his left arm out from under her. "I've been like that all night and I haven't attacked you yet."

Isabelle turned over and blinked to find his face so close to hers. She hadn't dared in her father's study, but now she took the time to peruse him.

He'd lifted himself up to prop his head on his left hand. Though she knew he couldn't have had much sleep, he looked exactly as he had yesterday—strong and tireless and intense. His hair had come free from the long ponytail he wore tied at his nape and his straight black hair brushed past wide shoulders to spill incongruously over her pale pink frilly pillow slip. His hair was thick and had the sheen of health, so black there were blue highlights. Her hands itched to touch it.

Suddenly, she remembered his erection, and what he'd said.

"All *night?*" she asked huskily before she could stop herself. Her eyes widened and she could feel a fiery blush bloom on her face.

"All night," he confirmed soberly. A corner of his mouth lifted and she was fascinated by the changes in his face. It was such a strong face, the features clean and sharp. That half smile made him even more wildly attractive. She was suddenly aware of her heart thumping in her chest.

"Ouch," she whispered.

"You better believe 'ouch'." He reached out and brushed away a few strands of her hair. His hand was large, easily double the size of hers, lean and strong. The raised veins of an athlete coursed along them, along his muscular forearms and up the huge biceps.

Everything about this man was outsize. Leaning on his side, his shoulders were so broad he blocked her view of the window on the opposite wall. He was bare-chested and the sight of the large, hard slabs of muscle made her stare. A mat of thick black hairs covered his chest, narrowing to a broad stripe over his flat stom-

ach. Luckily for her heart rate, the sheet covered the rest. She'd
had enough excitement for the year.

He studied her soberly and seemed pleased with his perusal.
"You're looking better. Are you up for some breakfast?"

Isabelle wrenched her mind away from what the sheet might
be covering. The memory of what she'd felt with her bottom—a
long, thick column as hard as steel—made her blush even harder.
"Yes, I—" She stopped and frowned. "Actually, I don't think
there's much to eat in the house. I've been too busy lately to do
much shopping."

"I suspect your house just grew some espresso beans and
croissants."

She smiled. Since she'd been a small child alone in the house
with a severely depressed woman, no one had ever prepared
breakfast for her. "Is that right? Would this be from the same tree
that grew cream of tomato soup and Merlot?"

He inclined his big head. "The very same. Stay here." He bent
and kissed her lightly on the lips and rolled out of bed, his movements powerful and graceful. He was out the door before she had
time to react.

He'd kissed her. In her father's study she must have wondered
how his kisses would taste, because her first thought was—*so
that's what it's like.*

It had been the merest breath of a kiss, his firm lips just brushing hers, and she had felt it to her toes.

It took her a moment to calm her senses and by that time, the
rich smell of excellent coffee had wafted into the bedroom and
she discovered, to her surprise, that she was hungry.

Minutes later, he walked into the bedroom carrying a tray with
a steaming cup of coffee and a plate with two croissants.

Isabelle sat up, plumping pillows at her back. Nicholas set the
tray on her bedside table and sat on the edge of the bed. He unfolded a large linen napkin with a snap, placed it over her lap and
handed her a cup. It was bone china with a delicate rose print.

Isabelle fingered the napkin. "Does that tree grow linen nap-
kins and—" she ran her hand around the rim of the cup, "Rosen-
thal china?"

"Limoges," he said. "Absolutely. And that same tree is going
to grow some lunch in a few hours."

She sipped the excellent coffee and sighed in pleasure. "It will
probably be delicious, judging by this coffee, but I'll have to pass,
I'm afraid. I've got a luncheon date for noon."

"No, you don't." Nicholas's deep voice was calm as he cut a bite of the croissant and lifted it into her mouth. Startled, she bit into the warm flaky pastry and nearly moaned at the buttery taste. She chewed, swallowed and frowned. "What do you mean—"

"Open up," he ordered, and delicately held another bite before her mouth. She opened it to ask what he meant about her luncheon date and he tipped the morsel in. She chewed quickly and swallowed. "What—"

"You had an appointment with Nancy Ruger at the Blue Lagoon. I called her up an hour ago and cancelled the date. She'll get back to you."

Isabelle sat up straighter. "How on earth—"

"Easy. Your organizer is right next to the phone. You very efficiently put your appointments and the phone numbers on each day. I've cancelled all your appointments for the next three days."

"How dare you do that!"

His eyes glittered. "You'd better believe I dare. You need peace and quiet. The last thing you need is to go skittering around town in this weather." He gestured out the window at the gray, sullen sky and steady rainfall. "All I did was make sure you'll have the opportunity to get the rest you need. You need rest, Isabelle. One way or another I'm going to make sure that you get it." His voice was calm. That and his measured movements reassured her on a level deeper than words.

And he was right.

She hadn't been looking forward to the lunch with Nancy Ruger, a colleague from the station. If truth be told, she wasn't looking forward to her other upcoming appointments, either. She was tired and ached all over and the idea of taking it easy for a few days was immensely appealing.

Somehow, Nicholas Lee knew that. She should be angry at him. He'd been high-handed in rearranging her life and he certainly hadn't apologized for changing her schedule. But the knowledge that he'd forced her to do something she should have had the good sense to do for herself pulled the punch of her anger.

He was watching her closely, his expression so intense the skin was pulled tightly over his broad, high cheekbones. She couldn't begin to read the meaning of all that intensity, except for the fact that it was focused tightly on her.

Amazingly, even in the full light of day, the irises of his eyes were almost the same color as the pupils. She'd never seen such black eyes before. Most dark eyes had color in them—it just

Lisa Marie Rice

didn't show up except in sunlight. Nicholas Lee's eyes were as black as midnight.

His skin was dark, too, a strong olive with no ruddy undertones. She couldn't tell if he was deeply tanned or whether it was his natural skin tone. Maybe he had some Native American blood in him, which would explain the thick, straight black hair and his coloring.

She was staring at him. To cover her embarrassment, she took another sip of coffee.

"Is the coffee good?" he asked softly.

He had an unusual timbre to his voice. It was deep and rich, with bass undertones that set up an answering vibration in the pit of her stomach. She nodded her head jerkily.

"Let me find out for myself."

Before she could understand his intention, he leaned forward and put his mouth over hers, slanting to open her lips. This time it was a real kiss and she shivered as his tongue met hers, sliding over it, exploring her mouth. He bit lightly at her bottom lip, licked it, then licked into her mouth. She couldn't open her eyes, she couldn't move. All she could do was open her mouth helplessly to his as his lips and tongue gave her a honeyed pleasure. She heard a soft noise and realized, dimly, that she was moaning deep in her throat. She shook and her hands clenched in the covers. His tongue swirled deep and withdrew. His mouth lifted, settled, then lifted again. He pulled back and gazed at her. Her eyelids felt heavy; it took great effort to open them. She stared back at him, numbly.

"God, yes, it's good," he whispered, and covered her mouth again.

This time she participated fully in the kiss, opening her mouth under his, raising her hands to rest them on the iron slabs of muscle on his shoulders. When his tongue met hers again, she dug her nails into his shoulders. There was no give to his skin at all. He was pure steel.

She breathed in deeply, her nose next to his cheek and drew in a heady odor of soap and male musk. His eyes were closed and she saw that he had thick, blunt black lashes.

She couldn't see anything more because her own eyes drifted closed. It was as if all her senses were concentrated on her mouth and she couldn't drum up enough energy to keep her eyes open.

With each beat of her heart, with each stroke of his tongue, she slid further down in the bed. Because she couldn't stay upright. Because his hard body was pressing down on hers.

He groaned and, dimly, she realized he was as affected as she was. He was hard everywhere she touched—the muscles along his shoulders, his biceps, the penis she could feel digging into her thigh.

She should draw away, but his mouth was too delicious, stroking heat into her, his taste too heady. She drifted dreamily, drugged with sexual heat as he explored her mouth.

He withdrew the barest breath away and she sighed in disappointment, but he immediately placed his lips on her jawbone and nipped lightly.

She jerked with surprise, with pleasure. Her breathing speeded up as his mouth moved to her ear, where he traced the delicate whorls with his tongue.

His thick hair fell like a cloud around them, encircling them in a private black embrace.

She felt cool air on her breasts and looked down. He'd unbuttoned her nightgown and spread the wings wide.

He lifted his head and she shivered at the heat in his eyes. Arousal had turned his harsh features even starker, his normally dusky skin flushed with blood. His hand was gently stroking her breast, his thumb slowly circling her nipple.

Before the sluggish thought formed in her mind—*I should protest*—he'd bent his head to her breast and she gasped as he took the tip into his mouth.

He cupped her breast, suckling strongly, and the sensation was so intense it was like a white hot wire drawing her towards his mouth. This wasn't a gentle suckling, like a child's, but a grown man's tugging with such strength she thought she would faint from the overwhelming sensations.

Isabelle looked down and found herself aroused by the contrast of his black head on her breast. His hand looked darker, even more powerful, against her white skin.

Isabelle let her head fall back as he moved to her other breast. The rain had stopped, as if the world had hushed to make way for the sounds they were making—her soft pants, his harsh groans, the erotic pulling of his mouth at her breast.

She was too wrapped in a sensual haze to protest when a strong hand stroked her leg. First her calf, his hand so large it easily met around it, then the back of her knee, then slowly, slowly up the inside of her thigh. He was using his teeth and tongue on her nipple, tugging sharply, and she was on fire.

At the first gentle hint of his hand, her shaking thighs fell apart.

He pressed his large, warm palm over her mound and she sighed with pleasure.

Nicholas lifted his head. "Look at me, Isabelle," he said softly. She lifted heavy lids to meet his eyes burning into hers. The air felt cool on her breasts, still wet from his mouth. He was breathing heavily, his chest expanding like a bellows. His body gave off waves of heat and hers felt as if a furnace burned just beneath her skin.

A large, blunt finger circled her flesh, stroking the folds. He couldn't help but feel her arousal, feel her hot wetness and she saw satisfaction in his lowered lids, in the flush of red over his cheekbones. His mouth was wet, lips slightly swollen from her kisses. He unfolded her as gently as a flower, petal by petal and her womb clenched.

He pushed a large finger into her heated center, barely at the entrance, and her hips arched to take more of him.

"That's it," his low, deep voice crooned. "That's it, open for me, love."

He moved his finger deeper and circled her clitoris with his thumb. He slowly withdrew his finger and slipped a second finger in. She gave a high cry and her thighs trembled.

"God, you feel so hot and tight, love. Like a virgin. You haven't had a man in you for some time, have you?"

She couldn't breath. She was burning up. He slid the two fingers gently in and out and then slowly separated them. She whimpered.

"Isabelle? How long has it been since you've had a cock here?" He thrust his fingers hard and she writhed. His fingers felt as large as a penis. Her whole body was trembling.

"Not—" she licked her lips. "Not since college."

"Good," he murmured, increasing the rhythm of his strokes. "My cock will be here soon. When you're ready. In the meantime, you're going to get used to my hands and my mouth on you. You'll come over and over again before I take you, and you'll be ready."

He circled her clitoris again, hard, and Isabelle exploded. She clenched helplessly around his fingers as his mouth ground into hers. Her fingers dug into his biceps as he continued stroking, harder and harder as she climaxed. She cried out, but his mouth covered her moans as she kept clenching around his fingers.

He knew just how to touch her, just how hard and how soft, to keep her on the edge, in helpless spasms of pleasure so blinding it was almost painful.

She finally subsided, exhausted, and lay back in his arms. He withdrew his fingers and touched her nipples, wetting them with her juices. He bent and licked them and she jerked. She couldn't possibly be feeling desire again, but she was.

Isabelle had never lost control of herself this way, hadn't known she could. It was exhilarating and frightening. She still shook with the intensity of her release. Her eyes closed and her hands fell to her sides. She could still feel the echoes of her orgasm in her lower body.

Nicholas kissed her closed lids. "Sleep now, love," he said in his black magic voice and she surrendered, sliding into darkness.

Chapter Five

"What do you want from me?"

Nicholas looked up from the book he'd taken from Isabelle's bookshelves.

He'd been pleased, but not surprised, to note that her tastes matched his. Her bookcase could have been his. He chose a book he'd read many times, noting from its well-worn look that she must have read it over and over again, too.

Isabelle stood in the doorway of the bedroom, eyeing him warily, too tense, too taut to move into the living room where he sat on the couch.

She held herself stiffly, arms crossed over her waist. Her face was expressionless, as if she were holding herself against him, determined not to give in to him in any way.

He'd let her sleep the morning and the afternoon away, knowing she needed it, both for the rest it would give her body and because her mind needed down time to process the violence yesterday.

Kevin had stopped by again leaving supplies and Nicholas could heat her up a late lunch or early dinner at any time.

"What do I want with you?" he repeated, putting the book down, raising his eyes to hers. She stood there, the woman who haunted his dreams, rumpled, delicate, fragile. He had never been vulnerable to anyone or anything but he knew in the deepest recesses of his heart that she could bring him to his knees. "I want to fuck you," he said calmly.

She winced.

Nicholas used the crudest expression to hide what he wanted to say with all his heart. *I want to love you. I want you to love me back. I want to court you, I want you to be mine forever.*

He'd come up from the dregs, from a rat-infested tenement and a drug addict mother who sold her body for a fix. But though he'd been born in poverty, he'd also been born strong and smart and ruthless. He'd used all the strength, power and cunning nature had invested him with to build an empire. He was rich and powerful beyond even the dreams of most men. He could have anything in the world, satisfy any appetite, save one.

He couldn't have Isabelle for a lifetime. A week or two at the most was all that fate would give him.

He got up and slowly walked towards her. He didn't take his eyes off hers. "I want to fuck you so hard and so often you'll forget what it's like not to have me inside you. I want to make you scream with pleasure, over and over again. I want to fuck you so much your body will be molded to mine, your cunt shaped to my cock, your skin smelling of me. I want you to forget where you end and I begin."

He stopped in front of her. Her eyes were huge as she scrutinized his face, as though trying to see what was behind his hard words.

He reached out to untie the knot of her bathrobe and slid it off her shoulders. It fell softly to the floor in heavy folds. Isabelle drew in a sharp breath, the sound loud in the silent room, but she didn't stop him.

In a moment, Nicholas had the buttons of her nightgown undone to the waist. He lifted his hands to her shoulders and opened the nightgown. It slid, caught for a moment on her hips, then slithered to the floor to lie around her feet.

He wanted her more than he wanted his next breath and she wanted him back, just as much.

A lifetime of sex had taught him all about female desire. Isabelle didn't move, barely breathed, but she wanted him. Her cheekbones were flushed, the pupils of her eyes were so dilated only a shimmering silvery band rimmed the black. Her nipples were deep pink and hard. He reached out with one finger to touch her.

He loved the contrast of his skin against hers. Countless times he'd read descriptions of a woman's skin, but words paled against the reality of hers. It was incredibly fine-grained, as smooth as a child's and the palest ivory in color.

With the lightest of touches, he followed her slender collar-bones, the swell of her breast, the smooth pink aureole a shade lighter than the nipple, down to the full, womanly underside. She was so finely made; he ground his teeth together so hard they ached at the thought of those bastards who had attacked her.

Her breasts were amazingly large for so slender a woman—heavy, firm and high with nipples turned a deep rose with arousal. He smoothed his hand down over her other breast and cupped it, loving the full weight of it in his hand. He bent to take her nipple into his mouth.

She liked it when he pulled hard at her. She might not even have known that she liked his mouth on her that way. He remembered her soft gasp of surprise when he'd first taken her breast in his mouth.

She didn't have much sexual experience, that was clear. His fingers had barely fit inside her and she had seemed stunned, almost frightened, at her body's response. And yet, her response to him had been strong and immediate.

There was so much he wanted to show her. He knew, from his experience with an endless number of sex partners, that when he finally took her completely, they would fit like a lock with a key. She was made for him, for his hands and his mouth and his cock.

Nicholas slowly sank to one knee and gently urged her thighs apart with his hands. She had silky, pale blonde hair between her thighs, soft pink flesh peeking temptingly through. He couldn't resist the temptation and leaned forward.

"Oh!" Isabelle swayed and Nicholas clamped two hard hands on her hips as she tried to pull away.

"Not yet," he said huskily. "I need to know what you taste like here."

Like seashells, like a rose, like the dawn.

He moved his mouth gently on her, his tongue feeling the soft folds of flesh open up as he explored her sheath as thoroughly as he had explored her mouth.

He lost himself in her flesh, delighting in her soft textures, in the smell of her. For minutes, they stood there, his hands holding her up as he delved deeply into her. Suddenly, Isabelle gave a sharp cry and her hands clasped his head. She trembled violently and erupted in the sharp contractions of orgasm.

Nicholas stood up swiftly, catching her in his arms, and carried her to the sofa.

Much as he wanted her naked in his arms, she might be cold,

so he wrapped her in the soft teal blue blanket which had been draped over the sofa. Isabelle still trembled. She turned her face into his neck, as if she wanted to hide from him.

Nicholas settled her comfortably in his embrace and lifted her chin with a finger. Her eyes were closed. The color that had tinged her face with arousal had fled and now she was pale. He waited patiently until she opened her eyes and looked at him.

"Let me tell you the way it should be in a perfect world, Isabelle," he told her quietly. "This is our story. One night, when I'm depressed and have had too much to drink, I watch your program on TV. You're a beautiful, intelligent woman, with a fascinating take on life. I like the way you think. I like the way you look. You love books. I love books. I get someone to introduce us and then I ask you out. I take you to a nice restaurant and to a jazz club afterwards. We have fun. We're very attracted to each other. Maybe you're a little lonely, too, looking for someone. We click on a number of levels. I take you home and kiss you goodnight. It's a good kiss, a solid kiss. Both of us would like to take it further, but it's too early yet. We both know this is something serious, something worth taking slowly."

Nicholas bent to give her a gentle kiss on the cheek, his lips lingering over the smooth skin. When he lifted his head, he looked her straight in the eye.

"I've had a lot of sex in my life, Isabelle. I need it often and I've never had any trouble getting as much as I want." She was watching him carefully, intently. Her eyes, that stunning mixture of silver and blue, never left his. He shrugged. "Ordinarily, an hour after I've taken a woman out to dinner, I'm in bed with her. Then we have a hot affair for a week or two at the most. Sometimes less."

For a moment, Nicholas rested the back of his head against the sofa and closed his eyes. Hearing himself describe his own life depressed him. He'd had all the sex he'd ever wanted but it had never been enough to fill this gnawing emptiness inside him.

For so long he'd refused to acknowledge his loneliness, the desire for a connection. Connections were for other people. All his life he'd thought of himself as utterly apart from the rest of humankind. He'd been born that way and, he thought, he'd die that way.

And all along, like a powerful underground river, his need for love had flowed until it had found the right place to come up into the light.

Right now, he felt closer to Isabelle than he'd ever felt to any other woman. And he hadn't even been inside her yet.

It couldn't last. The connection had to be severed and his river had to dry up. But first, he was going to give himself a taste of what others thought of as their birthright—a chance at love.

Nicholas opened his eyes at the feel of Isabelle's hand against his cheek. Her gaze was soft.

"That sounds like a lonely way to live," she said gently.

He covered her hand with his, then turned her hand around to lace his fingers through hers. He brought the back of her hand to his lips.

"Very lonely," he agreed. "Still, you can't miss what you don't know. Only . . . in this perfect world, I realize what I'm missing and it's in my grasp. I find you and I'm not going to let you go. I take you out every night. I accompany you to your conferences and lectures. I call you several times a day to find out how you are. I meet your friends and colleagues and I make it clear to everyone that I'm staking my claim to you. Like now, in this other world it's mid-December when I start courting you and on Christmas Day, I give you a diamond and sapphire ring and ask you to do me the honor of becoming my wife. We marry on New Year's Eve and we finally make love for the first time that night, as fireworks explode all around us."

Nicholas looked at her lying in his arms. Gently, he opened the edges of the blanket a little, as if opening a present. Her skin shimmered like a pearl in its shell. "It is well worth waiting for," he whispered.

He closed his eyes for a moment and ran his hands down her body, knowing her now by touch as well as by sight. He fondled her breasts, ran his hand over her flat belly and stroked his fingers into the notch between her legs.

"I fill you with my seed so often that you get pregnant right away. Every night we make love and every day I watch your body change as you carry my child. Late in your pregnancy, I start taking you from behind, very gently, and you feel both me and our child moving in your body." His fingers delved deeper, loving the way she grew soft and wet for him.

Isabelle arched, legs falling apart to ease his way. He stroked her, listening carefully to the way her breathing speeded up, watching her eyes flutter.

"When our baby is born, I watch you nurse him and some-times I feed at your breast, too, and you climax. Then you hold us both in your arms and the three of us are together, connected by love."

Isabelle gave a sharp cry and convulsed, contracting strongly around his fingers. His heart pounded as he turned his head to kiss her fiercely.

She clung to him and moved her bottom in his lap. He knew she could feel how aroused he was.

Nicholas lifted his head and looked down at her for a long time, letting her see his pain and regret.

"But," he said finally, harshly, "that's not the way it's going to be. This isn't a perfect world, Isabelle, and I haven't lived a perfect life. I've been forced to do things I regret and I've made powerful enemies, chief among them Luis Mendoza."

"But—" Isabelle blinked, clearly trying to emerge from a sensual haze. "But he's a criminal, a gangster!"

"Yes, he is," Nicholas agreed calmly. "And I'm not. Or at least, not any more. We had . . . dealings when I was starting out."

"He's a drug smuggler." Isabelle looked at him soberly. "That's what the newspapers say."

"And a murderer," Nicholas agreed. He wasn't about to whitewash his background but he didn't want her confusing them. "I've never touched drugs, Isabelle, and I've never killed anyone. Other than that . . . I did what I had to do to survive. By the time I figured out what a psychopath Mendoza was, I had moved on. I didn't want anything more to do with him. But our paths have crossed and tangled enough times to make us rivals. I've bested him often and he hates my guts. He wouldn't hesitate to hurt someone who means a lot to me. That hasn't been a problem up until now."

Nicholas hesitated, aware with every cell of his body of what he was going to say. Aware he'd never said it before. Aware that he meant every word.

"No one has ever mattered to me before, Isabelle. I don't have any family. I have household staff but I rarely see them and they have orders to stay out of my way. I have sex partners but I don't have love affairs. So I've never showed a soft underbelly to anyone. I've never been in any way vulnerable to Mendoza because no one has ever meant anything to me. But now—now someone does."

Isabelle smiled and her hand tightened on his arm. "Oh, Nicholas."

"Wait," he said harshly. "There's more. That rosy scenario, the one where I court you and marry you and live with you? That's for another world, not this one. In this one, if I were to marry you, I'd be signing your death sentence. You'd be a living target every day and I would go insane trying to keep you safe."

Nicholas closed his eyes and the image of a broken and bleeding Isabelle swam against his closed eyelids. He shuddered. He opened them again and stared down at her.

"About the only way I could survive in any kind of shape would be to keep you locked up. Literally. Twenty four/seven. Never let you out. And even then I wouldn't feel a hundred percent secure, because Mendoza could bribe a member of my staff to kill you, or poison the water mains leading to the house or blow up the place with a bazooka. He'd find some way to destroy you to get to me."

She was watching him closely, as glowing and as beautiful as moonlight in his arms. He tightened his grip.

"You say your . . . relationship with Mendoza was a long time ago?" she asked.

Nicholas nodded.

"Don't you think he might have . . . forgotten?"

"No. Mendoza's not the kind of man who forgets. He wants to put his hands on my businesses. Not that he'd be able to run them. To be frank, he's not the sharpest tool in the woodshed, but he makes up in ferocity what he lacks in smarts. He's just a crazy murdering son of a bitch."

Isabelle listened quietly, silver eyes watching him carefully. "Surely you're smarter than he is."

Nicholas's jaw worked. "Oh, yeah, I'm much smarter than he is. That's not the problem. You don't need a genius I.Q. to pull the trigger on an AK-47. You don't need to be smart to plant Semtex in a car and have it blow up at the turn of a key. All you have to be is relentless and ruthless. And you better believe that is exactly what Mendoza is. The instant he realizes you mean something to me, you're a walking dead woman." He closed his eyes briefly, then opened them again. They were black and hot. "I wouldn't be able to stand it."

Isabelle's face was colorless. He knew she was smart. She didn't doubt his words and he knew she could easily imagine the situation. She didn't even try to conjure up rosy scenarios, and he respected her for that. But her next words shocked him to the core.

"What if I were willing to accept the risk?" she asked quietly.

"No!" Every muscle in his body rejected the notion. He tightened his arms. "There's no question of that. I won't gamble with your safety. We have to accept the situation as it is, Isabelle. And the situation is that we can have a hot affair for a while—ten days, two weeks. No one will blink at that. So that's what we'll do. And on New Year's day we'll go our separate ways." Nicholas drew in a deep, shuddering breath. "We'll never see each other again. I'll make sure of it. But I'll also keep an eye on you. Watch over you. I'll leave you a way to get word to me and if you ever need my help, you'll have it, no questions asked. You have my word."

He didn't say that he'd make sure she would never want for anything again. Isabelle would reject the notion. But it soothed the ache in his heart to know that he could do this for her.

He'd rather give her a husband and children, but he'd learned long ago that pining after what was impossible led to heartache and nothing more.

"So, that's the way it is in the real world." He deliberately made his voice hard. "We can only be together for a short time. I want you to move in with me until the end of the year. I'll accompany you to the station and your book presentations and out to dinner and to concerts. We'll go wherever you want to go. We'll do whatever you want to do. We'll have as much sex as two people can have and still remain standing. We'll spend New Year's Eve making love. And on New Year's Day we say goodbye. That's what I can offer you. That's *all* I can offer you. Will you accept?"

Nicholas could almost feel the intensity of Isabelle's gaze. Her eyes moved slowly, giving off glittering silvery shards of light with each movement, looking deeply into his. Her gaze roamed over every inch of his face, as if to measure his resolution.

Nicholas was used to hiding his feelings. Until Isabelle, he'd have denied having any feelings at all.

So now he showed Isabelle the smooth, hard facade of his resolve. She mustn't have any illusions. They would be fatal. To her and to his sanity.

He had to keep her safe. He was guilty of many things in his lifetime, but bringing harm to Isabelle would never be one of them.

"What will it be, love. Yes or no?"

Suddenly, Isabelle expelled her breath and softened in his arms. She brought a hand to his cheek and a silvery tear slipped out and coursed down a smooth, ivory cheek. She held his gaze with hers and he could read everything of her character in it.

Strength, courage, understanding.

She tried to smile but it was a weak effort, and it broke his heart.

"Yes," she whispered and lifted her mouth to his.

Chapter Six

"Are you ready?" Nicholas asked quietly two days later, his hand on Isabelle's front door. "I want us to make it home before it starts snowing again."

Isabelle glanced up at Nicholas standing in the darkened foyer. His face was in shadow but she didn't need light to see him. Those strong features were etched in her memory forever. Everything about him was imprinted on her consciousness, on her senses, on her skin, and would be until the day she died.

She was leaving the house for the first time since the attack. Nicholas had insisted that she needed the time to recover and he'd been right. She finally felt fully herself again.

He'd stayed by her side constantly. Three times a day, a tall blond man named Kevin delivered box after box of marvels: books, magazines, videotapes, exquisitely prepared food and a selection of the finest wines. Nicholas had insisted on feeding her himself. She'd almost forgotten what it was to feed herself, to bathe herself, to dress herself. For the first time in her life she'd had someone to take care of her.

She'd been utterly pampered and loved from head to toe, over and over again. He'd used only his hands and mouth while telling her, in excruciating detail, just how he would take her completely once they were in his house. She shivered at the memory.

He glanced at her out of midnight eyes. "Cold, love?" he rumbled. "Maybe I can do something about that."

He reached down to one of the magic boxes Kevin had delivered and pulled up the sealing tape. He unfolded the flaps and pulled out something soft and blue. A flick of his hand and it billowed out—a rich silvery blue cashmere coat by Valentino. He held it up. "Here, try it on."

Stunned, Isabelle shrugged into it, her fingers lingering over the lushly soft material. It came to mid-calf and enveloped her in soft folds of warmth.

"Nicholas," she breathed. She brushed her hand down a sleeve. She'd never had anything as fine as this in her whole life. "Oh, I can't possibly—"

"Now, love." Nicholas started buttoning the coat up. "I hope you're not going to say something silly like you can't accept it. Not when I sent poor Kevin all over town yesterday looking for exactly the right coat. And then I had to listen to him complaining bitterly that shopping for a woman isn't in his job description. He told me in no uncertain terms that I owe him, big time. So, after all of that, you're not going to refuse it, are you?"

Isabelle smiled up at him and sighed. She pulled the collar of her coat around her neck, her fingers lingering over the soft material. "I guess I can't. But it's a very . . . extravagant gift. I don't know what to say."

"Try 'thank you'," he suggested, taking her hands.

"Thank you."

"You're very welcome." He smiled one of his rare smiles, lifting her hand to his mouth. "The color matches your eyes. You look so beautiful you take my breath away." He bent to pick up her suitcase. "If you're ready, we can go."

The snick of the door closing echoed sharply in Isabelle's heart. She had a sense of a door closing on the whole first half of her life. She would be a changed woman the next time she walked through that door and back into her apartment on the first day of the year.

She was a changed woman already.

Somehow, Nicholas had unlocked something in her she hadn't even been aware of. It wasn't just the sex, though God knows that was shattering enough, even the foreplay he'd restricted himself to.

No, it was more than that. It was the closeness, the connection. She'd grown up with two parents who were too embroiled in their own emotional messes to pay any attention to her. And then after her father had abandoned them, she'd been so involved in coping with her mother's depression and illness that she hadn't really had time to form close friendships or date. After her mother's death, it had taken her years of hard work to pay off the worst of the debts.

Her few affairs had been unsatisfactory and she was almost resigned to living alone and without passion.

The response Nicholas had been able to effortlessly coax from
her body astonished her. With him, she'd discovered a new side to
her nature. An entirely new dimension to life.

It was as if she'd only gone through the motions before, but
now . . . now she was living life to the fullest. Her time with him
was almost frighteningly intense. And knowing that she would
barely have a chance to open the door on this new dimension of
life, glimpsing the warmth and excitement and hot pleasure on the
other side, when that door would be slammed shut again in her
face forever, broke her heart.

Nicholas had been very, very clear what the condition for their
affair would be—they would live together for a short while, they
would be lovers in the most complete sense of the term, and they
would part on the first day of the new year, never to see each other
again.

How would she give him up?

Isabelle had grown used to Nicholas, to sleeping in his strong
arms, to having his mouth and hands on her, to having his tall,
powerful frame as a bulwark between her and the world. How
would she could survive the new year?

By living minute by minute. For now, Nicholas was with her,
and she intended to store up memories for a lifetime.

They walked out of her apartment building and she glanced up
at the sky.

It had been raining steadily for the past two days and the forecast called for heavy snowfalls over the Christmas season. The
rain had stopped by the time Nicholas handed her into his car, but
the clouds overhead looked bruised and sullen, heavy with foreboding, like a part of Isabelle's heart.

Excited as she was at the thought of living with Nicholas for a
few precious days, of finally feeling him inside her, of being completely and fully his, she knew she was committing herself to
heartbreak.

"What are you thinking about?" Nicholas asked as he started
the engine.

Isabelle turned her head to study his profile. Like everything
else about him, it was sharp, clean, strong. "About afterwards,"
she said simply.

He froze, his hand still at the key. Slowly his head lowered until his forehead touched the top rim of the steering wheel. He closed his eyes. "Isabelle . . ." he murmured. "Don't."

She reached out to put her hand over his and lay her head on his shoulder. "Oh, Nicholas," she whispered. "I can't help it."

Nicholas turned to catch her in his arms and kissed her fiercely, wildly. His lips crushed hers, his teeth clashed with hers as he ate at her mouth, bruising her, in a kiss of possession, not arousal.

His arms were so tight she could hardly breathe, but she didn't care because she was holding him just as tightly, her hands running madly over the strong muscles of his shoulders, over his hard neck, into his thick hair which always surprised her with its warmth. It was so black she instinctively expected it to be cold to the touch.

She was arched against him in his arms and she frantically wished she could get rid of the layers of clothes separating them. It was desperation more than passion. She needed to feel his skin against hers and be reassured by his strong steady heartbeat.

She'd never been held so much by another human being. The touch of his skin calmed her on a deep level. She could hardly sleep now unless her hand was resting on his massive pectoral, right over his heart, the beat strong and reassuring.

The feel of his hand on her breast, even through her bra, sweater and coat, made her jump. Though she responded instantly, she pulled back a moment and rested her forehead against his. They were both breathing heavily and several moments passed before she heard herself say words wrenched from the very core of her being.

"I'm going to miss you, Nicholas," she whispered. "So much."

Isabelle looked up and saw his jaw muscles bunch. He didn't answer her, just turned his head to look out the window at the sky. There was silence for a long moment.

"We'd better get home before the storm breaks," he said finally, gently pulling her arms away.

They drove through the streets in silence.

Isabelle had no idea where Nicholas lived. He was a very rich man. She imagined he would have an upscale residence in an elegant part of town—a mansion on White Oak Drive or a luxury condo in Brixton Heights.

To her surprise, Nicholas drove along the river, straight out to the industrial district. She tried to think of why they might be here, but she drew a blank. There was nothing but dark concrete and brick buildings, huge parking lots with trucks lined up like soldiers, two-story steel fences.

Ten minutes down a deserted road flanked by warehouses, Nicholas pulled a remote control from his jacket and pressed a button. He slowed and she could see massive iron gates in a tall concrete wall slowly opening out. Nicholas drove through the gates and into an industrial lot.

Isabelle turned around. Behind them, the gates slowly closed. It was as if she were entering a different realm, leaving her old world behind.

It *was* a different realm. She could see what looked like an abandoned factory and warehouse. Nicholas pulled into what would have been the loading bay, back when the place was a going concern.

Before her was an immense structure. Only a few stories high, it was so wide she had to turn her head to take it all in. Broken windows, cracked pavement, weeds growing up through the cracked asphalt. There was a desolate air of abandonment about the place.

Isabelle couldn't begin to imagine what they were doing here.

Nicholas brought the car to a stop next to a steel panel set in the wall. A halogen lamp just over the panel was the only illumination in the entire area encompassed by the walls.

He got out, took her suitcase from the trunk and came around to open her door. Taking her elbow he guided her to the panel in the wall. It could have been a door, except there was no doorknob and no hinges. It was in a better state of repair than the rest of the building—a slab of polished blue-gray steel.

Nicholas set her suitcase on the ground and pressed his palm against a small square glass pane inserted about five feet off the ground.

To Isabelle's astonishment, the pane flashed a violent green and, a second later, the steel panel opened with a pneumatic hiss. She swung her gaze up to Nicholas and a corner of his mouth lifted.

"Security scanner," he said, and ushered her into a large steel cubicle.

The door hissed shut and the entire cubicle fell quickly. She hadn't been expecting the cubicle to be an elevator and staggered slightly. Nicholas steadied her with his hand for the duration of the ride and with another hiss, the door opened again.

Isabelle had no way of knowing how far beneath the earth's

surface they had gone but she suspected several stories, maybe six or seven, given the speed of the drop.

Nicholas had his arm around her waist and moved her forward by the simple expedient of stepping out himself and half-carrying her with him.

"Welcome," he said simply.

She'd never seen any place like it.

The house had obviously been excavated out of the cliffs rising high over the south side of the river. Limestone cliffs, she remembered reading in school.

She was in an atrium at least three stories high, with a vaulted ceiling, black and white marble flooring and a striking Chinese rug. Massive enameled terracotta pots housed lemon and orange trees, ripe with fruit. She could smell their clean tang from across the enormous room.

As soon as the elevator doors opened, a massive crystal chandelier lit up, banishing the gloom of the day. There would still have been enough light to see by since the entire back wall of the house was floor to ceiling window, affording a breathtaking view of the cityscape and roiling river three hundred feet below. Isabelle could see the McClellan Tower and the Solara Building lit up across the river.

"This is magnificent," she said with a breathy sigh

Nicholas took her coat. "If you go to the right, you'll find tea waiting for you."

She didn't need to be asked twice. She turned right, crossing the great hall, into what was obviously a living room.

As she walked in, lamps lit up, picking up highlights. Everything she saw was luxurious and in superb taste—the artwork, the immense area rugs, Chinese vases.

The room was huge, divided up into separate areas by the furniture. Again, one entire wall was floor to ceiling window. On the left wall was an enormous fireplace, easily twenty feet long, flanked by a comfortable-looking black leather sofa and matching armchairs. A fire was burning brightly and a silver tea service gleamed on a trolley.

With a sigh, Isabelle sat down. She loved fireplaces. She hadn't had a fireplace since she had been a little girl living in her father's home.

Nicholas sat next to her, placing a cut crystal decanter with a brown liquid on the coffee table. "Don't bother pouring for me," he said lazily. He poured from the decanter instead, the smell of good whiskey filling the air. "I have my own tea."

"I see you do," she smiled. Isabelle sipped as she watched Nicholas out of the corner of her eye.

He unbuttoned his jacket and sat back with a sigh. He looked . . . relaxed. Like a king who had finally come back to the palace after a war campaign abroad.

Oddly, for a room that was both enormous and sumptuous, it was also soothing. Maybe it was the dramatic view out an entire wall, where you could watch the city at work and play, like a living painting, or maybe it was the crackling fire in a fireplace big enough to roast an ox in, or maybe just the leather sofa which was unusually comfortable, but Isabelle found herself slowly relaxing.

This house—this kingdom—was where she would spend the most intense ten days of her life. It was where she was going to leave her heart.

Nicholas lifted her hand to his lips. "The entire house is yours while . . . while you're here," he said quietly. "Go anywhere you want, do anything you want." With the hand that held the whiskey he pointed to a console on the coffee table. "If you need anything, press the button at the top. That's for Kevin. He'll interface with the staff."

The staff. Isabelle looked around. Of course. A house this size would need a big staff to keep it running smoothly. "Where is everybody?"

"The next level down. Four people besides Kevin live downstairs in mini apartments. But don't worry. For the next ten days, everyone has strict orders not to come up here unless I call. I want us to have privacy. I want to be able to make love to you anywhere, at any time. You ready to continue the tour?"

She nodded, her mouth suddenly dry at the images his words conjured up. She put her tea cup down with hands that shook and stood up on wobbly legs.

They went through room after room. A magnificent study, a truly astonishing library, with built-in bookshelves two stories high reached by wooden catwalks. A dining room like a cathedral. And always, always, the back wall floor to ceiling windows showcasing the city on the other side of the river. The windows had no drapes.

"Don't you wonder about privacy?" she asked.

"No. The glass isn't transparent on the other side. It's like a one-way mirror. It's also polarized so I can blank it whenever I want to block out sunlight. And it's bulletproof." He ushered her into another room. As always, the lights dimmed as they left a room and came on as they entered the next.

Isabelle gasped.

Nicholas looked down at her and smiled, his eyes heavy-lidded. Her thighs clenched. She knew that look. It was the look he got just before playing her body like a musical instrument. "This is the bedroom," he said softly.

It was the only room she'd seen which was carpeted. A thick, dark green mantle, like a lush lawn. Another huge fireplace, burning with some fragrant wood, was set in the left hand wall. In the sudden hush, she could hear the crackle and pop as the resin in the wood exploded. In the far corner, so far away she thought she would need binoculars, a door opened onto rich bronze-colored tiles. A bathroom.

Louvered doors covered most of the right hand wall. She supposed they would be the closets.

Here, too, were bookshelves everywhere, filled with what she imagined were his favorite books.

Deep burgundy leather armchairs were angled in front of the fire. There was a Louis XVI secretaire cabinet she had sighed over while reading an auction brochure, knowing she could never afford it. It had been sold for $60,000 to an anonymous bidder, she remembered reading.

At last, she turned to the bed, heart pounding. Obviously custom-made, it was easily double the size of a king, massive and . . . and *there*.

His voice was deep in her ear.

"That's where we're going to spend most of our time. And most of the time we spend there, we'll be making love. I want to be inside you."

Isabelle's heart stuttered.

"But first," he murmured, "we have to get you settled in, calmed down. Fed. Relaxed."

She would never be relaxed again. How could she be when just the thought of what they were going to do on that oversized bed was enough to make her mouth dry and her knees tremble?

"Why don't you put on something more comfortable?" Nicholas asked.

Isabelle swallowed and tried to get her nerves under control.

"All right." She looked around. "You'll need to carry my suitcase in here, please."

He walked her toward the wall with lacquered louvered doors, a large hand at her back. "That won't be necessary." He reached around her and opened two doors wide. "I've got more or less everything you might need."

Isabelle blinked. The built-in closet, like everything else in the house, was huge, tall and deep. Rack after rack shimmered with the most exquisite collection of clothes she'd ever seen. She reached out a hand to touch a silver lamé evening jacket. Armani. In her size.

"The clothes are new," Nicholas said quietly. "Not another woman's. I ordered them while I was at your place."

The barest glance showed that all the clothes were in styles she would have bought herself if she'd had the money. The color palette was hers, too. Silver, all shades of blue, moss greens, pale peaches. There was easily over a hundred thousand dollars' worth of clothing in that closet. Probably more.

"Is that what you were doing with your laptop?" she asked. He'd sometimes sat hunched over the keyboard while she puttered around the house. "I thought you were making megabucks on the stock market."

"I *was* making megabucks, but I was also asking the boutiques in town to scan and email me some models I thought you might like."

She looked up at him, her heart turning over in her chest at the sight of that strong, impassive face. No, not so impassive. Oddly, he looked slightly anxious, as if wondering whether she'd like what he'd done.

"They're yours," he said, placing his hands on her shoulders. "Afterwards . . ." he looked away and his jaw muscles bunched. "Afterwards, I want you to keep the clothes."

She didn't make the mistake of protesting. She sensed this was too important to him to refuse.

Isabelle stepped forward, putting her arms around his strong, lean waist and leaning her head against his shoulder. Automatically, his arms went around her. "I'd rather keep you," she whispered.

She could feel his big body jerk and his arms tightened fiercely. He was bending down to kiss her when the black console on an English marquetry side cabinet buzzed. With a sigh and a light kiss, Nicholas released her and pressed a button.

"Yes, Kevin. I'll be right there."

Nicholas turned to her, dark eyes penetrating. "I'm sorry, love. Kevin has strict instructions to contact me only if something important comes up. I have to go see what's happened. Take your time settling in. I ordered dinner to be served in the living room in front of the fire if that's okay with you. We'll meet in about an hour." His mouth tilted up in a half smile. "There's a pale pink silk knit outfit in there. I imagined you wearing it your first night here. Would you wear it for me?"

"Of course," Isabelle said softly. He bent to give her a swift kiss and she watched his broad back as he crossed the large room, the king on his way to check that all was well in the kingdom.

Nicholas stopped at the door and turned around. "Oh, and Isabelle," he said, black eyes boring into hers, "don't wear any underwear."

Chapter Seven

"It doesn't look good, boss."

Nicholas looked down at the papers Kevin had handed him. The pile was thick, but he was quick and in five minutes he understood what Kevin meant.

Separate incidents, but taken together, they were ominous and presaged an assault on RexLine, his largest holding, a sprawling warehouse and shipping complex along the docklands forty miles downriver.

Several hefty payments made into the bank account of the managing director of RexLine. Twenty people suddenly quitting and twenty new hires with ties to Mendoza. Four companies with complaints that goods which had left RexLine's loading bay on container ships had never arrived.

"What do we do?" Kevin asked.

Nicholas appreciated the 'we'. He had no doubt that Kevin took this assault on RexLine personally.

He was fiercely loyal and Nicholas trusted him with his life. More—with Isabelle's life.

"Fire Fred Hamlin," Nicholas said. "And make sure the IRS gets a copy of his bank statements. Keep an eye on the twenty new hires and fire them in batches of two or three. Say we're restructuring. Hire extra guards and have them work undercover in admin and as workers. And, Kevin . . ."

The young man looked up. "Yeah?"

"Thanks."

Nicholas had been taken off guard for the first time in his life. These were facts he should have caught himself.

It showed him what a fine line he walked. He couldn't afford distractions, ever. Much as he would like to be just an ordinary businessman, he wasn't. Not by a long shot.

The three days he'd spent wrapped up with Isabelle had been three days he hadn't been paying attention and he'd almost paid a hefty price.

God, how he wished his life were different. He'd been forced to do things Isabelle would be appalled at. But he'd done what he'd had to do. He was what he was. Nothing could erase the past.

Mendoza would try to come after him and anyone he loved for the rest of his life. And if something ever happened to Mendoza, there would be another enemy to replace him.

Had he held a faint glimmering of hope that he could some-how keep Isabelle with him, this turn of events had brutally plunged him back into his world. There was no place for Isabelle in it.

Which meant, Nicholas thought, as he strode out of his study, that he'd better enjoy every second of Isabelle while he had her.

Isabelle walked into the living room an hour later.

She'd taken a long, luxurious bath in Nicholas's amazing bathroom, so opulent it was decadent—as large as her living room and kitchen taken together. And the luxuries: a whirlpool, tub as large as a child's swimming pool, multi-headed water massage shower in an enormous glass-brick enclosure, heated towel racks, tanning bed, sauna, connecting exercise room and what seemed like acres of cultured marble countertop.

She'd lain in the whirlpool for almost half an hour, her head against the rim, feeling the water massaging her muscles until the tips of her fingers started wrinkling.

She felt both excited and uncertain as she made her way to the living room. Tonight they would make love fully and she didn't know if she could take it. She breathed deeply at thought of the coming night, of finally having sex with Nicholas.

Foreplay with Nicholas was so exciting she sometimes thought her heart would stop. Last night she had lay naked and spread-eagled on the bed while Nicholas suckled hard at her breasts, his hand moving between her thighs, for what felt like hours. She had climaxed so intensely she had actually lost con-sciousness for a second or two. Afterwards, she lay completely exhausted in his arms. They listened to the wild drumming of the rain outside her window. Nicholas's slow stroking started turning sensual again and she had protested she had nothing left.

"Oh, yes you do," he'd whispered and brought her to another shattering climax with his hands.

He wouldn't let her touch his penis, but she'd felt it, long and thick and hard. That penis would penetrate her tonight. Finally, she'd feel him inside her.

Isabelle's knees weakened at the thought and she had to grab on to the back of a chair for a second. She knew his size, his stamina and his skill and her heart thudded heavily at the thought of the two of them in the heat and darkness of the night, rolling around on that massive bed.

She was wearing what he'd asked her to. The long pale pink silk skirt with the thigh-high slit whispered sensuously around her legs as she walked.

Nicholas certainly had an eye for what suited her. The outfit was simple—a long buttoned tunic over an ankle length skirt. The luxury was in the delicate color and sumptuous silk knit which flowed like water over her skin.

As Nicholas had asked, she wasn't wearing underwear and she felt completely naked. The smooth silky material highlighted rather than covered her body. She felt wicked and decadent, unused to feeling her breasts swaying lightly without a bra, to being able to see her own nipples, to being aware of her bare genitals as she walked.

She was aroused by the friction of the silk over her bare skin and by the thought that she was so completely accessible to his hands and his mouth.

She stopped at the living room door. Through the open doorway, she could see a long table set for dinner in front of the roaring fire. Those invisible servants, she thought. A white damask tablecloth swept to the black marble floor and a large silver candelabra gave off the only light other than the fire.

She saw him across the large room and her heart rate picked up.

She would never forget the sight as long as she lived. He was in shadow, standing to the side of the massive fireplace, a large hand on the carved granite mantelpiece, the other curved around a glass of amber liquid. He was lost in thought, head bowed.

Just like that, she thought, as she committed the scene to memory. *That's how I'll remember him.*

Outlined against the fire, tall, immensely strong, graceful.

In his underground palace, he looked like a king of ancient times. A monarch of the underworld, strong and powerful but cut off from the world above.

As if he sensed her, Nicholas's head rose suddenly and she heard his sudden intake of breath. Across the distance, his eyes met hers, shadowed and piercing, taking in every detail of her appearance.

His gaze was enough to arouse her completely. As his eyes moved down her body, she could feel her breasts swell, her nipples harden, her sheath grow moist and aching.

He started towards her, walking slowly. His boots might have made a slight noise on the marble flooring but she couldn't hear anything over the pounding of her heart. Her breathing grew shallow as he came up and stopped, so close she had to tilt her head back. He took her hand and lifted it to his mouth.

"You look beautiful, Isabelle," he murmured. "Just as I thought you would." Holding her eyes, his big hand reached out and touched her breast, molding his hand around it, thumbing her nipple. "I imagined you wearing this, and me touching you, just like this."

Isabelle's breath caught. His hand seemed to shoot fire from her breast to her womb. The feeling grew so intense it frightened her, as if he and he alone possessed the secret button to switch her on.

She had been dead, lifeless before she had met Nicholas and now he seemed to have the power to catapult her into a new, frighteningly sensuous world. Her head fell back and she licked her lips as his hand caressed her other breast.

She needed to get herself back again. She straightened and pulled away, walking blindly to the huge window.

It had started to snow, fat lazy flakes for now, drifting slowly and melting before they hit the window pane, but the weather forecast was for a heavy snowfall during the night. The night she would spend in Nicholas Lee's bed.

Even more than before, she felt as if she had been sequestered by the Lord of the Underworld and taken to his subterranean fortress, spirited away from the bustling world she could see across the river.

Nicholas appeared at her back, looming over her. Their eyes met in the reflection of the dark window. She looked pale, insubstantial against his dark strength. He was a head taller than she was, his shoulders almost double the width of hers. Dressed entirely in black, he was like a dark frame for her—a pale column in pink silk.

In the window, she watched him as he pulled a box from his pocket.

"Don't turn around," he whispered. Still holding her gaze in the window, he fixed an earring to her left ear, then the other to her right ear. The earrings were long pendants, a brilliant white which shone brightly in the dark pane, brighter than the floodlights of the city towers.

Isabelle was very much afraid they were diamonds.

"Nicholas, I can't possibly—"

"Shhh."

"Really, I—"

"Not a word," he murmured as he placed his hands on her shoulders, still looking at her reflection, endlessly. She felt like Persephone in Hade's kingdom, helpless in the Dark Lord's grasp.

"You're so lovely," he whispered.

Still holding her gaze, he started unbuttoning the tunic, his hand moving slowly but steadily down. With a gentle flick of his wrists, it slipped from her shoulders. He covered her breasts with his hands.

Watching him touch her and feeling his large, powerful hands caressing her breasts filled her with erotic sensations. He opened his hands and she could see her erect nipples between his fingers. Slowly, slowly, his hands ran down her rib cage, then around to her back.

She couldn't see what he was doing but she could feel and hear. The soft silk skirt loosening, then falling with a whisper to the floor. The sharp hiss of a zipper and his steely erection pressed against her back.

She was completely naked. She watched, and felt, as his hand covered her mound. He was wearing a black sweater; his powerful arm and hand bisected her white belly. Isabelle's breathing grew erratic as he moved through the folds of her sex, stroking her, coaxing moisture from her.

Nicholas bent his dark head to her neck, kissing and sucking and bestowing light nips. Isabelle's legs started shaking as he inserted one long finger inside her, then two.

"I wanted to wait until after dinner," Nicholas whispered, his hand moving slowly inside her. She trembled but she wasn't alone.

His hand was shaking and his breath came in low pants.

"We were going to eat, and then I was going to carry you into the bedroom, undress you slowly and love you half the night before putting my cock in you. But I can't wait," he said harshly.

Holding her apart with two fingers, he bent his knees and she could feel him sliding forward, hot, heavy, enormous, barely inside her. "Brace yourself against the window," he said hoarsely.

She bent forward, her palms against the cool pane of glass, and cried out as he thrust into her, slowly, endlessly, until she could feel the rough hairs of his groin against her bottom. He stretched her—she could feel the tip of him pressing against her womb.

Slowly, slowly, he withdrew then thrust again, then again and again, setting up a heavy driving rhythm, one hand holding her under her breasts, while the fingers of his other hand stroked her clitoris in time with his thrusts.

He curved around her, like a massive falcon mantling its prey. She felt encased in his dark, powerful grip. The sensation was indescribable, impossibly intense. For an instant, she looked up and saw them in the reflection. She hardly recognized herself—lips puffy with arousal, eyes lost.

Her earrings and breasts swayed as he took her, moving faster and faster as he continued a driving rhythm, pounding into her.

His fingers moved sharply and Isabelle cried out, her orgasm so piercingly strong she thought she would die. He kept rocking inside her throughout the spasms, harder and harder until he, too, stiffened and cried out and poured himself endlessly into her.

Her heart beat in time with his and she knew she would never be the same again. Nicholas was wrapped around her, still shuddering. Isabelle didn't know how long her legs would hold out, how long she could hold his heavy weight.

Their labored breathing sounded loud in the large, silent room.

Nicholas slowly straightened, eyes closed. He pulled out of her so slowly it brought tears to her eyes at the loss. His eyes opened and met hers in the dark glass. Stooping to pick up her clothes, he bent to kiss her neck and then dressed her gently, as if she were a child.

Isabelle's muscles felt like water. She would never have been able to dress herself. She was still quivering inside.

Le petit mort, the French called the moment of orgasm. The little death.

Truly, she felt as if her soul had fled her body and then had come back, transformed. Every sense was amplified—she could feel the air moving in and out of her lungs; Nicholas, strong at her back; she thought she could see every snowflake now drifting in waves from the sky; she could hear the fire, the soft crackle sounding like a loud roar to her too-alive senses.

Gently, Nicholas turned her around and walked her one step backwards, until she bumped her back against the window. His hands bracketed her face and his eyes bored into hers.

"I couldn't wait. I wanted our first time to be in bed, but I simply couldn't wait."

He bent and touched his lips to hers in the gentlest of kisses, softly softly. Isabelle held on to his forearms as he kissed her endlessly, tenderly, as if it were their first kiss. As if they hadn't just had the most raw, carnal sex of her life.

Gently, slowly, the kiss went on forever. She was floating in his arms, her heart lifting. Tears pricked behind her eyelids, the sensation was so sweet. Her heart swelled as he kept the kiss light, oh so light and gentle, as if he were courting her with his mouth alone. As if he hadn't been in her a few minutes before.

He lifted his mouth a moment and she remembered to breathe. "All night, Isabelle," he whispered against her temple. "I'm going to make love to you all night long."

Isabelle's hand crept up to cup his cheek. She felt so buffeted by emotions—the excitement of his lovemaking, the fierceness of his sensuality, shock at his astonishing tenderness.

"But first," he smiled, "I'd better feed you." Nicholas took her hand and led her to the table. He seated her and lifted the silver domes covering the oversized platters. Wonderful smells drifted up and Isabelle smiled dreamily. All her senses were going to be pleased tonight. He deftly uncorked the champagne and poured.

He tapped her glass with his, the clear crystal ring of the glasses quivering in the air, and she sipped. It was icy, dry, delicious. "To us," he said softly.

"To us," she echoed.

The only light came from the huge fireplace, casting a warm intimate glow over the table. The rest of the room was in shadow. The only noise came from the crackling, popping fire and the ting of silver against china. Outside, the snow silently swirled wildly. Isabelle wished suddenly, fiercely that it would just keep on snowing, for days, weeks, months. She wished they could be snowed in forever, just the two of them.

"Open up," Nicholas ordered and her smiling mouth opened. They were at dessert, a luscious tiramisù.

Another spoonful. "Again."

Isabelle shook her head at the spoon heaped with chocolate and cream. "No," she said on a sigh. Delicious as it was, she was full.

"Had enough?" His voice was a deep rumble. He put the spoon down.

"Yes, I—" Isabelle jumped as he pulled aside her skirt and placed a large, hard hand on the inside of her thigh. Her breath came in on a long, shaky stream as his hand moved up then down to caress her knee. He slowly trailed his fingers back up again and stroked the folds of her sex.

Oh God. She couldn't think when he did that. He stroked her vulva slowly, delicately, and she could feel a rush of moisture there, making her slick. His hands had worked magic on her before, when that was all she knew of making love with him. But now that she had felt his penis in her, knew how hard and thick it was, knew how it could fill her . . . *oh God.* She whimpered as his thumb slowly circled her clitoris.

Nicholas leaned over and kissed her, his mouth slow and hot. His tongue mimicked what his hand was doing. Slowly penetrating, then retreating, leaving heat and longing in its wake.

Needing an anchor, Isabelle curved her hand around the strong column of his neck.

"Open for me," he whispered. She didn't know whether he meant her mouth or her legs. She opened both and was instantly rewarded. His mouth slanted over hers, biting her lips, then plunging his tongue deep into her mouth. His fingers penetrated her harder, deeper. He pulled her tightly against him as he lifted his mouth from hers. His fingers kept stroking strongly, the rhythm increasing as he watched her. Isabelle's mouth was open as she tried to drag more air into her lungs. She was burning up, on the knife's edge of exploding.

"Don't wear underwear while you're here. Ever." Nicholas's voice was low and deep. "Wear things I can unbutton easily, pants I can open quickly, skirts I can pull up. I want you open to me, day and night. I want to be able to fuck you anywhere, any time."

He circled her opening again, now completely wet with her juices. His eyes never left hers. When his thumb brushed her clitoris, Isabelle cried out, shaking. "Nicholas!"

"No! Not yet. I want you to come with my cock in you."

Nicholas surged to his feet, sweeping her up in his arms. He strode quickly to the bedroom as she clung to him, almost too dazed to realize what was going on. The bedroom, too, was in shadows except for the fire burning in the grate. Nicholas quickly stripped her and put her down on the bed. She was grateful for the cool sheets against her back. They anchored her, brought her back from the fevered place of pleasure she'd been drowning in.

Good.

She wanted to remember clearly every moment with Nicholas. She'd waited 26 years to feel this way and deep in her heart she knew she would never experience anything like this, ever again. These were memories she would take out and examine during the long lonely years stretching endlessly ahead of her. She wanted to live these moments to the fullest.

Nicholas looked down at her in his bed for a long moment. Isabelle knew that he was fixing this moment in his memory, too.

Without taking his eyes off her, he shucked off his shirt. His hands went to the buckle of his pants. Isabelle watched in fascination the bulge and play of muscles as he stripped, letting his clothes fall soundlessly to the thick carpet.

He was magnificent. A male animal in its prime. The power and grace evident in every line of his big body took her breath away. He was the only man alive who could turn her liquid with desire.

The fire burning at his back rimmed his body in an orange glow, like an eclipsed sun. He leaned down to grasp her ankle, as if even that short separation from her body were too much to bear. His engorged penis lay flat against the hard muscles of his abdomen, reaching almost to his navel. He was as beautiful here as he was everywhere else. He opened his hand to run his fingers along her leg, tracing her calf, trailing up her thigh, then cupping her mound.

Isabelle opened her arms and legs and heart. "No foreplay, Nicholas," she whispered. "I don't need it. All I need is you."

With a groan, he lowered himself over her. He braced himself on his elbows and entered her with one hard thrust. She cried out in surprise and shock. He held himself still. "You okay?" he whispered.

She couldn't answer, couldn't form the words. Her body did the speaking for her as she began the sharp contractions of orgasm. He smiled down at her and started moving—slow, deep thrusts, as steady as the sea tide. His heavy movements inside her prolonged the contractions. Her thighs opened wider and she locked her ankles behind his back, her heels riding his buttocks as he moved inside her.

She was drowning in mind-numbing pleasure. Isabelle held him as he rode her, her arms barely reaching around the immense shoulders. The muscles along his back felt as hard as concrete slabs. A drop of sweat from his face fell on her shoulder and she opened her eyes.

Nicholas's face was taut with concentration, jaw muscles bunched, eyes tightly closed. He was controlling himself, holding himself back.

Isabelle turned her head and licked his ear, smiling as he shuddered. She arched herself even more tightly against him, rubbing her nipples against his chest, rotating her hips, curling her fingernails into his back. Nicholas trembled and another drop of sweat fell on the pillow.

"Let yourself go, Nicholas," she whispered.

"I'm . . . afraid I'll hurt you," he gasped.

"The only way you can hurt me is by not loving me. Love me, Nicholas, love me hard."

Her words were like a starter gun to a race horse. He bucked, then started hammering into her. She shuddered with the force of his thrusts, opening herself to him as completely as a woman can.

As she held him, as she listened to his groans, as she felt his heart pounding next to hers, she knew, with exultation and despair, that she had never been as happy as this before. And never would be again.

Chapter Eight

New Year's Eve

Our last night together, Nicholas thought as he searched the depths of the glass of whiskey in his hand. There were no answers in the amber liquid as to how he was going to live without Isabelle. However much he tried to drown his rage and grief in alcohol, it wasn't working.

He stared at the door to the bathroom, waiting for Isabelle to emerge. They were going out tonight for the first time. They hadn't left his house and they hadn't seen another human being in the past ten days. Tonight was a commitment Isabelle had taken months before. She had offered to cancel and he'd been tempted, but she needed to move on with her life after he pushed her out of his. It wasn't fair to ask her to forego something that would further her in her career.

Nicholas would have ripped the heart out of any man who tried to stand between him and Isabelle. The irony was that *he* was that man. He would find the strength to put Isabelle out of his life, even though his heart felt as though it were being ripped out of his chest. Taking another huge gulp of whiskey, he savored the burn down to his stomach.

He contemplated another useless swallow when the door to the bathroom opened. Nicholas looked up and his breath tangled in his throat.

She floated towards him, graceful as a princess, lovely as moonlight. She had on a long silver beaded jacket over a floor-length multi-layered chiffon skirt, her long, slender legs barely visible through the layers of sheer material.

There wasn't a man alive who wouldn't try to make her his and, after tonight, Nicholas thought bleakly, after tonight any man was free to try. Free to fuck her.

He heard a crack and glanced down blankly at his hand. The smell of spilled whiskey drifted up to him. He'd crushed the shot glass.

"Oh, Nicholas," Isabelle said in dismay. "You've hurt yourself. You're bleeding." She rushed back into the bathroom and came out with a cotton towel.

Nicholas stared down at her shiny platinum hair as she bent over his hand to bandage the small cut. She had her hair up in a complicated style and had put on makeup. Already she looked different from the woman he'd shared his heart and his bed with for the past ten days. The makeup emphasized that she was going back out into the world now, after having been secluded with him.

She was going back out into the world where men would look at her and desire her.

Isabelle's eyes widened as Nicholas rose on a rush.

"Nicholas?"

He couldn't touch her hair, kiss her mouth, as he wanted to. He could only touch her where it wouldn't show. He stroked the soft skin of her neck and felt the life pulsing through a vein. How many times had he touched her, caressed her, stroking, feeling her skin warm under his touch.

"Yes," she murmured, knowing from his touch what he wanted. She exhaled softly, her head falling slightly to one side, a rose too heavy for its stem.

He reached out to unbutton her jacket and her eyes closed. "Isabelle." His voice was the merest whisper as he slid the jacket off her shoulders. It fell soundlessly to the carpet and her lace bra followed.

He cupped her breasts. He loved the heavy feel of them and had spent hours fondling them, suckling them. Her eyes closed as his thumbs rubbed over her nipples.

"Christ, you're lovely." His voice came out low and rough.

When they came back tonight, he intended to get in her and stay in her all night but now, right now, his hunger was sharp-edged, as if he'd never had her and would die if he couldn't enter her *now*.

He couldn't get the image of another man's hands touching her, another man's cock inside her, out of his head. It drove him crazy and his hands turned rough as he opened her skirt and pushed it down.

She had on sheer silk stockings held up with lace garters and panties. With a low, maddened growl, he ripped her panties off and pulled her to him. He turned with her held in one arm. With the other he swept his desk clear. A vase and books thudded to the carpet but he was beyond caring as he lay her down on the smooth cherrywood surface.

He stopped a moment, checked by the sight of her long pale figure laid out like a sacrifice, naked except for the garter, the stockings and strappy sandals. He was hard as a rock, his penis straining to be inside her. "I need you, Isabelle," he muttered, opening her legs by stepping between them. "I need you so much."

Her eyes opened and their gazes locked. "I'm yours, Nicholas," she whispered. "I always will be."

His own eyes closed in pain. His hands shook as they traveled up her long legs. His thumbs opened her and he dropped to his knees.

She was as beautiful here as she was everywhere else, smooth folds of skin surrounded by fine gold hairs. The pale pink lips he'd entered countless times slowly deepened in color as he stroked her gently. He watched as his fingers coaxed the cream of arousal from her. Her back arched and she moaned as he slid first one finger then a second finger into her, touching her as he knew she loved to be touched.

He brought his mouth to her and heard her sharp intake of breath. He kissed her deeply, exactly as if he were kissing her mouth. His tongue circled her clitoris then slid lower to plunge back into her vagina. His thumbs opened her wider as his tongue imitated his cock. Isabelle's thighs shook and she suddenly cried out and pulsed against his mouth. He could feel, taste her climax. Rising swiftly, he opened his pants and thrust into her hard, gritting his teeth to keep still as she continued climaxing.

She'd thrown her arms up over her head and lay stretched out before him, pale and slender, impaled on his cock. Her breasts shook with the force of her wildly beating heart. The pulsing of her vagina matched her pulse beats and he could feel himself become impossibly harder inside her.

As the contractions faded away, Isabelle opened her eyes. "God, Nicholas," she whispered, sounding dazed.

"Rise up," he said harshly and waited until she levered herself up on her elbows. "Look at us." He used his thumbs to open her more fully to his gaze and hers. "Look."

Flexing his buttocks, he pushed with the force of his hips until he felt the tip of her womb. He clenched his jaw and pushed further. The hairs at the root of his sex meshed with hers, jet black and pale gold. He ground against her, opening her up even more to his possession. "Mine," he gritted, his voice guttural. "All mine."

"Yours," Isabelle breathed.

They stared at each other, joined in every way a man and a woman could be joined, sex to sex, heart to heart, gaze to gaze.

Nicholas was the first to look away. He closed his eyes and leaned back. His hands gripped her hips hard enough to bruise and he began thrusting with all the strength of his body, hard and fast, in a hammering rhythm which he knew would have hurt her if she hadn't already climaxed. For all the force of his thrusts, he could feel her sheath soft and wet and welcoming.

His passion was too violent to last. A hot wire flashed down his spine, his back prickled. It was as if a freight train barreled into him and he erupted in her, jetting in wild spurts so intense he shuddered under the impact. His orgasm seemed to last for hours as he shook and groaned and spilled into her.

His knees were trembling as he pulled slowly out of her. Amazingly, he was still semi-erect even after that shattering orgasm. He could never get enough of Isabelle.

Capable of gentleness at last, his fingers closed over hers and he pulled her slowly up. Her fingers clutched his, silver eyes wide in a pale face. She'd been as affected as he had by the intense sex. A pulse beat wildly in her throat. He lowered his lips to lick along the vein, teeth closing on the nerve in her neck. Isabelle arched, moaning.

Nicholas slid his other hand around her back and down to her buttocks, helping her off the table.

"This is our last night together."

"I know." She shuddered.

His voice was strained to make its way past the constriction in his throat. "Men will look at you tonight, but you're not going to be aware of them. You're only going to be aware of *me*." He bent to pick up the beaded jacket, ignoring her bra which had fallen nearby. He slipped the jacket up her arms and paused. Arching her over his arm, he suckled slowly at one breast, then the other. When he finally lifted his head, her nipples were wet and distended, flushed a deep pink. He pulled the jacket up over her shoulders and buttoned it, his knuckles brushing against the soft skin of her breasts.

"They'll be talking to you and you won't hear a word because you'll be feeling your nipples against the material all night. All you'll be able to think about is my mouth on you, sucking hard."

She drew in a sharp breath.

He kicked away her torn panties and held her skirt open. Shakily, she stepped into it, one hand on his shoulder to balance herself.

Nicholas slid his hand under the skirt and felt his semen on her thighs. "And all evening," he whispered, his voice harsh and ragged. "All evening you'll feel my come in you and you'll remember my cock moving in you, filling you." He moved his hand further up and caressed her, slick and warm.

"When no one's looking, I'm going to take you around a corner and touch you like this and make you come." He bent his head to her neck as his finger explored her sheath. His voice was a mere breath against her skin. He could smell her sweet fragrance and the smell of sex. Other men would smell it, too, and he intended to make sure that there be no doubt about the man she'd had sex with. He pressed more deeply into her until he felt her sharp intake of breath and then a moan. "You won't think of anyone but me." His thumb circled her clitoris and he shuddered. "No one but me, Isabelle. No one."

She tugged sharply at his hair and he lifted his head. Her pupils were dilated and her hand trembled as she caressed his cheek.

"There *is* no one but you," she whispered.

Our last night together, Isabelle thought five hours later as she and Nicholas stood outside his house for the last time.

She looked up at that hard, beloved face, drinking in his features. After tonight, she'd never see him again. She bitterly resented having had to share him these past hours.

They'd been to an elegant reception at the Marriott, hosted by a major publishing house. She'd been the keynote speaker. Isabelle would have given anything to spend her last evening alone with Nicholas but the contract had been signed six months earlier. This night was significant if only because this was the first and last time she'd been in society with him.

For the past ten days, they hadn't set foot outside his palatial fortress. Each day, he'd offered to take her anywhere she wanted to go. To the finest restaurants. To first run movies. To all the most popular plays, including those for which tickets were impossible to find. He'd even offered to hire a jet to take her to Aruba for a few days.

When he'd asked, her answer was always the same—*I want to stay home with you*. His face always relaxed at her words.

They hadn't needed the outside world at all. Both of them had been perfectly content to spend their time together watching videos, playing chess and going for a swim in his heated indoor pool as the snowflakes drifted past the window.

And making love, endlessly.

She remembered his hard words, and how shocked she'd been at them.

I want to make you scream with pleasure, over and over again. I want to fuck you so much your body will be molded to mine, your cunt shaped to my cock, your skin smelling of me. I want you to forget where you end and I begin.

It had been nothing less than the truth. Her body was so attuned to his, she couldn't begin to understand how she could live without him. But somehow she would have to because this time tomorrow night she'd be back in her own home, alone.

Isabelle shivered as Nicholas put his palm to the scanner and the entrance door hissed open.

She stepped slowly forward. The next time she crossed that threshold, she would be leaving. Forever.

Snow had fallen all evening, but now the clouds had cleared and a million bright stars shone, remote and cold and beautiful. The deep mantle of snow reflected the light of the full moon, almost as bright as day.

They descended, Nicholas's hand at her waist. He'd never been more than a hand span's distance from her all evening. She shifted and felt her nipples brush against the heavy silk of her evening jacket.

He'd been right. His lovemaking had sensitized her body so much that she could hardly think of anything but being possessed by him. She felt him everywhere—her breasts, her belly, between her thighs.

She'd given her speech and, judging from the applause and the delighted look of the author and his publisher, she'd been successful. She had made literary small talk with two editors, a journalist-turned-book reviewer for the *New York Times Book Review*, a world famous publisher, and the editor-in-chief of the local newspaper. They, too, had shown signs of interest in what she was saying, though she couldn't remember what had come out of her mouth. She didn't care about Mailer's retro machismo or the structure of Joyce Carol Oates' latest novel.

Not with Nicholas brushing his hand down her arm, standing so close behind her she could feel his body heat, his arm around her waist.

The slightest sway brought her up against that powerfully muscled body. All it took was one glance out of heavy-lidded eyes and she could feel her body preparing itself for him. Her nipples beaded and she had to clench her thighs against the sharp desire, so sensitized by his lovemaking just moments before leaving the house that it was almost as if she could still feel him, hot and hard and deep inside her.

She'd found it impossible to concentrate on anything but him.

Before midnight, he'd quietly suggested they leave and she'd agreed, relieved that the charade was finally over. She wasn't interested in talking to or being with anyone but Nicholas.

There would be time enough tomorrow to have pleasant cocktail party conversations with her wide circle of acquaintances.

The rest of her life, in fact.

She wasn't going to cry.

She'd promised herself that. It would only make her anguish deeper and make Nicholas suffer. She didn't want to do that. She loved him.

Of everyone there tonight—the best and the brightest the city and the state could offer—the only one she'd really wanted to talk to was Nicholas.

She wanted to know what he thought about the book she'd presented and its overly anxious author, she wanted to know whether he'd found the Senator's prissy wife as ridiculous as she did and whether he agreed that the champagne was too sweet.

Isabelle could spend the rest of her life with only Nicholas and be happy.

Pity she wouldn't be given the chance to find out.

Her eyes stung with unshed tears and she lifted her face to his, wanting—no, *needing*—his touch. He must have been watching her because he immediately bent to take her mouth. She opened to him, reveling in his taste, familiar and yet wildly exciting, like nothing she'd ever tasted in her life.

The elevator came to a smooth stop and he lifted his head, dark eyes glittering. "Isabelle," he said, his voice low and rough. "I—"

The elevator doors slid open. The chandelier came to life and Isabelle looked out into the atrium and cried out in shock.

Nicholas went past her in a rush, a dark lethal shadow, moving so quickly he was a blur.

Isabelle could hardly take in what she was seeing. Kevin—Nicholas's right hand man—lying in the center of the marble floor in a pool of blood, half his head blown away.

Nicholas pulling aside a painting and slapping his hand against a panel. A flash of green and then he was pulling guns out of a safe in the wall. Isabelle didn't even have time to see how many weapons he had pulled out when, with another slap at the panel, the room was plunged into darkness.

She felt a strong hand clamp down on her arm and then they were running. Despite the darkness he ran straight, pulling her after him. She didn't even have time to protest. Loud reports echoed in the huge room as bright flashes seared the darkness.

Someone was shooting at them.

Nicholas plunged to the ground, rolling with her, ending up against a wall, his body protecting hers. Bullets hit the wall above them, where they'd been a second before. She closed her eyes as plaster dust rained down.

"They're all dead, Lee," a harsh voice with a faint Hispanic accent called out. "Everyone's dead in this house and you and your lady friend will be, too."

Nicholas's hand tightened on her arm at the sound of the voice. His entire body was hard and tense.

"When I start shooting, run with me to the living room. The door is five feet to your right." Nicholas's voice was low in her ear, so soft the sound couldn't possibly carry. She put her cheek against his and nodded to show she understood. His mouth touched her ear. "On the count of three."

He tapped her arm once. She tried to draw in her breath without making any noise. He tapped again and she pulled up into a crouch.

Three.

They were up and running, Nicholas a strong presence at her back. Slamming the door open, he pushed her through, turning for a second, weapon drawn and streaked a continuous blur of fire into the room. Isabelle heard him grunt, then heard a scream as he hit one of the men in the atrium.

He pulled the door shut behind them, Nicholas twisting until she heard the loud, solid click of the lock. A fusillade of bullets whined harmlessly against the steel door and Isabelle blessed Nicholas's obsession with security. They were safe for the moment.

Nicholas pulled something from his jacket pocket and re-loaded his gun's magazine, the movements practised and smooth. The magazine slid home with a soft click.

"Lee!" The deep voice outside sounded maddened. "You're a walking dead man. You and that woman you've got there—you'll never walk away. I've got Semtex and I'm going to blow that door right off its hinges. And then I'm coming in after you, you fucker. And then I'll take over your business—me. Luis Mendoza."

Nicholas took her arm and rushed her towards the fireplace.

There were scrabbling sounds on the other side of the door and Isabelle drew in a terrified breath as she leaned her hands against the wall for a moment. Shock must be running through her system because she saw red.

No, her hands really were red. She looked down with a frown. How . . .

Nicholas staggered and she almost slipped as she took his full weight for a second. And then she saw the bloody mass that was his side.

"Oh my God," she breathed. "You're hit."

Her hands and her whole right side were drenched with his blood. Frantically, she bent to rip a large strip out of her skirt. She bunched the material against his side to create a pressure bandage, cursing the fact that her terror made her clumsy. She ripped another piece of skirt and tried to wrap it around his waist.

Nicholas's hands stopped her. She looked up, numbly, terrified to see the pallor beneath his dark skin.

"Don't do that, love," he said gently. "It's not necessary."

"What do you mean?" He must have lost even more blood than she thought. "We've got to pack your wound."

"Isabelle . . ." Abruptly, Nicholas's legs gave way. He slid down the wall next to the fireplace, leaving a trail of blood, and Isabelle kneeled next to him. There were loud scratching noises on the other side of the door and Isabelle could hear the voices of at least three men, maybe more. The whine of a drill started up.

"They're setting the charge," Nicholas said. He leaned his head against the wall and closed his eyes. Isabelle reached around him to tighten the bandage. Blood had already seeped through. She worked frantically, hoping the bullet hadn't taken an artery or a vital organ.

"You have to go," Nicholas said. His voice was weaker now,

his breathing labored. He grunted in pain when she pressed down on the bandage, hoping to stop the steady flow of blood. Beads of sweat appeared on his face.

"Are you crazy?" She took his hands and her heart gave a lurch. They were stone cold. Nicholas, whose body was a furnace. "Come on, stand up," she said. "You can do it." She tried to fit her shoulder under his arm. Tears ran down her face and she wiped them on his sleeve. "Come on, darling. Get up."

Nicholas didn't budge. Slowly, he reached into his pocket, grimacing with pain. He pulled out a gun and pressed it into her hand. It was small, gray, light. He curled her hand around the stock.

"That's a Colt 22, Isabelle. It's a semi automatic. All you need to do is aim and keep pulling the trigger. Put your thumb here—" he guided her hand and she heard a small ominous snick. "The safety's off now. It's ready to shoot."

Isabelle opened her mouth and he put a finger across her lips, leaving bloody stains. His eyes bored into hers, willing her to pay attention.

"Mendoza won't stop until I'm dead and he'll have to kill you, too. I won't—" Nicholas broke off and his jaw muscles jumped as he struggled against the wave of pain. "I won't let him. Listen, Isabelle," he said with urgency, his voice a harsh whisper. "Next to the fireplace is a secret passage out of here. Press the third wood panel and it opens up. At the end of the passageway is a keypad. The code is 7928. Press the numbers and then run as fast as you can. Four minutes later, this house will blow up. You have to do it quickly before Mendoza gets here. Mendoza has to die now, otherwise you'll never be free."

Isabelle stared at him numbly. He was asking her to . . . "No!" she cried. "I'd kill you, too. I can't do that, Nicholas. Don't ask me to."

"I'm a dead man already." He gripped her arm, his fingers digging into her flesh. "Do what I say, Isabelle," he gritted. "I can't risk having Mendoza leave here alive. He'll come after you. You'd never—" He gasped and gritted his teeth. *"Do what I say, dammit!"*

He was sweating profusely now, lines of pain bracketing that beautiful mouth. Isabelle studied his face, the face of the man she loved. She'd never thought to have love in her life, but now she'd found it. Nicholas was the greatest miracle of her life.

No way was she going to lose him.

She was going to have to move quickly. The drilling on the other side of the door had stopped. She had no idea how long it took to set charges, but she suspected not long. Soon, Mendoza and his men would come blazing through the door.

Standing, she picked up the gun Nicholas had been using. It was huge, heavy and lethal-looking. She knew it was fully loaded.

Whipping off a tablecloth, she barely heard the sound of broken crockery and a pewter bowl rolling around on the marble floor. She bunched the tablecloth at Nicholas's side, taking away the bloody bandage. Holding the bloody material carefully, she wrung the bandage as she walked to the window, leaving a trail of blood spatters a blind man couldn't miss.

There is no such thing as bullet-proof glass, she remembered reading. Only bullet resistant.

Let's see if you resist *this*, she thought, bringing the muzzle of the gun up until it rested against the pane and pulled the trigger. The massive gun bucked in her hands, but she kept it pressed against the pane, moving it in as large a circle as she could. The blasts rang in her ears and her hands became numb as she kept pressure on the trigger.

Finally, she ran out of ammunition. A circle of holes starred the dark pane. She had no idea if her idea would work, but she was willing to die trying. Isabelle looked around desperately for something solid and heavy. In the corner next to the door was a wrought iron floor lamp. She pulled out the plug and dragged the heavy lamp to the window.

There was a sudden silence from the other side of the door. It could only mean one thing. The charge had been set and Mendoza and his men had backed away so they wouldn't be hurt by the blast.

She had mere seconds left.

Holding the lamp in front of her like a battering ram, Isabelle charged at the window, striking the pane in the middle of the circle. The stars widened but the pane held. Panting, she backed away and charged again. Diagonal cracks appeared. She charged again and . . . *yes!* Chunks of pane fell away. Wielding the floor lamp like a bat, she swung again and again until an opening three feet across had been created.

Outside the door, she heard a male voice cry out. "Twenty."

She had twenty seconds.

Running back to Nicholas, she crouched down to look into his eyes. Though his face was pinched and white, his gaze was sharp and aware.

He reached out with his big hand and caressed her face, leaving a bloody trail. "God, I . . . love you."

"I know, darling." Isabelle managed to get the words out past the huge lump in her throat.

"Go now, Isabelle." His voice was a mere whisper.

"Nicholas," she said. "You're going to die."

He nodded and closed his eyes.

"And I'm going to die, too."

His eyes snapped open again. "No!" he croaked. "Get out of here!"

"Ten!" a man called from the other side of the door.

"Both of us are going to die and then we're going to live again. Somewhere far away. We're going to start a new life together somewhere else, where no one knows who we are. We're going to leave our past behind us. But first you've got to get up, Nicholas." Isabelle bent down to him and tried to lift, grunting with the strain. "Help me here."

He shook his head.

"Nicholas," she whispered. "*Please*. I'm not leaving here without you."

His eyes looked intently into hers and she knew he could read the truth of what she said. She wasn't leaving without him. Either they lived together or they died together.

He gritted his teeth and Isabelle gave up a silent prayer of thanks as his legs bunched under him and he stood. He shook, but he managed to stand on his own two feet. She walked them to the side of the fireplace.

"Five!"

With her shoulder under Nicholas's arm, she reached out and touched the third panel. Nothing.

"Four!"

She started to panic when suddenly it swung smoothly open. She stared into the dark corridor.

"Three!"

Nicholas staggered and Isabelle braced herself against the wall. "Nicholas, *please* . . ." she whispered. "We have to make it out together."

"Two!"

"If you love me, Nicholas . . . *move!*"

"One!"

Nicholas lurched forward and Isabelle half-carried, half-dragged him through the door. It hissed shut behind them as a muffled explosion sounded in the next room.

Isabelle shuffled forward as fast as she could. Nicholas's arm was heavy around her shoulders and she bore most of his weight. She didn't know how long she could last but was grimly determined to take him with her or die in this corridor.

"They're going to think we escaped through the window. It's a straight drop down but it's dark and they won't know if we had equipment with us or not. Put your left foot forward, Nicholas, then your right. That's wonderful, you can do this, darling. You're the strongest man I've ever met. Did I ever get a chance to tell you how much I love you?" She sneaked a glance up and saw his lips curve faintly in his pale face. He shook his head.

"I didn't think so. There wasn't any point before, was there? We were never going to see each other again, so what was the use of telling you that leaving you was going to break my heart? Keep moving, Nicholas, you can do it."

She kept talking, hoping to distract him. He shuffled along like an old man, barely lifting his feet. The corridor stretched before them on a sharp incline, dimly lit with a few neon lights. She had no idea how long this passage would go on. However long, though, they would walk it.

"My best friend in college went on to get a degree in medicine, did you know that? She lives about twenty miles from here." Nicholas's eyes were closed. "Open your eyes, Nicholas, and listen to me."

He looked down at her, eyes slightly glazed. She shook him and he swayed. It was terrifying to see a man as powerful and vital as Nicholas look so weak. "Listen to me, damn it. Listen. We're going to live. We're going to go to my friend and she'll take care of that bullet wound and I'll take care of you until you recover. And then you're going to get us some false documents and we'll get out of the country. But right now, my darling, I need for you to walk out of this place. I need you to help me. Can you do that? I love you so much and I don't want to live if you die and I need you to help me *now*. Can you do that?"

"Yes."

Isabelle closed her eyes in relief. His voice was weak, barely a croak, but she heard his determination. She had no idea where he found the energy, what depths of reserves he had to dip into, but miraculously, he straightened.

She nearly gasped in relief as some of the pressure lifted from her shoulders. She hurried them as fast as she dared. Nicholas staggered but was upright.

The nightmare trip up the steep incline seemed to take hours. She dripped with sweat and Nicholas swayed on his feet when she finally saw the steel door at the end of the corridor.

Wheezing, she leaned against the corridor wall for a moment, allowing her screaming muscles a chance to rest, then pushed away again.

A thump came from far behind them and Isabelle's heart clenched. Her red herring hadn't fooled Mendoza and his men for long. He'd found the secret passageway and they would be coming through any moment. They were strong, healthy men. She had no idea how long the corridor was but they would come up running.

"Nicholas." She glanced at him. He was slumped against the door, breathing hard. "Darling, do you have the keys to the car on you?"

Opening his eyes, he stared blankly at her. She didn't think he understood what she'd said. Hands shaking, Isabelle reached into his pants pocket, sending up a prayer of gratitude as she felt a key chain and the remote control to open the gates.

From behind them came the sound of an explosion. Isabelle felt the heat and the rush of air. She punched the numbers into the key pad and pushed Nicholas out the door. They were at the entrance. Some god was looking down at them and protecting them. Nicholas's Lexus was only three feet away.

By her side, Nicholas lurched and fell to the ground. Isabelle fell on her knees beside him. Frantic, she put her fingers to his neck and cried out as she felt a thready pulse. He was unconscious, not dead, and she sagged in relief.

She still held a section of tablecloth and ripped the last piece into a long thin strip. Grunting, she turned Nicholas over on his back, terrified at his waxen pallor. *Please God, let him live*, she repeated to herself over and over.

Twisting the strip to make it more resistant, Isabelle tied his wrists together, looped his tied hands around her neck and shuffled forward, pulling his body after her. The snow lay heavy on the ground and it must have been at least ten below but she was sweating profusely by the time she dragged him to the car.

Grunting, terrified, she managed to get him up and into the back seat. Running around to the driver's side, she got behind the wheel just as the door to the corridor opened and men spilled out.

Isabelle took off with a squeal of tires and the driver's door still open, punching frantically at the remote control to open the gates.

Shots sparked off the reinforced steel gates as the men started shooting. She slid on the ice and a bullet went straight through the back window and out the front window of the passenger seat scattering shards of glass all over the car. She brushed the glass from her lap, barely noticing the cuts in her hands. The blood made the steering wheel slippery and she tightened her grip.

She accelerated hard, aiming at the gates. She didn't dare stop and prayed that a bullet wouldn't blow out a tire. Sobbing, she drove straight towards the still-closed gate, stabbing at the remote.

Slowly, the gates started opening. Another bullet hit the back of the car and she almost lost control. She floored the accelerator and shot through the gates with barely an inch to spare.

Skidding wildly on the icy road, Isabelle fought the wheel as the car made a complete circle. She had no idea which direction she should go in. All she knew was she had to get away *now*.

The wheels spun, then bit into a rough patch and she shot down the street. In the rear view mirror she could see the first of Mendoza's men run out the gate. He stood in the middle of the road and assumed the gunman's stance, feet braced apart, weapon held in both hands. She watched in the mirror, knowing he was close enough to take them down. The man brought the weapon up and steadied.

The explosion ripped the calm night air. The gunman was blown sideways as a bright flash nearly blinded her. A fiery cloud rose up into the night sky, followed by smoke billowing up. The roar came a second later.

Isabelle concentrated on the road ahead and was astonished to see an explosion on the horizon, ahead of her instead of behind her. She wondered if she was hallucinating, then recognized the stars and pinwheels and brightly colored bursts of joyful light.

Fireworks.

It was midnight. The new year had begun.

Isabelle drove into the sparkling night.

Epilogue

A thousand people had seen Isabelle Summerby and Nicholas Lee together at the Arkana Publishing Corporation reception at the Marriott and had seen them leave together. When no trace could be found of Isabelle Summerby, it was assumed that she had gone home with Lee and perished in the blast.

Isabelle Summerby's tragic and untimely death shocked the community. Her TV station, WKRC, dedicated a ten minute special to her memory.

The police investigated the explosion, but no tears were shed at the deaths of Nicholas Lee and Luis Mendoza. The case was considered closed.

Six months after the explosion, a couple travelling on Maltese passports settled on Kondalu, a tropical island an hour away by plane from Fiji. The mysterious couple kept very much to themselves. The locals knew only that the husband seemed to have more money than God and was crazily in love with his beautiful and bookish wife.

About the Author:

Lisa Marie Rice is eternally 30 years old and will never age. She is tall and willowy and beautiful. Men drop at her feet like ripe pears. She has won every major book prize in the world. She is a black belt with advanced degrees in archeology, nuclear physics and Tibetan literature. She is a concert pianist. Did I mention the Nobel? Of course, Lisa Marie Rice is a virtual woman and exists only at the keyboard when writing erotic romance. She disappears when the monitor winks off.

Flights of Fantasy

❧❧❀❧❧

by Bonnie Hamre

To My Reader:

I am thrilled to be back in a Red Sage collection! Since my first two Regency novellas in Secrets 1 and 2, the collections have generated fantastic reader appeal and I have to tell you, I'm impressed.

I hope you'll enjoy this story about a stressed-out, seen-it-all contemporary woman with a very specific fantasy, and a determined, no-holds-barred man . . .

Chapter One

Chloe Atkinson dropped her duffel bag on the dock and stared. She'd been wondering what to expect, but never in her wildest fantasies did she dream of a sea-going Taj Mahal. It was too late to catch it on film now, but maybe she'd have another chance to capture the sunset tones of russet, peach and rose washing over the sleek silhouette of the yacht anchored in Monterey Harbor.

"Ma'am?"

She glanced behind her. A young man dressed neatly in dark pants, dark tie and a white shirt with nautical insignia on shoulder epaulets, looked expectantly at her. "Ms. Atkinson? Mr. Yancy is expecting you. You're the last guest to arrive."

Guest wouldn't exactly be the right word. Hostage? Blackmailee? What word would explain her being here or else, as her boss at the news service put it. "Chloe, you're falling apart at the seams. Your photos aren't worth a shit, your writing sucks."

"Sheesh," she'd protested. "Don't they teach you anything in those touchy feelie seminars you go to?"

"Touchy feelie is what you need. Go swim with the dolphins, commune with a seagull. Come back at the end of the week like your old self, or get a job somewhere else."

"You want me to interview this guy?"

"Nope. He doesn't do interviews."

"Then why me? Why ask a journalist if he's not going to talk to me?" Her boss had just shrugged.

"Ma'am?" the young man prompted.

"Yes," Chloe sighed. "Lead the way."

He helped her into a glossy launch, then stowed her camera cases and duffel bag aboard, treating her well-traveled luggage as though it were Vuitton's finest. She'd brought her cameras, her laptop and some books she hadn't gotten around to reading. She planned to hole up in her cabin, sleep, read, and shoot a few pictures. That should satisfy her boss and get him off her back.

Pleased with her plan, Chloe sank back against a banquette bench as the young man smoothly edged the launch away from the dock and headed across the bay. A few drops of salty spray flicked across her face. She looked behind her, watching the sailboats in the marina, Cannery Row, Fisherman's Wharf, and the green forested hills of the Monterey Peninsula recede, severing the connection to her everyday world.

The launch slowed as it approached the boat. Chloe swept her gaze from one end to the other, noting the three decks, shadowy now in the dusk, water frothing from an idling propeller, windows showing lots of light. The word *Fantasy* was written in fanciful lettering across the stern. For sure a rich man's plaything, but maybe it wouldn't be too much of a hardship. Excitement bubbled within her. "That's some boat!"

The young man grinned. "We call it a yacht."

"Oops. Yacht it is."

A few minutes later, after welcoming her aboard, a crewman led her across the main deck into an elegantly furnished salon, down a short, narrow hallway, and opened a door. "Your stateroom, ma'am."

She stared at the creamy woodwork and opulent ivory furnishings, at the huge bed dominating the lavish room. "Oh, there must be some mistake!"

"No, ma'am. This is the stateroom you were assigned."

Her eyes widened. "Are they all like this?"

"The staterooms on the lower deck are each different, ma'am." He gestured to a phone. "The buttons will call your stewardess, the galley or any of the staterooms."

The young man left, closing the door softly behind him. Chloe stood in the middle of the room and slowly turned to take it all in. Unbelievable. Fantuckingfastic. She'd slept in tents, on the bare ground, in the back of trucks and sometimes, three to a bed. Having this all to herself was indulgence beyond belief. This was a room made for sex. Pity she had no lover to share the cozy conversation area formed by a plush loveseat, two armchairs and a coffee table. Or frolic in that decadent bed.

She ran her fingers over the silky white duvet, tempted to snuggle into the plump pillows clustered against the padded headboard. Behind the bed, twin swags draped a large window overlooking the dark water.

Lamps on either side of the bed shed a mellow glow. Several doors led from the room. She tried the one nearest her and found it locked. Another stateroom, no doubt. Underneath her feet she felt a fine tremor, the rumble of engines. Touching the band on her wrist, she hoped it worked. She'd never been on a cruise before, didn't know if she'd get seasick. For that matter, why this one?

She'd been assured that everything was on the level, that her host, Mr. Yancy, was well known with a spotless reputation. Though he preferred to keep a low profile due to the nature of his business, she had nothing to fear. All she had to do was rest. She was due a break, after pushing herself, going after the telling story, the perfect picture, for too long. She was supposed to put work out of her mind and be pampered.

She grinned. Pampering she could handle. Comforts like these, after time in the field where amenities like hot water and flushing toilets were scarce, felt almost surreal. But good, very good. Since she had to be here, she was going to enjoy every bit of this treat. Who knew if she'd ever have another chance?

Chloe kicked off her sandals and sank down on the bed. The fabric under her bare feet was soft, silky and sensuous, a tactile reminder of the difference between her lifestyle and this plush boat, er, yacht. Above her head, the lowered ceiling had hidden light sparkling on reflective tiles . . . sheesh, mirrors! Now that she looked, she saw her body in a dozen different angles. Just as she'd thought. This was a room for lovers. What a waste.

The knock at her door had her up and crossing the deep pile carpet to open the door. A young woman wearing a white shirt with nautical insignia with trim black pants smiled at her. "I'm Lisa, your stewardess. We've brought your luggage, ma'am."

Chloe stood back and watched a crewman stow her camera cases in the closet. He left her duffel bag on a luggage rack.

Lisa closed the door behind him. "I'll unpack and then press anything that needs a touch up."

"That's not necessary," Chloe protested. "All my clothes are wrinkle free."

"We'll see, shall we? Have you seen the activities schedule?" When Chloe shook her head, she gave her one.

Chloe scanned the itinerary. First night, cocktails and buffet.

Okay, she could handle that. She'd need to meet her host and make polite noises. Each morning had a buffet breakfast served on the boat deck, whatever that was, followed by discretionary recreation, then a buffet lunch, more activities, dinner, evening entertainment and a midnight supper. She pulled the waistband of her slacks away from her body. If she weren't careful she wouldn't fit into these by the time she got home again.

There were several "fantasy" activities with no descriptions. Her eyebrows lifted. Thanks, but no thanks. No doubt someone being cute, playing on the yacht's name. She stifled a chuckle. She could imagine playing with several very wild fantasies but none of them were likely to come true. It was a good thing she had an alternate strategy in mind.

In short time, the stewardess had unpacked and put away everything but her long black skirt, the red silk tank top, and the black jersey dress that went everywhere with Chloe. "I'll just take these with me while you get ready for the Welcome Reception," Lisa said. "What will you wear tonight?"

Chloe hesitated. "What do you suggest?"

Lisa held up the black skirt and tank top. "These will do very nicely. Tomorrow is more formal." She looked distressed. "Is this all you brought for evening?"

"It's all I own," Chloe admitted. There wasn't much call for fancy dress when she was working.

Later, after a shower, and an uncharacteristically long time spent brushing and doing up her long black hair in a simple knot, she applied her makeup and dressed in the outfit Lisa had returned. She stood back to see herself in the long mirror over the dresser. She never wore makeup on assignment in war-torn areas, but now she'd applied her own war paint. Blusher enhanced her pale complexion, drawing attention to her black eyes and lips that she'd painted a bright red. Dangling silver and onyx earrings completed the look. Grinning at her reflection, she flicked her thumb up in approval. "Looking good."

Chloe left her cabin, following the sounds of voices, a deep male laugh and the tinkle of glass and ice to the salon. She paused in the doorway to get her bearings. Like her stateroom, this room looked inviting and lush, yet definitely masculine. The furniture was oversized in bold, earthy colors, the sculpture and works of art a mixture of modern and American Indian motifs. The young man who'd escorted her aboard stood at the bar, mixing drinks and pouring champagne. Beyond a laden buffet table, groupings of furniture offered comfort and conversation.

In the middle of the room, a tall redhead in a skin-tight red dress flirted with three men clustered around her. One man, taller than the others, stopped a glass halfway to his mouth at Chloe's entrance. He put the glass drink down, then moved toward her.

"Chloe, it's a pleasure to have you aboard."

She looked up into his lean, dark face, cheekbones starkly carved, a wide slash of mouth, obsidian eyes beneath black brows. Light from the wall sconces gleamed on his skin, highlighting the bronzed tones of his shaven head. She suspected it was vanity that prompted him to keep his beautifully curved head on display. His face was ruggedly compelling and intriguing, one the camera would love. She didn't do commercial portraits, but he'd be an excellent subject. As she studied him, thinking about camera angles and lighting, she realized he examined her as intently.

"I'm Yancy," he said.

"Of course." She extended her hand, recalling what her boss had said about her host's professional accomplishments, his vast wealth, and his rapid rise to a position of power and influence. "Thank you for inviting me, Mr. Yancy—"

"Just Yancy," he interrupted as he took her hand. He smiled broadly, making a little dimple appear in one cheek.

"While I'm here, maybe we could do an interview?"

The dimple disappeared. "No interviews. Ever."

"Then why am I here?"

"You don't remember me?"

She narrowed her eyes and looked up past his broad shoulders covered with custom-made suiting, to his face. He smiled at her, softening the no-nonsense lines of his mouth. One slightly crooked tooth marred the perfection of otherwise even white dental work.

Her breath felt trapped in her chest at the way he stared at her, expectantly and oddly demanding. It was her business to remember faces, but she couldn't place his cryptic, intense face. Quelling the strangest urge to run her fingers over the curve of his head to learn if it was as smooth as it looked, she retrieved her hand from his warm grasp. "We've met?"

"A long time ago." His smile warmed his black eyes. The dimple deepened, giving him the look of a mischievous boy. "You sat at the front of the room, I was at the back. I think I paid more attention to you than to Mr. Braganti's theories—"

She wrinkled her brow in concentration, then made the connection. "You were in my poli-sci class? But that was in college, years ago!"

"It took me a while to find you."

"Why would you want to do that?" She took a step back, putting space between them. Just because he knew her college class schedule didn't mean he'd actually been there. She'd encountered stalkers before, met men who expected her to trade her body for an inside scoop.

"Relax. You're among friends."

Friends? Hardly. Did he think his money gave him the advantage? She put more space between them.

He smiled, as if he'd guessed her thoughts. "I've wanted to get to know you, but the time wasn't right. Now it is."

"Right for what?"

"For you."

"That's ridiculous. We've never even spoken."

"We'll remedy that on this trip. There'll be plenty of opportunity to get to know each other." He touched her elbow. Did she imagine that slight caress? If not, it just made her more uncomfortable. "Come, join my guests."

Friends? Hardly. She glanced at the others, saw strangers and returned their curious looks, then glanced behind her. Oh, no! Two men she'd never thought she'd see again entered the salon. She stiffened. First Yancy keeping tabs on her, then ex-lovers? "What's going on?"

"As soon as everyone else is here, I'll explain." Yancy nudged her forward, urging her across the thick carpet.

She stood her ground. "I want to know now. Why am I here?"

Yancy studied her. She didn't temper her expression. If she looked stubborn and demanding, tough.

"Fair enough," he said quietly. "If you still have questions later, then we'll talk."

As he moved forward, she heard a quick laugh and turned to see two women come up the stairs from a lower deck. The smaller one was dressed all in black, her black hair cropped close to her skull. The taller one wore her hair in multi-colored spikes. Her grunge outfit and heavy boots were a stark contrast to the hedonistic furnishings.

Behind them, as if choreographed, came two blondes. One had hair so pale it looked white, falling in a straight cut that emphasized the delicacy of her face. Next to her, the one with a no-nonsense short haircut looked sturdy and sensible.

If Yancy wanted to get to know her better, why all these people? Chloe stood rigid with her back against the wall, as far away from her ex-lovers and Yancy as she could get. Yancy looked around, as if counting noses. A man rose from a corner seat and caught his eye. Yancy nodded and went to stand in the middle of the salon.

"First, let me thank each of you for accepting my invitation aboard the *Fantasy*. It's short notice, I know, but I'm pleased you were able to clear your schedules." He noted each face, smiling an individual welcome.

Looking directly at Chloe, he continued, "Please sit, make yourself comfortable. The steward will offer you a drink, then leave. When we are alone, I'll have a few things to say."

Chloe accepted a flute of champagne, then perched on the arm of a chair upholstered in bronze suede. She looked at the other guests as inquisitively as they regarded each other, all the while avoiding the eyes of the two men standing by the door leading to the deck. Even though she didn't look at them, she sensed they were staring at her. Why now? And why together?

With her career taking her all over the world, she'd never been able to give a relationship the care and attention it needed. Yet, the two times she'd been swept into thinking that this time, with this man, it might work, she'd been wrong. Absolutely wrong.

Why were they here?

After the steward left the salon, Yancy resumed his welcoming speech. "There are a few safety regulations which the Captain will explain later. Until then, I have some suggestions to ensure your enjoyment during the five days you'll be aboard." He paused, as if waiting for complete attention. "I've already said this to a few of you, but I'll repeat: the first rule is confidentiality."

Chloe's head snapped up. Several of the other guests looked puzzled.

"That's right. Discretion, for your ease of mind. If you are not already known to each other, you may use only your first names," Yancy continued in a firm voice. "What you do after we return is up to you. In a minute, we'll introduce ourselves, and mention our chosen occupations, but beyond that, no shop talk. You are here because you are at the top of your professions, over-stressed, near burnout, and need rest and recreation. You need a complete change of scene." Chloe noted he looked directly at her. "Understood?"

She inclined her head and looked at the other guests. Some looked puzzled, others smiled and nodded.

"As you came aboard, you received the itinerary for this cruise. No doubt you're wondering what the surprise and fantasy items are?"

More nods.

"You'll have to wait to find out." Yancy's grin was unexpectedly contagious, and most of the guests laughed. Chloe rubbed her fingers over the soft suede. Oh, what she was going to email the boss when she got back to her stateroom. . . .

"There are some items aboard for your pleasure. TVs, DVDs, stereos in each of the staterooms as well as here in the salon. Don't bother to try the phones except for onboard calls. If there is an emergency, the ship's crew will handle it, but as my guests, you will not be allowed contact with your offices. That includes web connections and mobile phones."

Chloe's head snapped up. Yancy dismissed her protest. "You'll find protected sunning areas on deck. Clothing is optional." He ignored a few raised eyebrows. "There's a library in the small den, with cards, board games and such. We'll anchor at selected spots twice. We have scuba and diving gear aboard, WaveRunners, Zodiacs, snorkeling, fishing and exercise gear. If you need lessons in using the equipment, certified crew members will instruct you."

Several men looked eager with the promise of adventure. The redhead tossed her hair back in a curly swathe.

"Okay, to start the introductions, I'm Yancy. I've been fortunate enough to do well in aviation, but the sea is my passion. I spend as much time sailing as I can."

"My name is Saul, I'm in banking. This is your boat?" a tall, dark man asked.

"The *Fantasy* belongs to me, yes." Yancy nodded to the man on his right, the one who had risen from the corner.

"I'm Mark." A blush climbed his throat and stained his cheeks, matching the strawberry blond buzzcut. "I'm in electronics."

Yancy nodded to the woman next to Mark.

"My name is Ali," the black-haired woman all in black said. "I'm in . . . communications, I guess you'd call it."

"I'm Shelly," the brunette with the multi-colored hair spoke next. "I'm in theater."

The blond man next to her looked like a farm boy straight off the wheat fields, but his voice as he introduced himself was cool and sophisticated. "I handle imports and exports. You may call me Perry."

"Is that your real name?" the redhead cooed.

"Possibly." He looked her up and down. Even from several feet away, Chloe noted the way his glance lingered on the tight red dress. "What's yours?"

"Lane. I'm in advertising."

"Obviously," Perry murmured with a glance at her breasts.

The sturdy blonde woman laughed. "I'm Wynne, a pediatrician. I don't expect any of you to need my services."

Relaxing a bit, Chloe chuckled along with the others. The delicate platinum blonde waved her fingers. "Nor mine, I hope. I'm what you'd call a legislative reformer."

"Your name?" Saul asked.

"Tracy."

Yancy looked around. "Only three left. Who'll go first?"

The compact man in the doorway stepped forward, flashing an engaging grin. "I'm Adam. I fly Yancy's test planes."

Chloe looked away, afraid that his grin would melt her insides as quickly as it had at the experimental airshow she'd covered three years ago. A recently retired Air Force jet jockey then, Adam had swept her into a heady, short-term affair that had left her gasping for air. She'd thought at first that he might be the one, but their relationship fizzled when their schedules kept them apart. She hadn't seen him since they'd agreed to go their separate ways.

"Ladies first," came the deep voice of the man at Adam's side. Chloe flicked a glance his way and automatically adjusted the slit of her long black skirt to cover her thigh. He'd always admired her legs, claiming them to be the secret weapons she kept hidden under her serviceable twill pants. "I'm Chloe, a photojournalist."

Several pairs of eyes turned to her in recognition. Yancy intervened. "No questions."

Did he really expect his guests not to talk about themselves? Chloe looked at him curiously as the others turned expectantly to the last guest.

"Brad," he said in authoritarian tones. "I sometimes consult for Yancy." About what, Chloe wondered. Why did Yancy need military expertise for his aviation business? She could understand Adam, but Brad was not a flyer.

Yancy stepped to the middle of the room again. "Good, now we all know each other. Have another drink, eat, indulge yourselves."

He looked from one guest to another. "That's the prime rule for the *Fantasy*. No limit, anything goes. Anything legal, that is."

Laughter followed him as a number of the guests mingled, refreshed their drinks and congregated around the buffet table. Chloe edged closer to Yancy. "What gives?" she murmured. "Am I the only one here who isn't a stranger to the other guests?"

Yancy's dark eyes lingered on her face, moving from her eyes, to her mouth and back again. "Confidentiality, remember?"

Chloe hissed. "Why are Brad and Adam here?"

"They're valued associates. They need a break, too."

"Just keep them away from me!"

"Tell them yourself. Here they come."

Chloe stiffened. At her back, she could feel the heat of Brad's body much as she'd felt it in dark, dangerous places when he'd protected her with both his person and his weapons. He spoke her name.

Reluctantly, she turned and looked into his deep, blue eyes. Combat had etched lines around his eyes and mouth, but couldn't lessen his appeal. If anything, he looked tougher, more in charge in his civvies than he had in battle-stained camouflage.

It wasn't fair that her body should respond so quickly. Not after the struggle she'd had to forget him. She swallowed hard. "Brad."

"It's good to see you, Chloe."

Adam shot him a glance. "You two know each other?"

Brad didn't take his eyes from her. "We met in the Middle East," he said in his clipped voice.

Adam made a sound in his throat as he studied her quizzically. "When was that, Chloe?"

"Several months ago," Brad answered for her. His lips thinned as he turned to Adam. "Something to you?"

Yancy's eyes narrowed as he watched the two men, his body tensed for action. Chloe was aware of his changed breathing as they waited for Adam's answer. Though he said nothing, Yancy was in command, virile and, she was appalled to realize, exciting. Under her thin silk top, her nipples felt full.

Adam put up his hands and gave them his trademark grin. "Nope. Chloe and I were over long before that."

Brad gave Adam a long, considering look. Chloe knew she should leave them to their macho posturing, but she was rooted by her sudden arousal. She hated the thought that it was caused by the thrill of Adam and Brad fighting over her. Whatever she'd shared with each of them was over. Adam by mutual consent, Brad abrupt and brutal. Her scars from that encounter still hadn't healed. She couldn't imagine either one wanting to start something up again, so why the attitude?

Yancy took her arm and led her away. "Let's get something to eat. The chef is particularly talented with seafood."

Chloe noted the smooth transition from a man ready for action to urbane host. Moving away from his grasp, she said, "Thank you, but it's not necessary. I'm leaving."

Yancy gave her a quizzical look. "Haven't you noticed?"

"What?"

"We're underway. We sailed almost an hour ago."

"Oh, no!" She'd forgotten she felt the engines start up. "Turn around and take me back."

"Can't do that, Chloe. If you don't want to have anything to do with Adam or Brad, don't. Ignore them, do as you please. Make new friends. Lots of interesting people aboard." A slow smile lit his face, coaxing her out of her anger. "Or spend time with me. Forget about them."

She glanced over her shoulder at the two men staring at her with tight faces. "Oh, sure."

Chapter Two

Chloe rested her wineglass on the deck railing. A thin band of fog obscured the horizon, and far above her head, the stars winked at her. The breeze coming off the water was cold, but she welcomed the fresh air.

There was something going on here, undercurrents and emotions she sensed, but couldn't quite identify. It made her uneasy to know that Yancy had more on his mind than providing a stress-free break from work. She believed the other guests were strangers to each other, but why had Yancy invited her here with Adam and Brad? Yancy had to be aware they knew each other, since he hadn't been at all surprised at her reaction to seeing them.

It had to be a set-up. Had he brought her on board to play matchmaker, to patch things up between her and an ex-lover? If so, he was way off base. She'd learned her lesson. When—and if—she was ready for a new relationship, she wasn't going to settle for anything less than everything. She craved excitement, yes, but she also wanted something deeper. She wanted more than the passionate affairs she'd had with Adam and Brad.

As for that, how did they come to work for Yancy? She wouldn't have expected either to give up his military career. What had Yancy offered them to resign? Or had he? He was a puzzle. More than once she'd looked across the room and found his intent gaze focused on her. What was he thinking?

"Here you are."

She didn't need to turn to recognize Brad's voice. "I'd rather be alone."

"Tough. What are you doing aboard?"

"I was invited." She glanced at him from the corner of her eye. "What's this all about? Why me, why those people?"

"I have no idea. I'm as surprised as you are. Waste of time when I've got other things to do."

"Same here. But I got told no cruise, no job."

"The agency would let you go? No sweat. The others would snap you up in an instant."

"Thanks." Brad made her feel confident, secure, but then he'd always been able to do that. Except when he'd left her without a word. "So why did you come if you're so busy?"

"Yancy calls the shots."

"I would have thought Yancy would only hire flyboys. What's a Marine like you doing for him?"

"Ex. No shop talk, remember?"

"Same old Brad. No comment, no excuses, no good-byes."

He stiffened, standing almost at attention. "That couldn't be helped. I had orders."

"Oh, well, that's all that matters, right?"

"You know I would have told you if I could. I didn't like leaving you."

"And that's why you called me the very first chance you had, to let me know you were alive and I could stop worrying."

He flinched at her bitter tone. "I can only say I'm sorry." He edged closer and touched her shoulder. "We're here now, we can forget about that and get on with things."

"Wouldn't that be convenient?" Chloe moved away and crossed her arms. "Just throw off our clothes and hop in the sack. Oops, I forgot. We didn't get to do that too often, did we? Just get off enough to get it off. No, thanks."

The glow from the salon lighted the narrowing of his eyes. "We had something good going. Why the cold shoulder now?"

It had been good while it lasted. They'd come together, so quickly and completely; she'd thought that maybe she and Brad were destined to be together. How wrong she'd been.

"It's over, Brad. If you'd wanted a warm reception you should have called me when you dropped your uniform." She emptied the last of her wine over the side rather than dashing it in his face. "See you." She placed her glass on a table and moved away. "On second thought, keep away from me."

He took her arm, halting her. "Can't do that, honey. I didn't have anything to do with getting you aboard, but now that we're together again, I'm not letting you go."

"Too late." She moved out of his grasp.

"Is there someone else? Another lover? What do you do, change men as often as you do your film?"

She recoiled. "I cried for you once. I'm not going to do it again."

"There won't be another time. I swear."

"No need for that. Leave me alone."

"Not a chance."

Chloe felt his gaze on her as she strode across the deck to the lighted salon. She didn't look back. She entered the room at the same time the captain introduced himself.

He made a few general remarks, then cleared his throat. "In case you are wondering, the *Fantasy* is a power yacht. Our cruising speed is fifteen knots, and we normally have a crew of ten aboard. This cruise we're down to nine, but we'll do our best to make sure you have a pleasant, safe cruise. We're air-conditioned for your comfort when the fog isn't around. We carry more than enough fuel and water, can make more fresh water, so you needn't worry about bathing.

"Our zodiacs do double duty as lifeboats, and we have lifejackets for everyone. Your steward will show you where they are located in your staterooms, and show you how to put them on. We have more in all of the public rooms." He gestured at a cabinet and a crew member opened it to reveal a storage locker with bright orange lifevests. "If you hear the warning siren, put on a life jacket and meet on the boat deck. At once!

"We don't carry a medical team aboard, but if you need something, your steward will know what to do. In cases of emergency, we can land a Med Evac helicopter on the aft sun deck. In any case, we won't be far offshore." He looked stern for a moment, then smiled. "If there are no questions, I'll say goodnight."

As the captain left, Yancy stood and tapped at the side of his crystal glass for attention. "Welcome again to the *Fantasy* and all she has to offer. Don't forget you're here to relax and recharge your batteries. I'm going to say goodnight now. Sleep as late as you wish. Have breakfast in bed or join us here for buffet until nine. You don't want to miss the entertainment planned for breakfast."

Ignoring raised eyebrows and the buzz of conversation, he followed the captain below. Saying nothing, Chloe made her way across the room and entered the narrow hallway leading to her room. A woman's brittle voice followed her. "Why does she get that stateroom?"

Good question, Chloe thought. Why was she the only one here, and all the other guests on a lower deck? She went on to her cabin, opened the door and found her bed turned down, a designer chocolate on the pillow, and a bottle of mineral water with a crystal tumbler on her bedside table. The lamps were turned low, spreading an inviting glow over the cream colored sheets.

As she turned to close the door, the stewardess, Lisa, appeared. With a few words of instruction, she helped Chloe try on the life vest and re-hung it in the closet. She gestured at the bed. "I'd have put out your nightgown, but I didn't find one."

"That's because I don't wear one." On assignment she'd often had to sleep in her clothes.

Lisa grinned. "You'll find a terry cloth robe in the bath."

Chloe thanked her, and after Lisa left, she undressed, cleaned her face and slipped under the covers. She wriggled and stretched, enjoying the luxury of silk sheets on her bare skin. The fabric was cool, sensitizing her nipples and falling gently between her opened thighs. For a moment, she allowed herself to remember making love with Brad. The few times they'd been able to find a bed and be totally naked had allowed her to play with his fit body. His physique and training gave him stamina, and he'd been a powerful lover, bringing her to orgasm again and again.

Much of the heat and fierceness of their passion was owing to the dangerous times, the risk and the heat of battle going on around them. Sometimes she'd longed for lingering foreplay, the escalating need, the sweet torment of holding off just one more moment. No matter how many times she came, sometimes she'd hungered for more, to have every one of her needs fulfilled.

It wasn't likely that total immersion in physical gratification would fill the empty space in her heart, yet sometimes she'd wondered what it would be like to make love with more than one man at a time. How would it feel to indulge all her senses at once? To have every bit of her body caressed, stroked, kissed?

Her nipples peaked, firming in anticipated pleasure even as her center warmed and went liquid. Contrary to Brad's accusation, she hadn't made love since he'd left her without a word.

Tough, Brad had said. Tough, she told her body.

Adjusting the pillows behind her head, she settled in with a book. When the phone rang, once, twice and again, softly but insistently, she stared at it, willing it to stop, then reluctantly lifted the receiver. "Hello?"

"Chloe, sorry if I've woken you. Can you talk?"

"What is it, Adam?"

"I didn't get a chance to tell you how good it is to see you again. Surprised me, but it feels fine. How have you been, sweet lady?"

Chloe relaxed into the pillows. Nobody but Adam had ever called her that, ever even thought of her in that way. Sweetness wasn't a trait that would get her ahead as a photojournalist. Persistence, determination and a knack for getting to the truth of the matter: those were the traits she cultivated. Yet, every now and then it felt good to be complimented for her softer, feminine nature. "I'm surprised to see you, too. When did you go to work for Yancy?"

"About a year ago. He made me an offer I couldn't refuse. And that's all I'm going to tell you."

She heard the laughter in his voice. If there were planes to fly, he'd be first in line. "So, what's this cruise all about?"

"Dunno. Yancy came in one day, big smile on that poker face of his, gave his secretary a list of people and told her to get the invitations going."

"Why? Why these people? Why me?"

"Beats me. He keeps his plans to himself. All I know is he handpicked everyone here."

"Are we the only ones who know each other? From before, I mean?"

"I think so. In fact, I met Brad only a week ago. Didn't know he'd be here until I found we're sharing a stateroom."

Oh, no. Two gung-ho, macho men bunking in the same room. Both of them having a history with her. Both of them pawing at the ground when they found out about the other. "Sounds like bad news. Can you get another room?"

"Nope. Only six of them, and they're all full. Yancy's already in the crew quarters—"

"He is? Why?"

"Well, I'll be . . . you're in the owner's stateroom, Chloe. Yancy gave that up for you."

She sat up straight. The covers fell, leaving her breasts bare. "Why did he do that?"

"You don't know? This gets curiouser and curiouser."

"I had no idea." She pleated the sheet with her fingers. "Something's fishy."

"Why don't we put our heads together and see if we can figure it out?"

"Now?"

He laughed. She could just imagine his big grin, the crinkles around his hazel eyes. "I guess that's out by the sound of your voice. See you at breakfast? We can talk then."

They hung up a few moments later. Chloe sank back under the covers, confused and suspicious all over again. Adam's pleasant manner and quick grin often fooled people into thinking he was mellow and easy going. He wasn't. He liked to be in charge, to dominate the situation, to have all the answers. It wasn't like him not to know what was going on.

Why had Yancy brought them all together like this?

Chapter Three

Chloe considered the eggs, potatoes, bacon, sausages, fresh fruits and pastries displayed on the dining table. She placed a slice of melon on her plate.

Adam joined her. "Is that all you're going to eat?"

"No." She added two strawberries and some sections of orange. "This is."

He added bacon and eggs to his plate. "You'll be hungry by lunchtime."

"Better than not fitting into my clothes by dinner time."

He scanned her from tip to toe, his gaze lingering where her red fleece sweatshirt covered her breasts, then moving indolently down her torso, past her khaki shorts to her bare legs and sandaled feet. "You can always take them off." He grinned. "Remember, Yancy said clothing is optional."

"Oh, sure!" Chloe rolled her eyes but she laughed.

Adam replaced the silver tongs on the toast platter and turned to look at her again. She felt his gaze crawl over her body. All at once, she felt naked, poised under him while he took his time touching, kissing and licking her, stroking her into mindless passion. "Stop that!"

He gave her another quick, engaging grin. "Let's take our plates out on deck," he suggested. He led the way past groups of breakfasting guests to the side door, slid it open and gestured her through.

She hesitated between the warm salon and the cool, misty deck where fog and the plaintive cry of gulls were their only company. It was June, officially summer, but her clothes weren't warm enough for the annual summer fog. "Your eggs will get cold out here."

She stepped back inside and found a pair of empty armchairs and waited for Adam to join her. Some of the other passengers nodded and said good morning. Perry, the farm boy with the sophisticated voice, winked at her. She smiled back.

"One man at a time, if you don't mind, sweet lady."

Chloe smiled. His words reminded her of her thoughts last night, how she'd fallen asleep dreaming of fantasy lovers.

Adam ate his eggs. "Okay, so you don't know why you're here, and in Yancy's stateroom, and I have all sorts of ideas."

She leaned forward. "Like what?"

"Like why would he make sure you have the biggest bed aboard unless he plans to share it?"

Her fork clattered across the china and dropped to the floor. "I don't even know him!"

He handed her the utensil. She placed it and her plate on the coffee table in front of her. "There has to be another explanation."

"Like what? Why would he make sure we all understand this is a confidential, fantasy cruise? No last names, discretion all the way around? Sounds like he's set the scenario for a no-holds barred, sex-til-you-drop week. And baby, that's okay with me."

She glanced at the other guests. "They're all strangers."

"We're not. And," he gestured at the couple sitting on the couch, "they won't be much longer."

She followed his gaze. Perry and the redhead, Lane, huddled close together. Lane wore tight red leggings that didn't leave much to the imagination. Her nipples were clearly defined under a striped red and white tee shirt as she leaned into his body.

Chloe whispered, "She looks like the barracuda type. Maybe someone should warn Perry."

Adam grinned. "He's a big boy. He can take care of himself." Chloe bit back a smile. By the looks of Perry's tan Dockers, he was a very big boy.

"And check out those two." Chloe looked over her shoulder. Saul stared intently into Tracy's pale face, listening closely as she spoke. It was hard to believe that they'd met just yesterday. Or had they?

"Bet you a buck those couples will be in the sack by lunchtime." Chloe snickered. "I don't take sucker bets."

"We could steal away ourselves. Make use of that big bed, run a tub—"

"How do you know so much about my room?"

"Been aboard before." He saw her look and continued quickly. "Business meetings, nothing like this. All guys."

Chloe just looked at him, but he was saved an answer when Yancy and Lisa entered the room. She carried a silver bowl and stood just inside the door while Yancy made his way into the center of the room.

"Good morning. I hope you slept well. Our captain tells us the fog will burn off shortly, and we'll have sun and warm weather for the afternoon. We're cruising to our first anchorage and expect to reach it sometime during the night. To make it interesting, we're going to have a little contest. Anyone who guesses the time of our arrival, as clocked by the captain, wins a prize."

"And what's that?" called Ali. This morning, she wore black again; a short miniskirt and belly baring top displaying a black bead in her navel.

"All the prizes on this cruise are selected first for the occasion, second, for the sex of the winner."

"His and her prizes?" Wynne asked. Her jeans and navy blue cotton sweater only hinted at curves.

"His or her prizes," Yancy corrected. "If they choose to share, that's up to them." Laughter rose up as Lisa moved around the room, handing out paper and pens. "Write your guess and sign it," Yancy instructed. "I'll give you this much of a hint. We'll arrive while you're sleeping." He gave them all a wolfish grin. "While some of you may be sleeping."

Chloe frowned at Adam. "This is sounding more like a frat party every moment."

Adam nodded. "Probably going to get raunchy."

She took pen and paper. Firmly, she wrote, 1:35 AM while I am sleeping. Alone. Chloe.

Adam glanced at her slip of paper. "That definite, sweet lady? I may have something to say about that." He jotted down his estimate and folded the slip of paper before she could see what he wrote.

The stewardess collected their guesses and left, taking the silver bowl with her.

Yancy rubbed his hands. "Good. Now, your time is your own. Play, nap, enjoy yourselves. I'll see you back here for lunch."

Chloe watched him leave the salon, enter the passageway leading to her, no, his stateroom, then rose and followed him. She caught up with him as he was turning the key in a closed door. "May I have a word with you?"

"Sure. Come on in." He opened the door and gestured her in. She stepped into an office. Bookshelves held leather-bound volumes and a selection of antique nautical equipment. Yancy went to sit behind a curved expanse of cream-colored wood that served as a desk. Behind him, an open laptop and some file folders waited for his attention.

"You're working but we can't?" she asked.

"I make the rules. My guests need a break. I don't." Yancy gestured to the plush couch facing the desk. She sat, sinking deeply into supple copper suede, as he eased back in his large, rust colored leather desk chair. He seemed relaxed in black trousers and a tan knit shirt that set off the shadowed planes of his face.

"What's up, Chloe?"

"I want some answers."

He spread his hands. "Ask."

"First, I understand you gave up your cabin for me. It's beautiful, and I thank you, but you should take it back. I can sleep somewhere else."

"With whom?"

"By myself, of course!"

"There are no other sleeping accommodations available. You'll have to stay where you are."

She leaned forward and placed her hand on his desk. "Why invite so many people that you have to give up your cabin?"

"I didn't have to." He looked at her hand, then at her mouth. "It pleased me to do it."

"Why me? Why am I on board?" She put her hand in her lap, covered it with the other. "I've been wracking my brain, but I just don't remember you. Are you sure you knew me?"

"We didn't speak, but I knew you." His gaze roved over her face, dropped lower, then returned to meet her eyes. He smiled. "You weren't quite so thin then, and you wore your hair longer than now. Sometimes in a pony tail," he gestured at the back of his head. "But most often hanging down your back. Like black satin. You wore jeans, but I really liked one of your skirts. It was long and had flowers on it and with it you wore a yellow sweater. It looked soft."

She remembered that skirt. Black, ankle length, with little daisies scattered here and there. She'd loved that angora sweater. She shrugged. "You could have seen pictures."

"True, and someone could have told me that you argued with Braganti about third world countries and their right to make their own decisions. But they didn't."

"Okay. So you were in class with me. So were a lot of other people. I can't place you."

"It might come to you." He settled back in his chair, and linked his fingers behind his head. She noted once again the breadth of his chest, the swell of muscle under his clothing. She licked her lips. His breath hitched. His gaze lingered on her face, particularly her mouth. They stared at each other until Chloe broke the connection.

"Why wait all these years? You could have arranged to meet ages ago. Why this cruise?"

"I told you." He dropped his arms. "I wasn't ready. Now that I am, I thought I might as well give you the chance to relax and unwind while I was at it."

It sounded reasonable on the surface, but she was sure there had to be more to it. "What do you mean, you weren't ready?"

"Let's say that I didn't have much to offer then. Now I do." He made a vague gesture that took in the whole yacht.

"Impressing me with your money?"

"Something like that," he agreed on a dry note.

"That doesn't say much for me. Makes me sound like a gold-digger."

He chuckled. "You're not. Otherwise that playboy prince might have had more success with you."

Her mouth dropped open. She found her voice. "You have been keeping tabs, haven't you?"

"Only because I wanted the time to be right."

"For what?"

"Perhaps I'll tell you later, after I see how things go."

"You're confusing me."

"Good. Now, if you'll excuse me, I have work to do."

She stood up, dismissed and frustrated. She pointed at the closed door. "Where does that lead?"

"To the owner's stateroom." He studied her face. "It's locked."

She nodded and left his office. Instead of rejoining the others, she went to her room. Knowing that it was Yancy's usual quarters made her uneasy. She could see him here, his large body at ease, slipping naked between the sheets. She swallowed hard, imagining his burnished skin against the ivory sheets, his body dark against her pale flesh.

Hers? Where had that thought come from?

Now that it had, it slipped insidiously through her, warming her, making her skin quiver. Or was she only responding to his blatant interest? Either way, she felt overheated, stifled by his presence even though she was alone. She needed air!

She glanced out her window. The sea looked flat and gray, with an occasional white cap creating a contrasting color, white froth flicked into peaks by wave and wind. There was nothing unusual about it, but maybe she'd get some atmospheric shots to steady her nerves and clear her head.

Eagerly, Chloe took out her cameras, and checked her equipment. Photography wasn't only her occupation, it was her passion. She inspected lenses and light meters, filters and battery packs, then made sure she had all her repair equipment with her. She had become adept at fixing her own equipment since camera shops came few and far between in the field. She took what she wanted and securely repacked the rest.

Alone on the sundeck with nothing but the cool breeze ruffling her ponytail and chilling her bare legs, she took a few deep breaths, expelling her fantasies of Yancy and drawing in moist, salt-laden air. She turned in a circle, scanning the horizon. A still-weak sun was burning off some of the fog. A thin, dark line looked like coastline, but wasn't worth the film. Behind her, the wake streamed steadily and white against the grayish-green water. The churned up colors caught her eye for a moment, then receded.

Far out to sea, a small dot might have been another boat.

She sat on a padded bench seat, out of some of the wind, checked the light meter and looked over the side. Water rushed by, rising and falling with the boat. She moved to the front, and peered over the railing, to the front of the boat. The prow, as the captain had called it.

She aimed her camera as a crewman walked across her field of vision. In his uniform, wearing a black windbreaker, he offered contrasting color against the white ship and the gray sea and sky. He looked up, saw her and called a greeting. She lowered the camera and waved.

She snapped a few more shots, then repacked her camera gear and headed for the lower deck. She met Yancy as he was coming out the door to the salon. His shoulders all but filled the doorway. Instantly, the fantasized sight of him naked swept through her, tantalizing her with the imagined feel of his bare skin against hers.

He held out his hand. "I'll take that."

"What?"

"Your camera. I thought I made it clear that this cruise is confidential. That means no photos. No working. Give me your camera."

Sensual thoughts disappeared in a flash. "I wasn't working, just amusing myself. You did tell me to enjoy myself, remember?"

"Not by taking pictures. You can have your gear back when we dock. Hand it over, please."

She'd never been stripped of her cameras while she was on assignment, never been confronted by angry officials who denied her the right to capture on film what the world needed to know. Acting purely on instinct, she swung her camera case behind her back.

He reached for it. His long arms went around her. She felt his torso, his muscled arms enclosing her, his hands on hers. She tried to wrench free. His grip tightened. She became aware of her breasts pushing against him at the same time he did. She felt her nipples harden, felt his cock thicken and rise against her belly. Her eyes widened as he went still. Heat spread up from her nipples, climbed her throat and clogged her breathing. He looked down, she looked up.

Camera bag forgotten, they stared at each other. His black eyes were intent on hers, his face a mixture of determination and awareness. She tried to step back. His arms tightened, then dropped. His gaze never left hers.

He blew out a breath, fanning her temple with warmth. "The camera."

Without another word, she handed it to him and fled, not slowing down until she reached her room. She closed the door behind her and breathed hard. Her breasts were still flushed and sensitive. What was happening here? She'd sworn off men, and here were Brad and Adam wanting to renew the passion they'd shared with her. Here was Yancy, striking new sparks. She ran her tongue over her lips and licked away salt. What would his mouth taste like?

She headed for the shower, adjusted the temperature to cool and stepped in. She scrubbed her skin, then turned her face up to the water, letting it pelt on her temples and closed eyes. Gradually, her body chilled and she turned off the water.

She dried herself, drew the warm terry cloth robe around her and wrapped her head in a towel as she entered the bedroom.

"Are you all right?" Brad rose off the bed.

"What are you doing here?" she demanded. "How did you get in?"

"Your door was unlocked. You seemed upset, so I came to see if I could help."

"He has some nerve!" she exploded. "Taking my camera away from me!"

"Is that all?"

"Isn't that enough?" She whirled, looking for the rest of the equipment she'd left in the closet. All her camera cases and gear were gone. So was her laptop. "That rat!"

"Who?"

"He came in here and got all my camera equipment when I wasn't looking! Even my laptop!"

"You'll get it back."

Chloe ignored his soothing tone. "What gives him the right to take my things!"

Brad reached out and pulled her down on the bed next to him. "Don't you remember the meaning of the word discretion? Yancy's protecting all his guests."

"I didn't take pictures of them. Only the water, the sky and a crewman. What's the harm in that?"

"Nothing in that, I agree. Next time, who knows? Yancy's just making sure there isn't a next time."

She narrowed her eyes to a slit. "Whose side are you on?"

Chapter Four

"You don't sign my paychecks." Brad laughed. "C'mon, re-lax." He toppled her over on the bed and came down to rest on her. "Forget it. Your cameras will be safe."

He was heavy on her chest, his mouth inches away from hers, his breath mingling with hers. Chloe breathed in his aroma, a discreet mix of subtle aftershave and his unique scent that had never failed to turn her on. Still didn't, she realized in alarm. She pushed at him but he didn't budge.

"What gives, sweetheart?" His index finger traced the *Fantasy* insignia embroidered on the breast pocket of her robe. She felt his touch as though she were naked. "We've got a little unfinished business to take care of."

Maybe that accounted for her crazy hormones. Maybe an un-acknowledged yearning for Brad made her extra susceptible to Yancy's powerful masculinity. "I didn't want to come on this boat with a bunch of strangers, then I find you here, and . . ."

"Adam," he supplied dryly. "Old home week."

"And Adam, and I thought I was over you—"

"How about Adam?" He slipped a hand between the folds of her robe and caressed the underside of her breast.

"That was over long ago. Don't do that." She pushed his hand away. "I can't think."

He came back and nuzzled her throat, then her ear. "Don't think, just feel. I've missed you, missed this. Let me love you." He cupped her breast, then kissed his way down from her ear, past the hollow in her throat, to the moist valley between her breasts. "You smell good. I've dreamed of the taste of you in my mouth."

"Oh," she sighed. She should insist he stop, shouldn't start up with him again, but not now, not when what he was doing to her felt so good. With his hands and mouth on her body, it was hard to recall why she was angry with him, or how rejected and alone she'd felt after he'd left. His cock rode up. In a moment, he'd pulled the edges of her robe apart.

He licked her belly, sampled her and slipped a finger between her folds. She knew he'd find dampness, from the shower, from the arousal she couldn't hide. With his thumb on her clit, and a finger inside her, he teased her, prompted her, encouraged her. "That's it, baby. Show me what you want."

She moaned, she sighed, she wriggled. She opened. He drew back long enough to shuck his clothes, pull a condom from his pocket and slide it on.

"Now, baby?"

For the moment, the heartache she'd suffered for him disappeared. All she knew was the wrenching desire to be filled, to be consumed. "Now."

He lifted her legs, anchored them around his waist and drove into her with the sureness of lovers. He set the rhythm, thrusting and withdrawing as her ankles locked about him and her heels dug into his firm ass. With his elbows locked, arms braced against the mattress, he gave himself up to the moment.

Her hips rose, sucking him deeper, deeper still, until she felt she'd burst. She clutched at his shoulders, pulling him closer, trying to kiss him, licking whatever she could touch. Sweat popped out on his brow, dripped down his chest and made their bodies slick. She panted, he breathed laboriously. She cried out, he groaned. Her inner muscles clamped down, held him tight, refused to let him go as she convulsed around him.

He came an instant later, his entire body in spasms. He held himself still in her for a moment, then pulled out and dropped beside her. With his eyes closed, he fought for breath. "Damn, baby, even better than before."

She drew her legs free. Her thighs still trembled. Breasts heaving, she rested, her face close to his chest. He'd made her come, so good, so hard, and they hadn't even kissed. He'd always been a physically demanding lover, using her body hard, sometimes roughly, but always leaving her sated. This time was no different, but as her reason returned, she realized there was something missing.

She thought back to the times they'd made love knowing that

at any moment fighting would erupt and they'd be separated. As her breath evened out, it came to her.

The feeling of connection she'd shared with him then, when danger surrounded them, was gone. Then they'd made love. Now, they'd had sex. As satisfying to her body as it was, it wasn't enough. She sighed, feeling the emptiness expand within her.

A short nap later, Brad rolled to a sitting position, He placed his hand on her hip, running slow circles over it, down her belly, back up and down her bottom, tracing a line between her cheeks. "Mind if I use your shower, baby?"

She opened her eyes, edged away, and closed them again. "Go ahead." He patted her butt and rose. Chloe didn't hear him leave, but when she woke several hours later, bright sun flooded through the window and bathed her in a warm, golden glow. She stretched, feeling lazy and lax, even as she thought of the best way to tell Brad that their affair was over. For sure this time, over and done with. Her choice.

She showered again, glad the captain had said fresh water was no problem, and drew on her favorite black and yellow tankini. She covered it with a yellow tee shirt, and left her stateroom for the deck. Maybe she'd find a quiet corner, stretch out, grab some rays and think about her career. Commune with the seagulls, as her boss had ordered. Now that she thought about it, there was something that didn't make sense about his insistence she accept Yancy's invitation. She could have found a quiet beach nearer home, snuggled into the sand and watched just as many seagulls there as here. Why aboard the *Fantasy*?

She crossed the dining area of the salon as one of the stewards cleared lunch. She paused, suddenly ravenous. He caught her hesitation and asked if he could bring her something. Shortly after, she was lazing in a comfortable deck lounge, a crab salad on a tray on her lap and a large glass of iced tea at her side. The sun was warm and a windbreak kept the breeze off her body as she finished her salad and placed the tray on the deck. She pulled her tee shirt off, and after applying sunscreen, she stretched out and closed her eyes.

She recalled her orders to rest, recover her edge and go back to work as sharp as she had been, or else. Or else what? What else was there but her work and her passion for recording the human situation? What else demanded so much of her and satisfied her so completely? At least it had until lately. She hesitated, afraid to admit the truth even to herself. She'd returned from her last assignment tired, dispirited and weary. The never-ending supply of misery was getting too much for her. She was burned out. She needed to find some good will, some joy, to balance out the ugliness . . .

"You missed lunch."

Chloe opened her eyes to see Ali wearing a black tank suit and a towel draped over one shoulder. "I took a nap."

"You missed the vote."

"What was it this time? How long it takes the anchor to get pulled up?"

Ali giggled. "We voted whether we wanted to cruise around or continue with Yancy's program."

"And?"

"The vote was 10 to 1 in favor of the program."

"Oh?" Chloe sat up. "Who was the dissenting vote?"

"Mark. He discovered sailing. Can't talk of anything else now."

Chloe laughed. "It's peaceful out here. I'd have voted with Mark."

Ali shrugged thin shoulders. "You might be sorry. Yancy mentioned something big." She walked off and stretched out on a mat.

"She's right." Adam hunkered down on the polished deck by her chair.

Chloe turned to him and made a face. "Don't tell me you're taking part in those juvenile games?"

"I'd be stupid not to, when the prize for one of them is an all-expenses paid week in Fiji." He named a very expensive, very exclusive resort.

Her lower lip dropped. Adam tipped it up with a finger. "Looks a little different now, doesn't it?"

She batted his finger away. Yancy had to be extremely generous to ask everybody aboard and then give away a week in Fiji. He didn't appear to be flaunting his money, but she couldn't deny his largess. "I wish I knew what was behind all this. What does Yancy expect from us? Why is he doing this?"

"Who knows? Stop thinking like a reporter." Adam rose and pushed her legs aside to make room for him on the lounge. In baggy swim trunks, his body tanned and fit, he was attractive as ever. The warmth of his bare thigh pressed against hers made her remember how he looked nude. He was compact everywhere but his groin. She raised her glass of tea to her lips and drank deeply.

Adam ran a finger down her leg. "You're looking good, sweet lady. Very fit."

"Must be from carrying heavy equipment and running from bullets."

He glanced at her, hazel eyes sparkling. "Or bouncing about with our ex-marine? Someone works fast."

She drew her leg to the side. "No comment."

His grin flickered with a touch of resentment. He touched her leg again, lightly. His finger followed the curve of her thigh into the shadow between her legs. She stiffened and closed her legs. "Open," he coaxed. "Remember how it used to be? We could make it happen again."

"No," she murmured, even as her insides shifted and melted. He'd always been able to arouse her with just a touch, keep her humming and melting until he allowed her release. How could he do that now, when she was still sated from sex with Brad?

His finger burrowed deeper, then his entire hand slid between her clenched thighs. Remembered sensations from past lovemaking swept through her, leaving her wet and shaken. She put her fingers on his wrist. "Stop."

He took his hand away, then sprawled the length of the lounge, resting on his elbow. "Yancy says no shop talk, so I can't ask what you've been doing. Can't tell you about me, either, so what's there to talk about?" His slow grin went from engaging to suggestive. "Since we're on board to relax, let's play together."

Playing with Adam had been a favorite recreation of hers. She remembered stripping him out of his flight suit, yanking down his shorts and sitting on his lap. Other times, he'd liked to take her from behind, her head and shoulders on the bed, bottom elevated, while he played with her body, plucking her nipples and teasing her clit while he pumped into her. At times, they'd used bedroom toys until he'd exhausted her into begging him to stop.

Chloe flicked a glance at him. He looked relaxed, lying back on an elbow, head cocked as he watched her. The sun glinted on his fair hair, bringing out a hint of red, lighting his trim body with a touch of gold. His wiry physique was right for the cockpit, and just the right size and stamina to pleasure her for hours. Deliberately, she swung her gaze from him and looked out to the horizon, where cobalt water met the hazy blue of the sky. Overhead, traces of clouds scattered and reformed.

It was a peaceful sight, calming and eternal, but it did nothing to soothe the clamor within her. How could she be thinking of sex with Adam again, when they'd agreed to have nothing more to do with each other?

"Go away, Adam." She opened her book. "If I have to de-stress, I'm going to do it alone."

"That's why I saw Brad leaving your room with a big smile on his face?"

She frowned at him. "Is this what this is all about? A pissing contest?"

"No." He shook his head. "No contest, sweet lady. You know I don't operate that way. I don't share." He rose to his feet, stretched, and ambled down the deck. Chloe watched him join a group playing dominoes. He perched on the arm of Ali's chair, said something that had her lifting her face to give him a flirta-tious smile.

Chloe shook her head and turned her attention back to her novel. She read a few pages, then let the warmth of the afternoon coax her into sunbathing.

Voices and laughter flowed around her, barely breaking her sun-induced drowsiness. She heard an appreciative whistle and opened one eye to see the bare-breasted redhead, Lane, easing the bottom of her bikini down her legs, revealing a closely shaven mound with a center strip of red curls.

Chloe closed her eyes. For all Yancy's words about profession-als at the top of their fields, some of his guests were beginning to act like adolescent show-offs. How quickly the professional ve-neer wore off, revealing basic sexual natures. The laughter got louder, the jokes bawdy. All this extravagant leisure was eating away common sense. Sighing, Chloe sat up, gathered her things and left the sun deck.

On the main deck, Yancy, Mark, Wynne, Brad and Tracy sat comfortably around a table littered with glasses and coffee cups. Brad gave her a slow smile. Yancy beckoned her over. "Black and yellow. My favorite colors." His eyes invited her to share in the shared memory. "Join us."

She drew up a chair and sat between Yancy and Wynne. A steward appeared to clear the table and offer refills. Yancy said something to him. The steward grinned. Chloe decided she liked the easy-going way Yancy treated his crew. Evidently he didn't need to rely on his wealth and position to command respect. She watched him talking with his guests. They were sought after for their expertise, according to Yancy, but he surpassed them all. She wasn't sure how she knew this, but she knew it was true.

A burst of laughter had Wynne cocking her head at the upper deck. "What's going on up there?"

"Not much, unless you like exhibitionism."

Mark flushed. Wynne smiled. Brad winked at Chloe and stood. "Maybe I should check this out."

"Down, tiger," Tracy murmured. "I'm sure there's nothing you haven't seen before."

Brad wiggled his eyebrows. "But not those particular nothings."

They laughed. Yancy turned to Chloe. "Are you settling in? Comfortable?"

"Yes," she responded, noting that somewhere during the day she'd lost her anger at his high-handed confiscation of her cameras. "Some of the company may be a little immature, but the *Fantasy* is fabulous."

"You don't like the other guests?" Yancy asked.

"Not much. Present company excepted, of course," she added hastily as Yancy grinned.

"I'd guess regressing is a reasonable reaction to huge amounts of stress," Wynne said, echoing Chloe's earlier thoughts.

"Careful," Yancy warned. "No shop talk."

Wynne nodded. "Just an observation. If we all didn't do the work we do, coiled up tighter than a spring, then we wouldn't fly loose quite so easily."

"I can understand that," Tracy agreed. She wore a floppy hat to protect her face, but from the shadows, her light blue eyes sparkled. "If we weren't who we are, we wouldn't be here. Thanks, Yancy."

"Right," Mark mumbled. "I need the break. Sometimes I get so tied up, I forget to eat."

Tracy nodded. "It's the way we are." She paused, then spoke slowly. "If we had a choice, would we be anything different?" She looked at Yancy. "If you could be anyone or do anything besides who you are and what you do, what would that be?"

Yancy crossed one long leg over the other, then lifted an ankle to rest on the opposite knee. In baggy, well-worn Bermudas, shirtless and barefoot, he looked like a man who did nothing but sun and surf all day. Chloe leaned a little closer to hear his answer.

He strummed an imaginary guitar. "A musician. Rock group, even a roadie. Anything to do with music."

Wynne laughed. "I can see you in a band, dressed . . . hmmm, with your features and coloring, I'd say dressed like an Indian . . . sorry, make that Native American."

Yancy grinned. The dimple popped out, making him look younger, more approachable. "You wouldn't be far wrong. Crow."

"You're Crow?" Mark asked. "Man, that's something else."

Chloe sat back and studied Yancy. She had the strongest urge to poke his dimple, to see what he would do. What he would feel like. She kept her hands to herself, yet looked her fill. He was deeply tanned, his belly flat and well muscled. There was only a hint of hair across his pectorals and none arrowing down his stomach, but she had no trouble imagining what lay beneath his shabby shorts. Despite her sensual awareness of his body, an image formed at the back of her mind.

Of course, she should have noticed it before. If she'd continued to study him through her mental camera's eye, she'd have realized why his high cheekbones, slanting brows and deep-set black eyes teased her memory. Now she had a faint recollection of a longhaired guy in black braids, a band around his forehead, sitting in the back of the political science classroom, silent and intent. "I remember!"

Yancy smiled.

"Remember what?" Brad asked, looking from Chloe to Yancy and back again.

Yancy waved his question away. He held Chloe with a look as a tangible, private connection grew between them.

Now that she remembered him, she also recalled that he'd been active, in . . . what was it? Something to do with his heritage, a protest group, probably.

He'd come a long way. She couldn't look away from his dark-eyed gaze, or draw back from her awareness of him as more than host, more than a sexually attractive man. What had he been doing all these years, to become such a powerful, wealthy man? What would it have been like to have known him then, to follow his rise to prominence?

"What would you be, Chloe?" he asked softly.

"I don't know," she murmured, still dealing with her curiosity about Yancy. She knew it was more than her journalistic training that had her wanting to know everything about him. He appealed to her on so many different levels. What was happening here?

"Chloe?"

She noted the others waiting for her answer. "I've never thought—oh, I know. I'd be a painter, live somewhere beautiful and paint huge, colorful canvasses. Like Georgia O'Keefe."

Yancy smiled, teeth flashing white against his bronzed skin. "You do know people see erotic images in her paintings?"

"People see what they want to see," she retorted. Now that

he'd mentioned it, Chloe visualized some of O'Keefe's most famous paintings, calla lilies and iris and poppies all with overflow-
ing color, fluid lines and suggestive female shapes. To be able to
paint like that, to imbue contours and forms with symbolic interpretations, to meld her love of photography with vibrant art, that
would be heaven. To express her own sexuality in paint and imagination, that would be sheer bliss.

Aware of Yancy's gaze still on her, she lifted her ponytail to
cool her nape. His eyes dropped to her breasts, lifted high by the
motion. She was glad she'd worn the tank to her bikini, glad that
the high neckline covered most of her chest. And then she wished
she'd worn the tiny little top, the one that cupped her breasts and
held them up for all the world to see. For Yancy to see.

"I like you in yellow," Yancy murmured.

Brad made a noise, low in his throat. Chloe saw the expression
on his face, and rose smoothly. "I think I've had enough sun. I'll
see you all later."

Brad rose, too, "I'll walk you to your quarters."

"Just a moment, Brad," Yancy intervened. "There's something
I'd like to discuss with you."

Brad's lips firmed. "Sure." His voice sounded relaxed but as
Chloe entered the salon, she knew he'd have questions for her
later.

Questions she didn't know how to answer. Didn't want to answer.

Chapter Five

Chloe scanned her reflection in the mirror. The long-sleeved matte jersey dress was her basic black, the skirt draping softly to her knees. The bodice had three hidden snaps that either closed the vee neckline at a modest level, or unsnapped to bare her skin almost to the waist. A hidden bra supported her breasts no matter how much skin she chose to reveal.

She released the top two snaps. The jersey parted to reveal the cleft between her breasts. She undid the last, and the bodice fell completely open. She straightened her shoulders, pleased with herself. With her hair up and a few tendrils curled around her temples, her appearance was chic and sophisticated—a far cry from the usual multi-pocketed vest and khaki twill slacks she wore on assignment.

Brad thought so, too, she noted when she entered the salon as drinks were being served. He moved quickly to her side. "You look fantastic, baby."

"Thanks."

He put his hand on the small of her back to guide her to the bar. "Drink?"

"A small one," she agreed as she looked around the salon. "Looks like some of the others have been drinking all day."

"No doubt." His thumb stroked her spine. "Nothing else to do except go around in circles."

She eased away from his hand. "Aren't we on our way to some mysterious location?"

"We've passed the same headland three times today."

"I hadn't noticed."

"Maybe you're not as attuned to mapping coordinates as I am, baby."

"Listen, Brad, I need to talk to you."

"We're talking."

"Privately."

He studied her expression, then nodded. "Your stateroom?"

They started across the salon, pausing as the steward tapped a gong, calling them to dinner. The table was lavishly set with an ivory damask cloth, heavy silver and white china with a gold and cobalt trim. Crystal stemware sparkled. Chloe stopped. "Later, I guess."

Brad nodded, his eyes lingering on hers. She read his curiosity easily.

"Place cards." Shelly held hers up to show the sleek outline of the *Fantasy* with her name written in ornate calligraphy. "Here I am, Brad, you're next to me."

Brad held Shelly's chair, then looked at the card next to his. "Chloe?"

She sat as Mark took his place on her right. He whispered, "All those forks and things." He touched one. "How are we supposed to know which one to use?"

"Follow my lead," she whispered back.

"What are you two plotting?" Yancy asked as he placed himself at the head of the table.

Mark flushed. Chloe smiled. "We're admiring the silverware. It looks very elegant."

Yancy lifted an eyebrow, holding her gaze, but she said no more.

Across the table, Wynne sat at Yancy's left, then Saul, Tracy across from her, Perry and Ali with Adam sitting at the other end, opposite Yancy. Drawn into conversation, Chloe realized she was enjoying herself. The other guests were intelligent, in touch with world events and not afraid to voice their opinions. Table talk was lively as the steward served the meal, course after course of exquisitely prepared dishes. The chef had used fresh seafood, local produce and Monterey wines, and by the time he prepared zabaglione at the table, she could only savor a bite or two.

She lifted her wineglass. "Compliments to the chef for a wonderful meal."

"Hear, hear."

The chef inclined his head. "My pleasure." He was still smiling as he left the salon.

The steward topped wineglasses, poured coffee or tea and set out liqueurs with thimble sized glasses on a silver tray in the middle of the table. Next to Yancy, he placed the same silver bowl Chloe remembered from the evening before. She stifled a sound of derision. Not another silly game.

The steward placed a slip of paper and a pen by each guest, then left quietly. Yancy cleared his throat. "I see some of you are curious. No doubt you're wondering what pleasures await you."

Chloe groaned. Yancy laughed. "It's not that bad, I assure you. If you remember your bedtime stories, some of them involved magic lanterns and genies who could grant three wishes."

Chloe noted the increased interest on Lane and Ali's faces as they leaned forward to hear Yancy's explanations.

"Now, I'm no genie, and this," he held up the silver bowl, "this is no magic lantern, but we'll see what we can do about making a fantasy come true. Take a moment, think of something you've always wanted, no matter how wild, then write it down."

"Like what?" Mark asked.

Shelly giggled. "Like your deepest sexual fantasy."

"Or your childhood dreams," Wynne added.

"Seriously?" Saul inquired.

Yancy nodded. "Whatever you desire, short of a trip to the stars. Even I can't arrange that."

"No need," Tracy said. "I think I can come up with something more earthly."

"Or earthy," Perry added as the others laughed.

Chloe held the pen in her hands, gazing at the slip of heavy white paper. What should she write? She'd already mentioned her alternate dream of painting. The other guests seemed to have no trouble. One by one, they wrote, folded their papers and dropped them in the silver bowl.

Adam caught her eye and winked, then wrote quickly. He dropped his paper in the bowl and sat back in his chair to watch the others. Next to her, Brad shifted in his chair, then printed in neat caps. She glimpsed his words, felt her eyes widen and averted her gaze. Lane and Perry exchanged passionate glances, then wrote. They added their slips of papers to the growing pile. Lane reached in and swished the papers around. "There, no one will know whose paper is on top."

"Except there are still two to go," Perry reminded her.

Two left. Yancy and herself. He held her gaze for a moment, his eyes dropped to her mouth, then to the deep slit of her neckline. She felt her nipples peak, her breasts warm as warmth coiled low in her abdomen. He smiled, a tiny, thin smile that told her he knew what he was doing to her. That he intended to do more than seduce her with his eyes.

She wanted that. Wanted him. The more she learned about him, the more fascinating he became. He triggered intimate thoughts, visions of lovemaking. A mental picture of Yancy, naked and aroused, grew in her mind. Would he be as superb a lover as he was a seducer? Given the way he made her feel right now, she had no doubt he'd be a virile and demanding lover.

Abruptly, she knew what she would write. It could be the frank and sensual surroundings, her increasing awareness of Yancy as a desirable man that prompted her sexual fantasies, but why not be honest? No one would know it was her wish. She shielded the paper from curious eyes and wrote, *I want to be made love to by three men, all at the same time*. Without looking at any one, she folded the notepaper and dropped it in the bowl.

Mark handed the bowl to Lane who gave it to Yancy. He shuffled the papers around. "Now, no one knows. I'm not joining in. Wouldn't be right to draw my own fantasy, now would it?" He poured himself a snifter of brandy and then pushed the tray forward. As it came down the table, some poured themselves a drink, others passed.

Chloe sipped her coffee, keeping up a pretense of casual unconcern, talking and laughing with the others, but her gaze went repeatedly to the bowl. What had the others written? What if they were as simple as tickets to a ball game? A hidden crush? What if the fantasies were read out loud? She bit her lip. How could she have written something so private, so secret? How could she retrieve her note?

At last, Yancy tapped his crystal glass. The tiny tinkle caught everyone's attention. "Now, according to the rules I've made for this evening's entertainment, all the fantasy wishes here are anonymous. If you want to reveal yours, that's up to you. As I stated before, in the way of genies everywhere, I'll read three wishes, but I'll grant only the third one."

Ali leaned forward. "When?"

"On board, if possible. Else as soon as practical. Does that suit everyone?"

Saul took another sip of port and nodded. Tracy made small patterns on the damask cloth with her demitasse spoon. Adam cleared his throat and sat straighter. Ali shrugged.

Brad sat motionless. Chloe could hardly breathe.

"Ready?" Yancy asked. He drew the first slip of paper, read it and laughed. "Wish number one: I'd like this cruise to go on for another week." He looked around the table. "Wouldn't that be fun, but sorry, no."

Chloe dropped her hands in her lap. They were shaking so hard she was sure everyone would see. Yancy opened the second note. "Wish number two is in two parts: a) can the captain marry us and b) can we use that week in Fiji as a honeymoon?"

Yancy looked around the table. "Congratulations, whoever you are, and sorry, no to both questions." He waited for the laughter to die down, then reached in and ruffled the remaining wishes. He pulled one out and held it up, unopened.

Chloe's fingers clutched at her thighs. What were the odds Yancy would draw her note? She shouldn't have written that—should have written something casual, something she wouldn't have to worry about, hoping it wouldn't be granted.

Hoping it would . . .

"Now, the last wish. Remember, if this is in my power to grant, I'll do it." He unfolded the slip of paper, read it and smiled, long and slow. "Wish number three: I want to be made love to by three men, all at the same time."

A hush fell over the table, then Lane demanded, "Who wrote that?"

"I'll volunteer!" Perry said.

Chloe said nothing. She couldn't say anything. Her throat closed. Her heart beat so fast she was sure people could see it pulsing beneath her skin. She didn't dare look at Yancy. If she left the table now, people might guess who had made that wish. She made herself sit, smile at the ribald remarks, the assessing glances from woman to woman.

"One of you six ladies is in for the treat of your life," Saul said, as he looked from one woman to another. "Want to tell us who you are?"

"Confidentiality, Saul, remember?" Yancy intervened. "If the person in question wants to identify herself, or himself, that's their prerogative."

"Aha," Wynne murmured. "A new twist to the proceedings."

"How are you going to grant that wish, if you don't know who wrote it?" asked Mark.

Yancy looked at his guests, one by one around the table, as if trying to guess the fantasy wish winner. He picked up his glass and drank. "I have my ways."

Chloe felt her heart pounding faster. The merriment, the laughter, the lusty remarks all seemed directed at her. She pushed back her chair. "I think I've had too much wine. I need some air. Excuse me, please."

She had taken only two steps before Adam reached her. He took her elbow, opened the door for her and ushered her out into the cold night air. Chloe immediately shivered.

"You're cold. Let's go back in."

She ran her hands up her arms. She couldn't go back in, not until she'd gotten control of herself.

"Put this on, then." Adam stripped off his jacket and draped it over her shoulders. The warmth from it felt so good, so welcome, that Chloe burrowed into it, wrapping it around her like a life vest.

"That was some wish. Wonder who wrote it? Or how Yancy's going to make it come true?" He chortled and edged closer, putting an arm around her waist. "You're still cold. How about if I get you to bed, warm you up all the way?"

Chloe looked up at him. "What's this all about, Adam? Why this obsession with sex? We agreed it was over years ago. Why bring it up again?"

Adam dropped a kiss on her temple. "I guess I'd forgotten how good it was between us until I saw Brad pawing at the ground."

"You didn't want me before that, but because you think he does, now you do?"

He shrugged. "That about sums it up. I'd make it good for you."

"Sheesh." Chloe gazed out at the ocean, at the moonlight dancing on cresting waves, at the deep shadows in the troughs. "No way, Adam."

Chloe gave him back his jacket and left him standing at the rail. On her way to her cabin, she was passing the door to Yancy's office when it opened suddenly.

"Just the lady I wanted to see," Yancy said. He'd taken off his jacket, and loosened his black tie. His white shirt was rolled up at the sleeves and gleamed in contrast to the bronzed skin of his muscled forearms. "Have you got a minute?"

She averted her gaze from his broad chest, trying to ignore the heat coming from him. She made her voice cool and calm. "Nothing but time on my hands until we dock, but if you don't mind, I'd rather be alone."

"In a minute or two. Come in." He seated her on the plush

couch, then closed the door behind them. "Can I offer you a drink?"

"No, thanks. I've had more than enough."

He sat on the couch, far enough away that she didn't feel crowded. "I was worried when you left the table so suddenly. Are you sick?"

"No." She realized belatedly that she hadn't needed the anti-sea sickness wristband she'd forgotten to put on this morning. "I guess I'm a better sailor than I thought. I just needed some air."

"Were you upset by the fantasy thing?"

She felt her eyes widen. Could he be referring to her wish? "It's a silly game. No one is expecting anything of it."

Yancy smiled. "On the contrary. I've had a steady stream of men offering their services."

"Oh." She swallowed. "Well, I'm sure whoever wrote that isn't expecting it to come true. It seemed to be way out of line."

He reached over and plucked the silver bowl from his desk. "Some of the wishes were even more explicit. Take a look."

Chloe hesitated, then reached for a slip of paper. In feminine, upslanted writing, someone had written her desire to be bound and whipped. "Oh, my."

She took another, then another. Variations on sexual bondage, a man wanting a golden shower, a woman asking to be covered in warm wax. She tried to suppress it, but her imagination responded to the suggestive wishes. Her nipples grew hard. Deep in her belly, warmth curled and melted. Her inner muscles contracted, as if already enclosing a heated, hard cock. Her breathing altered, becoming faster, lighter.

Yancy watched her closely. "Want to tell me which one is yours?"

"I prefer to remain anonymous," she replied as she leafed through the written fantasies. She paused at the one where Brad had wished to pleasure six women at once.

"How is that possible?" she whispered.

Yancy moved closer to read over her shoulder. She glanced at him and caught his slow, tantalizing smile that made her think of cats and cream. "A man stretches out, and with his mouth, he eats one woman. Another rides his cock. He uses his hands and his big toes to fondle the clits of four other women until they come."

Chloe dropped the paper. Without any trouble, she imagined a man stretched out on the plush carpet, then realized it wasn't Brad she was seeing, but Yancy, his big body nude, hands, feet, mouth and cock busy. She imagined five women crouched around him. She was the sixth, riding his rampant cock. Her flesh warmed as she imagined him deep within her. Was his shaved head his own phallic reference to another, smooth as silk head? Her pussy muscles clenched.

"I can guess what you're thinking, Chloe," he said in a low voice that sent shivers down her back. "I wouldn't want any other women. Just you."

His eyes locked onto hers. With a fingertip, he traced the neckline of her dress from the pulse beating madly at her throat, down the edge of fabric to her waist, and partially up the other side without touching her skin. She waited, barely breathing, as his light touch focused all her attention on his hand.

At the valley between her breasts, he nudged the jersey aside and slipped his hand inside her dress. His warmth seared her. She glanced down, fascinated by the sight of his big, tanned hand against her pale flesh. He cupped her breast, squeezing lightly as she forgot how to breathe.

"Do you like that? I do," he murmured without waiting for her reply. "All evening I've been watching you, watching your breasts move under this dress, wondering what you feel like and now I know. Soft, warm, trembling, your nipple already hard in my hand. I wonder how you taste."

He reached behind her neck and undid the long zipper. He slipped the dress off her shoulders. The soft folds drifted down, revealing her bare breasts. Chloe didn't have to look to know they were already swollen, tender at the tips.

He murmured appreciatively and nuzzled her. "I am going to make love to you all night."

"Do I have any say in the matter?" she managed as he flicked one nipple with his tongue.

"No." He raised his head. "You want this as much as I do."

She couldn't deny it. All the shared glances, the curiosity about his body, the intensity between them—all led to this moment. He bent to her breast again, his closely shaven head hot and smooth against her skin. The feel of flesh against flesh teased her, made her yearn, made her wet. She caressed his head, running her fingers from temple to nape, enchanted by his smooth heat.

She could feel his smile of satisfaction. She ran her hand down his cheek, felt his dimple and pressed her fingertip into it. He looked up, still smiling. She took her hand away and traced his lips with her tongue, then touched his dimple, poking the tip of her tongue into it. He moved quickly, catching her tongue in his mouth, nipping it gently, then settling into a deep kiss. She sighed into his mouth, then sighed again when he left it and ran his mouth down her skin.

His lips closed over her nipple, pulling it into his mouth. He pulled at it gently, alternating suckling with tongue strokes, round and round her nipple. He experimented with little nibbles until her nipple hardened in his mouth. He sucked harder then, pulling on her, stretching her. He raised his head, licked the tip and pushed her back into the soft cushions before he moved to her other breast. He suckled her as before, harder and longer, as his fingers plucked at her other nipple, keeping it hard. Aching. Needy.

Chloe closed her eyes and concentrated on the feel of his mouth on her, his warm wet tongue swirling around her areolas, a hand kneading her other breast. Warmth and wetness flooded her panties.

She tried to hide a moan, then opened her eyes when he pulled back. His face close to hers, his eyes fixed on hers, he commanded, "Don't hold back. I want everything from you. Give it all to me."

Cool air on her bare breasts chilled some of her fever. She retreated from the imperious tone. "This isn't right. I can't do this."

"You will." His eyes, seen this close, were very dark, almost obsidian. The whites were clear, a startling contrast to the rest of his face. "I've been waiting for you."

She tried to break the connection between them. "You could have gotten in touch."

"Not while you were sleeping with another man."

"I hadn't been . . ." She swallowed. "That is, until this morning—"

"I know about Brad," he interrupted harshly. "I allowed it since we hadn't gotten to this point ourselves, but not again. Stay away from him."

"Allowed it?" She pushed him away and sat up. "What makes you think you can tell me what to do?"

He lay back apparently relaxed until she noted the fierce look in his eyes. "When the cruise ends, you'll be staying with me."

She stood. "Dream on, fella. I have commitments to keep."

His gaze lifted from her breasts to her eyes. "Your only commitment will be to me."

Chloe refastened her dress. "That might be your fantasy, but it's not mine."

He stopped her at the door to the passageway. "You need time to get used to the idea, that's all."

"Listen. I don't know what your game is, but count me out. Oh, you're a good kisser, and you turned me on back there, but—"

"That's only the beginning, Chloe." He leaned closer, letting some of his weight rest against her. "There's more. I want you, and your body tells me you're ready for me."

His prick rose hot and hard against her. The thin jersey material did nothing to conceal her reaction. Her breasts peaked again as her nipples rubbed against the soft cloth. He pressed against her as he bent his head to trace the rim of her ear with his tongue. She quivered, held immobile not by his body, but by her own response. How could she want him, want another man, after being with Brad earlier in the day? "I can't do this," she repeated. "I don't have sex with one man in the morning, and another one at night."

He frowned. "You're not going to have sex with me. We are going to make love."

She edged away. "You know what I mean."

Yancy brought her back to him. "Are you afraid I'll think less of you? Or do you think less of yourself?"

Before she could speak, he kissed her. "I think very highly of you, Chloe. From now on, it's going to be my job, my pleasure," he corrected himself. "My pleasure to keep you satisfied. Whatever you want sexually, I'll provide. Everything. Anything else you want, I'll get it for you."

"Just like that?" She tried to snap her fingers and found them shaking too hard to connect.

He caught her hand in his, brought it to his lips and stilled her trembling. "Anything. Everything you want."

"Is this how you treat all your women?"

His grip tightened on her hand. His mouth firmed then softened into a slow smile. "You're the only one I've ever brought aboard the *Fantasy*. The only one I've ever wanted to do everything for, give everything to."

"How can you say that when we've never even talked?"

"I can say it because it's true. You weren't ready for me before now."

She tried to shrug off that statement, dismiss his words as the smooth, sweet syllables men used so easily. She failed.

She stared at his face, trying to read his expression, and saw only truth, as naked as his desire. Such a simple explanation from a complex man. His words had hidden meanings, ones that set off alarms within her even as they challenged her to be as honest with him as he was with her. He'd arranged this cruise, a fantasy world in itself, for her. How could she find fault with that? Chloe dredged deep, but found no guilt, nothing to prevent her from admitting the truth. She felt only warmth, a rightness that spread through her and burned out everything but her deepest needs.

She wanted Yancy. She wanted him in her, over her, anywhere and everywhere. This was her choice, her decision. Without a word, she lifted her hands and loosened her dress. As the jersey fell, she took her breasts and offered them to him.

He grinned. He drew her away from the door, locked it and turning, unlocked the way to her stateroom. She went through and waited, eyes on him, wanting only him.

He closed the door and came to her. With his eyes holding hers, he took off his tie and dropped it on the dresser. His hands went to the buttons on his shirt.

"Let me," she whispered. She undid the top buttons quickly, then slowed as she came to the middle ones. She put her lips to his chest as she parted his shirt and licked.

He groaned. Encouraged, she took her time with the rest of the buttons, kissing and licking his smooth chest, the ridges of his ribcage and the flat torso. He yanked the tails out of his pants and threw the shirt on the floor.

She laughed, blowing warm air on his belly, and unzipped his trousers. He sucked in a breath when she slid her hand in, found the opening in his shorts, and caressed him. He was slick and hot, pulsing in her hand.

She clasped him for a moment, enjoying the feel of his cock, anticipating what would come, then took her hand away and brushed pants and shorts down together. Only when he stepped out of them, did she realize he was barefoot. "How convenient," she murmured as she slid to her knees in front of him.

She took a moment to admire him. He was erect already, large, taut and when she placed a fingertip on the head, throbbing. She traced him from scrotum to tip, pleased with the way his cock expanded at her touch. She placed her palm under him, weighing the length and weight of his rod and smiled. When she placed her lips on the tip, licking away the drop of fluid and kissing him before taking him into her mouth, he shuddered.

Pleased, she took her time, learning him with intimate strokes of her tongue while she very gently took his balls in her hand. He was hot and heavy and hard. Murmuring her delight, she sucked him, drawing him deeper into her mouth, releasing him with reluctance, only to suck him back in. With the tip of a finger, she stroked the soft, sensitive skin behind his balls and slid up between his cheeks.

He groaned, breath coming fast, and lifted her to her feet. "No more now."

She made a face. He laughed softly and kissed the pout away. She opened her mouth to him, and he accepted, tracing her lips with his tongue, then entering, tasting her. He explored, leisurely at first with slow thrusts of his tongue, then more quickly, claiming her, a preview of what was to come. Chloe leaned into him, giving him what he wanted.

He brushed her dress from her hips, following its descent with his palms, murmuring when his hands found bare skin at the tops of her thighs. The dress fell as he brought his thumbs down the curve of her belly to rest on her mound.

She inhaled his scent and put her hands on his shoulder as he backed her down into the bed until she lay on her back, her legs open, extending over the side.

He stood between her legs, looking down at her with possessive intent. He moved back to slip her barely-there black silk panties off, crushing them in his fist and bringing them to his face. "My woman's fragrance." He held her eyes as he breathed deeply. "Now it is only for me."

She trembled under his gaze, uneasy with his claim to her, thrilled by the enjoyment he took in her body. He dropped her panties to the floor, and took her ankles, lifting and spreading them wide to expose her intimately. Placing her legs on his shoulders, he studied her intimate secrets as he ran his hands down her calves, then her thighs, stopping short of her exposed clit. She murmured her disappointment and arched her hips in invitation. He ignored her enticement, retracing his way up her legs. He turned his head to her ankle, outlining the small bones with his tongue while she quivered.

"My shoes." She wiggled the foot still wearing a high-heeled black sandal.

"I'll take care of them." He undid the strap and nudged it off her foot. He ran his thumb across her sole, chuckling as she flinched and tried to pull away. "Ticklish?"

"A little."

He closed his hand around her foot and pressed his palm firmly on her instep. She jumped as sensation sizzled up her leg. Yancy grinned. "I'll find all your sensitive spots."

She could hardly wait. Impatiently, she waited for what he would do next. He removed her other sandal, then let her legs slide down his body until they rested on the floor.

She gave him an expectant look.

"Would you like my tongue in you?" When she nodded, he sank between her outspread knees, keeping them apart with the width of his body. "Are you giving yourself to me, Chloe?"

She licked her lips.

"I take that as a yes?"

She clenched her knees around his shoulders. "Yes. Right now!"

His laugh gusted across her mound, and blew warm air on her plush folds. She quivered, waiting for his tongue, and when it came, lightly at first, no more than a delicate tasting, she quivered.

Yancy slid his large hands under her bottom to lift her to his mouth. His fingers kneaded her cheeks; his thumbs held her in place. He buried his face in her muff, inhaling deeply, rubbing his mouth across her mound. She closed her eyes, all her senses concentrated on her clitoris. When his mouth closed over it and pulled it gently into his mouth, much the way she had sucked on his cock, she whimpered.

He pleasured her with long strokes, lazy licks, even tiny nibbles on her flesh, pushing her ever closer to the edge. One thumb ran along the valley between her cheeks, going deeper with each pass until it rested on her rosebud. She clenched her buttocks.

"Open to me."

She made herself relax, unclamped her muscles and spread her legs wider for him. He dipped one finger into her warm juices, then eased the tip into her bottom even as he penetrated her pussy with his tongue. Wicked pleasure swamped her, feeding her craving for more. His tongue and his finger worked together, alternately driving in and withdrawing, propelling her even higher.

Speared with pleasure, she panted and arched her hips into his face.

"That's good." He kept up the dual thrusts for a few moments more, then drew back to push her across the bed. He followed her, resting his weight on her. He was heavy, but it felt good and right. Instead of being smothered or crushed, she felt enclosed in his warmth, protected by his muscular body. He worked his arms under her, lifting himself up on his elbows. He looked down into her face. "Is there something you like particularly? Anything you don't want me to do?"

Her mind was a jumble of sensations, of arousal. "Yes. No. Whatever you want."

He kissed her slow and deep as he positioned his rod at her entrance. He teased her by rubbing against her slit, then withdrawing, pushing into her an inch, and pulling back.

She trembled. She wanted him, wanted him deep in her. Wanted him right now. "Stop teasing me!" She grabbed his hips and tugged him into her, demanding more than the inch he'd given her.

He plunged, satisfying her demand, thrusting deep. His breath escaped him in a long, sibilant hiss as he sank into her. She cried out at his penetration. She'd never felt this way before, never felt so filled, never so involved, her muscles working with his, tightening and releasing as he plunged and pulled back.

It lasted forever. It was over in a moment. It was sheer heat and wild frenzy. It was madness. It was glorious. She came an instant before he did. Her orgasm went on and on, convulsing her inner muscles around him even as her hands gripped his shoulders.

He came long and hard, his body in spasms as he shot deep and high into her. His breath came in furious, hot gusts, scorching her face and temples as his face contorted with passion.

At last, he stopped coming. He dropped his head onto the mattress next to hers. His breath now was labored, deep pants that matched hers as passion ebbed. She clung when he would have rolled off her. "Not yet."

He stilled. As her breath evened out, she became aware of the length of his legs wrapped around hers, his smooth torso resting on hers, his breath slowing, and his cock still buried in her. She lifted her arms and drew him closer, nuzzling at his neck. The pulse in his throat beat hard and fast. He had his eyes closed and his mouth partly open as he recovered.

"I meant to make it last longer," he muttered.

She panted still. "Any longer and I'd have passed out."

He smiled. She watched an expression of supreme satisfaction cross his face. "Next time."

Chapter Six

Chloe woke slowly, dazed and drenched with lovemaking. She rolled over, aware of a slight ache between her legs, and smiling, reached out for Yancy. His side of the bed was cold. So he had left as early as he'd promised. After he'd kept his other promise to make love to her again. In fact, he'd made good on that one several times.

He'd also done something else, something that she didn't expect, and wasn't sure how to handle. He'd made her feel wonderful, of course, since he was an expert lover. He'd touched her, stroked her, lifted her high, held her tenderly as she collapsed, then caressed her, each time whispering impassioned love words, showing her with his body how much he craved her. More than that, he'd made her feel truly special, unique, and appreciated.

Laughter and a raised voice roused her enough to sit up and peer out her window. She blinked as two WaveRunners dashed past, cresting the waves and zipping through the troughs. They were here then, wherever this mysterious here was. She pulled a pillow up against the headboard and watched the antics as Mark and Saul played like little boys with a new toy.

When the phone rang, it took her a moment to tear herself away. "Hello?"

"Good, you're awake. I'm sending Lisa up with some coffee. Meet me on the deck in twenty minutes."

He didn't give her time to agree or to protest. She shrugged, then dragged herself out of bed and into the shower. She winced at the bruises on her hips, put there by Yancy's large hands while he'd pounded into her from behind, but the lingering pleasure obliterated the aches. Fantuckingfastic!

When she came out of the bathroom, still drying her hair, a pot of coffee, juice and a warm croissant waited for her on the coffee table. She poured juice and coffee, drank them and nibbled at the roll while she dressed in shorts, a tee shirt and athletic shoes.

Yancy was alone in the salon. He rose at her entrance and tilted her face up to his. "How are you? Not too sore?"

Remembering how he had used her body brought a flush to Chloe's breasts. "I'm fine."

"I wasn't too rough?" The thought of his hands on her body made her skin sensitive all over again. Her knees wobbled. She felt moisture gathering in her pussy even as her breasts felt heavier, more tender. She leaned closer to him, absorbing his heat and scent. "I loved it."

He smile was slow, possessive and hot. "Spend the day with me."

She looked beyond him to the guests gathered on the deck. "Won't the others need you?"

"They can take care of themselves." He ran a finger down her arm, barely touching the fine hairs that quivered at his caress. "I want us to be together."

She looked into his eyes, saw the scorching heat behind the obsidian gaze, and felt it burn deep. "Yes."

"Good. I'll take care of you."

And he did just that for the rest of the morning, as he helped her into a wetsuit, checking her gear, and went over the side with her. Their time underwater was magical, sharing the cold waters with him at her side, fins idly kicking them along, bubbles surfacing, enclosed in an alien world of their own.

At lunch, served on deck with plenty of finger foods and laughter, they found a private spot on the sun deck. He sat close to her, urging her to eat. "I can't," she complained. "I won't be able to fit into my clothes."

"I'll buy you more."

She looked at him appraisingly. He was serious, she could tell, but instead of pleasing her, his offer made her uneasy. "No, thanks. I take care of myself."

"I know that. You wouldn't be where you are, who you are," he corrected himself, "if you weren't fully capable."

"Meaning?"

He studied her face. "You have a delicate look to you. As if you'd break or shatter if touched. Many men would be deceived. I'm not. You're tough. Independent. I like that."

She was pleased. "I wouldn't get far in my business if I was easy to crack."

Instead of chiding her for talking about work, he looked at her thoughtfully. "You've had to deal with situations that would make others weak. Your pictures show that."

"You've seen them?"

"Who hasn't, Chloe? You're in all the newsmagazines, on TV, on the wire services. You see and you show the world."

She stared at him. He understood what she was trying to do. To make her photographs speak for people devastated by war and disease, for orphaned children who knew nothing about play and too much about death. The realization that he shared her vision warmed her to the core. Then she thought of the subject matter of her work.

He seemed to read her mind. "Don't think about it, Chloe. You do a great job, but put it aside now. Don't let it consume you."

"I can't forget what I've seen. What I've experienced." She closed her eyes to shut out the images of her last terrible assignment. "And I'm on the fringes. Those people live it everyday."

"That's what makes you so good at your job, but you can only do so much. Give it a rest."

"I can't. I see . . . things in my dreams. I think I'm losing my edge," she admitted.

"Maybe it's time to do something else?"

"I can't."

"Think about slowing down, at least." He cupped her cheek with the palm of his hand. "You don't have to make that decision yet."

She leaned into his warmth. "Thanks for inviting me aboard. Even if I wasn't very gracious, I appreciate it."

"I'm glad." He moved closer, faces almost touching. "I want you to forget all that ugliness. Relax. Let the water and fresh air do their job."

"They already are." She looked into his eyes. So dark, so compelling. "What's happening here?"

"What I've wanted for years." He eased away, straightened his shoulders. "You need to know that I've kept track of your career from the beginning. I've sweated out some of your riskier encounters, celebrated your achievements. When you won that award, I was in the audience."

"Why wasn't I aware of this?"

"Do you know everyone who admires your work?"

Put that away, it sounded reasonable. "No, but—" If she'd known this earlier, she'd have been convinced he was stalking her after all. An earlier question interrupted that unpleasant thought. "Did you get my boss to threaten me if I didn't accept your invitation?"

He frowned, the crease between his eyes deepening, making his features more severe. "He did that? Coerced you?"

"He said get myself on this boat or else."

"I didn't expect him to go that far."

She rose and went to lean against the railing, arms crossed over her chest. Having her suspicions confirmed made her stomach churn. She trembled with the force of her fury. "What did you think he'd do?"

"Encourage you, urge you to take a break, that's all."

"In return for what?"

He hesitated. "There was some mention of a new helicopter."

This was worse than she'd expected. "You bribed him with a new chopper? Paid him for his services?" Her voice rose. "For my services?"

"You demean yourself thinking like that," he said firmly. "I did it for us."

"There is no us. Thinking that is as much a fantasy as the name of . . ." she glanced at the deck below where Perry and Lane indulged in a deep, passionate kiss, "this love boat!"

He laughed. "Sex is a great relaxer."

"That's all it is to you? A way to burn off stress?" The thought cut deep. She'd been so happy this morning. Now, she felt cold, nauseated, as if the boat lurched in heavy seas.

"What is it to you, Chloe? You had affairs with Adam and Brad. What did they mean to you?"

Pride kept her standing upright. "That's none of your business."

He was on his feet in an instant. "You gave yourself to me last night. Everything you do is now my business."

She went rigid. "I didn't give you anything!"

Yancy placed a finger over her lips to silence her. "I asked you if you were giving yourself to me. You indicated yes."

"I did not!" Then she remembered. "That was just last night—just for sex!"

"No, Chloe." His voice was adamant, resolved. "It was more than sex, great though it was. You belong to me now."

"You're out of your mind! Just because you bribed my boss to get me here, because you set up this elaborate, sneaky sham, that doesn't mean a thing to me. I owe you nothing!"

"That's true." She looked up at him, absorbing the heat of his body, the faint tang of sweat mixed with his own unique scent, as he gazed down at her intently. His dark eyes were hooded, making his expression unreadable as he studied her face. Chloe felt her body react to his even as her mind revolted against his under-handed methods.

She shivered as a thought occurred to her. "If you didn't man-age to get me into bed, would you have tried one of the other women? Are they here as backups?"

His eyes narrowed. "You ask me that when I've made it clear that this whole cruise is for you?"

"If it's about me, why did you invite Brad and Adam? Did you know about them? And me?" When he nodded, she jerked back. "So you had them come to see how I'd react?"

"In a way. If you were glad to see them, or willing to resume an affair with either one of them, I wouldn't have stood in your way."

"And if I'd preferred one of the other guys?"

"The same. It was a risk I had to take."

"And now?"

"Now I'm not willing to share you." He scowled, his face darkening and looking very fierce. "I wanted to strangle Brad."

She blinked at his admission. "Jealous?"

"I don't like the idea of any other man with you."

Chloe raised her face to the cool breeze tempering the midday heat. She didn't know how to handle all the emotions churning through her. "I hate that you bribed my boss, manipulated me—"

"But? Do I hear a but there?" he asked hopefully.

"But, it is flattering that you went to such lengths to meet me. You could have arranged that without all this fuss."

"I could have. I wanted to give you a good time, a real rest, even if you chose not to have anything to do with me. I was pleased when you weren't happy to see Adam or Brad."

She remembered his smile when she'd demanded he turn around and set her ashore. Now she knew why he'd looked so self-satisfied. She thought of the time she'd spent aboard, of the passion she'd experienced in his arms. More than that, she re-called the way he accepted her work and understood her vision. That understanding was rare. She didn't want to lose it.

Yet, how could she balance the way he'd loved her with the way he'd manipulated her? She'd been beginning to think that there might be something special growing between them, but how could that be? Heady sex, lack of sleep and indignation had made a mess of her mind. Yancy's words, his methods and her feelings about him left her baffled. Hopeful, but confused. "I need to think."

"Why don't you take a nap? Sleep as long as you want. Oh, by the way," he said as she started for the steps leading to the main deck, "dinner tonight is casual."

She nodded. Once in her cabin, she kicked off her shoes and curled up on the bed. The sheets were immaculate and sweet smelling, but she could almost catch the heavy musky aromas of sex and aroused male. She remembered how Yancy had made her come again and again, giving her no respite. He'd taken her repeatedly, in a variety of positions, and each time she'd thought she could take no more, he'd proved she could.

Much later, as the sun set, Chloe dressed in slacks, a cotton shirt and her warm red sweater, then joined the group on deck. Darkness settled over the water with only an occasional whitecap breaking the surface. Candles in glass lamps glimmered over a buffet set up on tables, and many of the others were already enjoying their meal. She selected some seafood and a couscous salad before joining a group in a sheltered corner. Yancy, seated in another group, glanced at the empty chair beside him, then raised an eyebrow. He held her glance until she turned away, ostensibly to hear what Mark was saying about his scuba experiences.

The captain joined them for coffee. After a few sips, he pulled a slip of paper from his pocket. "We anchored here last night at 2:30. The closest estimate was," he glanced at the paper, then at the group. "I think Sam said 2:15?"

Saul stood. "Saul."

"Right." The captain waited while Saul and Yancy joined him. The three shook hands, then Yancy pulled an envelope out of the back pocket of his Dockers and gave it to Saul.

"What is it?" Ali called.

Saul opened the envelope, read the enclosed document and nodded his appreciation. He shook hands with Yancy again. "Thanks. I'll enjoy this."

"What, what?" Shelly jumped to her feet and rushed over to Saul. He showed her the paper, then held it up for all to see. Chloe scanned the writing, saw it was a certificate for a weekend cruise aboard the *Fantasy*. Saul and Tracy shared a look that left no one wondering who would be sharing the weekend with him.

At least two people were making plans for the future, Chloe thought as she returned to her meal. Someone handed her a glass of white wine. She looked up and saw Brad standing by her chair. "Thanks." He looked handsome in a dark sweater and jeans.

He folded into a cross-legged seated position at her side. "I missed you today. Thought we could do something together."

She didn't want to handle the complication of Brad now, but she had to. She should have talked to him last night as they'd arranged. She looked into his clear, open face. He looked so boyish and young, but she knew the steely determination and courage that had fueled his career in the military. He gazed at her now with the same concentration she'd seen so often before in the field. It made her feel like he was assessing the best way to reach an objective. It wasn't fair to let him think she wanted him back in her life. "Yesterday shouldn't have happened. It was a mistake."

"I figured that out. I thought you'd have the guts to tell me yourself instead of hiding behind the boss."

She winced. "I'm sorry, Brad. I . . ." Her voice faded as she interpreted his expression. "It wasn't anything planned."

"Getting even for getting left in the Middle East?"

His question cut her to the quick. Even though she'd known yesterday that there was nothing more for them, it hurt to know he thought so little of her. "You know me better than that."

He looked at her for a long time before answering. "What's done is done." He stood and began to move away, then turned back. "If you're going to spend any time with Yancy, you'd better be prepared to let him call the shots."

It was an effort to lift her shoulder in a semi-shrug. "I'll keep it in mind."

"Just be warned. He doesn't take no for an answer." He gazed at her for another moment, then moved away.

Chloe looked after him. Sighing, she gave her plate and glass to a passing steward, then rose quietly and went back to her cabin. She needed to think.

She opened the curtains to the window and curled up so she could watch the stars and the dark sea flowing past the sleek hull. They were underway again, to another surprise destination. It still amazed her that a group of very busy people, professionals at the top of their careers and much in demand, could drop everything to accept Yancy's invitation. And what's more, to drop inhibitions and behave so indiscreetly.

She jumped off the bed. After taking a moment to check her hair and makeup, she headed for the door and pulled it open.

Yancy stood in the doorway, his hand lifted to knock. "May I come in?"

His wide shoulders blocked her view of the hallway behind him. "I was on my way out to join you."

His smile lit up his face. "Yeah?"

"Yeah. I realized I've been hiding out here whenever I didn't like the conversation."

"Can we talk?"

She stood back to let him enter. He came in, shut the door behind him and waited. She gestured at the conversation area.

He flicked a glance at the bed but accepted her invitation and sat on the couch. She took a chair across from him, keeping her hands folded in her lap.

He smiled. "You're looking more rested."

"I napped."

"Good." He leaned forward, elbows on his knees. "I did some thinking this afternoon. Want to hear what I decided?"

She shrugged.

"Going to make this difficult, are you? Okay. I can handle that."

She waited.

"You're probably thinking I acted high-handed. Getting you aboard under false pretenses."

She nodded.

He grinned. "You'd be right. I'm not sorry, though."

"Oh?"

"Not when things are working out the way I'd planned. Hoped," he substituted as her eyes narrowed. "Are they?"

The warmth of his smile and the light in his eyes went straight to her heart. She prided herself for looking for truth in her work. She couldn't ask less of herself. "Yes."

In an instant, he was on his feet and pulling her up from her chair. He took her arms and wound them around his neck, bringing her close for a long, tongue-twisting kiss. Any lingering qualms vanished in the fervor of his greeting.

At last, they separated. He lifted her to nuzzle his face into her chest. Holding her close, he nibbled on her long hair as he took the few steps to the bed.

"I was afraid you wouldn't let me in."

"How could I keep you out?" She laughed and kissed his temples, the curve of his brow, the top of his freshly shaven head. She nibbled on his ear. "Why do you shave your head?"

He pulled back, his face almost comical. "You want to talk about my head now?"

She laughed at his expression. "Why not? I like your head." She brought it back to her and ran her tongue over the crown.

He shivered. "Maybe that's why."

"An erogenous zone?"

"Why don't you find out for yourself?" He slid her down his body, letting her feel how ready he was. She smiled and pressed closer. He kissed her again, then moved his lips across her face, relearning her contours with his mouth and tongue. She turned her head to catch his mouth, but he evaded her, and pressed kisses on her ear, tracing the contours, then down her neck.

When he reached the collar of her shirt, he nudged it aside to reach the pulse at the base of her throat. He pressed his lips there, pulling slightly, making her aware of her speeding heart rate. He ran his hands down her back, under her sweater and pulled her shirttails out of her slacks. His fingers were warm against her skin as he slid them up and undid the catch of her bra.

Just in time. Her breasts felt heavy, swollen with need. He pushed her sweater and blouse out of his way, and lowered his head. She expected him at her breast, but he surprised her by putting his lips on her torso and tonguing his way across her ribcage. She shivered. His hands were busy at her waist, undoing the clasp, lowering the zipper, and easing his palms inside.

He dropped to his knees and pushed her slacks off her hips. They fell to the floor, leaving her panties in place. He surprised her again by pulling the waistband just low enough to reveal her navel. Yancy pressed his face into her belly, licking in smaller and smaller circles until he zeroed in on her navel. His tongue delved into it, making her stomach muscles contract. He chuckled and blew into the tiny depression.

"You're driving me crazy!"

He looked up at her, a sparkle in his dark eyes. His grin promised her much more to come. "Good."

He pulled her down on the floor next to him, and eased the sweater over her head. He eased the buttons free, then slipped her shirt off one shoulder, then the other. He tugged her bra free, then put his hands into her hair and loosened the clasp holding it away from her face. Her hair came loose, tumbling over her shoulders. He clutched a fistful and brought it to his face.

"I used to sit in the back of that classroom and watch the sun on your hair. I wanted to touch it so bad I couldn't sit still."

"So why didn't you?" she breathed.

"I wasn't good enough for you."

She stared at him. "Not good enough?"

"I was just another kid off the reservation, in school on a scholarship, working every moment I wasn't studying. What did I have to offer you?"

"You could have let me make that decision," she whispered.

"I needed to do it my way."

She sighed. "Stubborn." Her breasts moved. With one hand still in her hair, he nuzzled his face into the valley between her breasts and licked her. She quivered. He took one taut nipple into his mouth and suckled. She shook.

With his mouth busy on her breasts, she ran her fingers over his shaven head, delighting in the smooth, warm skin. She touched his nape, felt his response and stroked him gently. He sucked harder, then lowered her to the floor. Swiftly, he stripped off the rest of her clothing leaving her naked while he was fully clothed.

The deep pile of the carpet was soft on her back. His mouth was busy at her breasts, leaving a trace of moisture, cool on her heated skin, as he suckled and nibbled.

She arched her back, giving him more. He played with her free breast, kneading it, flicking his thumb against the stiff nipple. He sat up and moved between her outstretched legs, draping her thighs over his. She was open to him, her mons pressed tightly against his groin. The fabric of his jeans rubbed against her pussy, stimulating and frustrating her at the same time.

Yancy ran his hands up her torso, lifting her until she reclined on her elbows. With his palms under her, his thumbs were free to play with her nipples, and he did just that. He lowered his head and licked.

She moaned. "Take off your clothes. I want to touch you."

"Soon." He kissed her open mouth, taking her complaints and whimpers. Flexing his groin against her, he teased her with his aroused cock. She dropped her head back, clay in his hands.

He shaped her, letting her down gently, moving back to rest his face on her stomach. He lifted her legs until her heels rested on the floor by his shoulders and lowered his head to her. She writhed in his grasp, eager to have his mouth ease her torment.

When it came, it was the barest of touches. She wanted his tongue in her, wanted his fingers in her, wanted his hard cock in her. Instead, he gave her butterfly kisses, his eyelashes fluttering against her engorged clit. She whimpered, then cried out as he brought her to the edge of orgasm, and retreated.

"I need you now!" she panted.

"Soon." He withdrew from her and stood. She took his out-stretched hand and allowed him to pull her to her feet.

Yancy held her close for a moment, absorbing her shudders, then scooped her up and deposited her on the bed. She lay back, breathing heavily while he undressed. He took his time, giving her time to calm down and imagine what would come next.

She moved off the bed to draw the covers back, then reclined on one elbow to wait for him. He put one knee on the bed, his aroused cock jutting out inches from her face. She licked him. His cock grew before her eyes, then in her mouth as she drew him in and using her tongue, stroked him slowly. He exhaled and flexed his hips.

She took him deeper, swirling her tongue around the ridge, flicking the little nubbin there, and taking pleasure in pleasing him. She felt the tremors in the long muscles in his thighs and with her mouth clasped around his rod, pulled him forward to lie on the bed next to her.

He let her play with his balls and cock until they were wet and hard, then gently pushed her head away. "Enough. I won't last."

"Come in me now."

"Soon." He rolled her over on her stomach, spreading his palms against her back and caressing her in long strokes from nape to thigh. She murmured, sinking deeper into sensuality as his large hands kneaded her cheeks. She pushed back against him, ex-pecting him to position her for entry. He lifted her hips, pulling them up until she knelt with her weight on her elbows. She moaned in frustration, then in embarrassment as he spread her knees as wide as they would go, leaving her open and exposed. She started to close her legs.

"Be still." He moved her back as he wanted her, then lowered himself until his face was on a level with her bottom. He took her cheeks, one in each hand, and gently widened the crack between them. "You are beautiful, every inch of you." He stroked a finger down the crack. "Your ass, your pretty little bud here," he tapped her anus, then moved lower and traced her slit with his fingertip.

"Here, your pussy." He dipped a finger into her, felt her wetness. "You are so responsive. So ready."

"Please," she whimpered. "I can't take much more."

"We've only just begun, Chloe. Before we're done, I'm going to see how much you can take. Give you more."

He blew on her inner folds, creating a cascade of ripples along every one of her over-sensitized nerve endings. She was so close! Her hands pulled the sheets as her inner muscles clenched. Her breath came hot and fast against the bed. She begged, she pleaded for Yancy to finish it, to give her release.

He lifted his head and drew back. Only then she became aware of knocking at the door. "No, no," she cried. "Ignore that. Don't stop!"

Yancy patted her on the ass. "I'll get it." He rolled out of bed and stepped into his jeans as Chloe collapsed into the mattress and drew the sheet over her body.

She heard low voices and turned to see Adam and Brad in the open doorway. Brad still wore his jeans and dark sweater, but Adam had stripped down to a pair of well-worn Bermuda shorts. He had a black briefcase with him. Brad carried a bottle of champagne and four glasses.

Yancy didn't seem surprised to see them. She rolled over and sat up, holding the sheet over her breasts. The silky material caught on her pebbled nipples, sending another quiver through her. She eyed the three men.

"What's going on? What are you doing here?"

Chapter Seven

Yancy turned to her. "I asked Brad and Adam to join us. We're going to fulfill your fantasy."

She felt her eyes widen. Her stomach lurched even as her breath caught in her throat. "How did you know?"

"I'll tell you later. May they come in?"

Chloe hesitated. "But . . . you said . . ."

"Later, Chloe," he said firmly. He gestured at the men in the doorway. "Should I send them away?"

Her heart beat so hard she could hear it. Her throat went dry. Her nipples ached and deep within her, something wild and fierce clamored for satisfaction. "No."

Yancy stepped aside to allow Adam and Brad entrance. He locked the door as Adam placed his case on the floor beside the bed. Her pulse fluttered as she glanced from that to Yancy and then to Brad and Adam.

Yancy took the bottle from Brad and opened the champagne. He poured and handed a crystal flute to Chloe, then to the other men. He lifted his glass in a toast. "To Chloe. May the reality be as good as her fantasy."

Her breasts felt heavy and hot, hot as the liquid between her thighs. She took a sip, then another.

Adam and Brad drank theirs down. Yancy swallowed, then set his almost full flute on the bedside table. Chloe set hers down too and looked at Brad. "I thought you were angry with me."

His face turned grim. "I was."

"Then why are you doing this?"

He studied her, as if memorizing the sight of her, rumpled and needy. "Why not?"

She swallowed. "You don't have to."

"I want to. End of discussion."

Yancy looked from Brad to Chloe. Satisfied, he opened the bag and beckoned Chloe nearer.

She scooted across the bed, careful to keep her breasts covered, and looked at the contents. Bedroom toys, the kind Adam enjoyed playing with, masks, vibrators, dildoes and a small flogger like the one he'd liked to use on her. He hadn't hurt her, but brought her sensitivity to a fever peak. She glanced up and saw him smiling at her. He was remembering how he'd used the furry side on her, how he'd wanted to use the leather side and she'd refused.

Yancy was watching her reaction, saw her flinch when she recognized the nipple and pussy clamps. "You have a choice, Chloe. Would you prefer the toys? Or the men? Or both?"

Her throat felt dry, swollen. "Men," she whispered.

"Louder, Chloe."

"Men!"

Adam closed the briefcase and placed it by the door.

When he turned back, Yancy asked, "You're willing to let Adam make love to you?"

Chloe's gaze flickered from Yancy to Adam and back again. Strangely, she felt no fear, nothing but excitement bubbling up in her. This was why Yancy had aroused her so thoroughly, made all her senses clamor for completion. He had denied himself, had teased and tormented her, bringing her body close to coming, then withdrawing, cooling her down to bring her up again. He was readying her for this, for three men making love to her at once. Her throat burned. "Yes."

"You're willing to let Brad make love to you?"

"Yes."

"You're willing to let me make love to you?"

"Yes."

"All of us together?"

Waiting for her response, Brad watched her with narrow eyes. Adam wore his jaunty grin. She looked into Yancy's dark eyes, drawn by the hidden heat. "Yes."

"Do you want a mask? So you won't know who is doing what?"

She looked at the three men. Each so different, yet so alike.

Masculine, virile, demanding, at ease in their bodies, and so attentive to hers. She licked her lips. "No mask. This is my fantasy and I want to see every minute of it."

Yancy laughed. "Bravo." His smile faded, and his expression grew implacable. "Those are the only choices you'll have tonight, Chloe. Until we leave this room, you are only to experience, to take. From now on, you give your body to us."

She was unbearably excited, could only nod in agreement as she looked from one man to the other. Yancy unzipped, let his trousers fall. He stood at ease, his erection still impressive. He reclined on the bed next to her, propping himself against the pillows.

Brad moved, catching her attention. She watched him pull the sweater over his head, fold it and place it neatly on the coffee table. His jeans followed suit. He wore no underwear. Semi-erect, he came to stand next to the bed, the heat from his body warming the few inches between them.

She rose to her knees, letting the sheet drop from her body. After a questioning look at Yancy, she ran her palms up Brad's legs and cupped his balls in one hand. She licked the tip of his cock, then drew him into her mouth and made him hard. He put his hands in her hair and held her head close to his body. She inhaled his scent and sucked greedily.

"Enough." Brad pushed her away from him. She looked up, saw his expression and knew he was already in the moment.

Chloe glanced at Yancy, saw him relaxed against the headboard, watching her impassively. Adam sat on the far side, undressed, watching her with his mouth partly open.

Yancy held out his hand to her. She went to him, taking it and allowing him to draw her down next to him.

He settled pillows at her back. "Comfortable?"

She nodded. She'd cooled down in the last few minutes, lost the frenzy that had her begging Yancy to take her. As if he sensed the difference, Yancy stood and Adam took his place. Adam turned her to face him, cupped her face with his hands, and then began kissing her. "I thought this moment would never come," he whispered into her mouth. Softly, he kissed her, tenderly at first, then with greater intensity as she opened her mouth to him. His rod swelled and grew hard against her belly.

She felt the bed dip as either Brad or Yancy settled behind her. One hand stroked her back, another her leg and foot. Whoever it was lifted her foot and kissed her toes, then sucked them one by one. She murmured her pleasure into Adam's mouth, then gasped at the slight pain in her toe as someone nipped it.

Adam ran a hand down her throat to her breast. He shaped it, testing its plumpness and gently squeezed. Her nipple hardened under his hand and she lifted her chest to give him more of her.

Chloe gazed over Adam's head to see Yancy at the foot of the bed, his tongue licking the arch of her foot. He looked up and winked. She remembered how aroused he'd made her earlier with his palm on her foot and when he did it again, her body hummed in response. Any trepidation she might have felt vanished in the warmth of his gaze, his dark eyes intent on her, and on her pleasure.

She felt moisture on her spine, and realized it was Brad, tonguing from her nape down to the base of her hips, following the curve of bone and flesh until he had her squirming. Adam latched on to her breast, holding her still for his mouth. Brad's licking gave way to tiny nibbles, barely felt amidst all the sensations in other parts of her body. She felt his finger trace the crack between her cheeks, then part her gently. He blew on the tender skin, creating frissons all over her body. She closed her eyes and gave herself up to pleasure.

Chloe felt Adam move and another body take his place, but she didn't open her eyes to see which man. It didn't matter any longer. Her inhibitions had vanished. All three had loved her well and often. She trusted them to know what enhanced her sensitivity, unleashed her sexuality, what drove her over the top.

The man at her breast pushed her shoulder, rolling her onto her back. He buried his face between her breasts, pushing them up to cradle his face. Hair brushed against her chin, so she knew it wasn't Yancy. Brad then, who liked to place his cock between her breasts and tease them both with his thrusts. She smiled as she felt him straddle her, his hot hard flesh sliding between her breasts and stuck out her tongue to lick him on the forward thrust. His cock pulsed and grew as she lapped at him. With a muttered curse, he pulled back.

Behind him, she felt someone part her legs. She waited expectantly for a tongue, for fingers, but instead, lips brushed up from her ankle, to her knee, turning it slightly to reach the sensitive skin behind it, then continuing up her thigh. She trembled in anticipation.

She inhaled as the lips reached the juncture of her thighs, waited eagerly for the first touch. It didn't happen. Instead, he repeated his ankle to groin touch, barely touching the surface of her skin. It drove her crazy. "Touch me!"

"Just feel, Chloe." Yancy's voice reminded her of her promise. She gritted her teeth as sensation after sensation bombarded her body. Every bit of skin felt caressed by knowing hands. Someone bent to her mouth, pulling her tongue into his mouth, then thrusting his tongue into hers, fast and hard, a taste of what was to come. She opened to him, to the man at her pussy and moaned with desire when at last a tongue flicked at her bud. It licked her folds, running along and between, licking her, then penetrating her.

At last! She quivered and arched her hips. With his mouth still busy, he put a finger into her. She inhaled, caught up in passion, then forgot to exhale as he slid in another finger, then another. In and out, bringing her to her peak again, bringing her so close. Abruptly, they stopped. She opened her eyes.

Brad lifted himself off her body. Behind him, Adam put his fingers in his mouth and sucked them clean. Heat rushed through her.

Brad put his hands on her hips and pulled her down the bed, making room for Yancy who positioned himself on his knees at the head of the bed. He put his hands in her hair as he looked down into her upturned face. "Okay?"

Flushed with desire, Chloe could only nod. He ran his hand along her temple, her cheek and down to her shoulder. "Get on your hands and knees."

Chloe did as instructed, lifting her knee to let Brad slide in under her. In a daze, she straddled him and looked into Yancy's face. He smiled at her and filled his hands with her breasts. He pulled her to him until her mouth opened and took his cock inside. He made a noise low in his throat as her tongue circled the head of his penis and her lips clamped around him.

Chloe felt Brad's hands on her hips, moving her so he could reach her. He placed his palm on her mons and pressed. Chloe gasped as she realized that behind her, Adam was stroking her bottom and worming a finger into her. She tensed.

Yancy stroked her head. "Relax, Chloe."

She didn't know what she felt the most. Yancy's cock thrusting lazily in and out of her mouth, Brad's hand busy on her clit, fingers penetrating her one by one, or Adam applying oil to her bottom. She pulled her mouth off Yancy and peered over her shoulder. Adam spread lubricant on his cock, too. He grinned at her. "Easy, sweet lady. We've done this before."

They had, and she'd enjoyed it, but now, faced with the realization that she was really going to have cock in all her orifices, warmth flashed through her body. Her pulse thrummed in anticipation. She sought Yancy's eyes, saw them half-closed with pleasure. She felt Brad's cock probing as he lifted her, then settled her down on him. She sighed as she took him deeply inside her. Imbedded in her, Brad stroked several times, his hands busy at her breasts. A moan escaped her lips.

Adam held her hips, bending her forward over Brad's torso. Yancy crouched to keep his cock in her mouth. Within her, Brad pulsed, holding back while Adam slowly and deftly entered her from the rear. He gave her time to adjust, stroking her bottom and stretching her before he continued until he was fully seated. "Aaah," he moaned. "That feels so damned good. Hot."

She felt full, stretched, quivering as her inner muscles clamped themselves around the two cocks. Her lips tightened around Yancy. Adam moaned again and gripped her hips hard, as if willing himself to wait until she was ready. Brad gave a tentative thrust as he dropped his hands to grip her thighs.

Adam pulled back as Brad pushed himself in, then between them, they set up an alternating thrust and lunge that had her gasping for breath. She couldn't think, couldn't see. She could only feel, thrust and counter thrust, heat and sensation consuming her. Pleasure seared her to the tips of her toes digging into the luxurious bedding. It was too much. Not enough. She was so close!

Steamy heat rose from the four bodies so tightly meshed. Every forward movement brought Adam's balls against her ass, the rhythmic strokes caressing her intimately, and pushing her against Yancy, who filled her mouth with his cock. His hands were busy at her breasts, shaping them, pulling on her nipples, and pinching them. She felt every touch, every caress, every upward movement bringing Brad deeper into her, completely fulfilling her desire to be made love to by three men at once. Wracked by passion, Chloe felt stretched beyond belief, every pore absorbing sensation, every nerve ending battered by gratification.

She could no longer move on her own. Impaled at every opening, she could only accept and respond. Her body moved at the will of the others. Her breath came fast, as fire scorched through her. She closed her eyes, giving herself up to passion, to each stimulation of her already wracked body. Brad's thrusts went ever deeper. Adam lunged into her, overwhelming her with heat, then came in a long, shuddering burst. He shook with the force of it, inadvertently shoving her deeper onto Brad's cock who eased his hand between their bodies and fingered her taut little bud. Instantly, fiercely unbearable pleasure shot through her.

She convulsed around Brad, her pussy muscles spasming so tightly around him that he yelled and shot high into her. She felt his pulsing orgasm prolonging her own. She'd been kept at such a fever pitch for so long that her orgasm went on and on, draining her completely. Behind her, Adam eased himself from her and dropped to the bed. Yancy held her head away from him, protecting himself from her gritting teeth. She slumped forward onto Brad's chest. He rolled her over, wedging her between his body and Adam's prostrate form. Their chests heaved as they fought for breath.

Chloe licked her lips. Something tugged at her attention, something lacking, but she couldn't imagine what. She'd think about it later, but now she was too exhausted to think clearly. She lay sandwiched between two lovers, eyes closed, dazed and sated.

A hand smoothed hair away from her face. She felt the tenderness and smiled before dozing. She woke as Brad eased himself from her, and drifted off as she heard the shower running. She stretched, moving away from Adam who still slept.

"Rest, Chloe." Yancy's voice sounded close by, but it was too much of an effort to open her eyes to find him. A few minutes later, Brad returned to the side of the bed. She sensed him, fresh and damp from his bath, as he sat beside her. She forced her eyes open as he picked up her hand and brought it to his lips.

"Bye, baby. Hope I made it good for you."

She murmured deep in her throat, smiling as he kissed her fingers. Sometime later, she heard the water running again, then felt herself lifted and carried into the bathroom. She opened her eyes when her bottom touched the warm water, and purred as it came up over her body. The scent of sandalwood drifted up as the water covered her mound, then her hips and waist and slowly rose above her breasts. "Thanks, Yancy."

"My pleasure." He cupped her face in his big, sure hand and smoothed her hair back from her temples. "Don't go to sleep in there."

Yancy left, leaving the door partly open. She heard the murmur of voices, the rustle of sheets and gave herself up to comfort.

The bathroom door closed. Expecting Yancy, she smiled and opened her eyes.

"Almost like old times, sweet lady." Adam hunkered down beside the tub. "Was it what you wanted?"

Chloe felt heat rise from her breasts. Unbelievable that she should feel modest after what she had done, and what had been done to her, but she felt exposed now. She nodded. Adam touched her face, ran his finger over her lips.

"Good. Be seeing you."

Chapter Eight

Chloe heard the voices buzzing even before she entered the salon. What were they doing in San Francisco? She glanced out the window at the distinctive skyscape of the city with the Golden Bridge in the background. And to think she'd been sleeping while they sailed under it. In spite of Yancy's warning, she'd dozed off in the bath last night, and when she'd wakened, Brad and Adam had gone and Yancy was putting her to bed. He'd kissed her and left. She'd been disappointed that he hadn't stayed with her, but was too exhausted to complain.

"How this?"

She turned toward the voice. Wynne placed a black baseball cap on her head. Ali considered it. "No, more at an angle."

Wynne adjusted the fit as Chloe noticed that everyone was wearing a black polo shirt with the *Fantasy* logo on the upper left. Several already wore the same cap. "What's going on here?"

Mark hoisted himself off the couch and brought her a shirt and cap. "Here's yours. Hope it fits since everybody else got first chance at them."

Chloe took the shirt. "What's this all about?"

"Dunno. Have to wait for Yancy."

Even as he spoke, Yancy appeared in the doorway. He looked rested, at ease, tapping a sheaf of envelopes in his hand. He wore Dockers with his black polo shirt and a black belt around his trim waist. The shirt set off his broad shoulders and the depth of his chest. It did more than hint at the power of the muscles it covered. Chloe knew exactly how robust he was, how he looked naked, how his muscles flexed when he made love to her. She couldn't tear her gaze away.

"Good. You're all here." He flicked her a private glance, then turned to the others. "Today's activities combine some fun and games, some competition, some dress up and—who knows what else?"

Shelly waved her cap. "Are we going ashore?"

"All in good time. Listen up, everyone," he instructed as Lane and Perry started whispering. "In these envelopes I have a hundred dollars for each of you." He held his hand up as the sniggers started. "Yes, I know, but you have to spend your money wisely. We are going ashore and you have until five o'clock to spend your bucks."

Lane snickered. "I can spend that in a minute."

"But then you'd lose the prize."

Ali leaned forward. "Explain."

"When we meet at five, whoever has bought the most souvenirs with their money wins first prize."

"Fiji?" Saul asked.

"That's the one," Yancy confirmed.

"Souvenirs? Like from those tourist places on Fisherman's Wharf?"

"The more the better," Yancy agreed over the buzz of conversation. Chloe looked around and saw how serious the guests had become now that the stakes were known.

Yancy's voice cut through the hubbub. "Now, please go back to your staterooms, pack something for this evening. Black tie. One of the crew will take your bags to the penthouse suite at the Hotel Union Square. We'll meet there at five. Until then, you're free to do as you please. Any questions?"

Tracy nodded. "Why the dress clothes?"

"My surprise," Yancy said. He looked around the salon, as if judging the expressions. "Have you been disappointed yet?"

Mark laughed. "You can surprise me any time you want."

"Okay, let's go!" Yancy watched his guests mill towards the steps leading to their cabins. He motioned Chloe to stay.

"Are you all right?" His voice was low and intimate.

She was sore and tender in her anus, but her body felt sated, well used and relaxed. She'd awakened this morning remembering what had jiggled at her mind last night. "I'm fine." She moistened her lips. "About last night—"

"We'll talk about it after everyone else goes ashore."

"That doesn't give me as much time as the others," she grumbled. "They'll have a head start."

"Did I forget to mention that you are excluded from this race?"

"But what if I want a week in Fiji?"

"All the time you want, Chloe. With me."

Put like that, how could she complain? She nodded. He left her and went to supervise the proceedings. Chloe sank into the deeply cushioned sofa and let her head again fall back against the pillows. If anyone had suggested that she'd have her most secret fantasy so completely and delightfully fulfilled, she'd have laughed herself silly.

She didn't feel like laughing now. Instead, she waited impatiently for Yancy to return, to be alone with him. Once, she would have thought making love with three men, indulging her fantasy, would have been mechanical and devoid of emotion. Maybe even demeaning. Now she knew it hadn't been that way at all, and she had Yancy to thank for that. He'd made it very special, tender and loving. He'd fulfilled her fantasy in ways she'd never have dreamed of. She wanted to share her happiness with him, wanted to savor the closeness between them.

She wanted to ask him why he alone hadn't climaxed last night.

She heard laughter coming up from below, then Perry saying, "I think I'll call my office while we're here."

"I will, too," Saul said.

"Not me," Ali rejoined. "I'm having too much fun."

Laughing, they passed Chloe and headed for the boat deck. Shelly lingered. "Aren't you coming?"

"In a bit. I'll catch the next launch." Chloe rested her head against the back of the couch and lightly dozed while the others were taken ashore.

A short time later, Yancy came back into the salon. Chloe opened her eyes as he sat beside her.

"You look very comfortable." He took her hand in his, playing with her fingers while he looked her over carefully. "Are you sure you're all right? We weren't too rough with you?"

"Sssh!"

"It's all right," Yancy soothed. "Everyone else is gone."

She looked him right in the eye. "I'm fine. Thank you for arranging . . . that. For making my fantasy come true, even after we had that fight." She waited for the lump in her throat to go away. "You made it very special."

"My pleasure," he said once again, and Chloe could see that he meant it.

"Where are Brad and Adam? I didn't see them with the others."

"They left the *Fantasy* soon after we anchored last night."

She questioned him with a look.

"They won't be back." He forestalled her question. "It's better this way. You won't be embarrassed or skittish around them."

"I'm not either of those things. I wanted to thank them."

"You trusted them with your body. That's thanks enough."

She accepted his harsh tone. It couldn't have been easy for any of them last night. She'd been so aroused and eager to come that she hadn't considered their feelings. Maybe they were embarrassed to face her. She'd have to think about that, and contact them privately once she was ashore again. Thank them, and make sure they understood this was a once-in-a-lifetime thing. There was no possibility of a repeat.

"What's got you frowning?"

She put her thoughts of Brad and Adam aside and focused on today. "I have to do some shopping for your fancy dress thing tonight. I don't have anything dressy enough with me."

"Don't bother. That's part of the surprise."

"You're planning to have me pop naked out of a cake?"

He laughed. "I hadn't thought of that. Tempting, but maybe another time."

"Then what?"

"Why don't you use put yourself in my hands and see what happens?"

"I'd rather you answered some questions."

"I can guess what they are. Can they wait?"

"No."

"Very well. I'll tell you anything you want to know. Come." He stood and gave her his hand. She took it and allowed him to pull her up and lead her back to her stateroom.

It had been thoroughly cleaned in her absence. There were clean sheets and towels in the bath. The room was scented with sea air and the fresh flowers on her dresser and the coffee table. There was no trace of anything that had happened last night. Yancy shut the door behind them. "Have you had breakfast?"

"No, but—"

He lifted a hand to silence her and picked up the phone. He ordered breakfast for two. Chloe glared at him. "Nothing like broadcasting this situation."

"There are no secrets from the crew. And it doesn't matter." He settled comfortably into an armchair. "Okay, what do you want to know?"

"Did you kick Adam and Brad off this boat?"

"They chose to leave on their own. Why are you surprised?" he asked when she made a dubious face. "They are discreet."

"Are you sure? I don't want what happened in here . . . last night, I mean, to get around."

"They will keep it to themselves," he assured her.

"I hope you're right." She paused. "Why did you go ahead and arrange that scene last night?"

Yancy crossed his legs, balancing one ankle on the other knee. One large hand smoothed his trouser leg down. "Yours was the third wish. I was obligated to honor my promise."

"Nobody would have known or cared if you didn't."

"Not true. I would have known. So would you. I don't intend to deprive you of anything you want."

"That's crazy, Yancy, you can't—"

She stopped speaking when she heard the knock on the door. Lisa entered with a tray in her hands. She placed it on the coffee table in front of Chloe and looked at Yancy. "Will there be anything else, sir?"

"Nothing, thanks."

Without the slightest indication that Lisa knew anything existed between them, she left. Chloe watched the door close behind her. Yancy poured coffee.

"You can't arrange my life. Make things happen the way you want."

"Eat your breakfast before it gets cold."

A tense silence grew between them while they ate. Chloe was hungrier than she knew and ate a soft-boiled egg and two pieces of wheat toast with blackberry preserves. She reached for an orange.

Yancy took it from her. "Let me."

She watched him peel the orange. His long fingers stripped the peel, delicately separating the sections. The aroma rose from the fruit, scenting the air with citrus fragrance. Instead of handing pieces of orange to her, he held one up to her mouth.

"You don't have to feed me."

"I want to. I want to do many things for you. To you."

She paused, her mouth partly open to accept the segment. "We have to talk about this obsession of yours, Yancy."

"Sure." He touched her lip with the orange and, automatically, she took a bite. A drop of juice dribbled down her chin. Before she could wipe it away, Yancy licked it clean.

Immediately, she wanted him. He knew it. He placed the orange back on the plate and led her to the bed where he tenderly undressed her.

"Your body fascinates me. You are stronger than you look. Your stamina amazes me. You took the three of us last night and never complained."

"Why would I complain when you were doing exactly what I wanted?"

He touched the bruises on her hips, and turned her to see the redness around her anus. "We were rough."

"Not you. You didn't even come last night. Why not?"

He pulled the sheets back and stretched her out with her hands above her head. He smoothed his palms over her wrists and down her arms to the curves of her armpits. He cupped her breasts, running his thumbs over her nipples, which peaked immediately.

"Why, Yancy?"

"I didn't want to share you."

"But you did. You brought Brad and Adam in here. You made my fantasy come true."

He smiled. "Was it good for you?"

"You know it was. I've never come so hard or so long. It was so much more, so much better than anything I'd dreamed about." She smiled at the memory. "You made it wonderful for me. So special. Only one thing was missing. I want to know why you didn't come."

"I thought I would, but at the last moment, I didn't want to be just another cock pumping into you." He moved her legs apart, spreading them so he could explore her intimately. He touched her clit, gentling his touch when she jumped. "Are you sore here?"

"Just tender."

He put his mouth on her. His tongue flicked out, soothing any rawness away. He probed her gently, his tongue and lips learning her all over again. He inhaled. "I love the way you taste. Your sweet smell."

She squirmed under his touch. He kissed her again, tongue stroking her into fevered arousal once more. When she whimpered, he stood and shucked himself of his clothes. He stood before her, naked and aroused. "This time I am going to come. This time you'll feel only me. Can you take it?"

"I want you. Only you." Her gaze intent on his erection, she opened her arms to him. He came into them easily, fitting himself against her. She was so wet he slipped into her easily and he began to make love to her, so slowly and tenderly that she felt nothing but his big, unfaltering body giving her everything she craved. He kept up his rhythm, building excitement while he kissed her face, her eyelids, her throat, everywhere he could reach. He pleasured every inch of her body, and filled her heart with tenderness, with love.

She blinked, clearing her eyes of tears and looked above them. The mirrored recesses reflected their bodies, his large bronzed one covering hers, his torso bending and his buttocks clenching with each thrust. She couldn't see much of herself under him, only her pale legs clasped around his and her hands clutching his shoulders, but it didn't matter. She knew how she felt.

She felt cosseted, surrounded by his heat and finesse. Her arousal peaked so slowly she wasn't aware she was coming until she did. He took it all from her, encouraging her with words and caresses, before he let his own orgasm overtake him. He stiffened in her arms, going rigid for an instant before his back arched and he came in great heaves. She sucked in every drop of him, taking as much from him as she had given him.

At last, he took the weight off his elbows and rested beside her. He pulled her close to him, and rested his head on her breasts. She stroked his temples, then smoothed her palm over his head. "Why did you wait so long?"

His breath gusted over her belly. "I didn't want you thinking of anyone but me. Be open to anyone but me."

She flicked a glance at her nude body, lying a-sprawl as he'd left her. "I couldn't be more open than now."

He chuckled as he ran a hand down her torso, caressing her skin from armpit to groin. She quivered under his touch. "Not just like this. Open to me in every way. No secrets between us." He stood and walked naked to the bathroom. She heard water running, then he returned with a wet washcloth.

He began to bathe her, gently reaching between her legs, wiping softly between the folds still sensitive from lovemaking. "I was reluctant at first to set up that threesome."

"Why did you do it?"

"I want to give you everything you want. You wrote your fantasy and I wanted you to live it. Last night, I wanted you to experience everything, feel every passion, feel every bit of your body put to use. I wanted to satisfy you in every way, push you farther than you'd gone before." He finished cleansing her and dropped the cloth on the floor. Turning back to her, he took her face between his hands and looked steadily into her eyes.

"I wanted to make sure you experience your fantasy. With me. I wanted you to have three men at once so that you'll never have to wonder again about it. So you won't have to turn to anyone else to satisfy your sexual needs. So you'll choose to stay with me."

"But why Adam and Brad? Why not any of the others?"

He grinned. "I was pretty sure you'd called it off with them. Even so, I thought you'd be more comfortable with men you already knew intimately."

"But if I hadn't agreed?" she pressed. "What if I'd wanted somebody else?"

His hesitation lasted only an instant. "I'd have arranged it."

"Maybe I'd have preferred someone new?"

"Not a chance I was willing to take. Not then. Not now." He paused. "Is there someone I don't know about?"

"No-o," she admitted, a little bit ashamed of herself for pushing the issue. These emotions were too new, too raw to handle them properly.

"How did you know that was my fantasy?"

Yancy looked very pleased with himself. "I made sure you got a heavier paper. I knew which note was yours by the feel of it."

"Sheesh! That's cheating."

"No. That's being prepared."

"What if I'd wished for something different?"

"Like what?"

"Oh, let me think. A new Jaguar? No, a new Mercedes—"

"What model? Color? I'll have it delivered."

She narrowed her eyes at him. "You're joking, right?"

"No."

"Are you trying to buy me, Yancy?"

He leaned back and relaxed on one elbow. "If I told you no, would you believe me?"

"After all this?" She waved her hand, meaning the sumptuous surroundings, the *Fantasy* and everything. "You've gone to a great deal of trouble and expense to set this all up."

"Worth every penny."

"I wish you'd called me."

"And say what?" He put his hand to his ear, mimicking a phone call. "Hello, this is Yancy. You probably don't remember me, but I've lusted after you since college and I want to entice you into spending the rest of your life with me?"

Chloe laughed. "I guess not. There are other ways though."

"I considered them all. Getting you here, relaxed, where we could get to know each other, that's worked out okay, hasn't it?"

"Very okay."

Hours later, after they'd made love again, napped and lay in each other's arms talking about everything and nothing, Yancy glanced at his watch. "Time to get going. We have to meet everybody at five."

"Do we have to?"

He gave her rump a swat. "I'm the host, remember."

"But I don't have a thing to wear!"

"Yes, you do." He pressed a button on the phone, and spoke into it. "We're ready."

He got up, dressed quickly and opened the door as Lisa arrived carrying a long dress encased in a plastic bag and several other bags imprinted with the logo of an exclusive boutique.

Yancy thanked her and took them from her. He turned to Chloe. "I'll leave you to dress or we'll never get out of here. Is an hour enough time?"

She stared at the bags in his hand. "What's in those?"

"You'll see." He winked and left. Chloe jumped out of bed and tore open the bags. Underwear, sheer thigh-high stockings, shoes and even a beaded evening bag. What was Yancy thinking? She picked up the phone and asked to speak to him. A moment later, she heard his voice. "Listen, Yancy, I can't wear these things!"

"Are they the wrong size?"

"I haven't even looked, but I can't—"

"Lisa checked the sizes for me, and I had an assistant pick them up. I don't know if there's enough time to exchange them."

She cut into his worried words. "That's not the problem! They're much too expensive! And if I wear them, you won't be able to return them."

"Why would I want to do that? You're mine now. It's my pleasure to give you beautiful things."

"I'm not yours . . ." but she was talking to a dead line. He'd hung up on her.

She replaced the receiver, thinking how she could accessorize her black jersey dress. She threw open the door and found her closet empty. She swore. He'd left her no choice. Or so he thought.

Chloe sank down on the edge of the bed. What was Yancy thinking? Arranging this cruise, buying her clothes and setting up that fantasy game just so he could fulfill her wish? Why was he doing this? Going to all this effort and expense? After the passion and the closeness they'd shared, did he think he had to pay her?

The thought soured her stomach. She considered staying in her cabin, demanding the return of her clothes, and putting an end to this fantasy cruise. She could go ashore in San Francisco, rent a car and go home. She could write Yancy a polite thank you note and chalk these last few days up to an unforgettable experience.

She could. But did she want to? Did she want to leave Yancy? Everything between them had happened so fast. The sex was out of this world, but more than cosmic orgasms were at stake here. Her feelings bewildered her. She wasn't used to dealing with so much emotion. Did she dare trust him? Or herself? Her track record with men wasn't good. Did she dare risk trying again with Yancy? But then, could she bear to leave him? The quickening of her pulse gave her the answer.

She bathed quickly, and applied her makeup with a shaky hand, so nervous that she jabbed herself with her mascara wand and had to start all over. She ran a brush through her air and pinned it up, not caring that tendrils fell in wisps around her neck and ears.

She picked up the fragile silky underwear. A whisp of a white bustier, a garter belt, and—where were the panties? She shook the bag upside down but nothing fell out.

Chloe slipped into the white underthings. She took the shoes from the box, glanced at the label and puckered her lips into a silent whistle.

Her whistle became a gasp when she opened the garment bag. Something white, something chiffon. Delicate, soft, feminine, tempting. She held the dress up against herself and sighed. Carefully, she lifted it over her head, and felt it float into place over her body. She stared at herself in the mirror.

She recognized the design, the Greek goddess look of wrapped bodice, one shoulder bare and soft folds wafting out as she moved, settling as she stilled. She was so focused on her reflection that she didn't hear Yancy come in.

His pleased murmur brought her eyes to him.

"You're beautiful, Chloe. That dress suits you." He stood behind her, placed his hands on her shoulders and smoothed his palms down her arms to her hands. He folded them under his across her waist and kissed her neck. "Stunning." He turned her to kiss her fully, his mouth taking hers thoroughly, sweetly and softly.

Her knees had softened by the time he withdrew. Such tenderness from a fierce looking man dressed elegantly in black from neck to toe, his freshly shaven head gleaming in the soft lamplight, made her tremble.

"There's just one thing missing." He reached into a pocket and withdrew a jeweler's box. He opened it, and tilted it so she could see the sparkle of diamonds, the luster of pearls. Her breath hitched. "They're fabulous."

He took an earring and held it to her ear. "Just what I thought. White, virginal."

"Hardly that."

"You are to me." His mouth tightened. "We start from this day. Fresh. A new beginning for both of us."

Chloe shivered. His gaze on her was intent, possessive. Without looking away, she took the earring he offered and put it on. She did the same with the other one.

He studied her. "Mine."

Chapter Nine

Chloe stretched, then curled herself more closely into Yancy's body. He slept soundly even as his arm tightened around her waist and his hand cupped her breast.

The evening before had seemed enchanted with tickets to the Black and White ball, a San Francisco tradition to support the San Francisco Symphony, next a late supper, dancing, and then sailing away from the lights of the city, still bright long after midnight.

Yancy had made it an extra special evening, surprising her again with his careful preparations and attention to detail. All the women had worn either black or white. Yancy had made a ceremony of awarding the grand prize, the week in Fiji, to Wynne for her accumulation of tourist souvenirs.

Amid clapping and laughter, Wynne explained, "Those years in med school taught me how to stretch a dollar!"

Chloe and Yancy had come aboard, talked for hours about themselves, their lives and their dreams. They'd made love and fallen asleep together. Now, she could tell it was morning by the soft light filtering through her window. The absence of engine noise told her they were anchored again for their last day of recreation before leaving the ship in Monterey that evening.

She tried to ease out of bed, but Yancy's grip tightened, then eased as he woke. "Going somewhere?"

"Shower. You didn't give me a chance to take my makeup off last night. I must look like a raccoon."

He opened an eye. "Yeah." He rolled over.

She whacked him with her pillow, and smiling, went to shower and dress. She took her time, working out the kinks as she let her thoughts float by. Today was their last day together, and she wanted it to be special. How to make it memorable, though, after all Yancy had already done, was a puzzle.

She shampooed and soaped, rinsed and dried while she considered. Scuba again, perhaps, as they'd enjoyed that. Maybe he'd let her try her hand at underwater photography. She'd brought a new camera just for that. Maybe he'd appreciate some photos of him as a thank you gift. It seemed so paltry after his largesse, but maybe once she returned to work, she'd be able to take some shots just for him.

Pleased with her decision, she left the bathroom, all steamy and scented, and found herself alone. She went in search of Yancy. He was not in the salon, or on any of the decks, so she took some fruit and a cup of coffee and climbed the steps to the sun deck where she settled into a deck chair. The yacht seemed quieter this morning with few of the guests up and around. She watched the water, almost calm now under the usual morning fog. Painting the sea this morning would be a challenge. Indigo, azure, cyan, slate, ultramarine . . . she ran the colors through her mind, matching them to the water, seeking just the right shades of blue. If she had her camera, she might be able to capture some of the hues for later, when she had her palette at hand.

"Why so thoughtful?" Yancy sat beside her, a steaming cup of coffee in hand.

She looked up, then back out to sea. "I was trying to decide what colors are in that water."

"Blue."

She laughed. "So it is. Which shade?"

He lifted his cup and drank. "Any color you want it to be."

"Wish I had my camera." When he made no response, she added, "If we go scuba diving today, I'd like to take some underwater shots, try out some things."

He lifted an eyebrow.

"Not people. Fish maybe. You, for sure."

"Me in goggles?" He laughed. "Maybe another time." He reached out for her hand and clasped it in his. Warmth spread up through her arm, to her heart. She wished the moment could go on and on.

"Quiet today," she commented. "Where is everybody?"

"Wynne had an emergency. Saul decided to stay in San Francisco for another day or so. Tracy decided she'd stay, too."

"I thought I saw something developing there. I wonder if they'll stay together?"

Yancy studied her. "I'm more interested in what's going to happen with us."

She looked back to study the water. "It's been a fabulous vacation. Thanks for inviting me."

"You're welcome. Now stop avoiding the issue."

She waved her hand in an airy gesture. "You know what they say about shipboard romances."

He looked pained. "Is that what you think this is? Fun and games at sea and see you sometime when we dock?"

She shrugged and made her voice cool, as though her insides weren't trembling, already missing him. "It's been an experience, that's for sure."

His eyes narrowed even as they glinted with anger. "Why are you making so little of it? I thought I'd made it pretty damn clear that I'm not letting you go."

"It's not your choice to make!" she snapped.

"What's making you so uptight, Chloe?"

"What's making you so persistent?"

He looked startled, then frowned. "Maybe I haven't made myself clear. I want you to stay with me. I want us to be together."

Her throat tightened painfully. She couldn't speak.

"Is it because I'm Crow? Absaroka, if you want to be precise. One of the bird people."

Maybe that's why he loved flying. She shook her head, denying his thought. How could he think she'd be prejudiced?

She looked out over the dark water lapping at the yacht's hull, feeling pulled two ways at once. She loved making love with Yancy, loved the way he aroused her and then satisfied her so completely. She loved talking with him, sharing experiences and viewpoints. She enjoyed his company. She'd never felt this intimacy, this connection, with any other man. When she let herself dream, she could see spending her life with him. It pained her to think she couldn't, but she couldn't live with his commanding manner.

It grated that he'd made decisions for her, even if she'd enjoyed the results of those decisions. That might work for the short time they'd been together, however, she couldn't see continuing in this unbalanced manner for any length of time. She was used to making her own decisions, to working hard, taking chances, and evaluating risks against the good she could do with her photographs. She couldn't change into a well-dressed mannequin, to be there when Yancy wanted her or to wait quietly in the background when he was busy.

She couldn't throw away everything she worked for, all the work she had ahead of her, just because Yancy wanted her, because he claimed she belonged to him and wanted them to be together.

She turned to face him. "I can't do it, Yancy."

"Can't or won't?"

"Same difference. I'm used to living my own life. Being independent and in control of my career. I can't toss that all over to be your . . . plaything."

"Plaything?" he said harshly. "Hardly that."

"What then? What do you think I feel like when you give me all these expensive things? When you insist I wear the clothes you choose—"

"I like to do those things for you. I want to do them. I will continue to do them," he added firmly.

"In return for what? Sex?"

He looked pained. "Hell, yes. And a damn sight more. Your company, your attention. You."

"Meanwhile I'm giving up my independence, my free choice, my work—"

"Who asked you to do that?"

"—my life . . ." She stopped in mid sentence. "You did."

"Where did you get that idea?"

"You said . . . you said you wanted me to stay with you, stay on board. Oh. Did you mean for another few days?" She considered her schedule. "I think I could manage that."

"Don't do me any favors, Chloe," he snapped. "I never asked you to stop being who you are. Why would I want to change you? Have you stop doing what you're so good at?"

"But—"

"I asked you to stay with me, yes. You belong to me and I expect a commitment from you."

"That's it!" she cried. "That's it exactly! You want me to commit to you, belong to you, and what is there in it for me?"

His face darkened. "What more do you want, Chloe?" he asked in a soft, even voice. "I'm already offering you everything."

"Anything money can buy, you mean! What about your feelings, your commitment, your heart?"

His eyes widened. "What do you mean 'my heart'? You've had that all along."

"What?" Her knees wobbled. She sank down onto a deck chair. This changed everything. Sweetness flooded her, pushing out her scruples and doubts. "You didn't say anything."

"What else would this be about, Chloe? Why would I arrange this fantasy cruise if I didn't want to do and experience everything with you? Why would I set up that threesome for you if not to please you?"

"Why, Yancy?"

"Because I wanted to see if my fantasy of marrying, you, making babies with you and living with you for the next fifty years had any chance of happening!"

Her eyes misted. "The words, Yancy," she managed through the lump in her throat. "I need the words."

He didn't hesitate. "I love you, Chloe. I guess I fell for you more each time I read your reports. I'm continually awed by the power of your photographs. You make a difference in the world. I want you to go on doing what you are so good at, but not to the exclusion of everything else. I want you to make a difference in my world. Our world."

It took her a moment to breathe properly. Her reservations vanished, making her wonder why she'd worried about losing her independence. Her heart full, she reached for his head, holding the smoothly shaven curve in her hand. She pulled his face closer, and kissed one cheek. "I." She kissed the other cheek, pressing another kiss into his dimple. "Love." She kissed his mouth, taking her time, savoring his taste, the way he parted his lips for her, letting her take charge. Eventually, she released his mouth long enough to whisper against it, "You."

"I love you, Chloe. Never doubt it."

She swallowed hard. "We've wasted so much time."

"No. Now is the time for us. Now and tomorrow. All the tomorrows." He kissed her slowly, promising her all the days ahead. "Will you stay with me, Chloe? Be with me, marry me, belong to me?"

She wanted to dance and sing. She wanted to take his picture, capture forever the tender, loving look on his face. She wanted it all, her work, her photos, him. More than anything, she wanted Yancy.

"Sheesh, fella. All you had to do was ask." Her voice cracked. She threw her arms around him, hugged him tight. "Yes, yes!"

He returned the hug in full measure, and then some. He released her only long enough to kiss her the way she had kissed him. Long, sweet and loving, giving her everything, committing himself to her.

Chloe sighed. "Some fantasies are worth the wait."

About the Author:

A degreed historian, Bonnie Hamre puts her travels in the US, South America and Europe to good use in her novels. Multi-published in contemporary and historical romantic fiction, Bonnie lived in a coastal resort town of California, and has recently moved to the Northwest, where new adventures await her. She is busy writing her next book.

To learn more about Bonnie's books, visit her website http://www.bonniehamre.com or write her at bonnie@bonniehamre.com.

Contents

Private Eyes

✺꙰✺

by Dominique Sinclair

To My Reader:

Come take my hand, allow me to lead you into private investigator Niccola Black's story, where passions are heightened by anonymity and she is thrust onto an erotic playing field with a powerful man she knows only as Gray . . .

Chapter One

"Oh, come on, done already? I bill by the hour." Nicci Black slid the gold plated, palm size binoculars into her Prada handbag, withdrew a tube of lipstick and a compact. She flipped open the mirror and angled it so she could view *the subject*, a Mister Winston Chandler, walking toward her, and smoothed on Raspberry Ice as he passed.

Nicci clamped the mirror shut and followed discreetly, unnoticed in the busy lobby of the historic 1920's hotel, the Alexis Marquee, located in the heart of Seattle's Queen Ann District. Winston spent forty-five minutes in a luxurious room, quite possibly a sexual Olympic record for him. Since the call girl would use the room he paid for to entertain men until the last minute of check out the next morning, Winston, in fact, got screwed twice on the deal.

A slight shift in position and the jeweled brooch pinned to Nicci's Channel jacket lined up with Winston, who was mopping sweat off his brow with a hanky. Pressing the sensor pad on the bottom of her index finger with her thumb, the micro digital camera embedded behind the jewel made the merest whispers, inaudible to anyone even if standing directly beside her. She took a few more shots of Winston for good measure as he bustled into the hotel bar, presumably for a stiff drink to help gather his wits before going back to the office.

"Job complete," Nicci said to herself, satisfied she had more than enough damaging photos. Combined with the thick file of surveillance reports and a list of eyewitnesses ready to testify, *Mrs.* Winston had enough to bury Mr. Winston in divorce court; if he were smart, he'd settle quietly.

Nicci strode through the lobby in the fashion of a woman with a purpose and goal, and out the glass revolving door. Slipping the parking valet her ticket and a twenty-dollar bill, she stood as erect as the hotel pillars to wait for her Jaguar.

Winston, and other men just like him, unknowingly paid for her sleek foreign car, her designer clothes, her Alki beachfront condominium. She made her living off their infidelities, their sordid affairs; or rather off the women who suspected and paid Nicci to bring proof.

Ironically, the women knew without the photographs, surveillance tapes and documents that their men had strayed. A woman knew the truth deep within her, in an intuitive place. Just like Nicci had known . . . which was why she disliked handing over the evidence to a teary-eyed wife, fiancée or girlfriend, who'd somehow maintained hope her suspicions were wrong. Nicci knew how damned bad it hurt to stare at black and white evidence—only in her case it had been Technicolor, live action rolling before her eyes, in her very own bed. *Derek with another woman.*

Yeah, it hurt. More than anything she'd ever experienced. But later, when she looked back on it, she asked herself if she would rather have not known, if she would rather have continued on with the niggling, the doubts, the suspicions in exchange for avoiding the pain.

The answer came a definite *no*.

A little wounded, a little more wise to the ways of men, a whole hell of a lot stronger and sure of the woman she wanted to become, Nicci knew getting out of the relationship had unequivocally been the right thing to do.

Opening *Private Encounters* provided her balm, an opportunity to get back at Derek and other men like him. Only twice in the five years since she opened *Private Encounters*, had Nicci taken a case and found the man in question faithful. Neither time did she take the client's money.

Impatient now for her car, Nicci tapped her foot. She wanted to get the photos uploaded to her computer and printed, then contact Mrs. Chandler to have her come in as soon as possible. Prolonging the agony wasn't Nicci's style. Once she completed an investigation, she handed over the file and moved on to the next case.

There was always a next case.

Her Jag rounded the parking garage. "Finally." Adjusting her bag strap, she stepped forward.

A sleek black BMW maneuvered in front of her car and purred up to the curb. Horns blared, fists waved out windows, all ignored by the valet who hurried over to the Beemer, tore off a ticket, stuck it under the windshield wiper and opened the door.

Nicci locked her jaw, slid down her glasses and glared, half wanting to shout that waiting in line was a skill taught in kindergarten. Manners kept her quiet, though she pierced a deadly glare. *If only looks could kill.*

The driver put one polished black shoe on the ground, a hand on the doorjamb and stood. Draping an elbow on the roof of the car, he looked directly at Nicci, capturing her with a galvanic gaze intensified by dark blue eyes.

In all honestly she was used to men looking at her, but long ago learned to ignore the glances of appreciation. Hadn't so much as taken a lover as climbed Mount Everest. Yet, the way this man, so suave and debonair, looked at her seemed . . . different. Possessive. As if he knew something she did not, or perhaps that she wanted to deny.

His gaze lowered to the pulse jumping at her neck, lower to her chest and languidly slid the length of her body. The cool autumn air warmed on her skin where his gaze caressed like stroking palms. Her breathing turned shallow, damp, husky. All at once, in a swirl of fleeting thought and turbulent emotion, she feared and craved the tiny rivulets of what could only be desire coursing through her.

He took his time to return his gaze to hers, and when he did, she received his silent message, a secret command. She was to be his. Her mouth parted, one silent word wanting breath, *yes.* Her reaction startled her, confused her.

He lifted a brow, giving Nicci opportunity to say it aloud. Only she couldn't. The little voice niggling inside her head reminded her Niccola Black didn't allow for men in her life. She'd gotten a whole lot farther in life alone and didn't need another Derek to promise the moon and stars and deliver emotional hell.

And still, her womanly body so long denied, was roused by this stranger who, with no more than a look, voiced its wishes. Wishes of seduction, of pleasure she instinctively knew he could deliver. Her mouth went dry. Couldn't she have one without the other, she found herself asking.

Her stranger turned his attention to the parking attendant, suggesting she'd hesitated too long. Only moments before Nicci felt enhanced, aglow. Now she stood barren of this stranger's sensuous gaze, shaken from the encounter and needing shelter from the unearthed desires stirring inside her. Now that he turned his probing gaze away it was easier to deny her reaction. Her steps sure and long to overcome the slight tremor in her legs, her sight on her Jag now parked behind his BMW, she refused to give into the magnetic pull commanding, daring her, to look into his blue eyes again.

She did give into one impulse, however; her thumb depressed the sensor pad on her finger repeatedly as she passed.

He stepped up onto the curb behind her and Nicci meant to pause only a moment. His hand reached out and touched her arm and she found herself lingering in the shadow of his potency. "Come with me for a drink." The deep cords of his voice spread warmth along her neck, the wisps of hair loosened from her French twist teased in its wake.

He moved his hand to her hip, splaying his fingers, the tips pressing into her stomach with just enough pressure to send sensitized rivulets ricocheting through her body and alerting every nerve ending.

Nicci took in a long, deep breath to calm the foray of awareness. Only the expansion of air in her diaphragm increased the pressure of his hand. He tightened his hold and eased her back until her hip brushed his solid thigh. Turning her head to the side to look at him, to tell him to release her, she met his eyes, hooded by dark lashes and focused on her mouth, visually parting her lips. His breath swirled with hers, moist, warm air intoxicating her. Whatever she planned to say a moment or two before drifted out of reach as her mouth lifted toward his, wanting contact, to dip the tip of her tongue in the cleft of his chin, run it along the strong line of his jaw.

His eyes darkened to the color of the ocean at night and he gazed deeply into her. "I'd like to know you."

She sensed he already knew the secret of her response to him. "I'm not that kind of woman." A low vibration of sensuality contradicted the words she spoke more for her own assurance.

"What kind are you then?"

She took a moment to compose the wild thoughts overriding her sanity, to remember the kind of woman she made herself to be. "One who isn't interested in anything casual, anything serious, or anything I'm not in control of."

"Hmm, that could be a problem." Amusement touched his words, lit his eyes.

"Yes, it could be."

"I like challenges."

"Do you now?" Her tone teased, prompting further exploration of the boundaries a dark part of her mind wanted to cross.

"Umm, humm."

Niccola Black didn't allow for seduction in her life, she forced herself to remember, scraping the corner of her bottom lip between her teeth. *God*, but if she did . . .

Suddenly afraid if she didn't go quickly she just might succumb, she stepped out of his touch and concentrated on putting one foot in front of the other toward her car.

"You'll wish you'd stayed," he said, as she slid behind the wheel of her Jag.

She shut the driver door carefully, almost providing an opportunity for him to catch it, stop her, convince her to stay. Instead, he dug his hands in his pants pockets as she put the Jag in gear and drove away.

Nicci didn't bother with the lights in her office, simply kicked off her high heels and shed her jacket. Unpinning the brooch, she tapped out the micro-camera from behind the jewel and set it on her desk. She drew her arms into her blouse, unhooked her bra and released heavy breasts.

As she ran her palms over her nipples, the buds responded, encouraged her left hand to trail down her hip to touch the spot the stranger's hand had pressed against. A pulse thrummed low and deep in her body as she closed her eyes and easily conjured up the feel of him standing behind her.

On a shivered sigh, Nicci withdrew her hands and collapsed into the desk chair. She sank into molded softness, the cool leather soothing her body and mind. After a moment, she plugged the micro-camera into the computer cable, clicked open her photo studio program and downloaded the digital files.

Instead of getting straight to work and going over Winston Chandler's photos, Nicci went to the shots she'd taken of her stranger. During their brief encounter, his dark blue eyes hypnotized her. Now she saw the man as a whole, still frame-by-frame as she had passed. Dark hair, the ends brushing a cream scarf draped over thick shoulders, black turtleneck stretched just slightly over a broad chest, black slacks over long, lean legs.

Years of noticing details, Nicci clicked on the photo to enlarge it. The license plate on the car, Washington State issued, with a local BMW dealer frame.

Too late in the day for a business meeting, too early for drinks, there was really only one reason a local man went to a hotel that time of day. The same reason she had been there, *afternoon affairs*.

The only difference, men got sexual release and she got paid.

Enlarging the photo again, she zoomed in on his left hand. No ring, no telltale white line that she could make out. Gold cuff links, initials blurred. Gold Rolex.

One call to her contact at the Department of Licensing and she'd have her stranger's identity.

"No," she said. She would never see her stranger again, never know his name, never allow herself to indulge in such dangerous fantasy, in thoughts of dropping her guard for sexual satisfaction. If she were to maintain the woman she forced herself to become, the woman who had everything she needed and more, she had to stick to her guns. *No men.* Not for pleasure. Not for emotions. It couldn't matter that her stranger evoked a craving in her so strong and so foreign to her it nearly made her weak.

Actually it did matter, it proved her point—men could only lessen her. And she would never be vulnerable to a man again.

On that vow, Nicci clicked open Winston Chandler's photos. The arousal her stranger bestowed upon her as an unwelcome parting gift dissipated as pictures of Winston's chubby hands squeezing his *by the hour* lover's ass as they entered the elevator came on the screen.

Nicci printed the most damaging photos, stored the rest on a zip disk, made a few notes in the file, then leaned back in her chair, debating on asking Mrs. Chandler to come in now or to wait until morning.

The phone rang, jangling her into the realization that night had set in. She snatched the receiver. "Private Encounters."

"It's the funniest thing, I'm standing outside your condo, dressed in a monkey suit, knocking on your door. Funnier still, you're not answering. But you are answering your office phone."

Nicci glanced to her wall calendar, to the clock and groaned.

"I cancelled my plans for the night so I could pretend to be in love with you and you've stood me up."

Cradling the phone on her shoulder, she thrust her arms inside her blouse, struggled to hook her bra. "Brad, you know how much I appreciate it, and you love doing it, so don't give me any crap. Got wrapped up on a project. I'll be there in twenty."

"Make it thirty. It's rush hour, babe."

"Shit." Nicci hung up the phone, grabbed her jacket. How could she have forgotten about her appointment tonight? *Easy.* She'd been preoccupied thinking about her stranger. Just one more reason to stick to her rule of no men, she couldn't allow for distraction. She had a job to do.

Hurrying out the door, she knew she'd be lucky to make it a few blocks through Seattle's streets, which were infamous for commuter travel gridlock, in thirty minutes, let alone across town. "Shit, shit, shit . . ."

Chapter Two

Dressed in her little black dress that never failed to be just right for any occasion, Nicci pretended to laugh at something Brad said as their bodies, silhouetted in the glow of seemingly a thousand candles, moved together like lovers on the dance floor. It was easy to pretend to be involved with Brad. A golden boy with a killer smile and soft eyes, a star football player in high school and a muscular body still to prove it, he was more than attractive.

She moved in a little closer and whispered in his ear. With a nod, Brad spun her eighty degrees to the right in time to the seductive jazz quartet.

"Perfect."

"Who is the sleaze bucket you're scoping out tonight anyway?" Brad asked, his voice for Nicci's ears only.

"The oriental man with the tattoo, a brunette on one arm and a redhead on the other." Nicci didn't make any indication toward the man, nothing to suggest he was under surveillance. To an outsider, Nicci and Brad appeared to be nothing more than two people whispering enticements.

"Can't say I noticed him, but I did notice the women. Take it his wife doesn't approve of his entourage?"

"Apparently she never agreed to concubines in the prenup. She *did* agree to a happy-go-lucky quarter million annual cash payment and fifty-fifty split of all assets in the adultery clause."

Tonight, Nicci's digital camera had an infrared lens to compensate for the low light and was nestled in the corsage on her wrist. She pressed the fingertip trigger several times, documenting the redhead holding a cherry out to Mr. Tan's thin lips.

"If I had that kind of money at stake, I'd either keep my pants zipped or slip my wife a mickey, have a threesome and tell her she initiated the whole thing in the morning."

Nicci shot Brad an incredulous glance and slapped his shoulder. "You wouldn't."

He nudged her with his hip. "You know me better than to even ask. Although I must admit, the atmosphere in this place is intoxicating. How did you get us into this little soiree, anyhow?"

She smiled up at him, batted her eyelashes and ruffled his caramel colored bangs. An exclusive evening club, *The Blue Velvet* required patrons to pay a handsome yearly membership fee and submit their guests to pre-approval. "You know better than to ask about my sources."

Brad laughed, and tightened his arm around her.

"The subject is moving to the northeast corner of the room toward the bar," Nicci whispered.

The band picked up the tempo with a mean saxophone solo. Brad gripped Nicci's hand, moved her across the dance floor in a terrible interpretation of a tango and repositioned her so the camera could capture its mark. If Brad were any better at this, she'd have to put him on the payroll.

Mr. Tan handed each of his women a glass of champagne.

"You know, if I were truly your date tonight, I would have to punch that guy out," Brad said.

Nicci's stomach lurched. If someone was onto her cover . . . "What guy?" She resisted the urge to spin around and look.

Brad dipped her, his strong arm supporting her lower back. She arched, quickly scanning the room, and whipped upright the moment she caught the steely look of—

Brad steadied her. "Know him?"

She bit her bottom lip, shook her head. "Not really." She forced her voice to sound nonchalant, though her mouth had gone dry. Her stranger. Here. Watching her.

"Either you do or you don't. The way he's been looking at you . . . if you were mine, I'd be jealous."

"If I didn't know better, I'd think you were a bit green," she teased, an attempt to waylay any further questioning.

"I've been half in love with you since the first moment I met you."

"Oh? Only half in love?" She clamped a hand over her heart, which was beating a little faster, a little harder knowing her stranger stood in the shadows of the room watching her. "I'm wounded."

The emotion in Brad's eyes changed from a comfortable old friend to wanting lover, and for several moments Nicci stopped moving, searching his brown eyes, unable to believe she missed his signals, that she didn't pick up on what she saw so clearly now.

The warmth of his hand pressed deep against her back, arching her upward. His breath warmed her cheek as he leaned his temple against hers. "I'm only half in love with you because when I hold you in my arms like this . . ." He lowered his head. "Or when I kiss you like . . ." Softly his tongue probed her mouth open.

Nicci allowed Brad's kiss, tasting his flavor and feeling his texture as he sought her hollows with gentle exploration, and she waited . . . for a spark, for the earth to shift, for a stir in her body . . . any sort of reaction, anything even remotely close to what her stranger evoked. *Nothing.*

Brad ended the kiss and leaned his forehead on hers.

She gazed up at him through hooded lashes, hoping this wasn't the beginning to the end of their friendship. He was the one who had offered a friendly shoulder when she first moved to Seattle after leaving Derek in a swirl of dust. He was the one who made her smile and laugh. He was there day or night no matter what she needed.

She realized now he had waited patiently for five years for her to see the truth of his emotions now displayed in his eyes. "Brad?" *How could she have been so blind?*

"I'm only half in love with you because it takes two for love to be real, for love to be whole." He cupped her cheek, keeping her from looking away. "When I touch you, your breath doesn't quicken, your eyes don't dilate. You don't burn for more or crave to know. I don't pretend otherwise, but I had hoped . . ." He dropped his hand.

Nicci gingerly wrapped her arms around Brad's neck, her chin on his shoulder. "You're a special man." *Sweet, caring, kind,* she added silently, knowing he wouldn't want to hear the qualities that made him friend material only.

"Maybe someday." His voice sounded like a frown.

"Yeah, maybe someday," Nicci agreed, and knew someday would never come. He'd been the first man she'd trusted since

Derek. Brad was her safe haven. She couldn't risk losing that. She thought he understood. "I'd like a drink."

"I need a double." He took her hand and escorted her toward the bar.

Mr. Tan had moved to a corner table draped in an indigo blue tablecloth and sat between his arm pieces. The women seemed to have been temporarily forgotten as he spoke to a man sitting across the table. The night was still young enough for business and pleasure and Nicci figured it would be sometime before Mr. Tan moved his ladies to more private quarters.

If she had *the subject* pegged right, and she usually did, the limo Mr. Tan showed up in would be where he took his pleasure. Men like Mr. Tan got off on doing a whore where they sat with their prim, proper wives on the way to the theater. The irony seemed to make the sex all the more exhilarating.

Had it been that way for Derek? Did having sex with another woman in the bed he shared with naïve little Niccola, who couldn't make love without the lights on, make the sex all the more exciting?

Nicci shook off the direction of her thoughts and made a mental note to get a list of Mr. Tan's guests for the past year at *The Blue Velvet*. Undoubtedly there would be a wealth of women's names that would make for great reading during the divorce proceedings.

Brad handed Nicci a long delicate flute of ginger ale. To everyone but Brad, Nicci, and the bartender, she appeared to be sipping champagne. Nicci wouldn't jeopardize her clarity on even a few sips of alcohol while on the job. "Thank you." She accepted the flute gratefully, trying not to be obvious in scanning the spot her stranger stood a few minutes before. *Gone.*

Brad downed two fingers of Scotch from a crystal tumbler. "No problem."

"I could use some air." Mr. Tan looked content enough to be left alone for a few minutes. "Join me on the balcony?"

"You better go alone, I'm feeling a bit sorry."

She touched his face. "I'm sorry, too. I didn't know." He smiled, his eyes full of sorrow. "If the subject-"

"I'll let you know if he goes anywhere."

Nicci opened the heavy mahogany double doors and stepped into the damp night, drawing thick air deep in her lungs. The lights of Seattle twinkled through the fog. Somewhere in the distance a ferry horn blared. Without a wrapper, her bare arms and back instantly chilled. She welcomed the quick composure.

The clarity lasted only a moment. Suddenly she felt as if she stood in a mystical forest and like a unicorn she could sense danger. She slowly turned, drew in a sharp breath when she saw him leaning casually against the brick wall. He didn't move or speak, simply held her gaze through the darkness for a moment that spanned an eternity.

He finally pushed off the wall, his defined jaw set, and moved toward her through the mist swirling and dancing like virgin angels around his black tuxedo. His blue eyes focused on her, probing. "Did you think of me while you were in his arms?"

He knew she thought of him, Nicci heard it in his measured tone. *He knew* she wanted him to be the one in her arms on the dance floor. He shared her secret thoughts.

She turned from him, leaned against the balustrade and stared out over the Emerald City, held her breath as his footsteps moved toward her, then slowly expelled as his warmth radiated like a warm quilt on a winter night.

"I thought of you," he said, his words a Chinook against the delicate shell of her earlobe.

Involuntarily, she leaned toward his heat, until her backside framed his front. Nestled against his solid planes, her head resting just under his collarbone, Nicci's body rose and fell in rhythm to his breathing.

"Who are you?" she asked, though she'd persuaded herself earlier it would be best not to know. The pads of her fingers imprinted the rail and melted a thin layer of October frost.

He buried his firm lips into her hair, just above her temple. "Do you really want to know?" His right hand reached around and wound his fingers between hers, strengthening her support on the rail. "I don't think you do. It excites you to not know me." His other hand slid across her abdomen, pulling her taut against him.

Nicci's little black dress gave no barrier to the efficacious downward slide of his hand, nor to the pressure of his prominent desire awakening against her bottom. The spice of his cologne, the building heaviness in her breasts, the want to move her hips just slightly against his manhood, suggested he might be right. Maybe it was what drew her to him, the anonymity, a safety net from what she feared she wanted and knew she wouldn't allow herself to have.

"What do you want from me?"

His mouth touched her neck. Sensations ebbed and flowed through her body. "I want you. All of you." He unwound his fingers from hers, tilted her chin upward and to the side. He laved her neck with his tongue, his mouth moving in slow, languid nibbles to the point of her pulse, where her desire beat wildly out of control.

She closed her eyes, reeling in the intense tingles spreading from her neck to the tips of her breasts, effervescing lower and knew she should say no . . .

"Here. Now." Cool air rushed over her neck, drying her skin as he spoke deep tones just behind her ear, his warm, moist breath circling and spiking a shudder. "I want to take you. Again . . . and again."

Nicci arched her back, wanting more contact, craving more touch. "I don't even know your name."

He ran the side of his large, powerful hand down her throat in a touch so soft its caress was lighter than a breeze, yet stirred sensations deeper than a storm. His hand drew down between her breasts, over her rib cage and she sucked in her stomach as his hand tickled over her hipbone.

She turned around to face him, to look in his eyes, to tell him, *yes—*

The swoosh of the balcony doors opening sent music spilling out onto the crisp night. "I didn't know you had company."

Oh, god . . . Brad. Nicci stepped away from her stranger, feeling as if she were on the other end of her surveillance.

Brad looked beyond Nicci's shoulder as if he couldn't bear to see into her eyes. "The . . . ah, it's time to go."

Nicci understood both the message and the pain in his tone. She thanked him with a smile for remembering not to expose her undercover identity, and emphasized an apology with her eyes. He couldn't know it, but the apology extended to breaking the trance her stranger seemed to hold her in with his eyes, his words, his touch. How close she'd been to making a mistake. "Thank you. I'll be right in."

Brad nodded, stepped back through the doors.

Unable to look at her stranger, unsure if she would be able to leave if she met his deep gaze, if he touched her again, Nicci smoothed her dress. "I have to go." She stepped toward the doors.

He grabbed the strap of her evening bag, eased her backward. Her body fit against him like a puzzle piece, completing the hard planes and angles with the soft curves of her body. "Stay." It was a command. She wanted to obey.

"I—I can't."

He moved her purse out of the way, nuzzled her even closer. "Come to me later," he said, his breath jagged against her ear.

She bit her bottom lip to keep from asking where and shook her head.

"I'll be waiting."

"I can't," she whispered, and pulled free. Slipping through the doors, knowing the succulent desires her stranger awoke in her would never be experienced again, mounted a mournful ache. Yet it was an ache that reminded her, again, of what she had to lose.

⁂

By the time the valet got her Jag brought around, Mr. Tan's limousine was out of sight. "I need to see if I can pick up his scent," Nicci told Brad as she hailed a cab for him. Silently she damned herself for the moments spent on the balcony with her stranger—it cost her Tan's trail. She loosely hugged Brad and gave him a kiss on the cheek before he climbed inside.

The look in his eyes as she shut the door made her feel a little blue and she wished she had words to make their relationship the same as it was just hours before. If only she could be attracted to a man like Brad, maybe she wouldn't have to guard herself so carefully.

⁂

Nicci drove through the sloping downtown streets of Seattle searching the dark loneliness of desertion, hoping to pick back up her surveillance. Outside of a few people staggering from a night club, or a homeless man bundling up against the late fall chill, she saw no sign of life.

Rain began to plummet, and in the emptiness of her car, the swipe of the windshield wipers the only sound, her stranger's words reverberated deep in her womb, stirring a desire far from squelched. *Come to me . . . I'll be waiting . . .*

The stirring turned to small pulses. Rationality began a dueling match against the quivering heat of need.

"You don't even know his name. You don't know him," Nicci told herself.

Your body knows his touch, the feel of his mouth, the scent of his seduction, answered her lust.

She glanced at the dashboard clock. "He's probably left *The Blue Velvet* by now anyway."

The Alexis Marquee popped to mind. *He's waiting for you*, replied the voice of her carnal want.

"Don't do it, Niccola Black. Don't go there." She wouldn't sacrifice herself for pleasure. A one night stand. With a man she didn't even know. And yet, turning the car in the direction of home left her wishing herself brave enough to take a chance.

Chapter Three

Nicci quietly shut and locked her condominium door. Although mentally exhausted, with her vision blurring, her body wasn't listening to her brain's signal. Sensation still hummed, sensitized skin where her stranger touched her tingled and the lonely places where he had not ached.

Unstrapping her high heels, she kicked them across the hardwood floor. They thunked and rolled. She hooked her thumbs under the elastic band of her thigh high black stocking, slid it down, hobbled on one foot maladroitly and pulled the netting off. Her stranger would have taken his time removing the stocking . . . His large warm hands would have moved over her thigh, to her knee . . .

Nicci rolled down the second stocking, imagining the feel of his touch as her hands moved excruciatingly slow, gently massaging the length of her leg, the way *he* would have. Her hands smoothed over the muscle of her calf, pressed small circles with her thumbs along her foot. He would have knelt before her, looked up at her with oceanic eyes darkened with desire.

The slow throb deep in her womanly body heated to a thrum, weakening her as she created the fantasy. She leaned against the entryway wall, pressed her palm to the tempestuous stir in her lower belly.

"Touch me," she whispered, her breath turning ragged, her hand inching lower, toward the pulsing stream of silver heat cresting deep in the apex of her thighs, and beyond. Her knees weakened, her breasts filled with a rush, her nipples taut, aching and begging. She fisted a handful of skirt at the hem, her other hand splayed the orange peel texture of the wall, the pads of her fingers digging in.

Her breath became shallow, uneven rasps as she imagined her hand was her stranger's exploring the soft, sensitized skin of her inner thigh, moving toward her silky heat. Her other hand left the wall, moved to the V neckline of her dress at the same moment the other slid under her damp panties. She nestled her finger through the curling hair and slid deep into the valley of her engorging folds.

Yanking her bra down, she revealed her breast for her hand to cup. She thumbed her nipple. Through hooded lashes, she watched as she touched herself the way her stranger would have.

Her undulating body slid down the wall until she sat on the cold floor, knees bent and her heated juncture open wide. She discovered the throbbing point buried above her cleft, gasped as she unveiled the hungry nubbin. She clamped her eyes shut, thrashing her head as she envisioned her stranger kneeling before her, placing her legs over each of his broad shoulders and his mouth replacing her touch.

Nicci's stomach muscles clenched. The pads of her fingers dug into her breast, nails biting half moons as a molten contraction liquefied her, depleted her of strength to do anything but clamp her hand between her legs and feel the pulsating ride of her orgasm, the vision of her stranger abandoning her, leaving her alone.

Nicci had never touched herself before, never walked through the gate of seduction, into the garden of sin where the soil was fertile and the sunshine scorching. She'd been too afraid of what she'd find there, that she would end up like her mother who used sex as a means of support—one "uncle" after another staying for various periods of time, a day, a week, a month.

By the time she was sixteen Nicci knew her mother's true colors. Graduating a year before her class, she left home at seventeen for college and never looked back at the single-wide trailer or her mother. All Nicci took with her was a bag of second hand clothes, self-imposed virtues and a determination to become a real lady. And then she met Derek, fell in love and learned the hard way that men didn't want a lady, they wanted a whore.

Now, as Nicci lay spent on the floor, a strand of her blonde hair stuck to her parched bottom lip, she could only think to blame him, her stranger, for making her lust. Only she didn't feel dirty, didn't feel a whore. If anything she felt as if she discovered a new part of herself. She discovered pleasure was wonderful, enjoyable, that she was still Niccola Black, just as strong, just as secure. Her entire body glowed.

Yes, she wanted to experience this again, and again, a thousand times, with her stranger, the man who unearthed delights she didn't know possible. She smiled, realizing there wasn't even a residual trace of doubt he would take her to heights of orgiastic pleasure. She wasn't her mother, she wasn't the same naive young girl she'd been when she met Derek. She was Niccola Black, the woman her stranger desired.

Nicci hauled herself off the floor, her inner thighs trembling, knees weak. She wanted to know, to walk on the other side of the stone wall of the secret garden she'd never dared even peek over before. She wanted her stranger to be the one to touch her, to make her body coil. For the first time in her life she wanted without the restrictions of her past.

Pouring a glass of water, Nicci drank deeply. Tomorrow she would find out who her stranger was, find out everything about him, and if he was nothing more than what he appeared, a sexy man offering her carnal pleasure, she would, for the first time in her life, let go and enjoy being a woman.

Chapter Four

Nicci woke, her body scintillating after a night full of vivid dreams that took her on a journey of sweet seductions and carnal delights in her stranger's arms. The need to be touched stirred a flowing throb against the pressure of her thighs. Lazily she ran her hand over a breast, down her stomach toward the dampness and parted her legs.

No . . . Nicci gripped the sheets, fisted and clamped her legs together to snub the lustful quake. This time she would wait for her stranger, for the plateaus she instinctively knew only he could take her. Only thinking about him, the touches she dreamt about, made the tiny pulses throb harder. The dampness between her legs grew warmer. Her hips began a slow rhythm, creating delicious pressure between her legs. Her hand released the sheet and slid between her legs to cup her mound, legs pressing tighter together.

Rolling onto her back, giving into the need, her legs fell open as she worked her hips to the stroke of her finger between her folds, delving into the sheer fire of her sheath, out again to slick her nubbin with her moisture. She cupped her breast with her other hand, the sheet still tangled in her fingers and worked her nipple with the flannel and thought of her stranger as her stomach coiled and she bucked upward, an orgasm shuddering through her.

Once the sensations subsided, Nicci stood on wobbly legs to shower and dress. Only when she touched her body to wash, to lave on lotion, to cup her heavy breasts nearly bruised in her lace bra, to dab perfume, her body begun to blaze its hunger again. She wanted to savor each tantalizing pulse, to linger her hand in exploration. The only thing stopping her was the need to find her stranger before she lost her brazen strength.

"First things first," she said, clamping on pearl drop earrings as she stood before the mirror, "Mrs. Chandler's report." She smoothed her black and white pinstriped linen skirt-suit, determined to focus on the day's agenda.

Or, she thought, turning to look at her bottom and running a hand over the arc, she could call in the plates from her stranger's car to her source at the DMV, and find out who he was now . . .

Her palm rounded her buttock, fingers probing toward the spot beginning its quiver around the bend, stretching the fabric of her skirt to make contact. Heat washed through her like a sauna as the tips of her fingers pressed against swelling lobes.

Hips rotating slightly against her hand, the friction of cloth against dampness creating an escalating moan from deep in her throat, Nicci watched in the mirror as she bent slightly over, thrust her hips upward and slid her skirt covered fingers under her panties and brought herself to culmination. She witnessed the point the heat became an inferno, the tortured bliss in her eyes, the drop of blood that spilled from the clamp of her teeth on her bottom lip, and loved the way release shuddered visibly through her, head to toe.

Nicci cleansed the musky scent of sex off her body, changed into a pair of black slacks and low, form fitting burnt orange sweater with a thin satin trim, which seemed to flame to life the squelched vixen she never knew she could be. She took off the pearls and dug through her jewelry box for chunky gold hoops.

Well past the time she normally left for the office, Nicci dumped the contents of her beaded evening bag onto the kitchen counter and began stuffing items into her Prada handbag. Car keys, compact, lipstick.

"What the heck?" She picked up a wad of bills clamped with a gold money clip, ran her finger over engraved initials, G.T.

She unhooked the clip, flipped the c-notes one by one, and counted to two thousand. An Alexis Marquee hotel room card key fell on the counter.

She cocked her head to the side, locked her jaw. *Her stranger*. She didn't know which insult stung the worst, that he sought to buy her favors, or that she was only worth two g's. Either way, she suddenly felt no better than her mother. She'd justified her actions, convinced herself she was nothing like her mother, and yet here she stood looking down at payment for sex.

"Bastard." All night, all morning, she'd fantasized about him, and he'd thought her nothing more than a prostitute!

She wouldn't be abased by the likes of him or any man. Nicci stuffed the rest of what she needed into her bag and slammed out the door.

Nicci stood in the hotel hallway, hand raised to knock, anger bubbling to the point of explosion. She knew she shouldn't have come, but damn her stranger for taking away what she thought to be a wonderful discovery and turning it into something ugly. She wouldn't just cower away like she did with Derek, her stranger would hear exactly how she felt about his proposition. She would shove the money in his face. Niccola Black didn't come with a price tag.

Nicci slid the keycard into the slot above the door handle and entered, *she was invited after all*. Closing the door behind her, but not quite latching it, she scanned the room. The suite lacked suggestion that he'd been up yet. No aroma of coffee or room service cart. No newspapers spread on the Pembroke table. No jacket or tie draped over the cream colored camelback sofa ready to be put on before heading out the door.

The room appeared impeccable, as if uninhabited at all. Maybe he'd come and waited for her, then finally gone home—

To what?

A wife, kids?

The thought surged her anger further. She wouldn't be some man's satisfaction while his family waited at home.

Nicci laid her coat and handbag on the floor by a cherry wood tea table and headed stealthily for the bedroom, her footsteps quiet over the hand-woven Oriental rugs as thoughts ran rampant on what she would say, already feeling some satisfaction standing up for herself.

Hearing the faint spray of the shower beyond the door, Nicci carefully opened it and stepped inside the bedroom. She glanced to the bed and back stepped, covering her mouth with her hand to stifle a gasp.

A nude, dark skinned woman lay sprawled on the bed, the

white sheet tangled about her long, lean chocolate colored leg. Her sleeping hand languidly cupped the breast of another woman, this one nestled deeper in the blankets but for the breast and blonde head snuggled deep in a pillow. An empty bottle of wine and two glasses were on the bedside table, a pair of skimpy fuchsia pink satin panties on the floor.

Nicci didn't need to be a private investigator to figure this one out.

The shower shut off, the old pipes gave a groan and a squeal. Nicci stilled, hoping neither woman woke. Reaching behind her for the door handle, she planned to get out before anyone knew she'd been there. Just as she slinked out of her bedroom when she walked in on Derek.

No, she thought with a whip of righteousness. Her stranger would hear what she came her to tell him, just what she thought of men like him. Nicci marched across the bedroom, not caring now if she woke the women, and stormed into the bathroom.

Thick, pine scented steam dissipated with the whoosh of fresh air from the open door, clearing the air enough to see her stranger tightening a thick monogrammed towel around his waist. He looked up at her, no signs of embarrassment or shame, seemingly at ease with the situation of having two women in his bed and trying to pay for a third. A self-satisfied smile tugged that damned sexy dimple on his freshly shaven cheek.

Nicci pulled the wad of bills from her bra where she'd tucked it, and without breaking eye contact, fanned them under her chin, cocking her head toward the bedroom. "My, my, my . . . looks like I'm too late for the party."

The mordant tone she used to mask her anger didn't appear to faze him. He simply turned toward the fogged mirror and ran his hands through his wet hair. "You could never be too late." The muscles in his broad back and upper arms flexed.

"Use it to pay the whores in your bed for another night then." Nicci threw the bills at him. "I'm not for sale." She spun, grabbed the brass knob.

"Stay."

She jolted to a stop, his word a command and her body its slave. Slowly pivoting, she drew out the movement as she tried to regain a semblance of control over her reactions.

He had turned back around, the money lay at his feet soaking up sloshed water. It would have been satisfying to see him on his hands and knees scooping it up. Instead, he stood like a sphinx, the money seemingly as insignificant as a peasant bowing at a king's feet.

"Stay?" She laughed bitterly. "To think, I wished I'd allowed you to seduce me last night."

"The money was an incentive to make you come."

"No pun intended?" Nicci fisted her hand, remembering why they called her "Lefty" in high school, and wondered if she could still land a solid blow. "Thanks, but I'll pass." She yanked the door on her way out.

He caught it with his hand just before the big slam she intended as the finale to her show of righteousness, and thrust it wide. She made it one step before he took her by the elbow and hauled her back into the hot, humid room, kicking the door closed behind them.

He backed her against the glass shower stall. "I have never paid for a woman in my life until last night. I needed to be with you. If I insulted you, I'm sorry. I assumed—you were here, at the hotel yesterday, but the valet said you'd only come for a couple hours."

Nicci pushed against his broad chest with both palms. He snared her wrists and pinned her hands above her head with one of his own, stilled her kicking by wedging himself between her legs.

The intensity of his eyes bound her as tightly as his hard body. "And last night." His jaw tensed. "The only type of women who go to *The Blue Velvet* are—what was I suppose to think?"

"Damn you." Though she couldn't blame him for assuming her a prostitute, it stung. She'd thought the connection that passed between them had been special, unique, one of a kind.

He pressed harder, her blouse dampening from the shower drops, his minty breath fire on her temple. "I wanted you so much—enough to do something I'd never do—something I've never done."

The ridge of muscles just under his pecks were solid against her breasts, her chin rubbed the sprigs of dark chest hair as she snapped her gaze upward. "So much it took two women to cure the ache?"

He let go of her. Blood rushed to her numb hands and she flexed them for circulation as he backed up a step. "I didn't touch those women." His voice toned conviction.

Nicci scrutinized him, attempted to find a sign of mistruth.

His eye contact didn't waver. "Nothing happened—that I was involved in."

Too bad she didn't have her portable stress analyzer with her. He might have the ability to hide the effect of his lie on the outside, but vitals were a lifeline to the truth. "So what, you're a voyeur?" She stepped forward, jerking her shoulder back to avoid contact as she meant to barrel past him and out of there before she was inclined to believe any more of his lies.

He swung up his forearm in front of her, pressed his palm on the wall and leaned his weight into it. She thought about ducking, figured he'd just stop her another way. "A business associate sent them over as a wedding gift. It was late, I was tired."

Nicci bit the inside of her cheek, crossed her arms below her breasts. "Okay, you're forgiven for the lesbians." She gave a smart smile. "When hell freezes over for being engaged."

"Damn it." He jabbed his hand through his hair. "I'm not really engaged."

"Nice try, I'm not that gullible." Dodging to the right and quickly to the left, she rounded past him. This time she made it past the women in the bed, still cozied up like kittens, out of the bedroom and half way across the suite.

"I'd like to explain," he said, his voice reaching out and slowing her steps.

Nicci stopped, lingering her hand on the back of a goose necked armchair and contemplating why any of this mattered. *Why she wanted to believe him.* "Fine then. Let's hear it."

"It's complicated."

"I'm listening."

"I used the engagement to explain why I wasn't interested in the lady my associate provided for me last night. Apparently he interpreted that as I would prefer something a little . . . less public."

She really should just go. "Why weren't you interested?"

"I had this connection with the most stunning woman yesterday afternoon." He came up behind her, his breath teasing her nape. He lowered his head, droplets of water from his wet hair absorbed through her sweater onto her skin as his lips touched her shoulder. "She intrigued me, lured me. Made me want to break the rules."

Shivers coursed through her body as his concoction of pine soap and minty breath played havoc with her mind and body. Splaying his hand around her throat just under her chin, he tilted her head back. Her pulse tattooed wildly against the pressure of his fingers.

"I wanted her." His free hand tangled in her hair.

"I—" His feral control over her body aroused a primitive want too swift and heated to suppress, still she had to try. "—I don't play games like this."

He ran the tips of his fingers down her throat. "I want you. It's as simple as that. No games. No rules. Just this . . ."

Through hooded eyes she watched his hand arch over her sensitized breast, massage deeply. Her mouth dropped open, released a little moan instead of telling him for her this was anything but simple, that this was more than she ever dared.

"Your body was made to be touched. Allow me to touch you, taste you."

Nicci arched against his length, her hands gripping his hips, bunching the towel and pulling his hardening manhood taut against her. *Oh god, touch me.* He was swelling for her and she wanted . . . "I don't even know your name." Her breath ragged as she rotated her hips ever so slightly.

"Gray."

Her head tipped back to the hollow of his collarbone, and, turning in his arms, repeated, "Gray," tipping her chin and raising onto the tips of her toes.

His eyes darkened as his sculptured, firm lips moved downward and met her waiting mouth. He explored her, deepened her already stirred passion. He pulled his mouth away and she lowered onto the balls of her feet. "You're so damned beautiful."

Unsettled being the focus of such carnal want, Nicci ran her hands up his forearms. She dropped her gaze to sweep the trail of dark, damp hair over the ripples in his stomach to the point it disappeared underneath the terry cloth slung low on his lean hips.

She swallowed thickly. "You make me feel beautiful."

His erection thrust beneath the towel, the pads of her fingers pressed deeply into the muscles in his biceps as a wash of feminine readiness responded to the thoughts of him filling her completely. He lifted her chin with two fingers and she caught desire flash through the midnight of his eyes before he claimed her throat with his mouth. Her nails bit into his arms. Soft lights swarmed her vision.

He lowered to the satin hem of her shirt, dipped his tongue under the neckline. His hands banded her waist, holding her, gratefully, for she might have fallen.

The towel loosened, dropped silently over her foot. "I want you, too," she managed to say, her hands leaving his arms to clench his shoulders before beginning a dangerous descent.

Hot and molten, Gray's mouth suckled the tip of her breast as she cupped the stem of his erection, pulled along the length and, dipping her thumb in the moisture beading in the cleft, circled. She'd never been so brazen to touch a man. It made her feel powerful, in control of his desire. His teeth clamped her nipple as he sucked in a raw breath. His hands rounded her hips and palmed her buttocks, squeezing as he eased his erection from her hand, and lowered to one knee. Nestling his mouth at her junction, he laved and suckled over her slacks.

Nicci cried out, shivered, and clenched her nails into his shoulders. "Oh . . . Gray . . ." Her head lolled back, her bottom lip tucked under her front teeth as heat swirled and rushed to meet his attentions.

His hands slid around her rib cage, up to cup her breasts. He stroked her aching nipples. Gray slid her zipper down, parted her slacks and dipped his tongue to taste her through silk panties. Nicci's breath caught in her throat and she swayed a little further back, leaning into a woman's soft curves. Teeth nipped her earlobe, moved down her neck.

Nicci's gaze lowered as tendrils of black hair fell over her shoulder, and she looked at dark hands flattening her breasts. Gray laved her engorged nubbin and her eyes shuttered closed on a shivered sigh. Her body liquid, she relaxed and sank into the sensations.

Supple, moist lips touched the corner of her mouth. A tongue drew along the underside of her upper lip before entering her mouth. Long, soft fingers wound in hers and coaxed her hand to touch a rounded globe, a hardened nipple thrust against her palm. Nicci jerked her hand away, opened her eyes. The blonde woman stood next to her. Nicci couldn't quite grasp the reality of it. She slowly glanced to the dark hands fondling her breasts, down to Gray suckling her . . .

"No," Nicci said, torpidly fighting away the complex sources of pleasure.

Gray glanced up, looked to one woman and then the other, to Nicci, and she could tell he had been no more consciously aware of the women's approach than she. "I want only you." He pressed his thumb against Nicci's throbbing nubbin, drew a finger between her heated valley. "But if you . . ."

The dark skinned woman ran her hands down Nicci's belly, stretching her fingers on either side of Gray's. "We can all find pleasure," she said with an exotic purr, her mouth hovering naughtily behind Nicci's ear.

The nude blonde walked behind Gray, squatting so her knees were on either side of him and reaching around his waist, took his erection in her hand and bit his shoulder while looking up into Nicci's eyes.

Nicci's body still hummed with sensation and she wanted so very much to experience everything she'd denied herself, but did she want this?

Gray shrugged the blonde's mouth away and Nicci glanced down to the hand gripping his manhood. There was no pleasure dewing the tip, no thrusting against her hand. He wanted only Nicci. "No."

"Leave us," Gray said with no leeway in his tone for argument.

The women obeyed, joining hands and walking back to the bedroom. Nicci's cell phone rang, seemingly a signal that she was on the opposite side of the playing field and that she needed to get back to comfortable territory. "I have to go," she said and pulled free of Gray. She drew up her slacks, adjusted them into place. Before she could change her mind, she lifted her handbag off the top of the tea table, scooped up her jacket, opened the door and walked away.

Chapter Five

"Let me know if there is anything more I can do for you, Mrs. Chandler," Nicci said as she showed her client to the door, having given her the full report and photos on Mr. Chandler's *extracurricular* activities.

"Thank you," Mrs. Chandler replied and stepped into the hall.

Nicci stifled a yawn and closed the door. Feeling like she'd been pulled from the depths of hell, in late the night before . . . her surreal visit with Gray that morning . . . delivering the final report to Mrs. Chandler . . . an appointment with Mrs. Tan in a little over an hour . . . she would have preferred to go home and crawl in bed with a good book. Instead, she plopped down in her desk chair and pulled up the Tan file on the computer.

A few minutes later, her office door swung open and a young woman paused in the threshold. Since *Nicci Black, Private Investigator* wasn't painted on a pebble glass door window like the movies portrayed PI offices, usually only clients with an appointment came to her office. However, the woman wearing a turquoise sleeveless silk dress with a mandarin collar, raven black hair pulled severely away from her face, lips painted dark red, thin eyelashes over almond shaped eyes seemed confident to be in the right place.

While considering asking the woman to come back another time, the businesswoman in Nicci quickly chimed in and overrode the need for some R&R. She clicked save and powered off the monitor, stood and offered a pleased-to-meet-you smile as she beat back another yawn. "Welcome to Private Encounters. I'm Nicci Black."

The woman's dress fit her slender, tall body like a tailor-made glove and showed her long leg on a slit to the thigh. Nicci moved around her and shut the door, then waved her hand to the seating area. "Would you like to sit down, Ms. . . ." Nicci prompted.

The woman began to stroll around the office, running her hand over bookshelves, the back of the desk chair, reading the degrees and certificates framed and hanging on the wall. Nicci noticed what looked like a dragon tattoo on the back of her neck.

"Is there something I can help you with?"

The woman finally turned and smiled for a long moment. Her nose was slightly flattened to a flare at the nostrils, her cheekbones high and her eyes cold, impassive and focusing intently on Nicci as if she were a curiosity. "Yes." She pulled a slender gold box from a brocade slingbag, opened it and took out a long dark brown cigarette. She lit it with a matching lighter, flaring a sickly sweet clove scent.

Nicci scurried to find some sort of an ashtray. She discovered a shallow candy dish, emptied out the mints and placed it on the coffee table.

The woman strolled over, flicked her ash without even a passing glance to see if it made the mark. "Do you know what it is like to have the man you love cheat on you?" The question was rhetorical and spoken in monotones, almost as if she were outside herself. "Do you know what it is like to have the man you've given your heart to succumb to the evils of another woman?"

"Ms.—"

"Do you?" Her coolness quivered just slightly and she arced a delicately plucked brow.

"Ms.—"

"Vanessa."

"Vanessa, please sit and we'll talk about how you're feeling and see if my services can aid you in resolving your situation."

"You make it sound as if I've come to you for mental help." She took a long drag off her cigarette, exhaled and crushed the butt in the candy dish, where it smoldered a thin wisp of gray. "Shall I lie on the sofa?"

Nicci waved the smoke away and ignored the latter comment. "In a way, my service is help. I'm the beginning of the truth. If someone you love is violating the trust of your relationship, and consequently your physical and mental health, you need to know. You have the right to know."

"Oh, I already know."

"Suspecting and proof are very different. My investigations are very thorough so my clients understand the depths of the infidelity."

Vanessa finally sat on the sofa. "But I am not a client, am I?"

"You have nothing to be ashamed of in seeking help." Nicci perched on the edge of the chair across from Vanessa.

"Oh no, I have nothing to be ashamed of." A long grim smile slid across her face. "Tell me about Nicci Black."

Referring to her in third person seemed a bit odd, however Nicci understood the women who came to her for help were in a fragile state of mind—this one perhaps a bit more so than the usual client. "I have a BA in Psychology, spent five years as a—"

"Your credentials are hanging on the wall, Miss Black. Tell me about you."

Nicci shifted under the woman's intense gaze. "I prefer to keep my personal life separate from work."

"Do you?"

"Yes," Nicci answered quite firmly, overtly aware of Vanessa's skeptical, almost accusing tone. Perhaps she was too fatigued to handle a new client today after all. "Forgive me. You caught me at a rather bad time. I've got an appointment—" Nicci stood, grabbed a brochure. "Here is some basic information on my services. Why don't you go home, mull over everything? If you feel you are ready to proceed forward, then you can *call* for an appointment and we'll discuss the next step."

Vanessa stood, didn't give the brochure even a quick glance. "I have learned enough, for now," she said as she left without another word.

※〜(℃Ｘ)〆※

Nicci met Mrs. Tan behind a beautifully painted silk screen in a little oriental restaurant off First Avenue called the Empress. Mrs. Tan liked the traditions of her Chinese ancestry, but was American in every other aspect. After the tea was poured and the brightly robed waitress bustled away, Mrs. Tan made polite conversation for several minutes.

Nicci answered about her day, commented on the weather, agreed the tea was good. Working on a five thousand dollar retainer and billing one-twenty-five plus expenses per hour, she should allow Mrs. Tan to chatter all day, but her pride in business ethics demanded she bring Mrs. Tan around to the reason of the meeting.

"You had something to discuss?"

Mrs. Tan lifted her delicate teacup with a hand that began to shake. She sipped noisily, a dribble of tea spilled down her blouse. "I want to know what else you've uncovered," she said, returning the cup to the saucer.

"As I explained before, I can't reveal any more information than I already have until I've completed my investigation." Nicci had confirmed the affair, but to make the case solid for a divorce, she needed proof in as many forms as possible. For each piece of evidence she gathered, some high-priced lawyer would get two thrown out of court.

And, having just learned Tan possibly had an illegitimate child some twenty years before, Nicci needed one hundred percent certainty, not speculation before sharing this news with Mrs. Tan. The more she investigated, the clearer it became that Tan possessed a completely separate life from that which he shared with this wife.

"It is very hard to look at him and pretend everything is okay."

"I know, which is exactly why I want to wait on delivering the details. You could jeopardize both the surveillance and my safety by accidentally saying something to your husband in a confrontation."

Mrs. Tan lowered her gaze and folded her pudgy hands on the table. "I understand."

Reaching over, Nicci squeezed Mrs. Tan's hand reassuringly, and then stood to leave.

"Before you go?"

"Yes?"

"I shredded your business card, so my husband wouldn't come across it, but I have a friend who would like to contact you."

"Of course." Digging through her handbag, pocket after pocket, Nicci frowned. "I seem to have misplaced my little folder of cards."

"The next time we meet will be fine."

"Your friend, is her name Vanessa?"

"No. Why?"

"Nothing. I'll be in touch."

Nicci ordered a double mocha latte from a little drive thru after she left Mrs. Tan. The tea just didn't cut it when a good shot of espresso was needed. She still had a party to attend that night. If she were going as a social guest, she gladly would have passed. Climbing into bed by eight o'clock with a bag of microwave popcorn, strawberry soda and falling asleep to Casa Blanca sounded much more appealing.

She paid for the coffee and blew into the cup as she maneuvered her Jag back into traffic. This party was at Tan's *other* estate. The estate Mrs. Tan didn't seem to know existed. Nicci had paid a source rather generously to get her inside. She took a long sip of java and set the Styrofoam cup in the dash holder. Tired or not, she'd be at the estate tonight.

Which reminded her, she needed a new cocktail dress. Which brought around the memory of the night before . . . the way she had touched herself.

In the light of day it seemed surreal the pleasures she found in the darkness, as if it had been someone else. Only it had been her, with a wanting for a stranger urging her on. Her discovering things about herself she didn't know possible. Her wanting to experience, finding the strength to dare, understanding her needs did *not* make her like her mother.

And then this morning at the suite, her stranger named Gray . . . she never wanted so much. Never thought it possible to trust even her body to a man again. And yet, she'd been willing to give it to him, no games, no rules. Didn't that make it simpler? No expectations, no chance for pain. Only pleasure.

Heat pulsed deep in her body, a mounting of pressure. She clenched the steering wheel and her vaginal muscles even tighter, hoping to snub the stir, as she changed her direction and headed for some downtown shopping. The tightening of her inner self only made her body beg to be filled with a man's fullness.

Not just any man, *Gray*.

❧༺✿༻❧

Two hours later, a rare break in the clouds allowed for a patch of light to shine through. Used to gray skies and rain, the Seattleites blew dust off their sunglasses and put them on, the bright ball in the sky offending their eyes like vampires emerging from a casket at high noon. Nicci protected the dress bag as best she could while bumping shoulders with the Friday afternoon crowd along the sidewalk.

Her cell phone began to ring. Digging it out of her handbag, she flipped it open. "Nicci Black."

"I would like to hire you, Miss Black."

Nicci recognized Vanessa's voice, though it sounded even more impassive than during their earlier meeting. "There is a contract to go over, my fees to consider, options to discuss—"

"Your office, one hour."

Vanessa sat on the sofa taking long drags off her clove cigarette as Nicci pulled out a laminated 9X12 service menu. "I have several plans to choose from," Nicci said, pointing to the list of services on the left side. "I would recommend this if you suspect your husband—"

"Fiancé," Vanessa said, enunciating the word with precise finesse.

"If your *fiancé* is suspected of having an affair and your goal is to confront him with proof, Plan A includes three hours of my time "training" you on what evidence to look for, ways you can find out if he's cheating."

"Such as?"

"For example, I can show you how to do a cell or beeper phone switch. We switch his cell or beeper with an identical match for the day and you receive his calls and messages. These types of electronic devices are usually the method of contact by the other woman."

"Move on."

Nicci bit the inside of her cheek. "Plan B is similar, but a little more detailed. It includes the "training" of Plan A, but also involves planting some surveillance and recording equipment either on his person or surroundings."

"Humm," Vanessa sounded approvingly.

"I have watches with digital cameras, desk lamps with audio and visual. You get the idea. The data is sent here, to my computer, and I follow up on what is recorded and provide a report of who, when, where, why, etcetera."

"Would I be able to receive the data directly?"

Nicci waited for Vanessa's exhale of smoke to clear. "Theoretically, I could set it up so the information is sent directly to the client."

Vanessa's eyebrows spiked in interest.

"I don't recommend it. Sometimes, even when a woman thinks she is prepared for the truth—"

"I would want the data." Vanessa took the last drag of her cigarette and then crushed the butt in the dish.

"The report is for your personal use. However, I feel compelled to stress that I don't recommend—"

"Noted."

Nicci stifled a sigh. Vanessa wasn't going to be a compliant, "listen to the PI and follow her advice" kind of client. Money was money, and she supposed the challenge of maintaining patience could be a growing experience.

She smiled. "The flat fee for this plan is five hundred dollars, plus a deposit on the surveillance equipment. For additional hours, I bill one twenty five, plus expenses."

Vanessa leaned forward, touched the menu with a French tipped nail. "Plan C?"

"Plan C is the most extensive. The client is not involved beyond providing basic information, name, age, occupation, list of friends, that sort of thing. I take over from there with a detail oriented investigation that includes personal surveillance, photos, eye witness accounts, physical evidence . . . I recommend this in situations where divorce is imminent, when making a solid case of infidelity is the goal."

"Or to know every detail about the tramp." Vanessa lifted her gaze off the menu and focused deep in Nicci's eyes.

Maintaining the connection, Nicci said clearly, "I won't be used to seek revenge on a third party. That is not the goal of my operations. I *will* alert the authorities if I feel—"

"If you didn't take this whole private eye thing so very seriously, I might be offended you would even dare suggest I would engage is such a plot."

Nicci leaned back, pretended a moment of contemplation when in fact she knew exactly what she was going to say. "I think it best if I terminate this meeting right now."

Vanessa pouted, sticking her bottom lip out with the skill of a scolded three year old. "Oh, you don't really think I would harm someone, do you? I am just a woman who wants to know the truth." She sniffed, her eyelashes lowered. "If I gave the wrong impression, I'm so very sorry. It's just that I've never had to deal with something like this before. I'm rather beside myself."

The act was either very good, or Vanessa was honestly distraught. Nicci pulled out several tissues from the box of Kleenex she never allowed to run out and handed them over. "I'm the one who should be sorry."

"So," Vanessa dabbed her eyes, "how much is plan C?"

Try as she might, she couldn't get a handle of what motivated Vanessa. "Five thousand retainer. One twenty five an hour. Expenses. Out of town is a thousand a day, estimated costs upfront."

Vanessa wadded the tissue.

Nicci flipped the menu over. "There is also an Ala Carte menu." If she was going to get home in time to dress for the party, Nicci needed to get Vanessa wrapped up and out the door.

Vanessa ran her finger down the list of services. "I rather think the digital watch is clever. I want the data directly, I do not wish my fiancé to be made a spectacle of."

"I work discreetly. Everything is kept strictly confidential."

"Of course."

Nicci felt like she was being patronized, and couldn't muster up another fake smile.

"I would like to handle the situation myself."

"Vanessa—"

"I am a strong woman, Miss Black. It is living with the unknown, the suspicions, that I can't deal with."

Nicci caved. She knew too well what Vanessa was going through and couldn't blame the woman for wanting to take a stand and handle the situation herself. She couldn't imagine having to share the scene with Derek in her bed with another woman with someone else, a stranger no less. "I will program the digital files to be transferred over the Internet to a password secured site."

"Perfect."

"I can have it ready for you tomorrow."

"Today."

"I have an appointment."

"I'll pay extra to have it now."

If it got this woman on her way, then so be it. Nicci took the needed contract forms from her file cabinet, handed them to Vanessa along with a pen and told her to fill out the agreement while she programmed the watch.

Chapter Six

Nicci eased her Jag behind the procession of limousines, Rolls Royces, Porches and other classic cars polished to a shine and waiting to be parked. A valet opened her door with a sweeping gesture. "Madame." He took Nicci's hand, assisted her out and escorted her around to the sidewalk.

"Thank you." There were no porch lights and the curtains were drawn on all the front windows of the four story, white pillared brick house that sat over four hundreds yards off the main road and was secluded by a thick laurel hedge. Pulling her wrapper against the chill of evening, Nicci followed a trail of low-lit golden running lights along a stone sidewalk and up steps to the front door. She knocked.

An elderly man with sleek salt and pepper hair opened the door. "Good evening."

"Good evening," Nicci replied and stepped forward.

He sidled in front of her. "I must regretfully inform you that an invitation is required."

"Oh, I—I'm Dahlia." She kept her gaze on his, didn't waver for even a moment as he scrutinized her. The password for entrance she'd paid for better be legit—

He bowed and scooped his hand grandly for her to enter. "Welcome, my Lady Dahlia. Your servant awaits you."

Right-o, her servant. What kind of party provided personal servants? She stepped into the marble foyer where white tapered candles provided the only source of light. She shed her wrapper, handed it to the butler and waited to be led in the right direction.

"Your mask?" If this man had any personality, he hid it well.

"My mask?"

"Your mask," he said flatly. He had to be an Adam's family descendant.

"I, um, guess I forgot it." Nothing like being prepared. She outta scoop a hundred back from her source for this.

He gestured toward a room off to the right. "You may select a mask of your pleasure from the assortment of extras." Nicci stepped into the sitting room. "You may hang your clothes in the armoire. When you are ready, I will show you to your servant."

Nicci nearly choked. "Excuse me?"

"Which part did I lose you at, my lady?"

"The clothes part. You mean my wrapper, you want me to hang my wrapper?" She made to take it back from him.

Nicci turned toward a soft tinkling sound that preluded the appearance of a nude woman, who seemingly stepped out of the shadows. It took Nicci a long moment to realize the woman was real . . . alluring, sensual . . . *real.*

A turquoise feathered mask covered her eyes and angled over half her face. Thin bands wrapped around her neck and upper arms like golden snakes. Her small breasts with dark areoles held firm as she moved forward. Three golden chains with an assortment of charms dangled around her midriff. A diamond twinkled from her belly button, lighting the way to burnt red curls marking her womanly juncture.

Nicci rushed her gaze away, fighting against a sudden and terrifying response to the woman's exotic beauty.

"Bernard, I will take care of our guest," the woman said. "Perhaps this will be her first time. Hmm?" She took Nicci's hand and led her into the room.

Nicci hesitated. "I'm not, I shouldn't have—"

The woman placed her finger to Nicci's mouth, pressed gently. "*Shhh*, there is nothing to be afraid of," her voice soothed. "You may do as much or as little as you are comfortable with."

"You don't understand—"

The woman smelled of sweet jasmine. She pressed against Nicci to whisper in her ear. "Here, you are Dahlia." Twining her fingers in Nicci's again, she urged her gently forward. "If you are not enthralled, if your passions are not heightened, you are free to leave at any time. Come, come and see first before you decide."

Nicci allowed herself to be pulled to a dressing table and sat down. Just last night she'd wanted so very much to explore her sexuality. *Here you are, Dahlia.* Just last night she'd wondered what it would be like to be someone else. *Here you are, Dahlia.* Just this morning . . .

The woman unpinned Nicci's French twist and fingered her blonde hair loose. She then lifted a gold beaded mask with a large chrisom rose in full bloom at the left temple and set it gently on the bridge of Nicci's nose. Three swags of tiny pearls looped under each eyehole, cool against her cheeks. The woman tied silk straps, securing the mask then ran the pad of her finger down Nicci's cheek.

"You are beautiful, Dahlia."

Nicci closed her eyes as the woman slid down the zipper of her black dress. Soft, silky hands pushed the dress off her shoulders and down her arms, jewels tinkled a siren's song, hypnotizing.

She cupped Nicci's breasts, admired them in the mirror. "Your body is lovely."

"I'm sorry." Nicci shrugged out of the woman's touch. "I can't . . ." She lifted the bodice, held it over her traitorous nipples.

The woman stroked the tips of her fingers over Nicci's shoulders. "My affections do not please you?"

"It's just that, I shouldn't have come." The Tan investigation brought her here. Mrs. Tan was paying her to be here. And truth be known, a part of her wanted to know, to compare, to experience. What was there to be afraid of? She had only herself to face. She would no longer look in the mirror and see her mother's sins. "I am curious and wish to stay, but I would like to keep my clothes on."

The woman nodded. "Very well." She zipped Nicci's dress. "I will take you to your servant."

꠸ᕤᖇᕤꠋ

Thankfully, Nicci wasn't the only one who preferred partying with her clothes on. She estimated half the guests mingling in the terrarium in the center of the house were dressed. Albeit, some of the attire barely covered and others wore lavish costumes ranging from Regency gowns to Egyptian togas. The only constant were the masks, elaborate to elegantly simple.

Nicci's feathered friend disappeared into the crowd, assuring her that her servant would come soon. "To hell with the no alcohol on the job rule," Nicci murmured, needing something to get her through the evening. She snatched two flutes of champagne off a passing waiter's tray and guzzled, lifting her gaze to the glass roof of the terrarium. The moon, full and bright, loomed directly above like a voyeur in the night.

Nicci set down the first empty flute, started on the second glass. A warm, tingle spread through her and she welcomed the wooziness as she casually scanned for a sign of Mr. Tan.

"My Lady Dahlia."

Nicci turned toward the man who silently approached, taking her time to appreciate his long blonde hair brushing past thick shoulders, his chest glistening gold and sculpted with the finest pecks, to the strips of white fabric tied around his muscular arms, and lower—*gracious*—to his manhood erect beneath loose, thin, white cotton trousers.

"I am ready to serve you."

She glanced up to his face, overlooked in her visual feast of his glorious body. Cleanly shaven, dark brown eyes behind a plain white mask, a smile on a firm mouth made for kisses. "Serve me?"

"Ah, my Lady Dahlia has never been serviced before?"

She shook her head and glanced to the center of the terrarium where a woman bowed at the feet of a group of male musicians. They played with strange instruments filling the room with twangy, earthy music. A brawny dark man began a steady pound on a drum he held between his knees, and the woman's body began undulating upward, seemingly worshipping, offering her lush, ripe body to the rain of notes.

"My Lady?"

Nicci turned to her servant—to the man—he was not her servant! "I—" She licked her parched lips, lifted the champagne flute and tilted her head hoping for one last drop to moisten her mouth.

The music picked up tempo. The high tones of a flute drifted over the beat of drums. The woman danced wildly, seductively. Nicci's head began a slow spin, the moist terrarium air wrapped around her throat, drenched her lungs with thick, suffocating air.

Her servant took her hand, lifted her palm to his mouth and circled it with his tongue before pressing his lips firmly. "Dahlia, allow me to serve you."

She stared down through little white lights strobing around the edge of her vision. A rush of heat, a wave of dizziness. She swooned.

"My Lady." He began to work hot, moist kisses up her arm.

"I—" Why couldn't she just open her mouth and stop him?

"I am hard and ready for you. I want to serve you, Dahlia."

Her gaze left his, floated to other men dressed similarly, walking around, touching women, allowing women to touch their swollen pistons beneath the flimsy gauze as if testing their size and strength.

Over there, a servant bent his head to suckle the small breasts of a woman as she laughed and talked in a gathering of friends.

And there, a woman touched herself, then motioned for a man to follow . . .

Pleasure, passions. Ready, ripe for the taking.

"Dahlia."

No . . . Nicci, struggling out of an abyss of honeyed delight, listened to the little voice in her head telling her she did not want this. "No." The music became louder, her word drowned out on the exotic high tempo.

In the corner of her haziness, she saw great double doors swing wide. A man entered the room with the grace and power of a five foot six dragon, *Mr. Tan*. Nicci cocked her head to the side, her foggy brain reminding her Tan was the reason she'd come to this place.

A woman came to Mr. Tan from the left, another from the right. Where was her camera? Nicci couldn't remember, didn't try to recall as her servant knelt on one knee, cupped her thighs and began to massage with thick, strong hands.

Her lashes lowered behind the mask. Her mouth parted. She reached out and took a lock of her servant's hair, twisted it around her finger. She could fist her hands in his glorious hair while she rode his body to pleasure like a succubus in the night.

The crash of cymbals, the plucking of a guitar . . . how could she entertain such a wicked thought? "No," she said again, her voice weak.

Her servant nuzzled the inside of her knee with his mouth, his hands working up to the curve of her buttocks.

Her body was betraying her. She couldn't find the will nor strength to fight the heat radiating to her nerve endings. She closed her eyes and sighed.

"This woman is not for you." The deep, commanding voice broke through her abyss of pleasure.

Nicci forced open her eyes, which seemed to have cemented shut in the short time since she'd closed them. With great effort she tried to focus, blinked several times to restore clarity.

Gray . . . She might have sighed his name aloud, might have kept it to herself like a delicious secret. She smiled and reached for him, trying to keep her vision from wavering. He didn't wear a mask, no costume. Just obvious displeasure etched on his handsome features. Her hand fell like a branch of a mighty oak in the dead of winter.

Her servant stood, bowed slightly. "I am this woman's servant for the evening."

"I shall see to her needs."

The servant nodded and disappeared as quietly as he'd approached, leaving Nicci to face Gray alone.

She wondered why he was here, but could only focus on the pulse between her legs.

Gray took the empty champagne flute she forgot she held, set it aside and then took her by the elbow. He drew her back against his chest, lifted her onto her tiptoes and moved her into a darkened alcove.

"What the hell are you doing here?" His breath steamy on the shell of her ear. His fingers dug into her arm.

Nicci didn't dare pull away. Words of explanation flitted about in her mind as if on the back of a hummingbird. None would materialize on her tongue. "I—" She couldn't tell him she came for a client. "A friend told me about this place, and I was curious."

He crushed her chest with his forearm. His heart pounded against her shoulder blade. "Curious? So curious you're willing to allow a strange man to touch you?"

The force of Gray's words reprimanded her. She feared his punishment, and yet . . . her arousal blazed imagining the sinful ways he could torture her.

"Did you want him? Would you have taken him right here in front of everyone?"

She shook her head. "No." The denial quivered, making the doubt she harbored seem brutally acute.

"No?" He thrust her legs apart with his knee. "You were standing like this for him. Did you like it?"

Nicci thrashed her head away from the hiss of Gray's words. "No."

"No?" His reached under her dress, pulled her high cut panties over the arch of her bottom so they stretched across her thighs. "He wanted to take these off you, would you have let him?"

A jolt of passion seared through her, even as she silently damned him. "No."

He fisted the swatch of panties and ripped them away, then

slid his hand around her leg, cupped her inner thigh and lifted her leg until she sat upon his slightly bent knee. "No?" The arm around her chest loosened, his hand draped her throat.

"No," she repeated, moving her hips slightly to feel his hardening shaft against her naked bottom. The flaring heat deep inside ached so intensely to be filled, she reached around and gripped him at each hip, pulling him taut as the tiny pulses demanded bolder action. Arching, rotating, she slid along him, across his engorging maleness, the heat of him throbbing against her.

Gray took in a hiss of breath, stifled a groan.

"Humm," Nicci dropped her head against his shoulder, rolled it to the side and nipped the stubble along his jaw. "I need you—"

Gray brought his half wild gaze to her eyes beneath the mask. She rotated against him again, watching his eyes darken and his breath hold as he fought against the friction.

"No." The one word seemed to cause him grave pain.

She needed him to take her over the edge, to free her of the incredible pleasure-pain radiating from deep inside her to the outermost petals of her sex. She wouldn't take no for an answer.

Nicci bit the corner of his lower lip, ran her tongue over it to soothe. "Oh, yes. Inside me, Gray—" She banded his left wrist, guided his palm between her legs and pressed him against her dampened folds. "Why are you resisting me? Isn't this what you've wanted?" Running her fingers to twine between his, she pressed into the delicate valley of her pleasure and worked him through the damp hunger. "I've imagined you touching me like this." Her other hand found the snap of his trousers behind her, yanked. She pawed for the elastic of his underwear, dug her hand underneath and cupped his erection.

Gray shuddered. She felt the power of it at every point their bodies were connected. She began to stroke his length in time with their joined hands between her legs, and watched his tension build, muscles bunch.

"What's wrong, Gray? Afraid you'll lose control?" She teased, taunted. "Afraid you already have?" God, how she wanted like she never wanted before.

He pushed her off his body, yanked her around and backed her against the opposite wall of the alcove with brute force. "I'm always in control." The feral penetration of his eyes, the hard set of his features made Nicci fear that she pushed too far.

With a growl, Gray lifted her, wrapped her legs around his

hips, and pressed the weight of his body against her, crushing her to the wall. His erection jutted against her, teasing her entrance.

"Now, Gray." She couldn't move to guide him into her core. She ached for release so intensely she barely kept herself from crying aloud like a beast howling at the moon. "Now," she whimpered.

He lifted both her arms above her head, wreathed her wrists with his powerful hand, and then clasped his other hand over her mouth. The pads of his fingers dug into her cheek as he thrust his engorged shaft deep into her body, biting his bottom lip and tensing his jaw as he forced her to take all of him.

Her velvet walls gripped him, drew him even deeper as an onslaught of contractions released a forceful orgasm. He drowned her scream with his mouth over hers and kissed her until the initial release ebbed into aftershocks.

"Now," Gray said, easing his hips to withdraw his length and then pushing back into her with exquisite slowness. "I'm going to ask you a couple of questions, my nefarious beauty, and I want the right answers."

She flashed her gaze into the hard concentration of his eyes, forgot what she meant to find there as he drove into her again.

"Do you understand?"

Questions? Answers? Nicci shook her head, locked her knees around his waist tighter, cognizant only of the rhythm of his body beating into hers. Her mask slipped free of the knot and fell to the floor.

"Tell me what I want to know and I'll protect you." He lowered his head to her breast, suckled a nipple she didn't realize had been so cruelly left out. She wanted him to rip open her dress and feast. Instead, he took the nipple in between his teeth and bit hard enough to cause alarm bells to jangle through the sweet ringing of another orgasm. "Lie to me and I'll be forced to get what I want the hard way."

Nicci struggled to free her arms. "What do you want?" Her traitorous body kept responding to the strokes delving deeper with each powerful thrust. Quite suddenly, she realized there was more to Gray than the outer layer of a seductive stranger. "Who are you?"

He slid his hand between them, unhooded her delicate nubbin and commanded it into submission with delightful pressure. A long slow withdrawal of his shaft and a final thrust home, Gray collapsed his head on her shoulder as his orgasm momentarily possessed him.

Nicci thrashed her head to the side as her own orgasm disintegrated her into a thousand shards. She gasped for breath, for sanity, completely defenseless against the shattering contractions, hating what he did to her, hating that she'd never experienced anything so intense. Hating that she wanted it again.

For a long moment she could hear nothing but their gasps for air. Finally, Gray moved his head to study her. His manhood remained buried deep within her. His weight held her against the wall. "How long have you been working for Li Tan?"

"I—" Her muscles tightened, even those in her slick channel. "I don't know what you're talking about."

Gray slid from her, released her hands and allowed her to stand on her own wobbly legs. "Why is Tan paying you to follow me?" He adjusted his pants, zipped and buttoned.

"I don't work for Li Tan."

"My hotel, *The Blue Velvet*, tonight."

"Our meetings have been nothing more than coincidence."

"Let me motivate your cooperation a little bit. Federal investigators are positioned outside waiting for my signal. Now, you can cooperate with me, or I'll allow them to haul you off to jail with the rest of these people. You can spread your legs for a prison guard to get an extra fifteen minutes in the yard, while your attorney works to get you a deal."

Her mouth dropped open. "You're FBI?"

"The innocent act worked once, not twice. DOMIS."

She played the letters of the acronym and came up blank.

"Department of Manufactured Illegal Substance. Does Tan know who I am?"

"I wouldn't know."

Gray shoved her against the wall. "If you withhold information that puts any of my men in jeopardy, I'll kill you with my bare hands."

"I'm a private investigator." With every bit of strength to hold onto a semblance of pride, Nicci held her head high, straightened her dress with a shaky hand and gave him her PI license number.

"Who hired you?"

"I'm bound by client confid—"

Gray shoved her again. Her head whipped backward and rammed the corner of a picture frame. "Fuck client confidentiality. Who hired you?"

"Mrs. Tan. She suspected her husband was having an affair."

He jabbed his hand through his hair, lifted his sports coat lapel and spoke in a low voice, "A blonde woman will coming out the door within the next sixty seconds. I want her followed to a safe distance and then picked up. Hold her, peacefully, until I arrive. Everyone else, maintain your positions."

Nicci squared her shoulders, stepped away from Gray, refusing to allow any of the emotions combating inside her to take over. The most prominent defied her will and heated her cheeks, glaring as bright as if someone stuck a "fool" tag on her ass. The most erotic, sensual, glorious encounter of her life had been nothing more than a licentious interrogation tactic.

Nicci made it three steps out of the alcove when a cold, foreign hand grabbed her forearm. She whipped around and stared down into the black eyes of Mr. Tan. He bowed his head, keeping his gaze locked with hers. "Ah, Gray, you white devil, how sinful of you to keep this peach all to yourself."

Chapter Seven

Gray stepped forward, laid his palm on Nicci's lower back. "Do you blame me for wanting the most beautiful woman here tonight to be exclusively mine?"

Tan finally took his ebony eyes off her and shifted over her shoulder to Gray. "I would have preferred you shared."

"You should know by now I can be most difficult to make a deal with."

Tan removed his hand from Nicci's arm as an approving smile split his thin mouth into a grin. "Ah, yes, you do drive a bargain. Bring your lady friend, we must celebrate."

Gray's fingers pressed into Nicci's back, the muscle in his forearm bunched, though in her peripheral vision she noted his face remained unemotional. "Thank you for the kind offer, but I'm afraid I was just leaving," Nicci said politely.

"You will stay." Tan's apathetic tone provided no leeway for refusal.

Nicci glanced up at Gray, silently imploring him to defy Tan.

"My companion and I would like nothing more than to celebrate," Gray said in a pleasing note. "However, my terms have not yet been approved."

"I have arranged to make it so." Tan snapped his fingers to the tall redheaded woman Nicci was certain to be the same woman from *The Blue Velvet*. The redhead crossed the room, her ivory beaded gown shimmering with each long legged step and her voluptuous hips swayed. She linked her arm with Tan's, and they started forward.

Gray pressed Nicci to follow.

She did, fearing with each step she took that she was following the five foot six dragon to his lair.

The mingling guests parted like the Red Sea to make a path for Tan, many of them bowing as he passed in the fashion one would for a king. Nicci casually scanned the terrarium, creating a mental blueprint of the house, noting exit doors and estimating where the corridors would lead. Located windows large enough to break and climb through if necessary, columns and furniture that would block bullets should she need cover.

Satisfied with her plan for safety in the worst possible scenarios, she scanned the guests. So many . . . mass panic could break out when Gray's men barged in, hampering their mobility to back up Gray. So many . . . enjoying fantasy and pleasures.

She had a small taste of that sexual possibility and even now, knowing the truth about Gray, she wanted to be his lover, to be in his arms exploring passions. Instead, she was in the wrong place at the wrong time, following in the path of danger and she had no choice but play along.

And play along she would, the only difference in undertaking an undercover role this time was that she had an emotional involvement.

She said her mantra in her head, "Nicci Black doesn't allow for seduction in her life," knowing it was much, much too late to listen.

She saw her servant sprawled on a cream-colored chaise lounge, his head propped on chrisom and gold throw pillows. A woman kneeling beside him serviced his manhood with her mouth, another woman stood with one foot beside his hip on the lounge, her head tipped back as he worked her sex with his hand. His teeth were clamped over his bottom lip and his eyes followed Nicci as she ascended a flight of marble stairs behind Tan.

"Would you like your servant returned to you?"

Nicci jerked her head up. Mr. Tan, three steps above her, stared down at her with a bemused smile. "I, uh—"

"No, she would not," Gray said. He pressed Nicci forward again.

"And what if I want my servant returned to me, Gray?" she queried sweetly. If she had to play the part of Dahlia, who was here for sinful pleasure, then Dahlia she would be.

"Excuse us a moment," Gray said to Tan, who nodded and finished the climb to the second floor landing. "What the hell are you doing?"

Nicci wrenched her arm free of Gray's band of fury, silently triumphant to witness his jealousy. "If I have to be caught in this raid, I might as well enjoy myself before it happens," she hissed under her breath and then smiled adoringly up at Tan.

"What's that suppose to mean?"

"Since what I *thought* we had going between us was, in fact, an illusion, I might want to find someone who is actually interested in me."

The planes on his face hardened, accenting the chiseled beauty of him. "You will do no such thing."

She gave a little wave to her servant, then batted her eyes at Gray innocently. "Why not?"

He gripped her jaw between his thumb and forefinger, forcing her to look at him. "The only man who will be touching you tonight is me. Understand?"

"What does it matter what I do and with whom?"

Dark, thick clouds scudded through his eyes with flashes of lightning. "This situation takes precedence over anything personal, but let me assure you, you will be mine."

"Why I would allow you to even touch me after this?"

Gray lowered his head and kissed Nicci, a strong, passionate kiss that branded her with his flavor and texture, drew sensations from deep in her core, and brought them to life with promises of wicked delight. He ended the kiss, running the pad of his thumb over her moist mouth.

"You'll allow me to touch you because you need me to touch you." He started up the steps, leaving her to follow like a little lamb to the slaughterhouse.

And she did, no longer sure which held more potential for danger, being caught up in a raid on Tan, or knowing she would give Gray anything he asked for, so long as he fulfilled her need.

"She has much passion," Tan said with an approving smile.

"Yes." Gray held his hand down for Nicci, raised an eyebrow and smiled with carnal delight. "Many passions I have only begun to explore." He took her hand, kissed the back of it, his gaze traveling the length of her arm leaving goose bumps of pleasure. "Which is why I'm hoping we can conclude our arrangement soon."

Tan laughed as Nicci put her hand over her heart Scarlet O'Hara style and exclaimed, "If you make me wait too long, I just might call for my servant after all."

"Don't even go there again." Gray's tone was light, but Nicci received the warning in the pressure of his fingers as he wove his hand with hers.

Tan led the way to a formal dining room. The great doors were swung shut and locked by two men dressed as servants, though their build was much brawnier than the ones pleasuring guests.

In the center of a long polished mahogany table was a nude woman sitting crisscross, leaning back on her palms, the peaks of her small breasts thrust upward, her head back, cascading black hair to pool on the table. As Tan passed, he plucked a stem of grapes off an array of fresh fruit draped off the woman's body.

Tan sat at the head of the table, Gray to his right, Nicci next to him. The redheaded woman stood behind Tan, running her finger along the brightly colored tattoo of a dragon that wound from Tan's shoulder to his hand.

A formally dressed server came around and poured champagne. Tan raised his glass and everyone followed suit. "To a prosperous future."

Gray echoed the salute.

Nicci brought the flute of champagne to her mouth.

Gray put his hand on her knee and squeezed. "No more champagne," he whispered.

Feeling Tan's black eyes tearing her way, Nicci ran her fingers through Gray's hair at the nape and didn't question Gray's order.

"Tell me, Dahlia, have you enjoyed the evening?"

"Very much."

"It is your first time visiting us, yes?"

"Yes."

"Yet, you are familiar."

"Oh?" Nicci cocked her head toward Tan, pretending to reflect as she debated on just how much she should reveal about her attendance. If she stuck to the truth, she was less likely to be caught in a lie.

The redheaded woman ran her palm down Tan's chest, whispered something in his ear. Tan nodded, slowly lifting his eyes to Nicci. She knew the woman recognized her.

"No." Nicci forced herself not to look to Gray for a prompt. "We haven't met. However; I did see you at *The Blue Velvet* the other night. That's where I met Gray."

"I thought she was one of your girls," Gray said, taking a strawberry from a bowl nestled between the nude woman's legs, dipping it in a fondue pot of white chocolate and holding it out to Nicci's mouth.

She opened like a baby bird, cupping her hand under her jaw
to catch juice and blobs of chocolate as she bit into the ripe berry.
She chewed slowly, closing her eyes and feeling immensely grateful Gray provided her with an excuse to be silent and not say anything that might contradict his undercover identity.

"Hah! If she were one of my girls, I would not have given her
to you. She is far too beautiful. Possesses an innocence I would
take my time to corrupt."

Nicci stifled a shudder.

"She is not an easy one to corrupt," Gray's tone held approval.
"She didn't respond to being offered money for her favors very
well."

Tan laughed, a high pierced *hee hee hee* that ranked right up
there with fingernails down a chalkboard. "You have not learned
much from me, have you, Gray? Never stoop so low as to pay a
woman, it makes you weaker than they are, allows them the means
to control. One hundred dollar, suck your cock. Two hundred dollar, sit on your lap." Tan gripped a lock of the red head's hair and
pulled her downward as he scooted out his chair to make way for
her between his knees. "No, you don't pay for women, Gray. A
man must know what a woman wants, give it to her and then make
sure she remember who has the power to make it all go away."

"Touché." Gray lifted his glass in a mock toast.

Nicci snatched her champagne flute and took a long swallow
before Gray banded her wrist with his fingers and lowered her
hand. She licked a spilt drop of wine from her bottom lip, needing
something to quench the dry shock thickening her mouth as the
redhead worked Tan.

"You see." Tan turned his beady eyes to Nicci, gripping the
armrest of his wooden chair, his knuckles turning white. "It is why
I provide servants for my guests. Nobody has to pay for what they
secretly wish for. There is only mutual satisfaction."

"And what do your guests secretly wish for?" Nicci asked as a
warm fuzziness started spreading through her again, starting in
her stomach and radiating outward. Heat pooled between her legs,
yet she recognized it was not the crude display of Tan's sexual
gratification playing out before her, rather an un-stimulated response of her womanly body.

"Ah, a woman who asks good questions." Tan's eyes shuttered
closed a moment as he drew in a quick rush of air. The redhead
slowed the pace of her sucking, allowing Tan to regain control
over his body. He seemed to relax again. "My clients wish to not

feel guilt in their passion of the flesh. For example, as a woman is lying beneath her husband assuring him his tiny dick is pleasing her, she is wishing for a dark and dangerous man to come rip off her skirts and bury his enormous cock inside her. Here, she can have that, and anything else she desires."

Something, Nicci realized, must be in the champagne. Something stimulating her sex drive and clouding her thinking, which was exactly what Gray had been trying to warn her of. "Don't you believe women would prefer romance?" Nicci asked, thinking some potent mixture of romance and sin held the key to happily ever after.

"Ah, Gray. You have indeed found a fresh one."

Gray ran his hand down Nicci's leg. "Indeed."

Whatever was affecting her heightened awareness of her sexual self surely explained her reaction to her servant's attentions earlier. The drug seemed to strip away her inhibitions. Allowed her to succumb to desires she would have normally suppressed. Or rather suppressed until she met Gray.

Her response to Gray at every encounter was more potent than any drug, more alive than any manufactured substance, more passionate than masked interludes. She responded to Gray because her body instinctively knew the absolute pleasure he would deliver, that his body would bring completion to hers. The drug might have made her bolder, more courageous to ask for what she wanted, but the heights he took her to were launched from a deeper place than a mood altering substance.

Gray lifted another strawberry, dipped it and dangled it in front of her mouth. As she tilted her chin to take it, his lips intercepted and seared her with a kiss that confirmed her thoughts accurate.

A guttural sound came from Tan and Gray ended the kiss, saying against her mouth, "Finally," and plopped in the berry.

The redhead stood from between Tan's legs and he dismissed her with a wave of his hand. She left the room silently as the waiter returned with a dome-covered platter. He set it before Tan, lifted the lid, uncovering what looked like a rack of specimen vials, each filled with an amber colored liquid.

"Let us conclude our deal." Tan zipped his trousers. "Would you like to sample?" He raised a vial, swirled the liquid and studied it in the dim light. "It is the best blend so far."

Gray reached into his inside jacket pocket and removed a fat white envelope.

This is it, Nicci thought, and reached tentatively over the

woman's leg into the bowl for another berry to keep herself from showing any anxiety. She dipped the berry, lifted it toward her mouth.

"Or perhaps right about now your lady friend can attest to the potency, *humm?*"

Nicci looked from Tan to Gray, the berry suspended in mid air.

"She has not had but a sip of champagne," Gray said, "but I assure you we will have some later, *in private.*"

"I believe if you reach between her legs right now, you will find her already liquid with need. The chocolate has been enhanced as well."

Nicci laughed delicately, biting into the berry and licking her lips Dahlia style. "How very naughty."

Tan reached out for the envelope, Gray drew it back toward his chest. "Where is the rest of my order?"

Tan nodded to the guards. In unison, they swung the doors open and the redhead woman stepped forward. She walked to Gray, pulled him from the chair and arched her body along his length. Taking the envelope, she handed it to Tan and then began to lead Gray from the room.

Nicci started to rise from her chair.

"Sit," Tan said and then waved the guards to follow Gray and the redhead.

"Gray?" *He couldn't just leave her.*

"It's okay," was all Gray said before leaving Nicci startlingly alone with Tan.

The doors shut. Abruptly, Tan scraped his chair back, stood. Nicci flinched.

"Ah." Amusement twinkled in Tan's coal eyes. "You are like a frightened little doe." He withdrew a vial from the rack, swirled it. "I like just a touch of fear in women." He walked slowly around the opposite side of the table, his impassive eyes honed in on her like a target.

"Where is she taking Gray?"

"He'll be back soon. Suggestions on how it would be best to pass the time?" He was on her side of the table now, slithering toward her like an eel.

"Gray wouldn't like me to pass time in any way that doesn't

involve him." She smiled sweetly, hopefully naively. "I'm sure you understand."

Tan said he'd enjoy corrupting her. The way he was looking at her, it was quite possibly on his *to do* list. She wasn't licensed to carry a gun, didn't think it would ever be necessary, keeping her practice to domestic relationships. She never thought she'd be caught up in the middle of a drug raid, left alone with a sexual predator . . .

If she got out of this, she'd take the necessary classes and fill out the forms. *A little snub nose would be quite comforting right about now.*

"It is Gray who understands the hierarchy of my business. It would be considered an honor if I chose to pleasure his woman."

"I'm not really his woman. I'm just—"

"You're not going to fight me, *are you, Dahlia?*" He stood beside her, ran his fingers through her hair. "I do hate to commence such a lucrative deal with violence."

She needed to stall him, buy enough time for Gray to be led to the shipment and call in the troops. "I was rather hoping you'd take the hint I'm not interested."

"You do not want to offend me, Dahlia."

"You're right, I don't. So how about we just forget this whole conversation took place. You go sit back down and we'll talk about the weather—"

Tan gripped a handful of Nicci's hair and yanked her head back. As she yelped, he emptied the vial into her mouth, half the sweet liquid went down before she could spurt out the rest and clench her lips tightly closed.

"Do not patronize me." Tan lowered his head, his thin lips on a direct path for hers.

If she wasn't so worried about blowing Gray's investigation, she'd kick Tan's ass before she'd kiss him.

In the distance, a woman shrieked. Tan paused, his face pinched and contorted.

Footsteps thundered outside the door, sounding like a herd of elephants rushing the marble stairs.

The raid was going down, *now.*

Tan pulled Nicci upward by the hair, held her against his body as the doors flung open. Four black clothed agents aimed assault weapons. The nude woman on the table leapt off, sending fruit flying as she screamed hysterically and dodged under the table.

Gray stepped between the agents. "Li Tan, you are under arrest for manufacturing and distributing an illegal substance."

"I'll kill her before I let you take me," Tan sneered.

"I don't think so." Nicci rammed her elbow into Tan, grabbed his arm, bent over and hurled him over her shoulder. He landed flat on his back with a satisfying thud on the hard marble. With an inhuman groan, his black eyes rolled into his head.

The drug Tan poured down Nicci's throat took effect. She swooned, focused on Gray's blue eyes, smiled and then passed out.

Chapter Eight

The following evening on the six o'clock news, Nicci recognized herself in the background as one of Gray's men brought her a cup of coffee while she sat huddled in a blanket on the front steps of Tan's mansion. No one else would be able to recognize her, it was dark and the camera focus was on the HAZMAT team dressed in white spaceship looking outfits entering the house as DOMIS agents hauled out handcuffed party guests.

The newscaster, a solemn looking man with wire rimmed glasses told the abbreviated version of how Li Tan manufactured the sexual drug in a laboratory set up in the basement. Thanks to "the agent working undercover" a list of over a hundred other "business partners" Tan had associations with, were served with search warrants, resulting in more arrests.

She'd given her detailed statement at least a dozen times before contacting Mrs. Tan in person at three a.m. to tell her the fate of her husband. She finally crashed into bed at five to sleep off the residual effects of the drug and slept the entire day.

A knock sounded at the door, jolting Nicci into instant hope. *Gray.* She looked out the peephole and covered her stomach to keep the disappointment from overwhelming. She slid open the deadbolt, unlocked the door and allowed Brad inside.

"Hey you," she said playfully, shutting the door behind him.

He set a basket on the kitchen table, unloaded containers of food. "Don't 'hey you' me. I saw the news this morning. I've pounded on your door every hour all day. I was ready to break it down." He took a lid off pasta, another off sauce and heaped it onto a plate he took from her cupboard, knowing her kitchen as well as his own.

"I didn't think anyone would recognize me." Her stomach growled as the delicious scents assaulted her. She hadn't bothered with anything before collapsing in exhaustion.

"I'm not just anybody." Brad set the plate on the table, ordered her to sit and eat as he fixed a large glass of ice water. "I want you to quit."

Nicci swallowed her first bit of nourishment before she could enjoy the burst of tomato and spice. "Close Private Encounters?"

"You could have been hurt last night. What in the world were you doing going to a place like that? You could have at least taken me along." He uncorked a bottle of wine. "Drink the water and I'll allow you half a glass. You look terrible."

"Gee, thanks. I couldn't take you along. And as much as I appreciate your concern, we both know a certain amount of risk comes along with my work."

"Risk?" Brad slammed his weight into a chair, crossed his arms on the table and shook his head. "You know how I feel about you, Nicci, and I'm not going to pretend otherwise." He held up his hand to stop her from speaking. "I know you don't feel the same for me, but damn it, I can't just stand by and let something happen to you."

She reached over and took his hand, rubbed her thumb over his knuckles. "I'm sorry. I had no idea any of that stuff was going to go down. I was on Mr. Tan for completely different reasons and got caught in the middle of the raid. Things like this don't normally happen."

"Just like you don't normally make out with an undercover cop?"

"I didn't know he was working undercover. I didn't know anything about him—" Nicci broke off, her excuse so incredibly lame and hurtful. "Damn it, Brad. I don't know what it was with him. I'd met him earlier in the day, just bumped into him and had this strange connection. And then he was at *The Blue Velvet*, and he just possessed me. I've never felt anything as strong as that before, and I'm sorry I don't feel that for you."

"So what are you saying, this was some kind of 'love at first sight' bullshit?" His pain rode on his tone like a Harley.

Nicci pushed spaghetti around her plate. "No," she admitted. There were no fuzzy warm feelings of love for Gray. "It was an intensity that plateaued anything I have ever felt before, anything that I knew could exist. It was erotic and dangerous and everything I never knew I wanted to feel."

Brad stood, nodding. "For a private eye, you sure are blind."

"What's that supposed to mean?"

He walked to the door, gripped the handle. "Your describing something the rest of us only hope to find. What the rest of us call love is just a delusional state of mind we get on in hope that it will materialize into what you are describing."

She tried to laugh, she sounded like a choked chicken. "How many bottles of wine did you drink today?"

"Not even a glass, but I wish to hell I'd been drunk when I sent him away."

"Sent who away?"

"Mr. Undercover, whatever the hell his name is. I cold cocked him in the jaw, threatened to call the police." Brad rolled his eyes. "Yeah, I know but I was operating out of jealousy, not thinking clearly. Anyway, I finally said you specifically told me not to let him bother you and he left. So, you see, I wish I had been drinking, because then I'd have an excuse for acting like an ass."

"Gray was here?" Nicci tried to temper the excitement she felt bubbling up.

"He said that if you changed your mind he would be at the same place until morning. He didn't say what place, and I really had no intention of giving you his message so I didn't ask and—"

"Brad," Nicci stood and walked over to him and wrapped her arms around his waist, "I forgive you, and I love you. You've been here for me and I appreciate it more than you can ever know."

He kissed her forehead. "Be careful, for me?"

"Yes."

Brad slid from her arms and left.

⁂〰(ૐ)〰⁂

Nicci's whole body went numb as she stood face to face with Gray in the entryway to his suite. If she could move, she might have run, might have flung herself into his arms, might of done a thousand things besides stand there, immobile and unable to come up with a cognizant thought, let alone words.

All she knew was that what she'd experienced with Gray couldn't have been imagined. The connection. The consuming fire. The slow burn.

He braced a forearm on the doorjamb above his head, his bruised jaw tensed. Doubt began creeping in. What if he'd come to her apartment earlier because he needed another statement? To tell her, *Gee, it's been fun, but . . .*

The world shrunk to the space they shared and slowed to a long pause as she waited for a sign on how to proceed. He showed no outward emotion, his face remained stolid and his eyes dark, unreadable.

"Gray?" Nicci lifted a hand toward him, wanted to feel the stubble on his jaw, to run her fingers through his hair. If she could just touch him . . .

He clasped his fingers around her wrist, led her into the suite, letting the door slam shut on its own.

This was the end, Nicci realized as she followed him, panic clutching her chest. If he had taken her to his bed, she would have laid for him, greedily taken any pleasure he was willing to give her before he said goodbye. Instead, he led her through the suite to the master bathroom, let go of her hand and turned the spigots on the old-fashioned claw foot tub.

He tested the water with the back of his hand, plugged the drain, and then turned to her, cupped her face in his palm and kissed both her eyelids softly. "Did you sleep at all?"

She sighed, letting go of all the worry, all the doubt. "Hmm, yes. Several hours today."

He trailed his hands down her arms to her waist, slid his palms under her T-shirt and lifted. "It wasn't enough. You still look tired."

The steam from the bath dampened her skin. He dropped the shirt to the floor. Her breasts, confined to her bra ached to be released, touched, kissed . . .

He unsnapped her faded jeans, slid them over her hips and she gave a passing thought that she should have changed into something sexier. Memorable. *Next time.*

Gray kneeled before her and kissed her stomach, slipping her jeans the rest of the way down. She lifted one foot at a time out of the denim, her hands braced on his broad shoulders.

His heated mouth chartered a dangerous course to her panties, his tongue moving in lush circles evoking a series of damning tickles and absolutely delicious craving. "Gray," she whispered, her nails digging half moons into his shoulders. "I want you."

He slid off her panties, stood and slowly turned her. She held up her hair as he unfastened her bra and slid the straps down her arms, his fingers light as butterfly wings. Every tiny hair on her arm stood up and quivered. "You're beautiful, *Niccola*."

"You've checked up on me." And knowing it pleased her devastatingly.

"Routine."

"Funny." She angled her head and shot him a curious glance. "Nothing about you has seemed routine."

"I was buried undercover. There is no protocol when your life and those of others are at stake." He cupped her breasts in his palms, lifted as he stroked her nipples with the rough pad of his thumbs.

"Anything, any means, to catch the bad guy?"

"Something like that." He nibbled her shoulder.

"Am I just a casualty of justice at any cost then?"

"No."

"Then what am I?"

"You knew the moment I touched you the first time."

Yes, she knew. *His*. He branded her that very moment. "I want to hear you say it."

"You're mine." Gray scooped his arm under her legs and lifted her off her feet. She draped her arm around his neck and devoured the flexing of his strong arms and chest against her bare flesh. "And by the time I'm done with you, Niccola Black, any doubt you may have will be gone."

She tipped her head back, offering her throat for his hungry mouth to taste. "Never be done with me, Gray."

"Never." The word vibrated, his breath hot against the column of her throat. He lowered her into the tub with gentleness, soaking the sleeves of his sweater. "Relax for awhile. I want you refreshed and strong. Ready for a long night."

Nicci leaned her head back against the porcelain and sighed, the water enveloping her body and soaking away the tension. "Hmm . . . I might stay in here forever."

His dark blue eyes flickered and a smile tugged a dimple. "No, you won't. When you're ready, come to me." He pulled the sweater over his head as he walked out.

Hair brushed sleek down her back, a fluffy white towel secured around her chest, Nicci padded barefoot through the bedroom to find Gray. He stood at the living room window, hands dug deep in his trouser pockets as he looked out over Seattle.

"They call it the Emerald City," she said, slipping a wet strand behind her ear, imagining how it would feel to run her hands over Gray's body. To feel his hardened planes beneath her palms, rake her nails down the length of his back, wrap her legs around his lean hips.

"I wanted to go to the top of the Space Needle before I left," he replied, reminding her just how little she knew of him, where he came from, who his family was. It was also, she supposed, a gentle way of telling her he would be leaving.

"How long before you go?" She met his gaze in the reflection off the glass as she moved slowly toward him, the soles of her feet sinking into the plush carpet.

He pulled his hands out of his pockets, rammed his fingers through his hair. "Too soon."

Too soon . . . How could she give up what she'd only begun to find?

He turned, leaned against the windowpane. The city twinkled in the backdrop, the tip of the Space Needle pointed up just beyond Gray's shoulder, the stars above shining in all their glory on a clear, crisp night.

He would be gone soon, this night would be theirs forever. "Then let me have you for as long as I can," she whispered in a smoky soft voice and brazenly dropped the towel.

"No." Gray pushed off the window, his focus on her mouth. "Let me have you." His gaze lowered to her throat, her breasts. "Completely." He stepped forward, emptying the space between and replacing the air with feral want, intent. "Trust me. Surrender to me, Niccola."

To surrender—her body, her mind, her heart? She backed up, matching his stride until the corner of the wall nipped her back and splayed her hands on either side of the wall. *To trust*—her body, her mind, her heart? "I—"

"*Shh.*" Gray touched her mouth with his finger, ran the pad over her lip, obscuring the shape. "My pants."

Nicci could obey his command, would allow for this pleasure of the flesh, as long as she kept her mind and her heart out of it. She unfastened the slim black belt with nimble fingers, slipped the trouser button through the slit and slowly slid the zipper down, the back of her fingers brushing the length of him through cotton Hanes. The veins in his mighty organ pumped blood, thickened, swelled him to a rigid state.

On a swift intake of air, Gray yanked the belt free of the loops, twisted it around his hand, his eyes portraying an oceanic turbulence. A smile tugged the corner of her mouth. She wanted to be the wind to blow him off course, the ship that chartered him to new seas, a mystical creature of the unexplored depths who guided him.

Parting the open V of his trousers by sliding her hands on either side of Gray's erection, she slid her palms over his hips, under the band of his underwear, over the arch of his sculptured buttocks. Her body pressed against him, enticing, warm, damp.

Hmm, a little moan caught in her throat as she slid his pants down, her mound pressed against his gloriously lean, muscular leg as she bent her knees, moving downward. Excruciatingly slow, every course hair on his leg tangling briefly with the soft, dewy hair of her womanhood.

Balanced on her haunches, the wall against her spine, knees open wide, Nicci helped Gray step out of each pant leg. Running her hands up the length of his calves, her mouth pressed the inside of his knee, his thigh. Hot breath over his manhood . . . stomach . . . chest.

He crushed his mouth over hers in a fierce, hungry kiss, effluent primal passion released in an underscored urgency. She dug her fingers wildly through his hair, fisting and releasing strands. She teetered, breathless, suffering from orgiastic delirium when the kiss ended.

Gray rolled her off the corner so she faced the length of the wall, took her arms and placed each hand on the smooth floral printed wallpaper above her head. Tiny gold threads pressed into the pads of her fingers. He nudged her legs apart until she stood spread eagle to the wall.

"You're not surrendering to me, Niccola. Not cooperating." He ran his hands down her sides, over the curve of her hips, smoothed down her legs. "You're not concealing anything, are you?"

Yes. "No." *I will never surrender completely to you, only to your carnal delights.* She could barely breath as his hands worked up the inside of her thighs to the juncture of her dampened heat and palmed her mound. She gasped, shuddered, tilted her pelvis back and upward, wriggling against his hand.

"Your full cooperation is necessary." He slid his finger inside her tight sheath. Another. Nicci cried out, bucked against him. Gray drove deeper. "Otherwise I'll have to treat you as a hostile suspect."

"Tell me . . ." She wanted to reach around to his hips, pull his erection jutting against her buttocks deep inside her. "How exactly do you treat a hostile suspect?"

"With any means available."

"Show me." Gray pressed the pad of his fingers to the upper lining of her tender wall, stroked, begged her to come hither. Her nails clawed, her breasts bounced heavily with the rocking of her body, her nipples brushing the wallpaper.

Pressing upward with constant pressure inside her, Gray rolled her nubbin between his thumb and forefinger, squeezed. "Think you're tough enough to take it?"

She bit the inside of her arm to keep from screaming out as the point of climax climbed higher.

"Answer me, Niccola.

She nodded, resting her head in the crook of her arm.

"Trust me, surrender to me?"

"I can't," she whispered. "Not completely."

He released her nubbin, blood rushed, tingled, throbbed. He slid from her sheath, emptying her of the supple pleasure—a punishment in itself. He snatched her wrist, twisted her arm behind her back, the other, and wrapped the belt around her wrists, binding them together in a loose knot.

Gray pulled Nicci away from the wall and walked her toward the wing-backed chair, sat her down. Took one leg at a time and put them over the armrests with a gentleness defying his intent. The petals of her sultry sex bloomed, fragranced the air with her sweet, honeyed scent.

He kneeled before her, his jutting erection teasing her body into small pulses of invitation to sample her nectar. He gripped the back of the chair on either side of her head, the muscles in his arms wrought iron. "Ready to cooperate?"

"I can't."

He thrust his thick length into her, entering completely and held taut. His eyes penetrated hers as deeply as his manhood her body. "Do you want more?"

"Oh—" *god* "—yes."

He eased out until the tip of him nestled in her valley and then drove back into her. "So do I." She gasped, clenching the muscles in her channel to draw him even deeper.

"Tell me what you want." He withdrew again, this time completely, his erection jutting upward, slick with her dew.

"You."

Guiding his erection to un-hood her nubbin, pumping the slick head against the engorging need, Gray slid his length over it, downward, teased with the tip again. "What do you want, Nicci?"

Heat flooded through her, washing her in sensation like a mighty wave, yet she drowned in need for completion. "I—" Her words caught in her throat as he leaned his head down and flicked a nipple with the tip of his tongue. "I—"

"I can't do anything until you tell me. Cooperate, Niccola." He took her nipple in his mouth, suckled, pulled the pearl with his teeth, circled away the pain with his tongue. "Trust me, surrender . . ."

She fisted her numb hands, wanting to refuse. He was demanding more than her body, drawing out the raw edges of hunger to a breaking point where she was forced to confront everything Gray evoked in her. Every emotion, every desire. So intense, so right. One night to find the completion she denied herself.

Ultimate completion required her to trust, to surrender. To give her body, mind, heart without fear of what pain may come when he left. To give without fear she would become like her mother. "Make love to me, Gray."

Gray brought his mouth to hers, initiated a languid exploration of texture, taste as he worked the knot loose behind her back and untied her hands.

She linked her arms around his neck, wrapped her legs around his hips. "Make love to me," she repeated, as he stood and carried her to the bedroom.

Chapter Nine

The sheets tangled around Nicci's legs when she woke were scented with the musk of sex, a delicious reminder of the night making love to Gray. She stretched her sore muscles from the tips of her toes to her fingers, then grinned like a fool at the slice of sun peeking through the heavy brocade curtains. A perfect morning after, one that could only be made better if Gray hadn't roused her before dawn to say he needed to leave for a few hours.

It wasn't a permanent goodbye, yet.

Slipping from the sheets, Nicci went to the walnut dresser to rummage for a t-shirt to put on, she'd find her clothes later. She pulled the top drawer open, took out a white Hanes, lifted it over her head and slid her arms through. Noticing her hair in the mirror above the dresser, she fingered out the tangles, smoothed some of the wild flyaway.

The top of the dresser was a catastrophe of personal items. *Gray's things.* A bottle of cologne. Shaving kit. Cuff links. A handful of coins scattered. A different watch than his Rolex . . . She picked it up—dark clouds scudded in off Puget sound, blocked out the sun—and Nicci's heart thudded to the floor as she recognized the watch.

She threw on her clothes and fled Gray's hotel suite. She needed to get to her office, shut down the Internet site receiving the digital files from the watch. Maybe, just maybe Vanessa hadn't downloaded . . .

Inside her Jag the sweet, musky scent of sex permeated, a constant slap in the face. How could she have believed Gray, fallen for his lies? Glancing at her reflection in the rearview mirror, to the dark circles dug under her eyes, her swollen lips, her cheeks raw from Gray's morning stubble, hair a tangled mess, she wondered how could that be safe, responsible Niccola Black, who vowed to never trust a man again, to never be seduced, to never—never—never—

It seemed so outer world, a different realm. This couldn't be happening to her.

She parked in front of her office building, leapt out of her car and ran up the steps. Thank god it was Sunday, no one to witness her half crazed dash through the lobby and into the elevator. Her legs were trembling, heart palpitating, her breath labored and yet she swore she could hear the watch, which she'd stuffed into her handbag before leaving the suite, ticking.

The elevator doors dinged open. Nicci rushed down the hallway toward her office, finding the right key on the ring as she went. Looking up, her steps slowed, her office door stood slightly ajar. Approaching cautiously, steps silent, heart beating wildly in her ears, she held her breath and inched the door open . . .

The lights were out, just as she'd left them. Nothing appeared ransacked. But standing before the window in a pink cherry blossom Cheongsam dress—

A rush of dread churned in Nicci's gut, she was too late.

Vanessa turned. The morning sun dulled in the cloudy sky behind her formed a halo, as if accenting Nicci's sin. "Miss Black."

"Vanessa, I—" What could she say? *I spent the night making love to your fiancé . . .*

She closed her eyes. *No*, not love.

Sex. Gray had sex with her, used her and she'd believed the erotic desires were a predecessor to something deeper, something more.

Even as she stood there she couldn't make it *not* feel right, and yet she knew she must be in a space of denial like so many of her clients. Only Nicci had become the woman her clients hired her to find. She'd become someone like her mother.

It seemed impossible. Gray felt right. "I had no idea, Vanessa. If you would have told me his name from the beginning—"

"Oh! But you had already sunk your nails in by then."

"What do you mean?"

"Don't play innocent with me, Miss Black. I saw you, and those women in Gray's suite, corrupting him."

No. Oh, God—

"You are nothing more than a fucking *whore*. Gray was different, until you." Vanessa's face contorted into an ugly, sardonic twist as she lifted her hand and pointed a pistol, taking aim at the center of Nicci's chest.

Nicci stepped backward, her eyes riveted on the barrel. "Oh. God. Vanessa, don't—"

"You took Gray away from me, waylaid his lust like the rest of them."

"Okay, yes, I was there, but it wasn't the way it looked." *Think, think, think*, there had to be a way out of this sudden twist in the nightmare. "You be honest with me. Why this drawn out game?" It worked in the movies, if she could stall Vanessa by getting her to talk, maybe she would be able to gain the upper hand and avoid being shot. "How did you even find me?"

Vanessa reached into her slingbag, tossed a bundle of Private Encounter business cards at Nicci's feet. They scattered like crashed dominos.

When she left the suite Friday morning, her purse had been *on top* of the table—"You searched my purse."

A wobbled smile slid on Vanessa's mouth, her finger tightened on the trigger.

Nicci wondered if Vanessa was gathering the courage to shoot, or just wanting a moment to triumphantly rein fear. She wasn't ready to bet on either just yet.

Since her first meeting with Vanessa she couldn't put her finger on her motivation. And there lie the key—

What exactly was Vanessa's motivation to hunt Nicci down, to go through a pretense of being a client . . . For that matter, what kind of woman would have walked out of a hotel suite, leaving her fiancé with three women . . . A woman engaged to an undercover agent *might* have enough understanding to know that work could put him in such a predicament. Very doubtful.

Nicci knew enough cops to know an undercover agent would never allow his fiancée near him during an investigation, especially one involving a sexual predator like Tan.

Which meant Gray's involvement with Vanessa had formed undercover . . . The traditional Chinese clothing . . . the dragon tattoo . . .

Vanessa was linked to—

Nicci nearly laughed in relief, would have, save the gun still pointed at her. Gray had used Vanessa, she'd been his inside source to the Tan investigation. "Did you really believe Gray would marry one of Tan's concubines?"

Vanessa's face paled to an apathetic ash gray. "How do you know Tan?"

"Gray arrested him two nights ago."

Vanessa's arms grew slack. The gun lowered a mere inch. "Gray," she shook her head slightly, "arrested my father?"

It took Nicci several moments for the revelation to sink in, even though she'd heard rumors of an illegitimate child. Vanessa's black hair and eyes were the only obvious genetic gift from her father, her Caucasian mother's genes clearly dominated to provide the light skin and height.

"You're wrong. Gray is going marry me. I had to stay away for a little while, until he had the money from the deal." The confident woman Vanessa projected herself to be wilted like a jaded flower, almost seemed to be speaking to herself. "Father can't know. He'd never let me leave. I'm the favorite, Father says the men like me best. I sweeten the deals. But Gray is different, he doesn't want me to pleasure him, but I must trust him, obey or he won't take me away."

Vanessa cocked her head to the side, a lost puppy like expression settling on her face, the gun lowered until it dangled by her thigh. "I couldn't tell Gray I came to the hotel, that I saw, that I knew you were a private investigator. He would have been mad at me, he would have left without me."

A light rap sounded at the door. "Hey, Nicci?"

Gray. No! Nicci wanted to shout that Vanessa had a gun, didn't want to remind Vanessa she held it.

"You better be here after what I went through to get your neighbor to tell me where your office is." The door swung open. Vanessa's teary eyes moved to Gray as he entered. "Why did you leave the hotel—Vanessa, what the hell?"

"Hello, Gray."

"Where's Nicci?"

"I'm here," Nicci said. He glanced to where she stood. "Everything is okay." She used the voice she would to a baby fussing. Soft, cajoling . . . "Vanessa is a bit upset. It seems she has the wrong impression about your relationship."

Vanessa's eyes whipped back to Nicci as she raised the gun. "Shut the hell up, Miss Black."

Gray stepped toward Vanessa, his hand outstretched. "Let's go somewhere and talk."

"You love *me*, Gray. Me."

"Vanessa." He took another step toward her. "Give me the gun."

"You're going to take me away."

"Put the gun down. Your father is going away for a very long time. You're safe now. Free."

Vanessa shook her head. "You loved me. Until she came along." Her finger squeezed the trigger. The world dissected into a million slow motion pictures as the bullet blurred toward Nicci.

Gray lunged, snatched Vanessa's wrist and thrust her hand upward, the consecutive bullets meant for Nicci firing into the ceiling as the first slug entered, lifting Nicci off her feet and hurling her against the wall.

Nicci slumped downward to a heap on the floor. Her framed PI license fell, shattered glass spewed. Nicci's eyes shuttered closed.

Chapter Ten

Nicci struggled out of a groggy, drug induced sleep. Lifting her heavily lidded eyes and licking parched lips, she rolled her head to the side and smiled. *Gray.* She thought she'd dreamt him when she woke during the night. "You're here."

He rose from the chair, leaned down and kissed her forehead. "Where else would I be?"

"Back, Quantico?" It hurt to speak but the pain constricting her heart had nothing to do with the bullet wound. It would have been easier if he left without saying goodbye.

"There's another matter I need to take care of."

A glow radiated through her, wiping out the ache of her wound, she would have a little more time with him. "Thought all, loose ends, tied up?"

"In the Tan case, they are. He's going down for a very long time for drug manufacturing, distribution and a whole slew of sexual deviancies. Vanessa has been taken to a facility for abused women and will receive counseling."

"So, why here?"

He smiled, took her hand and kissed the back of it. "I met this intriguing woman, and it seems she has stolen something from me."

Curious now, Nicci tried to inch upward on the pillow. "What, she take?"

Gray cupped the back of Nicci's head, gently lifted her mouth toward his, careful not to hurt her bandaged shoulder. Before his lips met hers, he whispered, "It'll require a full investigation to be absolutely sure, but it seems she's stolen my heart."

About the Author:

Dominique Sinclair, who also writes contemporary and romantic suspense as Jewel Stone, lives in rain-drenched Western Washington State. Her home is nestled in the lush green forest of tall evergreens and ferns, providing her with the beauty of nature surrounding her while she writes full time.

Private Eyes is Dominique's first erotica piece and she can't help but wonder, now that she's walked through the gate of seduction, into the garden of sin where the soil is fertile and the sunshine scorching, if she can ever turn back again . . .

Come visit Dominique in her sensual, seductive, sinful world of erotica romance at: www.dominiquesinclair.com *Or for bold, exotic, seductive romance:* www.authorjewelstone.com.

The Ruination of Lady Jane

※(✿)※

by Bonnie Hamre

To My Reader:

What a pleasure to be in the tenth collection with another Regency-era tale of passion and propriety. The dictionary defines ruination as "destruction achieved by wrecking something," but oh my, how splendidly satisfying when accomplished by an expert in the sensual arts. Enjoy!

Chapter One

The country, 1816

"Lady Jane still has those spots, I gather?" Havyn Attercliffe, the once not-so-Honorable, asked idly. Since his return from India, a mere seven weeks before, he and his elder brother Neville, Lord Grantham, had been renewing their familial relations with some degree of accord. "Are you keeping her hidden until they disappear?"

Seated behind his desk in his library at Grantham Lodge, Grantham shot him a narrow-eyed look. "Why do you ask?"

Havyn settled himself more comfortably in a large leather armchair. "We've discussed the estates, the country's sorry situation, my travels, your neighbors. Why not your ward?"

Grantham nodded.

"What of her, then?"

"Now that she is two and twenty," Grantham replied in his usual stiff manner, "she has removed herself to my town house. She spends much of her time with Lady Howden, who was kind enough to undertake her introduction to Society."

Havyn recalled Lady Jane's unruly dark hair and black eyes, as well as the olive cast to her complexion, an unfortunate disadvantage in a society that lauded fair hair, porcelain skin and blue eyes. Havyn almost felt sorry for the chit. Ugly, spotty, and when last seen, bearing too much flesh on her short, stubby person. "With her appearance, it's no surprise that she gathers dust on the shelf."

Grantham sent him a chiding look. "She has improved since her debut."

"If you say so," Havyn murmured. "How does she occupy herself?"

"The usual pursuits. She assists some benevolent societies."

"Indeed." What else was a spinster of no looks but ample fortune to do but help the less fortunate? "Very charitable of Lady Howden to take her on."

Havyn remembered the stir Justin, Earl of Howden's marriage had caused among the *ton*. The fair lady had conquered the erstwhile rake quite suddenly. Whispered comments had him enslaved by her skills between the bedsheets, but seen in company, the countess was all that was above reproach. He wondered if she was ripe for an affair. If she agreed, he'd be sure to make it a pleasurable experience for them both.

With exquisite discretion, of course. No point in creating gossip when he had important business at hand. He'd come home to ensure his rightful place in Polite Society. He and Grantham had made their peace, and now, having proved his worth, he was eager to blend his life as an English gentleman of means with the knowledge and wealth acquired abroad.

One unexpected but supremely gratifying result of his enforced time beyond the sea was his perfecting of the sensual expertise known as *Kama*. His attention to erotic delectation and fulfillment had brought him and his bed-partners much satisfaction. He thought of one of his particular favorites, *jrimbhitsasana*, recalling the last time he'd had a lover's back bowed over scented pillows while he knelt and fitted her to him. Imbedded deeply in her *yoni*, he'd been able to play with her breasts and belly while he prolonged their sexual congress.

Smiling with the memory of pleasured feminine moans and cries, Havyn twirled the brandy in his glass before lifting it to his nose. He inhaled with pleasure as he considered his brother's unfortunate ward. "There have been no offers for Lady Jane, I collect?"

Grantham eyed Havyn for a moment, as if considering his answer, or weighing Havyn's interest. "On the contrary. There were a number of offers. I rejected them."

"I would have thought you'd have accepted the first and been done with it. And her."

Lord Grantham stiffened his shoulders. "She's always been headstrong but I know my duty." Older than Havyn by a decade, Neville had succeeded to the title when Havyn was at Eton, and felt his responsibilities heavy on his shoulders. He arranged some papers on his desk, as if ordering his thoughts as well. "Her father entrusted her welfare to me. None of the young bucks who presented themselves met with my approval. I can not allow her to go to some disreputable fortune seeker."

"I'd forgotten the size of her estate," Havyn murmured. "That explains her popularity. She comes into her fortune with her marriage?"

"Indeed. Or if not married, in three more years. Her father was quite explicit on the matter. He left meticulous instructions."

Havyn nodded. "No doubt he suspected she'd need it for her spinster years."

"Not necessarily," Grantham responded, with a fleeting expression of satisfaction. "I have recently accepted an offer. Lord Yarwoode."

"Yarwoode?" He searched his memory for details. "That old goat?" Havyn's jaw dropped. "Surely you could do better, even for Lady Jane."

Grantham's lips firmed. "He is settled—"

"Thrice widowed, or is it more by now? And how many children?"

"—In possession of his own estates, and is willing to overlook her temperament."

"In favor of her abundant supply of guineas, no doubt."

"Your sarcasm is misplaced." Grantham looked unsettled. He stood, paced to the window, rocked on his heels, then turned to face his younger brother. "And so is she."

"I beg your pardon?"

"Lady Jane has disappeared." His countenance became more severe. "She is not at any of my establishments, not at Howden House in the country, not at their town house, nor with friends."

"How can she go missing? Isn't she chaperoned?"

"Naturally. She gave everyone the slip on Bond Street. No one has seen her since."

"Since when?"

"Three weeks ago."

"Good God, Neville. You've looked for her?"

"Of course, we have!" Grantham harrumphed. "We've had inquiries made, we've searched everywhere we can think of."

"Who is we?"

"Myself. Howden and Yarwoode, too. All very discretely, naturally."

"You've questioned the household staff?"

"Yes. And the stablehands, and the outside servants. No one has any information."

"Demands for ransom?"

"None."

"No delayed notices in the *Times* of a marriage in Gretna Green? Or by special license?"

"Not hers."

"What has Yarwoode done?"

"Nothing openly. The engagement is not yet announced."

"I see. Worrisome, to say the least." Havyn remembered the persistent little girl dogging his heels, a nuisance with her incessant questions. "Still, one can't help but admire her spirit."

Grantham harrumphed again. "She has that, to be sure. But, if she is not recovered soon, and in good health," by that, Havyn knew he meant unsullied, "Yarwoode might cry off."

"So much the better for the chit."

Grantham gave him an assessing look. "Who else, of good reputation, would have her with her reputation in tatters?"

"Who else is wife-hunting? Desperate?"

"I am troubled." Grantham ignored Havyn's questions as he paced his library. "I don't know how much longer her absence will go unnoticed." He stared out a window, as if searching the grounds for his elusive ward. "Where can she be?"

"Wherever she is, she timed her flit well." Running his fingertips across the smooth old leather of his chair, Havyn considered the situation. "Funds?"

"She has them." Grantham returned to his desk, sat and flipped through a ledger. "Her quarterly allowance had just been paid. She has taken most of it."

"How far can she go?" Havyn considered. "She's bound to fritter it away and be obliged to return, bonnet in hand, begging forgiveness."

"I doubt that," Grantham's voice was dry. "She has always been determined and frugal. No doubt she squirreled some away."

"In expectation that she would flee?"

"More likely for her pet charities, but who knows how women think?"

Havyn allowed himself a small smile. In Polite Society, women were restricted to inane remarks. In private, to his great pleasure, women were treasure troves of information. At least, so he had found them on his travels. No doubt English misses were still ignorant of intelligent conversation. He wondered if Lady Jane had absorbed any of the education Grantham had provided. Knowing his brother, it would have been excellent. "When did you accept Yarwoode's offer?"

"A month or so ago."

"And she's been gone almost as long. That didn't leave her much time to make arrangements." Havyn felt a flicker of admiration for a woman who could make and carry out a plan on short notice. Her actions showed a quickness of mind and determination, two traits he respected. "It's clear she doesn't want to marry Yarwoode."

"So she wrote."

"You haven't spoken with her?"

Grantham set his lips. "No. I refused her an audience."

"Why?"

"I can't bear feminine wiles or tears."

"I don't remember her as a watering-pot." Havyn concentrated, trying to recall if he had ever seen Lady Jane cry. For all she had nipped his heels like an unshakeable terrier, he'd never seen her shed a tear. "When did she write? Before or after she ran away?"

"Several days before." Grantham had the grace to look discomposed. "I see now I should have spoken with her, but then I thought she was merely indulging in a pique and could be brought round."

"You were wrong."

Grantham's brows grew together in a dark frown. Once that look was enough to make Havyn uneasy. He remembered the last occasion when he had been the recipient of his brother's frowns.

Six years ago, Havyn had been standing stiffly in front of the large mahogany desk. He'd kept his working eye focused on the painting above his displeased brother's head, but that hadn't helped. The disappointed look on his father's portrait had made him feel dismally at fault.

His other eye had been swollen shut. Blooded, bruised and in disgrace, he'd been sent down from Oxford. Whoring, gambling and excessive drinking were the usual reasons for dismissal, but in his case, some foreign prince's whelp had accused him of cheating at cards. He'd done no such thing, of course, but had no proof. When he brought counter charges against the young lordling, thugs had beset him. He'd fought back but had been badly beaten. His tutors and the powers behind the famed college walls had refused to believe his protestations of innocence. If he'd started in the petticoat line, a practiced much disapproved of at Oxford, then it must follow that he'd be equally depraved at the card table. And so he had found himself at twenty, standing unsteadily before his elder brother, accused and disbelieving.

"Havyn, you are in grave danger," Grantham had stated.

"What?" he'd scoffed. "It's a damned hum."

"False accusation or not, your safety is at stake."

"I didn't cheat, Neville."

Grantham sighed. "I believe you. Still, you didn't help the situation by losing your temper and provoking fisticuffs."

"I planted more than one facer, you know." His mouth hurt to speak, but he kept himself upright by force of his will.

Grantham eyed his injuries. "Perhaps the outcome would have been different if it had been a fair fight."

"I'll see him at dawn. Without those ruffians backing him up, he won't be so ready to sport his canvas."

Grantham stood and came around the desk. "It's not a matter of an appointment at dawn. You'll get a bullet or a knife in the back when you least expect it."

Havyn forced his one working eye to focus. "You're trying to scare me off."

"I'm trying to keep you alive, fool." He placed his arm around Havyn's shoulders and eased him into a chair. "You'll leave first thing tomorrow. I'll notify you when to return."

Havyn attempted to hide the pain of his broken ribs. "I'm not going anywhere until that toady retracts his accusation."

Grantham seated himself behind his desk, his expression weary. "Consider this your Grand Tour."

"Everyone will think I've debunked. That I *am* a damned card shark."

"Let people think as they will. It will be forgotten with the next scandal."

"Then why should I be sent abroad? I could purchase a commission, instead."

Grantham had been implacable. "I prefer you alive, Havyn."

Havyn had resisted further, but Grantham had him out of the country, with a generous bank draft, the next day. Most young gentlemen of the *ton* took their year-long Grand Tour to broaden their views with experiences abroad, but he'd considered his journey another expulsion. Exile.

With Napoleon making himself busy on the continent, Havyn

had reluctantly gone farther afield. He'd begun his tour in Greece, exploring the ruins, gone on to Turkey, avoiding the border squabbles with Greece, and then made his way slowly overland through Persia and the Ganges plains.

In India, he'd been charmed, intrigued, at times repulsed, and ultimately converted to much of the Indian beliefs. Rather than continuing immediately on to the Orient, he'd traveled leisurely about that vast continent, absorbing the knowledge and the culture. Ignoring Grantham's summons to return after his accuser had been discovered cheating at cards, confessed other instances and retracted his accusations against him, Havyn had preferred to delay his return.

He didn't want to go haring home with his tail between his legs, or as the hot-headed youth he'd been, but as a man of worth and respect in his own right. Thus, he'd immersed himself, consulting the sages and ultimately taking for his own some of the tenets that now shaped his life. Eventually, when Grantham's demands that he return home became more frequent and imperative, he'd made his way to China and thence to England by sea. He'd spent his time since his return re-acquainting himself with his brother and considering how best to implement his goals.

Now, Havyn turned his mind to Lady's Jane's flight. How could a young woman, raised almost in isolation, elude her companions and disappear from sight? Who had helped her escape? Or, more likely, and far more dangerous to her person, had someone whisked her away from her companions? To what purpose? And was she still alive? If alive, still innocent?

Havyn felt his blood run cold. "What did she write?" He'd seen young girls sold into slavery. True, Lady Jane was no young girl, but a full-grown woman. Still, the prospect made him fear for her. "Did she give you any idea of her intent?"

"None at all." Grantham drew a note from the desk drawer and read it. "She states that she has no desire to marry Yarwoode, no wish to raise his minor children or subject herself to his attentions. She is quite vehement on that point."

"I don't blame her. He must be above twice her age." Havyn shook off his concern for her. By the sound of her note, Lady Jane was quite capable of minding her own best interests. The thought of bedding Yarwoode would send any sensible woman fleeing in the opposite direction. "But how does she know about a man's attentions?"

"How do I know?" Grantham replied testily. "Maybe she

learned something from Lady Howden. How does any woman learn anything?"

Havyn shrugged. In his experience, women learned much from each other, and more from their lovers. Quite often, they taught their partners a thing or two. In fact, he himself had learned many of the sensual arts from women. "You don't know much about the fair sex."

"Nor do I care to."

"No wonder you are still unmarried."

"Don't sneer." Grantham made a quelling noise. "That means you are still my heir."

Havyn shrugged. "No doubt when the time comes, you will have done your duty to posterity."

"No doubt."

A moment or two passed, with Havyn imagining Neville engaged in the dutiful act of procreation. He visualized a faceless woman in a voluminous, modest nightgown and Neville in and out as fast as possible without a thought of mutual pleasures. He wondered if Neville would accept a suggestion or two, possibly the congress of the cow? He took another sip of brandy, relishing the aroma as he imagined his brother on his knees pumping into his wife from behind. No, likely not. "So what are you going to do about Lady Jane?"

In turn, Grantham studied his younger brother. Havyn had once squirmed under that cold, assessing glare, but now he returned it without a qualm. The years abroad had strengthened his character as much as the harsh Indian sun had bronzed his once pale flesh and bleached some of the brown from his hair, leaving it streaked with lighter shades. Squinting into the bright light had left creases around his eyes, now a more startling blue in his sun-browned face.

His London tailor had tut-tutted at his clothing. In addition to being out of style, it was also outgrown in the chest, shoulders and thighs, and loose in the waist. Years of labor, of climbing peaks and riding hard had created a solid physique, which his tailor had delighted in displaying without need of padding. With his new, fashionable wardrobe and his thick hair shaped by his valet into the latest style, Havyn was poised to make his return into London society.

When Grantham broke the stare, Havyn glanced around the room, again pleased with the proportions, the tall bookshelves lining the walls, and the windows open to the grounds. The sound of gardeners scything the expansive lawns was as pleasing as the scent of freshly mown grass floating in with a soft, summer breeze. He had missed this on his travels.

He rose, giving the globe on its stand a whirl as he passed, seeing the countries he'd explored roll under his hand, and strolled around the room. He glanced up at family portraits, at framed maps of the world, and at the set of paintings he'd sent home from India. Pleased that Grantham had had them hung, he studied their bright colors. The costumes and poses were totally foreign to the darker tones of the library. Just as he'd been drawn to that exotic life, he found himself drawn again to the brilliant gold and orange hues glowing against the paneled walls.

The man and woman portrayed reclining on plump pillows, garbed in rich silken robes and adorned with jewelry, were not discussing the next day's menus. Rather, they contemplated their coming sexual union, and no doubt the man reflected on which of the many positions he would employ. The woman's smile promised him great enjoyment. Havyn remembered mastering the common positions, and then the advanced ones requiring flexibility and stamina. His groin tightened pleasurably in memory of those more erotic and gratifying sensations.

"Havyn."

He turned to face his brother who now smiled, making Havyn wary. He knew that expression. Grantham had some plot afoot.

"Have you plans for the immediate future?"

"Not exactly," he answered cautiously. "I thought I'd examine a few country properties, and perhaps a place in town in preparation for the winter season."

"No engagements?"

"None at all." Havyn waited. After a moment, he added, "Thus I am quite at your disposal."

"Excellent." Grantham smiled again, a tight little smile that did nothing to alleviate the severity of his countenance. "You will find Jane. Track her down and return her to her proper place."

"I?" Havyn blinked in surprise. He was ready and willing to undertake any task for his brother, and by extension, for his ward, but this?

"You. I have plans for the chit, and I will see them in place."

"What plans?"

Grantham frowned at Havyn's question. He took a moment to respond. "I intend to announce her engagement to Yarwoode at my annual summer house party." He gave Havyn a level look. "It wouldn't do for the bride-to-be to be missing."

"Indeed, but you expect too much of me. I know nothing of her habits, her customary pursuits," Havyn stated. "I've been gone too long."

Grantham nodded. "Precisely. You won't be hampered by misconceptions. You have the time and no one will suspect what you are about."

"I wouldn't know where to begin."

"Did you not stalk a leopard until you found his lair and killed him?"

Havyn conceded the point. "But Jane is not a leopard. She's a lady, bound about with restrictions." He had been thinking of her as some bothersome lap dog, not as a sleek jungle cat.

"That is true. Yet, from your own accounts, you loosened your strictures, learned to live among the natives and adopted their habits. You learned to hunt. Use that knowledge now to hunt her down."

"She's not a wild beast!"

Neville, Lord Grantham, waved away his protests. "She has gone to ground. Find her."

Chapter Two

She no longer had spots.

Havyn strolled past the fishermen who mended their nets on the quay at Whitby, a small Yorkshire fishing and shipbuilding port, and studied her with satisfaction. He'd have her back to Grantham Lodge soon enough to quell any speculation of her disappearance.

Lady Jane wore a simple high-necked gown of blue serge covered with an ample white apron. An unfashionable gray bonnet tied with a loose bow under her chin covered her hair. A steady breeze, smelling of salt and fish, rumpled a row of ruffles on the bonnet and drew attention from her face, but Havyn was not so beguiled.

She might have put away her fine clothing and donned the garb of a villager just as a leopard learned to live undetected among humans, but Havyn was not fooled. He had been looking for a short, stout miss with a blemished complexion. That's how he had described her to the shops and establishments on Bond Street and the smaller surrounding streets. No one had recognized her by that description, claiming forgetfulness after so many weeks. When he offered a coin and described a young lady of good dress and manner, he had much better luck.

He had traced her to Holborn Street, where she had taken all the inside seats for the stagecoach bound for Edinburgh. He'd questioned that, wondering who had made the purchase for her, but it made sense. Having the interior of the coach to herself saved her from unpleasant remarks, censure and the attentions of the two male passengers who rode outside. She was quite alone, but that didn't mean she hadn't been forced in some manner.

It surprised him to learn that she had a fair amount of baggage stowed in the boot. This was no impulsive, spur of the moment flight, but one organized and assisted. She had to have had aid in removing her trunks and portmanteaus from his brother's town house, but none of the servants would admit to any knowledge of her departure. That was to be expected, for if any admitted to helping Lady Jane, it would mean instant dismissal, perhaps even a charge before the magistrate.

Taking the chance that this unidentified woman was his quarry, he made his own travel arrangements. Choosing to track her as she had traveled, and foregoing the services of servants who might broadcast his search, Havyn rejected Grantham's loan of his travelling coach and followed her route by stage. He had inquired after her along the way at inns and overnight stops. It hadn't been easy, not after some weeks, but enough people along the way had remembered a young woman traveling alone in a public conveyance to point him along her route.

With the passing of each day, he realized he'd been hasty in predicting she'd soon return home begging forgiveness. An admiration for her cleverness and determination grew together with his concern for her well being, particularly when he'd lost her by description in York. He'd spent a few bad moments until someone recalled a young lady who had left the stage and taken a slower conveyance to the coast garbed not in fine clothes, but in servant's dress.

He'd found her by happenstance this morning as he'd roamed the waterfront, intrigued by the calls and speech of the Yorkshire fishermen. He took a moment to readjust his conceptions of her. Lady Jane was still short in stature. Her complexion, though still darker than was fashionable, had undertones of rose and her cheeks were smooth and unblemished. Her face was round, with a dimple in her right cheek that flashed as she spoke, and a seductive look to her full lips.

He enjoyed the sight of her while an unbidden curiosity about her person crept into his thoughts. He tried to brush them away, but they refused to be discarded.

She still had too much flesh on her bones, but it was arranged attractively in a generous bosom and hips. That generosity made her waist seem smaller, definitely hand-spanable. Her lush, womanly figure reminded him of the *houris* who had entertained him in India. Blood shot to his head, then to his groin.

A man would have to be insensate not to be enthralled by the sensual, voluptuous look to her. He licked his lips. He was no callow youth to be thunderstruck by an attractive, seductive woman, but somehow, the transformation from the ugly duckling he remembered to dark swan stunned him just the same. He repressed a laugh. Not a yapping dog, nor a jungle predator, but a luscious bird of exquisite plumage.

No wonder she'd had so many offers. Grantham had mentioned rejecting her potential suitors, but hadn't specified the number. Men must have flocked about her, competing for her favors. With her looks and her fortune, it was a wonder she hadn't been married long before this. Yarwoode was damned lucky.

Unless, of course, that alluring exterior concealed an unpleasant disposition. He remembered her childish single-minded attachment to him, one he'd carelessly brushed away. Grantham had mentioned her willful temperament, but had she become a veritable virago? Had his brother concealed the truth about her? What else had he not revealed?

One thing was certain. He'd said not a word about his ward's allure. Why had Grantham not mentioned she'd become a beauty? True, she didn't fit the *ton's* predilection for milkwater misses, but she had fire and spirit. He liked that in a woman.

She'd proved her mettle by giving her chaperones the slip and traveling halfway across England. He couldn't recall any proper miss exhibiting such enterprise or daring, and couldn't restrain his growing admiration of Lady Jane. Admiration be damned. He blew out a frustrated breath. He had anticipated temper and perhaps a plea for help. He had considered suitable responses to withstand these, but he had not anticipated a struggle with his own sensual nature.

It could not interfere with his charge. No matter his approbation and sudden, startling lust, he still had to return her, untouched, to Grantham.

Havyn watched her for a few moments more. He couldn't tell much about her hair, covered as it was by that ugly garment, but her dark eyes sparkled in the morning sun and her wide smile displayed even, white teeth as she haggled over fish.

He had to smile. Quite a picture Lady Jane Ponsonby-Maitland made, one that would cause titters among Polite Society. She was with an older woman, dressed much as she was, but creased and red of face. He dimly remembered the older woman from his nursery days.

Lady Jane appeared to be enjoying the bargaining. Several of the fishermen smiled at her and called out encouragement. When the older woman sealed the transaction, Lady Jane broke into laughter and fished in her reticule for coins to pay for their purchase. Turning back to town, she took the older woman's arm.

They came his way, looking for all the world like two villagers headed home to cook their fish. He stepped into their path, swept off his fawn beaver top hat and bowed. "A good day for marketing, is it not, Lady Jane?"

She stopped short. She paled, her mouth opening though no sound came out. Her fingers clenched on her companion's arm. She took a step back, then another, and would have turned to run had her companion not grabbed her hand and stilled her flight.

"Easy, Lady Jane, easy," he soothed, as he would have calmed a fractious beast. "I mean you no harm."

"How did you find me?" she panted, as though she'd run a long way.

And she had. She'd run a long way from London to this tiny village, a long way from her position in Polite Society to this . . . whatever she was masquerading as.

"I am sent to find you by my brother, your guardian. Lord Grantham."

"Attercliffe?" She narrowed her eyes at him. "Is it truly you?"

"Indeed." He gave her another bow. "Havyn Attercliffe."

"Quite so. Ridiculous name."

"But mine." He grinned. "We all have our burdens to bear."

"I collect all too well."

As she should, with the consequences of her unseemly flight looming before her. "Are you well? Has anyone harmed you?" He scanned the men on the quay, looking for danger. "Were you forced to come here? Or stay against your will?"

Surprise flitted across her features. "I am quite well. I am here because I wish to be."

Havyn felt his muscles ease. "I am relieved to find you unharmed. Grantham was quite concerned on that score."

"You may relieve his mind as well. I am here of my own accord."

"He will wish to hear that from you in person." He waited for her to say something. She did not. "How long will it take you to make ready to leave?"

Color rushed to her cheeks. "You may leave as soon as you wish."

He glanced around them, saw they'd attracted the attention of fishermen and villagers alike. Several had moved nearer to hear better.

He gestured her away from the growing group of onlookers. "Very clever of you to choose a fishing village for your hideaway, but you are wanted at Grantham Lodge."

She didn't budge. "I am staying here," she stated, her voice sharp.

"Then we have a problem, don't we?" He smiled, keeping both his manner and his tone pleasant though her stubbornness irked him. "You won't go and I can't allow you to remain."

Her companion said something to her in a dialect so broad he could barely take her meaning. Jane shook her head, then at a repeated whisper, scowled, then shrugged her shoulders.

"Oh, very well." She glared at the gathering crowd, then at Havyn. "We can't talk here. Come to the cottage."

He offered her his arm, which she refused by stalking ahead, tugging the older woman behind her. He was left to follow, an insult he didn't mind very much as it afforded him the chance to watch her posterior under her skirts. It swayed most attractively, making him wonder about the flesh underneath the blue serge. Instead of the mincing steps affected by young ladies, she walked with a natural stride that set her skirts swinging and gave him a view of nicely turned ankles. He grinned. She might have donned rough, workaday clothing as a disguise, but she hadn't given up her stockings. They shimmered when the breeze lifted her hem, and he found himself wondering if her skin would be as silken as her hose.

He trailed behind the two women as they made their way through the streets, past a ropery, building yards, taverns, fine houses built by prosperous shipowners, and then along narrow streets with smaller red-roofed houses until they came to a cottage along the river Esk. He paused, taking in the surroundings. The river flowed past curving banks, where cliffs rose on either side with more of the town perched atop the rise. All in all, a very pleasant view. The older woman held open a gate for him, while Lady Jane strode past to open the cottage door.

He entered, removing his hat and bending his head to avoid a painful knock on the low frame. Blinking to adjust his sight in the darker interior, he noticed a table and chairs set before a low fire.

The rough walls were whitewashed and an old, serviceable carpet covered a portion of the stone floor. A cupboard, dishes, pots and pans marked the cooking area of the spotlessly clean room, and through a half-open door, he spotted a low bed draped with a coverlet.

"Sit, sir," the older woman said, gesturing to a ladder-back chair at the deal table.

He did as she bid, studying her face all the while. "I know you, don't I?"

Her face broke into smiles. "And here I was wondering if you'd remember old Anna from the kitchens at the Lodge."

"Anna, of course! You used to bring up the nursery trays."

"Aye, sir, that I did."

"Always with an extra treat, if I recall."

She nodded. "You liked your biscuits, you did."

"Do you make them now for Lady Jane?"

"She won't have them. Appetite's gone right off, it has." Her smile drooped. "Shame it is, making a young lady marry against her will. Many a night I've held her while she cried."

He glanced at Jane, who looked mortified by this revelation. "Recently?"

"Nay, the weeks she's been here she's kept her misery to herself. It was while she was no more than a babe, orphaned with no one to love her or care that she had dreadful nightmares."

"Hush, Anna," Lady Jane implored.

Havyn eased back against the wooden chair and studied Lady Jane's expression, picturing her weeping in the comfort of Anna's arms. He'd never have guessed it, but then, he was learning more about her by the moment. "How did you manage your way here? No, let me rephrase that. I know how you managed, for I followed you every step of the way. You showed determination and originality."

She shrugged, but he could see his remarks pleased her.

"You had help?" Again, he surmised the answer, but waited for her explanations.

She glanced at Anna, then away. She toyed with the bow at her throat, then slowly untied it and removed her bonnet. He saw now that her once unruly hair was contained in a neat bun at the nape of her neck, with only a few tendrils coming loose to curl around her ears. It was an effort to keep his hands to himself, when he was tempted to tuck a curl away and feel the soft swell of her earlobe.

"Who helped you, Lady Jane?"

"I won't tell you, for I wish them no trouble."

Anna stooped to place a kettle on the fire. She rose, dusting her hands. "I bain't afraid to say I helped her."

"That is obvious, Anna, but who else? Who packed her trunks and saw them to the stagecoach? Who bought the tickets?" When the old woman said nothing, he turned to Jane, frustration in his voice. "Surely you didn't do that by yourself?"

"No." She took three cups from the cupboard and placed them on the table. Sugar and milk followed, then when the kettle boiled, she made and served tea. In silence.

Havyn watched her pour tea as though she graced a drawing room. Her actions were elegant and calm, a decided contrast to her ungracious manner. He lifted the cup to his lips. Strange, how good it tasted in these rustic surroundings. Not a biscuit or a cucumber sandwich in sight, but Anna cut him a slice of dark bread both moist and delicious.

He finished his tea and bread. "Thank you, Anna." He rose from the table and looked about him. "Is there a place where we can talk?" he asked Jane. "Privately?"

"I have nothing to hide from Anna."

"Perhaps not, but I would prefer to speak to you alone."

She glanced away from him, her mouth set. "I prefer not to speak to you at all."

"Am I such an ogre, then?"

She turned back. Something flickered in her eyes, gone too quickly for him to identify. Lady Jane looked to Anna who nodded encouragingly. Shrugging, she gestured to the door. "We can walk a short way onto the moor."

"Very well." He held the door for her while she donned her homely bonnet. The scent of old roses in the cottage garden wafted in, reminding him of the extensive rose gardens at Grantham Lodge, but for some reason, this fragrance was more immediate, headier. He inhaled deeply.

He held out his arm, and this time she took it. Her head came only to his shoulder, the bonnet rim concealing her face. Her hand on his arm was warm and steady. She wore no gloves in keeping with her workaday costume and he felt her touch as though there were no fabric between her fingers and his flesh. He glanced down at her slim hand resting on his blue superfine sleeve and wondered if it would be as assured if their skin was not separated by layers of clothing. He smiled at the thought of stroking her skin as he led her onto the dusty lane. "Which direction?"

She turned them away from Whitby. They walked in silence past some cottages until they were clear of habitations. Havyn pondered several approaches to make her see reason and return where she belonged. Her refusal was unladylike, defiant, yet he couldn't pick her up, toss her over his shoulder, and hold her, by force if necessary, on the long journey back to town.

He sighed. Neville had given him some indication of her stubbornness, but he should have figured it out for himself. She had been tenacious as a child, a trait that clearly persisted into her womanhood. It took willpower and determination to plan and execute a successful escape. He respected those traits, and found his reluctant admiration growing ever stronger. Still, he couldn't let his esteem, or his lust for her person, prevent him from carrying out his task. How was he to overcome her obstinacy and persuade her to return her to Grantham?

Damn Grantham for placing him in this position!

Beyond the trees, he saw the face of the cliffs from which the moors stretched inland, a vast, open space that had seemed interminable on his journey here. She led the way over a low rock wall and began to climb a steep path. "I like the view from the top."

He moved to her side, and took her elbow to assist her up the incline. "You seem to have found your way about remarkably well."

She shook off his hand. "Anna often told me of her home and I walk here almost daily."

"You came to Anna seeking refuge."

She nodded.

"But now you are discovered. Now you must return."

"I am happy here."

He sighed. He knew what it was like to leave a dwelling of contentment, and he wished it might be otherwise, but she had no choice. "This is foolish, Lady Jane. You must return to your rightful home."

"Never." Her voice was firm, absolutely resolute.

"You are used to much better."

She continued upward. She had a limber grace to her movement, climbing easily where others might trudge and pant. He wondered if she wasn't going to answer him, but at last, she slowed her pace. "Better, perhaps, but none more welcoming. I know I am wanted here."

"You are wanted at home."

"Home?" She turned to face him, scorn on her face. "I may be 'wanted', but not for myself, merely as a pawn in the marriage mart."

He had no answer to that. She was absolutely correct, but that was the way of their world. "Many people make the best of things, find happiness in honoring their duty."

She gave him a decided snort in response. "I have already found that to be untrue. Grantham is the most unhappy man I know."

He was astounded by her insight. Neville did bury himself in his duties. He couldn't remember the last time he'd seen his brother smile.

However, allowing himself to be distracted from the discussion at hand did no good. He tried another approach. "You'd rather live with a servant than have your own servants waiting upon your comfort?"

She frowned. "The servants have treated me with kindness. That is the greatest comfort. Others," and Havyn knew she meant his family as well as the *ton*, "have not been sympathetic."

"I am sorry to hear that," he said with genuine compassion. He remembered with regret his own neglect and unkindness toward the child she had been. He should have been more understanding and generous to a lonely waif. She'd been orphaned, sent to live with a man who had little time for her. He hadn't helped by shaking off her company as often as possible.

Add to that her unprepossessing appearance as a child and her temperament, she must have gathered early on that she had only herself for company. She might even have formed a dislike for herself, and certainly a distrust of Grantham. And himself? He should have exerted himself in her company. Still, those times were past and could not be undone.

For all she might not know it, he and Lady Jane shared a situation. They must both put aside their pasts and look ahead to the future. While his represented the realization of goals and dreams, hers was not as pleasant, yet neither of them had any choice. Her future had already been decided.

He regretted being the one to deliver her to it, but once he'd accepted Grantham's request, he was bound to see it done. "I must take you back."

"I will not go."

It was his turn to frown. He wasn't used to being contradicted. She made him uncomfortable, even angry, something she appeared not to notice as she continued climbing, leading him up to a broad cliff overlooking the North Sea.

A wind from the water blew steadily, billowing her skirts about her as she held on to her bonnet but did not slow her pace. At times, the wind pressed her garments to her body, and he took careful note of the ample swell of her bosom and the curves of her waist and hips. Her legs seemed straight and strong, and he already knew she had sweetly turned ankles. No doubt her calves were as pleasing.

He followed her lead, his thoughts exploring her intimately. He wasn't pleased with her and he couldn't enjoy her physically, but that didn't stop his thoughts. His *lingam* swelled uncomfortably in his tight buckskin trousers. The loose robes he had grown accustomed to wearing had concealed an engorged state, and not for the first time, he wished he were back in India.

Setting his mind to his present task, he clasped his hat to his head as they approached the sheared off walls of a large church.

She slowed and pointed across a wide swathe of green. "Those are the ruins of St. Hilda's abbey. The clerics who lived here must have faced difficulties and succeeded." She turned to face him. "So shall I."

He bit back an impatient retort as he tried to find the words to persuade her to return willingly. He studied the broken spires, the roofless walls, gathering calm. "Shall we approach?"

"Yes." She led the way again, taking him into the shadow of the walls. The wind dropped, allowing them to lower their voices.

She sat on a low cropping of stone that had fallen long before from the ruined walls. He sank down into the grasses beside her. "Do you come here often?"

"When I wish to think."

"It does seem to be an ideal spot for reflection. I wonder if you have given any thought to your situation."

She turned away, very obviously ignoring him.

"Why don't you face me? Here I am, willing to help if you'll let me—"

"Help? Hah," she scoffed, but she did turn around. "My guardian sent you to fetch me home like a lost parcel." She lifted her chin. "I refuse to be fetched."

"You may refuse, Lady Jane." He didn't bother to hide his annoyance. "But it will do you no good. You will return to Grantham Lodge with me. My brother expects you at his house party to announce your engagement to Lord Yarwoode and there you will be."

"I will not."

"Cease your protests, Lady Jane. Neither of us has any alternative."

"You have no choice? You?" She whirled to face him. "Are you dependent on your brother for funds that you must do his bidding?"

He restrained his temper at the insult. "I am my own man. With my own fortune and responsibilities."

"Yet here you are, demanding I return with you. What have you to gain from this errand? Has Yarwoode spoken to you, secured your support?"

He spoke through gritted teeth. "I am acting on Lord Grantham's behalf. I have nothing to do with Yarwoode."

"Yet you expect me to marry him," she snapped.

"I don't care whom you marry, Lady Jane," he retorted. "All I have contracted to do is see to your safe return."

"And I wish nothing to do with you, Lord Grantham or Yarwoode. He's a swine!"

"Quite so." It was difficult to argue with her when she held so many points in her hand. She was obstinate, yet he couldn't help respecting her.

Nor thinking about her naked.

Her clothing attempted to disguise her natural shape, but he was positive it would be lush and womanly. Exactly as he liked a woman to be. He didn't care for this situation one bit. It distracted him from his duty and created a discomfort in his belly. To be attracted to her, understand her revulsion, be sympathetic to her plight and yet have to take her back and hand her over to another. He sighed and leaned back, looking up into the cloudless sky, studying the strength of the broken walls, the jagged edges dark in contrast to the clear blue of the heavens. What was he to do?

After a moment, he dropped his gaze to her.

Like the ruins of the abbey, her profile belied any softness. She had a straight little nose, a firm chin and a broad forehead. Dark curls escaped her bonnet to fling themselves against her temples. She seemed very much at home on the moor and oddly appealing. Innocent and yet earthy, a combination hard to resist. She seemed unaware of her allure, ignorant of the physical reaction she caused in him. It seemed a pity all her charms should go to another man. Yarwoode, of all people! He couldn't fault her reasons for running away. Yet . . .

"There is something you must consider, Lady Jane." He softened his voice. "You must preserve your good name. Grantham and Yarwoode are concerned for you. Even Lord Howden has made careful inquiries into your whereabouts. My brother has kept this quiet, but even he cannot protect your reputation once you are found out. Everyone must soon know that you have gone missing. You must return before your reputation suffers."

"Who cares about that? No one! All they care about is my wealth, how much I'll bring the man who can stomach the idea of marrying me!"

He flinched. She spoke the truth as she knew it, but why did she think she suffered from ill looks? Had no one ever told her she was ravishing? Or that Grantham had refused a number of offers for her? He debated contradicting her, then said, instead, "Yarwoode seems to have no trouble in that regard."

She muttered something under her breath, something quite unladylike and extremely rude. "Don't you understand?" Her voice rose. "The very thought of Lord Yarwoode makes my stomach churn! I can't bear to be in the same room with him. How am I to bear him in the bedroom?"

He took a step back, shocked by her awareness of what would happen once Yarwoode laid claim to her.

He was appalled at the burning jealousy he felt at the image of Yarwoode's hands on her. Not just his hands, but his mouth, and rot the bastard, his rod.

No. That was not going to happen. Yarwoode would not lay a finger on her.

"Very well. I accept that you have no wish to marry Yarwoode. Now you must make Grantham understand your aversion. Only he can put an end to your engagement."

She scowled. "I have already informed him."

"He mentioned your note."

"Before that. I spoke with him when Yarwoode began courting me." Her scowl deepened. "He brushed me aside as if I were no more bothersome than a buzzing fly."

"Why wouldn't he listen to you?"

"I cannot say." She yanked a flower out of the ground by its roots. "One would think that a woman my age is quite enough advanced in years to know her own mind, but no, Grantham quotes my father's instructions and I must comply!" She all but spat the last word. "This is all Grantham's fault!"

Havyn wondered about that. Perhaps Grantham could have been more understanding, less autocratic. Why did he insist on Yarwoode when surely there must be other men, honorable men, who would appreciate and care for Lady Jane? Surely one of them could be brought to snuff. He sprawled in the wild grasses and studied the changing sky as he let his mind consider the situation.

"If you must marry, must it be Yarwoode? Would not another fiancé do as well?"

"Who? Every other offer has been refused out of hand."

So she knew. "Rakes and fortune-hunters as Grantham described them."

She shrugged.

"Perhaps you would allow me to speak to my brother on your behalf. Once he understands your disgust of Yarwoode, he will—"

"I am pained to tell you that you are quite wrong. He knew that before he accepted this offer. Why should he change his mind now?"

Havyn remembered his own conversation with Grantham on that matter. His brother had seemed quite unconcerned with Yarwoode's age, his offspring, or even his reputation. He could and should have done better for his ward. "Still, there is no harm in trying, is there?"

She blew out a breath. "You must know Grantham never reverses his decisions."

Havyn recalled his brother's refusal to allow him to stay in England. There had been no persuading him then, either. "You have a point," he conceded. "But surely you wish to marry?"

She narrowed her eyes at him. "Another old man? An impoverished rake who needs my fortune?" she scoffed. "I think not. If I ever marry, it will be to a man I choose."

"Is there someone you wish to marry? Perhaps formed a *tendre* for?"

She adjusted her apron at her waist and smoothed the folds over her lap. "No one who would have me." She sounded wistful, almost sad.

"Ah, so there is someone you care about."

"No." She flicked a glance at him, then busied herself pulling up another wildflower. "I love no one." She shredded the stem.

Havyn searched his mind for another argument. "You have responsibilities. Those of your position," he reminded her gently. "You cannot ignore those."

"Can I not?" she cried. "I was a responsibility to your brother and he ignored me."

He sat up to make his point. "He housed you, clothed you, educated you."

"True. And how often did he speak with me? Inquire about my well-being? Did he ask if I was content in his care?"

Grantham had answered those questions himself by his attitude toward her. Havyn wasn't sure of the particulars of how she had come to be Grantham's ward. He himself, as a boy, had not been welcoming, but to his credit Grantham had accepted the responsibility.

"For that matter," she continued in a rush, "did you even acknowledge my existence?"

"How could I not? You followed me everywhere." Yet once he had gone away to school, he had ignored the little orphan left in the nursery. He hadn't even answered her carefully penned letters, something he regretted now. On the occasions when he had been at Grantham Lodge, he had avoided her assiduously. After his expulsion, he had never thought of the child, alone and isolated, in the old schoolroom. She must have been very lonely.

He glanced at her. She was a child no longer, and if Grantham hadn't sent him after her, he'd still be ignorant of the changes in her. And untroubled by his responses to her. Damn her for being such an enticement. Since he'd seen her laughing on the quay this morning, she had slipped past his guard with her supple and tantalizing body. He understood the physical appeal, an age-old primitive male response to a sensual female, but it was more than that. He enjoyed the challenge of her disposition, at once rebellious and sensitive. He sensed there were deeper facets to her nature and found himself eager to discover them.

In short, he liked her. And liking her, caring for her well-being, he wanted more for her. She deserved better than Yarwoode. She deserved a man who would see her as a treasure, a woman to be cosseted and adored all the days of her life.

"I beg your pardon." He stood and made her a bow. "I was unkind to you."

She wasn't mollified. "It can make no difference now." She stood, shook out her skirts, and with her long stride, began walking toward the cliff's edge.

He followed her. "Lady Jane." When she looked over her shoulder, he continued, "Think of children. Surely you can love any children you have, no matter who sires them," he suggested, but she would hear none of it.

"I refuse to bring children into this world unless they have both a mother and father to care for them. My children must know they are loved and wanted." Her lip trembled. "They must have security."

Ah, of course she would think that. Most parents happily consigned their progeny to the care of nannies and tutors or governesses while they went about the business of amusing themselves with whatever took their fancy. Yet, with Lady Jane's childhood a lonely, sorry one, of course she wanted better for any child of her own.

As if she'd heard his thoughts, she stated, "I will bear none unless their father loves me above all else and I love him."

Ah, she laid herself open to a questionable lot. "And if you don't find such a paragon? What will you do then?"

"Better not to marry than marry and be unhappy." She kicked at a stone in her path. "I will continue to devote myself to good works, or some such."

Such a waste! All her enchantment shriveling away if she remained a spinster. She was meant for a man's bed. Pity it wouldn't be his. Pity he couldn't have just a taste of her before he consigned her to her fate.

Something must have shown on his face for her expression softened, becoming even more seductive and captivating. Her gaze lingered on his mouth, then flicked to his eyes. She stared at him, her dark eyes locked with his, as they stood face to face on the windy cliff.

A curl escaped her bonnet. Without volition, his fingers found it, tucked it away and stayed to caress the soft lobe of her ear. She sighed, closed her eyes for a moment, and then opened them. She looked astonished. In terms of endearing gestures, it was only a small matter, but to look at her eyes, large and liquid, one would think he'd given her a fortune.

Or a rare tender moment.

"My apologies," he murmured automatically.

She shook her head. Refusing his apology or clearing her mind?

His throat constricted. He knew better, yet he lifted his hand and stroked her cheek, his fingers gliding down the soft, smooth curve. She swallowed, her throat working under his touch as he continued the caress down the side of her neck, his finger coming to rest on her shoulder.

The material felt rough to his touch, not the silk or delicate materials she should be wearing. Under the fabric, he felt the slender bones, the quiver of her muscles.

Her breathing quickened. She trembled under his touch. Her tongue flicked out and licked her bottom lip.

All he knew of society's strictures deserted him. He forgot she was promised to another man, forgot her innocent state, forgot all but the feel and look of her. He pulled her close, then closer still.

She gasped as her full breasts pressed against him. He could feel her heart race even as his began to beat harder. The vein at her temple pulsed, her lips opened as she stared, wide-eyed, at him. He had to bend his head to feel her breath against his face, but it came, quick and hot, inflaming him.

He had to taste her.

The urges he'd restrained since meeting her surged forward. He kissed her, demanding entry, applying his seductive knowledge until her lips parted under his and his tongue slid into her mouth.

She moaned as her head fell back under his onslaught, but she didn't move out of his arms. She stood still, her arms where they'd fallen at her sides. At last, he lifted his head and stared at her. What had he done?

She should have slapped him, boxed his ears, yet she did neither. She was innocent, a stranger to desire, yet she didn't appear to mind his dizzying leap into passion. With her lips parted, her eyes half-closed, she appeared dazed. Her eyelids fluttered, then lifted. She looked him straight in the eye.

Havyn waited for her angry remonstrance.

She took a short breath, then a longer one. She exhaled. Moistened her lips. "Kiss me again."

Chapter Three

"No."

"I want you to. I liked it."

"You are promised to Yarwoode."

She recoiled and took a backward step. He read the pain of rejection in her face and wished he could kiss it away.

Her expression changed, returning to wonder as she touched her mouth, her finger touching the tip of her tongue, as though she could still feel him. She licked her lips. He forced himself to look away.

"I wondered what it would be like," she murmured. "I might never feel that way again. Please, kiss me."

That she could want more from him after he'd behaved so dishonorably! Havyn inhaled deeply, searching for the strength to deny her.

"Please, Mr. Attercliffe."

He was lost. How could he deny her soulful request? This time, however, the mastered training of *Ananga-Rana* came to the fore, and he bent to his task of kissing her with all the finesse he could muster.

He kissed her mouth with courtesy, keeping his touch gentle, belatedly taking time to let her know his taste and smell. He used the tip of his tongue to ease her lips apart, then explored the fleshy softness of the inside of her lips. When she gasped, instead of plunging in, he withdrew. She trembled within his arms. As he loosened his grip, expecting her to move out of his embrace, she astounded him once more by sliding her arms under his coat and around his waist. The heat of her palms sifted through the fabric of his waistcoat and shirt to warm his spine. He stiffened, struck by the immediacy of his response. She was an innocent, yet apparently the skills of feminine seduction came instinctively to her.

He smiled at her, then kissed her temples, her cheeks, her forehead, then her neck, and pushing her bonnet off her head, behind her ears. Her trembling increased as she followed his mouth with her own, reaching for his lips. When at last he gave them to her, she sighed and tentatively, with great daring, touched them with her tongue.

He savored her curiosity and her awakening to passion while he inhaled her fresh, sweet breath and tasted *nirvana* on her lips. Gradually, reason intervened and he forced himself to retreat. She had to be lonely in her life, and if he was the first man to show her some small attention, perhaps her first taste of passion, no wonder she was hungry for more. The thought of accommodating her was tempting, but he couldn't accept what she didn't know she offered.

"Lady Jane," he whispered against her lips, "you don't know what you are doing."

Her eyelids drifted open. "I am kissing you," she murmured. "I quite like it."

He smiled. "As do I—"

"Kiss me again, then."

Wishing he could do exactly that, he set her apart from him. "That leads to lovemaking."

"It does?" she asked in a dreamy voice. "How very nice."

He had to laugh. "Yes, it is very nice. With the proper partner, it is more than nice."

"Are you the proper partner?"

Havyn took a deep breath. The cut of his buckskins had become uncomfortably tight. He could feel himself straining against the buttons, and if she cared to look below his waist, she would see precisely how improper he was. "You should save this for your husband—whoever he might be."

"I want you," she murmured as she strained on tiptoe to kiss him again.

She could have no idea what she suggested. He ached. It would be only too easy to sink down into the wild grasses and take her. Abruptly, he released himself from her grasp. It was wrong of him to have kissed her at all. He stepped back, putting space and reason between them. The wind felt colder now against his chest. "That's impossible."

She swayed a moment, then recovered and straightened her shoulders. "Why? Why can't you be my lover?"

"Generally, it's the man who does the asking, Lady Jane."

"Who is to know or care who says the words? Think of it," she coaxed. "You could kiss me whenever you wanted. And I could kiss you, too."

He looked at her lips, full and lush and moist from his mouth. The idea was preposterous, of course, but the thought of kissing her at his leisure was tempting. Too tempting.

He forced the idea from his mind.

He had much to do yet in attaining *Moksha*, the enlightenment of the mind and spirit that would mark the fulfillment of the great goals of life. A woman, even one so appetizing as this luscious swan, would only hinder his pursuit of manly perfection. And though he ached to make love to her, he wouldn't offer marriage. Nor could he dishonor her with an offer to make her his mistress, not even if he offered *carte-blanche*.

He didn't wish to cause her further pain, but neither could he agree to this impulsive, improper proposition. "It wouldn't do," he said at last, very gently.

"Why not?" She wore her determined look again, which narrowed her eyes and mouth and, instead of being annoying, made him want to kiss her again.

"If we were to give into our inclinations, as pleasant—," *what a weak word that was!* "—as that would be, we would be forced to marry and I am not ready to take a wife."

"At all? Or just not me?" she asked, her voice betraying her hurt.

"Anyone," he said. "I have things I must do before I consider marriage." His heart softened. "And you, Lady Jane, don't want to leap from the frying pan into the fire."

She bristled. "I know my own mind."

"Just so. Then let it work for you. Think of something else."

She sighed. She looked out to sea, then back, a faraway look in her eyes. "I must act quickly before Grantham sends a notice to the *Times*." She sighed again, more deeply. "But that is not your concern."

"I have made it my concern, Lady Jane. Return with me and I will convince Grantham to refuse Yarwoode and cancel the announcement of your engagement at his annual affair or elsewhere."

"I wish I could believe it would be that simple." She looked wistful as she pursed her mouth. "Having once accepted Yarwoode's offer, there would have to be a compelling reason to now reject it."

"We'll think of something," he promised.

Her eyes gleamed as a small smile curved her seductive lips upward. Her posture lifted, her head tilted to one side as she eyed him thoughtfully. "Very well. I collect that you don't want to marry, but we could be engaged, could we not?"

He had told her to think of something else, but not this! "That's not likely since Grantham has already accepted Yarwoode's offer."

She wasn't put off. "Not if we had a prior engagement."

He laughed. "Prior? Since when?"

She approached him and placed her hand on his chest. "We could have had a secret engagement before you left the country."

"When you were what?" He shouldn't encourage such a ludicrous notion, but devil take it, he enjoyed her lively imagination. "Fifteen, sixteen? You were still in the schoolroom."

"The very reason it was secret!" She all but crowed with delight. "See? If we've been engaged all this time, Yarwoode can't have me now."

"I doubt my brother or Yarwoode would be put off by such fustian nonsense."

"It could work," she insisted, with a coaxing smile. "Every one knew I followed you about, made a cake of myself where you were concerned. It wouldn't be difficult to believe that we had conceived a *tendre* for each other." She pressed against his chest. He felt her fingertips burning past his coat, waistcoat and linen shirt all the way to his skin. "All you'd have to do is refuse to release me from my promise to you. Yarwoode would have to withdraw."

He moved her fingers away. "That is if Grantham believes you. When he told me about Yarwoode, if we were engaged, he would have expected me to say something."

She pursed her lips in a delectable moue. He restrained the urge to kiss the pout from her mouth. She brightened. "Not if you wished to see me first, to find out if I still desired to marry you. He would respect your sensibilities."

"Perhaps. But what happens when we don't marry? After all, if I've been away all these years, surely I'd be in a hurry to claim my bride?"

She smiled. "Especially when she likes to kiss you?"

He laughed again. Funny, he couldn't remember laughing quite this much in a very long time. "Especially then."

She tilted her head again and pursed her lips. "We could say that we are allowing each other time to become re-acquainted. After all, I have grown up while you were away."

"And delightfully so." He was enchanted with this display of feminine wiles.

She looked taken aback. Had no one ever complimented her on her looks? After a moment, she regained her argument. "After a time, when Yarwoode is no longer a threat, we could say we don't suit and call it off."

"What's to prevent Yarwoode from renewing his suit? Or my brother from accepting his offer again?"

An expression of distress crossed her lovely face. "Hmm. Perhaps he could be put off?" Her look turned thoughtful, then impish. "I know! We could be found in a compromising situation."

Another reference to knowledge young women weren't supposed to have. Was Lady Jane not as innocent as she appeared? She'd kissed him without artifice, but perhaps she'd been acting? His voice turned harsh. "What do you know about those?"

"Oh my, it was all the *on dit* last Season when a young lady was found with her groom. No one would tell me the particulars." She looked disappointed, as if considering the possibilities. "At any rate, the groom was dismissed without a character and she was ruined. Just ruined! No one would have her then." She looked hopefully at Havyn. "Couldn't you ruin me?"

Oh, he could. With delight. He stalked away from her. At a safe distance, he looked back. "You don't know what you're asking. There are rules, Lady Jane. If you were known to be ruined, no other man is likely to make an offer for you."

She waved that objection away. "Since I would marry only for love, the man who loved me would accept me as I am."

He blinked at her logic. "You have no assurance on that matter, Lady Jane. Fortune hunters might not care that you were not an innocent. Indeed, they would be careful to make you think it was a love match." He studied her face. "Think of something else."

"Nothing else will work. Please, Mr. Attercliffe. It would only be for a short time."

"How short? Do you mean for this temporary engagement to last until you come into your estates?"

"Oh no!" Her forehead creased delightfully as she considered the possibilities. "Just until Yarwoode looks elsewhere. Then we could part. Until then, I'd make few demands on you."

"Really?" he drawled. "How few would those be?"

She flushed. "Well, that is . . . none but the usual . . ."

"And those would be?" He knew the polite rules of courtship as well as she must, but he wondered what notions her creative mind would come up with.

She waved a hand in dismissal. "Your company of course. Society must see us together to accept our engagement. You must be attentive to me and I must . . ."

"You must be seen to be properly submissive to your future husband. You must accept his guidance in all things." He spoke in a teasing manner, just to see her reaction, which wasn't long in coming. Nor surprising.

"Oh, bother all that! You must appear to be madly in love with me. Me," she insisted. "Not my dowry or my fortune."

Naturally she would want that after a cold, lonely childhood. His heart ached for her, but he kept his manner light as he approached and took her hand. Raising it to his lips, he pressed a kiss on the back of it, holding it just a moment longer than propriety allowed. "Like this, you mean?"

Her fingers trembled. "Like that. If you were to kiss me, in a place where people might think we have gone to be alone, but actually chosen so that we might be in view, that would be good, too."

"You wish me to press my attentions to you where we might be discovered?"

"Oh, yes! It would be infinitely better if ours was seen as a love match."

To do as she wished meant he would be leg-shackled before the week was out. He dropped her hand. "You are quite foolish, Lady Jane. You have been reading too many romanticals. Only in one of those novels would you find such an insane notion."

She bristled. "Do not poke fun at my expense. I am not deranged. I want you to pose as my fiancé for as long as it takes." Her imperious tone matched her stiff pose. All she needed was a crown and a scepter.

He laughed. "No."

"What harm can it do? We'll protect each other. Surely you know that all the Marriage Mart will have its eyes on you? You've come back from . . . wherever," she said with a wave of her hand.

"From India and points East," he supplied.

She looked curious, but continued, "Extremely wealthy. You are, aren't you?"

He nodded. He had invested wisely in tea, in gems and sumptuous silks and fine Kashmir wool. He had traveled in style, but most of his income had gone into his London accounts. He had achieved his first goal, *Artha*, wealth and material well being, quite on his own. That would go a long way to ensuring his acceptance into Polite Society again.

"And by the looks of you, a swell of the first stare. You possess a certain mysterious air with your darkened skin and piercing blue eyes. The ladies will be quite desirous of your company."

He laughed. "You have been reading too much!"

She narrowed her eyes at him. "You aren't already married, are you?"

He shook his head.

"There you have it. You're wealthy, presentable, and eligible. You won't last a season with all the caps set on you."

"I have no choice in the matter?"

"None whatsoever. Before you know it, you'll be riveted. Willing or not, some matchmaking matron will have you married before the Season ends."

"On that you are quite mistaken," he retorted. "I will not be forced into a marriage I don't desire." His words echoed in his mind. Unlike Lady Jane, he could choose his mate.

She advanced on him with her quick stride. "Then help me! Don't force me into this marriage with Yarwoode."

He evaded her hands, knowing that if she touched him again he might not resist. "Lady Jane, you put me in an untenable position. I've told you I have no wish to marry, yet you insist on a situation where marriage would be the inevitable result."

"You could refuse." Before he could speak, she rushed on, "It's different for a man. You can do as you please."

"To a degree," he admitted, remembering a time when decisions had been made for him. And yet, it was not the same. Despite being exiled from England, he had had the freedom to seek his own goals and desires, whereas Lady Jane never had such freedom.

"Nevertheless, there are duties and expectations. You would be ruined for life, unacceptable to Polite Society, and I would not be welcome in any of the homes of my acquaintances." In addition to being excluded from drawing rooms, he could be shunned by investors, thus putting *Artha* at risk and damaging his search for *Moksha*. He looked her straight in her dark, lustrous eyes. "That is too high a price for either of us."

"Upon my word, sir, I had no idea you were so cowardly."

He drew himself up to his full height. Towering over her, he made no effort to conceal his rancor. "You insult me."

She glared back at him, her eyes narrowed. After a moment, her expression softened. "I beg your pardon, Mr. Attercliffe." She moistened her lips, drawing his attention away from his ire and placing it completely on those full, delicious lips. "My situation quite makes me forget myself. I was dreadfully rude. Please forgive me."

He wanted to do much more than forgive her. Despite his care for his goals, he wanted her. He wanted to taste her, to disrobe her, to view her nakedness from every aspect. He wanted to cup her breasts, slide his palm down her stomach to her mound, caress her bite, and touch her intimate places. He wanted to pierce her, explore all her orifices, put his tongue in her mouth again, in her ears, her belly button, and her *yoni*.

He ached thinking about it, imagining how it would be to have both upper and lower congress with her, of the sounds she would make in the throes of passion. He wanted to teach her the delight of *auparishtaka*, the oral pleasures lovers bestowed on each other.

He could do none of this.

He was charged to return her to his brother, her guardian. Though the instruction had not been given, he understood the necessity of returning her still a virgin, still a marriageable miss.

"It is impossible." He turned her back to the path. "We'll speak no more of it."

Chapter Four

She gave him no peace. On the return to Anna's cottage, he tried to close his ears to her incessant pleas. Finally, beleaguered beyond endurance, his control snapped. "Quiet!" When she stopped abruptly, both her words and her pace, he took her by the shoulders and facing her, gave her a slight shake. "You drive me to distraction. Have you never heard of the womanly virtues?"

"No one considers me a woman," she retorted and broke his grip. "Lord Grantham orders me here, there, like a child, or one of his servants. Yarwoode regards me as a possession he wishes to acquire. You don't credit me with knowing my own mind." She looked up at him and spoke vehemently. "I'm not a child."

"No," Havyn agreed with an astonishing tenderness that went marrow deep. He released her. "That you are not."

Her chin went up. "Then treat me like a woman. Allow me to know my own mind."

If the time were different, if he didn't have goals he must accomplish, he'd consider offering for her himself. Even irked with her defiance, he was beguiled by her spirit. And her lush form. It was hard to forget how her body, with her full bosom and hips made to cradle a man, had nestled against his, mocking his resolve to return her home untouched.

She moved closer as if she knew his thoughts. Her hands rested on his sleeves, then slid up to his shoulders as she pressed herself against him. "Mr. Attercliffe," she whispered, "I need your help."

Her lower lip trembled. He ached to nip it with his teeth, bite her hard enough to show his displeasure, then suck the tiny hurt away. He was a man trained in the erotic arts and captivated by his admiration for her. He knew very well that she used his sensual nature against him, but he couldn't fault her for offering what he so much desired. Yet, if he continued in sympathy, to allow her to stand so close to him, it would be more difficult to put her aside.

Her hands crept up around his neck. He inhaled her sweet fragrance. In response, his body tightened as he forced himself to endure her closeness and ignore his lust. He managed to keep his resolve until her fingers crept beneath his shirt collar and stroked his nape.

With a groan, he acknowledged both their needs. His hand strayed lower on her back, resting on her hip. His fingers opened and squeezed gently, as he enjoyed the lush, giving womanliness of her. She snuggled closer, making a low sound of pleasure in her throat.

Bloody hell. If she was this responsive, standing, with all their clothes on, what would she be like, naked, resting on silken sheets and velvet pillows? He could think of nothing but *avidarita*. He tortured himself with the thought of her lying on her back, wearing nothing but her jewels, her legs raised, feet pressed against his chest, leaving her open and exposed to him while he sat between her thighs and enjoyed her. With her ample bosom and shapely hips, he imagined her a voluptuary, a woman intent on experiencing every nuance of passion. His chest constricted, all blood left his head for his greedy *lingam*, and he had to close his eyes and imagine the grim face of his brother before the enticing vision left his mind.

His throat went dry. He ached for her, yet having her wasn't within his plans.

She lifted her face. "Lord Grantham won't acknowledge anything but a prior engagement as sufficient reason to refuse Yarwoode once he's accepted his offer. Even Yarwoode must accept that."

She was right. Bloody hell. In that moment, looking down at her beseeching eyes, her mouth reddened from his kisses, Havyn knew he'd lost the battle. Most uncharacteristic of him to be swayed by a woman's emotional temperament, but he was as intrigued by her character as he was hungry for her person. God help them both, but he was consumed with tenderness. With lust.

"You must realize, Lady Jane, that only our word of an engagement between us is insufficient." He sighed inwardly. It wasn't what he had intended to do, but it was what he must now do. So much for his honorable intentions of seeing her back safe and innocent. So much for his determination to let nothing hinder his efforts to attain *Moksha*. He looked beyond her, to the Yorkshire moors. The vast expanse of hill and dale, rocky tors and endless sky made him realize again the futility of raging against nature. It wasn't in his character to cause distress or pain to creatures less powerful than himself. *Moksha* would have to wait. He braced himself. "We will have to prove our attachment to each other."

Her eyes brightened. She cast him a hopeful look. "Oh, thank you!" Her face clouded over. "But how are we to do that?"

He thought for a moment, then grudgingly voiced the only sure solution. "We must be discovered in *flagrante delicto*."

"How is that?"

"We must be discovered in an intimate situation."

"Truly? You will make love to me?" Her smile started small, grew larger and reached her eyes. They sparkled. Her dimple deepened. She was utterly enchanting. "When?"

Her pleased expression made him uneasy, and he hastened to add, "It will be sufficient to give that impression, without actually—"

"Oh, no! It must the real thing," she said firmly. "There must be no mistake."

Havyn groaned. "Lady Jane, it is bound to be that."

"What if I am examined, Mr. Attercliffe? What if I am found to still be untouched, what then? I'll be a liar." She propped her hands on her hips. "A *married* liar."

He couldn't help it. He smiled at her.

"We shall leave for York, but along the way we'll stop at an inn." Her face lit up. "There you can ruin me!"

Havyn laughed, a bittersweet sound of regret. "You needn't sound quite so happy about it."

She turned her face up to him, her gaze searching his face. "Will it be so very terrible for you?"

Terrible? No. Heavenly was more like it. He ached to place his hands and mouth on her, to undress her slowly, revealing every bit of her voluptuous person. He thought of various techniques to slowly prepare a virgin, then thought better of it. With her willingness to lose her maidenhead, he would have to restrain her haste to make sure she achieved her woman's pleasure.

If only he survived.

His soon-to-be paramour dashed ahead with unladylike

alacrity, rushing into Anna's arms as she waited at the cottage door with a concerned expression.

Lady Jane hugged her. "Anna, I have the most remarkable news."

Anna looked from Jane to Havyn and back again.

"Mr. Attercliffe and I have renewed our engagement."

"What?" Anna's mouth dropped. "Be that true?"

Lady Jane nodded her head, smiling beatifically. "Yes. We must return to Grantham Lodge at once to make the news known."

"Oh, my lady." Tears gathered at the corners of Anna's seamed eyes. "Why didn't you tell me you were already spoke for? And to Master Havyn. You should have told his lordship and put an end to Lord Yarwoode."

Jane managed a creditable sniff of her own. "I couldn't until I was sure that Mr. Attercliffe and I were still of one mind."

Havyn watched this scene with narrowed eyes. For a man who prided himself on achieving *Dharma*, the judgement and responsibility of a well-ordered life, Havyn felt himself whirling through disorder. He chafed at losing control. From now on, he would wrest back the power in their association and do things his way, the proper way.

He straightened his shoulders, removed his hat and entered the small cottage. He turned to Anna who still wiped her eyes. "Lady Jane will be leaving in the morning. Will you have her ready for an early start?"

Anna smiled broadly and fondly. "Oh, to be sure I will, sir."

He bowed to Jane. "I shall await your pleasure in the morning, then."

"Until tomorrow." The dimple in her cheek deepened as she flashed a conspiratorial grin at him. "I can hardly wait."

Chapter Five

Wait she had to, thought Havyn, as they bumped along the road leaving Whitby in a southwesterly direction for York. The route took them over moorland, up hill and down dale, through forests and open spaces where naught but the earth and sky met the eye. All seemed peaceful.

Not so within the coach. Rather than sit comfortably opposite him in the hired conveyance, Lady Jane pressed close to his side and leaned into his body with each bend and sway of the coach, teasing his senses with her light fragrance, and taunting his self-control with the warmth of her breast against his arm.

Her face bright with curiosity, she asked question after question about his travels. Where had he gone and what had he seen? Where had he stayed? How had he journeyed? What foods had he eaten? How had he gotten so brown?

She listened avidly, and when he wished to deal lightly with some of the more unpleasant aspects of his tour, she pressed him until he gave her the information.

The time passed quickly, but at the first coaching stop, Lady Jane leaned closer and whispered, "Here?"

Havyn shook his head but did not answer. On his journey to Whitby, he had noted few inns with decent accommodations. This business might be less than upright, but he wanted something better for her than rough fare and an uncomfortable bed.

At the third coaching stop, Lady Jane looked desperate. "Here?" she repeated.

"Here," he agreed and helped her from the coach. She descended gracefully, then stretched her neck and head to relieve strained muscles. Havyn wished he could relieve the strain on his muscle as easily. She had put away her rough clothes and donned her own fashionable garments. Her brown traveling dress was simply cut, of the finest material, but the drab color did nothing for her dusky complexion. No doubt she or her *modiste* believed the severe cut and color would minimize her shape, but they were wrong. She needed brighter colors to set off her magnificence. Only her yellow hat with its jaunty ostrich feather tickling him in the nose, complimented her spirit.

He watched her, enchanted by the delicacy of her throat. He intended to sample it, to run his tongue from her chin down to the hollow where her pulse beat. He could almost feel it pulsing hotly against his tongue, taste the sweetness of her flesh.

She waited while he dealt with the coachman, then the landlord, arranging for a private parlor, and then escorted her up the stairs. The landlord preceded them, listing the pleasures of the inn's kitchens and fine, locally made ales.

Lady Jane didn't appear to be listening. She flicked a glance at the landlord, then another at Havyn, who saw the small trembling of her lips. He questioned her with his eyes.

She wet those lips, then nodded and glanced quickly away. So, she was nervous, then. After all her insistence that he bed her and ruin her for Yarwoode, now she was apprehensive?

"If you have changed your mind, we should continue our journey," he suggested.

She swallowed. "No, no. We must stay."

The landlord cast them both a suspicious look, but wished them well after Havyn pressed a coin into his hand.

Havyn closed the door behind the innkeeper. "Will this do?"

The room was surprisingly large. A Turkish carpet covered a portion of the oak floor, and a massive cupboard stood near the door. A fireplace on one wall faced a large bed, thick with feather mattress and plump pillows. A table rested before a window that looked out over miles of open, heather-covered moor. Chairs beside it invited the occupant to dine and enjoy the view.

Jane wandered around the room, touching the candles on the mantle, lifting the coverlet to find clean linens on the bed, peering behind the screen in one corner, next pausing at the window. She nodded as two porters brought her luggage in.

Havyn shook his head at the amount, then watched as his own joined the pile. He gave each porter a coin, and at last, they were alone. He locked the door.

With her face in shadow from the sunlight streaming through the window behind her, Havyn couldn't see her expression. He moved closer, saw the fine tremor of her hands and said softly, "This is no good, is it? Let us be on our way."

She shook her head, seemingly gathering her resolve. "No. I want this."

He tried reason once again. "It will be sufficient to have shared a room. Everyone will believe the worst."

"No. There must be no pretense."

"Very well. I've told the innkeeper to send up refreshments in an hour or so."

She nodded and started to untie the bow under her chin.

"Let me play lady's maid." He untied the bow of her fashionable bonnet and lifted it from her head. She made a small sound, then stood quietly as he ran his fingers through her thick, dark hair looking for pins. He loosened her hair. "So soft, silky to my touch," he murmured as he shaped her head with his palms and tenderly massaged the nape of her neck. She murmured deep in her throat as she bent her head before him.

This small gesture of submission gratified him. Though the independent and comely lady might not understand it all yet, he would soon show her how agreeable it was to submit to his guidance.

He raised her head and kissed her. As before, her lips, then her mouth, were sweet and welcoming. In moments, she opened for him and let him in. He took his time, teaching her the thrust and withdrawal to come when *yoni* accepted *lingam*, and the sweet fever of anticipation. When she linked her arms around his neck and leaned into him, letting him support her, he smiled and drew her closer. The kiss went deeper as he explored her mouth, licking the roof, drawing her tongue into his mouth to suck on it, making her gasp and break off the kiss with a startled look.

"Are you shocked, Lady Jane?"

Chapter Six

Wordlessly, she touched her lips, swollen now and pink from his kisses. She nodded, her heavy-lidded eyes intent on his.

"We do not have to continue." It cost him to say that, for now that he had a taste of her, he wanted more. He wanted all of her.

She took a step back, then another. Slowly, without looking at him, she fingered the fastenings on her spencer, undid it and pulled it first from one arm, then another. She let it drop to the floor.

He inhaled. Her shapeless blue serge gown and the voluminous apron she'd worn yesterday had only hinted at the shape of her bosom. Seen now, in the close fitting muslin gown she wore, although it was demurely cut at the neckline, the curve of her breasts made him ache to touch them. Yet he waited to see what she would do next.

She turned her back to him. "Undo me, please."

Havyn did as she asked, his fingers handling the fastenings with ease. As he loosened her gown, revealing her skin inch by inch, he kissed her neck, then her spine, and down until he met the fabric of her chemise. She wore no stays to support her breasts, pleasing him.

She pulled the gown and chemise from her shoulders, letting them drop to her hips. Bare now to her waist, she stood before him, waiting. He smoothed his palms over her shoulders.

"You have beautiful skin, Lady Jane. Soft and smooth." He lowered his face to her spine and inhaled. "Fragrant." He licked. "Tasty."

She squirmed and when he thought she'd move away, she surprised and delighted him by turning in his arms and lifting her mouth to kiss. "You arc tasty, too."

He bent his head and kissed her. She nestled closer, her breasts fully against him. Without breaking away from the kiss, he slid his hands between them until he cupped her breasts. Gently, ever so gently, he traced her nipples.

"Ooh," she murmured. "Do that again."

He lifted his head and watched her face as he cupped her breasts more fully, taking the weight of them in his palms, squeezing softly. Her mouth parted, her eyes half closed as she absorbed the sensation. She breathed more deeply. Her nipples hardened and gently he pulled at them, enlarging them.

Her eyes popped open.

"Do you like that?"

She moistened her lips. "It quite takes my breath away."

He had to smile. "This is only the beginning. Shall I help you with the rest of your clothing?"

Her face paled, then went pink as a flush rose from her breasts to her cheeks. "Is it necessary?"

"It is. During the intimacies of a man and a woman there should be nothing hidden."

"You will remove your clothing as well?"

"I will." He shrugged out of his tight coat, unbuttoned his waistcoat and loosened his neck-cloth. He ached to undo the buttons on his buckskins, but kept his hands above his waist. She watched, wide-eyed, as he hung up his outer clothing on pegs.

Next, he pulled his shirt off over his head. "Now we are equal."

He wasn't sure if she'd display a missish dismay at his bare chest, but once again, she surprised him. She eyed him, then lifted her hand and with the tip of her finger traced the line of his collarbone, then followed the curve of muscle down his arm. He forced himself to stand still under her explorations, even as his muscles tensed. "Your skin is brown."

"I know. Does it offend you?"

"No." She poked at the hard pectoral muscles of his chest, then ran her hand down to his waist. "Your hair here is soft."

"Is it?" He mimicked her motion. "You have beautiful soft breasts. I wanted to touch them the moment I saw you."

She crossed her arms over her chest. "They are too big."

"To the contrary." He had to exert a little force to loosen her arms and move them to her sides. "They are perfect. Made to pleasure a man. Made to pleasure you."

"Truly?"

He lowered his head to her, gently touched his tongue to the tip of her nipple. He tasted it, wet it, and covered it with his mouth. "Some day a babe will suckle here, and its father will feel both jealous and proud. You should feel only happiness and enjoyment. Cherished."

"Ah," she exhaled, pushing more of her nipple into his mouth. He pulled the rest in, and with a swirl of his tongue, taught her to take pleasure in her breasts. He sucked a bit harder, elongating her nipple, then raised his head. "I want more of you."

"As you wish," she murmured, though it was more gasp than measured agreement.

He smiled then. Possessively. With that consent, she acquiesced to anything he wished. He wanted it all. He gestured at her gown hanging from her hips.

She swallowed. He watched the motion of her throat, then dropped his gaze to her rose pink nipples. She flushed, but grabbed the fabric at her waist and pushed it all to the floor. Standing before him only in her shoes and stockings, with her breasts and softly rounded belly at last exposed to him, she appealed to his eye as well as his *lingam*. He pointed a finger at her feet.

She bent, untied her garters and let her stockings drop, then kicked off one shoe after the other. He suppressed a chuckle. She might have enjoyed her respite with Anna, but she was accustomed to her maid retrieving her clothing. He did that for her, hanging her gown and spencer carefully on a hook next to his coat. He placed her underthings in the cupboard and turned to her.

She had her hands crossed over her belly, hiding her most intimate places from him. He didn't reprimand her, merely moved behind her and put his arms around her. Placing his hands over hers, he inched them apart. He caressed her fingers with his, calming her as he whispered, "One of the things I noticed immediately about you is your glorious form. You are shaped as a woman should be, with bosom and hips to cradle a man. You are a sensual delight."

She lowered her head, scanning her shape. "But . . ."

"But you are not like other women, I know. They may be slender and willowy, and all that is fashionable, but you, my sweet, have the body of a woman. A body made for love."

She searched his face, as if looking for truthfulness. Who could blame her if she agonized over being short and too plump when all about her she saw women who refused to eat properly lest they gain flesh? He gazed back, smiling reassuringly, hiding nothing of his admiration from her.

"Truly?"

"Truly. You are like the women of the East. Sultry and formed as women are meant to be. You must take pride in your womanliness, Lady Jane. It is what makes you beautiful."

She exhaled. Havyn knew that along with her breath, she expelled a lifetime of worry about her shape. She turned her head and gazed up at him. "I shall remember that."

He kissed the last syllables away, taking her promise into his mouth and adding his own to it. While he kept his share of the bargain to ruin her for Lord Yarwoode, he would also teach her pride in her body.

He turned her in his arms, kissing her anew, this time allowing her more of himself. He not only drew her tongue into his mouth to suck, but placed his at her disposal. Smiling inwardly as she accepted the invitation and sucked on his tongue with enthusiasm, he spared a thought for the men of the *ton* who had let her get away. Fools.

She drew her mouth away. "Oh, I never knew kissing would be like this."

"Indeed. You have a great deal of experience?"

"Of course not. Surely you can tell how green I am. The only kisses I knew were cold, dry and uninteresting." She pursed her mouth. "Did it take you very long to learn how to make your kisses warm and wet?"

He had to laugh. "I practiced with great regularity until I got it right."

"I must do the same then."

"Only with me." The demand popped out before he considered his words.

She eyed him gravely, as if weighing his claim. He, too, searched within himself and could not contradict his declaration. At last, she nodded. "Teach me more."

"Have you always been this forward?"

She considered that with her head tilted to one side. With her hair hanging free, one lock curled around a breast, she looked adorably pensive. "I have always pursued knowledge. What else was I to do, hidden away with no friends?"

His heart ached for her. He made his voice light and easy.

"Well, you have me now to be your tutor. Are you ready to begin the lessons?"

She smiled, the dimple in her cheek flashing. "Haven't we already made a start?"

"So we have. You appear to be a promising scholar. I warn you, you might be thoroughly tested."

Her dimple appeared, then disappeared as she assumed a studious look. "Shouldn't you be properly garbed? Or un-garbed?"

"Quite so. I'll put it right." So saying, he sat to remove his boots, Hessians now that the top boot so favored by the French was out of fashion. He placed them neatly, side by side, while she waited and watched.

He stood and undid the buttons of his buckskins. Her gaze followed each movement of his hands. He watched her watch him, noted when her eyes grew bigger as his *lingam* rose and pushed at the flap. He inched the trousers down his hips, down his thighs, removing with them also his long drawers, something his tailor insisted upon so as not to ruin the line of his buckskins, even though he would rather have done without.

She swallowed convulsively as he bent to pull the tight skins from his legs. His valet usually accomplished this for him, saving him from an undignified display. He flicked a glance at her from the corner of his eye. She appeared entranced with the exposure of his naked ass. What would she do when he stood and she got her first real look at him?

He'd always prided himself upon the length and breath of his *lingam*, of being a horse man, as Eastern lore described, rather than a hare or an overly large bull man, but it was sure to create consternation in an innocent maid. Slowly, he righted himself.

She made a noise deep in her throat. "Oh," she whispered, her eyes big and round. "Oh."

"Do I frighten you?"

With her eyes intent on his *lingam*, still growing under her rapt gaze, she licked her lips. Heat seared him. Blood rushed to his member, making it longer, redder, harder.

"Oh," she repeated. "Does that hurt?"

Did she mean him or her? "It doesn't hurt unless it fails to find satisfaction," he said, opting to believe she meant him. She would find out for herself shortly. He hoped he could make losing her innocence as painless as possible.

She looked at him, then down at herself. Suddenly, a question occurred to him. "You do know what is about to happen?"

She gave him an unsure look. "You mean to put th . . . that inside me."

"Exactly. This is my *lingam*." He took it in his hand, letting it rest on his palm as he showed himself to her. "Once you are prepared, I'll put it into you. Into your *yoni*."

"My . . . ?"

"Your *yoni*." He gestured at her lower belly. "The most intimate, secret part of you."

She seemed to accept that, but her gaze was still riveted on his shaft. "It's so big." Her hand crept forward. She yanked it back. "It will never fit."

He smiled gently. "You will be surprised. Shall we ready you now?"

"If you are sure. . . ." Her voice trailed away as she stared at him. Unbelievingly, he grew even longer. Harder.

He took her hand and placed her fingers on the head of his member. It leapt with approval. She jumped and tried to draw her hand away. He held her quivering fingers securely in his, then moved them as one, in effect stroking himself with her hand, first on top, then in circles around the eager head, and finally, underneath, touching the small nib of flesh, the source of so much pleasure.

Inadvertently, his breath hissed in. His *lingam* jumped.

She pulled her hand back. "I'm sorry."

"Don't apologize for giving me joy." He waited a moment. Waited while he exerted self-control. Waited while she called on her courage and curiosity. "Touch me again."

"Like this?"

Her small hand caressed him with delicacy, retracing the path her fingers had taken before. When his cock began to throb in her hand, he thought she'd release him, but instead, she tightened her palm. Instinctively, he pushed forward into her grasp and couldn't hold back a moan.

She raised astounded eyes to his, then looked down again. A small drop of fluid appeared on the head. He expected her to be repulsed, instead she touched it with her fingertip, then smeared the liquid around the tiny opening.

"My God, you were born to be a *houri*!"

"What is that?" she asked without letting him go.

He took himself out of her palm. Guiding her to the bed, he pulled back the covers and placed her, sitting, on the edge of the bed. "A woman of perfect beauty who brings paradise to her lover."

She began to shake her head, but he touched his finger to her lips. "You are exquisite, Lady Jane. Never doubt it." He spread her knees and stepped between them.

When she tried to close her legs, he edged closer, holding them open with his body. "Now it is my pleasurable task to prepare you for my *lingam.*"

Again she tried to speak, but she spoke into his mouth as he pressed kiss after kiss on her. In a matter of moments, she was kissing him back, taking his kisses on her temples, her cheeks, her chin and returning them ten-fold. When he kissed her throat, she tossed her head back, exposing herself to him. He licked his way from her chin to the hollow at the base of her throat, feeding on her rapidly beating pulse, encouraging her with his murmurs of appreciation.

He shaped her shoulders, slid his hands down her arms to her hands bracing herself on the mattress. He took her hands, placed them on his shoulders and bent his head to her breasts.

One after the other, he suckled. He licked. He traced each tiny whorl with his tongue. He pulled her pebbled nipples into his mouth, teaching her by example how he would like her to suck upon his flesh. He nuzzled her cleavage, blew on the wet trail his tongue created.

He placed one hand on a plump bottom cheek to hold her still as she began to wriggle. The other hand was on her hip, slowly sliding down and across the curve of her belly, each time lower, until, with his thumb, he outlined the shape of her mound. She tensed, but with his whispered words of reassurance, she relaxed, slowly, slowly, while he burrowed through the curls to flesh and stroked. Gently, ever so softly, tenderly, he stroked first one side of her labia, then the other, a barely there touch. He licked her throat, tracing her pulse with his tongue, coaxing and teasing until she sighed, and her lower lips opened to him.

Deftly, he inserted the tip of one finger and swirled it around the edges, urging her to relax, to accept. He kept her occupied with deep, tongue-lashing kisses, assaulting her maidenly reservations with mouth and hand, until at last, she moaned deep in her throat and fell back on the bed.

Her thighs were wide open to him now. He bent, studying her little bud, applying just a bit more pressure, a little more depth to his finger. With his other hand, he stroked her breasts, played with her nipples and her navel, followed the line of her ribs to the shadowed pit of her arm. He stroked tenderly there, too.

She widened enough for him to insert another finger. With two, he began an easy in and out thrust, drawing from her the sweet juices telling him he would soon be feeling more of her. More and more until his *lingam* was buried to the hilt in her succulent *yoni*.

Her head moved restlessly on the bed. He had her pinned and primed, but at any time, he was ready to release her if she wanted it. She didn't appear to, as she arched her hips in the age-old female signal to her mate.

"Your body invites my *lingam*, my sweet. I am going to come into you now."

In answer, she half raised her knees, and finding no purchase from the air, pushed back until she rested her heels on the edge of the mattress.

He moved over her, centering himself between her legs. "Just so." He lowered himself and probed. "Do you feel the tip of my *lingam* requesting permission to enter?"

Her eyes widened. Her mouth opened. She nodded.

He pushed just the tip in. "Now, it begs a welcome. Will you allow that?"

Her pulse raced madly in her throat. "It's big. Too big."

"Never fear. You were made for this. Put your arms around me." He pushed in another inch, then another. He bent his head and suckled at her breast. He nipped her nipple, and when she yelped, busy with the small pain at her breast, he entered her completely.

She drew in a sharp breath, one he drew from her in a deep kiss, absorbing both her exhalation and her pain. Her feet drummed on the mattress. Her hands clenched on his shoulders, her nails digging into his skin.

He held still while she adjusted to the size of him. When her inner muscles relaxed slightly, he drew back. "Now your *yoni* has learned its purpose. My *lingam* is eager to know it better."

"Will it hurt again?"

"Perhaps a little, but it will grow easier. Truly," he added in anticipation of her next question.

She smiled. How quickly she learned that alluring, seductive female look of invitation. He kissed her, and with her tongue in his mouth, he began an easy, gentle thrust. Her *yoni* accommodated him as she learned the rhythm. In and out, each time deeper, each time a bit faster, until her hips worked with his and her muscles clenched around him.

His breathing grew faster, hotter. She panted, searching for a release as yet unknown to her. He thrust deeper still, pushing her up the spiraling curve of pleasure, until, at the apex, she opened her eyes, gazed deeply into his, and convulsed around him.

Her spasms continued, provoking his. His back arched, went rigid as he thrust one final time, the tip of his *lingam* piercing deeply inside her, and with a hoarse cry, he emptied himself into her care.

Her hands fell from his shoulders. She lay limp beneath him, her eyes closed, breathing fast. He couldn't leave her, not yet, not when his *lingam* had found its home, not when her sensitive *yoni* still grasped him greedily. He eased himself down on his side, rolling her with him so that they faced each other with his cock buried securely. He could feel the tiny tremors still shaking her inner muscles. He took a deep breath, filled with satisfaction and a hunger yet unappeased.

Her eyes opened slowly. "I am ruined, then?"

"Without a doubt."

"I am so glad." He thought she would sleep as her eyes drifted shut.

Instead, they popped open. "Shouldn't we make sure?"

Chapter Seven

Lady Jane woke some time later with a prodigious appetite and requested a meal, which she consumed quite slowly. For every bite Havyn fed her, he kissed her, so the meat went cold, the wine sat untouched and the clotted cream for her strawberries ignored. A kettle on the hob kept water hot for tea. She didn't seem to notice any of that. She reclined against the pillows, the sheet puddling at her hips, opening her mouth when prompted, for either a kiss or nourishment.

"Tell me more about those naked statues," she murmured when her mouth was free.

"I collect you like hearing about naked men and women," he teased. When she made a face at him, he grinned. "Very well, then. The temple at Konarak, also in the jungle, has the same type of statues adorning the outer walls."

"It seems most unspiritual to have statues of men and women, er. . . ."

"Enjoying the intimate physical aspects of lovemaking," he supplied.

"Quite so."

He tempted her with a ripe strawberry. The aroma filled his senses, competing with the sensual smell of her still moist flesh. "Consider that the lovers depicted, and in the most close and passionate manner, are sharing both a sexual and a sacred love."

She bit into the strawberry. A bit of juice dripped down her chin. He promptly lapped it up, then took the rest of the berry from her lips with his teeth.

She swallowed and licked her lips. "Tell me of the positions."

"There are hundreds of statues," he cautioned.

"Perhaps one or two of your favorites?" she suggested with a sly smile. "Perhaps six?"

"You are a minx." He laughed. "There is one of a standing couple, looking at each other with smiles of great tenderness. He has one foot resting on the wall behind him for balance, with one hand at her waist, the other lifting her leg over his upraised thigh. She leans into him with her arms clasped around his neck."

"And he is in her?"

"No doubt."

She licked her lips again. "Might we try that?"

"We might."

"Another?"

He thought of the ones where the man stood with his lover, always referred to as his wife, upside down with her knees hooked over his shoulders and her arms clasping his bent legs. His hands lifted her outstretched thighs while he bent his head to her *yoni* and drank her juices. No, not that one. Lady Jane wasn't quite ready for that. Nor was she ready to crouch between his open thighs, allow him to rest one foot on her upraised knee, and bend slightly forward from the hips while she sucked his *lingam* dry. The statues depicting many lovers at once enjoying each other's bodies were also too advanced. As eagerly as Lady Jane absorbed the lessons in lovemaking, she would be shocked to hear of lower congress, no matter how it stimulated the lovers.

In response to his thoughts, his *lingam* stirred and lengthened. "One statue depicts the woman resting much as you are now, her back supported by pillows." He moved, whisking the sheet from her, and eased her legs apart. "The man comes between her limbs, like this," he instructed as he knelt on one knee and lifted her leg to rest upon his thigh. "Now that she is open to him, he presses his chest to hers and unites their private parts. Thus," he said as he entered her with one sure thrust.

Her head fell back on the pillows. She gasped, "And then?"

"He enjoys her as much as she does him. In the statues, both are smiling." He thrust again, deeper and harder. "Will you smile for me now?"

"Oh, yes . . ." And she did, all the while he entered her, now deeply, now barely penetrating, all the while he caressed her chest with his and pressed kisses on her smiling mouth.

He, with his greater experience and control, was able to restrain his *lingam*, and prevent spilling his seed. She, however, a novice and unaware of the benefits of prolonging lovemaking, came in a great gush very quickly.

Havyn took her cries of joy into his mouth, then pulled back slightly, allowing her legs to fall to either side of him. While she recovered, he caressed her breasts, her belly and the soft undersides of her thighs.

She murmured, deep in her throat. "No wonder those statues smile."

He laughed.

"You must tell me more."

"Haven't you heard enough?"

"Not yet. All those funny names. I want to hear them all. Remember you promised to show me, too."

"You will recall that I did just that a moment ago."

She stretched, arching her pelvis at him. "And now I want more."

"Very well, greedy thing. I shall describe a few more common positions. We shall each choose one to practice. Very fair." More than fair, he thought with a grin. While he was accustomed to being in charge of lovemaking, it excited him to have her take so ardent an interest. With her eagerness to learn more, he was completely agreeable, avid even, to be her teacher.

Havyn moved out of the way and rolled her to her stomach.

"I shall take my turn first," he said when she grumbled. "We have already agreed that your breasts are perfection, my sweet. Now we shall admire your buttocks."

She tried to roll back over. He stopped her with one hand.

"These curves entice me. So full, so tempting." He ran his palm over one plush cheek, then another. He trailed a finger down the dark, hidden cleft. "They are rounded, soft, a cushion to sit upon, and a cushion for a man."

She squirmed and turned her head. "How so?"

"Like this." Taking care not to hurt her, he pulled her legs slightly apart, fitting himself between them and over her until her body fully supported his. He reached forward and took her hands in his and extended them over her head. Stretched then, from outflung hands to toes, his body resting on hers, he whispered into her ear. "See now how your entire body is a pillow for mine, and your buttocks a soft cushion for my belly. Do you feel this?" he asked as he arched his back, pushed his *lingam* down between her fleshy cheeks and searched for her entrance. Having found it, he inserted his *lingam* and gently, easily, made love to her until she moaned and her *yoni* muscles clamped around him, refusing to let him go. "This is the elephant posture."

"You're making that up." Her giggle worked itself down to his *lingam*. "Where is the elephant's trunk?"

He moved her outstretched hands from side to side, mimicking a swaying trunk.

She sniggered. "And the rest of the beast?"

"Don't you feel it?" He thrust mightily into her.

Her laugh turned into cries of delight. "Don't stop."

He held himself still a moment. "Perhaps we should try the congress of the bee."

"You jest," she panted. "A bee is too little. Please, more!"

He resumed his thrusting. With her soft bottom against his groin, the depth he reached in her *yoni*, he couldn't restrain his need. Arching his spine, his head bent back, he came at such length, and so copiously, he was mindless with the primitive possession of the male animal. He shouted, drowning her cries.

Barely aware, completely sated, he slumped to his side, taking her with him, still imbedded deep within, back to belly, and slept.

When he woke, he was alone in the bed. Splashing noises behind the screen told him where she was. He stretched and lay back, supremely comfortable and content. For all he knew this to be a mistake, a great wrong he did her, the ruination of Lady Jane was an entirely pleasurable enterprise. Who would have, or could have, guessed that the oft-forgot little orphan girl would grow up a courtesan at heart?

He heard her push the screen aside and watched her walk to the fire. She rattled the kettle, then added more water and replaced it on the hob. She glanced at the bed and saw him watching her. "Oh, good, you are awake."

"How long did I sleep?"

"Not long." She smiled. "Poor Mr. Attercliffe, I've quite drained you."

He laughed. "And so you did, but fear not. I shall recover shortly." His groin tightened. "Perhaps sooner than you think."

"What shall we do now?"

He sat up in bed. Through the windows, the afternoon sun poured a golden haze into the room. The glow on her skin tempted him to taste her warm, fragrant flesh again. "Come here."

Her hips undulating, breasts swaying proudly, she came to

him with her body erect, spine straight, shoulders thrown back and a greedy look on her face. "It's my turn now."

She sat next to him and couldn't hide a wince.

"Are you sore? Have I hurt you with my attentions?"

"Perhaps at first, but I am quite all right now."

"Let me see."

She retreated, her hands covering her mound as she stood.

"Don't be silly, Lady Jane. After all we have done, and intend to do, don't you think this modesty is misplaced?"

Her hands trembled. Her chin quivered, but she came forward, hands slowly dropping until her rounded mound, with its riotous crop of dark curls was within his reach. He inserted his hand between her thighs, slowly easing them apart, and with delicacy, gently opened her fleshy lips and exposed her to his gaze.

She had washed the stains of lovemaking away, leaving her petal pink, but slightly red where he had used her, and totally inviting. Bringing her closer, he kissed her belly, then each hip bone, and back to her navel. She squirmed under his touch. He placed both hands on her hips to hold her still and placed little suctioning kisses over her belly. She quivered under his touch but didn't move out of his grasp. His kisses grew bolder, a bit more intense as he kissed lower and lower and sought her most intimate place with his tongue. She gasped, then exhaled in a long slow breath of pleasure as he found her bud. He nuzzled in her scent, and then lifted his head, a slight frown on his face.

"What? Is that wrong?"

Chapter Eight

He kissed her flanks. "Nothing is wrong between lovers, my sweet."

"Then why do you grimace?"

He ran a fingertip atop her bite. "I prefer a woman's body to be hairless."

Her eyes grew round. "But that is not natural." She glanced at her legs, then her mound, where dark hair hid her *yoni*. "I can't help that."

"But I can. Will you allow me to shave you?"

She blinked. "Shave me? Women don't shave!"

"Perhaps not shave," he agreed, smiling a little at her scandalized protest. "In the East, women denude their bodies to please their lovers. Their reward is greater satisfaction when their lover presses kisses all over their skin."

"Truly?"

In answer, he pulled her to him and kissed her breast. He ran his tongue around her nipple. He sucked one into his mouth, then, maintaining the suction, pushed at her nipple with his tongue, almost losing it, then sucking it back in again. He felt her chest quiver with her increased breathing. He smiled. "Do you like the feel of my lips and tongue on you?"

"Oh," she sighed, "you must know that I do."

"Imagine how my tongue would feel here . . ." he touched her armpit. "Or here . . ." he stroked the back of her knee, smiling as she wriggled under his caress. "And here . . ." he reached between her labia to stroke her intimately.

Her legs opened of themselves, offering her to him. She closed her eyes and nodded.

He pulled himself away from her. "You won't regret it." He rose from the bed and rummaged in his luggage. He returned in a few moments with his shaving gear and placed it on the bedside table. He spread towels across the bed, then motioned her down on them. He brought two bowls of water and set them next to his shaving things.

He lifted his ivory-handled cutthroat razor. "Do not be frightened. If I had the lotions or creams Eastern women use, you might be less apprehensive, but by the time I use this, you will be ready." Next, he dipped a cloth in hot water, wrung it almost dry, and wrapped it around her calf. She winced a bit and raised questioning eyes to him.

"I'll start here, so that you grow accustomed."

She gave a slight nod. He interpreted it as nerves, curiosity and a desire to please him, all of which gratified him. While the cloth prepared her skin, he stropped his razor under her cautious watch and tested the edge. Next he mixed up lather in his shaving cup.

When he thought the cloth had done its job, he removed it and applied lather to her calf with his shaving brush.

"That tickles!" She sniffed. "Sandalwood. That's why your skin smells so pleasing."

He grinned. "As yours will. Now watch." He opened his razor, handle up, and applied the broad, sharp edge to her leg. He stroked gently down, removed the blade, rinsed it and tested his work. "Look, see how smooth your skin is."

She ran a finger down the shaved patch. "That didn't hurt a bit."

"Of course not. I don't wish to harm you." He repeated his actions on her other leg, and once satisfied with its smoothness, he took one arm and positioned it above her head, exposing her armpit to him. "Don't move." Gently, he soaped and shaved her, careful not to exert undue pressure or nick her skin. When he had scraped all her underarm hair away, he rinsed her clean and kissed the hollows of her armpit.

She squirmed and giggled but left her arm where it was as he kissed and licked the freshly shaven skin. "You taste delicious. A bit soapy, but delicious."

While he soaped and shaved her other arm, and then her thighs, he talked to her again of his travels. She listened, agog or aghast at some of his tales.

"Do you mean that cattle roam freely? In the streets? No one retrieves them and puts them back in the fields or dairy sheds?"

"Quite so. The cow is sacred."

She giggled. "That is absurd."

"To many Indians, the cow is the symbol of motherhood. She nourishes with her milk, provides butter for cooking and eating, and is protected as the symbol of charity and generosity. This virtue extends to matters of the flesh, thus the congress of the cow is the most spiritual, when the male worships the female."

She appeared unconvinced but seemed more interested when he began to speak of the women he had met.

"Did you make love to them all?" she asked.

"Of course not." He added fresh lather to a section of leg and re-shaved it. "At first, I was a pupil, learning certain skills. As I perfected my own technique, I added some of my own interpretations." He rinsed the razor, kissed her leg from ankle to knee as he stroked ever higher, accustoming her to the sensations.

She licked her lips. "Tell me."

"I am going to show you shortly." He paused to rub his finger over the entrance to her *yoni*. "Once you are ready for me."

When her limbs were closely shaven, he refreshed his water and stropped the razor again. She watched him, wide-eyed. "You don't mean to shave my head, do you?"

He grinned at her. "Absolutely not."

She swallowed. "Then . . ." Her glance flickered down.

"Yes," he said firmly. "I want to taste you, lick you, nibble on you."

She watched his razor fly against the leather. Swallowed again. "You will be careful?"

He noted she didn't deny him, merely request he not cut her. "I will be even more careful. Open to me."

The muscles in her upper thighs clenched, closing her legs, then, drawing a deep breath, she opened them wide.

"Good. Now hold still."

He applied a warm cloth, then lathered her. Intent on pleasing as well as denuding her, he let the brush tickle her bud, penetrate the outer regions of her *yoni*, and play against the extremely sensitive area around her anus. All the while, he praised her. "It's a pity you can't see how beautiful you are, your legs open to me, your *yoni* calling to me. Even your rosebud here," he said as he rimmed her anus with the shaving brush, "is interested in my touch."

She murmured a protest.

Havyn pressed a kiss on her belly. "The *yoni* is the most secret part of a woman, the part a man yearns to know, to claim as his own. Once a man knows his woman's intimate fragrance, he could pick her out of a roomful of women with his eyes closed."

When he could apply no more lather, and she lay relaxed and limp, he applied his razor. Sliding gently down one side of her labia, then the other, he shaved her. He took his time, assuring her with his tender touch and calm voice, though his *lingam* jumped and pulsed, ready to claim her once more. Once or twice, he inserted his finger into her and circled her inner muscles, provoking them into clasping his finger with a firm grip.

Pleased, he stropped his razor again and bent to his task. At last, her body was as hairless as she had been as a babe. He rinsed her thoroughly, taking time to ease the cloth into both her *yoni* and nether opening to cleanse her of all lather. She was by now so accepting of his touch that she allowed everything he did to her. She moaned with pleasure as he flicked her little bud with his thumb and slid a finger into her. "This is for upper congress," he instructed, then inserted the tip of another finger into her anus. "Here is for lower." He waited a moment, then added, "Many find lower congress stimulating."

She tensed, then relaxed the tight muscles, allowing him to play.

Pleased with her response, he set his shaving gear aside and lay between her legs. Beginning with her ankles, he kissed where his razor had been, replacing the touch of finely crafted cold steel with his hot mouth and tongue. Her moans grew louder, her body restive as he tongued her behind her knees, finding those exquisitely sensitive spots, then up higher, lapping in bold strokes, ever closer and closer to her waiting, moist *yoni*.

He alternated the long tongue laps with short strokes, wetting her skin and working his mouth and lips over the moist skin.

She moaned and writhed in his arms. "You torment me!"

He lifted his head enough to promise, "I shall do more."

He placed his hands on her knees, holding them open for him and bent his head to her again. He nuzzled her for a moment, inhaling both the scent of his sandalwood shaving lather, and the fresh clean aroma of woman. Then, before she could wriggle away, he put the tip of his tongue at the entrance to her *yoni* and licked upward over her bud.

She screamed.

And screamed again when he licked one side, the other, and twirled his tongue around her bud. She jumped, tried to pull his head away from her, tried to stop the sensations he knew must shock her, thrill her. At last, she stopped trying to evade his flicking tongue and gave herself up to her pleasure. Pleasuring him.

He gave her no rest. His tongue busied himself with her *yoni*. His senses inhaled the taste and the fragrance of her, his mouth sucked on her all the while he gently probed her anus then boldly thrust first one, then two fingers into her *yoni*. Her cries gave way to moans, to her hips arching under his touch. "Oh, please, no more," she begged. "Aaah . . . don't stop!"

Chapter Nine

Havyn tucked her hand into the crook of his elbow and led her down the cobblestone street. She had protested getting dressed and grumbled at leaving the intimacy of their room at the inn, but he had insisted they needed fresh air.

He led them around the square, pointing out this building and that, and then down an inviting side street where he helped her over a style onto a path circling a wooded grove. When he was sure that no one could overhear their conversation, he stopped her.

Turning her to face him, he studied her face under her silly little hat with cherries on the brim. "Shall we rest a moment?"

"I'm hardly an invalid needing to rest," she retorted, still peeved.

"I thought you might be a trifle chafed." He looked down into her face. "I haven't been as gentle as I should have been."

She glanced away, then back at him. "I have no complaints."

"Nor I. Your skills will soon exceed those of the most accomplished *houri*."

Her dimple flashed as she gave him a smug, cat-in-the-cream smile. "I promised you wouldn't regret ruining me."

Her words reminded him that their idyllic time must come to an end. Regretfully. "So you did. I only hope you never will." He pressed a kiss to her temple. "Shall we discuss the next stage of our plan?"

Her eyes questioned him.

"Now that you are properly 'ruined'," he said with a satisfied grin, "have you thought what we should do next?" He had a plan in motion, but he wanted her to voice her own thoughts.

She gazed out over a field ripe with barley. "Do you think we should continue on our journey?"

Absolutely not. Now that he had succumbed to her arguments and quite delightfully introduced her to the erotic arts, he had no wish of cutting short their time together. Not even by a second, though he knew it must happen soon. But not yet. Every day he became more entranced with her, unwilling to let her go. "Shall we?" he asked, pleased that he kept his voice cool.

She toyed with the fastenings of yet another spencer, this one in a pale blue that did nothing for her features. Had he the dressing of her, he would choose vibrant colors that set off her complexion and flattered her succulent form. He waited, not so patiently, while she considered.

"Please, let us stay here. I collect Anna will send word to the Lodge, and when we don't arrive, someone will set out to find us." She smiled up at him. "Then we could be found in fragrant delic . . ."

"Flagrante delicto," he corrected with a laugh. "An excellent plan!" He didn't mention that he'd taken a moment to pen a quick message to his brother and sent it off by post stage. It shouldn't be too long before he or Yarwoode sent a coach to fetch Lady Jane home.

It was necessary, he reminded himself. He'd miss her company. She was a delightful companion, both in and out of bed. Ah, bed . . . Before they were discovered, he would instruct her on more of the lovemaking arts he'd perfected on his travels. With her aptitude, she'd master them quickly, giving them each time to enjoy them and each other. He wanted every moment of pleasure. Who knew how much time they had before their interlude was interrupted?

And what would he do then?

He pondered the question through a meal served to them in the private parlor he'd reserved, but found no answers, only more questions. The meal was simple fare but well prepared and served with discretion. He sat across from her at a small table before the fire, enjoying both his mackerel with fennel and mint and the candlelight dancing across her face. In the muted light, her eyes seemed larger, more lustrous, and her smile, coming often with her laughter, added spice to their dinner.

"There I was," he recounted, "sitting like a tailor on a silk cushion, with my legs uncomfortably cramped under me. A meal fit for a king was laid out on the table with golden goblets, fragrant flowers everywhere, and I couldn't eat a bite."

"Why not?"

"It was blistering hot, and my clothes bound me so tightly I feared I'd suffocate."

At her questioning glance, he continued. "The other guests and the rajah himself wore loose robes, nothing constricting." He grinned. "Even the serving girls wore loose clothing."

Her eyes rounded.

"The next day, a servant brought some local garb to my rooms. It was a gift from the rajah and I donned it without regret."

"What was it?"

"Loose baggy pantaloons, a silk coat or tunic of sorts, fitted to the waist and then loose to my ankles. Soft leather boots. A turban round my head. Like this," he gestured with a wrapping motion about his head.

"How very odd."

"How very cool. It made much more sense in that infernal heat." He drank some ale. "Shall I tell you what the women wear?"

She nodded, her eyes large and curious.

"First, no corsets or undergarments. They put on loose skirts, which are actually a long piece of cloth which they wrap around their middles until they make a very tidy dress."

"And their . . ." Lady Jane motioned to her upper torso.

"Ah, with the climate in mind, the ladies bare their midriff and wear a garment, much like your spencer, with short sleeves, and no collar. With a rounded neckline," he added, gesturing at her bosom. "Sometimes they wear a longer, more closely fitting tunic like a man's but I preferred the short tops."

"You would!"

He laughed. "In the privacy of their rooms, the women don't wear a shawl, or veil, covering their heads." He paused. "When they practice the sexual arts, men and women wear nothing but jewelry on their necks, arms and hands. Even their feet."

"You jest."

"I do not. A woman's dowry is in her jewelry. When she wears it for her husband, she takes satisfaction in her worth. A man takes pride in adorning his wife. Gold chains, pendants studded with gems, armbands also with gems, and on their toes and fingers, many rings. Indeed, the ankle band is connected to the toe rings with many fine gold links."

She said nothing for a moment, her face still as she thought. "You mean like those paintings at Grantham Lodge?"

He drew his brows together. "You saw them?"

"Of course. I often borrowed books from my guardian's library." She paused to reflect. "The people in those paintings looked as if they knew a secret. I often wondered what it was."

"You know now. They are lovers, contemplating how next to please each other." He smiled, thinking of how next he would please her. "Perhaps he is thinking of making love to her when she wears nothing but her gems."

"It must be very uncomfortable."

Perhaps, but if he were at home, with all the wealth he had brought back from his travels, he would show her. More than show her, he would bedeck her from head to toe in exotic gems and fine gold chains. He imagined her, gold at her neck, her waist, her navel, dripping from her wrists and arms. Toe rings connected to the chains at her ankles. A jewel fitted to her navel and another in her *yoni*. Emerald or ruby? He swallowed hard. His *lingam* rose and requested prompt attention. He noticed she had stopped eating some time before. "Are you satisfied?"

She shook her head no.

"I mean, have you finished your meal?"

She didn't look at her plate. Instead, she rose. "I am ready to retire."

He rose quickly, too. She glanced down then, saw the bulge growing larger behind his buckskins and smiled, a heady, ravenous smile. "Shall we go up?"

Grinning, he escorted her with more haste and less grace than befitted her rank. He unlocked the door to their room and stood aside to let her enter.

She paused on the threshold, staring at the bed, freshly made with clean linens, at the flowers, gladioli and lilies from the innkeeper's garden, and candles, candles everywhere.

The room glowed with flickering lights, the scent of blooms laced the air, and the bed welcomed. She entered the room, her face entranced. "You ordered this?"

He nodded, gratified she found it pleasing.

"Thank you, Mr. Attercliffe."

He closed and locked the door behind them. "Surely by now you might feel free to use my given name."

"Havyn . . ." She ran into his arms. "Oh, Havyn!"

He waited while she sniffled, then handed her a clean white

handkerchief. How odd that she could handle rejection with anger and pride, but a tender gesture set her to crying. He kissed her temples, licked away her tears and eased her lips apart with his tongue.

She caught her breath, then pulled his tongue into her mouth and sucked on it. The kiss grew deeper, hotter, unrestrained until both panted, drew quick breaths and fed on the other again. He felt her knees quiver, took her weight upon himself and held her still while he ravaged her mouth and in return, fed her increasing hunger with his own.

At last, gasping, they drew apart. They stared at each other, a smile blossoming on her face.

"I want to learn more. Teach me more positions."

"You must be devilishly sore by now, Lady Jane."

"No. You must ease this ache in me. Why does my belly ache? My breasts burn?"

"That is desire. Your body craves mine."

"Do you feel the same?"

He took her hand and pressed it against his groin. "Indeed I do. More than my belly aches for you. My *lingam* begs for your touch."

"Teach me," she commanded. "Teach me the cow position!"

He hesitated. That would require her assuming what she no doubt would consider a very undignified position. It would be best to ease her into it. "Would you undress for me, please?"

She did so with alacrity. He had to laugh. Shy, modest Lady Jane had disappeared, replaced with an eager *houri*. He removed his own clothing, hanging both his and hers from the pegs.

He looked over his shoulder to see her rummaging in her portmanteaus. She brought forth her jewelry box. Ah, so she had taken his words to heart. How he wished he had some gems to give her now.

She drew both some pearl earbobs and a matching necklace. "Will this do? I'm afraid I have only a few things with me. Most of my jewelry is in safekeeping."

He took the pearls from her and fastened them on her neck and earlobes. He bent a little closer and licked the edge of her ear, tracing the whorls with the tip of his tongue. He held his breath, careful not to breathe in her ear, while he pulled the lobe, pearl and all, into his mouth and sucked.

She exhaled, her body going lax against his. He put his arms around her, holding her facing away from him. With his palms, he cupped her breasts, tweaking at the nipples until they hardened and grew longer, then with his mouth on her neck, sucking in and nibbling, he smoothed down her ribs, her hips, circled her belly and, while she breathed harder and faster, teased her closely shaven bite.

He circled her mound with his fingers, drawing ever closer to her *yoni*, until at last, his fingertip pressed between the smooth nether lips and tickled her bud. "Does this excite you?"

She squirmed her buttocks against his belly. "You must know it does."

"Bend your head." When she did, he removed her pearls, and slid them down her chest, around her breasts, pushed one in her little navel, then draped them over her mound. He slid the pearls across her bud and over her *yoni*, then between her thighs and up between her soft, fleshy cheeks.

Her bud grew as he fingered it. It hardened, mimicking his own greater member. He played with it while she grew restive and moaned.

"You are so responsive, so easy to please." He paused, considering his next words. "You can do this for yourself any time you wish."

"Truly? With my pearls?"

"Or your hands. Shall I show you how?"

She moved her shoulders against his chest. "I would like that."

"Come, then. Take your hand, like this," he covered her hand with his and stroked down her belly. "That's right. Now your finger, here . . ." He guided her index finger to the one side of her labia. "Start here. Find the stroke that feels best to you. Either here on this side, or the other. Or alternating sides." He demonstrated, using her finger to touch herself. At first she balked, then as if realizing the pleasure she denied herself, allowed him to instruct her.

"Have you ever touched yourself here?"

"Oh, no!"

"There is nothing wrong with it. Pay attention, now. You will find yourself getting moist, making it easier to touch yourself and more pleasing. Do you notice that yet?" He asked but he could answer for himself. Her woman's juices were seeping, allowing her finger to slip easily over her increasingly sensitive skin.

He increased the pace of her strokes, from the bottom of her *yoni*, up along the lips, flicking gently at her bud, then gently rimming it. Her breathing increased. A flush rose from her breasts.

He changed the direction of their fingers, circling her anus, rimming it with her fingertips while she squirmed, next her bud now without touching it, then with the sides of her labia with their fingertips. She moaned and moved her hips in time with their hands.

"That's it. Is it pleasing to you?"

She nodded, her luxuriant hair caressing his chest. His *lingam* felt like it would burst from the need to bury himself deep within her.

"Just a bit more. Now, easy, gently, touch yourself here." He tapped the bud directly. She caught her breath, then took the motion from him and pleasured herself without his guidance. "You can please yourself any time you wish. You won't need a lover to give yourself satisfaction."

"But nothing makes me feel how I am with you." Her hips rotated, grinding against his pelvis, exciting him beyond control. Quickly, he took her hand away from her *yoni* and bent her over completely so that she supported herself on her hands and feet. Before she could utter a word, he widened her stance, then moved closely behind her, and with one hand on her hip to hold her, the other replacing hers at her bud, he entered her with one quick, forceful thrust.

"Aah . . ." She tried to pull away, shake him off her, but he held her still. "No, get off me!"

"This is the congress of the cow," he grunted between thrusts. "Imagine that you are the sacred cow of India, and I am the bull!"

"I didn't know it would be like this!"

"Relax, my sweet. Allow me to worship you."

She subsided, her cries dwindling to whimpers, then murmurs.

His thrusts grew longer, deeper, faster. She held herself perfectly still, her head almost to her knees. Gradually, so slowly he wasn't sure he felt it, her hips moved as she began to take pleasure in being taken in this manner. Her movements gained force, then swiveled, her buttocks pushing back against his groin as she moaned and cried her ecstasy. She convulsed around him, her inner muscles working furiously, pulling and clenching his rod. He came in a great, thundering rush, almost blinding him with pleasure.

He staggered, making her stumble, and they collapsed together to the floor.

He lay dazed, almost insensate while she was pinned beneath his greater weight. At last, her squirming efforts to move out from under him penetrated his senses. He pulled himself out of her and rolled to the side. "My apologies," he gasped. "Are you hurt?"

She sat up, her breasts heaving and her face red. "I can't believe that . . . that was so humiliating, to be used like . . . like an animal!"

His eyes had drifted shut but he forced them open. "I take it you didn't like the congress of the cow?" He ignored her splutters, preferring to recall her cries of pleasure. "It is a particular favorite in India."

"Not to me!"

He smiled lazily. "I was quite overcome with satisfaction. As were you."

She ignored his reminder as she got to her feet and vanished behind the screen. He heard water splashing, thought he should get up, but just a moment more. The floor wasn't all that uncomfortable. His eyes closed.

He heard her rustling about, felt her pacing through the movement of the floorboards, then heard something he couldn't quite identify. He forced himself to open his eyes.

She had opened her *necessaire* and taken her scissors to a pale green spencer. He watched in astonishment as she snipped away, first the sleeves, then the collar. She held it up, nodded in satisfaction, then put it on. The sleeves were ragged, the bodice buttoned to just beneath her breasts and the neckline uneven, but he loved it.

He waited, watching to see what she would do next. She rummaged through her portmanteau, taking out clothing, scanning it and dropping it to the floor. At last, she held up a voluminous, demure white nightgown with ruffles on the sleeves, at the buttoned up neckline and on the hem. She tore at it with her hands, then when the material didn't give, grabbed her scissors and went to work. Bits of fabric floated down to join the shambles on the floor. She cut off the bodice, then slit open a side seam, leaving only a length of white cloth. Intent on her task, she didn't see him watching while she wound it around her hips.

He laughed. "You look like a raggedy Indian woman."

She whirled around, her expression a mix of pride and insecurity. "Is this how they wear it?"

"Somewhat. Silks and a proper cut make a difference, but I am charmed that you did this." He sat up, stretched and got to his feet. "I wish I had some silk to wrap around you. Scarlet, I think, with gold thread. You would be magnificent."

Her eyes widened. "Truly?"

"You would put every other woman to shame." He nodded. "As it is, your efforts demand a reward."

"What kind?"

"What would you like? Silks? Jewelry?"

She waved those offers away. "You."

"Even after I humiliated you with being a bull to your cow?"

She glared at him, then dimpled and smiled. "I have rethought my reservations about that position."

"Ah—"

"To reward me for my change of mind, you must place yourself at my disposal."

He opened his arms. "I am here."

She stayed where she was, looking like an innocent waif playing dressup in her butchered clothing. Then she smiled, and the look changed to a seductive siren luring men to her sensual lair.

He went willingly, eagerly.

Chapter Ten

Two days passed while they rarely left their bedroom at the inn. Content with the coins Havyn provided, the innkeeper sent up meals, the chambermaids refreshed their room and all left them in peace.

Lady Jane rolled over and sat, with her legs crossed beneath her. Her *yoni*, red and pink and deliciously tempting, was completely exposed to him. "I want you to teach me something . . . something wicked."

He blinked. "Wicked, how?"

"I know you didn't describe the more shocking temple statues. You thought I was too innocent to learn about all of them. Well," she propped her hands on her hips, "I'm innocent no longer. I am a completely ruined woman."

He laughed. "Indeed you are. Thoroughly ruined."

"So there is no reason not to complete my education." She paused, then added wistfully, "Who knows if I shall ever know such pleasure again."

He wished he could reassure her that she would indeed be pleasured again and again, as often as his *lingam* would cooperate, but who knew how much time together they had left? He kissed her instead.

When he released her sometime later, both breathless, she said, "You have been showing me how to make love, showing me how to please myself, but there must be something I can do to please you."

Oh, there was, there was. "Pleasing you has given me great satisfaction."

She licked her lips. "What do you do when you are alone and want to pleasure yourself?" She glanced at his *lingam*, which had been resting quietly, recuperating, on his thigh. Under her gaze, it lifted its head and made its presence known.

Havyn covered himself with his hand.

"Do you touch yourself?"

Her question, posed so innocently, made him pulse. What had happened to young proper English misses in the years he'd been abroad? Had they all decided to throw modesty aside? Or was he fortunate enough to have discovered the only one who made his blood sing and his senses reel?

"You do, don't you?"

He nodded.

"Show me how."

How could he ignore this command when his *lingam* echoed the demand? He moved his hand, revealing his member already grown and hard. He placed his palm under his cock, then gripped himself. With a motion grown familiar from much usage, he pulled out, stretching the skin to all but cover the head, then back, sliding his fingers over the shaft, stroking the most sensitive underside of the blunt, rosy tip.

She moved closer, dropped to her knees to observe. She watched him stroke, one, twice more, while she learned the motion he favored. "Let me."

Without a word, he moved his hand and surrendered his *lingam* to her. She took it hesitantly, reverently, shaping her hand around his full length. She looked up at him with wide eyes. "You are soft, like satin, but hard inside."

He swallowed. "Touch me like this," he instructed as he placed his hand under hers and once more taught her self-pleasure. "As you did before, but this time, add a stroke. Yes," he inhaled sharply. "That's the way."

At first, she was cautious, doing only as she was shown, but gradually, she gained confidence and began experimenting. He bore it well, though she tormented him beyond measure, watching him closely for his reaction. She even dared skim a finger across his sac.

"Those are my ballocks," he murmured. "Touch them gently or you could cause me distress."

"Like this?" She circled one with a finger, then jumped when the ball inside moved. "Oh!"

"That is good. Very good," he hissed as his belly contracted. "You have an exquisite touch." Before she could ask, he reassured her, "Truly."

She smiled. "Thank you. I collect that being ruined is infinitely more fun than being proper."

He had to laugh. "That is not what the *ton* wants you to think. You are supposed to wail and cry and bemoan your fate."

"Oh bother all that! Now that I have discovered what this is all about, I have nothing to bewail. In fact, I shall continue being improper."

"No doubt one day your husband will have something to say about that."

At his words, she fell silent, reminded no doubt that Lord Yarwoode expected to be her husband. She let his *lingam* lie restless in her palm, then jumped up and went to the window. She seemed heedless of her nakedness as she rested her face against the cool windowpane. In the quiet, he could hear laughter from the taproom below and noises from the stable and courtyard, but they appeared not to bother her.

He couldn't see her expression, but he berated himself for introducing reality into their sensual cocoon. He rose and went to her. "I apologize. That was thoughtless of me."

She sighed and turned into his chest. He drew the curtains together, shutting out the night and enforcing their enclosed feelings.

"I don't want to think beyond this room," she whispered.

Her breath touched his chest, much as her words touched his heart. He could continue being locked away from the world with her for an indefinite time, but eventually, they would have to face two angry men. He hoped they took their time in finding them, but he couldn't count on that. Shortly, she would have to accept the consequences of her ruination.

She had been right when she stated that it was different for men. His conduct would raise eyebrows, a titter or two, perhaps even banishment from some salons, but in the end, he would be no worse for the experience. He stroked her bare, silky back. "Come to bed before you get chilled."

She looked up at him, her eyes solemn, seeming undecided for a moment, then shrugged. "Shall we continue the lesson?"

He was staggered by her determination. Her courage. Lady Jane was a precious jewel, deserving to be treasured. He embraced her for a moment, then led her to the bed.

They snuggled under the covers. She took him in her hand

again, and stroked him as before, but he could tell her heart wasn't in it, and removed his *lingam* from her grasp. He turned her away from him, lying spoon fashion, his hand across her belly, her buttocks nestled against his thighs. "Sleep now, my dear."

Sometime during the night he awoke, to find her leaning on one elbow, gazing raptly into his face. All the candles but one had fizzled out, leaving just enough light to see her intent expression. "Was I snoring?"

"Just a bit."

He realized that the covers were off, that he was bare to the knees, his *lingam* rising proud and high against his abdomen. Her small hand had him firmly in her grasp.

"It occurs to me," she said solemnly, "that if it pleasures me to have your tongue on my . . . *yoni*," she managed at last, "it might pleasure you to have my tongue on your—"

"*Lingam,*" he supplied promptly. "It would indeed."

She scooted down the bed until she was at eye level with his *lingam*, that impatient fellow who kept waving his head at her. "What should I do?"

He forced himself to sound calm. "Whatever you wish to do. Except bite."

She giggled. "Upon my word, do you think I would do that?"

"It has been known to happen to a man whose lover is unhappy with him."

"I am not unhappy," she assured him with a grave face.

"Then I am much reassured." He waved at his groin. "Whenever you are ready."

She paused, her hand poised over his lingam. She frowned, as if thinking hard. Then, tentatively, she circled the tip of his rod as she had done before, then pleased with herself, she slid her hand around it, holding him with her thumb on his head. He forced himself to remain still, watching her watch him.

She slid her palm down, gripping him at the base, feeling his pulse jump and skip about in happy expectation, then with her other hand, cupped the head of his *lingam*. She squeezed, gently at first, and when he didn't protest—how could he when it felt so deuced good—she brushed her palm over the head, making circles.

Suddenly, she jumped and pulled her hand back. She stared at the drop of liquid on the tip of his *lingam*. "Did I hurt you?" she whispered.

He managed not to groan. "On the contrary. What you see is merely my body readying itself to enter yours."

"It's good, then?"

"Very, *very* good."

"Shall I continue?"

"If you wouldn't mind." He had to smile, such courtesy came naturally to her, as free and spirited as her generous nature.

With growing confidence, she applied herself to her self-appointed task. She cupped her hands around him, slid them up and down his shaft, girdled the tip and laughed when he moaned. She took no mercy on him.

Eventually, she grew even bolder. Havyn thought he'd expire from the touch of her hands, but when she cast him a questioning glance, then bent her head and circled the rim of his *lingam*, he knew at once that he'd entered Nirvana. She echoed some of her hand movements with her tongue, discovering for herself the little head was exquisitely sensitive. She flicked it with her tongue, laughed when he jumped, then set herself to teasing him with delicate strokes, tiny little nibbles that inflicted no pain, only made him harder, longer, mad for her.

She slid her mouth down his rod, taking it in her mouth as deeply as he could penetrate. She gagged a bit, then released him slowly, drawing her lips over his receding member, then sucking him in again, this time less deeply, but with greater firmness. She swirled the tip in her mouth, and with a provocative glance at him, reached between his open thighs and stroked his ballocks.

At last, he could take no more. "Enough," he gasped and moved her head away from him. "You will make me spend in your mouth when my *lingam* desires your delightful *yoni*."

She looked first disappointed, then interested. Very interested. "What shall we do this time?"

"Whatever you desire."

Her eyes were dark in the flickering candlelight, the dimple in her right cheek flashed, her full lips smiled provocatively. "What is your favorite of all positions?"

He paused to consider. "There are many I favor. Some are very difficult if you haven't trained your body to be flexible."

"Describe one," she demanded instantly.

"Ah, let's see. The man sits, balancing his weight on his hands placed behind him. He opens his legs, and the woman, facing him on hands and feet, bends away from his torso." She looked confused. "She offers her *yoni* to his mouth, and reaching back, spine bent in a curve, her body almost in a circle, takes his *lingam* in her mouth. Her forehead rests on his thighs. They give each other mutual gratification."

Her eyes widened as she visualized the contortions involved. "That's impossible!"

"Not if the woman is very supple."

She shook her head. "That won't do," she said firmly. "Tell me another. One we can do."

He grinned. "As you wish." He found candles and lit them from the dying one as she made impatient noises. "I want more light to see you."

He moved back, resting his head on the pillows. "For this one, I shall be prone and you shall be in command."

"I? How?"

He laughed. "In Indian lore, men are classified by the size of their *lingams*. They are hares, bulls, and horses such as myself." He saw understanding grow as she glanced at the size of his growing rod. "Now, since I am a horse, you shall ride me."

He lifted her and placed her on his thighs. Her legs opened on either side of him, as she sat with her weight on her knees. "That's it. The beauty of this position is that I can play with your breasts." He demonstrated as he spoke, cupping her luscious breasts in both hands, thumbing the nipples, tweaking them, making her shiver. Her hair, long ago tousled from bedsport, cascaded over her shoulders and clung to his fingers. He took a moment to wind a silky curl around her velvety breast.

"I can also play with your dainty little bud, here." She moaned as he stroked and teased her, her eyes fluttering closed. "Pay attention, Lady Jane."

She opened her eyes and held his with a heavy-lidded look.

"Now, when you lift up, like this," he instructed with his hands on her hips, raising her, "you can command your horse with your knees." He lowered her slightly, releasing one hand to guide himself to her glistening *yoni*. "You choose how deep you wish me, how fast, how slow you wish to take me into you. You command your mount, my lady."

She took him an inch at a time into her *yoni*. She sighed, threw her head back, then brought it forward to watch his member disappear into her. She laughed. "I like this!"

His fingers delved between them to find her bud. He stroked it once, twice, making her gasp and quiver. "Let me!" She pushed his hand away and inserted her own, touching herself, then circling the base of his *lingam*. In and out he went, doing her bidding, now barely penetrating her, next thrusting deeply, taking his instructions from her. She shook with the pleasure wracking her body. "Oh, it quite overwhelms me!"

In a moment of desperate delight, she convulsed around him, her inner muscles clasping, clenching, milking him dry. He shot up into her with such fervor, he realized he'd emptied his soul into her keeping.

She trembled. She cried. She fell forward onto his chest, losing herself to tears. They came, hot and heavy, soaking his chest. He stroked her hair, her back, her buttocks, murmuring soft words meant only for her. Still crying, but softer now that the intensity of the moment ebbed, she rolled to her side. He rolled with her, keeping her clasped closely to him.

"I'm sorry. I hate being a watering-pot, but I don't know what it is about you that brings out this behavior."

He understood. Reaction to deep emotion, physical sensations she'd never experienced before, and a growing realization, and acceptance, of her own worth as a woman. All these things in a short period of time. It was no surprise that her emotions were heightened. "Not to worry, sweet," he soothed. "You can sprinkle me whenever you wish."

She laughed, then hiccuped. "What a bother I am to you."

"What a delight you are to me."

His contradiction set off a fresh flow. She turned away from him, and buried her face in the rumpled sheets. He allowed that for a moment or two, then scooped her in, spoon fashion. "Sleep now. You deserve your rest."

As he did. It amazed him that he had such stamina and vigor with her. When he'd agreed to her plan to ruin her for marriage to Lord Yarwoode, he'd thought he'd take her innocence, compromise her, and then face the consequences without any personal involvement. How wrong he'd been!

Chapter Eleven

They had returned from an early morning stroll on the heather covered moor. Lady Jane had scampered about, heedless of her virginal white muslin gown and blue spencer which she'd worn with a wide-brimmed straw hat with matching blue ribbons streaming behind her in the breeze.

Havyn had sat on a rock, watching her with an amused smile as she gathered great armfuls of heather. He kissed away a scratch on her hand, then opened her spencer to press kisses on her exposed bosom. At his instruction, she'd omitted the lacy wrap that would otherwise cover her properly, befitting the time of day. "You taste delicious."

She raised her mouth to his. "You always say that," she murmured against his lips.

"I always mean it." He opened her mouth with his tongue, then with lazy sweeps, explored her mouth thoroughly. "You are a succulent morsel. I could devour you."

She laughed. "You've already done that. I have your teeth marks on my sit-upon."

"You do not. I did not bite your bottom." He reached for the hem of her gown. "I shall correct my oversight, now that you mention it."

"Perhaps not," she danced out of reach with a mischievous laugh.

"But I am hungry," he complained.

"Perhaps later, if your breakfast doesn't satisfy you."

"Perhaps I won't want to then," he teased and raised his face to the sun. The English sun felt weak after years of the intensely bright, hot sun of India, but it warmed him anyway. The breeze was cool, bringing with it the scent of the heather, wild grasses, and farther away, crops almost ready for harvesting. In time, the wind would chill, the fields lay fallow, and winter would lie thick upon the ground, but now, his time with Lady Jane was an idyll.

One he didn't want to end.

They strolled, avoiding the marshy bog areas, talking of this and that. Havyn told her more about his travels, how he had climbed portions of the Himalayas and gazed upon the snowy peaks with awe. He described the Eastern customs and the long sea voyage home. Lady Jane listened, asked intelligent questions and entranced him with her interest, before telling him of her work with her various charities.

How lucky some man would be to have her as his lifelong companion! Regret tainted the delight her company gave him. Their time together must soon come to a close. All too soon.

Still regretting their private intimacy must end, Havyn escorted her up the inn stairs to their room to change her gown before their meal. As before, he played lady's maid, undoing her fastenings and reclining on the bed to watch her complete her toilette.

She had removed all but her stockings, and held one leg up to examine the tear at one ankle. "Oh, bother."

Her upraised leg gave him a clear view of her shapely mound and pink *yoni*. He swallowed. His *lingam* leaped to attention. He rose and went to the little table. "Come here," he said thickly.

She glanced up, surprise on her face, then at a glance, took in his engorged condition. "Now?"

"Now."

She came to him obediently, a question on her face. With one hand, he unbuttoned his buckskins and lowered the flap. His red sprang free. She touched it, ran her hand down the shaft, then up to circle the head. "But you are still clothed."

"And you are naked." He turned her, bent her over the table. He slid his hand over her bottom, pinched it lightly, and when she jumped, kissed the tiny hurt away. He rubbed his face against her smooth, plump cheek, bit it and delved between her parted legs.

Finding her moist and ready for him, he murmured his appreciation and played with her nether lips for a moment, while she squirmed and tried to get up. "Stay there."

He took his *lingam* in hand and bending his knees slightly, probed between her legs until he found the entrance to her *yoni*. In a flash, he entered, embedding himself deeply. She gasped in surprise and he answered her with a gratified moan.

He began a steady rhythm, in and out, feeling her at first tense, then surrender to the passion and gradually pushing out her bottom to make it easier for him. No longer fretting at the submissive position, or worried about humiliation, she grasped the table edge for support, held immobile by his body while he claimed her again and again. And again. He closed his eyes, giving himself up to the moment, but his hands were busy, stroking her cheeks, then finding her bud, stroking and pulling it until she shattered around him.

He came then, too, pulsing madly within her, hot and hard and urgent. He rested, still held by her yielding body, chest heaving.

She made a little mewling sound, and he realized he must be too heavy on her. Reluctantly, he pulled back and out. She inched off the table, and stood, a little unsteadily. Turning her to face him, he studied her dazed expression. "Did I hurt you?"

She shook her head slowly from side to side. Her eyes never left his. "I didn't know I could feel that way . . . I felt you touch my heart."

His broke.

He could say nothing, but look at her and wish that he could tell her how much she had touched him, how she was making him reconsider his situation. In seeking fulfillment of the great goals of life, he credited himself with achieving three. He repeated them to himself, wishing to impose order and calm where his heart beat madly.

One, he had a fortune in his possession as ordained by *Artha*. Two, he had achieved the sensual pleasure and physical fulfillment of *Kama* many times over. Three, he had believed himself to have found the judgment and responsibility of *Dharma*, as required for an well-ordered life.

He sighed. Lady Jane had thrown his best laid plans into complete disorder. He had yet to achieve *Moksha*, the fourth and greatest goal of enlightenment of mind and spirit that bound the previous three goals into a satisfying, contented whole life. With his newfound doubts and immoderate acts, *Moksha* seemed even further away.

His actions here with Lady Jane were not those of a man of ordered judgment. Rather, he had thrown reason to the wind and acted with the mad, impulsive haste of an importunate lover. There was a price to pay for that and he reconciled himself to paying it, no matter the cost or difficulty. He could do no less and consider himself an honorable man.

Deep in contemplation, he found a cloth, moistened it, and cleansed first her private parts, then his own. He redid his buckskins, pushing down his errant *lingam* that boasted it could still perform its pleasurable duties, and helped her dress in a fresh, clean gown.

"I had thought you had too much baggage, sweet, but now I see you have need of everything you brought."

She shook out the wrinkles in her day gown. "I didn't quite expect, however, to be wearing nothing so much of the time."

He laughed and called for their meal. They spoke of this and that, broadening their knowledge, and at least on his part, his delight in her lively, intelligent mind. The time slipped by as they lingered at the table.

"How is it that you are so well-read?" he asked.

She glanced around as if Grantham were there to overhear. "When my guardian was not at home, I went into his library and read his books."

"As I recall, there is nothing but history and philosophies."

"Oh, there is much more than that. I couldn't translate all the words, but I found the French plays quite amusing."

He remembered some of the more risqué ones. "Did you take the meaning, then?"

"Partly." She colored delicately. "Some of it has become quite clear since I met you."

He laughed. "Very happy to oblige your understanding."

She laughed too, then yawned, covering her mouth with her hand. "Oh, my. I find I am fatigued. All that fresh air and exertion this morning." She gave him a coy, seductive glance. "I think I'd like a nap."

"Excellent idea." He smiled even as he felt his *lingam* jump for joy.

Once again abed, naked and relishing the soft breeze through the open window, he lay back with his head propped on his arms. "You aren't sleeping."

"Neither are you." She touched his erect rod, caressing the head with a fingertip. "In fact, you look most decidedly alert. Are you always this way?"

He considered how he should answer. How could he tell her that his stamina was both the product of his never ceasing desire for her and long practice in the sensual arts? He knew how to pace himself, how to prolong desire and postpone fulfillment while he ensured that his lover came copiously and often. At last he settled for the simplest answer, the simple truth. "I am with you."

She smiled contentedly. And yawned, her eyes drifting shut.

He kissed her open mouth, then lifted his head. "Put on your jewels."

Her eyes popped open, all sleepiness gone. She hopped out of bed, rummaged in her portmanteau and brought back her jewelry case. "You choose."

"Everything." He took his time, placing the pearls and another simple necklace around her neck, bracelets on her wrists and arms as high as they would go, and wound a gold locket around her ankle. He added rings to her fingers, and one on a toe. When she was garlanded, he sat back, pleased.

She looked at herself and shook her arms, making her adornments tinkle. "I look silly."

"You are ravishing. I think, in honor of your yawns, I will take you in the yawning position."

Her eyes grew bigger. "How?"

"You'll see." He gave his shaft a stroke or two, testing his readiness, but as always, his *lingam* was enthusiastic and able. "Lie back, make yourself comfortable."

She did, tucking a pillow under her head. "And now?"

He sat at her feet, spreading her legs. "Open for me."

She obeyed, giving him access easily, with no hesitation or resistance now. He had taught her well, he reflected, judging by the eager look on her face and the delicate flush rising from breasts to throat. He touched the pulse there, feeling it cavort under his finger.

He traced a line from throat to belly to *yoni*, feeling her skin soften and grow moist with her womanly juices. He played for a bit, amusing himself while she grew restive. When he judged her ready, he lifted her legs, tucked a pillow under her bottom and draped her knees over his shoulders.

She exhaled sharply. "Wha . . . at?"

"Be quiet."

She closed her mouth, but her eyes remained open, fixed on him as he continued to tease her bud and nether lips. He smiled down at her. "You should see yourself now. Adorned with your jewelry, your skin lit by the sun, open to me. You are a lovely dark swan."

She sighed deeply. "Truly?"

He flicked her little bud with his finger and thumb in reprimand. "You mustn't question me, Lady Jane. You must believe in
your beauty."

"If you insist." She smiled up at him. "You make it easy to believe you."

"See that you do," he said, intent on angling his *lingam* at just
the right mode to rub against her little bud. He stroked several
times, alternating between soft, beguiling caresses, and harder,
bolder, demanding strokes. She responded immediately, her
thighs quivering and her *yoni* growing hot and wet under his
touch.

She gasped at a particularly inventive stroke, then tossed her
head back. Her hands clutched the bed covers. The breeze dried
the sweat forming on his brow but didn't cool his ardor as he continued stroking her to fever pitch.

"Please, please, I need you!"

He held back a moment more, denying both of them the pleasure he knew they would feel the instant his *lingam* kissed the interior walls of her *yoni*. At last, he could wait no longer, and with
a forceful thrust, entered her deeply, fully, imbedding himself to
the hilt.

She screamed. He shouted.

He didn't settle into one motion, but experimented, testing her
responses first as he thrust straightforwardly, next as he rotated his
hips in a circular motion, feeling his *lingam* revolve against her inner muscles. He withdrew all but the head, then slowly eased back
in. He used his *lingam* to tease her bud, making her cry out again,
then slapped her lightly with it, making her gasp, then demand
more, more, always more.

He bent to his task. Holding her legs apart, he pounded into her,
demanding everything from her, giving her his all. Sweat dripped
from him onto her. She released the bed covers long enough to rub
it into her breasts, panting and shaking all around him.

He waited, desperate for consummation until she orgasmed,
convulsing so hard he feared for his shaft, then came himself in a
tumultuous gush, shooting deep down into her. Breathing heavily,
he closed his eyes and gulped air.

Her legs quivered and shook against his chest. He eased one
down, then the other, holding them still against his flanks as he remained in her a moment longer. Her throat worked convulsively
as she drew in air. Her breasts heaved, the nipples still large and
engorged.

He lowered himself atop her and suckled like a babe, seeking nourishment and reassurance. She held his head, stroking back his hair from his temples while their breathing gradually evened out and they slept, holding each other in perfect contentment.

Havyn dreamed of days and nights as exquisite as this, and in his sleep, settled his future.

Chapter Twelve

Lady Jane Ponsonby-Maitland, the erstwhile modest, virginal young woman, lay stretched naked across his body, feeding him small bites of cake from their tea, which had been delivered earlier. The tea had gone cold, and the cakes beginning to dry at the edges, but Havyn didn't care. He felt supremely lazy, unable to move a muscle after their prior exertions.

They had napped after their strenuous efforts with the yawning position, perhaps that was why it was so named? Then they'd woken, and sent for tea, but had forgotten it to make slow, lazy love.

He nibbled a bit of cake, then her finger. He swallowed the crumbs, then pulled in her finger and swirled his tongue around it.

She laughed. "You are insatiable."

"It's all because of you. I can't get enough of your sweet flesh."

She raised up, resting her weight on one elbow. She bent her head and traced his nipple with her tongue. "You are tasty, too. I find myself ravenous for you."

"Excellent. Make sure you continue to feel as hungry." He made himself more comfortable as noises from the innkeeper's courtyard drifted through the window. He ignored them. Coaches came and went all day. Horses clopped on the cobblestones and ostlers called to each other. "You've been a very apt pupil of the erotic arts. Are you ready to be tested?"

She snuggled closer. "The spirit is willing, but the body—"

He laughed. "Very well, then, we shall have an oral examination."

"Umm, as long as I don't have to move."

"Tell me then, what is the *yoni*?"

"That part of me that belongs to you," she answered promptly.

Surprised, pleased, and feeling a definite surge of masculine pride, he stroked her back. "Correct. What is the *lingam*?"

He wasn't surprised when she answered, "That part of you that belongs to me." He might argue the point, but why bother? So long as they were ensconced in this love nest, why cloud the air with the differences between the sexes?

"What is the congress of the cow?" He had to raise his voice against the loud, angry voices rushing up the stairs from the inn's tavern below. Did no one have any respect for lovemaking patrons? "You behind me with me on my hands and feet."

"Does it please you?"

"Not at first, but it became quite . . . splendid."

He chuckled. "Nicely put. What do you like the best?"

"When you are in me. I can't think of anything then but how good, no, how *excellent* it is."

"I think you may have a passing mark coming your way, but you must be more specific." He tapped her on the bottom to get her attention. "Your favorite position?"

He heard loud footsteps on the stairs, then on the wooden hallway floor. Coming this way. Oh, devil take it, he had forgotten to lock the door! He tensed, listening.

He didn't have long to wait. The footsteps paused outside their door. Loud pounding. "Havyn Attercliffe! Lady Jane!"

She reared up, panic on her exquisite face. Her eyes grew big and round. Her face went pale. "Oh, no, not now! Not so soon!"

He jumped out of bed, threw the covers over her, and struggled to get his buckskins on. They caught at his knees, devil take it, then at his hips. Not a moment to lose!

"Attercliffe! Open this door!"

"A moment," he called back. "Give me a moment."

"Now!" The door flung open.

Lady Jane squealed and buried her head under the covers.

Havyn forced his rod behind the flap and mis-buttoned.

Neville, Lord Grantham, stood in the open doorway. His mouth hung open, his face a mottled red.

Lord Yarwoode stood at his shoulder, mouth flapping like a landed trout.

All was silent for a moment. Then all hell broke loose.

"What the devil are you doing here with my fiancée?" shouted Yarwoode.

"Havyn! What is the meaning of this?" demanded Grantham.

"Out, out!" Havyn ordered.

"I'm not your fiancée!" Lady Jane proclaimed in the most unladylike, strident tones. "I refuse to marry you!"

Havyn cast a quick glance at her. She had uncovered her head and knelt in the bed with the bedsheet up to her breasts, looking for all the world like a dark swan arising from the mist. Suddenly, he thought of all the animals he had thought of in connection with her: a pesky dog, a leopard, a swan. He recalled the congress of the cow and that of the elephant. He couldn't help it. He laughed.

"Havyn!" Grantham and Lady Jane cried in unison.

"Attercliffe!" Yarwoode bulled his way into the room. "This is no laughing matter."

"Indeed it is not." Havyn regained his composure. "If you two will wait for me in the downstairs parlor, we can discuss the matter there."

Yarwoode shot angry looks at Lady Jane, who shot daggers back. He glared at Havyn. "I shall expect satisfaction."

"Oh bother all that!" Lady Jane cried. "He's already quite satisfied me!"

"Lady Jane!" the three men shouted as one.

"Well, he has. I'm a thoroughly compromised woman. Absolutely ruined," she announced with supreme satisfaction.

"Downstairs, if you please, gentlemen." Havyn made shooing gestures at the door. Grantham gave a great sigh, but went.

Yarwoode left as well, throwing dark, menacing looks over his shoulder.

Havyn locked the door behind him. "Well, that didn't go quite as I expected."

She sat with a plop. "I wanted more time with you."

"As I did with you." He sat on the bed beside her. "I'll go down and smooth their feathers. Yarwoode has seen that you are now *absolutely ruined*," he quoted with a faint smile. "He'll be all bluster at first, but he'll be on his way soon enough."

"You won't let him hurt you?"

"Of course not. He'll see reason."

"And your brother?"

Havyn sighed. "He might be more difficult."

She cuddled close to him. "I want them to go away and leave us alone."

"They can't do that, sweet." He stroked her hair back from her face and kissed her temple. "You'd better dress and start packing. I'll be back as soon as I can."

He rose and completed dressing, as formally as though he were going on trial. Which he was, of course, but he was confident of the outcome. Yarwoode and Grantham would foam at the mouth a bit, demand he do right by Lady Jane, and he would agree. They would be married by special license, and the dark swan would be his, all his.

Satisfied both with his plan, and his cravat, Havyn dropped a kiss on Lady Jane's cheek and went to meet his fate. He heard something hit the door on the other side and grinned. Life with her would be a constant adventure. Her temperament and spirit would never bore him. Her passion and eagerness to make love would keep him content and satisfied. Her quick mind and willingness to speak her mind would keep him entertained. What more could he want?

Very pleased with himself, Havyn entered the private parlor with a smile on his face. Grantham had seated himself at the table, head propped on one hand while Yarwoode paced with a heavy tread from one end of the room to the other. "Gentlemen?"

Both turned to face him. Yarwoode began shouting at once. Grantham merely looked at him, severe displeasure written across his countenance.

It was his quiet voice that Havyn heard, not Yarwoode's ranting. "Havyn, I entrusted you to find and return Lady Jane."

"And I was on my way."

"With a rather lengthy stay at this inn?"

Havyn winced. He sat across from his brother and poured them both ale from the foaming flagon he'd had sent in. He sipped, his brother ignored the offering.

"Shall I explain?"

"No explanations are necessary, Attercliffe! You've compromised my bride-to-be. How are you going to make amends?"

"Marry her, naturally."

"She can't marry you! She's engaged to me."

Grantham sighed. "I would have wished this resolution otherwise."

Havyn wondered at his brother's expression. Disappointment, to be sure, but something else? "This is as Lady Jane wished."

"Never!" Yarwoode exclaimed. "She's not a demirep, but a lady, through and through."

"I agree completely. She's also a lady who has no wish to marry you. As she's told you." He gestured to each of them.

"You had better explain yourselves," Grantham said in a quiet voice.

"I tracked her down as you requested, Neville. I found her in Whitby, a little fishing village on the coast. She'd gone to ground with Anna, the kitchen maid who had befriended her as a child." He paused, waiting for his brother to speak.

Grantham said nothing, merely gestured for Havyn to continue.

"She didn't wish to return. Indeed, she was quite adamant on that point. She begged me to assist her, to help her avoid marrying Yarwoode, and I agreed."

"But you could have spoken with me," Grantham said. "You didn't have to compromise her."

"I suggested that, however Lady Jane thought I might not be forceful enough to change your mind, or that you were obdurate on the subject. Having heard your thoughts on the letter she penned you, I believed she had a valid point."

"You didn't have to fuck her!" Yarwoode yelled.

Grantham looked offended. Havyn certainly was. He advanced on the older man, fists clenched. "You will speak of Lady Jane with courtesy."

Yarwoode wisely put up his hands, palms out. "No offense to the lady. After all, I mean to make her my wife."

"You'd want her after she's been compromised?" Grantham asked.

"She's a spirited filly. Even if he," said with a truculent glare at Havyn, "has broken her in, of course I want her."

"You can't have her," Havyn shot back. "She's mine."

Grantham held up a finger. "Perhaps we should let Lady Jane decide."

"An excellent idea," said Havyn. He settled back to wait while his brother sent a message asking her to join them. There wasn't a doubt in his mind that she would choose him.

Chapter Thirteen

Lady Jane entered the private parlor looking serene and supremely confident. In the last few days, she had become a woman, feminine, seductive, and aware of her worth. Proudly, she held her head high, and her shoulders back. Her hair was neatly brushed and arranged in a becoming knot at her neck, displaying her throat to advantage. She wore yet another gown, this one suited to an afternoon visit, which didn't make the best of her complexion, but Havyn didn't care.

He had seen his lady to her best advantage, naked, her dark hair a-tumble about her shoulders and luscious breasts. What she wore in company detracted from her appearance, but maybe, on second thought, that was to his advantage. The fewer men who eyed his woman with appreciation, the better for their health.

He rose and escorted her to a chair. She sat with perfect aplomb, smoothing her gown over her knees and folding her hands in her lap. She glanced from man to man, but spoke to Grantham, "You wished to speak with me, sir?"

"Indeed. Lord Yarwoode has indicated that this . . . adventure of yours will not affect his offer of marriage." When she looked astounded, Grantham clarified, "He still wishes to marry you."

Yarwoode cleared his throat. "So I do."

"I will not have you." Her voice was firm and decisive.

Havyn smiled at her. "You do not have to concern yourself about Yarwoode. You will marry me."

Her eyes lit up. Her smile grew and grew as her dimple deepened, tempting him to poke his tongue into it. "Truly?"

Yarwoode came forward. "Now see here, Lady Jane. We have

an agreement. Tell her, Grantham," he demanded. He turned back to Lady Jane. "I am willing to overlook this escapade of yours." His voice sounded strangled, as if he forced himself to be reasonable and pleasant. "Once we are married, I won't hold it over you. I can't be more generous than that."

Lady Jane seethed. "How very kind of you, Lord Yarwoode. You can keep your generosity to yourself. I will not marry you."

"You still refuse me?" Yarwoode queried, his face darkening with anger.

Grantham stepped between Lady Jane and Yarwoode. He bowed in stiff apology to her. "I was wrong in attempting to coerce you." He turned to Yarwoode. "My ward rejects your suit, Yarwoode." He hesitated, his mouth working before he forced out the words. "Evidently I misunderstood her refusal as missish quibbles." Pausing for effect, he then continued, "I expect no word of this to get out. Neither I nor Howden would be pleased if it did."

Havyn added, "And as Lady Jane's husband, my displeasure would be great."

Yarwoode glared at Grantham, at Lady Jane, then furiously at Havyn. "I'll be gone, then." He strode to the door, flung it open and left, leaving the door ajar behind him.

Havyn closed it, a sense of satisfaction filling him.

"Oh thank you, my lord," Lady Jane burbled at Grantham, her face wreathed in a huge smile. She wrapped her arms around her guardian's middle and hugged him.

"Quite all right. No need to make such a fuss." Grantham stood at stiff attention, his expression a mix of consternation and embarrassment. One hand came up to pat her awkwardly on the shoulder. "I had plans for you, but you have arranged your life to suit yourself. You shall have my blessing."

Lady Jane smiled tremulously and hugged him once more before moving back. Grantham gave her an uncomfortable smile in return. Havyn looked on, pleased with the signs of rapprochement between his brother and his bride-to-be.

Grantham flicked a stern glance at Havyn. "Why did you not mention your intention to marry my ward in your message to meet you here?"

Lady Jane looked stricken. She raised wounded eyes to Havyn. "You wrote him? From here?" Her voice cracked. She turned away, shoulders slumping. "How could you? I thought we were happy together. Content to be only with each other . . ."

"We were. We are," Havyn amended quickly. He touched her shoulder, turning her back to him. "We shall go on being content together when we are married."

She looked pensive, disappointed somehow, as she resisted his intention to draw her closer. "Why do you wish to marry me, Mr. Attercliffe?"

So he was back to being formally addressed. This was not good, not at all his expectation. Damn Grantham for exposing his actions.

He glared at his brother. "A few moments alone with Lady Jane, if you please."

Grantham hesitated, then as if realizing she could not be any more ruined, nodded stiffly and left the room. He closed the door quietly behind him.

Havyn turned back to Lady Jane. "Allow me to explain."

"As you wish."

No lady of the *ton* could have done that disdainful look any better. Havyn searched for the right words. Sending that missive to Grantham was a huge error. He should have procured a special license and married her before they could be discovered. "You are displeased with me," he said at last. "Was not our plan to be discovered?"

"Do not mince words or try to lessen the damage you have done to me, sir."

"My apologies." The words crowded his throat, allowing him little room to breathe. Eating humble pie didn't suit him at all, but dine on it, he would. "I realized soon after I sent that message to Grantham that I had erred. My only excuse is that I wished to be sure that he would discover us, and keep the news of your compromised status to himself."

She eyed him with a narrow, suspicious stare. "Is that the truth?"

"I swear. I was afraid that if our activities became the latest *on dit*, you would suffer from the resulting gossip. I would have been talked about, to be sure, perhaps even ostracized for a time, but in the end, I would have suffered no permanent damage to my reputation. You, on the other hand—"

"Would be ruined for life, I know."

She appeared slightly mollified, but Havyn knew there was more. There had to be, for she wasn't looking at him with the loving expression he had come to rely on. To crave.

She paced from the table to the window overlooking the stable yard. The view was not inspiring. Coaches, drivers, ostlers, horses standing weary or waiting to be hitched. Dust and straw and horse piles on the ground. What could she find so interesting that she stared out the window for some moments?

"Yarwoode will keep his tongue," he offered. "He won't risk facing my wrath."

She shrugged a shoulder. At last she turned, but stayed where she was. "I asked you before. Why do you want to marry me?"

"We are as good as married, right now. We only need to formalize our union."

"That doesn't answer my question!" Her voice rose. "You said nothing about marriage before my guardian and Lord Yarwoode burst in on us. Now you take it as certain that we shall marry."

"Are you forgetting, my sweet, how we have been occupying our time? You may already be carrying my child."

Her mouth opened with a quick gasp. They had not discussed or taken precautions, an error on his part, but one he wished to rectify with marriage as soon as possible.

"I forget nothing! If I am increasing, I shall . . . I shall think of something." She glared daggers at him. "I remember you stated, quite vehemently, that you have no wish to marry." She narrowed her eyes. "Pray inform me what has changed your mind."

"A very good question." He approached her, intending to take her in his arms and proclaim his feelings for her. He would explain his quest for *Moksha* and she would appreciate his reservations about marriage. They would be married as quickly as it could be arranged.

He stopped when her glower pinned him to the floor. Instead of his explanations, he found himself fumbling with his words. He managed to say, "I find that we quite suit, and I am looking forward to spending my days and nights with you."

"Such a tender proposal," she mocked. "And all for naught."

"Surely you can't mean to refuse me?"

"Exactly that."

Chapter Fourteen

Havyn flung himself into a comfortably plump armchair in his apartments at Carlton House, his latest letter to Lady Jane crumpled in his hand. Like all the others, she'd returned this one unopened.

She was willful, temperamental, stubborn, opinionated and spiteful, and by God, he missed her. She was loving, and gracious, sultry and lustful, womanly and seductive, and he craved her.

Devil take it. There was only one thing to do. He'd given her three weeks to come to her senses and agree to marry him. She'd refused to see him, but now, his patience was at an end. His dark swan belonged to him, and he was going to claim her.

He jumped up, yelled at his valet to hurry, and when the man added yet one more box to the increasing amount of baggage already stored by the door, Havyn stood, checked his cravat in the hall mirror and marched downstairs to his hired coach.

Ordinarily, he'd take his new phaeton, but not with all his necessities for an extended stay, if that were necessary to convince Lady Jane. When all was stored away, Havyn climbed in and gave the orders to go.

Hours later, he strode through the entrance hall at Grantham Lodge, waving away Grantham's butler and barely acknowledging a number of the *ton* gathered in the salons. Devil take it! He'd forgotten this was the week of Neville's annual house party. Why hadn't he canceled the damn affair? He paused outside Grantham's library to knock once, then fling open the door.

Seated behind his large desk, Grantham sat penning a letter.

He raised his head. "Ah, Havyn. I expected you earlier. You'll find her in the garden." He bent to his task again, dismissing Havyn.

With that permission, Havyn grinned and set out for the gardens.

He sighted her strolling a path between the formal flowerbeds. The fragrance of sun-warmed blooms perfumed the afternoon, but all his senses were concentrated on her. She moved with poise and confidence, a woman sure of herself. He gritted his teeth, pleased to see her proud and beautiful, yet craving her for himself alone. She was elegant and graceful in a dainty white muslin gown embroidered in green, a darker green shawl dripping from one shoulder, her wide straw hat with matching green ribbons tied loosely at her bosom. Ah, that bosom . . .

It was apparent, even from this distance, that the two men dangling after her were entranced. Young Corinthians, by the looks of their tight coats and elaborate cravats. Anger surged through him. What was she doing, enticing men to ogle her bosom?

She hadn't noticed him, so he started down another path, behind the topiary, stopping every so often to track her progress. To be reduced to peering through shrubbery!

He paused, forcing down his jealousy with a deep breath. He had achieved *Dharma*, he could proceed with order and reason, curbing his emotions lest he frighten her away. Or more likely, inflame her temper again. That wouldn't be so terrible, he thought, recalling her spirited looks and flushed cheeks. If he could break through the chilly silence between them—

"There you are, Mr. Attercliffe. Grantham said we should expect you any time now."

Did he? Forcing back a scowl, Havyn turned to see who had greeted him. He spied the Earl and Countess of Howden approaching. She was radiant, her fair hair and skin a perfect foil for her husband's dark, possessive eyes. The earl scanned the gardens, glowering at any man who dared admire his wife. He once had been known as a rake, and an excessively randy one at that, successfully avoiding leg shackles until he'd rescued a snowbound woman and her infant niece. Looking at Lady Howden, Havyn could understand why any man would want to take her under his protection.

Vaguely, Havyn recalled wondering if Lady Howden would entertain an affair with him, but it was quite beyond the pale now. Even if she hadn't been increasing so obviously, he had no thoughts for anyone but Lady Jane. *His* Jane. He wanted to find her immediately but courtesy demanded he answer and linger to converse.

He swept Lady Howden a polite bow. "I had business in town."

He turned to the earl. "My thanks to you and Lady Howden for taking Lady Jane under your wings. And for keeping her journey north to yourselves."

The earl and his lady exchanged a speaking glance. Howden turned to Havyn. "You did not do well by her."

Havyn stiffened. "I mean to make it right now. If she will have me."

Lady Howden sent him a sweet look. "You will have your work cut out for you, but you have our blessing." When her husband said nothing, she added, "Doesn't he, Howden?"

Justin, fifth earl of Howden, frowned at his countess. Then he smiled, a man who could deny his wife nothing. "If you say so, Sarah."

The look Lady Howden sent her earl was one Havyn craved from his lady. He shifted his weight, impatient to be gone. The Countess glanced at his feet, then at his face, a smile quirking her lips. "I believe I saw Lady Jane headed for the pergola."

Havyn expressed his thanks, bowed once again and all but ran down the path. Behind him, he heard Lady Howden laugh. He didn't care. He had to speak to Jane now.

Avoiding other guests who strolled through the Grantham Lodge gardens, along the grassy paths or rested on benches under the shade of old oaks, Havyn made his way quickly to the pergola on the far side of the lawns.

He entered, pleased to find it empty and cool in the heat of the afternoon. He circled the enclosure, watching as Lady Jane approached. He smiled when she stopped and dismissed the men with her. He couldn't hear their voices, but he could tell by their expressions that the two men wished to continue escorting her.

She waved them off, and wandered slowly along a path through the rose garden. She paused to admire a bloom here, remove a spent blossom there. When she entered the pergola, a fragrant white bud held to her nose, he was waiting for her.

"Good afternoon, Lady Jane." He swept her a handsome bow. "A fine day for gardening, is it not?"

She dropped the rose. "You!"

He retrieved it for her. "Indeed. Did you think I would accept my *congé* by letter? Or the lack of one?"

She refused the rose and turned to leave. "I have no wish to speak to you."

"But I must speak with you. I am glad you came the rest of the way by yourself."

She drew her shawl higher up her arm, covering herself. "You have been spying on me?"

"Not spying. It wasn't difficult to notice those two drooling over you, like pups with a bone."

She went rigid. "You can have nothing more to say to me."

"But I do." He put his hand on her arm to detain her. "Am I to expect an heir?"

She tried to shake off his hand. "I am not increasing."

"Ah," he murmured, strangely disappointed. They had time yet, and perhaps it was better this way. She would know he married her for herself, not for the sake of a child. And no one would count their fingers when his child did make an appearance. He slid his hand down to hers, then took her fingers and lifted them to his lips.

"I've missed you, sweet. You are more beautiful than ever."

"Indeed."

He brought her closer and took her lips. She tensed, held herself stiff and still, refusing him any enjoyment.

He stepped back just enough to allow a small space between them. "You are displeased with me, I see."

"Your powers of observation are as acute as ever." Her tone haughty, she turned away from him.

How he admired her spirit. He suppressed a smile. "As is your enchantment."

"Such pretty words." She flicked a glance at the entrance to the pergola. He moved to block the way. "Let me pass."

"After you hear me out. Please?"

She sighed, but sat on one of the cushioned benches lining the latticed walls. He sat near her, not touching, but close enough to inhale the sweet fragrance of her skin. In the shaded light her eyes looked large, lustrous, and distressed.

"I must offer you an explanation," he began cautiously. "I find my life since I met you perplexing." At her dismissive look, he hastened to add, "You know that in the last few years, I have traveled, had adventures both pleasant and dangerous, and met a number of people who had a great deal to teach me.

"Some of that knowledge I have shared with you." When she

flushed, and looked delicately away, he continued, "The pleasures of the flesh, *Kama*, and there is much more to share. Together," he stressed. "We have not made a child yet, but we will. It is part of my plan."

She flicked him a glance, her head tilted to one side. "You take it for granted, then?"

"Do we intrude?"

Not again! Did his brother's guests have nothing to do but interfere with his affaires? Havyn cast an annoyed glare at the man who dared interrupt him, then quickly stood. "Your Graces." He bowed at the couple surrounded by a number of guests, men and women alike.

The years since Havyn had last seen the Duke and Duchess of Sutherland had not blunted their impressive appearance. Havyn noted the Duke still received the lion's share of coy feminine glances from women who might have thought that the few strands of white at his temples only added to his feral attraction. He'd filled his nursery with cubs who took after both parents in determination and arrogance. At his side, the Duchess, stunning in dark blue with her still glorious chestnut hair piled atop her slender neck, smiled warmly at him.

"I haven't seen you in quite some time," Antonia, the Duchess of Sutherland, said to Lady Jane.

Lady Jane curtsied. "It is a pleasure to see you now, Your Graces."

Havyn stepped back to allow the Duke and his Duchess to enter the pergola.

The Duke glanced around. "You are alone, I see."

Havyn chafed at the disapproval in the older man's tone. He recalled the *on dit* about the merry chase the duchess had led him before their marriage and searched for a memory. Wasn't there something about the lady's quest for a lover? If so, Sutherland must understand his impatience now to be private with his own woman. "Lady Jane and I have some matters to settle between us," he murmured for the other man's ears alone.

Sutherland studied him. "You have Grantham's approval?"

"He sent me out here."

Sutherland nodded. "Are congratulations in order, then?"

"A trifle premature, but I will accept them for both of us. Hopefully." Havyn glanced at Lady Jane, deep in conversation with the duchess, who looked at her husband, and smiled. Havyn noted the tenderness between them and ached for the same for Lady Jane and himself. How long must he do the polite before he was left alone with Jane?

"Come, my dear," Sutherland said to his wife. "We have kept these two long enough."

The duchess gave Havyn a long, considering look, then whispered something to Lady Jane, who after a moment, nodded her head.

Rising graciously, the older woman took her husband's arm and allowed the Duke to lead her, and their following entourage, away from the pergola.

Havyn let out his breath. Turning to Lady Jane, who watched him approach with a cool look on her face.

"I hope we are not to be interrupted again," he said. When she said nothing, he asked, "What did the Duchess say to you?"

"She inquired if I wished to be private with you."

And she had agreed! Havyn sank down beside her. "Thank you." He swallowed, suddenly nervous. "Will you listen to what I have to tell you?"

"If you wish."

Havyn could wish for more enthusiasm, but at least his lady had consented to stay with him. He took a deep, steadying breath. "I take nothing for granted where you are concerned, my sweet," he assured her and took up where they had been before the interruption. "There are four goals a man must achieve in his life. One is *Kama*, which we have enjoyed together, another is the accumulation of wealth and material possessions to ensure his wife and children want for nothing. That is *Artha*. A third is *Dharma,* judgment and reasoning to make his life, and that of his family, well-ordered and secure." He paused, watching her reaction.

Her gaze intent on him, she nodded for him to continue.

"I considered that I had achieved those goals, some to greater degree than others."

"Like *Kama*?" she suggested with a faint smile.

"Like *Kama*," he agreed, recalling with warmth how well and how often they had practiced the arts of sexual congress together. How they would again, if he was successful in wooing her. He forced his focus away from his expectant *lingam* and back to his explanations. "And *Artha*. I have the means to support a wife and family. I have bought a town house which is undergoing renovations at the moment, and am looking for a suitable country property."

She waved those away as if owning establishments counted for nothing.

"My sense of *Dharma* was somewhat lacking when I agreed to the plan to ruin you for Yarwoode."

She jumped up. "So you regret helping me?" she snapped, her icy manner melting under her ire.

He took her hand and pulled her back down, this time closer to him. "Never. However, I should have used reason and courted you properly. Then we could have rejected Yarwoode's suit without exposing you to gossip."

"You would have done that? Truly?"

Her questioning glance opened his heart to her. "I knew as soon as I saw you that I wanted you. I just didn't know then to what extent."

"And now you do?"

He sidestepped the immediate response. "The fourth, and greatest goal I wished to achieve is called *Moksha*. That," he said, forestalling her question, "is a complicated spiritual tenet by which a man searches for enlightenment, a reason for living, a higher plateau, perhaps."

She wrinkled her brow. "It sounds nearly impossible to achieve."

"Perhaps not, if one has the right incentive." He watched her carefully. "According to the Indian sages I consulted, *Moksha* means liberating the mind and soul to meet its maker."

She looked distressed. "Surely you aren't contemplating—"

"Dying?" he supplied, pleased with her concern. So she did care for him. At least a little. "Not for a very long time, my sweet. And until then, with you only *le petit morte*, the loss of awareness one feels with a perfect climax."

"Ah." That she could understand.

"I believed that I could achieve *Moksha* only if I were unattached emotionally to another human being. Specifically, to a woman. Oh, I planned to marry and have children, but I thought I could do it without involving my heart."

Her eyes went huge.

"I was wrong," he hastened to add. "Since you left me at that inn, I have done a great deal of thinking. Do you want to know my conclusions?"

She nodded, her gaze intent on his.

"I now believe that finding *Moksha* means liberating my mind and soul of everything but living my life with the perfect companion. It means devoting myself to her well-being, her perfect state of being, of giving myself up to her completely, and in accepting her entirely as she is."

She waited, the tiny pulse at the base of her throat fluttering.

He lowered himself to his knees. He lifted the rose to his nose, pressed a kiss to the dewy bud and offered it to her.

She took it!

Havyn inhaled to steady himself against the euphoria coursing through his veins. "You are the perfect companion I wish to devote myself to. Will you do me the greatest of honors and consent to be my wife?"

Lady Jane Ponsonby-Maitland slipped off the bench onto her knees next to him. Tears came to her eyes. "Why do you wish to marry me?"

"I just told you."

"The real reason, Mr. Attercliffe."

"Because I don't want to live without you," he confessed. "Because, devil take it, you are my heart. I love you."

The dimple in her cheek flashed as she threw herself into his arms. "Havyn, oh Havyn, that's all I needed to know!"

Epilogue

Lady Jane raised her arm and looked at her hand in the flickering candlelight. "It is a vulgarly huge diamond, Havyn. I quite adore it."

He sat back on his haunches, still dripping sweat. His bride wore nothing but jewelry, from the beaded headband holding back her unruly dark locks, the necklaces dripping gold and gems at her throat, the gold chains at her waist, wrists and ankles, to the rings on her fingers and toes. As she mentioned, her wedding ring was ostentatiously large, befitting his very large *lingam* still buried deeply within her.

He took her foot resting on his shoulder and kissed the sole then slid her toes into his mouth. When he was done nibbling on the tips, he let her foot slide down his chest, coming to rest on his thigh.

He fingered the gold chain on her ankle. "You look like a sated *houri*, and yet you still haven't answered my question."

She pursed her lips. "And which one was that? I accepted your proposal, promised to honor, love and obey you," she frowned at the latter. "What else was there?"

He grinned. "At the inn, before we were so rudely interrupted, I asked you to describe your favorite position."

She lowered her legs to the rumpled silk sheets and pulled the velvet pillows from under her upraised buttocks. "Hmm, I am mad for the congress of the cow, for the elephant, and I adore riding you, my darling, for you are such a spirited steed!"

He laughed and moved within her, finding just the right spot to make her gasp. "And your favorite?"

"I even like the lower congress, when your *lingam caresses my bottom, but. . . ." She drew him down until he stretched his legs out behind him and rested his weight full upon her.*

She kissed him, taking her time, teasing him with running her tongue around the shape of his mouth, between the seam of his lips, opening enough to suck in his tongue and suckle it. At last she released his mouth and gazed at him with heavy-lidded eyes. She stroked her hands down his spine and cupped his buttocks, pulling him deeper into her.

"I like this position best, when I can look into your eyes and tell you how much I love you."

"Ah, Jane, my sweet, my love. I thought ruining you would be the ruination of me, but instead, you are my Moksha, my salvation."

About the Author:

A degreed historian, Bonnie Hamre puts her travels in the US, South America and Europe to good use in her novels. Multi-published in contemporary and historical fiction, Bonnie has recently moved to the Northwest, where new adventures await her. To learn more about Bonnie's books, visit her website: www.bonniehamre.com *and join her newsletter list at* http://groups.yahoo.com/group/bonniehamre. *Bonnie, busy writing her next book, loves to hear from her readers!*

Code Name: Kiss

❧⁂❧

by Jeanie Cesarini

To My Reader:

With all the events unfolding in the world right now, I wanted a little hope that good will triumph in the end. That desire inspired my muse and brought Lily and Seth's story to life. Code Name: Kiss allows fantasy to thrive under some very tough conditions and proves love can grow even when people must make hard choices about what's most important in life . . . "Peace on earth and good will toward all men."

"Clear to go."

Hour Four: 1227 hours

In my head, I could almost hear my mission commander's voice clearing me for action. Almost. Seth Blackthorn was halfway across the world at the moment, safely ensconced in our Washington D.C. command headquarters. He'd deemed audio contact on this mission an unacceptable risk, so I only had the memory of his voice to spur me into action now that I'd infiltrated the target site.

"Clear to go."

His voice would be deep silk with that hint of upper class Maryland. Even in memory the man was an anchor to cling to, and as much as I hated to admit it, I could use one.

My name is Lily Justiss, operative number 6390, and the only *real* voice I could hear right now was that of an older, heavily accented man over an intercom system.

"Stand still."

I came to a halt in the middle of the bath chamber, aware that the owner of the voice was watching me on elaborate monitoring equipment, along with the other guests in attendance at this all-important strategy session. The emir might be with them as well, but I didn't think so. That one was too careful. He'd likely remain sequestered deep within the labyrinth of this palace-turned-secured-military-facility until the gathering of his commanders, his *Shura*, got well underway. Just a guess.

"Disrobe," the command reverberated as if the small chamber had the acoustics of a cavern.

"Clear to go."

Gaze fixed on the tiles forming a mosaic sunburst at my feet, I took a steadying breath and raised my arms. Slim, oddly feminine hands appeared, fingers brushing against my skin. Slow, smooth motions that unfastened my veiled garments, lifted away the silk, a layer at a time.

Each departing veil exposed me in what quickly became a test of breathless torture. The caress of humid air along my shoulders . . . my breasts . . . my stomach . . . I could feel every inch of my bare skin as it was revealed for public viewing. My heartbeat thumped loud in the bubbling quiet.

I didn't need to see my audience. I didn't need to hear the roughness of male breathing or the shuffling of booted feet. I was bared to the tiny eyes of the surveillance cameras. To men who gauged my worth by every inch of unveiled skin.

I'd have felt more in control if I'd have known the positions of those cameras, but I wasn't permitted to glance around the room. Slave women in this Middle Eastern world weren't granted that sort of freedom, which meant my job was to stand here compliant while this beautiful eunuch unfastened my waistband. I guessed what was coming and forgot to breathe.

He drew the filmy trousers down my legs, inch by agonizing inch, lending drama to an action meant to tantalize my audience.

Lily Justiss. Operative number: 6390. Mission: swallow.

The term had originated in Russia, during the Cold War when Americans were a lot more honest about the need for a black operations intelligence agency keeping in touch with the pulse of world events. The days of the Cold War were over. Nowadays we told ourselves that the global community had evolved to the point where we didn't need black operations. *Right*.

Mother Russia might not be holding her finger poised above the nukes . . . Now radical terrorists had the job. Like cockroaches they scrambled around for nuclear leftovers from countries vacillating between Western good will and lightning-fast falls from grace.

Life would be a lot simpler if we didn't arm our enemies.

But the bottom line . . . it didn't matter whether the term "swallow" originated with us or them. Playing this role meant I'd infiltrated a military compound as an operative who would use sex to trap my target. So I did my job and held still while those soft hands untied the fastenings of the chemise that was my last defense against my audience.

I stared at those sharply cut mosaic tiles on the floor. Yellow.

Gold. Orange. I resisted the adrenaline fueling my thoughts along dangerous paths, reminding me of circumstances that needed no reminder. I was being watched. Yellow. Gold. Orange. Pink.

I stood in the temporary headquarters of Islamic militant Nabi Ulmalhameh, the self-proclaimed emir of an extensive terror network called Husan al Din, or the Sword of Faith. This man had devoted his life and his substantial resources to eradicating the heretics from the Holy Land.

I was a heretic. An *American.*

Yellow. Gold. Orange. Pink. Scarlet. Under the guise of sex slave, I'd infiltrated the emir's borrowed palace in a country rich in oil-processing wealth, but morally bankrupt in a Muslim extremist regime that sanctioned all forms of terrorism.

My current location: Qahtrain, an island country physically cut off from the mainland by the surrounding Persian Gulf. Barely three-point-five times larger than the whole of Washington D.C., this island also cut me off from Command, and Seth. Yellow. Gold. Orange. Pink. Scarlet. Wine.

My mission objective . . . I had several actually, each one contingent upon the one before it, a ladder I must climb to reach my ultimate goal—contact with the emir.

The chemise fell away. I stood there freshly scrubbed, lotioned to satin perfection and finally, utterly nude. The eunuch gathered up the collapsed silk from the floor and left me standing with my eyes lowered, my arms outstretched.

I tried not to imagine the sound of male breathing, the laughing comments men might make when facing the promise of sex. I hadn't known silence could echo.

Inhaling slowly, I put Seth front and center in my mind, a desperate attempt to keep panic at bay. Thinking about him comforted me, felt as natural and familiar as breathing.

I thought about him a lot, *too* much since he didn't see me as anything but a fellow operative and sometimes trainee. His rejection didn't dampen my fantasies though. Seth Blackthorn was the one indulgence I allowed myself. A guilty pleasure I'd stopped feeling guilty about a long time ago.

"Lower your arms and turn slowly."

I did as commanded, feeling leering gazes as if each left behind a dirty residue on my skin. That these men weren't present in the room meant nothing. One of them would claim me, and with any luck, it would be the man I'd been sent to make contact with.

Xavier Jareb—mission objective number one.

Jareb had made my passage into this compound possible. He'd leaked the information about this thirty-hour window when the emir would surface. Xavier Jareb was a Sword of Faith commander who'd turned defector-in-place for the good old U.S. of A.

At the moment, I hoped our mole was on the other end of the surveillance monitor liking what he saw. *Really* liking it. Not that I was so eager to take one for the home team, but if I failed to make contact with Jareb, my remaining mission objectives would be moot. I'd simply be at this gathering for the ride, hoping to catch a glimpse of the elusive emir while playing sex slave to whatever commander wanted to prove his moral superiority over the West on my body.

"Arouse her," the command echoed over the intercom.

The eunuch rose from his submissive pose nearby and stood behind me. I tried not to wince when his hands made contact, long fingers rounding my shoulders gently, a gesture, perhaps a kindness, as if he was asking permission to touch me.

I responded by clasping a hand over my heart. I held it there for one breath. Two. Hoping my audience would perceive my action as a sign of nerves, I held the pose for a third breath. A fourth. I vibrated with anticipation. And fear.

The commanders on the other end of the surveillance monitors, men who considered themselves holy warriors with divine permission to murder by ambush, torture devices and explosives, would likely be entertained by my reaction.

But the one commander who mattered—Xavier Jareb—would recognize the signal. I was the contact he'd been waiting for.

"Clear to go."

Lowering my hand, I kept my gaze fixed on the floor, my mind focused on how Seth's voice would sound if I could hear him. I nodded to give the servant permission.

The eunuch slid his hands along my shoulders, a caress of excruciating slowness. Sweeping aside my hair, he exposed my neck, dragged his palms over my skin, forbidden touches that shouldn't have made me shiver, but did.

He swirled his fingers along my breastbone, the tops of my breasts. My nipples peaked to tight tips, and I imagined how I must appear to my audience. My nude body showcased by his veiled one. His dark hands, a striking contrast to my fairness. Would the cameras detail the sweat glazing my skin?

My most basic mission objective was to establish a credible cover, but I wasn't entirely sure how to do that right now. The eunuch's touch distracted me, made it difficult to assess the situation. I wouldn't have thought that such glancing touches would scatter my thoughts so completely, would make me so aware of my body. My breathlessness was surprising the hell out of me, it was grudging . . . *unwelcome.*

He pressed so close now I could feel a whisper of his smooth muscle through his veiled garments. I had no clue what he intended, how far he'd been instructed to go to get a response, so I simply braced myself. But I couldn't have prepared for his tongue dragging a rough-velvet stroke along my nape.

I imagined it was Seth's kiss invoking this crazy fluttering low in my belly, told myself it was the heat of his breaths caressing that sensitive juncture between neck and shoulder. If I just pretended that he stood behind me, his mouth skimming along my skin in an open-mouthed glide, I could explain my reaction, the way my weak knees left me swaying uncertainly.

Firm thighs parted wide enough to cradle my bottom and steady me. A silk-covered chest with hard nipples pressed into my back, and I put distance between us again, but didn't get a chance to catch my breath before he aimed his next volley.

Flicking his tongue lightly, he timed the motion with those of the fingertips he traced along the undersides of my breasts. He stroked my skin like he might have fingered a harp. His mouth curved, a smile I could feel against my skin.

And when he rolled my nipples between his fingers, the suddenness of the move took me so off guard that I gasped. A sound that echoed through the bubbling quiet like I'd tossed a stone down an empty well.

His touch ignited every nerve in my body, and I could only breathe deeply to manage the sensation.

I needed to get a grip. I'd been sent to perform for an audience, and I would. This was my chance to prove myself. Seth had gone out on a limb to put me in the field. He believed I was the best operative for this job—young enough to entice the commanders, yet skilled enough with undercover work despite my youth—even though I still hadn't completed my training.

I *was* the best woman for the job, and I'd prove it by not freaking out now. I just needed to keep my head and watch for unexpected opportunities to accomplish mission objective.

So keeping my gaze on the tiles, I played the model slave, as if being aroused by a eunuch for the entertainment of internationally wanted criminals was all in a day's work.

Yellow. Gold. Orange. Pink. Scarlet. Wine. Blood.

I really wished this felt like a normal day's work, but somehow those long fingers and the vision of eight terrorist commanders were coloring my day differently. I'd be fine if I could stay focused on the man I'd much rather be performing for.

I wondered what he thought about me standing nude with my eyes downcast and legs spread, a strange man's mouth and hands teasing me with touches that aroused me against my will.

I focused all my thoughts on Seth Blackthorn, my intelligence officer—I told myself it was his clear gray gaze raking over me, making me feel every inch of my bare skin, my tightening nipples, my moist sex.

Because from half a world away, via satellite signal, he was watching.

"Move to the first mark."

Hour Five: 1310 hours

Seth tapped the spacebar to bring up the image of the satellite projection onto the displays in his monitoring station. Pixels converged to create Lily's image, a striking vision of sleek curves and pale skin that nailed him back into his chair as he tried to steel his body's response.

He shouldn't let the sight of her affect him this way. He was a professional, but watching her slim form arch away from the male servant, her straight hair slice across her shoulders in a white-blonde wave, made his chest constrict. Even on flat screen monitors, Seth could see the heightened color of her face, a blush that contrasted with all that fair hair playing peek-a-boo with her breasts.

Willing himself to observe the bathing chamber in its entirety, he forced his gaze from the location of one surveillance camera to the other. The Qahtrainian royal family had spared no expense in turning their summer palace into a fortress to protect Ulmalhameh and his men. They were as devoted to their cause as he to his.

Devoted enough to send Lily into the hot zone.

As intelligence officer, or control, for this mission, his job was to monitor the progress of both Lily and their mole, to make tactical decisions to ensure their safety and facilitate their efforts to accomplish mission objective.

Kiss the target.

Hence the code name. Lily was in possession of a cutting-edge transmitting device developed by American scientists, the Wizards as they were known throughout the intelligence community, to deal with the reigning issue of the new millennium—terrorism. Made of a polymer that rendered it invisible to the naked eye, the Kiss of Death earned its name from the unique method of application. Lily wore the device stored inside a false crown. When she made contact with their target, she would use her tongue to maneuver the device onto her lips and *kiss* it onto his skin.

Simple. Undetectable. And highly effective, as it would make the elusive leader of the second largest terror network in the world visible to American reconnaissance satellites and a missile lock should mission objective suddenly be upgraded from retrieval to termination.

Best case scenario would be to bring Ulmalhameh into Command before his termination. Seth intended to extract intel about Husan al Din that only its leader could provide. He intended to disable this network to the ground and wanted no other radical stepping into Ulmalhameh's place to continue the "holy" war that left terror in its wake, piles of bloody bodies and screams that rang out around the globe.

Bringing Ulmalhameh in before his termination would also send a message to his followers and similar organizations that black operations were alive and well in the West. A message Seth believed gave them leverage with terrorists who tended to get cocky when the superpowers were limited to lengthy diplomacy as their first call to action.

He imagined those military commanders right now, men who were being treated to this same erotic show. No doubt they were enjoying Lily's pale beauty and skilled performance—a perfect combination of innocence and surprised arousal.

Seth told himself the show was for Ulmalhameh and his *Shura*. He had to ignore the refined satellite image that detailed the way Lily's full breasts quivered when the servant tugged on her nipples, stretched the blushing peaks until Seth could practically feel the touch half a world away.

As control for this mission, he should be objective. He wasn't. Watching Lily submit to a stranger's commands . . . Seth should be observing her actions tactically. Unfortunately, he found himself preoccupied by how beautiful she looked. His lack of focus annoyed him. This wasn't the first time he'd had the problem while working with her.

Inhaling deeply, he lifted his gaze gratefully from the monitor when a knock sounded. "Come in."

The door opened and Jayne Manning, a senior level operative and Command's resident psychiatrist, appeared, a vision of professionalism with her conservatively bobbed hairstyle and silk suit. "Van Brocklin told me you'd gone into seclusion."

"Too many distractions in System Ops."

"A lot of active missions." She headed toward a chair in front of his desk, not bothering to await an invitation. She'd obviously come for a reason. "You're monitoring Lily?"

He nodded.

"How are things going?"

Her gaze shifted over his shoulder and he realized that Jayne had a bird's eye view of his monitoring station. Resisting the urge to minimize the screens, Seth frowned. Feeling protective of Lily when he'd sent her halfway across the world to deal with Ulmalhameh and his *Shura* was irrational.

"She's getting ready to move to the first mark."

"Good for Lily. How's she holding up?"

Seth recognized the question was double-edged—not only had Jayne come to check on Lily's progress, but she'd come to evaluate him. "My uncle sent you."

"Yes."

"Official capacity or a personal favor?"

"Both, actually. I'm in charge of oversight—"

"Oversight?"

She inclined her regal head, letting her expression reveal absolutely nothing to hint at a hidden agenda. But Seth knew one thing from his years as an operative—neither Jayne Manning nor his uncle, the director of this covert intelligence agency that answered directly to the President, ever operated without a laundry list of motives.

"It's your first mission as control," Jayne pointed out. "Surely you don't question the need."

No, Seth didn't question the need for oversight. But he'd met too much opposition to his strategy for this mission to put much stock in her casual reply. "My history of field work tracking Husan al Din factions makes me the most qualified officer for this job."

"Which is why the director assigned it to you."

The director. Seth recognized a retreat to maximum safe distance when any of the senior level operatives referred to his uncle as "the director." He braced himself.

"While the director has every confidence that you're the best officer for the job, Seth, you've chosen to make some very bold moves," Jayne said. "Understandably, he's chosen to monitor the situation closely."

And to step in if Seth got in over his head. Jayne didn't say that out loud. She didn't have to. It was in her steely tone loud and clear.

"Why psychological? Tactical oversight makes more sense."

"Not necessarily. Just like you've made strategic choices about this mission, the director chooses where to direct his attention with oversight."

"So he's monitoring my emotional performance."

"Yes, he is. He feels responsible for Lily's safety. And yours." She allowed her expression to soften. "On the personal side, *your uncle* has asked me to make myself available. Given the unusual circumstances of this operation, he thought you might find me useful to talk to as events unfold."

"What specific events is he worried about?"

"Sending Lily into a high-risk situation under her cover was a tough call to make. He wants to support you in any way he can while you're dealing with the effects of that choice."

"He thinks you can help me maintain control so I can do my job properly."

"Why does that surprise you?"

Because Seth hadn't entertained the idea that his emotions would factor into the equation. "Sending Lily in as a swallow was the last thing I wanted to do," he admitted. "I ran sims and feasibility studies for every other scenario. I couldn't even come close to finding one with this potential for success."

She nodded.

"Sometimes our jobs require a price," he said. "We don't question that. We wouldn't be with this agency if we did. We have a chance to bring Ulmalhameh into custody and we take it. I understand that. So does Lily. My uncle and every one of his advisors agreed."

"None of which makes the reality any easier to deal with."

Seth gazed back at the monitor, watched the servant retreat from Lily in response to a verbal command from an unseen man over an audio system. Not Ulmalhameh, whose voice he'd heard before on various prerecorded media releases, but an older man. Most likely Ulmalhameh's mentor, Khalid ben Sarsour. A man Ulmalhameh would never have surfaced without by his side.

Lily took a deep breath that relaxed her visibly, and Seth

silently encouraged her. He'd asked her to do a dirty job and she'd taken it on with a level of determined professionalism that only reinforced his belief that she was their best chance for mission success. She'd make contact with their mole, and gain access to Ulmalhameh. She'd kiss their target and Seth would bring them both in safely. The agency would retrieve Ulmalhameh and start dismantling Husan al Din from the top down.

The end justified the means.

And Seth had never felt the bite of that belief more than when Lily stood in that bathing chamber halfway across the world. With her eyes cast down in the manner of a slave, she waited for the man who would claim her, waited to see if their mission would proceed as planned . . .

Seth found himself reaching for the mouse, fingers poised over the infrared device in case he needed to upgrade a perimeter unit to extract her from the inside of that military compound. A battle he would rather fight than leave Lily in the care of another terrorist for the duration of this meeting.

Staring at the monitor, he squelched any doubt. Mission objective now rested in the hands of their mole, a man who'd double-crossed the leader he'd sworn to serve. All Seth could do was be ready to protect Lily, will her his strength, as they waited. . . .

The door to the bathing chamber swung wide. Seth saw Lily startle at the sound, but to her credit she held her position, her gaze fixed on the floor. But he could see anticipation stretching tight across her shoulders, in the rapid rise and fall of her breasts.

Her immediate future strode through the door one booted foot at a time, long muscular legs aggressively chewing up the distance between them. Seth's suddenly moist fingers slipped on the mouse, startling him from his assessment of the bold figure in camouflage. A tall, bearded man with a powerfully physical build that Seth recognized instantly from their covert meetings.

Xavier Jareb.

"She's moved to the first mark." Withdrawing his hand from the mouse, he wiped his sweaty palms on his slacks.

"Congratulations," Jayne said.

Both her neutral tone and her sentiment irritated him. This wasn't a contest where he needed to prove himself. Operation Kiss wasn't about rationalizing his decisions to his superiors; Operation Kiss was about eliminating a terrorist—another Osama bin Laden—before he paid them a visit on American soil.

The only person who needed to prove himself today was

Xavier Jareb. He would have to prove his trustworthiness and his value before Seth would exfiltrate him from Husan al Din and bring him in to seek asylum in the United States.

Only sheer stubbornness helped him focus on the monitor.

Xavier Jareb looked like a cookie-cutter terrorist dressed for the prom. He was rough around the edges, more comfortable slithering on his belly through a sewer with several pounds of ordnance strapped to his back than inside a bathing chamber. But he'd been scrubbed and his fatigues pressed to knife-point creases. A vital man, his aggressive build and dark features contrasted sharply with Lily's fairness.

Folding his arms across his chest, Seth watched as the man raked his gaze over Lily for the first time in person. He came to a stop directly before her, towered above her, but Lily held her ground, eyes on the floor where their feet almost touched. Steel reinforced boots to bare toes. Master and slave.

Seth wondered what Jareb thought of Lily, of the way she trembled, a shiver that rippled along her long, slim curves . . . did he think he'd been rewarded from the U.S. government for his work this past year and a half?

Jareb dragged an assessing gaze down her body. He gave a nod of approval, definitely pleased with his new slave. But there was something else in his face, too. Amusement, perhaps, that the crazy Americans would send a beautiful woman into the hot zone to do a man's job.

Spearing dark fingers into her hair, he forced Lily to lift her gaze, incredible eyes so deep a blue they looked violet. The move forced her to arch backward. Her hair shimmered out behind her, a wave of blonde that fell to her thighs. Her breasts thrust high in the air. The rosy tips, still hard from the eunuch's attention, speared toward Jareb's crisp shirt eagerly.

But there was nothing eager about Lily's expression. She submitted to the man's examination, but not with the controlled performance that Seth had expected. He'd briefed her on how to handle Jareb, and she wasn't following the script. She seemed uncertain. Her hesitation was coming through in her performance, the first sign of nerves he'd seen since she'd been transported with the other women to the island.

Seth hadn't considered what this job might cost her. And peering into her face, so shielded behind careful detachment, he knew that it would cost.

Jareb didn't seem to notice. The man was too occupied with

surveying the terrain of sleek curves that stretched out before him. He traced his fingers along Lily's jaw, down into the scoop of her neck, his exploration thorough, as if savoring every inch of her soft skin.

Jayne would notice, though. She wouldn't miss the way Lily held herself rigidly in Jareb's grip, a tightness that sharpened every muscle until it radiated an almost brittle intensity. As though she might shatter with another touch.

Nor would Jayne miss Seth's reaction, though he was forcing a detachment as careful as Lily's, a detachment he wished like hell he was feeling.

But how else could he feel when Jareb's black eyes projected his hunger for Lily across a satellite signal and half the world? That he intended to satisfy that hunger on his slave's not-quite-willing body.

Seth braced himself when Jareb bypassed Lily's shoulder to splay his hand over her chest. Pressing his palm flat, he seemed to be testing her heartbeat with that touch, fingers aimed toward her breasts, an obscene contrast of dark skin and light.

Lily's expression never changed, but her mouth parted around a gasp when Jareb slid his hand over her breast and idly thumbed her nipple. The breathy sound invited Jareb's black gaze back to her face, his concentration broken by the sound. And whatever he saw in her careful expression intrigued him, because he squeezed her nipple hard enough to make her flinch.

"Lily's handling herself very well."

Jayne's voice startled him, and Seth turned to face her, needing a break from the sight on the monitor. "She's struggling."

"Yes." Jayne gave him a look of mild curiosity. "Do you question whether she'll manage the job?"

He gave a curt nod. Lily might not like what she had to do, but she'd do it. He'd never questioned that when he'd argued her case to his uncle and the agency's top-level advisors. He didn't question it now with Jareb's hands on her.

Jayne nodded. "I'm sure she'll calm down once she's more familiar with our mole and what to expect from him."

Seth guessed she meant to offer reassurance, and he wanted to tell her not to bother. He was a professional, too. He was reconciled with what he'd asked Lily to do.

The end justified the means.

Somehow he couldn't get the words past his lips. Which had everything to do with sitting safely in his office while Lily operated in the hot zone far away.

"Kiss me, fair one," Jareb said, dragging Seth's attention back to the display. "Show me how grateful you are that I am your master."

Time slowed to a crawl as Seth watched Lily reach up to cup Jareb's bearded face between her palms. She seemed almost grateful for the chance to act, as if action was easier than idly submitting to the man's touch.

Urging Jareb's face toward her, she slanted her full mouth across his, obeying his command. He issued a growl low in his throat and hauled Lily up against him, her bare curves molding into those knifed creases.

Her hands fluttered against his face as Jareb assumed control of their kiss, his beard masking her expression from view, his jaw working as he devoured her mouth with a focus that made Seth grind his teeth in frustration.

Lily stiffened visibly when Jareb's free hand left her breast to begin a kneading descent down her ribs, over her hip. Jareb explored her at his leisure, smoothing his palm over the firm curve of her bottom, dragging a fingertip along her cleft.

Seth imagined the satin smoothness of Lily's skin, could almost feel the strength of the slender fingers she dug into Jareb's beard, a grip as if she was hanging on for dear life.

And when Jareb thrust a hand between her thighs, she shivered, a full-bodied motion that made her sway sharply against him, made her react with what looked to Seth like more fear than arousal.

Gripping the arms of the chair, he dug his fingers into the leather to resist the urge to reach for the mouse. Just one click to abort this whole mission . . .

Seth jerked to attention when Jareb broke their kiss to gaze down at her with what looked like surprise. Tightening his grip on her neck, he forced her to lean back even farther, an angle so severe she would have fallen without support. Then he positioned his fingers between her thighs and eased upward.

Seth jerked forward in his chair at the sound of Lily's gasp. His gut clenched tight as he watched a flush bloom in her cheeks as Jareb eased inside her with a move that was obscene in its intimacy.

Lily seemed poised breathlessly beneath him, as if she was waiting, so Seth waited, too, unsure for what. Jareb's reaction maybe, or for Lily to control her nerves and calm down. Maybe he just wanted his own heart to steady its beat. But he was struck by how startlingly vulnerable she seemed in contrast to the man who now held her, how exposed.

Her breasts rose and fell on a sharp breath as Jareb explored her, and his beard split with a smile that made his white teeth flash. He thrust again, an oddly gentle stroke this time, almost a caress.

Lily winced and steeled herself against his touch.

"Come on, Lily," Seth hissed at the monitor, as if he might lend her his strength by sheer will. "Don't go to pieces now."

"She'll manage," Jayne said, certain.

He resisted the impulse to glance her way, refused to spare himself the painfully intimate sight in front of him.

"She's frightened—" He broke off when Jareb bent his head to whisper into Lily's ear.

Though Seth strained to hear the exchange, he could hear nothing more than the whisper of their hushed breaths, and that more than anything drove home the depth of his powerlessness.

Mission *control*?

Seth had no control. Not while sitting halfway across the world while Lily subjected herself to this stranger's touch against her will—and this was against her will no matter how noble her intention to do her job.

Another rough whisper. With a violent blush scorching her cheeks, Lily nodded in response to Jareb's question.

The man gave a lusty laugh. Withdrawing his hand, he traced a fingertip up her smooth abdomen, leaving behind a trail of her body's moisture that glinted in the light. "You will now come to my bed, fair one. I would savor the emir's generous gift."

Lily pressed her eyes tightly shut, trembled.

Seth shot forward in his chair. "I'm losing her, damn it, and I can't do a thing to help her." His voice sounded harsh, frustrated, unfamiliar. "She's scared to death, like she's never let a man touch her like this before."

"There would be a reason for that."

Jayne's cool tone impacted him like the blast from an assault rifle. And when her words finally penetrated, Seth snapped around to look at her, ground out the only question that mattered. "And why is that?"

"Because she hasn't."

The name Nabi Ulmalhameh meant prophet of war. The man who'd recruited him to become that prophet had gifted him with the name and he'd born it humbly for most of his adult life. But when Nabi Ulmalhameh thought of himself, he was the emir, a ruler of the sons of Allah, men who fought their Jihad to expel the heretics from the countries of the Holy places.

He had followers from all over the world. Several governments had donated land and resources so he could set up facilities to bring in experts on guerrilla warfare, sabotage, and covert operations to train his recruits. In the years since he'd committed his life to creating a Holy army, he had mobilized nearly 10,000 fighters to their cause.

"Moving among the living again brings you great pleasure, does it not, my son?"

The emir turned away from the wall of surveillance monitors he currently watched to find the man who was the father of his heart entering the room with painfully slow strides.

"It does indeed, my father." Covering the distance between them, he took Khalid ben Sarsour by the arm and helped him to the chair he'd ignored to pace off his own restlessness. "Duty keeps me so active that I never realize how solitary my life has become until I'm out breathing fresh air again."

"Which is precisely why we're here. You will choose new faces to bring into your household and inhale a moist healing breath. Your soul cannot be allowed to wither."

A much-needed breath, the emir silently agreed. For a man who commanded so large an army, he lived an isolated life in a high-tech stronghold—seclusion born of necessity to protect himself from the Americans, who'd made it their holy calling to hunt him. Emerging to confer with his *Shura* in person was a risky, unavoidable, and, yes, welcomed venture, despite the tragedy that had forced him above ground.

Khalid was dying, a cancer that ate his bones. At his insistence, they would recruit a man together to replace him, to be the emir's arm in a world in which he could no longer function without great risk to himself and their cause.

The emir understood the need, though he knew no man would ever replace his heart-father. Not as a trusted advisor. Not as a beloved friend. Khalid ben Sarsour was a simple man with great vision. He would be missed.

"I have seen to the pairing of your commanders with the

slaves," Khalid said. "They are grateful for your generosity. You are pleased with their choices?"

The emir clasped his hands behind his back and scanned the monitors displaying the various security zones where several of his commanders made the acquaintances of their women. "I find a few of their choices interesting."

Khalid laughed. "Quiet Boghos choosing that green-eyed hellcat surprised me. I would have thought him more suited to that raven-haired beauty with the excellent manners."

The *submissive* beauty with the excellent manners, the emir silently corrected. Had Khalid felt up to choosing a slave of his own, he'd have likely installed that very beauty in his bed. Khalid, for all his faith and vision, was an older generation man with very simple tastes—he wanted his women on their knees eager to please.

The emir though, like his quiet Commander apparently, enjoyed the challenge of making his women submit. He added the hellcat to a list of potentials to fill his own harem.

His gaze trailed to the monitor where Commander Jareb was leading the American away to his apartment. The emir's gaze had strayed frequently to this woman, an oddity with her white hair and pale skin. But her eyes sparkled like bright jewels, and her tall, willowy form was pleasing after a diet rich with the small darkskinned women from his part of the world.

"You look to the heretic with interest, my son," Khalid said, missing nothing as usual. "Jareb does well to show her the proper place of slave."

"He seems to be making his point."

Commander Jareb hadn't allowed the woman to robe herself before leading her through the palace. The effect pleased him. She followed Jareb with her gaze cast at his heels, seemingly perfect decorum, but her manner bristled with pride. Another arrogant American. She was clearly uncomfortable with her nudity and irritated by that discomfort.

He couldn't help but enjoy even such a small victory.

Ironic that he should find an American within his grasp now, and an innocent one. For the emir had recognized what his commander had—this woman, for all her bravado and impeccable manners, was yet unskilled with the language of her body.

Khalid was right. She did interest him. Not sexually but as a curiosity. He enjoyed the challenge of taming his women, usually preferring to be amply rewarded, not required to put forth more effort to train an innocent.

But he could appreciate the appeal of this one with her un-yielding pride, and the emir appreciated the chance to observe his commander handle such an unusual slave. A test of character.

The emir felt the weight of the task before him. Choosing the right man to replace Khalid would ensure the continued success of their Jihad, but the wrong man could complicate an already complex situation and endanger all they'd worked for.

So the emir would test his *shura* in the only ways he could. He would watch his commanders handle their slaves. He would watch them interact with their peers. He would listen to their ideas at council. He would assess their loyalty, their moods, their person-alities. Then with Khalid's help, he would choose.

Far more pleasing was the task of selecting slaves for his harem, which needed new blood. He'd left the mother of his only sons with the task of cleaning his household, a job he knew pleased her. She would command her rivals' deaths and, upon his return, would reign like a queen over his new harem.

His gift to her for giving him strong sons.

But until his return to seclusion and the inevitable passing of his beloved friend, the emir would savor these moments among the living. He would meet the challenge of choosing Khalid's succes-sor. He would watch his commanders rule their slaves and see how well the slaves pleased their new masters. He would savor these rare moments of freedom from the cause that dictated his life.

Khalid was right. His soul couldn't be allowed to wither.

"First Contact."

Hour Six: 1405 hours

I kept my eyes on Jareb's feet as he led me through the palace, for once appreciating the subservient pose that spared me from meeting the gazes of those we passed . . . servants and lesser officers who'd come to serve the emir.

The position also saved me from the sight of Jareb from behind, all long-legged strides, lean waist, broad shoulders, and the memory of the way he'd kissed me, touched me.

Instead, I marked my steps, counted the doors and archways that passed in my periphery to determine a layout of the place. I wondered what Seth thought about my performance so far. I'd wanted to be bold, competent, but I'd been nervous instead. I was trying to talk myself out of the nerves now. Seth had briefed me on how to handle Jareb, but I hadn't told him about my lack of actual sexual experience. If I had, one of two things would have happened—he'd have refused to send me on this mission or he'd have sent me anyway.

The first I couldn't live with professionally. I didn't want to know that best case scenario for ridding the world of a monster had been thwarted because of my virginity.

The second reason was more personal. I simply couldn't face such blunt proof that Seth didn't care about me at all.

So I'd detailed my sexual explorations with my various boyfriends, omitted the relevant details and 'fessed up to Jayne Manning instead. She'd conducted my psych prep for this mission and had assured me I could handle the job. Since she'd recommended me to the director, I'd taken her word for it.

"Don't dwell on it, deal with it," was her favorite saying.

I would deal. It was my job. Simple.

Jareb came to a stop in front of a door and waited while a male servant swung it wide. He never acknowledged me as he swept inside the room, instructing his servant to run a bath. Then they both disappeared through another doorway—the bathroom, I presumed—issuing directions about preparations for a feast that would be taking place tonight. I stood inside the doorway, taking in the well-appointed suite—or what I could see of it in my periphery.

Two doorways, likely the bath and a bedroom. The outer chamber had comfortable leather furniture grouped between a stone fireplace and a magnificent view of a blooming courtyard with a fountain. From what I could see, Jareb had been put up in a suite in keeping with the style the Qahtrainian royal family hosted their guests.

Except for the surveillance cameras. Always the cameras. Constant reminders that I was here to perform. Now that the commanders had chosen their slaves, our audience had dwindled down to the emir and his nearest and dearest. Khalid ben Sarsour, for sure. And Seth. He was treated to a front row seat for this show.

I tried to pinpoint the cameras' exact positions, took in all I could without appearing too curious. Concealing my gaze beneath the fall of my hair, I listened to the voice of the man who controlled the next all-important hours of my life.

Until today, I'd only seen Xavier Jareb in grainy surveillance photos from various bombings and hijackings. He was a hard man, lean, dark and exuding an edgy, dangerous energy that had contrasted so sharply with Seth's polished demeanor.

Two sides of black ops—the bad guy and the good guy.

Jareb lived on the edge, in the trenches, terrorizing an entire world in the name of his faith. Seth was equally passionate. He lived on the edge, went into the trenches and used power as his weapon, made split-second decisions that affected the course of global events.

Both men believed what they fought for was right.

Both men were willing to die for that belief.

But Jareb had claimed to have a change of heart. Or so we presumed. There was no way to be one hundred percent certain that he wasn't a provocateur luring us into a trap. Seth had run sims to assess the possibility. He'd maneuvered Jareb into a situation where he'd had to risk himself by passing along pertinent information to assist us.

Even so, there was no telling how much these terrorists would sacrifice to get inside our agency. No doubt in my mind that the Sword of Faith would drop big bucks setting up elaborate operations only to sabotage their own efforts—and kill their own men—if it meant getting us to trust Jareb.

And here I was cut off from Command, and Seth, at Jareb's mercy, *trusting* a known terrorist we *hoped* was a defector.

Sometimes I wondered why it had never occurred to me to consider another line of work. I mean, just because my parents were deep-cover ops didn't mean I'd had to become one. . . .

Jareb returned, dismissed his servant, and then we were alone again. Except for the cameras. Always the cameras. And Seth. I wondered if he was experiencing even a fraction of the nerves I was right now. Probably not.

Jareb left me standing beside the doorway. I could see him when he sat on the edge of the sofa to unlace his boots, and my heart began a slow, hard pounding when I realized he was stripping. The boots went first. Then the socks. I was grateful for my long hair, which hid so much of my face from view.

Not that Jareb bothered to glance my way. He didn't. He was too busy peeling away his dress fatigues and folding them into neat little piles. But I knew Seth wouldn't miss a thing, and I was determined to present myself as assured and in control to recover from my not-so-stellar earlier performance. Jareb wasn't the only one with something to prove around here.

"Come," he said, a sharp sound in the quiet, a sound that made my hard-pounding heart issue a jerky beat.

Dodging flashes of his dark legs and tight butt, I followed him into what was indeed a bathroom, and from what I could see a spacious one.

"You will bathe me."

Nodding, I told myself I was ready to get this show on the road, and a bath would give inspired new meaning to the term "first contact." I'd much rather deal with the matter at hand than keep dwelling on what might happen. All this teasing was winding my nerves way too tight.

Lifting my gaze, I searched for the supplies I'd need to complete my new mission objective. Give a terrorist a bath.

I found soap and shampoo in the vanity; linen in a cabinet near an amazing shower stall with wall jets, a rock garden and a window that, like the tub, presented a view of the courtyard.

He stepped into the huge garden tub, still filling from the tap with steaming water. He was indeed hard and lean, the definition of his tightly muscled body severe. A man who lived a desperate life on the edge. Yet he was oddly striking, unreal almost, his definition cast in the rich bronze skin tone of his heritage. He looked stark in the late afternoon sun streaming through the windowed wall.

Muscles shifted, a rippling display of lean power as he gripped the edges, lowered himself into the water. He sank down to his neck, rested his head back against the rim and closed his eyes. His sigh echoed through the bathroom, a sound that made me suspect he was having a day much like my own.

I knelt on the tiled step of the tub, a careful motion meant to keep from disturbing him. I awaited my command to begin my task, suddenly more aware of my nakedness than I'd been walking bare-assed through the palace halls.

It was a lot harder to pretend I was in a fantasy with Seth when I was kneeling barely a foot away from a nude Jareb. His broad shoulders broke the surface with his every breath, his corded neck glistened as water sluiced off his skin.

We were so close I could detect a hint of scalp beneath his brutally short hair, see the glossy sheen of that stubble, another gift of his ancestry. His profile was sharp—strong brow, deep-set eyes, straight nose—and the trimmed beard was the only thing to soften the lines of his jaw, to temper a look that struck me as death sculpted in bronze.

Put an assault weapon in this man's hands and his appearance alone would scare hostages and send bystanders running for cover.

I tried to imagine what he might look like clean-shaven and dressed in those custom-tailored power suits that Seth often wore for political appearances. Or those tuxes that made him look so high-ticket and incredible during black-tie functions.

I couldn't. Jareb was simply too ethnic. Too *menacing* to civilize in my imagination. And too damned close. I'm sure my imagination would have improved dramatically with distance.

I waited. My knees ached on the tile. I forced my spine straight, my shoulders back even though the position turned the tub's edge into a shelf that showcased my breasts. I inhaled slowly, exhaled as deliberately, determined not to let adrenaline get me winded. Each second ticking past was agony.

I waited some more. Mentally prepared myself. At least I thought I was. When Jareb opened his eyes and turned to stare at me, I jumped at the suddenness of his move. No matter how much

I'd been expecting his gaze, I was completely unprepared for the reality of it.

I caught a glimpse of impossibly black eyes before averting my own to show respect. It didn't matter. Jareb knew I'd been checking him out. Just as I knew he was checking me out. I could feel that gaze as if it was knifing the distance between us.

And suddenly his face entered my field of vision. I registered his sharp features and determined expression as he leaned toward me purposefully. Or, more accurately, toward my breast. His tongue lashed out to scrape across my nipple.

My breath hitched hard, a sound that managed to shriek above the running water. My chest rose and fell sharply, unwittingly driving my nipple toward his lips again.

He didn't even blink. He just sucked that peak into his mouth, an unexpected pull so deep and complete it was just shy of painful. I couldn't be sure whether it was that feeling or the answering pulse low in my gut that made me gasp aloud.

Jareb hung on. His mouth fastened onto my skin in a vision of shocking eroticism that might have been happening to someone else if not for the corresponding reaction swelling inside me.

His black eyes met mine over the pale expanse of my skin, and I recognized the first glimmer of emotion in those inky black depths. Triumph. Satisfaction.

This man liked his control over me, evidenced when he flicked his tongue across my nipple and sucked deeply again, a painful pull that made me yelp.

That hurt. And I could do nothing but ride the sensation until it passed. This was a test to see what I was made of. I could tell by the way he watched me, the way he searched my expression for some sign of weakness.

I didn't give any. I held my face blank. Jayne had told me to expect my body to react, a physiological response to stimuli that had nothing to do with whether I was enjoying myself. So I kept my gaze averted in what I hoped was enough respect not to get me busted with the emir on the other end of the surveillance cameras. I wasn't worried about Jareb at the moment. If he was a defector in good faith like Seth believed, then he'd cut me a little slack since any hope he had for a decent future rested in the hands of my superiors.

If he was a double-crosser, I was dead anyway. And if I was going to die, I'd prefer to go *before* playing his sex slave.

I didn't let Jareb see that in my face, either.

But he must have found what he was looking for because he ended our little battle by swirling his tongue around my nipple as if to soothe away the pain he'd caused. Sitting back, he lifted a hand from the water and extended it to me.

I stared blankly, not grasping what he wanted me to do.

"Come," he said in a gravelly voice I hadn't heard enough yet to find familiar. "Unless you expect me to stand like a child, you must be inside the tub."

Great. Just great. But there was *something* in his voice . . . An edge of exasperation maybe, not hostile or resentful but as if he was saying, "You foolish Americans know nothing."

That tone got me past my paralysis.

Sliding my fingers into his, I was immediately struck by the roughness of his skin, the contained power in his grip. I forced myself to rise before him, so aware of his gaze that I could feel my movements keenly—my right leg unfurling, accepting my weight as I balanced from kneeling to standing, brought my left leg under to steady me.

My imagination seemed to be back in force because I could practically feel his gaze rake down my body. First stop . . . my breasts, one nipple still wet and aching from his mouth. Second stop . . . my sex, which had been denuded of any protection I might have felt if I'd still had some pubic hair.

No such luck. I got to feel the air brushing my exposed folds as I climbed the tiled stair, stepped on the rim and lowered myself onto the ledge.

My bottom slapped the tile and lucky Jareb got an award-winning crotch shot as I let my feet slip into the hot water. I sank down and knelt so I didn't land full against him. I thought I'd be glad for the water to cover my nudity, but all at once I could feel his bristly legs as he spread them wide to make a place for me. Warm, wet muscle nestled me between his thighs, trapped me with the startling feel of our bodies touching.

My foot pressed against his calf and my knees bumped his, but to my surprise, I was most aware of the hand he still clasped around mine. The way his strong fingers had twined through my own was a simple gesture that somehow struck me as more intimate than our tangled legs.

It was ridiculous, I know, but I didn't have time for analysis. I got to business instead. Only action would help me now. I extricated my hand with a relief wildly out of balance with the moment.

"Don't dwell on it. Deal with it." I reached for the soap.

My hands trembled as I lathered a washcloth and decided where to begin. Having the terrain of an unfamiliar man spread out before me sent logic flying out the window, but I felt better when Jareb sank back against the tub and closed his eyes, obviously content to let me proceed however I saw fit.

I decided on his feet, hoping our audience would interpret my actions as another mark of respect for my master. There was something about distance that appealed to me.

Scooting to the opposite edge of the tub, I turned off the water and reached for Jareb's ankle, directed the solid weight of his leg into my lap.

Average American citizens read daily newspapers that report global events, events that while interesting, don't stop them from heading into their offices or dropping off their kids at school. And that was exactly the purpose of black ops—to keep the threat far away so our citizens would be safe on home soil. A job getting tougher and tougher every day. Impossible even sometimes. Unfortunately.

But the distance the average American citizens keep between their daily routines and terrorist activities wasn't a luxury I enjoyed, which put a whole different spin on the bad guys.

When I looked at Jareb, I expected to see a fanatic whose life ambition was to murder heretics—he who dies with the most points wins. I'd studied the manipulations of terrorists, seen the devastation they caused up close and personal. But as I worked the washcloth in soapy circles between Jareb's toes, along his arch, over his calloused heel, I saw a man.

He had faint indentations around his ankle from where his socks had imprinted his skin. Waffles, my mom had called them, like the pillow lines I'd get on my cheek after a nap.

This different perspective threw me, *unsettled* me, so I focused on my task, trying not to dwell on it. I worked the lather up a strong calf to his knee. I began the process over again with his other leg.

Jareb kept his eyes closed, appeared relaxed. Good. My entire purpose in life now was to please this man.

"Don't dwell on it. Deal with it."

Thank you, Jayne Manning.

Swallowing hard, I soaped the washcloth again and braced myself for the inevitable trip onward. Looked like Jareb was anticipating that trip, too, because he drew his knees higher, allowing me 360 access to his thighs.

One of us was familiar with this bathing routine.

But I was a fast study. Working the lather in slow circles over hard muscle, I noticed the way the glossy hairs on his thighs floated up in the wake of my strokes, lifted away from his skin on the current. I told myself that this was practice for my fantasies about Seth, experience. And who knew . . . maybe one day his feelings for me would change.

A girl could hope, couldn't she?

I did. At least until Jareb exhaled a breath that interrupted my reverie, and I found his eyes still closed and his fierce expression somewhat diminished with relaxation.

Score one for me—I was pleasing my master.

His groin splayed open, an obstacle that would invariably need to be tackled as there was no place left to go but up. I couldn't seem to span that final distance though. I couldn't reach out to take his maleness into my hands, conquering this last obstacle. I couldn't bring myself to find out if he was responding to my touch.

So I took the path of least resistance, instead. Bypassing his lap entirely, I proceeded along the safe terrain of his rippled stomach, his waist. The only negative here was proximity because my knees suddenly pressed into those hard thighs, my damp breasts swaying forward as I worked my way up the furred hollows and ridges of his chest.

I imagined that one day I might touch Seth this way. And if I did, I wouldn't be jumping from his thighs to his chest and skipping all the good stuff in between.

The thought almost made me smile. Almost.

But reality intruded when I was forced to stretch full against the wrong man to brace a hand on the tub ledge to support myself. I worked the lather over his broad shoulders and into the crook of his neck with the other. I had to awkwardly switch hands to continue along the other side. While I accomplished this little maneuver, my thigh pressed high into his and I answered my own question.

Jareb was indeed reacting to my touch.

His penis thickened and my gaze instinctively shot to his. He'd opened his eyes and was watching me with one brow arched. The last thing I wanted to do was face him with that growing erection between us, so I took defensive maneuvers and focused on the smudges beneath his eyes, the hollowed cheeks, the flare of his nostrils when he inhaled.

He had full lips that might have been sensual if I could have imagined them smiling. I couldn't. I'd seen them stray from that grim line only once since we'd met—when he'd discovered proof of my inexperience. Not what I'd have called a real grin. But he had been surprised, I thought, and pleased.

Yet I remembered the taste of his mouth, the way his lips had spread over mine, tasting, devouring, laying claim to me as if he had every right, as if he'd been waiting.

And when I thought about it, the longing made sense.

Jareb was as aware as I was that we were under surveillance, and his position was even more tentative than my own. He walked a tightrope between the emir and Seth Blackthorn. Between his past and his future. Could I really blame the guy if he wanted to take advantage of what might turn out to be the last pleasant hours of his life?

I couldn't. Jareb was a naked, virile man, and I'd been sent in to serve him. To pleasure him. To perform for the emir and oddly enough for Seth, too. He was assessing my performance as carefully as the emir was.

I was doing my job. I was familiarizing myself with Jareb's body and brushing up against him in all sorts of places that would arouse any living man.

At the moment, Jareb was alive and well.

And he knew exactly how hard I was working to keep up my performance. The arched brow gave it away, I think. It was a curious look, quizzical almost, as if he was defining my character in much the same way I was defining his.

I wondered if he was having any luck. I supposed that when one thought about a black op swallow from a heretical government, one understandably wouldn't expect a virgin.

Well, I'd never fit the developmental norms. It was that fact, along with speaking the language, that had uniquely qualified me for this mission. It was what reminded me I *was* uniquely qualified for this mission while I sat naked in a bathtub with a terrorist.

Settling back on my haunches, I reached for his hand, laving my soapy attention between his calloused fingers, his ragged nails. He'd closed his eyes again, and I breathed a little easier. At least until I ran out of things to wash except for his crotch or his back.

Procrastinator that I was, I slipped my hand around his neck, urging him away from the tub. He sat up without comment, and I shimmied around him, careful to avoid brushing our slick bodies together, and positioned myself behind him.

I scrubbed his back vigorously, found that broad expanse of smooth skin a safe zone on turf where every curve brought me some place I didn't want to be. I retreated to grab the shampoo and proceeded to work a lather into his short hair.

I'd meant to slip away so he could go under and rinse out the shampoo, but he caught my wrist before I could go anywhere. I inhaled sharply, a gasp that shocked the quiet, as he pulled me toward him, sealed my wet body against his. My breasts crushed his back, my abdomen cradled the curve of his buttocks. Our thighs molded together back to front.

In this moment, not black ops or religious beliefs or even culture could steal the primitive awareness that he was a man and I was a woman.

My heart throbbed hard. My nipples hardened against my will. His pulse jumped in his throat, a fluttering beneath his dark skin that told me he was aware of how I reacted to him.

"Kiss me."

Though I'd known the command would invariably come, I hadn't expected to be relieved when it did. But action seemed the lesser of two evils right now. Anticipation was killing me. Anticipation and knowing that Seth was watching.

Shampoo dribbled from his hairline near that pulse, and I lowered my mouth to his skin, pressed a close-mouthed kiss along his neck to catch the lather.

He shivered, his grip tightening on my hand for an instant, before he dragged me around him in a series of erotic motions that brushed soapy skin against skin, shifting muscle against muscle. I went with the motion, my body unfurling against his.

I felt him gather against me and knew what he intended even before he made his move. I caught a sharp breath before he dragged me under water, using the buoyancy to agilely reposition himself around me, so that I was trapped between his thighs.

We came up with huge gasps. The water had rinsed the shampoo from his hair, and he settled back against the tub again, with me in his arms. I was trapped, half-submerged, unfolded against him so my breasts crushed his chest, my stomach cradled his erection.

I could feel every inch of his hard body against me, making my body tighten in places I hadn't realized would react.

"You're not through washing me yet." His voice was rough gravel in the quiet.

Unfortunately, I wasn't, which meant a hand job for him.

Avoiding his gaze, I reached for the washcloth, forced to stretch full against him for support as I soaped the cloth. I knew he could feel my nipples hard against his chest. He could probably feel my heart pounding double-time, too. Maybe he knew I was nervous. I don't know. I only know that when I slid back down the length of his body, I could feel every inch of him against me. He wasn't nervous.

Maneuvering to my side, I reached for his erection. Although why that suddenly felt like a refuge, I honestly couldn't say. An illusion of control, maybe?

I slipped my cloth between his thighs. He was big, uncircumcised, and so dark his skin looked almost purple. He sucked in sharply when I touched him, and his erection swelled impossibly larger, banging against my wrist as I lathered him.

I soaped with tentative strokes, resisting the urge to gaze into his face, couldn't confront what I'd see there.

Awareness that mirrored my own.

Oddly, as much as I clung to the memory of Seth to get me through this moment, I couldn't seem to picture his face right now. I was too distracted, too unnerved by the way I felt, *aware* when I hadn't expected to be, didn't want to be.

I'd come prepared to act, to fake my way through this mission. I'd been comfortable with the thought of a physiological response. But I hadn't counted on *feeling*, *reacting*. What I felt seemed to be a little more than tissue responding to stimuli.

"Don't dwell on it, deal with it."

Jayne had a point. So did Jareb. If I was going to wind up dead, I'd rather go out doing my job, proving myself a professional. Proving that Seth had been right to believe in me.

I laved the soft cloth up his shaft, over the swelling purplish head, the skin stretching with life beneath my fingers. I focused on his reactions rather than my own, reminded myself again that I was here to please him.

When I delved lower, his buttocks parted easily to my touch, and I felt a moment of triumph when his erection swelled. Even wielding such a small power over him gave me back some control in a situation where I felt powerless. A control that grounded me, centered me.

"Touch me with your hand," he said, a guttural command.

Withdrawing my fingers from the cloth, I touched him more boldly, amazed that I could handle these liberties. With slow soapy swirls of my fingers, I tried to give him what he was looking for.

Dragging my fingertip down his cleft, I felt the crinkled ring of nerves and pressed lightly, my soapy finger intruding barely. Jareb shuddered, a full-bodied motion that brought him against me, and I jumped, enough to make water splash over the rim of the tub.

"I shouldn't confuse innocent and shy with you." His words were another harsh bark of sound in the quiet, and I just froze, unsure how to react when I was lying here with my fingers intimately caressing this man's ass.

Seth hadn't briefed me on what to do in this scenario.

He hadn't needed to. I had a new teacher now, and he sank down onto my fingertip, his body giving another heave as he managed the sensation, his raw groan vibrating through me.

Heat ignited in my cheeks, a blush I could feel from the tips of my breasts to the roots of my hair. I'd made my little power play and had been caught. There was only one thing to do now . . . I lifted my gaze.

Laughter glittered in those dark eyes, vital and alive. I felt speared by the sight of it, hadn't known a man who lived in the shadow world of terror and death could still have laughter.

"What say you, Atiya?" His gruff words somehow sounded gentle with his bright eyes. "You do talk, don't you?"

"Atiya?" I understood the word but not his context.

"It means gift." He eased off my finger, his nostrils flaring. I slipped my hand out from between his thighs, trying not to look embarrassed and flustered.

I didn't manage either. Jareb was too amused by me. He lifted his hand to my temple, smoothed away a tangle of wet hair, his knowing smile keeping my blush alive.

"You have been given to me as a gift, Atiya, and I'll instruct you how to please me. We begin with another kiss."

Threading his fingers around my neck, he urged my face towards his as his lips parted . . .

I could even taste the laughter on his mouth.

"*Mission Variable.*"

Hour Seven: 1537 hours

Seth watched Lily. She lay stretched out on the bed in Jareb's suite, her first real sexual encounter a sacrifice on the altar of government espionage.

"We discussed sexual strategy, Jayne. I grilled Lily about her experience. She's young. I was concerned about her handling this part of the job. We talked about the men she's dated."

There'd been a level four comm operative she'd seen for nearly a year. And more recently an op from munitions. Seth had known Lily hadn't had an opportunity to date outside of the agency. During the years when most young women were dancing at proms and throwing sorority parties, she'd been immersed in a training program that encompassed everything from survival skills and tactical strategy to psych prep and global analysis.

"How is it I didn't know she'd never had intercourse?"

Jayne met his gaze. "She's had enough sexual experience to discuss the topic intelligently without sharing that detail."

"Why? Her inexperience is a mission variable."

"You'll have to ask Lily that question."

"I should have known."

"You should have," she agreed simply.

As control, the responsibility of knowing fell squarely on his shoulders. "You knew, yet you approved her mission ready while you were still giving me grief about strategy."

Jayne steepled her hands, adopted a contemplative look Seth recognized from countless hours of psychoanalysis over his career. "My *grief*, as you call it, was about sending Lily in as a swallow. I care about her. So does your uncle. If there had been any other approach, we'd have preferred taking it."

"There wasn't."

"Agreed," she said. "And Lily is a professional committed to doing her job. Your uncle and I both believe her inexperience will serve us well in two areas. She's got a thirty-hour window to plant the transponder. That won't happen unless she can get into a situation to kiss the target, which means she has to catch his attention. Her innocence can help her stand out from the other slaves."

"The second area?" Seth asked.

Jayne met his gaze above her fingertips, looking resigned. "Given her lack of experience, I thought it would be kinder for her to go in unaware of the potential aftereffects. She thought she could just hold her breath to get through a distasteful job. I'm afraid it won't be that simple. She expects a certain amount of physiological reaction to sex, even sex with a stranger, but she can't really know how she'll react. We'll deal with her emotions as they come up, when she's in from the field."

Seth glanced at the display. The satellite array presented a 360 overhead of Jareb's suite where he and Lily stretched out on a bed. She lay on her side, her hip sloping out from her narrow waist in a tempting rise of pale skin. Her heart-shaped bottom angled smoothly into long, long legs.

A gift, Jareb had called her. Seth hadn't known how generous he'd been.

If he'd realized the extent of Lily's inexperience, would he still have sent her? Like Jayne and his uncle, he'd been counting on her youth and innocence to entice Ulmalhameh. But would he have asked her to sacrifice her virginity?

Lily must have questioned his reaction, too, otherwise, why wouldn't she have told him?

"Now I have something to ask you," Jayne said. "Why is this bothering you? Lily's virginity is a casualty of this operation. Unfortunate, yes, but she was willing. I don't see a problem."

"Do we have the right to ask this of her?"

Jayne frowned. "You were willing to send her in to have sex with our mole, and perhaps even our target to accomplish mission objective. Why is her virginity changing the scenario for you?"

Leave it to Jayne to zero right in on the heart of the matter.

Leave it to Jayne to ask a question he couldn't answer.

"It just does."

"You need to give that some thought."

Seth shifted his gaze back to the monitor, grateful Lily's long hair blocked out the sight of her face. It was hard enough sitting here, watching.

"I'll think about it," he said. "*After* I figure out how to deal with the fact that I've asked her to give her virginity to a terrorist." To a zealot who'd made his career murdering innocent victims for the glory of his God.

Xavier Jareb had professed to see the light. Seth believed him. He'd have never risked Lily otherwise. But his conviction of Jareb's redemption didn't erase the possibility that the man could get up from that bed, wipe the come from his dick and turn her over to Ulmalhameh to be tortured.

And it would take Seth twenty-one minutes just to get a team in. More time to extract Lily.

While Ulmalhameh raped her, tortured her, executed her.

"Keep in mind that Lily's a professional," Jayne said. "She was reared in the field. Technically she has more experience than you or me."

True enough, but knowing Lily's history didn't take the edge off. It might make her more pragmatic about the realities of surviving fieldwork, but he didn't feel the same when he watched Jareb touch her. There was nothing pragmatic about how Seth felt right now.

He wasn't being rational. Lily's upbringing in the field was exactly what had qualified her for this mission.

In the days long before Norplant, her parents had been field ops undercover as a married couple. When their mission had resulted in an unexpected pregnancy, to everyone's surprise they'd announced they'd fallen in love and wanted reassignment to see the pregnancy through and rear their child together.

Thus began a deep cover operation that had lasted nearly two decades. Lily's father had been a linguistic anthropologist. He'd taken his family to the far reaches of the world under the cover of researching the languages of primitive tribes while he and his wife flushed out drug lords.

They'd lived the life they loved and reared their only daughter to love it, too. They'd trained Lily at their knees until their deaths in the line of duty when she'd been sixteen.

Seth's uncle had been a close friend who'd honored his promise to bring Lily into Command until she reached the age of majority and decided what to do with her life. To Seth's knowledge, she'd never considered anything but working for the agency. His uncle oversaw her training and had agreed—albeit reluctantly— that Lily was their best chance for success with Operation Kiss, whether she'd completed her training or not.

Now Seth understood his uncle's reluctance, and he sat there with his gaze glued to the monitor, watching the scene unfold before him with careful deliberation, his penance for not having known the truth about Lily. If she had to live it, then he would be with her, watching and listening.

"Come, Atiya." Jareb issued a low groan that echoed halfway around the world. "You please me *too* well."

Damned straight. The guy practically vibrated as he dragged Lily up the length of his body, her bare curves stretching in a sleek arc of pale skin.

Seth forced his gaze to Lily's face. Moisture gleamed on lips swollen and red, casting her features into sharp relief. Her expression was set in fine detail, exquisite, almost angelic. Her mission objective meant submitting to this stranger. Her life depended on her ability to play a role that forced her to sacrifice everything.

And she did, willingly. The perfect field op.

Seth was far less than the perfect control.

Watching her perform the services he'd sent her in to perform made him ache in a way he didn't want to ache. Lily subjecting herself to Jareb's commands wasn't remotely erotic. Yet his body responded. Despite the logistics of a scene he'd rather not be watching.

He violated Lily with his arousal. With the way he wanted to be the man caressing her slender curves, tasting her skin. The way he couldn't control his reaction even though Jayne Manning sat on the opposite side of his desk.

He betrayed her by wanting to be the man underneath her. He wanted to drag his erection between her thighs. Pull her forward and catch her nipple with his teeth. To watch her react, her slim body tremble, her swollen mouth part around a gasp, her eyes shutter closed.

Seth wanted to drag that surprised sigh from her lips. Yet he was the man who had to feel grateful that Jareb was taking the time to explore her innocence with her, allowing her the opportunity to feel arousal. Given the situation, the man could have so easily taken his pleasure with no thought for Lily.

If Seth were the perfect control, he'd have considered Jareb's actions a sign of good faith in their arrangement.

He felt angry instead.

"Jayne," he said, determined to salvage what he could of his responsibility to Lily. "When you mentioned the emotional after-effects of this mission, you meant that Lily would have to deal with sexually responding to Jareb, didn't you?"

Jayne nodded. "She was convinced she could handle this part of the job. Cavalier almost. She went in to perform for the man, but I don't think she realized she might really respond to him."

"She's human. Given the logistics, it's to be expected. A more experienced woman would know that. She would capitalize on it during her performance."

"Yes. But that's not our case with Lily. She's young, and Xavier Jareb is a terrorist who is guilty of crimes she's been reared to abhor."

"She's doing what she must to make contact. It's her job. She'll rationalize."

"Yes, I agree. But you seem certain that her job will be enough to support her actions. I don't think it will be."

"What are you worried about?"

"That she'll have to rationalize her actions emotionally. She'll question why a man like Jareb can arouse her."

Seth frowned. He'd been meticulous in his examination of this operation's tactical. But his best efforts had left holes in his strategy. Jayne was right. Lily was an emotional woman who would have to explain her reactions to Jareb in some way.

The realization that his best efforts hadn't been nearly enough struck a hard blow, one Seth would ultimately have to deal with, too—after Lily was safely back in Command.

But right now mission objective was ensuring that she made it back in one piece. "What else have I missed?"

"I'm surprised you haven't guessed yet."

He exhaled heavily, too familiar with Jayne's tactics to ask again. She wanted him to figure out the answer and would make him rephrase the question until he blundered onto an epiphany. Yet too much was at stake for him to indulge in lengthy self-exploration. He needed to understand, and Jayne's surprise seemed to be key here.

"I didn't take into account my own emotional responses."

She inclined her head, silently crediting him with correctly recognizing the answer so quickly. "How do you feel about Lily responding to this man?"

"I shouldn't feel anything except concern that I missed a critical element in this operation, that my people might suffer as a result."

"You're human." Jayne fed his own words back to him, but they did nothing to rationalize his oversight.

So Seth kept his attention fixed brutally on the monitor, forced himself to hear Lily's every soft gasp as Jareb skillfully coaxed her to respond while she pleasured him.

He kept his gaze locked on Lily, watched her grow flushed with her awareness, and didn't allow himself to blink.

"Intact and proceeding normally."

Hour Nine: 1758 hours

I arched back on my hands, my fingers digging into the hard muscle of Jareb's thighs as he stroked his erection against me. I held my breath waiting for that one inevitable stroke. I stared down at his bronzed chest, frozen, my every muscle poised on the edge. Just waiting.

But he kept up that steady stroking, playing with me while he slipped his other hand between us. His finger found my clit and rolled it around, and I sucked in a gulp of air that almost choked me.

"You like that, Atiya." It wasn't a question.

The sensations flooding through me hindered speech for a moment. I felt edgy and on fire, every inch of my skin awake with new sensations. I finally lifted my gaze, figured I'd earned the right. "I thought you wanted me to pleasure you."

That would have been easier.

"I would savor your innocence. To rush our pleasure would be a waste." He rolled my clit harder, and the wave of sensation that plowed through me dragged another gasp from my lips.

His black eyes glittered. "I would make your body alive so when I take you in earnest, you will respond in a way that pleases me."

"The patient approach." The words simply burst out, a knee-jerk response to the look in his eyes, a look that made me aware of my hands digging into his thighs, intimately, as if I needed to hang onto him. I did.

"Sometimes patience yields the most reward."

And he was determined to be patient. I seemed to have become a challenge. He worked that bundle of nerve endings between my thighs. Lazy sensation coiled my insides tighter and tighter. My breasts grew heavy, receptive, as if I could feel the air through my skin. My sex gave a clench that I wondered if he could feel, guessed he could because he raked his hardness along my folds purposefully, a deep stroke that made a wet sound in the quiet.

He pressed inside just enough to make me shudder, a preview of what was to come. My body stretched enough to accommodate the swollen head of his erection, a pressure that sent goose bumps spraying along my skin, a pressure I could feel everywhere.

I breathed deeply. I reminded myself that it was natural to react this way to Jareb. Our situation was tense, dangerous, and even if adrenaline hadn't lent an edge to our responses, the possibility of winding up dead would have. Jayne had told me I might respond. I was.

I told myself that I could add this experience to my repertoire of Seth Blackthorn fantasies. I was always open to new ones, and my virginity had become sort of an issue anyway. I'd just turned twenty—way past time to get the deed done.

Since I didn't really believe that Seth would ever see me as anything but the ten-year-old he'd met so long ago, *who* did the deed had lost a lot of its importance.

At least my virginity would go for a good cause.

Jareb kept thumbing my clit until I writhed on top of him, unable to stop riding that sensation. His erection stretched me just enough to be a constant presence, a fullness that made my body tingle with intimate awareness, made me want to keep sinking down to feed this growing ache inside.

I wondered if Seth was enjoying this performance. I was accomplishing my mission objective, pleasing my master and putting on quite the show. Jareb touched my body skillfully, but with such an intense desperation, I couldn't forget that at any second the door could burst open and guards could drag me away, a casualty of faulty intel and a bad choice of friends.

Nor could I deny that I was feeling desperate enough to be glad Seth sat on the other end of that bouncing satellite signal, watching. I wanted him to see what might have been his if he'd only opened his eyes to see me as a woman. It was a petty thought, but I was lucky to be thinking at all right now.

My body was on fire so that I could barely remember that the man who touched me was a terrorist. It was the man not a terrorist who thumbed my clit until I arched against his hand to explore this awakening inside me. The man who kept crowding his hardness into my wet heat. The man who made me cry out as he arched his hips and finally pressed inside, forcing my body to take him one grudging inch at a time.

Then the deed was done. It didn't hurt. I felt . . . *full.*

Very anticlimactic really.

Or maybe it only felt that way because I'd forgotten to breathe. But when Jareb dragged his hands toward my breasts, I remembered. Sucking in a huge breath, I was overwhelmed by the feel of his hands on me, his body inside mine. He didn't move, didn't thrust, and I think he must have been giving me a chance to become used to the feel of him.

His features had sharpened with his arousal. His chest rose and fell quickly. I could feel the tenseness of his muscles beneath me, and I waited for him to show me what to do. He brought his thumbs to my nipples and tugged, sending a sizzle shooting down to that place where our bodies joined. Arching his hips, he pressed deeper into me, not a real stroke, but more pressure, more fullness. He tugged again. Another sizzle, and my insides started to melt.

The feeling was so unexpected . . . my thighs suddenly felt boneless and I swayed forward, braced my hands on his shoulders, a move that pressed my breasts into his hands. He pinched my nipples this time, made me shiver.

"Ah, Atiya," he ground out, and I could hear the tightness in his voice, realized he was struggling to keep control. "You please me."

I wasn't sure how to respond, couldn't reply because he kept thrusting into me with those barely there strokes, awakening me in ways I hadn't realized I could be awakened.

Apparently no reply was necessary. He slipped his arms around me with whipcord strength. He pulled me close until I lay full against him. I could feel his thickness inside me more deeply than before and barely registered the unexpected intensity before his mouth caught mine hard, his lips almost bruising with demand. My mouth parted beneath his and then his body tensed, and he began to move for real.

I gasped, that first hard stroke forcing the air from my lungs. He caught the sound with his kiss and moved again. This time the sensation was stronger, swelling. He thrust again, and again.

Sliding his hands down my back, he locked them onto my hips, taught me how to move, how to ride the motion . . . It was like a dance really. Moving together, my breasts glided over his chest as the strength of each thrust forced me upward along his hard body. It was intrusive, overwhelming, but there was something inside me, a feeling that made my muscles melt, made me arch back against him, looking for . . . *more.*

I grew flushed and achy, breathless from our tangling tongues, the constant pressure of having him ram inside me, those hot strokes that seemed to build to a crescendo. His muscles tightened and I could sense the explosion about to come.

Tensing, I waited as he dug his fingers into my bottom, locked me hard against him. Then he growled and exploded, and the sheer force of his release dragged a cry from me, too.

Just like that it was over. He collapsed, clinging to me, pulling me across him like a sweaty blanket. My legs sprawled on either side of his and my heart beat in double time, matching his rhythm. While my body still tingled, still glowed from the unfamiliar sensations, I knew something was missing. There had to be more for this act to live up to its press.

Then again, I hadn't really expected fireworks with a terrorist, had I?

I had.

I stifled a desperate laugh. I was such a mess. Yearning for Seth all these years. Trying to find some shred of redemption in this mission. I was a woman with healthy desires—I needed to get my head out of the clouds and start paying attention to my needs, work on curtailing the fantasies and stick with a real relationship. . . .

Of course *now* I could suddenly see Seth's face in my mind—along with the way I must look on his display. Boneless, bare-assed and sweaty as I rode Jareb's heaving chest.

I wondered what Seth was thinking now. Was he pleased with my performance? Or relieved that guards hadn't stormed me while I'd been preoccupied in our mole's bed?

Did he *finally* see me as a woman?

Jareb's gruff voice dragged me back to reality. "What has you so deep in thought, Atiya?"

Great. Pillow talk. "I was wondering when slaves get to eat around here," I whispered into the curve of his neck.

He laughed, a real laugh that shocked me by the joy of the sound. Raising his fingers, he caught my chin and tilted my face upward. I was surprised to find such amusement mirrored in those inky eyes.

"You pleased me, Atiya."

I couldn't explain it, absolutely refused to dwell on it, but some part of me was glad.

The emir had long since vanquished his restlessness and sat down beside Khalid to watch his commanders' performances. It was companionable work with much discussion and laughter—the assessment of men in their pursuit of sex provided a fascinating glimpse of the man himself.

But it was sad work as well. Khalid would never admit it, nor would the emir dishonor his heart-father by mentioning it, but he recognized the slump of the older man's shoulders. He saw the circles around his eyes and the strain at his mouth. The afternoon had tired Khalid. He would need to rest before the council began and the commanders presented their visions for the future.

But despite his weariness, Khalid had been the entertaining companion he always was. And each laughing comment, each moment filled with fellowship and purpose drove home how much the emir would miss these moments.

There were so many years between them. The emir had grown to manhood beneath his heart-father's guidance, couldn't fathom life without hearing his wise words or pondering the meanings that forced him to analyze new angles, envision new possibilities, conceptualize a world abiding the *Sharia.*

His heart-father had helped him see past doubt and fear, helped him be a man worthy of his Holy Purpose.

Now he would walk the path alone.

"Do not look so troubled, my son," Khalid said, reaching a once strong hand across the distance. "You have men of value in your command. We shall find someone of worth."

He took Khalid's hand. True, they would appoint another to Khalid's place, but not one of the men he'd watched on these monitors today possessed the value of the old man at his side.

Not one could ever hold such a place in his heart.

All of his commanders had behaved exactly as intended— utilizing this time until the council's gathering at sunset to satisfy their lusts. They'd watched each joining on the various display monitors, assessing, reassessing, and in certain situations, finding themselves surprised by the commanders' interactions with their slaves.

Boghos hadn't made the first cut as Khalid's replacement. He hadn't tamed his hellcat so much as allowed her to tame him, which came as a shock since the quiet commander was so manipulative in strategy and bloodthirsty in battle.

"A man ruled by his woman is weak," Khalid had said.

The emir agreed, but he had been impressed with the hellcat. She was lush of form and strong of character. She'd slipped easily into the role of master when Boghos had revealed his weakness. She'd brought him to his knees with her lush curves and knowing touches before allowing him release.

The hellcat stayed on his short list. Taming the fiery beauty would be a challenge to amuse him for some time to come.

Commander Fahd had turned out to be an unpleasant disappointment as well. He'd chosen the submissive, a woman, as Khalid had observed, who was mild in temper and eager to please. But Fahd had preyed on her gracious spirit, had enjoyed her terror while forcing her to submit to his cruel lust.

Where was the challenge in bullying the weak?

Though Fahd was a man with a gift for rallying recruits to their cause, his sadism presented a flaw too easily exploited. The emir needed no such vulnerabilities in his network no matter how constant his demand for new followers.

But this woman would accompany them back to the compound, too. Not to grace his own harem, but as a parting gift to bring Khalid pleasure in his final days. His heart-father would enjoy her gentle hands, her kind smiles and her soft voice to ease the pain of his passing.

"Do not lose hope." Khalid squeezed his hand reassuringly. "There is much to be told by a man and his lust. The council has not yet started and we have already learned a great deal about your men."

"I haven't seen much to give me hope, my father. Pedestrian sex. Petty power mongering. A strong man reduced to a woman. What have you witnessed that I have not?"

"You are pleasantly surprised by Jareb and his heretic, are you not?"

"You do not think his handling of the American . . . sentimental?"

"Bah, no." Khalid scowled, an expression that gathered his withered face into a fist. He withdrew his hand and waved it impatiently at the monitor. "Jareb might have intimidated such a proud woman. Fahd certainly would have demanded her submission. Boghos wouldn't have known what to do with her."

The emir resisted the urge to smile. "Not a good match, I agree. Boghos would still be hard as stone waiting for that proud innocent to figure out how to master him."

Khalid's face softened. "Like he commands his men, Commander Jareb sees with an eye to the future. He might have intimidated the heretic, but he exercised intelligence instead. He distracted her with a bath and allowed her to explore her innocence. He subjugated her and won her to his side with guidance and patience. She pleased him and would gladly do so again. Fahd would have to beat his woman bloody to get her to submit to his perversions once more."

Xavier Jareb had denied himself the pleasure of seeing a healthy fear in the heretic's gemstone eyes, a denial that couldn't have been easy with her spread out tempting and naked against him. Their enemy. "You are right, of course. Commander Jareb has proven himself clever and controlled. He shall remain on the list for now."

Khalid nodded his approval. "The heretic?"

"A waste of cargo space." The emir laughed. "I have room for four more women in my harem. I'd surely kill that arrogant slave before long, leaving me an empty place. Who knows when I'll have the chance to rejoin the living again to replace her?"

"Insightful as always, my son."

Khalid wouldn't think he was all that insightful if the emir confessed that his mind had awakened to the idea of peeling away the heretic's innocence, of making her body respond in lust. Jareb had indeed manipulated his slave skillfully, arousing her until she touched him freely and sighed sounds of pleasure, but he hadn't brought her to completion.

The emir found himself intrigued with the thought of tackling that contest himself. To peel away her pride like her innocence. To humble her by making her a slave to her desires. To hear her beg to be taken by a man her Western world looked upon as an animal. To watch her cringe in shame afterward.

Unfortunately she would never properly accept her place as slave and the emir's patience had definite limits.

Casting his gaze at his heart-father, the emir smiled. Khalid was right. The council had not yet begun but he had already learned much. Not only about his *shura*, but about himself. He did have life left inside him, and knowing that his soul hadn't withered gave him new hope for the future.

"Bona fides."

Hour Twelve: 2000 hours

Seth slugged back the dregs of ice cold espresso. The unexpected mouthful of grinds made him wince, but he swallowed hard to clear his throat, appreciated any distraction to keep him alert.

He hadn't slept since first receiving Jareb's intel about the window of opportunity, and the long days since had finally pushed his brain dangerously close to overload.

Or was his reaction to watching Lily responsible?

She knelt in front of Jareb who sat on the bed. Her long hair hung heavily down her back, shielding her body. A servant presented Jareb with a tray stacked with a variety of jeweler's boxes and he reached for one and explained, "The emir has asked his *Shura* to gift our slaves according to their performances."

Flipping open a long velvet box, he said, "Lift your hair."

Lily raised slim arms and gathered the white-blonde sheet away, gifting them all with a choice shot of her beautiful body still flushed from sex.

Jareb withdrew a necklace that sparkled with diamonds, good-sized gems if he was reading Lily's surprise right. Slipping the piece around her throat, Jareb affixed the clasp and twisted the necklace into place.

"You have pleased me well this day, Atiya."

Lily lowered her hair, brought her fingers up to touch the necklace. "You are most generous."

"Now here's a twist," Seth said.

Jayne shifted her gaze from the monitor to him. "What?"

"Ulmalhameh is testing the women, or his commanders. I'm betting on his commanders."

"Assessment."

Seth set the Styrofoam cup back on his desk, all traces of exhaustion gone. "I had intel from Black Cell recently that biochems changed hands with Husan al Din. My people haven't confirmed yet. I didn't think Black Cell had access to that kind of power, but with the breakdown of Iraq, I could be wrong. My guess is Ulmalhameh has some operation in mind that he needs to place a man in charge of. The *right* man."

"You think this council is cover to find him?"

"Thirty hours to personally assess his commanders. Watching them interact with each other. Testing them with the women. It fits. Ulmalhameh hasn't surfaced in three years. He can't bring his *shura* to his safehouse without risking its location."

One thing was for sure—something had dragged Ulmalhameh from his hole and that something was big.

Seth considered the possibilities as he watched Jareb slip a ring onto Lily's finger, another piece to match the necklace. Earrings and a bracelet followed before he instructed, "Sit back, Atiya. Give me your ankle."

Lily braced back on her hands, and Jareb's gaze crawled possessively up her shapely leg before he fastened an anklet around her ankle.

"You knew watching Lily with Jareb would bother me," Seth said to Jayne. "That's why my uncle sent psychological oversight instead of tactical."

She nodded.

"Why, because I'm calling the shots this time?" *His* feelings shouldn't be a mission variable. He wasn't the one risking his life in the field. He was safe in Command, assessing, making decisions, doing his job.

"I've executed this scenario before, Jayne. Not as control of my own operation but as a field officer in command. I've sent other operatives, both female and male, into similar situations. Why should this time be different?"

"Only you can answer that question."

Seth watched Jareb pull Lily to her feet, an erotic unfolding of sleek curves and smooth skin. A sight that drove a knife-sharp stab of awareness through him. A sight that made him feel raw.

He stared at the screen while Jareb pressed a kiss to Lily's bowed head, recognized his answer in the way he could practically feel her tremble. A physical response.

"It's Lily."

Seth bowed his own head, protecting himself from the sight on that monitor, of actions taking place half a world away. Actions he'd commanded.

The end justifies the means.

Or it had *before* he'd known Lily was a virgin. *Before* he'd finally understood how much he cared.

Massaging the sudden ache in his temples, Seth tested out a realization that didn't feel like such a surprise anymore.

"How did I miss this?"

Jayne shrugged. "Suffice to say you don't deal very comfortably on these emotional levels."

"Both you and my uncle recognized the signs."

"You work very hard to keep your distance with Lily. Too hard sometimes. It's noticeable."

Except to him. He'd been tossing distance between them as if that would cure the awareness he hadn't wanted to feel. He'd been lying to himself that she was just another operative.

She was so much more.

Dragging his gaze back to the monitor, he watched servants drape her in the veiled garb of the palace and hurry her from Jareb's suite. He recognized her relief in each liquid stride as she passed through the corridors, her bowed head that she seemed struggling to hold up. He could practically feel her exhaustion as she was taken back to the harem, where she was immediately herded into the baths.

Other slave women had gathered. Four so far. Lounging around the pool, various pieces of jewelry adorning their nudity. They watched Lily as she was undressed, apparently interested in the booty she'd brought from her master. A raven-haired Frenchwoman got in her face to inspect her jewels.

"Pink diamonds?" she said, her dark gaze scanning each piece of Lily's set. "How did you rate such a rich prize?"

Another brunette woman with golden skin, whom Seth recognized as the native of Jordan, came to stand by her side. "You must have pleased your master."

Lily only smiled, lifted a hand to her necklace and handled the piece. Seth got the impression that she was uncomfortable being crowded by two naked women.

"What could you possibly do to earn those exquisite gems?" There was no missing the resentment underlying the French-woman's words. While she wore an equal number of pieces, her own stones were rubies.

"I gave him my virtue," Lily said.

The Jordanian woman whistled. "There's a rich gift. How did you manage to hang onto it for so long?"

Lily shrugged. "My former master frightened my suitors. No one dared to touch me. It was frustrating, really."

Her former master?

She had no former master in the cover he'd worked up for her. Why was she improvising? He didn't see the point. But there was something deadpan in her expression . . . Then it hit him. Lily was referring to *his* uncle. Her master here at Command.

Her experience with men had been limited to the agency. A function of proximity and age. She'd come in from the field when she'd been barely sixteen and training had consumed her life ever since. When Seth thought about it, the fact that his uncle was personally training her must surely factor into her dating choices. It took a certain kind of man to tackle dating the big boss's protégée.

Her lack of experience made a little more sense now, and here was an unexpected glimpse of the woman who affected him in ways he hadn't wanted to be affected, who'd made him run for cover rather than deal with his feelings toward her.

Until now, when he held her life in his hands.

"Looks like Jareb will be in council all night, Seth," Jayne said. "Lily will spend the next few hours grooming. Why don't you go catch some rest? You have to stay sharp."

He glanced beyond Jayne to the door, envisioned the barracks where he could close his eyes and escape in sleep.

Nodding, he stood, but couldn't make the door. If the situation changed, it would take time to get back to his office, more crucial seconds to be briefed. . . .

"I'll catch a few here on the couch."

Jayne didn't look surprised. Circling the desk, she sat in his chair and said, "I'll wake you if anything changes."

He nodded. Sinking down onto the plush leather, he toed off his shoes and stretched out.

Sleep didn't come. The lack of stimuli only freed up brain space for his thoughts to race. For questions to demand answers.

Like how long had he been running from the truth?

Why had he run?

His weary mind served up memories of Lily . . . He remembered a ten-year-old who'd lived in the field with her parents and conversed with an intellect that had amazed him.

As a young recruit new to Command, she'd always been eager to test her skills, to do whatever she must to prove herself.

As a woman, she'd agreed to go undercover as a swallow to catch their target, had sacrificed her virginity without giving him a chance to object.

Why?

He'd questioned her bona fides from the start, had needed to understand why she'd willingly play a swallow.

He knew Lily believed in their cause. She believed the end justified the means. The same could be said of all the agency's operatives. Seth believed it. Jayne and his uncle had reinforced the position by approving her for the mission.

Squeezing his eyes tightly shut, as if he might block out the images in his head, Seth asked himself if they'd had the right to ask Lily to give her virginity to the cause.

The only answer he had was the memory of her on top of Jareb, her beautiful body swaying erotically, her pale fingers digging into his dark skin.

He'd been single-minded and zealous in pursuit of his beliefs. And it struck him that there was another man who was just as single-minded, just as zealous. That man, too, believed the end justified the means.

Nabi Ulmalhameh.

Seth had masterminded a terrorist cell to radicalize Islamic groups from all over the Middle East and create new groups where none existed. He advocated the destruction of the United States and a way of life he saw as a threat to Muslim societies. He supported terror fighters in all the world's problem spots: Afghanistan, Algeria, Bosnia, Chechnya, Eritera, Kosovo, Pakistan, Somalia, Tajikistan. . . .

The U.S. State Department had a fact sheet on Husan al Din that listed incidents including the murders of a dozen U.S. servicemen in Yemen on a humanitarian mission to deliver food to starving Muslim people.

A car bombing against the Egyptian embassy in Pakistan that had killed over thirty Americans, Egyptians and Pakistanis.

A plot that Seth himself had thwarted to blow up an airliner in an assassination attempt on the Pope.

Nabi Ulmalhameh used terror to fight for his cause.

Seth had used Lily's body to fight for his.

Did the end justify the means?

It was the first time he'd ever asked the question.

"Move to the second mark."

Hour Twenty-Five: 0900 hours

My thirty-hour window was ticking away, each minute tightening a chokehold to accomplish mission objective—kiss the target. At this rate, I'd never even get near enough to the emir to pick him out in a crowd, let alone affix a tracking device. The council had lasted the entire night, and I had only just returned to Jareb's suite to assist in his bath—no funny stuff. No time, he'd informed me, which struck me as odd since I'd bathed, groomed, eaten and slept presumably for round two.

I wasn't complaining.

I'd also become acquainted with the other women through the night, and some of their comments had raised a question about what the emir had planned for us at the council's end. Given the conflicting information the women had received, I suspected we would be considered liabilities and disposed of accordingly.

I was almost sure of it after Jareb told me that we'd be attending a farewell feast.

One big room where we could ID the emir and his *shura*.

Major liabilities.

Unless the emir considered the inferior sex too inferior to be a security threat. I didn't think so. The man hadn't evaded capture this long by leaving his safety or that of his organization to chance.

Fortunately, I felt refreshed after my few hours sleep, more focused on mission objective than I'd been after my encounter with Jareb last night. He looked tired by comparison, and I wished I could have asked him questions about the council.

No dice. I could only trust that he hadn't blown my cover, which meant that Seth's instincts about him seemed on target. And if Jareb still proved to be a defector in good faith by the end of the thirtieth hour, he'd debrief and we'd have the information, anyway.

Jareb emerged from the bath, looking tired but impeccable in traditional Islamic garb—a white *thobe* with a matching *ghutra* covering his head.

I, on the other hand, wore loose silk trousers that weren't so bad, as they covered me almost to my ankles, but the open vest left my arms and breasts exposed—about the only skin visible since a veil covered the lower half of my face.

My jewels, however, were on display for the world to see. I supposed they ranked me in some fashion. But for whom? The emir? I didn't see anyone around here caring if the women impressed each other.

When the show was about to start, Jareb swept past me without a glance, and his servant motioned me to follow. I fell into place behind him, my heart rate jumping into gear as we traveled through the palace, away from the residential suites and the harem.

We arrived at a great hall. From what I could see from my sucky vantage point, the hall had been decked out lavishly, complete with armed soldiers standing at attention along every wall. A long table for the commanders occupied one side while a throne-like dais had been arranged at the head of the room, surely meant for the emir and his advisor. Above this dais hung a banner with the words:

La ilaha illa-llahu, muhammad rasul allahi.
There is no God but God, Muhammed is the apostle of God.

Adrenaline worked a number on me—I was almost in. At this very second, Seth would have the comm techs in System Ops downloading satellite images of every person in this hall for evaluation.

Several of the commanders—with their slaves in tow—were already seated. Servants milled around. At the very least Seth would have visuals on the emir's most trusted commanders, and as a bonus, he could listen in on any conversation within earshot of my signal. A definite improvement after the night's idleness.

Jareb took a seat at a long table across from this throne. He exchanged pleasantries with the man seated to his left while I took my place behind him. On my knees, naturally, ever ready to serve.

Within minutes, the eight commanders, accompanied by their slaves, had congregated at the table. The energy in the hall rose to a crescendo or maybe it was just my nerves making me feel that way. I jumped when a ringing bell signaled the guests to attention, a move that didn't go unnoticed by Jareb. He glanced back as he rose, and I took a steadying breath, willed myself to calm down. I couldn't blame the guy for being antsy. We'd reached critical mass, and he was taking as big a leap of faith here as I was. He was trusting Seth to extract him, trusting me not to do something stupid to get him busted by his compatriots, but I was a professional and wouldn't do anything without just cause. Even if not being able to look around the hall, to watch the new arrivals was just about killing me . . .

The commanders raised their voices together in greeting. From the corner of my eye, I could see Jareb bow slightly, clasp his hand to his breast in a gesture of respect.

The emir had arrived.

I was in. Now all I had to do was watch for an opening to make my move. And in that moment, I could feel Seth's approval, sense his faith in my abilities. I was another step closer to our target. Another step forward in our war against terrorism.

The emir answered the greeting, beginning with deep-throated pleasantries one might expect from a king to his followers. I recognized his voice from public statements and declarations he'd made through the years, pre-recorded messages that usually wound up in the hands of the media to claim responsibility for death and destruction.

He gave his men a pep talk. Better to die in the service of Islam than whore for the infidel and all that. Personally, I was more impressed by the ceremony of the whole affair. And the deference the commanders paid their leader.

Jareb was putting on a damn fine show. Or what I hoped was a show. Twenty-five hours might have passed with the man on good behavior, but I wasn't ready to trust him just yet.

He wouldn't earn that privilege until *after* our extraction.

The meal finally began. A formal affair the caliber one might expect when entertaining a king, or an emir as it was. Adrenaline heightened my every sense, helped me to concentrate on everything around me, despite my disadvantaged eyesight.

The emir conversed with his men, sounding genuinely jovial, which came as another surprise. I was reminded of Jareb last night. Our sordid encounter had shattered my notion that terrorists were monsters and not men, but even so, I still didn't find ascribing human qualities to mass killers that easy.

It seemed too simple that the only difference between us and them was a choice.

Time passed. One course yielded to another. I began to feel a growing sense of disbelief that a chance to make my move wouldn't come. That the bell would ring to signal the end of the meal, and the emir would slip away until want or necessity drove him above ground again in who knew how many years.

Leaving him free to kill in the interim.

That simply wasn't acceptable. I was too close to let him slip away. So I listened.

I waited.

I willed something to happen to give me a chance to cover the absurdly short distance separating me from him. Perhaps the emir would want entertainment and command a striptease. Or give our masters lap dances. Whatever. I was getting desperate.

Still nothing.

By the time the thick black coffee in tiny ceramic cups arrived, I knew the only chance I was going to get to make my move would be the one I made myself.

I took a deep breath . . .

Jareb made mention of a meeting in Serbia where some mutual acquaintance had apparently given the assembled commanders a good chuckle. The emir laughed at the reminder, a hearty laugh that rang through the hall, overrode the sounds of the servants shuffling around, the clinking of ceramic cup on saucer.

I made my move.

I lifted my gaze and peered at the emir, a gaze I hoped would be interpreted as a glance from a curious, ignorant woman.

A gaze I hoped would draw the soldiers' attention.

I recognized the emir immediately. He looked leaner, older than the surveillance photos I'd seen of him during mission briefing. Seth had told me the photos had been taken during his last surfacing three years ago. Perhaps the long night had contributed to the circles around his deep-set eyes, the strain that seemed to weigh heavily on his brow. He wore a gold-edged *bisht* over his *thobe* and the effect was regal.

I recognized his companion, too. Barely. Khalid ben Sarsour, the emir's mentor and long-time friend, had aged dramatically from the photos I'd seen. He was an older man, approaching seventy, but he didn't look good. His dark skin had the ashen look of ill health. His face was gaunt. His eyes flat and dull. A big man shrunken like a dried fruit.

I lowered my eyes again.

And waited.

My pulse thudded so hard that I could barely hear the booted feet ringing out over the tiled floor. When I did, I held my breath and waited, just waited, hoping I hadn't blown the entire mission.

Rough hands grabbed my arms, jerked me to my feet.

Jareb glanced at me as the two soldiers dragged me away, and I could read the surprise in his gaze, the anger.

The hall had fallen eerily quiet, a silence louder than my runaway heartbeat, a thunder that vibrated through me, made my knees weak, my feet stumble.

One soldier jerked me up hard, and at a command from the emir, he detailed my crime in a gruff voice for our audience.

Though I kept my head lowered, I could hear a chair scrape against the tiled floor, knew the emir had risen. I tried to keep my breathing steady, didn't want fear to distract me.

"Move to the second mark."

I could hear the command in my head as if Seth had spoken it aloud, and I clung to him like an anchor. An image of him standing in System Ops flashed in my memory, a hundred such images. His sculpted face frowning in concentration at his computer while viewing new intel. Scaling a corrugated tin wall in obstacle training, all athletic grace and tightly coiled power. Naked and awesome as his sleek muscles brushed mine and we found egress from an underwater cave. Laughing, his smile alight in those penetrating gray eyes, as he bulleted to earth by my side during my inaugural skydiving exercise.

Watching as I had sex for the very first time.

I wondered what he'd looked like then, would never know. But in that instant it was enough to feel him by my side, on the other end of a bouncing satellite signal.

In my periphery, I caught the emir circling the table, and as he appeared in front of me, the soldiers forced me to my knees before they stepped away. His commanding presence angled down to the lower half of his *thobe* and his feet in sandals.

"What have you to say on behalf of your disobedient slave, Commander Jareb?" the emir's voice boomed out above my head.

I knew better than to break my silence, another mark of respect as great as a lowered gaze. I kept my mouth shut, didn't beg forgiveness or offer defense.

"I have no explanation, sir, save the West has not properly taught her of the importance of humility."

"Yet I see from her jewels that she has pleased you."

"Until now."

I heard the emir give a snort of laughter above my head.

"Come, commander. Discipline your slave then."

In the corner of my eye, I could see the soldiers lift their heads toward the table, knew Jareb was on his way.

I saw my window.

Several gasps echoed around the room as I sank to the floor, my tongue working frantically to release the device that had been affixed to my second bicuspid. Nearly prostrate at the emir's feet, I smoothed the Kiss of Death into place on my top lip. I heard the shuffle of booted feet lurch into motion, expected at any second to be ripped up from the floor. Or shot.

The emir must have recognized my action for the submission it was because a sharp clapping rang out above my head, made me jump. The boots halted. Silence fell again.

My move. I leaned forward, lifted my veil with one hand while wrapping the other in the hem of the emir's robe. Time felt like it crawled backwards as I pressed my lips between the straps of his sandals, against his warm skin in an open-mouthed kiss . . .

Mission objective accomplished.

The adrenaline rush made me dizzy and I closed my eyes as I was lifted to my feet, not roughly. Jareb.

He directed a servant to lift my hair, and I could feel the watchful eyes of the emir, the commanders, the rest of the women, and Seth, as he twisted the heavy necklace around my throat, unfastened the clasp.

Then I understood. He would publicly strip me of my jewels, of my rank—his judgment that I was no longer worthy of favor.

I had the inane thought that the women, particularly the Frenchwoman, would cheer that I'd made such a stupid mistake. But they were no longer of any interest to me.

Mission objective accomplished.

I wasn't clapped in irons. I wasn't beaten as an example. I was simply stripped of my jewels and escorted from the hall by two soldiers. It was all very civilized really.

Now all I needed to do was stay alive for six more hours so Seth could extract me.

I hoped.

"Operative burned."

"Upgrade your team to standby." Seth transmitted the message to the team leader of his first extraction unit, his gaze fixed on his monitor as Lily was shoved roughly into a cell.

The steel door clanged shut, an echoing, tinny sound buffeted by twelve-inch thick stone walls. The lock clicked. Approximately ten-by-ten feet square, the stone cell had a rusted vent in the ceiling and no furnishings.

Except the shackles bolted to the wall.

"If you send your team in now, Lily is as good as dead." Jayne's calm tone and true words grated.

"I know. But I need a twenty-one minute lead to get on that island. I want my people ready to move. Those soldiers can break Lily's neck in a second."

"In which case your perimeter team will make no difference whatsoever." Jayne acknowledged pragmatically, before adding, "She did very well, Seth. You were right."

"Is that supposed to make me feel better?" he snapped, turning toward her. "Or are you just trying to distract me?"

She speared him with a hard look. "I'm reminding you to keep your head. Lily's done her job. Now it's your turn to do yours. Extract your operative and your defector safely so you can bring in your target."

"I intend to."

Unfortunately Seth had no intel about Ulmalhameh's plans for departure at the end of the council, so he had two perimeter units in place, each prepared for his best projected scenarios.

He hoped that Jareb would be transported off the island so his team could intercept on the mainland without incident. Lily's extraction was still a question mark. Perhaps the slaves would be permitted to accompany their new masters, in which case Lily would be intercepted with Jareb.

But if Ulmalhameh considered the slaves a liability . . . Seth's team was on standby, ready to infiltrate the palace to extract her by force.

Reaching for the intercom that was his direct link to System Ops, he made the connection and instructed Van Brocklin to begin preparing his new team and readying a transport.

"For Ulmalhameh?" Jayne asked.

Seth nodded, shifting his gaze back to the monitors, between Lily in her cell to Ulmalhameh, who'd been reduced to a red blip by the tracking device.

He should have felt something to see Ulmalhameh on his display, his agency locked onto a target Seth had been after for the past six years. But he felt nothing more than a terrible sense of impatience.

"What are you planning, Ulmalhameh?" Seth silently asked, unwilling to declare open war on the palace while any hope remained of extracting Lily and Jareb peaceably—his best chance to bring them home safely. He wouldn't risk firepower unless he had no other choice. To know, he needed answers.

He made another call to Van Brocklin for an update on his team's assembly, estimated the time until the transport would be flight-ready. Then he gazed back at Lily.

She'd sunk to the floor, hands crossed over her knees. She looked both contemplative and tired, and he wondered what she was thinking. Did she know he was on red alert? Would she trust that he'd move heaven and hell to extract her safely?

Or was she questioning why she'd ever agreed to this mission at all? She could have easily refused. Declining this mission wouldn't have even been noted on her record. And given his uncle and Jayne's initial arguments against his plan, no one would have thought the less of her for her refusal. Yet she'd not only agreed, but had sacrificed so much to accomplish mission objective.

"Why, Lily?" he silently asked. "Why?"

She believed in their cause, and her unique upbringing had taught her to place duty above everything. He remembered the young girl she'd been when they'd met, how amazed he'd been listening to her talk about fieldwork at the absurd age of ten.

He still remembered that bright-eyed child, social and energetic, easily answering his uncle's questions about crackdowns in mountain retreats and drug busts in jungles. Seth even remembered feeling envy. She'd had a lifetime to become what he'd always dreamed of being—an operative.

He hadn't thought of Lily again until she'd shown up in Command after her parents' deaths. He could still see her in his memory, a teenager who was too tall, too lanky, as if she hadn't grown into her body yet.

But she had grown . . . into a young woman who blushed whenever he'd touched her elbow to assist her from a car or escort her into a meeting . . . into a recruit, who was driven to prove herself, eager to please . . .

Now he stared at the display at a woman who risked her life, had sidestepped the truth about her sexual experience to go on a dangerous mission.

All because she believed in their cause?

Or had she gone because he'd asked her?

The emir waited as his soldier unlocked the cell door and stepped aside to let him pass. The heretic stood against the opposite wall in the manner of an obedient slave, but he didn't let her deceptive pose fool him. She was arrogant, this one. Her eyes might be cast down, but her shoulders were squared with pride, her posture erect with challenge.

She was also lovely. The veil covered all but her gemstone eyes, but her garb allowed him the freedom to peruse all the smooth pale skin between her neck and her naval, let him admire the full curves of her breasts.

He had a final test to make before deciding this one's fate. Nodding to his soldiers, the emir watched as they covered the short distance across the cell, each forcibly grabbing an arm to drag her away from the wall and toward him.

Unsurprisingly, the heretic didn't cringe away or resist. She lifted her chin a notch, but the veil made a lie of her defiance. It trembled on the edge of a deep breath, a sign that she wasn't as composed as she'd have him believe.

Pride, so unbecoming in a woman.

But that was what he was looking for—a sign of nerves beneath her arrogance. Did she fear him? The sight of her on her knees at his feet in the hall earlier had aroused him and the challenge of making her submit had been growing ever since.

He stripped the veil from her face.

She startled, but didn't pull away. Rather, she quickly braced herself, revealing self-control and strength of will. Her eyes flashed amethyst fire. She'd recognized his game.

Ah, yes. A definite challenge to tame this one. *If* he chose to accept.

Perhaps.

He flipped away the vest that half hid her breasts from his view, took in the firm fullness, the rosy nipples.

Lovely.

Slipping his fingers around a soft curve, he squeezed hard, testing the warm weight in his hand. She shivered in reply. Defiance perhaps. Or fear.

With a glance the emir directed his man to unfasten the belt at her waist, watched as he unthreaded the embroidered silk and dragged it away. The trousers collapsed, baring her long white legs to his gaze, the smooth belly, the pouting mound of her sex.

She wasn't lush like his usual women, soft curves that a man could grab and sink into. No, she was athletic rather than soft. A combination he hadn't imagined to find attractive.

Yet he still felt stirrings . . . He didn't know why. Her beauty perhaps, or simply her poor attempts at submission.

Motioning his soldiers to turn her around, he ran his hand over the satin curve of her cheeks, tested the firmness of thigh beneath the smooth skin. He trailed his finger along the cleft, slowly, deeply, parting her cheeks suggestively.

She trembled again. Definitely fear.

Wrapping a hand around her waist, he hauled her back against him and ground his groin into the firm flesh of her backside. He swelled in response. The reaction he needed to make his choice. He could indeed enjoy the challenge of humbling this slave, even if his patience ultimately cost him an empty place in his harem.

"Prepare her," he commanded before leaving the cell.

"Exfiltration compromised."

Hour Twenty-Nine: 1246 hours

I wasn't sure how long I'd been left to roast in this hot cell after the emir had left. Another two hours, maybe. Long enough for my whole life to flash before my eyes and to work up a good sweat in the confines of this stifling room.

But I wouldn't allow myself to give in to doubt. Whatever happened next, I could count on Seth. He monitored my situation, doing what he did best—assessing, strategizing, safeguarding. If there was any chance at all to get me out, he would.

I wouldn't let myself give in to worry about what the emir had planned for me either. Whatever it was, I wouldn't like it.

Nor would I let my thoughts drift to Xavier Jareb. He was a topic I couldn't tackle just yet. Not when I needed all my focus to keep panic at bay.

So I kept doubt under control by thinking about—surprise!—Seth. Not the Seth in Command who was currently coordinating his perimeter units to safeguard my life, perhaps even pulling together his mission to capture the emir. I thought about the Seth in my fantasies. The dream man who saw me as more than a child, more than another operative. The man who wanted me as a woman. The man who cared about me as much as I cared about him.

I'm not sure what it is about him that fascinates me. Has *always* fascinated me. For some reason I still can't explain, I'd decided the first time we'd met that he fit my ideal of the perfect man. I hadn't changed my position ever since.

True, he was gorgeous with his black hair and quicksilver eyes. His sculpted features were so strong, yet somehow managed to be so beautiful that I sometimes wanted to reach out and touch him just to see if he was real.

But Seth is about more than looks—although once upon a time his looks were enough. When I'd first come to Command, I could barely talk to him. He'd look my way with those clear eyes, and I'd go straight to pieces.

Time and necessity helped me past that.

And the fantasies. It's not so hard to talk to a man you've imagined doing all sorts of things with, naked, in a bed.

I wiped the sweat from my eyes again and smiled.

But my smile disappeared fast when a key fitted into the lock. I got to my feet as the steel door ground open, its hinges protesting loudly.

The soldiers again.

"Come," one directed, and he hadn't needed to bring his assault rifle to convince me to follow.

I was led back to the harem where, with the help of two servant women, I was quickly bathed and robed. And I knew the instant I saw the formal traveling garb that I'd be making a trip outside the palace. And not a trip to the bottom of the Gulf in a sack, either. I was going out into the world.

I joined four other women similarly dressed for travel and immediately recognized Nora, the woman from Jordan, whom I liked, and the nasty Frenchwoman, whom I didn't. I hadn't ever exchanged words with the Portuguese woman, but she'd been quiet and well mannered during our time in the baths last night. The Russian woman, conversely, had been loud and friendly.

"You wait here," the servant instructed me and I took my place beside them and waited.

I was tempted to strike up a conversation with Nora to get an idea of what was happening, but the armed soldier at the door made me think better of the idea. Placing myself at risk was one thing, but involving the others when we were all vulnerable wasn't a chance I would willingly take.

We didn't wait long before more soldiers arrived. They led us through the winding halls of the palace and outside. The sun shone brightly and stung my eyes, and I inhaled deeply of the sea air. Whatever happened next, I'd gotten to breathe fresh air again. I was grateful.

We were escorted into Jeeps for a short trip to . . .

The instant I saw the airstrip I knew I was in trouble. A private jet was being fueled on the runway. If this was the emir's jet—and

I would have bet money it was—I had no doubt that he was on his way home, which meant I would have the dubious honor of accompanying him on the journey.

The only thing that saved me from panic was knowing Seth had a lock on us. He could track us into the emir's stronghold.

If, of course, we got there. The emir might simply intend to use me and the other women as in-flight entertainment and then dump our bodies with the lavatory tanks.

We were herded up the steps into the jet and directed toward the back. I had a hell of a time keeping my gaze submissive between climbing the metal stairs, not tripping on my robes and maneuvering through the galley module.

I did manage to sneak a peek at the flight crew as we passed by the open cockpit door and then at the comfy arrangement where several men were already seated. The emir. A uniformed man I didn't recognize. Khalid ben Sarsour.

And across from Khalid sat Xavier Jareb.

My heart seemed to drop to my feet, and I almost stumbled on my hem. But I rallied and pushed past while one question echoed in my brain:

Had Seth been wrong about Jareb?

"In the wind."

"Van Brocklin, fuel the director's jet for a flight into the hot zone," Seth shot over the intercom.

"The director's jet?" Jayne interrupted his transmission. "Why not a transport?"

He spared her a glance, found her watching him curiously. "I'll need the equipment on my uncle's jet to monitor the teams in transit."

"*You'll* need the equipment? Seth," she trailed off with a frown, apparently understanding what he intended to do.

"Ulmalhameh will touch down somewhere in Serbia, Jayne. I've got a unit behind him, but he won't fly a straight route. He'll implement diversionary maneuvers as a precaution and touch down at least once before heading home. I plan to intercept."

"You're control on this operation. Your place is here."

He wouldn't debate. Not with Lily's life on the line. She was safely in the back of that jet right now, but her status could change in a second. There could be any number of reasons that Ulmalhameh had brought five slaves on his flight and none of them were good. "His stronghold is in the mountains—"

"You can't know that. We've also received intel that he's underground."

"Smoke." Seth waved his hand dismissively. "I've been playing cat and mouse with this man for six years. Trust me, he's in the mountains. I just need coordinates, and I'll have them shortly. Van Brocklin's monitoring cockpit transmissions."

"What is it you can do that your teams can't?"

"My perimeter unit is *behind* Ulmalhameh. Once I have the coordinates, I'll have team one intercept. I want them on the ground to greet the plane when he touches down. I know this man, Jayne. I know the kind of people he surrounds himself with. I want a smoking-bolt operation. I want total control of his air base and ground crew so I can apprehend him when he gets off that jet. Nothing to tip our hand in advance and give him a chance to escape. I'll stand the best chance of accomplishing that if I'm calling the shots on-site."

"You're control."

"You're right, and as control, I'm downgrading my status to action officer."

Jayne pushed her chair back from the desk and stood. Not an attempt to intimidate him, Seth knew, but a sign of how disturbed she was by his tactics. "Let your team intercept. Trust them."

"Not with Lily's life."

"She accomplished mission objective. If Ulmalhameh goes underground, we can find him."

"One word, Jayne: Waco. I refuse to be forced into a position where I have to storm his compound," Seth said, turning back to the display. "I won't risk Lily. Ulmalhameh doesn't get a chance to bury himself again."

"There will be consequences."

"One of them won't be Lily becoming Ulmalhameh's sex slave."

"Or Jareb's, either?"

He glanced up at her again. "I won't believe Jareb turned on us."

"But you can't be sure. Don't you think it'll be better to leave him in place to find out why he was promoted to be the emir's new right-hand man?"

"I'll find out. From Ulmalhameh. When I bring him in."

She braced her hands on the side of the desk and stared him down. "Fine, Seth. You've set your mind on a course of action. But you're letting your emotions get in the way and breaking protocol. I need to inform the director."

"Don't bother. I'll inform him myself."

Reaching for the phone, he connected, and within seconds his uncle was on the line, asking, "How's our girl doing?"

Seth gave him a sitrep to bring him current on the developments. His uncle listened and finally said, "I understand you feel responsible, but that's your job on this one, Seth. You're control. Command doesn't come without cost and sometimes that cost weighs heavily."

The end justifies the means.

Not always.

"My job is to see my operative home safely," Seth said. "I will."

Operation: Intercept

Sixteen Hours Later

My worries about becoming part of the mile-high club proved groundless. Our tour of the skies above the Middle East turned out to be a long one, with two landings and subsequent take-offs designed to mislead and confound any onlookers. The passengers on the emir's jet—myself included—were all too exhausted and cranky to engage in anything more than cat naps and grumpy exchanges with the flight crew as we squeezed through the ever-shrinking aisles on our trips to the lavatory.

During the first landing, several of the soldiers, out of uniform and costumed in traditional Muslim garb that rendered them anonymous, had disembarked with great ceremony while the jet refueled.

A similar ploy played out again during the second landing. This time our touchpoint was an Asian country—I could tell by the heritage of the groundworkers servicing the jet.

I knew these diversions wouldn't mislead or confound Seth. Compliments of me, he had a lock on the target and could follow us to hell and back again. I clung to that fact during the never-ending flight while using my time to assess Jareb's collusion with the emir.

I was still up in the air on that one.

He hadn't betrayed me yet I was sure. These men weren't stupid. If they knew I was an American operative, they would guess that Seth had sent me in monitored, which meant taking me to the emir's headquarters would give away his location.

And there was just something squeaky-new about the emir and

Jareb's interactions. All the exchanges I'd witnessed since our take-off from Qahtrain had given me the impression that Jareb was a welcomed guest, as if the relationship was blossoming into unexplored areas. At one point, the emir had cornered Jareb on his way back from the lavatory, and they'd sat down just a few rows away, where I could overhear much of their conversation.

They'd discussed making arrangements for Jareb to disappear from his life, so he could go underground without leaving loose ends. They planned an apartment explosion that would torch all his worldly possessions and stage his death. To the world Xavier Jareb would be dead and buried. No longer a threat.

Of course, there would have to be human remains to convince the local authorities that someone had died in the explosion. I couldn't help but wonder who would get that job. Would the emir simply appoint one of his soldiers, a man who would consider it his highest honor to die in the service of their jihad?

Once upon a time, I couldn't fathom that mentality, but after playing Jareb's sex slave for my own jihad, I had a little more insight. And a lot less room to cast stones.

When the jet began another descent, I prayed this was the final one. I was antsy. I had no idea how Seth would tackle my extraction now that Jareb had officially been upgraded to a wild card and I'd become a part of the royal entourage.

For all I knew, he would keep me in place. I'd go underground while he monitored activity at the Sword of Faith's headquarters and assessed Jareb. I tried not to think about another stint as Jareb's slave girl. Or worse yet, the emir's.

We descended into mountainous terrain, where snow-covered peaks thrust up suddenly on all sides of the jet. During mission briefing, Seth had told me about various reports placing the emir's stronghold in caves and mountain retreats. He'd believed the emir hid in the mountains, and I thought of him now, wondered if he'd allow himself even a moment of satisfaction. Knowing Seth, probably not. He'd be too busy working. Assessing whether to keep me in place or extract me. And what to do about Jareb? Exfiltration? Elimination? Decisions, decisions.

The jet landed, and I went onto hyper-alert when a patrol of armed soldiers disembarked. They soon radioed back with an all-clear and one of the pilots emerged from the cockpit. We were instructed to gather our things.

The emir's entourage, including Jareb, headed out first, but soon all the passengers had made our way through the bitter winds into a warm hangar.

A convoy of all-terrain vehicles was parked on one of the two runways, and the emir's soldiers began shuttling luggage from the jet while we waited. Obviously we'd be transported to our destination by land, but I was glad to stretch my legs before climbing into those vehicles for another cramped trip.

We formed a nice little parade when we finally departed the hangar. I expected the soldiers taking point and following up the rear.

I didn't expect the gunfire.

Our group had cleared the building but hadn't gotten halfway to the vehicles when the first salvo of shots pounded out. Shouts erupted. Several women beside me screamed. Soldiers went down in the front, and in the back, too, I'd bet, given our exposure, but I didn't turn around to confirm.

Soldiers immediately surrounded the emir, Khalid and the pilots. They returned fire. I couldn't see if Jareb was behind that protective wall of bodies, but of course no one gave a second thought to the women. We were left exposed. No way could we make it back inside the hangar. So grabbing Nora's arm, I dragged her toward a concrete barrier housing a power generator.

I yelled for the others to follow. Several leaped into action but the Portuguese woman froze where she stood. I shoved Nora toward cover, motioned for them all to hunker down beside the generator while I went back to grab our straggler. We managed not to get shot as I dragged her toward cover and hauled her down by my side.

We became part of a robed cluster, exposed if our assailants opened fire on us, but somewhat protected from stray bullets. There was simply no way to make it to the vehicles for cover without getting shot.

Gunfire streaked out from the trees around the perimeter. The human wall around the emir began to collapse. One of the soldiers went down near us, half his face blasted away.

The Portuguese woman collapsed in a dead faint. Nora screamed and scrambled backwards, looking like she was bolting back toward the hangar. Only she'd never make it. Whoever had ambushed us had the airstrip surrounded.

Grabbing onto her robe, I yelled at her to calm down. I don't think she heard me above the noise, but I fought with her anyway, refusing to let go, until the Frenchwoman came to my assistance and helped drag her back into the huddle of women, shielded from the sight.

I nodded my thanks and scrambled back onto my knees to assess the situation. All I could see were men in the trees, dressed in black camouflage, their heads covered, their features darkened. I had no idea who they were, but as they were shooting the bad guys and not us, I figured we had a common goal. And the emir apparently recognized the same thing because he didn't wait for the last of his soldiers to go down. He pulled Khalid into a roll and headed towards us, by way of the rifle the dead soldier had dropped.

Making a wild lunge, I managed to kick the rifle away, sending it spinning safely out of his reach. With a roar loud enough to hear over the gunfire, he thrust Khalid into the crush of women and came at me. I slammed back onto the tarmac so hard that my vision blurred, but my physical training served me whether I could see clearly or not.

Throwing my balance so he couldn't pin me underneath him, I clasped my hands together and brought them around. I made contact with the back of his neck, and he clearly hadn't expected the blow because it slowed him—just long enough for me to gain my knees. The damned robes hampered my maneuverability, but I brought my elbow around for another solid blow to his face. Luck was with me. The blow connected, and he lunged forward cradling his broken nose.

Launching myself onto him, I locked my thighs around his throat and shifted my weight forward. With his face pressed into the pavement, his nose bloody, he was struggling hard just to breath, but I held my thighs clamped around him for dear life. I needed to disable him only long enough for our assailants to make it across the tarmac.

A quick glance over my shoulder revealed that they were on their way, close enough to recognize that several carried tranquilizer guns, not assault rifles.

The good guys.

That was my last thought before I was dragged off the emir, my breath thrust from my lungs painfully as I was knocked onto my back by a hard male body.

Jareb.

It took me a second to realize that he wasn't trying to hurt me. He spun me beneath him in a hard move, shielding me from a soldier who was aiming a rifle my way.

Jareb had protected me from one threat, but now the emir was free again. His shock at Jareb's action transformed his bloody face into a mask of confusion. I was sure he couldn't decide whether Jareb had rescued him or betrayed him, and for an instant I thought he'd demand an answer, but his survival instincts were too sharp, too automatic.

He wrenched Nora in front of him, instead, using her as a human shield as our assailants rushed us. I grabbed at her robes, trying to wrestle out from beneath Jareb so I could free her, but with my legs pinned, I couldn't manage the leverage to break free. Then I lost my grip on her entirely as Jareb jerked me away.

I saw Khalid stagger free of the women, handgun raised, just as I felt the shot. The impact caught me hard enough in the side to rip me from Jareb's arms, but it was Jareb whose shoulder exploded in blood and gore as he rolled back onto the tarmac, suddenly limp. I heard a scream, Nora I think, and then black clad assailants rushed us, seizing the emir and Khalid, freeing Nora and taking control of the women, attending to Jareb, coming for me.

One knelt beside me, gathered me against him to check my wound. My head had grown too thick and foggy to react, my entire body suddenly boneless, but I looked up into his blackened face, into familiar gray eyes . . .

Seth. He'd materialized from one of my fantasies, dressed in camouflage. I found myself smiling, grateful for his image when darkness was crowding my vision. He'd been my anchor through this mission. I felt . . . *calm* to have him with me now.

His quicksilver gaze raked over me, both relieved and worried, a look I'd imagined a thousand times in my dreams.

A look that meant he cared.

I ignored the fact that he couldn't really be here. This was too great a fantasy, and I was totally bummed when I couldn't keep my eyes open anymore to enjoy it.

Agent of Influence

Forty-eight Hours Later

Seth dropped ice cubes into a ceramic pitcher, carried it from the kitchen through the chateau, a safehouse the agency kept in the French Alps.

This chateau had been his hideaway for the past two days while he and a nurse had tended their very sleepy patient. But the patient was finally awakening so he'd dismissed the nurse to take over the job himself.

He emerged in the doorway of a bedroom, where two walls of glass doors overlooked a frost-edged courtyard flooded with late afternoon sun. He strode inside and set the pitcher on the bedside table. After stoking the fire he'd kept blazing in the stone fireplace, he sat in the chair positioned beside the bed, where he'd passed long hours, watching his patient sleep.

Lily.

Her pale hair streamed over the pillows, gleaming strands against the dark bedding. Her beautiful face was so peaceful in sleep that he'd found himself content to sit there and watch her breathe, to gauge the steady rise and fall of her chest beneath the covers, to reassure himself that she was indeed alive and would soon awaken.

He'd come so close to losing her, before he'd even acknowledged the impact her loss would have on him.

He acknowledged how much now. Every rise and fall of her chest mirrored a breath of his own. His heart beat strangely hard, contingent upon how fitfully she slept. Faster when she grew restless. Calmer when she dreamed peacefully.

As he'd sat by her bedside, Seth had looked at how he'd distanced himself from his emotions. Forced himself to ignore how much he wanted her.

And he wanted this woman. Never so much as now when he'd finally admitted the truth, when he couldn't be sure what to expect when she opened her eyes and faced him, and the memory of Operation Kiss.

When he didn't know what to say. Honesty was all he had and he didn't know if it would be enough.

So he waited, needing her to open her eyes, to recognize him, to prove she'd recover and decide if she'd forgive him.

Then, finally, as the fire faded again in the hearth, her breathing grew shallow and she fought her way through the drugs to awareness. Her lips parted on a silken sigh. Her lashes fluttered open uncertainly then closed again, as if she wasn't yet sure she wanted to swap dreams for reality.

Seth steepled his hands before him, watched, waited, humbled by the way his heart beat faster when she exhaled a resigned breath and opened her eyes with a more purposeful gaze.

He could see awareness in those purple depths, wasn't surprised when she said, "You're here."

Her voice was a faint whisper, words exhaled on another sigh, a sound that filtered through the fire-sparked quiet, filtered through him.

He nodded.

"The airstrip?"

"Yes."

Something about that seemed to confuse her. A tiny frown rode her brows, but she just inclined her head, a movement that required effort.

"You should sleep, Lily," he suggested, though he wanted nothing more than to keep gazing into her eyes. "You accidentally took a tranquilizer dart intended for a two-hundred pound man. You'll feel better soon."

"The emir?"

He should have known she wouldn't be distracted from questions. Lily, always curious, always conscious of duty. "He's in Containment. At Command."

She tilted her head away, long blonde strands dragging across the pillow as she gazed through the glass doors at the frost-covered garden. "Where are we?"

"A safehouse in France."

"Why?"

A simple question with no simple explanation. "I wanted to debrief you away from work, where we could be alone."

She appeared to consider that, then asked, "The women?"

"All safe."

"Jareb?"

Naturally she'd want to know what had happened to him, but somehow her question still came at him sideways. His head filled with the memory of their roles in Operation Kiss. Stung.

"He took a bullet meant for you, so you winded up taking the tranq dart meant for Khalid ben Sarsour. Jareb's had surgery to put his shoulder back together. He'll recover."

"You were right about him then."

She kept her gaze fixed out the window, her profile backlighted against the harsh winter sun. That she wouldn't face him told Seth how much she'd needed to rationalize her actions, how much she needed to hear that Jareb hadn't betrayed them. Betrayed *her*.

He nodded.

"What will happen to him now?"

She wanted to know if she'd run into the man. She wouldn't. Not while Seth was in command.

"Jareb has stepped into Ulmalhameh's place as head of Husan al Din. He's agreed to work with us to dismantle the organization from the top down."

She faced him then, and he could read the curiosity in her expression, the hope. "You trust him?"

"I do. Seems safer to place my faith in our defector-in-place than allow Husan al Din to splinter off into radical cells." Jareb had earned this chance because he'd passed along the intel that had enabled Seth to capture the emir.

And he'd handled Lily with care.

Seth tried to read Lily's reaction in her heart-shaped face, wished he could help her find peace with this job. But Lily would have to accept Operation Kiss in her own way, in her own time. He intended to be with her while she did.

The end didn't always justify the means. Lily had taught him that and now he'd teach her, but not yet, not until she'd made peace with her memories.

"Anything else you need to know before you can close those eyes and do what you're supposed to be doing to recover?"

She met his gaze and nodded. "I don't understand why you were at the airstrip, Seth."

Here it was . . . honesty. He owed her nothing less. "I didn't trust anyone else to do the job."

"You were control on this mission."

"The title didn't matter. I was the best chance to get you out safely. I needed to be there, so I was."

In the purple depths of her eyes, he could see uncertainty. She didn't know what to make of his admission. He'd broken protocol and she wasn't sure how she factored into his actions.

Leaning forward, he brushed fine hairs back from her temple, let touch bridge the distance between them. Her eyes widened and the pulse jumped in her throat. He traced his fingers down her cheek, sought that thready pulse that gave him the hope he so desperately needed.

"Lily, there's a lot I need to explain. *Too* much to hit you with while you're groggy from drugs. Let's just say Operation Kiss helped me find the courage to stop lying to myself."

"About what?"

"My feelings for you."

The words just hung there between them, more intimate than even his fingers on her smooth skin. Her expression softened, and Seth hadn't realized until then how desperately he'd needed to see understanding dawn in her eyes, surprise, and pleasure.

"You care about me." It wasn't a question.

"Yes, Lily. I do."

The Debriefing

I slept again, only this time my sleep had that familiar dreamy feel of my fantasies. When I awakened, I told Seth I wanted to debrief. He argued that I wasn't ready, but I needed to make a place for what had happened. I wanted to clear my head so I could try and make sense of what he'd told me. How I felt to know he cared.

It took some convincing, but he finally retrieved his recorder from his briefcase. Then he sat on the bed and gathered me against him. I was amazed at how right I felt in his arms. Better than any fantasy, and I'd had some winners.

I relayed the story as it had unfolded in my point of view, told Seth everything he already knew.

Which was the easy part.

His questions were much tougher.

"You let me believe you'd had sex before, Lily. Why? Did you think I wouldn't send you on this mission?"

Explaining this one away meant admitting that he'd had the power to shatter me and hadn't even known it. But the encouraging, and yes, even pleased look in his eyes helped me find the strength to confess just how much I cared.

"I was afraid you'd send me anyway, Seth. I couldn't handle that, so I didn't give you the choice."

He'd tightened his arms around me, seemed to understand the things I couldn't say. How I'd wanted him to see me as a woman. How I'd hoped to feel better because he was watching, seeing up close what might have been his. How much I'd wanted him to care.

He didn't let go, which was good because telling him that I was experiencing conflict about my job was even harder. Though I'd understood what becoming a swallow would involve, I hadn't realized I'd feel as though I'd whored myself for my country. And if that wasn't bad enough, I'd responded to Jareb enough to confuse and humiliate me.

I told Seth that too, though I think he already knew. His translucent eyes grew all smoky and tender, and it was the tenderness that got me. Tears swelled inside, even though the very last thing I wanted to do was cry in front of this man.

But the drugs still had me under their spell, and I lost that battle.

His expression grew all soft around the edges when he thumbed the first tears away. I hadn't realized he could ever look this way, so gentle and caring. I'd imagined it, of course, but I'd never believed he'd let his guard down. Not for me. Yet he let my heart break in the safety of his arms.

I'd fallen back asleep to his promise that he wouldn't let me go again now that I was finally where I belonged.

He kept that promise. Every time I opened my eyes, he was there. And after we returned to Command, he stepped into that empty place in my life that had always been his.

In the Black

One month later

With Jayne Manning's help, I found a place inside me for Operation Kiss. The process had been more difficult than I'd expected, yet simpler in some ways. The difficult part had been dealing with the aftereffects of my response to Xavier Jareb, understanding my reactions, facing my regrets, learning not to cringe when I thought about him.

Simpler because Seth was with me. He'd promised to explain everything about how he'd come to his realizations about me, asked me to trust him until then. I did. It wasn't hard to wait, when I had something worth waiting for.

But I was eager to start our future together, a future I suspected would finally begin the day I found myself back on a jet bound for France.

He was also cryptic about this trip, and I still couldn't be sure we weren't on some errand for the director.

"This one's need-to-know," was all he'd say while driving me through the quiet countryside.

And when he pulled off the road into a lined drive that led to a very familiar chateau, I said, "I need to know, Seth."

He brought the car to a stop at the front door and cast me a smile that made my heart begin to pound. "I had Van Brocklin jam all visual."

"Really?" I tried to sound unfazed. "Until when?"

He opened his door and slid out saying, "Oh-dark-thirty."

The military shorthand for "sometime during the night" meant we were officially off-duty, and if Seth had arranged for leave, I knew I was right—our future was about to begin. "Oh-dark-thirty, hmm? Sounds like you've got plans."

He appeared to open my door, gazing down at me with a purely male look. It was a look he'd been tempting me with for the past month, a look that made me breathless. "I plan to make love to you, Lily."

I just melted inside and gazed up into his face, still amazed by the turn of events . . . by the possession in his expression, the hunger . . .

"May I kiss you?" He extended his hand, guided me to my feet.

My pulse fluttered crazily, and I was sure he could see how long I'd been waiting for him to ask. *Forever.*

An edgy look came into his eyes, a look that told me he'd been waiting too, anticipating . . . I had no words then, only a desire so deep, so familiar, so exciting. My fantasy was finally coming to life. Tipping my face toward his, I answered his question by catching his mouth with mine.

What I'd intended to be a long-awaited exploration exploded into wild discovery the instant our lips met. He had a sensuous mouth that I'd fantasized about a lot, but nothing had prepared me for the his tongue driving inside to tangle with mine, the clash of our breaths together.

He slanted his mouth to deepen our kiss, a kiss of possession that erased any lingering questions I might have had about his desire. He wanted me. I could feel his demanding breaths, the way he tested the limits of my willingness with his rough silk tongue.

I was *so* willing. I arched against him, and with those strong hands on my arms, he pulled me close, fingers digging into my skin. My breasts crushed his chest, a solid reminder that nothing but a few layers of clothing separated us, shielded my body from his.

As if I'd want to be shielded from my fantasies . . .

I was drowning in Seth. The taste of his groan against my mouth. The impact of his warm breath clashing with mine. The fresh male scent of his skin. The feel of the strong cords of his neck. The coiled strength in the hands he ran along my arms, my back, my hips. He anchored me against him, against that hard length of thigh he wedged between mine, forcing my legs to part while his hands held my bottom close.

I pressed against him in all the right places, wanted only to slip my arms around his neck and cling to him, to ride his thigh as awareness swelled inside me, the promise of even greater pleasures.

I could feel the length of steely erection growing against my belly, and there was something so delicious about this primitive proof of his need. That he wanted so much. Wanted *me*.

I tried to gauge the magic of the moment against the fantasy, but with his hands securing me against him, that male hardness branding me through my clothes, his mouth devouring mine hungrily, I couldn't remember my fantasies. I was overwhelmed by the reality of the man and my reaction to him. By the power of our chemistry together.

Skimming my fingers through his hair, I caressed the short strands that were so silky and thick. I needed to learn him by touch, wanted to explore my reactions, wanted to take liberties that I'd only dreamed about before.

Drifting my hands over his face, I held him closer, kissed him more deeply, and he gave another low groan, a gravelly sound. His erection swelled. His thigh rode between mine, a pressure that made the pleasure mount, made my insides converge into a pool of hot desire that made it impossible not to arch against him, a needy motion that begged for satisfaction.

"Let me pleasure you, Lily." His words broke softly against my lips, interrupting our kiss. The very idea that I might deny him after wanting him for so long struck me as funny.

And I felt like laughing, too, out of amusement, out of joy, but not surprisingly, I couldn't manage anything more than a sigh. "Pleasure me, Seth."

He lifted his head, not enough to break our kiss entirely, but enough to meet my gaze, and the wonder in his clear eyes was reward for my every fantasy, for so many nights spent yearning.

Then he trailed his mouth from mine, outlining my lips with whispery kisses, my cheek, my jaw, my ear, and in a sudden move, he scooped me into his arms. I gasped and hung on. He laughed and carried me into the chateau.

Straight into the bedroom.

A fire already burned in the hearth, which meant Seth had contacted the groundskeepers before our arrival. The windows had lost their frosted edges and the garden courtyard showed the first green hints of approaching spring. The bed was freshly turned down and I found the room even more welcoming than the drowsy memories of my last visit.

He lay me on the bed then stood over me, watching me with those clear eyes that promised so much. He reached out his hand and traced my temple, my cheek, my neck, a lingering touch as if he'd waited forever for the privilege.

I shivered as sensation rippled through me. This was arousal the way I'd never experienced it before. Seth's touch building my excitement, the anticipation almost painful in its intensity. The promise of pleasures to come.

"I want to see you naked." That hot command sent another wave of longing through me.

I smiled up at him. "That's exactly what I want, too."

Suddenly his hands were on me, pushing my jacket off my shoulders, dragging it down my arms. I let him control the moment, lifted my hair when he reached for the button at my nape, raised my arms so he could draw the shell over my head.

Kneeling before me, he wedged himself between my legs and reached for my bra. Suddenly we were nearly face to face and I could see his every move reflected in his expression . . . popping the clasp and sliding the straps over my shoulders, down my arms . . . peeling the silken cups away in slow, breathless degrees, revealing me.

His gaze trailed down my body. Though Seth had seen me nude before, not only on Operation Kiss but at different times during my training, he'd never watched me like this.

He'd never looked at me, and *wanted*.

A very male smile touched his lips as he unfastened my slacks. His warm fingertips brushed my skin as he slid the zipper open, parted the waistband. I lifted up so he could maneuver the slacks over my hips, taking my hose away until we both had what we wanted and I was sitting before him, naked.

He gazed down at me, his fully dressed presence and his hunger so real that I realized just how missish and innocent my fantasies had been. I'd imagined his reactions, his lust, but the hot look on his face was enough to make a blush rush up my neck and into my cheeks.

His lust was all male. His gaze moved like a living thing over my skin, a look that possessed every inch of me, of my body, of my reactions. That look held power and he knew it. He could arouse me with nothing more than the desire in his eyes.

And he liked that.

I liked it too. My breasts grew heavy, my nipples erect. My

body performed for him, showing him everything I'd always wanted him to see.

I wanted him. It was simple. *Right*.

"Touch me," I said.

He leaned close, forced me to arch backward as he pressed his mouth to my neck, kissed a tender path along my skin. His fingertips barely brushed my face as he traced the line of my jaw, the arch of my throat.

His hands slid down to circle my breasts, shaping them, cupping them in his velvet rough palms. He thumbed my nipples, an intimacy that stole my breath until I could only arch back on my hands to brace myself and press upward into his touch.

He trailed those fiery kisses lower, still lower. I knew what he intended and watched him draw near in exquisite detail, the breath catching in my throat as he lifted my breast up and his mouth parted . . .

He dragged his tongue over my nipple, a warm stroke that drew my gasp when I finally remembered to breathe. He sucked the hard tip into his mouth, a hot wet pull that arrowed through me like a lightning bolt.

I trembled.

He smiled, and sucked a little harder.

I would have come off the bed had he not held me pinned with his big body between my legs.

I writhed instead, savoring the feel of his mouth on me. I wanted to watch his expressions, to capture these moments in my memory. But I could only stare at the top of his dark head as he made love to my breasts with his mouth and hands.

Seth had promised to pleasure me, so he did.

His mouth suckled. His tongue laved. His teeth nipped. He aroused me until every nerve ending in my body awoke to his touch, until even the gusting of his warm breath on my skin made my belly swoop wildly.

And when I thought I couldn't possibly take anymore, he moved down my stomach, a path of moist kisses and purposeful caresses as he lowered his face between my legs. I watched his descent, refused to miss any part of an experience I'd envisioned so often. The sight of his dark head bent low over me, his big body wedged between my legs.

But for as much as I'd imagined this moment, I hadn't a clue what to really expect. He slipped his strong hands between my knees, parting them until I was spread wide open, my thighs impossibly pale against his broad chest. And then he just knelt there, idly skimming his fingertips along my sex, not enough to penetrate, but enough to separate the moist folds in a way that was intensely intimate.

Coaxing my clit from its hiding place, he rubbed it with a lazy circle that made me gasp. Then, lifting his gaze above the rounded mound of my bare sex, he flashed me a grin that sent the blood rushing into my cheeks. *Again.* And rushing to other places as well when my sex gave a greedy little clench.

Seth's smile told me he could feel my body's response. He rubbed again. And again.

The warmth that stole through me took control, chased away everything but the feel of his hands on me, the sight of his pleasure as he aroused me. Almost more intimate was his gaze, those clear eyes watching my body gather, tighten, open to his touch as though my senses had never truly been awakened.

They hadn't. Though I'd never had sex before Operation Kiss, I'd known arousal. Though my fantasies had been limited to the man between my legs, I'd experienced passion before. But never *ever* had I known a desire that warred so fiercely with my reason, possessed my thoughts, my body, my fantasies.

Only Seth had this effect on me.

And when his gaze slipped away and he lowered his face, I held my breath, waiting, just waiting . . . the feel of his stubbled cheeks between my thighs, his mouth on my skin.

He drew that little bud in with a soft pull, a move so erotic, so irresistibly sensual that my entire body melted with the power of the sensation.

Then his tongue joined the game. A devilish, very thorough stroke that made me gasp. He licked again, and I could only sink back against the bed, drive my hands beneath the pillows and hang on as my insides became a wave of sensation that mounted . . . building, rolling, waiting to break.

And just when I was vibrating, an undignified mass of quivering, needy skin, he slipped a finger inside me, a hot stroke that drove me to climax.

I recognized this phenomenon. I'd aroused myself often enough to the fantasy of Seth's mouth and hands on my body, his erection inside me. I'd brought myself to fulfillment before.

But my fantasy fulfillment had *never* felt like this.

What I'd experienced before had been a spark, a crackling flame, flaring hot then suddenly over. This was an explosion. A detonation of all my senses, a total consumption that left me thrusting my hips against his hand.

I was unable to do anything but clutch the comforter and let my body slow its motion on its own.

"Good thing I'm your superior," he said conversationally, resting his cheek on my thigh. "Nobody can tell me when to get you back to Command. I'll keep you to myself as long as I want."

My sex gave another clench, and I exhaled a shaky breath. His hand idly stroked like he had every right in the world to touch me so intimately. He did, and he knew it.

"You intend to hold me hostage in a French chateau?" My voice sounded faraway and dreamy. "Does your uncle know?"

"Yes."

"Yes?"

"He sent Jayne as oversight because he expected I'd have trouble monitoring your mission."

Psychological oversight. I hadn't known. "What kind of trouble?"

His hand stilled its lazy motion and his expression grew serious as though he kept his gaze fixed on the sight of our bodies joined, his tanned forearm against my thigh. "It started when you first got naked, Lily. I had to monitor the mission privately in my office. All the people in System Ops were getting on my nerves, making it impossible to concentrate." He gave a short laugh. "It didn't take long to realize I didn't want anyone walking up behind me to see you."

I waited, not sure how to respond to his admission. His frown revealed so much surprise, so much turmoil, so much emotion I'd never seen in him before. Seth routinely faced pressure and tragedy at work, but I'd never seen him look so troubled, uncertain.

"It was more than watching Jareb touch you," he said. "When I realized how inexperienced you were, it changed everything. I was struggling already, but knowing that I'd asked you to sacrifice your first time to the job . . . God, Lily—"

"You didn't ask, Seth." I stroked his dark head, wishing I could absorb his pain. I hadn't meant to hurt him, only to protect myself. "I didn't give you a choice."

"Jayne pointed that out, but it didn't make any difference. It was my job. I should have known before I put your life in Jareb's hands. I gave him all the control, and even though I believed he acted in good faith, when your life hung in the balance . . ."

Seth's eyes slipped closed and he exhaled shakily. "He could

have turned you over to Ulmalhameh. And I was so damn grateful that he wasn't ugly with you . . . I finally understood how much I didn't want you to be hurt."

"But your uncle knew."

He nodded, lifting his wry gaze. "Jayne said I worked so hard to keep my distance from you that they couldn't help but notice." He gave a hard laugh. "Everyone knew except me apparently. At least until it was almost too late."

I wanted to reassure him, tell him he could never be too late, but the emotion I saw in his face stopped me. He was struggling too hard. Though I wasn't sure how I felt about Jayne and the director finding our feelings for each other so transparent, I was glad they'd been there when Seth had needed them. I might not know him intimately—yet—but I knew him very well professionally. Facing his attraction to me, his uncle's protégée, had to have been . . . difficult.

"For what it's worth, I didn't know. I thought you saw me as a ten year old."

He grabbed the lifeline I tossed him with both hands, and pressed that devilish finger inside to disabuse me of the notion. "Surprise, surprise. I haven't seen you as a ten year old since you were ten."

"Seth." With a groan, I collapsed back on the bed, unable to face his laughter.

And the tense moment was broken. I was glad. We didn't need angst. I'd already reached my quota for the month, and I'd rather the man of my dreams keep proving he wanted me. There was still this whole orgasm thing to explore. . . .

"Make love to me, Seth."

His hand slid away and suddenly he was slipping out from between my legs, unbuttoning his shirt. Scooting upward on the bed, I swung my legs around and sat up, a more dignified position that gave me a much better vantage point to watch him undress.

I'd seen him naked before, but never like this. Not even my fantasies measured up to watching him hastily strip for me, his tanned, sculpted body fully aroused. For me.

Suddenly he was climbing onto the bed, kicking the comforter down, dragging me toward him. I draped my leg over his and straddled him, made myself comfortable with my thighs spread wide, his erection poised at the entrance of my sex.

We were face to face, closer than we'd ever been before. A view that let me see the diamond starbursts in his eyes, how absurdly thick the fringe of black lashes that ringed them.

He had a cowlick tossing his hairline into a curve along his brow, his thick black hair short, but shiny in the fading firelight. I found myself reaching up to trace his mouth, those full lips that had been the inspiration for so many wonderful fantasies. His skin was rough around his mouth, along his cheeks, as if he'd soon sprout a respectable stubble.

Finally I had the freedom to touch, to explore, and I grazed my hands down his neck, over his shoulders, explored the hard ridges of his arms, his chest. I pressed kisses into his hair, behind his ear, down the strong column of his throat.

I touched him, tasted him, and with an incredibly tender look that caressed me from the inside out, he indulged my need to explore. His eyes never left my face as I discovered his strong jaw, the faint indentation in the cleft of his chin.

"I've wanted to touch you for so long." I admitted, not remotely shy. I'd never felt guilty for my fantasies. Life was too short. I'd indulged in imagination what I'd never thought I'd have the chance to indulge in real life. "I fantasized about you, Seth. Did you ever have any clue how much I wanted you?"

He turned his face and licked my palm as it passed his mouth. A warm-velvet stroke of his tongue that made me shiver.

"I was attracted to you. So much that survival training was torture. You were wrapped around me naked, and I had no business feeling the way I did. I thought about you in ways I shouldn't have but told myself it was natural given the logistics. I was a man, and you were a very beautiful woman. I thought it was just physical. Until I was out of control with no choice except to analyze why."

Skimming my fingers through his hair, down his neck, over those broad, broad shoulders, I encouraged him to keep talking. I liked hearing how much he wanted me.

"I distanced myself for a reason, Lily. You tempted me, and when I thought about why you might have agreed to go on this mission, I suspected I wasn't the only one feeling that way. I hoped."

I smiled. If he'd had *any* idea . . .

"I hoped, too," I admitted. "I hoped you'd do this." I slipped my hand between us and caressed the swollen head of his erection against me, a glancing stroke that made him shudder.

Lowering my face, I pressed soft kisses along his shoulder, breathless at this new intimacy, unable to face the excitement in his expression as I admitted, "I had some very erotic fantasies about you, Major Blackthorn."

Another moist caress of that hot length. Another shudder.

"At least what I thought was erotic," I continued. "I'm thinking my fantasies are tame compared to the real thing."

"Really?" His muscles flexed as he pressed inside just a bit.

I gasped.

He smiled, pushed inside a little more. "Did you fantasize about how we'd feel together?"

Together.

I nodded, savoring the feel of his steely heat inside me. I knew a sense of rightness I could only have dreamed of.

This was my fantasy come to life. Even better.

"Love me, Seth."

When his gaze met mine, so familiar, so earnest, I was overwhelmed with the honesty I saw in his face.

"I do, Lily."

And then he was realigning himself between my legs, pulling me into his arms. He filled my gaze with the stubbled curve of his throat, the hollow where his neck met shoulder.

I could feel the head of that erection poised just inside me, and I arched against him, invited him deeper. My hands slipped around his nape to draw him into a kiss.

Our breaths collided. He rode my wetness before pressing inside, a slow heated stroke that made us one. I moaned as my body stretched to accommodate him and he caught the sound with his mouth, fed it back to me with a rumbling groan.

He held me and I knew he was as overwhelmed as I was by the reality of us together, our bodies close, our heartbeats racing in sync.

"Ah, Lily." Rocking his hips to draw back, he eased out of me, then slid back in, a long slow stroke that consumed me with its intensity. Again.

I lost myself in his body, in those slow, powerful strokes that jumbled fantasy with reality, somehow managed to be both.

He never slowed our wild kiss, savored my mouth possessively as though he'd waited forever for the privilege. His hands slipped from my hips up my waist, my ribs, caressing me as if he couldn't stop himself, as if he wanted to learn every secret to making me soar higher. He caught my hips and taught me his rhythm, tantalizing, forceful, *right*.

And then I could feel it, that swelling again. Seth seemed to know, because he quickened his pace. His mouth broke from mine, trailing urgent half kisses along my cheek, my temple. I could only meet his thrusts, skim my hands along his shoulders, his ribs, his hips, exploring, discovering.

My pleasure was building, rising inside me and he stroked me higher and higher, dragging my hips impossibly closer, showing me exactly how to move to feed the growing pressure.

His mouth was so close to my ear I could hear his every breath, the low rumbling that began deep in his chest. And he kept driving into me, whole bodied movements that dragged him nearly all the way out, before he plunged back, shoving the air from my lungs on low moans. His body flexed beneath my hands, and I hung on, the pressure building, my excitement rising. I wasn't sure what to ask for, but I knew he couldn't stop, not then, not when I was this close to coming apart.

I dug my fingers into his butt and arched into his thrusts. I could feel his body gathering, tensing, and when he went over the edge, a magnificent tightening of powerful muscle and male strength, I went with him.

"Love me, Lily," he whispered harshly.

I turned my head to kiss his mouth. "Always."

About the Author:

Jeanie Cesarini is an award-winning author of red-hot romances. She enjoys following her muse and looking for love, even in the grittiest real-life situations. She believes in happily-ever-afters. Not the "love conquers all" kind, but the "two people love each other, so they can conquer anything" kind. To check out more of her sensual Secrets stories and her other red-hot romances, visit her website at www.jeanielondon.com.

The Sacrifice

❧✦❧

by Kathryn Anne Dubois

To My Reader:

The Sacrifice is truly my most naughty tale to date so be forewarned . . . 'Tis not for the faint of heart! But the wicked Count Maxwell made me do it. Caught under his wicked spell, I was compelled to write his story.

In my first story in Red Sage I invited you to enjoy the chase, in my second to enjoy the capture, and in this to enjoy the forbidden.

Chapter One

Anastasia awoke with a start, blinking against the dank blackness that greeted her, struggling against images she couldn't control and of which she should have no knowledge. Dark sensual images that haunted her.

The coarse woolen blanket scraped the stiff tips of her nipples and drew a desperate moan from her lips. While she slept she had unlaced her linen shift. Her face burned with that knowledge and from the heavy moist pulse that throbbed between her legs.

Was she destined to take her final vows, in a mere three days hence, still plagued by forbidden thoughts and shocking desires? Surely Lucifer was tempting her mortal soul.

She flung off her covers and sank to her knees. The rough stone floor chafed her but she paid no heed. She vowed to persist all night if praying would deliver her from this awful curse.

Her sobs echoed against the walls of her sparse cell in the abbey but only a mocking silence followed. No guardian angel answered her prayers.

Yet, the life for which she was destined awaited her. She could never doubt that. Had she not prepared all her life for the holy nuptials which would make her the bride of the Lord?

To be raised in privilege allowed her to appreciate her sacrifice to live in poverty, and having been born a girl, obeisance had been her life. She could offer those gifts with a generous spirit.

Poverty and obedience, aye. But what of chastity?

While she had no carnal knowledge of men, she willingly offered the sacrifice of celibacy as well.

A thought startled her. Perhaps her prayer for deliverance had just been answered? For how *could* she offer the last as a gift? A gift that had no meaning since she had no knowledge of what she offered.

She sprang to her feet and donned her simple novice robes over her nightshift, then wrapped the heavy linen tightly around her head. She tucked her toes into small leather slippers, certain of what she must do.

Grabbing a small torch from its wall holder, she hurried to the circular stairwell leading to the back gardens. A snap of cold air bit her fair skin as she stepped out. Pausing after she passed the fishpond, she looked up to the sky. Dark clouds loomed ominous. She would have to move swiftly to avoid the storm.

Long before the first hint of sun teased the horizon, Anastasia found herself on a drawbridge, frozen with fear, standing before Hawkwood and its foreboding gates of iniquity.

Chapter Two

A streak of lightning crackled in the sky and the heavens let loose with a sudden downpour as though issuing a final warning.

Every novice at the Cloister heard rumor of the man who went by the irreverent title of Count Maxwell and of the dark sexual secrets that simmered behind these walls. Whispered admonishments filled the abbey of pleasures of the flesh lurking within the fortress.

She clutched her cloak tighter. It was soaked through and plastered her robes to her skin.

"Who goes there?" Immediately sentries blocked Anastasia's path. The two men-at-arms raised their swords and bucklers.

Anastasia hesitated, not knowing what to say.

"Is Count Maxwell expecting you?"

When still she didn't answer the guards exchanged a glance then spoke again. "Why are you here?"

How was she to explain that which she sought?

"Are you here to see *Ian Maxwell*?"

Such a noble name for so legendary a debaucher, Anastasia thought. She simply nodded.

They drew nearer, their eyes sweeping over her small wet frame, and then peered at her face, hidden beneath her hood. The younger man spoke in a husky voice and glanced at the other. "I'll take her in. You stay here."

They signaled above and the iron-studded portcullis lifted. Lightning flashed, jolting her. She misstepped and nearly fell but for the strong hold of the soldier who reached out to grab her. When she looked up, the castle's spiked turrets, like giant lances, silhouetted against the illumined sky. An army of ravens kept watch at each crevel. A shiver stole down her spine at the awesome sight.

"Hurry along, now," he scolded, firmly dragging her through the gatehouse and toward heavy wooden doors.

Within minutes she was entering a large antechamber. A single blazing torch cast ghostly figures along the gray stone walls, the flames forming shadows that mimicked a sensual dance, sinful in its promise. A bite of incense hung in the air, a scent so familiar it should have lent comfort but within these walls smelled sultry, hinting at heathen rituals and mystery forbidden.

The guard led her through a wide barbican that took them to the far end of the keep and then up the winding stairs of a tower. When they reached two floors up, she stepped into immediate warmth. The smell of white-ash wood filled the air. She looked to the blazing hearth that graced almost an entire wall. Volumes of books, equaled nowhere but in a monastery or abbey, bracketed both sides.

On a wooden stand in the corner perched a large hooded falcon, its feathered legs and sharp claws partly visible. It must be asleep, for the only sound was the soft crackle of dried sagebrush in the roaring fire. The soldier pushed her farther into what Anastasia assumed was Count Maxwell's private solar.

"'Tis a visitor, my lord." He cleared his throat. "Another one from the abbey."

Anastasia looked to where he directed his words. A man sat before a rough-hewn trestle table, head bent to paper, a large hound stretched out on the floor beside him.

Anastasia startled to see the hound suddenly raise his head and peer at her. She doubted the master heard their arrival, so deep appeared the man's concentration. His long tapered fingers encircled the clipped quill with which he wrote with a languid hand. The candles burning at each corner of his desk flickered light over inky black hair that fell in soft waves to broad shoulders.

"Count Maxwell?" The guard repeated.

So this was the master of the keep, thought Anastasia. The infamous Lord of Pleasure. A titled lord who had abandoned his vast holdings to seclude himself in these inhospitable mountains.

Even before her cloister, she'd heard tales of his power over women with indulgences he'd learned as the captive guest of a

Saracen sultan. Things whispered about under cover of darkness, stories of mysterious sensual practices forbidden by the church. Only those women obsessed by wicked demons were heedless of the warnings. No one was safe from falling under his spell.

It was said their desire for him drove them to madness in the end. But it was he who had disappeared, and thus remained a recluse, unrepentant and carrying on his sinful practices.

Without sparing a glance, the depraved Count answered his guard. "Give her to Duncan. He likes virgins."

Anastasia drew in a breath, stunned by his response. Did he sense her purpose?

How could he know? Perhaps her journey here was destined, fated by her guardian angel so that she would truly be worthy of her sacrifice.

Count Maxwell continued to concentrate on his script, but then spoke again in a deep velvety voice that stirred a disturbing response in the pit of her belly. Could the alluring power of his voice alone be a precursor of what was to come? It was no secret that the man dabbled in the mystical. Some declared him a sorcerer of unequaled power.

But to believe such would acknowledge a power as great as God. Anastasia would lend no credence to such a claim. He was simply a man with exceptional powers of seduction. But for that reason, she would not have come. And failure to remember that would do more than simply thwart her undertaking. It would lead her down the most forbidden of all paths. She had come to strengthen her faith and increase her sacrifice not abandon both.

Count Maxwell waved a dismissive hand. "Duncan could use the amusement."

Before she could wonder about Duncan, the guard took her arm to lead her away. When she glanced back, hoping for a final glimpse at the legendary warlord, her hood fell to rest on her shoulders. The hound reared up abruptly and started forward.

"Damascus, be still," the Count scolded.

The hound whirled on him and barked and then turned back to Anastasia. When the Count looked up, his quill stopped. His eyes met hers. Dark orbs, reflecting light from the banking fire, moved over her face and then suddenly flared with a primal need that sent flames to her groin. She stifled a cry, sure she had but imagined the exchange.

The falcon sparked to life, squawking and rattling its perch. Should the leather straps that bound its legs break, it would surely fly for Anastasia's head.

"Cleo," the Count growled. The bird quieted.

"Bring her here." He flattened his palms on the table and rose slowly, his gaze intense. Even from across the room, she could feel his power. The guard drew her back into the room until she stood across from the Count with only the table between them.

She lifted her eyes to his face but remained impassive, proud in her determination to end her quest and silence the senseless ache that kept her from her destiny.

Raw strength radiated from his tall frame. A muscle ticked in a jaw line that was sharp and shadowed with beard. But what drew her most was the deep cleft in his chin. It was the only softness in a face seemingly chiseled from the mountainside in which the castle was carved.

When he came from behind the table, her eyes involuntarily fastened on his rough tunic, opened down the front, revealing the taut smooth skin beneath. Dark hair curled over honed muscle. And then her eyes drifted below to his member, swelled to hardness, frightfully thick in his braies. She gasped on a shocked breath.

"Surprises me, too," he said silkily. He shot his guard an amused glance. "Not since I was a young squire have I hardened at the sight of a fully clothed woman."

He moved to open himself. She jumped back, jostling the guard braced behind her, her eyes wide.

Count Maxwell released a husky chuckle. "As much as I'd like to feel your lips on me, you need not fear. I'm simply giving myself much needed room."

He loosened the ties and then reached for her, cupping her elbows. "Come." He drew open her cloak, letting it fall to the floor. "Let's see what else you can do for this world-weary lord."

With a nod to the soldier, the man crossed the room and returned with a soft cloth while the count gently unraveled the long strips of linen cloth from about her head. She was still reeling from the notion of her lips on his male member when, with a slow hand, Count Maxwell began unwrapping her robes. Her heart pounded in inexcusable anticipation at the same time she knew that she would displease him. Her skin was as pale as dust and her breasts would barely fill a man's palms.

But when he drew aside the last of the cloth until she stood in just her thin shift, his nostrils flared. Even in her inexperience she recognized the signs of male desire and, to her disgrace, her pulse quickened with pride. The guard stepped closer. She shivered and then burned under the heat of their gaze. With the calloused pad of his finger Count Maxwell traced lightly the tip of one ruby nipple.

The contact made her breathless, the touch so wicked in its pleasure, she thought she would faint. The Count drew in a harsh breath and then in one swift movement he lifted her into his arms and brought her to stand before the fire.

He stripped her quickly, allowing her shift to pool at her feet. Despite her sacred mission, she crossed her arms and attempted to cover her small mound with one hand.

He grabbed her wrists. "Shall I bind you?" His voice was low and vibrated with arousal.

Would he do that? When she managed a small shake of her head, he released her hands. She clenched them tight to her sides in her struggle to obey him.

He knelt before her and with a gentle hand rubbed linen as soft as a baby's skin over her body, soaking up the last of the chill from her flesh. Then he threaded his fingers through her hair and draped it along her shoulders, allowing a few locks to settle on her nipples. She muffled a sob at the light friction, knowing it would soon pucker her nipples to hard points.

He sat back on his heels and stripped off his tunic. His muscled arms flexed with the movement and sweat glistened down the hard ridges of his chest. Her eyes were drawn to the thick scar that slashed from breastbone to hip. Another thin, silvery one ran along one shoulder. She had nursed and cared for many men in the infirmary at the abbey, and having been raised a lady, she often attended the bath of male guests as a show of welcome and honor, but never had she seen a man like this.

The sight of his battle-scarred body should have repelled her, looking as he did every bit the fierce warrior lord of legend. But smooth golden flesh, pulled taut over rippling muscle, aroused in her a female response she could naught control.

While she tried not to stare at him, his own eyes traveled over every trace of her body. The tip of his rod peeked from his woolen hose, plum red and wet, swollen with desire. She prayed for the strength to drag her eyes away but the devil himself must have locked her gaze. The moist flower of her sex opened against her will. When the guard drew up in back of Count Maxwell to look at her, she finally found the strength to break the spell.

She bowed her head in disgrace, torn once again between the desire to sacrifice herself and the desire to remain chaste. But if she failed in her task, the chastity she offered would be but of the worldly kind, simply a purity of the flesh, for her heart and soul stilled burned with desire for carnal pleasures.

The heat from the fire licked at her buttocks, making her skin feel far too alive and threatening every surface of her skin, now lit in a fever she couldn't control.

A large hand palmed her breast. She looked up into the heated gaze of Count Maxwell. He pinched her nipple between his fingers, causing her to jump with the pleasurable jolt. He smiled at her response and then did it again. She almost grabbed his wrist as flames arced down to her woman's place, but she remembered his admonition about tying her up.

He slid both palms over her breasts, covering them completely, his calloused fingers stimulating her sensitive flesh. When he pinched both nipples mercilessly she felt herself tumbling near the edges of restraint. A helpless sound escaped from the back of her throat and her head fell back.

She shivered, mortified, and struggled to control herself and return her gaze to him.

His expression was astonishingly tender. "You are beautiful in your abandon." He circled both nipples with his thumbs. "Have you never done this to yourself, little minx?"

A shocked breath escaped her. She shook her head in disbelief.

"Ah, yes," he murmured. "The vow of chastity, with which you struggle so."

How did he know?

"What is this?" A deep voice sounded behind them and a man as tall as Count Maxwell but as fair as he was dark framed the archway. He moved quickly to join them. "She is lovely," he murmured and boldly reached to smooth his palm over her belly.

Before he could touch her, she stepped back dangerously close to the fire. Count Maxwell's hands encircled her waist and pulled her back, the feel of his rough palms against her smooth skin, scandalous. Then to her horror, he slipped a hand to the downy patch at the juncture of her thighs and threaded his fingers through the golden strands. Heat pooled and throbbed between her thighs, wetting her shamelessly.

She bit her lip to keep from crying out and concentrated on

the large crossbow that rested on a row of corbels, its iron-tipped quarrel loaded through its bow. A reminder to Anastasia of the infamous castle sieges attributed to the barbarian count. He was a man of war . . . and death, his victories on the battlefield, legendary.

"She is a novice, Duncan." Count Maxwell held her chin, forcing her to look at him. "Are you not?"

She refused to answer, preferring instead to invoke the sacred vow of silence to lend her protection.

He murmured, his voice warm and silky, "A pity so lovely a creature would be stowed away in a convent." He trailed his fingers up over her belly. His palm skimmed her hip and then smoothed down to her thighs once again. "I perceive great sensual promise in this one, beyond what she, in her innocence, could possibly imagine."

No! Anastasia wanted to protest, but she struggled to keep her silence. She would not allow his knowledge of her base desires to command her. To acknowledge her weakness was to conquer it and rise to loftier aspiration.

"I see." Duncan raised amused eyes to Anastasia. "If anyone would know of great sensual promise, 'tis you, my lord."

Count Maxwell grumbled a response and then leisurely played his fingers through her soft curls with a gentle touch that heated her flesh. The heavy pulse between her legs beat viciously. A wicked voice within her urged him to slip his fingers lower but she successfully smothered it.

He reached behind and cupped her bottom with his other hand. "Her skin is delectable," Count Maxwell murmured, smoothing his hand along the curve where buttock met thigh. "Her curves supple, her flesh warm."

Duncan wet his finger and stroked along the tip of one sensitized nipple. She bit back a groan. "Her nipples are overlarge and ripe, enticingly erotic on such delicate breasts."

"Aye," Count Maxwell said, his voice low. "If she weren't cloistered, I'd wonder if she were of age. She'd be a difficult one to turn away."

She burned with embarrassment while both men, fully clothed, swept their gaze over her entire length.

"Turn her around, Ian."

With a gentle turn, she was facing the fire and listening to the soft murmur of their voices. Large hands settled on her buttocks and stroked along her curves. She closed her eyes against the sinful feel of male hands sliding over skin that had never seen the light of day, had never been touched. But the aching throb at her womanhood only grew stronger and became a powerful need that frightened her.

"Bend her over," Duncan murmured.

She caught her lip between her teeth to keep from protesting.

Using gentle pressure, Count Maxwell forced her forward and with one long finger stroked lewdly between her buttocks, letting the tip come to rest on her secret rose. She stifled a cry. Duncan murmured his approval as the Count pressed with the pad of his finger against the small opening. She stiffened and burned with humiliation, not understanding why he would do this and tried to squirm away from his touch, imagining how she looked to the hungry eyes of the men behind her. Even the guard still remained, poised behind Count Maxwell, drinking in his fill. The thought of her so exposed while the men discussed her caused her to burn with shame.

He held her hip with one hand. "Be still." He withdrew from the spot and then soon returned with his fingers wet and slippery. He smoothed the wetness around the tiny ring and then probed gently. She contracted hard against his touch, refusing him entrance, so horrified that he would do such a thing. Still, a heavy fullness pooled at the juncture of her thighs even as she shuddered at the aberrant act. Then he withdrew with a quiet sigh.

He turned her back around. She could feel the entire surface of her skin flushed rosy from the heat, from their lascivious perusal, and from her own agitation.

"Let us have a look, Ian."

Count Maxwell nodded.

She was bewildered, for they were already looking at her.

His meaning became clear when he dropped down beside Count Maxwell and placed his hands on her thighs. To her alarm, he smoothed back her curls with his thumbs and then spread her pink lips with two fingers.

"Open your thighs," he commanded her gently. She sucked in a breath and wanted to shake her head, no. But was not this what she must do? To know the meaning of sacrifice?

On a shaky breath, she spread her legs and closed her eyes, giving them full access. Duncan slid his fingers lower and the moment his flesh touched hers she ignited. He slipped around her swollen petals and it seemed that every sensation she had ever felt centered between her thighs.

She writhed in frustration, the pleasure painful as he petted her into a torturous ache that consumed her, his fingers exploring, sliding and pressing. A pleasure that often caused insanity, she reminded herself.

She suppressed a traitorous whimper and opened her eyes to see Count Maxwell and the guard watching Duncan spread her wider. The air against her newly exposed flesh stimulated her unbearably. When they all leaned in for a closer look, she thought she would die. Count Maxwell licked his sensuous lips. Then Duncan slid one long finger between her folds and it disappeared in her body. She gasped as small tremors of pleasure shook her.

He let out a low groan. "She is soaked and deliciously hot."

All three men's gaze fixated on his thick finger impaling her.

Count Maxwell's eyes glittered.

"And virginal tight," Duncan moaned, beginning to move inside her with slow shallow thrusts.

She stiffened around his invasion but too soon found herself shamelessly opening to the pressure. To be impaled before the men was humiliating, despite the fire that sliced through her as he increased the pressure and continued to probe deeper.

In an involuntary gesture, she clasped his wrist, not knowing whether she wished to stop the pressure or guide his finger deeper. A small sob broke from her lips. He stopped and with a leisurely caress circled his thumb up once above her center. The shock of pleasure was enough to threaten her collapse.

She grabbed onto the Count's shoulder to steady herself and felt a new rush as her skin met heated flesh. He reached up, his eyes still pinned to her center, and covered her hand.

"I cannot feel her maidenhood." Duncan thrust farther. "Aye, there it is." He gave an appreciative murmur. "I am going to enjoy—"

"Nay." Count Maxwell's voice came out on a harsh breath. He rose. "She is mine."

Duncan withdrew his finger from her burning center and scandalously licked it. He gave her bottom a pat and then rose, too.

Count Maxwell's gaze returned to her. "Tell me your name?" he said, his voice but a whisper.

The question surprised her as much as the gentleness with

which he spoke. His eyes moved over her face as he waited patiently for her response.

Something dangerous in her almost caused her to answer before she remembered the spell he would spin. She cast her eyes from him instead.

A low growl rumbled up from his throat. "Take her to my men," he commanded Duncan. "She is intent on exorcising her demons." He tilted her chin up. "Look at me." His eyes darkened. "They will touch you, stroke you, lick you, spill themselves on your lips if they desire. Do you understand?"

Anastasia could not respond even if she intended. She should flee now, but she could do naught but stare into the fathomless depths of his eyes.

Then in a tender gesture so at odds with his licentious words, he stroked his thumb along her cheek while he directed his next words to Duncan. "They are not to bring her to pleasure. That I save for me alone. You will bring her back to me to deflower." He turned fully to Duncan. "Understood?"

Duncan lifted a surprised brow. "As you wish, my lord." He gave a mocking bow.

Count Maxwell scowled, then tipped up her chin. "This is for what you came, is it not?"

She nodded. She wanted to tell him that it was only in knowing the pleasures of the flesh could she denounce them and offer up her gift, but she chose to keep silent.

Somehow her silence made her less culpable in this wicked pursuit in which she had embarked.

He frowned lightly, cradling her face. "You were raised in wealth," he murmured, studying her. "Your parents should never have cloistered you." He brushed an idle finger along the delicate line of her cheekbone. "Your skin is far too soft to have been reared otherwise, and though your eyes are completely innocent, you possess unusual erotic potential."

Anastasia drew back, rebelling at the sacrilegious notion at the same time she felt the awful conviction of his words. Her struggle with her base nature and the torturous claim it had on her body had haunted her for so many years. Was there no hope for her escape? She refused to believe she was prisoner to her desires.

And by whose authority did he hold such claims? He was but a man, like others. The disturbing power he held over her was of her body alone. And it was precisely for this, to free herself, for which she had come.

Duncan took her arm and gently guided her out and down the winding stairwell. It wasn't until he led her through the covered passage and up into another tower that she realized she was still naked.

Chapter Three

Laughter and music drifted up the winding stairwell as a lady's maid draped Anastasia in cloth of the sheerest fabric she had ever seen. The threads were tightly woven but delicate, like a fine web. She had touched the rare raw silk from the East but a few times, but this was lighter. She felt surrounded by mist.

The filmy fabric swirled around her body offering little modesty, the texture just rough enough to tease her nipples to sensitive buds. She wanted to squeeze the tips and relieve the restless tingle. She wondered suddenly if the Count's men would do this. The thought drew a shameful ache that throbbed heavy at her private center.

"Come," the young attendant said, guiding her out of the chamber and down the stone steps. The maid brought her through the inner ward and soon she stood at the entrance to a dimly lit banquet hall filled with smoke, its fabric walls draped in blood red.

Her eyes took in the rows of arched windows and finely carved stonework. A stone basin graced every wall. Only in chapels had Anastasia seen such basins and those were used strictly for rinsing the cup used during religious services. The largest window, facing the sea, was set with stained glass.

Only the finest cathedrals boasted such opulence.

As the maid drew her in, the sweet tangy smell of lavender and tansy reached her nostrils and then her eyes fully adjusted to the haze. When she beheld the immoral scene unfolding, she swallowed a gasp.

Voluptuous wenches draped themselves boldly along men's laps, some half dressed, their large creamy breasts exposed. Other men looked on with lecherous grins. More beautiful women sat on benches between men, the men's hands buried beneath their skirts and allowing the men to pour raw honey along their bosom and then lick the sweetness up with their tongues.

It was disturbing that all the men were fully dressed while all the women were in varying states of undress, as though the women served as slaves for the base desires of the men. As she stared, a woman flew by, chased by three men, her woolen skirts lifted high, her stockinged legs in full view.

"She's a naughty one, Rolphe," a large man called out, tipping a brass jug to his lips.

Pitchers of ale and wine littered the tables and the smell of warm yeast hung in the air.

To her horror the three men were now wrestling the wench to the ground. One pushed down her bodice while the other two rucked up her skirts. Anastasia was riveted. Her face burned with shame but she couldn't look away.

The woman squealed with laughter as the man beside her covered her nipples with his hands and mouth and sucked on her greedily. The men in front soon had her mons completely bared and one shoved his finger deep into her. Anastasia silently moaned, recalling how it felt when Count Maxwell touched her.

Then the man spread her lips and with his wet finger touched a shiny nub that rested at the apex of her sex lips. The woman moaned and arched to his hand.

Anastasia's mouth went dry as she felt a thick throb at her own sex exactly where this man was touching the woman. She bridled at the thought that she wanted to explore her own sex lips to discover whether she, too, possessed this little pearl and then nearly swooned when the man licked the woman between her legs. Anastasia's heart stopped when the woman screamed with pleasure and then spread her legs wider. Her large hips bounced off the ground.

Just as Anastasia was wondering what would happen next, the maid nudged her further into the room and Duncan drew up beside her. He smiled, his eyes settling on her nipples, rudely visible through the ivory bliaud. He gave each one a pinch, sending flames to settle at the flower of her sex. "You are aroused. That is good." She made an attempt to protest but he gave a soft chuckle. "You would no doubt enjoy the rings. You're very sensitive." He draped his arm around her waist. "Come, look around."

The sight that greeted her was more shocking than she could have imagined.

In the center of the room, thick furs covered the rushes and torches blazed, forming a circle of flickering light. Gracing its outer circle were more couples drinking and fondling. Anastasia was sure that one young flaxen-haired woman was deeply impaled on a man's lap. He was a giant of a man while she was delicate and small. Her finely boned hands flattened against his bare chest and her skirts spilled around his lap.

Upon closer look, Anastasia could see that the lovely woman was bared to the waist and the giant was plucking at her nipples. She shuddered and moaned and then squirmed on his lap, raising herself as though struggling to get off, but the pleasure glazing her eyes made Anastasia think not.

The giant tipped her chin. "Did I not tell you to stay still, Glenda?" His eyes gleamed.

"Nay, she is not listening, Ned," a voice called out.

"I'll fix that."

In one easy movement the giant lifted her off him. Anastasia nearly choked at the sight of his member, huge and thick, standing straight up, its red, purpled head slick and shiny.

Glenda whimpered and clawed at his chest, grabbing a fistful of chest hair between her small fingers.

"Och!" Ned squeezed her wrists until she released him. "You little vixen."

"Spank her, Ned. She's more than deservin', that one."

Ned chuckled. Anastasia was horrified to think that he would hurt the woman. Effortlessly, he lifted her again and draped her over the thick trunks of his thighs and tossed up her skirts, revealing her plump white bottom for all to see. Anastasia choked on a gasp. His bronzed palm nearly covered one satiny globe.

And then he leveled a slap that rang out on her tender flesh, followed by another. Glenda cried out and bit his thigh through the coarse woolen cloth. "God's teeth," he muttered, anchoring her wrists with one hand and landing another series of small stinging slaps that had her jumping and squirming on his lap. Glenda's cries turned to moans that caused the crowd to roar their approval.

Anastasia was shocked to see Glenda spread her legs and arch her bottom higher into his hand. Then to her amazement, Ned leaned down and kissed her flaming bottom, running his tongue along the reddened curves. He poked a thick finger into her womanhood.

She screamed and ground against his hand. Anastasia's breath completely stopped when he licked his thumb and plunged it into her bottom hole. She nearly swooned at the sight of his finger wiggling between her buttocks. Her own sex grew tight and hot.

The spell had been cast; she felt ready to burst and her nipples were aching. She reached up to soothe them before she quickly suppressed the urge and dropped her hands. But she couldn't stop watching Ned. He plunged into Glenda's openings over and over again, and Anastasia couldn't help thinking that might have been what Count Maxwell had wanted to do to her. She thought of his elegantly tapered fingers, his cleanly trimmed nails, and the warm feel of his palms.

She shut her mind to the image, suddenly confused as to her purpose. Had she come to know the pleasures of the flesh but not enjoy them? Yet, if she did not . . . enjoy it, how could it be a pleasure she would then willingly sacrifice for the rest of her life, in keeping with her sacred vow of chastity? She *must* derive some pleasure. But she must not lose her head. The wicked demon of carnality awaited to pull her down into its dark depths and keep her there. Surely this place was its testament.

By now Anastasia's entire body burned tight with arousal. The restless, all-consuming ache that had tortured her for so many nights reached unbearable heights.

Duncan breathed into her ear. " 'Tis time you enjoyed some of what you've seen."

Anastasia pictured herself turned over the giant's knee and she flushed as a new rush of moisture seeped from her sex.

"Come. I'll take care of you."

Duncan drew her slowly toward the sable pelts and flaming torches at the room's center. A hush fell over the celebrants. It was a silent reverence, as though they had approached a sacred spot—a silence not unlike that of prayer hour at the abbey. Then a low murmur of voices rose until Duncan lifted a hand.

"Our young visitor seeks our help. She wishes to know the pleasures of the flesh so as to better offer them up when her time comes."

Yes, Anastasia thought, grateful that Count Maxwell had understood and instructed Duncan to regard her mission gravely. Even the lecherous crowd nodded with sympathy. Still, she instinctively reached for her prayer beads, perpetually tied to her belt and wound around her fingers day and night, discarded now in her cell at the abbey.

As if to confirm her absolute spiritual nakedness, Duncan pulled on the laces at her shoulders, sending her bliaud to puddle at her feet. An excited murmur rose from the gawking crowd. She wanted to flee but couldn't, so transfixed was she by their blatant admiration. A full blush spread over her body as the crowd moved closer. More than one man stroked himself through his braies, and hungry eyes traveled along her naked skin.

"Do not worry. Count Maxwell has given strict orders that you're not to be ravished." Duncan must have sensed her unease, but misread its cause. "Apparently," he continued, "Count Maxwell is saving the pleasure of ravishing you for himself." His lips quirked.

A disturbing knot of desire coiled in her belly at the thought of Count Maxwell. Though Anastasia did not fully understand what Duncan meant, she sensed that Count Maxwell's orders also served to protect her.

Still, she must fortify herself. Soon she would sacrifice herself upon the altar of pleasure. When the deed was done, the test of her spiritual strength lay in her ability to then forsake, from that point on, all carnal pleasure.

"Jamie, Sven, Robert," Duncan called to three young men straddling benches and drinking from large flagons dripping with ale. "She needs experienced hands."

So, this would be her penance as well. She was to be pleasured before an audience. The fulfillment of her base desires that had kept her from her calling would be witnessed by all.

Duncan smiled and turned to the minstrel. "Play your most sensuous song. A song of promise and pleasure." Despite her nakedness, Anastasia stood proud, drawing courage from her conviction of righteous choice.

Duncan spoke to the guests. "Our young visitor is to be stimulated and aroused but not brought to pleasure." He pinched one nipple as he spoke, drawing a small helpless cry from her. She burned with embarrassment as the three men looked on in bewilderment. All were tall and wickedly handsome, though none conveyed the power of Count Maxwell.

"You heard me." Duncan smiled. "Count Maxwell wishes her ready . . . but only for him." He plucked both nipples between his thumb and forefinger, elongating their cherry tips. "A pity."

A stir of surprise filled the hall and renewed interest lit the crowd's eyes. They jostled each other for a closer look as the sweet sound of flutes filled the air.

"Be gentle," Duncan commanded the men before he stepped aside.

Robert, the largest of the three, caught Anastasia around the waist. "Come, little one," he coaxed, as he eased down to sit upon the furs, his muscled body half naked but for the tight braies covering powerful thighs. Her eyes drifted to the tight mat of copper hair dusting his chest.

She offered up a prayer before she obediently knelt down beside him. He lifted her onto his lap and slipped his hand between her legs. "Let us see what we have here." When he slipped a thick finger up between her folds, she strangled a moan.

Pleasure, pure and unbidden, lanced through her. Instinctively, she arched her hips into his hands. He laughed. "I'd say she's more than ready." He withdrew his finger and licked it. Then he dipped in again before turning her around to face their audience, her back pressed to his chest. Anastasia closed her mind against his wicked touch. He was smoothing back her tight curls and was teasingly spreading her lips for all to see. The wetness that seeped from her was impossible to stop. He hooked his knees under hers and spread her legs wide. The shock of it had her struggling from his grasp, but he locked her tightly in his grip.

Jamie, the youngest one, knelt before her. He leaned back on his heels. "Be still," he said and ran his fingertips over the heated flesh at her groin, his blue eyes feverish and his neck flushed to a deep red. He pulled down his braies and freed a massive organ that throbbed with life and jutted out from dark blond curls.

Duncan sprang forward and gripped his shoulders. The crowd chuckled while Anastasia stared, eyes riveted to the sight before her. Never had she seen anything like it.

"I'm not going to deflower her, man. But I'd like to feel those dainty lips on my cock."

"Just remember what I said."

Anastasia watched in sudden panic as he took his dusky member in hand and kneeled up between her outspread legs.

He guided it to her mouth. "Lick it a little," he explained, his voice soothing in its gentleness.

Her fear turned to curiosity at the smell of fresh male sweat mingling with leather, so different from the familiar smells of the abbey. On impulse, she leaned forward and licked the shiny head. He hissed and cupped her chin. "Aye, that's it."

She licked again, this time allowing her tongue to feel the smooth skin and to trace the large blue veins that traveled down his thick length. He was so warm and silky. His member jumped and bobbed even as he held it in his hand. In back of her, Robert was stroking her inner thighs, tracing his fingertips along the sensitive skin. A rush of heat swept through her, making her skin alarmingly alive and alert.

Then his fingers played with her swollen sex, stroking and petting her as she lay splayed open for all to see. But the hot pleasure she felt made her careless to their gaze and served as a powerful reminder of the hold carnal pleasure had over a soul. She was slipping under, going up in flames and prey to a dizzying sensation that she feared she could scarce control. But she would.

She would experience the pleasure without becoming its slave. This was the key, she was sure. Like a chant, she murmured the belief to herself over and over again.

She grabbed onto Robert's wrists in a weak effort to stay his hand just as Jamie pressed down on her chin and her mouth opened. In one smooth motion, Jamie slipped the large head of his sex into her mouth. She groaned with the shock. Robert's finger probed her center and then he inserted two, making her squirm and arch against his hand. She felt trapped but so alive. The entire breadth of her skin flushed to a fever.

Robert's fingers moved to her nipples to pinch and pluck as Jamie's cock sunk deeper into her mouth. Jamie let out a low guttural moan just as two lazy fingers traveled along her wet sex lips and circled around the delicate pearl that swelled and throbbed and that held so much of her pleasure.

When she screamed in delight, Jamie throbbed in her mouth and thrust in quick rhythmic bursts. "Holy Mother of God," he groaned.

Anastasia tensed at the mention of the mother of God.

Jamie pulled out of a sudden, his face contorting. Then he howled like the wolves she'd heard when she couldn't sleep. She watched in awe as his creamy seed spurted from his member in smooth arcs that splashed hot on her breasts. The sight of him throbbing out his pleasure and watching the thick milk drip off her nipples was torture. The burning tightness in her sex grew worse by the way Robert's slippery fingers teased her little bud and then skittered away to lightly brush her curls or smooth over her belly before returning to the tight center of her pleasure.

She clutched Robert's thick wrists and sobbed.

Robert kissed her ear. "Relax and enjoy it, little one." His fingers danced away to lightly stroke her thighs.

Jamie took the head of his cock and rubbed it along the tips of her nipples, stimulating the swollen flesh until she whimpered.

She jumped with pleasure at the feel of Robert's finger returning to her plump folds.

"Ah, you are a beauty," Jamie said, massaging his sticky seed into her skin. The salty seed that clung to her lips tasted of him. She licked up the drops and cried out in frustration.

Robert stopped his torturous petting as the third man, Sven, who had been watching, knelt beside her. He was dark and strong looking, like the Count, but without the Count's regal features and hollowed cheeks. She tensed, glancing up at Duncan whom she had come to think of as her protector in the absence of Count Maxwell. He was looking down at her, eyes glittering and roving over her naked body. But when she caught his eye, he gave her a nod of assurance.

"Lay her back," Sven demanded. Robert reclined back, taking her with him. The hard warmth of him braced behind her and his boulder-like arms that cradled her lent some comfort. His meaty hands slid up to cover her breasts.

Sven smoothed his palms down over her belly and then along her thighs, his gaze hot and settling on her swollen center. He licked his lips and gave a small growl.

"Don't hurt her," Duncan warned.

"Och," he grunted, waving his hand in dismissal. To her horror, he settled his face between her legs and his thick fingers spread her wide. The tiny aching pearl at the top of her lips swelled and throbbed as he peeled back her skin. He was so close she could feel his warm breath fanning the tiny bud.

He blew on her, hot steamy breaths of air that made her jump out of her skin. Coupled with Duncan's licentious stare and her audience's hushed murmurs as they drank and ate and watched the scene, her sense of shame came crashing back.

She was naked and spread out for all to see with a man blowing on her most secret place and another fondling her breasts. She felt ready to explode. Would this never end?

This restless reaching for something unobtainable? A wicked need that could never be filled, for which one only grew more desperate the more the need was fed? In *that* lay its evil, she was certain. The temptations of the flesh lured the body but left the spirit unsatisfied and yearning. She could stand no more.

She struggled against Robert's hold, but both men ignored her silent plea.

To her right, a stocky man bent a maid forward over a bench, flung up her skirts, and stroked the full rounded globes of her bottom. With a flick of his wrist, he took his thick rod in hand and plunged into her pink fleshy folds. She cried out her pleasure.

That's what Anastasia needed. That thickness plowing her, relieving the endless ache and filling her, ending it. She was caught in temptation's claws and it showed no mercy.

She grabbed fistfuls of Sven's hair, nestled between her legs. His wet tongue covered her bud. She bucked at the swift pleasure that gripped her and that sucked her body into a swimming tunnel of bliss. He withdrew.

She gasped and sobbed, straining toward him. He licked her delicately, sliding the tip of his tongue along her lips and dipping into her center for a moment before returning to stroke her little bud with a teasing touch.

She needed it harder and tried to grind against his face. Behind her, Robert's grip tightened, holding her still. Then he slipped two fingers between her lips and back up the crease of her buttocks, coating her with her own arousal. He placed a wet finger at her bottom hole and pressed. Anastasia's eyes widened with the shock even as her blood pumped thick.

"Ach, Robert," Sven said. "If you do that, she'll crest and Maxwell will have our heads."

"Nay, just once. A small poke. She's so tight." His thick finger pushed for entrance in her bottom as Sven's tongue returned to lick and swirl. The pleasure was scandalous, the hot ache torture.

Then Sven abruptly retreated. Her body rebelled and writhed against the loss. Robert's finger probed and stretched, wriggling for entrance, stimulating her to agonizing proportions. She groaned with the delicious pleasure-pain but it wasn't enough. She looked to see her reddened petals splayed open and wanting. It seemed the crowd had drawn closer. A rough-looking man studied her growing arousal and licked his lips.

"Can we touch her, too?" he called out.

Sven gave a lecherous chuckle and licked the evidence of her arousal from his lips. "Nay." He grinned and lowered himself again. She sighed with relief, so bereft and wanting, needing his tongue to soothe the restless ache.

He pressed his lips over her taut little kernel with a teasing touch. Then he suckled her. The force of it had her reeling. She screamed, spreading herself wider. Robert's finger at her bottom pushed through her tight entrance and sunk deep.

"Oh . . ." She arched up and shivered, her whole body igniting and gathering within. Robert's fingered pumped quickly and then both pressures abruptly withdrew—the one thrusting pressure into her bottom and the other powerful suckling of her netherlips. She cried out her frustration and flailed, kicking at her tormentors, but they held her still.

"You almost did it, Robert," Sven warned him.

Robert hissed, lifting her up off his lap. "Damn that Maxwell." He turned her swiftly to kneel before him. Instinctively, she pressed her thighs together, but Sven spread them apart again from behind and held her still. The cool air only increased the painful ache.

With rough hands, Robert pushed her breasts together and then knelt up and slid his thick rod between them. "What I'd like to do," he said, his voice rough and his harsh features twisted into a grimace, "is to poke your smooth little bottom." His neck muscles strained as he thrust before he throbbed out his pleasure. Thick milky spurts sprayed out, covering her mouth and running off her chin. He touched her mouth with his fingers and smoothed his seed over her lips. Then he collapsed onto his back with a groan. "God's bones, she's a vixen."

She was stunned anew by the degradation and lit to a fevered pitch of arousal.

All around her men stroked themselves, their members jutting out, red and angry, their eyes glazed with lust.

She tried to touch her little nub of desire but an arm wrapped swiftly around her from behind and stopped her. *Duncan.*

"Be patient, little one," he whispered. He took a clean cloth and tenderly wiped her face.

"Lucky Maxwell," Sven chuckled, rising to his feet, cock in hand. "Where might I find a willing wench?" He laughed and strode toward a circle of waiting women, their eyes lit with anticipation. Anastasia gawked at his gait, made awkward by his sex standing straight out from his belly like a lance, the red knob flushed and angry.

Duncan caught Anastasia up and lifted her into his arms. "Come, fair one, and seek your relief."

Chapter Four

As Duncan carried her through the hall, one male voice after another called out lecherous sneers describing what they would like to do to her. Whereas before tonight any thoughts of what they suggested would have had her cowering, now thoughts of male members penetrating her every orifice were shamefully arousing.

The need to be filled shook her with such an intensity as to make her cry. She tried to dip her hand down to ease her sensitive flesh, but Duncan kept her arms pinned at her side as he carried her, his lustful gaze traveling over her body as he held her.

She wanted to beg him to lay her down and touch her. She ached everywhere and began to understand the dark power of pleasure to seduce a person into a life of immorality. The knowledge only increased her convictions. It was in experiencing the unspeakable pleasures of the flesh and then forsaking them for a life of sacrifice lay the test of her true spiritual strength.

As though sensing her struggle with the demons of desire, Duncan gave her a smile marred with regret. "Ian gave clear orders to save you for himself. And no one thwarts his commands." He laughed. "Not even I."

The thought of the dark count claiming her frightened Anastasia for just a moment before shivers of shameful anticipation slid up her spine.

Duncan carried her up a long winding stairwell and toward heavily carved double doors. With a push of his shoulder he swung her into a candle-lit chamber, bathed in golden light and replete with burning incense. The smell of saffron and cinnamon sweetened the air.

Braced in the room's center loomed an iron tub. Smoky steam rose from its surface and moisture dripped down its sides onto layers of the Persian carpet that surrounded it.

Count Maxwell sat submerged, his dark head resting along its wide rim, the rich luster of his hair cascading in waves over the edge. A mellow light surrounded him and glanced off the sculpted muscle that covered his chest and along the powerful lines of his arms, resting now along the tub's sides. The torturous ache between Anastasia's legs began anew.

Count Maxwell opened his eyes at the sound of their approach. In the space of a breath, his gaze transformed from one of slumbering repose to a banking blaze. His nostrils flared.

Duncan eased her down to stand before him.

But Anastasia could take no more. Fearful now that the wicked count would pleasure her to even greater heights and then simply keep her wanting and aching for more, she moved back to Duncan's side and clutched at his tunic.

Count Maxwell sat up abruptly. "Have they hurt her?"

"Nay." Duncan gave a soft chuckle and pried her fingers off him. "But she's badly in need of relief, Ian. Her pleasure has turned to pain with the wanting."

"Aye . . ." His smoldering eyes softened. "Then she is well prepared." He reached around and cupped her bottom, making her jump at the scandalous feel of his calloused fingertips sliding over her skin.

He frowned. "Give her to me," he said to Duncan, his voice rough, his eyes never leaving Anastasia.

She returned his gaze, pulled inexplicably into their glittering depths, as Duncan picked her up and lowered her into the water.

She closed her eyes and let the comforting heat of the water surround her, mindful of the weight of his gaze and fearful that if she allowed herself to gaze upon him again she would be lost.

"Shall I bathe your princess?" Duncan quipped.

Count Maxwell grumbled for him to leave and moments later Anastasia heard the door close softly behind her.

The only sound that remained was the gentle stirring of the water between them and then his deep rhythmic breathing.

The air grew heavy and still, expectant. A tiny flutter sounded above her. She blinked her eyes open to see a small russet-brown nightingale, hovering high between the rafters, perch itself on one edge. Another soon joined it, jostling it a bit, perching itself so close to the other that they looked as one.

The feathered couple peered down at them, eyes gleaming, heads cocked in question.

Anastasia felt a smile form on her lips at such curiosity.

"That's Belle and Sam," Count Maxwell said.

Anastasia avoided looking at him, but she could hear the smile in his voice.

"They're lovers."

Anastasia's breath caught.

"Faithful lovers," he continued. "They'll have no others."

Anastasia wasn't sure if he was jesting or merely stating observation as she watched the small creatures snuggle together.

"Humans would do well to learn from such loyalty."

Anastasia looked at him closely. 'Tis true that as a novice Christ was her lover and she should take no others. Was he suggesting she had betrayed her sacred vows? She studied him, searching his expression for signs of censor, but all she saw was a trace of amusement laced with a tenderness that took her by surprise.

Her gaze soon strayed to the strong line of his jaw and then settled on lips that were full and soft against the dark scrape of his beard. His jaw flexed in response and then his eyes filled with undisguised desire that caused heat to stir once again in her belly.

"Come here," he said, reaching for her hand, his voice whisper soft, "'tis time."

She placed her hand in his, letting him draw her near.

His eyes moved over her face. "I will pleasure you," he said, cradling her face. He ran his thumb along her cheek, idly tracing the delicate bone under her eye. His eyes grew heavy lidded and the dark irises smoldered. "I will pleasure you with my lips and my tongue and, when you are ready, with my cock." Her pulse jumped at the thought of his cock breaching her, torn between the fear of such violation and the need for her restless body to be filled. Yet, she believed instinctively that he would not hurt her.

In an unhurried manner he locked his hands around her waist and drew her close, allowing his large body to surround her, his face so close his breath brushed her skin. He smelled of delicious male warmth.

He kissed her. Full on the mouth. A soft chaste kiss, so at odds with the sexual intent of his gaze.

He reached beside the tub and picked up a clear cup filled with ruby liquid. A glass cup, cut glass that shimmered with light. Spoils from the infidels. Her mind rebelled while her senses drunk in the subtle tangy scent.

He lifted the glass to her lips. "Drink, my sweet."

The tart taste turned pleasing on her tongue and then heated her throat as it glided smoothly down to settle in her belly, turning her body to liquid. When she drank more than half, he placed the glass on the stand beside him.

"'Tis enough," he murmured. "I want you at ease but conscious." He smiled against her lips and then licked off excess drops with the tip of his tongue, the touch so intimate she became lost in the feel of it. In a movement so smooth she hardly noticed, he slipped his tongue into her mouth and played with her.

Her breath caught at the sensual feel of his tongue, warm and smooth, tangling with hers.

Her sex throbbed.

He growled and sucked gently on her tongue then stopped and returned to teasing her, gliding his tongue along her lips with the lightest touch and then probing gently between her lips, making her chase his tongue for another delicious taste of him. She grabbed onto his shoulders and whimpered her frustration. Then he plunged deep again, stroking relentlessly along her tongue and inside the recesses of her mouth until he broke away.

He muttered a curse. "I'll not let a virgin lead me by the nose." He set her from him. "Stand before me."

Not understanding, she rose on shaky legs until the water stopped at her thighs. Sudsing his hands with lavender soap, he then skimmed his palms down her belly and between her legs.

"Open for me," he commanded, his voice hoarse as though he waged a battle with himself.

Anastasia knew about battles of the spirit but could not imagine against what this dark count fought.

"Open for me," he repeated with impatience.

When she opened her thighs wider, he closed his eyes on a sigh. And then he fondled her, petting her plump petals with slippery fingers and pushing a thick finger into her tight center. The pleasure was shocking. She opened wider, clutching his wrists and reaching for more as he cleaned her sex lips.

He soaped every part of her, teasing and probing as he did, pinching her nipples into tight little buds and slipping a soapy finger into her bottom as he cleaned her. She pushed herself into his hand each time with a restless whimper, begging for more.

Warm water splashed and rinsed her and then with a harsh groan his lips were everywhere, with a touch so tender she wanted to scream. He lovingly skimmed along her shoulders and the underswell of her breasts, his tongue caressing the taut skin that covered her hips and teasing the sensitive skin of her inner thighs.

He sighed, his breathing labored. "You are delectable." With gentle fingers, he spread her sex lips wide and touched her pearl with just the tip of his tongue. He groaned deep in his throat. And then it was too much. He suckled her, licking greedily until her knees weakened and she collapsed onto his lap.

He pressed his forehead to hers and drew in deep drafts of air as though he struggled for control.

"*I* am master in this sensual dance," he breathed against her lips. "Do you understand?"

She shook head.

He closed his eyes and sighed. "Of course you don't." He turned her effortlessly to straddle his hips. "'Tis past time," he murmured, the thick rod of his sex pressed against her splayed lips. She instinctively reached to grab him and shocked herself at the thick feel of it.

She looked down to the water's surface, wanting to see him.

He must have sensed her wish, for he responded by covering her hand and drawing it down his length. "'Tis best you don't see me," he said, allowing her nonetheless to measure his size with her hand. The tip peeked just above the water's surface, a pearly drop glistening on the purpled skin. The potent feel of him made her suddenly anxious that he would split her apart.

She pushed against his chest and shook her head.

But he would not permit it. He circled her waist with his hands. "The pain will be fleeting," he murmured, his eyes heavy-lidded and his voice low and soothing. "The pleasure much greater."

He lifted her easily and placed the large knob of his sex at her entrance and pushed steadily, sinking her down slowly, the feel of him stretching her frightening and wonderful. Until he met her virgin barrier.

A burn seared through her before he lifted her again. But she longed for him to fill her. When she grabbed onto his shoulders and bore down, he let her until she felt the tearing and stopped. She clutched at him and wriggled on his lap, crying out her impatience.

What was this torture? she quietly sobbed.

He gave a small smile. "Shall I fuck you?" he asked, forcing her chin up.

She blanched at his words even as they aroused her, and then to her horror she felt her very soul responding to the possessive way his eyes held hers.

Against her own will, she nodded, her eyes pleading with him to claim her.

Something primal flared between them. He anchored his hands on her hips and with a grunt brought her down swiftly, tearing through her in one sharp thrust, the pain it caused blinding.

The shock of it had her punching him and trying to lift herself off, but he impaled her deeper, even as she shook her head violently and cried.

"Shhh, be still." He gathered her against his chest, filling her completely, the pressure so shocking it caused her to tremble uncontrollably in his arms. He simply held her close and murmured nonsensical words that nonetheless soothed her.

Above them the little nightingales sweetly sung.

Soon the gentle lap of warm water against their entwined bodies was the only other sound. That, and the thumping of her heart.

"Shhh . . ." He stroked down her back and then along her bottom, the feel of his hard body and strong hands somehow protective and calming on her taut skin. The pressure soon became a pleasurable ache. He ran his lips along her forehead and then began to move, in shallow thrusts, rhythmic and gentle.

Oh . . . The feel of him sliding up inside her was heaven. She wanted more of it. She squirmed and writhed on his lap. He groaned and clutched her hips, raising her a little higher and thrusting deeper until he drew her down onto him completely, fully impaling her, only to withdraw and repeat the motion with a stronger thrust.

He grunted and plunged faster. The pleasure was unbearable. She gasped and met his thrusts with a force of her own.

He shuddered. "You like this, little minx."

His words fueled her desire but the shocking thought of what she was doing made her fill with erotic shame. She was as eager as him.

He slid his hand down over her belly and then between her legs, pressing his thumb over her bud.

Oh, my God. She looked into eyes hot with passion as he cradled the nub between his thumb and forefinger and rubbed it into a tight knot.

He pressed full lips to hers, licking the corners of her mouth with a gentle touch. "So succulent," he murmured.

With his ceaseless stroking her body ignited, gathering into itself, the pleasure so exquisite she drowned in it. Every inch of her skin was on fire. He stroked her bud harder as his cock stroked her center and then he slipped a finger into her bottom. He groaned and plunged his tongue past her lips, claiming her and thrusting high and fast.

She exploded then, in hot quick bursts of exquisite pleasure that raced through her body, radiating from her center to her toes and pleasing every fiber of her body. She cried out her release as waves of sensation shook her, melting her bones into blissful pools of delight that left her trembling.

She clutched him fiercely, sobbing against the strong wall of his chest.

Beneath her he tightened and swelled within her, his cock pressed deep against her womb, his body stiff and vibrating beneath her. With a growl of surrender, he gave a powerful thrust and pumped inside her, his seed splashing warm against her womb. The groan that strangled his throat frightened her.

And then he collapsed, sliding deeper into the water.

He gathered her into the strong fortress of his arms, his heart pounding wildly against her breasts.

The sight of this potent man collapsed in her arms stunned her. With the comforting feel of his lips pressing against her hair, she settled herself into his warmth and softened against him, wanting to somehow melt her body into his and become one. The thought terrified her as much as she craved it. The intimate connection of his body to hers seemed suddenly so much more than a physical joining. Her heart constricted at the thought of separation from him.

The room grew still. The fragrance of the sweet herbs returned to her heightened senses and mixed with his rich male smell. She licked the salty taste from his skin, the male sweat turning sweet on her tongue. The heat from their bodies and the water cocooning them melted them together, convincing her for just a moment that they *were* one. His palms still covered her buttocks, his finger deeply impaled and his cock still buried to the hilt.

When he let out a deep sigh, she wrapped her arms around him and snuggled closer.

Sometime later he stood, lifting her gently into his arms, and carrying her out of the tub.

He wrapped her in cool linen and dried her with care, running his lips along her warmed skin as he did. Then he tucked her into his bed and spooned her naked body with his. His body hair stirred her sensitive flesh everywhere they touched.

She must have slept for when next she awoke she was still beside him in his bed, her hair still wet and fanned across his damp chest. Her fingers tangled in the coarse dark hair sprinkled over muscles that were hard and unyielding beneath her palms.

When she raised her head, his arm tightened around her and slid down to her buttocks. But he was asleep. His thick wet lashes made little crescent shapes along chiseled cheekbones. His lips were soft and relaxed. Only his dark stubble looked menacing.

Of its own accord her hand drifted down his belly, under the soft linen coverlet. There she found the object of her fascination. He was thick even in repose and long, and so smooth and silky. She lifted the linen just a bit, and then couldn't resist pushing the cloth out of the way so she could see him.

He was dark everywhere. From the inky black hair that covered his groin to the heavy sack that rested between his thighs. She touched him tentatively, cradling his pouch in her small palm.

A groan issued from his lips and then to her astonishment, he began to grow. Her eyes widened. As though it had a life of its own, his sex came alive.

She wanted to taste him.

With gentle licks she slid her tongue along the dark purpled vein that ran down his thick length. Beneath her tongue he pulsed and thickened, the smooth skin turning hot on her lips. He stirred along the sheets and then she felt strong fingers sift through her hair.

A soft low chuckle rumbled from his lips. "God's bones, I must be in heaven."

At his words, she stiffened and then sat up abruptly, suddenly ashamed of her desires and not understanding how she had come to this. She wanted to flee.

His face darkened with concern. With the lightest touch he slid his fingertips along her jaw. "What troubles you? I meant not to upset."

How, she wondered, could such a wicked sorcerer show such tenderness?

Mesmerized by his haunting gaze, she allowed him to draw her down beside him. He stroked her face as he studied her. "So young to carry such burdens." He brushed her lips with his. "Give them to me," he murmured. "For this mission you have come to complete, let me help you."

She could only nod and watch him spread her out underneath him.

It was true what he said. She had come to experience carnal pleasure so her sacrifice would be sincere. She had to leave knowledgeable of what she offered.

"I shall show you how to pleasure yourself," he said, his voice low.

She let out a tiny gasp of confusion.

A small smile reached his eyes and, before she could stop him, he guided her hand between her own legs. She could feel her wetness and tried to look away from his probing eyes, but he wouldn't let her.

"Look at me," he commanded.

He skimmed his hand down her belly and along her thighs, spreading her legs as he went, her shame increasing when he bent her knees. The candles burning brightly hid nothing from him, but he moved as though what he was doing was as natural as breathing. She could feel her cheeks burning as he guided her fingers along her sex, drawing a small moan from her. When he dipped his finger and then two into her wet heat she groaned aloud. She was open and wet and couldn't help from shuddering around his fingers.

"Have you never touched yourself?"

She shook her head no.

"Of course you haven't. 'Tis time you did. I shall teach you to relieve the ache."

She snatched her hand back but he circled her wrist and drew her hand back to press her fingers along lips already swollen with desire. He separated her with his fingers.

"Your lips are dewy and red. The fragile pearl at the apex of your sex stands proud." She throbbed delicately under his licentious gaze and felt a new rush of moisture glisten along her lips. She could feel the tiny nub that caused such aching night after night swell.

When he thrust gently with two fingers up into her slippery heat she bit back a moan. Then he reached beside him for what looked like precious bath oil and anointed his thumb. When he smoothed it along her nub she arched off the bed with the sudden pleasure and groaned. While his fingers thrust, his thumb massaged.

"You can do this yourself." He pressed harder with his thumb and she stiffened further, spreading herself wide and arching her hips to him.

He was hard and throbbing, so powerful, as he knelt up between her legs. She wanted him.

She reached for him, beckoning with her eyes, but he grabbed the bottle of heated oil and dripped warm liquid along her mons. The warm contact along her sensitive skin made her moan and writhe, causing her breath to come in little bursts. He took her hand and spread her fingers along her sex. "Touch yourself."

She shook her head but the pleasure was fast overtaking her.

He teased her lightly with his fingertips, soft fleeting touches, gently probing in a way that was more torture than pleasure, only now Anastasia knew why. This unbearable ache with which she suffered could be soothed by him. She gripped his wrist and tried to make him press harder but he was too strong for her. Instead he snatched up her other hand and forced her fingers up between her sex lips. She closed her eyes and moaned, bucking against her own hand. He circled her sensitive bud while she continued to thrust with her own fingers, her sense of shame lost in the pleasure she so desperately sought.

He sat back on his heels, his eyes glittering, and watched her play shamefully with her own sex. She parted the plush lips gently with her fingertips and stroked along the stem of her pleasure, shuddering with the strokes, unable to stop herself, and reaching for the release she craved.

She pleaded with her eyes for him to help her. He licked his lips and wet his finger. Then she watched as he trailed his finger down the thick vein that ran the length of his arousal. She reached for him but he held her from him and placed her hand over her breast. "Play with yourself," he murmured, pinching one rosy nipple, pulling it gently and then plucking it harder. Her body shook with each hard pinch, but she couldn't take her eyes off him. She was desperate for release now. She wanted him in her and almost broke her vow of silence in protest when he pulled away from her.

Instead he dipped his finger into her again and ran her liquid around the sensitive head of his cock. A pearly drop of arousal oozed from him. She let out a low groan and touched herself, soon giving over to the unbearable pleasure. She sobbed aloud and watched his eyes brighten as she convulsed before him, her sex throbbing shamelessly and her nipples swelling to ripe hard peaks, her disgrace complete. She collapsed upon the coverlet and looked away from his penetrating gaze.

"Nay," he murmured, lowering himself between her legs. "You are beautiful." He cradled her face between his hands and then nudged her thighs apart. He entered her with exquisite gentleness. "I'll move slowly lest I hurt you," he groaned against her lips. " 'Tis too soon to take a virgin again but I can't help myself. I desire you above anything I have known." He pressed himself deep and rested against her womb, his breathing labored. He stilled, running his lips along her brow and then dropping small kisses along her eyelids. With a low guttural groan he throbbed out his pleasure and held her close. The warm liquid of his seed wept from where they joined.

For one mystical moment she felt they had transcended this mortal world.

"Perhaps I shall keep you," he murmured.

She smiled against his neck until the weight of his words broke through her blissful tranquility. She drew a cautious space back and searched his eyes, willing to see into the very depths of his soul. His gaze was warm and liquid, his lashes shimmering with moisture. He caught up a wet lock of her hair, lifting it off her neck, and then drew his fingers along the delicate line of her jaw, his gaze locked with hers.

The sharp angles of his face had relaxed and the candles threw a golden glow over the sweat that clung to the dark shadow of his beard. She wanted to scrape her palm against the rough feel of it.

He was beautiful.

And wicked. A bastard son and a warlord whose coffers overflowed with the spoils of the infidels and who ravished women in keeping with what he had learned in the Sultan's harem.

She prayed for deliverance.

He was the Lord of Pleasure. And she was no different than the hundreds of lovers who came before. An inexperienced young novice of no consequence.

"I shall make you my chatelaine," he said on a quiet sigh. He trailed a finger down her throat. "I will dress you in silk and jewels. Give you your heart's desire."

A clawing panic gripped her. And in return he would expect her to be his pleasure slave like so many others?

Too soon what she had done crashed down upon her. He had spilled his seed deep within her. He intended to keep her as his concubine.

And she? She had almost offered up her soul for his wicked pleasures. She had almost convinced herself they were as one.

She closed her heart and mind against the strong feel of him inside her and focused all thought on the Blessed Mother, her solace in despair, her rescuer in times of trouble. He slipped out of her and drew the coverlet up over their naked bodies. She murmured prayerful entreaties under her breath when he pulled her close and settled his lips in her hair. After a time she felt him blessedly drift off to sleep.

❊ꙮ❊

Slivers of dawn light poked through the shutters of Ian's chambers. He turned away from it and towards her delicious smell, eager to feel her warmth and caress her softness. But when he reached out to mold her to his side, his hand met with cool linen bedding.

He opened his eyes to see her gone. *Little chit*, to rise before he did.

He sat up.

A quick scan of his chambers told him that while her scent might linger, she did not. He tossed off the covers. Without clothes, she would hardly wander about the castle. Where was she?

He opened his door wide, still naked, and called for Bjorn, the night guard. When he got no answer, he started down the hall. He found the guard on the top step to the tower stairs, sleeping soundly against the wall.

Ian kicked at his foot. Bjorn sat up abruptly and then stood.

"Where is she?"

"Milord?"

"The girl," Ian repeated. "Where is she?"

Bjorn blinked. "I . . ." He glanced about.

Disgusted, Ian bounded down the hall to Duncan's room and pushed open the door.

Duncan was sprawled out naked on his bed, hands propped behind his head, a tumble of tousled red hair blanketing his groin. The body of the fleshy wench that belonged to it lay hidden beneath the covers.

"Duncan," Ian called to him. "Where is she?"

The buxom redhead who'd been warming Duncan's bed of late sat up abruptly, letting the covers draping her fall to her waist. Her large breasts swayed with the motion. She made no move to cover herself and her eyes dropped to Ian's cock. While years ago Ian would have welcomed a threesome, of late he'd grown even too bored for that.

Duncan gave a laugh. "God's teeth, Ian. Where is whom?"

"The girl." Ian grumbled.

"Which one. There are too many—"

"The novice from last night. With the blue eyes."

Duncan raised a brow. "She's not *here*, I can tell you that."

Duncan's bedmate gave Ian a small smile and beckoned him. Ian sighed on a muttered curse and closed the door.

A search of the kitchen and courtyard garden proved fruitless. When finally he questioned the sentries at the gatehouse, he learned that his virgin novice had left soon after he bedded her. The implication irked him. He thought he'd been gentle—as gentle as possible short of failing to breach her—and he knew she was pleasured. The way she came apart in his arms attested to such. Nevertheless, she chose to flee to a sterile passionless life of seclusion.

So be it. He was none the worse for it. There was no reason for him to go after her.

Just three days hence, Ian found himself pounding at the door of the abbey.

"Open up!" he growled just as Anne opened the shutter and scowled through the iron grate. She huffed out a breath and slammed the shutter.

Bolts slipped through iron studs and then the door opened a crack. "Ian Maxwell. Have you come to break down my door?"

"Anne." He nodded. "Am I not welcome here?"

The older woman gave him an amused frown. "Of course you are welcome. Though I'm surprised you wish to tread such hallowed ground."

Ian gave a snort.

"Come in." Anne swung the door wide. "Follow me."

After she escorted him into a small room, she whispered softly to someone in the hall. Minutes later, while Ian stared at the crucifix that dominated one wall, a small bird of a girl ushered in a tray of hot cider and sweet bread. She placed it on the scarred trestle table that took up the room's center. Anne indicated the plain wooden chair for him to sit. In all the years he had known Anne, Ian had not once set foot in the abbey.

Anne sat in the only other chair and took a sip of her drink before settling her speculative gaze on him. "What ails you?"

Ian looked at her bluntly. "I have come for a girl." He rested his hands on his lap.

Anne choked delicately and then reached into her voluminous robes, pulling out a linen cloth. She dabbed it to her lips. "While that does not surprise me, surely you know you have come to the wrong place."

Ian gave her a sour look, impatient to get to the matter at hand. "There is a girl here. She needs to come with me."

Anne raised a brow. "Which girl?"

Ian shifted uncomfortably. "I don't know her name. She would not tell me. No doubt she invoked that vow of silence along with all the damnable others."

"You'll not refer to sacred vows in that accursed language of yours." Anne wagged her finger at him.

"Fine, I will not. Now I need the girl."

Anne's gaze deepened. "How do you know of this girl?"

Ian avoided her gaze.

"She has lain with you?" Anne asked, making no attempt to hide her agitation.

"It makes no difference what has passed. I have come for her."

"And what of her?"

"What of her?" he stood abruptly, suddenly restless under her probing gaze. He would not allow her to make him feel like the street urchin he had been when she had rescued him so many years ago in the city outside de Ville.

Anne stood, too, flapping the long white bib that draped her and giving it a snap before tucking both hands behind it. "Does the girl have no say?"

Ian grumbled and began to pace.

"You come here demanding that I turn over one of my novices to you and expect me to obey?" She stiffened her back, drawing up her tall frame another inch. "Have not you and your men snatched up enough of my girls?"

Ian stopped pacing. "You know as well as I that most are here at the bequest of their parents, lords and ladies too idle to care for their own and rich enough to allow the church—".

"The money parents pay bears not on what I am—"

Ian sighed. "I meant no insult. I meant only that few girls see the church as their true vocation. Make no mistake about who is seeking out whom. *They* come to *us* and are free to leave."

"After you ravish them. You could turn them away at the outset."

Ian muttered a curse. "That's not bloody likely to happen."

"Indeed it has not." Anne snorted and then turned her back on him and walked over to the single window set high into the thick stone wall. The silence that followed was enough to choke him.

He appealed to the sense of fairness he had always admired in her. "I have never come to you and demanded thus, demanded anything," he said, his voice hoarse.

She lifted a shoulder.

"Just let me talk to her."

"You don't even know her name," she said over her shoulder.

"She is golden-haired and no more than eighteen, with eyes the color of a summer sky, skin pale as cream with no marks but for a tiny mole"—he pointed to a spot just below his earlobe—"right here."

Anne turned slowly and looked to where he indicated, her gaze weary. "I will speak with her. But it is the girl's decision. Come back in a fortnight."

"A fortnight!"

"*You* may rule that den of iniquity high up on your mountain, but I rule here."

Ian was not about to argue, for while he knew her to be fair and compassionate, she was also one of the most stubborn people he had ever known.

"Very well." He turned to exit the room but not before he gave a parting remark. "A fortnight and not a moment more."

She failed to answer.

"Not a moment more, Anne."

With her expression troubled and her lips forming into a tight thin line, she nodded her assent.

It was all Ian needed. For now.

But a fortnight later he found himself once again in the sparsely furnished room, glaring now at the wooden crucifix that mocked him while Anne explained why he could not talk to the girl. She would not even deign to tell him her name.

"Did you not tell her it was I who had come?"

"She wishes to be left to her prayer and service. She's expressed no wish for contact with the outside world. You are no exception, Ian. At least that is what I understand."

"She said that?"

"Your name did not come up though she's had ample opportunity to talk to me about what troubles her?"

"She is troubled?"

Anne let out an exasperated breath. "Not troubled precisely. Just not the same girl of little more than a fortnight ago. And it is little wonder."

" 'Tis why I need to speak to her."

" 'Tis maybe why I *shouldn't* let you speak to her.

Worse than Anne's dismissal of him was the empathy in her tone, as though she could read his soul, sense his bone deep need for the angelic nymph who had mesmerized him. From the first moment he glimpsed the girl he recognized her erotic potential and was seized with the need to explore it. The need haunted him despite his struggle to denounce it. He feared he would find no peace until the desperate need was put to rest.

But the need was purely sexual. Anne would not have empathized so readily if she knew that, and Ian was not about to tell her that whatever lofty ideal she might imagine was unfounded.

He repeated his request. "Let me speak to her."

"Do you love this girl?"

"Love?" Ian balked. "I have the barest knowledge of her."

"Precisely, and as such have no right to interfere in her intimate, private struggles."

"Struggles?" Ian said as a question.

Anne stiffened, her back ramrod straight. "Are you so jaded that you do not see matters of the heart? Have you no knowledge with what the spirit struggles? For all your desperation to see the girl, you have gleaned nothing from your need?"

Ian rebelled against her notion of desperation. He felt a powerful need to see the girl, it was true, but he was not desperate.

But he *was* fast becoming impatient.

"I've asked little of you, Anne, since you rescued me as a boy and I have repaid you a thousand fold in return. I'll not be so generous this winter when your crops are low if you thwart me in this."

Anne gave him a tired look. "Even I know you are not that jaded."

"I am. And I will help you no more. And I can't guarantee the safety of the girls that come to me from this point on if we can't reach an understanding on this matter."

Anne waved him off. "I know you too well, Ian. Take your idle threats elsewhere."

He slapped his hands onto the table. "God's teeth. I *will* see her."

"How?" She whirled on him. "Will you turn the abbey upside down?"

"If need be."

"And do what? Force her hand? How?" She turned her back on him, but spoke to him over her shoulder. "You should examine your soul for why you want this girl and then, if your motives are pure, seek to make yourself worthy. You cannot thwart God's will."

Ian boiled with anger. He didn't plan to marry the girl, he just . . . needed her. Why was Anne making a simple request to speak to her so difficult? He was getting nowhere with his threats but he would not give up. "I will do so, if you'll speak with her. Give her a chance to see me."

Her shoulders lifted and then fell in a long-suffering sigh. The silence that followed was suffocating. Finally she spoke. "One month."

Ian stifled a growl of protest. Of late, mere days had felt like months. A month would feel like a year. But what choice did he have? He muttered a string of curses.

"Your vile language—"

"Very well," Ian grumbled. "I'll wash my mouth *and* wait once again, this time for one month," he agreed.

Anne's gaze softened. "I know what is best in this matter, Ian. You have to trust me."

Ian gave a curt nod of farewell, neither agreeing nor arguing. He had always trusted Anne, but he knew not how long his patience could last.

❧❁❀❁❧

Mother Anne dabbed a cool cloth along Anastasia's forehead and once again held the cup to her lips and urged her to rinse her mouth. The tray of breakfast beside her narrow bed went untouched.

Anastasia had not been able to keep down any food for a month, her breasts were sore, and her bleeding had not come. No amount of prayer and penance had changed what Anastasia now had to face. She knew the Abbess Mother was waiting for Anastasia to unburden herself, but Anastasia was too ashamed.

"Anastasia," Mother Anne said, smoothing a tangled hair from off Anastasia forehead, "you are with child."

Anastasia burst into tears and covered her face with her hands but Mother Anne wouldn't allow her to turn away from her. She gently circled Anastasia's wrists and pulled her hands down. "Did the man who did this to you hurt you?"

Anastasia's eyes widened. "No." She shook her head. "He did not hurt me. It was I who hurt myself. 'Twas all *my* fault and now I am being punished."

"Hush, child. A babe is never a punishment, but a gift from God."

"Nay, Mother, I am being punished for my sins."

"You must tell the man who has—"

"No!" Anastasia sat up abruptly.

"Are you afraid of him?"

Anastasia nodded but then quickly amended it. "I'm not afraid of him, exactly, but I am fearful of seeing him. I can't see him again. And he would not want this babe."

"You don't know that—"

"I do, Mother, believe me. He's not the sort of man who would welcome such knowledge." Anastasia thought of the dark count, of the sinful practices he surrounded himself with. The life he led. While he may want her for his own carnal needs, a child could never live within his castle. He would send it away.

Anastasia vowed to herself at that moment that he could never know. No one would take her child from her.

"He has a right to know."

Anastasia looked at the Abbess Mother in horror. "You can't mean to make me go to him. Please, Mother, you don't understand."

The Abbess Mother looked at her sadly. "You need to search your heart, my child. Ask the Lord what is right. Trust in Him and believe that He will guide you, even if you don't fully understand what is being asked of you." She drew the woolen blanket up to Anastasia's chin. "Sleep now. Rest. And in your prayers ask for God's help. Believe that you will receive it."

Chapter Five

Two Years Later

"Are you sure I can't come with you?" Duncan asked.

"Nay," Ian answered. "I need you here at Hawkwood. The journey to my manor at de Ville will take weeks, and I've no way of knowing how long it will take me to free my poor Uncle John from the clutches of the young woman who has captured him."

"You mean the young woman who has cared for him so well in his illness and whom your uncle has spoken nothing but accolades this entire year?" Duncan chuckled. "She is a healer under Margaret's tutorage, the Abbess' old mentor. Surely the young woman is not so cunning as you think. Your uncle's letter spoke of true caring and companionship."

Ian waved a dismissive hand as he gathered up a stack of papers from off his desk. "Uncle John is sick and elderly and thought to be rich since I've left him as chief bailiff with no plans to return. We will see how long the *companionship* lasts once the little tart learns he is not the inheritor of my mill and quarry."

"Ah, such a cynic when it comes to love."

"No more than you."

Ian finished stuffing the last of his papers into a satchel. "Is Darius ready?"

"Aye, my lord." Duncan bowed and waved a hand toward the door. "The stable boy awaits your leave."

Ian raised a mocking brow. "Sure you don't want me to find *you* a wife on my journey? A young widow perhaps? To give you a son?"

Duncan frowned. "Find *yourself* one if you're so eager to have a wedding. I'll continue on here as I have and more the happier for it."

Ian knew that to be only half true. Duncan had garnered more than his share of female attention during his years at Hawkwood. But Ian also remembered a younger Duncan, upon both their return from the battlefields of the Crusades, and his happiness to be reunited with his young wife. It had been torture for Duncan to resist the charms of the Sultan's harem while they were captives but, unlike Ian who had indulged his every desire, Duncan had deprived himself. Duncan had since made up for that deprivation many times over throughout his years at Hawkwood.

It had been only one year after their return that Duncan had joined Ian here, vowing never to return to de Ville. His wife had betrayed him and was carrying another man's child.

Ian remembered well the day Duncan arrived. Ian himself had retreated to Hawkwood just months before, disgusted by his own treatment of the de Ville women who served him, regardless of their willingness. He had behaved as though de Ville was his own private harem. Even the men in their loyalty seemed to accept his right to do so. Ian could no longer allow himself to taint the very people he was sworn to protect.

He had fled to the abandoned castle and made his home and had welcomed Duncan's help. And then the help of the most tortured or cast out souls who had landed at his castle gates.

But that was a long time ago, and Duncan was through healing. Ian couldn't help thinking that he deserved more.

He looked at his friend. "You could do worse than father an heir?" Ian shrugged. "We both could."

In a rare moment of candor, Duncan eyed him. "True enough." Then he glanced away and spoke softly. "Mayhap we are too wicked? Good men would not adapt so many of the rituals from the East and call it enlightenment."

Ian lifted a brow. "Better that we bathe once a month and use animal fat for soap in favor of daily baths with olive oil soaps and the sweet herbs of the Persians?"

"All spoils of the infidels."

Ian simply shrugged.

"Will you be searching for her along the way?"

Ian hesitated a moment in lacing his satchel, but he did not look up at Duncan. It was unnecessary for Ian to ask to whom Duncan referred.

Ian had been furious when he continued to return to the abbey month after month, trusting Anne when she pleaded with him to be patient, only later to find that the girl wasn't there. At some point Anne had sent her away without telling Ian, claiming that time was necessary for God's will to be made manifest. Ian vowed never to forgive Anne for her deception.

When Ian glanced up, Duncan was looking at him expectantly, but Ian needn't answer. Duncan knew that Ian would be scouring the countryside for her as he journeyed and would continue to look for her until he took his last breath. The need for her still burned deeply within him.

A loud thump had Ian and Duncan turning to see Damascus bounding toward them. The hound jumped up and flattened his large paws on Ian's chest and lapped underneath his chin.

Duncan chuckled. "He was to be kept in the kitchen, busy with the backbone of a boar, while you slipped away."

Jamie came lumbering after him, wiping his hands on the large white apron draping him. "The devil's gotten into this one. 'Tis as though he knows you are leaving."

Ian scratched down the sides of Damascus' neck. The hound whimpered deep in his throat and then let out a yowl.

"I'd take you with me, but the journey's too long," Ian said. "You stay with Duncan and look after things."

Damascus licked Ian's face with long wet swipes and then dropped down and barked. When Jamie hooked his fingers around his collar and led him out with promises of a walk along the cliffs, the hound eagerly followed.

Minutes later Ian mounted his charger with his battle hauberk beneath his cloak and his broadsword strapped to his side. The silver-hilted blade he was never without lay hidden in his ox-hide boots. While the region was enjoying an uncommon respite from baron robbers, tribal rivalry simmered beneath its surface. And then there was the occasional renegade knight. A wise warlord stood ready with a well-aimed thrust of a blade.

Chapter Six

Anastasia hurried along the hard packed mud of upper gate street that led through the center of town, waving to the mason and then the shoemaker as they worked in their stalls, and greeting other familiar faces she passed along the way.

In the two years since she had come to de Ville at the urging of Mother Anne, she had treated almost everyone in the village at some time. Under Margaret's patient tutelage, she lovingly mixed herbs and ointments and strived to receive her patients as one would Christ Himself. Before the Abbess had sent her off to de Ville, she had counseled Anastasia to administer to both the body and the soul, and Margaret had seen that she did.

As she raced along, she smiled whenever she saw the cherub faces of the babies she had delivered. Those were her fondest duties and more than made up for those times when the skeleton of death refused to abandon his claim.

A gentle spring breeze picked up her woolen skirts and wafted the air with the smell of marjoram and feverfew, letting her know she was nearing the manor house.

Before the infamous Lord de Ville had abandoned his vast holdings to the care of his uncle, he had developed and maintained a large herbal garden filled with spices from the Near East. Though her mother and father had been lord and lady of a once thriving keep, until her time here Anastasia had never tasted the spices of cumin and ginger that grew so abundant in this garden.

But the garden had fallen into disrepair before she claimed and lovingly revived it. Many times she had discovered small treasures while tending the foliage. A large gold disk was imbedded in the garden's center. When she cleaned and polished it, she discovered etchings of fish and rings and other curious symbols running along straight lines surrounding its perimeter, the lines resembling those of a measurement tool. In one corner, placed in the center of the lungwort, stood a magnificently carved enamel vase scripted with fine lines running in patterns that almost resembled letters.

John had warned her to leave anything she found. She could restore and clear the gardens but not remove anything. Everything was to stay where it was. She knew that her intended husband harbored the hope that some day his nephew would return.

When the mud street turned to crushed stone she stopped, hesitating to go further. The fragrant garden lay before her, completely gracing the front of the lime-whitened keep. She looked up into the fine lattice windows on the second floor just above the great hall, adorning what she knew to be the private solar of John's nephew. John had refused to use it while his nephew was gone but made sure that it was kept clean and ready should he return.

Behind the polished horn panes she knew they deliberated her future.

Word had reached her that Lord de Ville had not been happy when he had received his uncle's missive informing him that he wished to marry, though Anastasia could not imagine why. She had cared for John throughout his illness and as such they had developed a fondness for each other, a friendship. One night when he questioned why she had never married, she explained to him that she had been a novice but was now in de Ville to search her soul for what God willed for her. She didn't share that the true reason she had agreed to come to de Ville was that she felt unworthy to stay since she'd been unfaithful to her vows. And she feared the Abbess deemed her unworthy as well. She had pretended to believe Abbess Anne when the Mother told her she needed time to heal herself and learn God's will, away from the abbey. The holy mother would not return Anastasia to her home either. Abbess Anne was convinced de Ville was where God willed her to be.

It wasn't long before Anastasia knew she could not return to the abbey with such a blemished soul. She felt that perhaps this is what God willed for her—to stay on as a healer in this small village. Margaret was ill and would soon be unable to carry on. Abbess Anne had given Anastasia her blessing and then John offered her marriage. While he was no longer a young man, with proper care, Anastasia knew that he might have some years ahead to live. He offered her a home and companionship and he needed her in the last days of his life. She vowed to do her duty to the people of de Ville and to make John a good wife.

With that calming thought, she hurried through the doors of the manor house and up the winding stairs, greeting Hannah, the maid, before she headed through the wide double doors of the solar to which she had been summoned.

John stood before the hearth next to a dark imposing figure of a man, dressed in fawn colored hose that hugged powerful thighs. He was turned toward John, dwarfing him as they spoke, his one arm draped along the mantle and fisting a shimmering glass. His other hand made an impatient swipe through his hair, pulling the long thick mane from off his face.

Her breath caught. Images flooded her. *Lord have mercy!* It couldn't be him.

She stopped in the middle of the solar, unable to move another step.

John came forward to greet her. "Anastasia."

She stared past him and watched as the man who had, in one unforgettable night, changed her life forever, turned slowly toward her.

He was as dark and forbidding as she remembered him. And more handsome than ever.

She held her breath and for one hopeful moment believed he wouldn't remember her. Surely the Lord of Pleasure could scarcely account for every girl he took to his bed, nor would he have noticed that she had fled his bed while he slept on that night. Before the linen where she lay had cooled, she was sure another had taken her place.

But her hope was soon dashed as the drink he brought to his lips stopped midair when their eyes met. Sinfully dark eyes, eyes she remembered so well, moved over her face.

She swallowed a gasp.

His jaw tightened. He slowly set his goblet down. After a moment's hesitation, he started toward her with slow, deliberate steps.

She stared open-mouthed, watching him, unable to breathe as the air surrounding her grew heavy and still. His own gaze never left her face.

John turned to her and cupped her elbow with a tentative touch. "Anastasia? Are you well?"

Count Maxwell stopped before her. In a movement so subtle it was barely perceptible, he raised his hand as if to touch her before he stopped himself. "Anastasia," he murmured, his eyes burning through her. "Your name is Anastasia."

The rough velvet sound of his voice and his distinctive scent wrapped around her and brought her swiftly back to that sinful night. She stifled a small cry and nodded in numb silence.

"Surely, I've told you her name, Ian. This is Anastasia Bedovier," John said, moving closer to her side. He took both her hands in his while she continued to stare. Count Maxwell's eyes dropped to their entwined hands. His nostrils flared.

"Let me speak with her alone, Uncle."

"Alone, Ian?"

"Aye." He ran a hand down his face and gave a quiet sigh. His eyes softened as he turned to his uncle. "Forgive me, but I ask for just a moment. I'd like to speak with her privately."

"Well, I . . ." John turned her to face him. "Is that all right, my dear?" he asked, his eyes clouded with concern.

She squeezed his hands and managed to find her voice. "I shall be fine. We will join you shortly."

"All right then." He nodded and turned to his nephew. "I shall be in the refectory." He left the room quietly, closing double doors behind him.

Anastasia stood frozen to the spot, her gaze fixed on the sweet rushes beneath her. She couldn't look at him. Already his nearness heated her body and sent her heart to beat wildly in her chest.

He tipped her chin up with his knuckle. "Look at me," he said, his voice rough.

She raised her eyes, her glance lingering on his powerful chest and then along the strong chords of his neck, past lips she tried not to think about and finally met his eyes.

The pain she saw reflected in his dark eyes startled her.

"Did you despise me so much?" he asked.

She swallowed a breath, bewildered by his question.

"You spoke not a word to me when we were together and when I reached for you at dawn, you were gone."

His words and the image they carried, even two years later, set her pulse racing. In the quiet night hours while she had tried to slip away, he had held her close, his arm wrapped around her and cupping one breast. Molding her back and buttocks to his powerful frame, he joined their bodies once again and took her with an urgency that shook her.

Even now her skin tingled with the memory. Desires she had

thought conquered came rushing back as her gaze dropped to his mouth. She remembered his taste.

He cradled her face with one hand. "Do you fear me?" he asked, tracing his thumb along the tip of her chin.

His voice washed over her like warm waves, making her think of his hands on her while they bathed, his gentleness, and then his passion.

She could not let him believe that he had hurt her.

Without thinking, she laid her palm along his cheek. The contact was like lightning. The maleness of his skin burned through her in one swift arc.

He sensed it.

He caught her up and before she realized what was happening, he was pressing his body to hers and kissing her. She startled at the feel of his arousal trapped between them and his lips urging hers open, his tongue seeking entrance. A sound strangled in his throat. His palm slid along the curve of her back and settled on her bottom, burning through her woolen kirtle.

Despite her resolve and the years that separated them, she melted against him, opening to him in every female way, her body yielding and turning liquid in his arms. Of their own accord, her arms gripped his shoulders, bringing him closer and her lips parted, her tongue seeking his.

He groaned, tangling their tongues and stroking with an urgency that scared her and then inflamed her. He tasted as she remembered. Sweet and strong, male, his texture rough and wet and so warm she wanted to cry. His scent of leather and sandalwood, suddenly so familiar, filled her. She throbbed deep and low as blood rushed to her groin and pounded.

Every memory, every sensation, every sexual dream that haunted her and that she had done penance for came rushing back.

The demons of desire she had struggled against and finally mastered reared their heads with just one kiss from him.

She fought now against Satan's trap and thrashed in his arms.

He released her and staggered back.

She pressed her hand to her mouth and turned from him, fleeing the room.

Chapter Seven

The lord's visit had the kitchen buzzing. The cook bellowed orders while the under-cooks chopped vegetables and plucked geese with vigor. The venison was pounded until tender.

Young scullion boys raced to fetch water and clean cauldrons while others sweated by the brazier, turning the pig on its skewer.

The entire village prepared for the return of Ian Maxwell, Lord de Ville. Some with elated anticipation, others with visible apprehension.

His barbarous acts of victory on behalf of the king were legendary and had earned him the title of warlord, his reward the near ruined village of de Ville and all its holdings.

The former lord had squandered what little the peasants produced, and upon the man's expulsion for treachery against the king, the new Lord de Ville gradually built his prize into a thriving town. He immediately planted orchards and gardens, built fishponds, and cleared land for the cattle and sheep he bought and then loaned to farmers for breeding so they could start their herds. Soon masons and carpenters were needed to build new homes as farmers thrived at market and merchants set up shop.

The warlord built his own quarry and mill in response to the need and soon peasants came from afar to work and then offer their allegiance to the new lord.

By the time Lord de Ville left for the Crusades less than a decade later, the town had become the most populated and prosperous village in the region.

But he had returned a different man. It was true that he brought spices and herbs from the Near East the likes of which they'd never dreamed. And he covered the great hall with beautifully woven rugs where everyone—farmer or merchant, serf or knight—was treated to a feast and entertainment at least once throughout the year. He ordered a library assembled and housed it in the merchant's hall for anyone who chose to learn to read, although they were few.

Then he had disappeared into the mountains, secluding himself with nary a word about when he would return. Now, six years later, they pondered whether he would stay and what it would mean.

Tonight the garrison was summoned and every notable gathered to honor John Conway's nephew. Although not related by blood, he had helped raise Ian who was the unacknowledged bastard son of a Frankish warlord and a lady's maid. Catherine Maxwell, of mixed Scots and Viking blood, had died in childbirth. Ian had been left to be raised by a collective of servants similar to the ones he now commanded.

But even as a child his uncommon strength and agility earned him the attention of a powerful knight who secured a place for Ian as a page of his lord. Later, the knight made him his squire. Ian repaid his debt years later when the knight had fallen captive to Saracen swords. The bloodied mud of the battlefield that day attested to Ian's vengeance. The Saracens hastened to release their hostage.

The rescued knight made sure word of Ian's bravery reached all of Christendom, but Ian himself would never speak of it.

Ian soaked now in a tub of sweet smelling oils. He rested his head along the tub's wooden edge, envisioning another bath and how smooth as silk Anastasia had felt in his arms, how deeply he had impaled her, had claimed her that night. His cock throbbed thick and hard with the memory, the fresh, hot water doing nothing to ease his mounting tension.

"Shall I wash you, m'lord?"

Ian opened his eyes. The young maid standing beside him had her gaze fixed on his throbbing shaft, partially visible beneath the soapy water. During his years at de Ville he had welcomed such suggestions. He had taught many a young maid, and older ones, too, how to clean and pleasure him at once. He had delighted in watching their awe as he exploded in their hands and then later between their breasts.

One eager young maid had heard tale of a magic elixir contained in a lord's seed that insured that a woman would not die in childbirth. When Ian pumped his seed into her mouth, she swallowed eagerly. Others soon followed.

Ian gazed at the young girl before him, fresh faced and hopeful. She had unlaced her long tunic. Pink stiff nipples poked beneath the course linen shift. She pinched one hard nub under Ian's watchful gaze, leaving him to wonder about her virginal state.

And then in one swift movement the shift slipped from her shoulders, taking the tunic with it to pool at her feet.

"Shall I join you, m'lord?"

Ian sighed, even as his eyes traveled over her naked flesh. He no longer wondered about her maidenhood. The flower of her sex pouted prettily beneath a muff of dark curls. A shimmer of moisture dripped down one smooth thigh.

He thought of his mother. Fourteen and carrying the child of the lord of the manor and left to die in childbirth.

"Kneel down beside me." He patted the tub's outer wall.

She dropped onto the heather and tansy that mixed with the rushes sprinkled along the floor. He thought of all the young girls he had seduced upon his return from the Crusades. All the wicked sexual tricks he had learned as the guest of the Sultan that he later taught to so many women of the village. And their misfortune when their husbands found out or when he no longer desired them.

"Have you not heard rumor of my sexual lechery? Has no one warned you to stay away?"

Her eyes blinked wide, the dark lashes shimmering from the steam. "I have heard many things." She peeked at him from lowered lashes. "But I do not understand. I want you to teach me."

"Teach you?"

"Of the pleasures of the flesh."

It would be so easy to simply take his ease with her. Lose himself inside her. She was so young, untried, or almost so. He was half disgusted with himself for resisting. But even after two years of celibacy, he had no taste for it. Not after what he shared with Anastasia. And now that she was so near, now that he had finally found her, he was determined to keep her.

Ian simply scoffed to himself at the maid's suggestion, wondering how many stories this young girl had heard. He had thought by now the stories would have died.

During his time at de Ville he had willingly fallen victim to woes of sexual discontent, had convinced himself he was helping the women of the village, maiden and married alike. He taught them the way to show their husbands how to pleasure them.

Of course this young girl was too young to know of his conquests. He wondered if her mother had been one.

At the same time he was sure that she was no child of his. No one was. He was more than knowledgeable enough to have made sure of that.

Except for that one night with Anastasia, that one very long night, when he had taken no precautions, simply took her, again and then again, as though she were his.

And then she had left him.

He sobered at the memory of the two long years that followed.

The maid stood and began to climb into the tub, but he anchored his hands onto her hips and stopped her. "Nay. Dress yourself and leave me. And do not let the wrong man touch you."

His stern tone had her scampering to her feet and gathering up her clothes. She slipped them quickly over her head and then scooped up her long dark hair into the coarse linen cap that she had discarded as soon as she came to prepare his bath.

"Am sorry, m'lord. Thank you." She bowed in deference and fled the room.

His erection subsided as he lowered himself into the warm water again.

But that wouldn't last.

At the high table in the banquet hall would sit his head garrison and his steward. Two seats to his right would be his chief bailiff, Uncle John, with Anastasia seated between them.

He thought of her pale skin, like new cream, and the light flush that rose to her cheeks when he looked at her. He remembered how she felt, from along the curve of her throat to the tender skin along her inner wrist and the moist silky folds between her legs that throbbed when he touched her.

He sighed heavily. This obsession with her had not diminished. He couldn't touch her tonight. He shouldn't touch her.

His uncle's heart was filled with such hope for their future. Ian had determined the seriousness of his uncle's illness and learned that it was uncertain the years he had left. Anastasia had taken good care of him and his fondness for her was evident.

He would not touch her.

Even though he knew she burned for him. Maybe as much as he did for her.

He muttered an oath.

He couldn't touch her now, and he couldn't hurt his uncle, but he *would* figure a way to have her . . . in time.

Chapter Eight

Anastasia clutched the jeweled vessel and drank more of the pungent wine than was wise. Still, the effort to calm herself before *he* entered the great hall attested worthless.

Churchmen in flowing brocade robes assembled at the low table just in front of where she sat at the raised dais. She knew each one of them. She glanced down at the exposed swell of her breasts. John had wanted her attired in her finest clothes in honor of his nephew. Although Anastasia had been raised in wealth, she enjoyed the freedom of the townspeople's simple dress.

Tonight, she wore a delicate linen tunic, its long train pinned to her sleeve. Her waist and hips were laced with gold and silver chains that matched the single gold chain and cross at her throat and the net that restrained her plaited hair. The thought that she would sit next to him in full view of the assemblage of priests had her taking another gulp of wine. She almost reached for John's ale beside her.

He touched her hand. "Are you all right, my dear?"

All she could manage was a weak reply as she patted his hand in reassurance. "Have you taken your tonic today?"

"Of course, despite that the lemon balm will ruin my taste for the grand feast before us. But Anastasia, are you sure all Ian talked to you about was your understanding that I had not inherited his wealth?"

"Aye," she lied. "He is just concerned that my intentions are honorable." She had to remind herself not to refer to his nephew as Count Maxwell, a title used only at his Hawkwood castle, although she wondered if John was even aware of that. Or that she might have known of his nephew since she'd been cloistered in the mountains near Hawkwood. Then again, he had never asked exactly where the abbey was located.

She gave him a small smile before turning her attention to the local troubadour who played a celebratory tune that wafted above the excited buzz of the guests. She didn't want him to see how nervous she was. While the servants bustled about refilling drinks from ceramic jugs, the smells of mutton and cabbage grew stronger. As the feast loomed near, the entire assemblage awaited a glimpse of their illusive master.

Anastasia wished she had paid more attention to the gossips when she'd first arrived. All she had learned in her tenure here was that he was very handsome, had never married or borne an heir, and had left without a word. Still, she often happened upon the women of the village whispering about him and young maids asking questions that drew nervous glances from the older women.

Knowing now that it was Count Maxwell, the Lord of Pleasure, about which they whispered, helped her to understand the dangerous mystery that surrounded him. She understood the power of his sexual dominance over a soul, the control of a woman's spirit he could exercise with just a look.

She couldn't let her base nature cloud her moral judgment as she did before when she struggled with her vow of chastity.

She had paid dearly then. God's retribution had been fierce. The baby that she carried and had loved had been taken from her. It took months for the holy mother to coax her out of her silence and draw her back to life at the abbey, but her heart had never fully recovered.

In the time that followed, although she had desired to sacrifice her life to God, she felt unworthy of the gift. The holy mother urged her to go to de Ville and use the healing arts to help the people of the village. The holy mother believed that Anastasia would find the answers to her prayers there.

Now that she had, she would not turn her back on her destiny again.

A hushed whisper befell the hall.

The trumpeter announced the lord of the manor and within moments the count strode through the open door, his black mantle swirling around his tall broad length. A glittering broach of precious gems fastened beneath his neck and held his mantle closed. Dazzling colored lights sparkled off its surface. As he came nearer, Anastasia could see a golden moon circled by a ring of ruby stars.

The guests rose as he strode down the aisle toward the dais. Blazing torches reflected light off black waves that tumbled to his shoulders and did nothing to soften the angular lines of his face and shadowed jaw.

He looked like a sorcerer and altogether too male to ease Anastasia's fears.

She held her breath as he approached the high table and then took his place without looking at her.

She tried to distract herself by watching the reaction of the crowd, but she could smell him. That rich dark scent that stirred the unfathomable need that she desperately tried to ignore.

She had made a sacred promise of chastity years ago that she had failed to keep. Just hours ago she had reminded herself of her vow to make John a good wife. She would not break yet another sacred vow.

Lord de Ville gazed upon his roomful of guests and raised his glass. The room fell silent. A new scent, subtle, that of saffron and cinnamon herbs blanketed the air, filling her with another memory she had tried to forget.

He spoke in a calm low voice, but still its deep timbre reverberated throughout the hall. "I thank you for such a warm reception and apologize for my long absence. But I see you all have hardly suffered." He swept his glance around the hall. "The fields have been fruitful and well maintained as I trust I will find the quarry and mill when I inspect on the morrow." He turned to his uncle. "I was wise to leave you to the care of my capable bailiff."

"Nay," a voice from the back called. "John's a good man, but we need your leadership. Come back to us, Lord de Ville." A chant rose and grew until he silenced them with a lift of his hand.

Tension creased his brow. "A fine feast awaits. Let us eat."

"How long will you stay?" yet another voice called.

He took a deep breath and Anastasia caught him glimpse at her from the corner of his eye.

He sighed. "Longer than I intended." He graced them with a smile that seemed to satisfy them. He then lifted his glass. "To de Ville and its capable vassals and serfs." When he took a drink, everyone followed suit.

A burst of activity ensued. In minutes, servants scurried up with plates, eager to serve the lord of the manor first.

He tapped his pewter trencher to signal for the serving to begin. Immediately trays of choice chunks of roasted swan and peacock and a steaming cauldron of pottage was presented to him.

His servant moved forward to test a sampling, in full view of the assemblage, a custom demanded of the cup-bearer to insure against poisoning.

The servants then waited on the lord before moving on quickly to the honored guests and then the lower tables.

Anastasia watched, along with everyone else, as he speared a slice of meat with his knife, dipped it into the spicy juice pooling in his trencher, and then took a bite.

He closed his eyes as he swallowed. Her eyes followed strong corded muscles that moved along his neck. She fought against the memory of how the rough texture of his skin felt against her tongue. She remembered his salty taste. The taste of fresh male sweat.

He opened his eyes and gave a nod. A burst of cheer shook the rafters and then the guests dove into their own food with gusto.

After a long pause, he acknowledged her and John, but then looked past her and spoke to his uncle. "'Tis a fine feast, John. You have done well by me."

John returned a troubled look but responded in kind. "Aye, a feast befitting you, Ian. They have waited a long time."

He gave a dismissive shrug and looked out over the gathering. "They do fine without me. Better without me." He picked up his drinking vessel and drank deeply.

"Anastasia told me of your talk." John covered Anastasia's hand with his. "You are assured of her intentions?"

Ian placed his jug down with deliberate care then gazed at her, though he spoke to his uncle. "She is an angel of comfort to you. I understand that now. And I see your happiness." His gaze turned heated. "'Tis truly what *you* want, Anastasia?" His voice was like a warm caress.

Anastasia's head began to pound. She hated deceiving John but she could never tell him what had passed between them. Yet, the ardent way Ian looked at her surely betrayed them.

When a servant eased between her and John, Anastasia turned a pleading stare and whispered. "Why must you do this?"

He leaned in close. "I have to know. Can you dismiss what passed between us, what still burns between us?"

"I cannot dismiss it. But neither can I embrace it." Her eyes begged him to understand. "I gave John my word. I vowed to care for him. He needs me."

"What of *your* needs," he breathed, his eyes moving over her face.

"Please, your lordship," was all she could manage.

"You cannot keep running from your desires, Anastasia."

"You have no right," Anastasia choked, fighting to keep her voice low. "What I desire is between me and God." Their lips almost touched but she could not back down. How dare he think he knew her own soul. While he continued his lecherous ways, she had struggled to keep his child, only to have it taken from her in the end. He knew nothing of her and her hopes and desires, nor what she feared.

She swallowed a lump in her throat. The air grew impossibly warm and heavy, the gala around them seemingly a distant festivity.

His breath was warm against her lips. "You may deceive yourself but not me." His eyes burned through hers. "Why do you deny yourself? And turn away from the truth?" he said, his voice barely a whisper.

His gaze dropped to her mouth. For one horrified moment she feared he would kiss her.

"M'lord?" A soft female voice sounded before them. Anastasia turned to see the sister of the village priest standing before Ian, a basket of plum petals in her hand and a seductive smile on her lips.

He frowned lightly. "Lorraine." He tipped his head.

"I have brought you a treat for your bath. I remember how you delight in the smell of crushed petals floating about in the scented oil." Anastasia was surprised that the woman stepped up without so much as an acknowledgment for Anastasia and then turned away from her. Just last season Anastasia had sat with her through a sentnight of false labor pains until she finally delivered her son.

Anastasia watched the exchange with mounting shame for, instead of attending to her betrothed who sat beside her, her heart was tight with jealousy. But she could naught look away.

He took the basket and thanked her with a small smile. "And your husband, Charles, how is he?"

The woman's eyes shuttered. She mumbled something about him standing watch in the gatehouse. When Ian nodded in approval, she scurried off.

To Anastasia's dismay, Lorraine's approach proved an invitation for others. No sooner had she left than a parade of women greeters approached the dais to welcome home Lord de Ville. The way in which they spoke to him and his response left no doubt of his past relationship with each and every one of them.

Had the women no shame?

Then Anastasia thought of her own slide into temptation. Thought of her headlong *fall* into temptation and chided herself.

It was with a sigh of relief that Anastasia watched a young knight grapple his way to the forefront, shield and sword in hand.

He stepped up before the dais and knelt on one knee before Ian. "Lord de Ville. I come to you from Anjou."

"With a message?"

"Nay, sir, I enter your homage wishing to pledge my loyalty."

Ian stood. The room grew hushed as people whispered what they'd heard.

"From who do you hail?"

" 'From Baron le Barre."

"Aye," he replied with the certainty of one who knew of the legendary Baron's overbearance with his vassals.

After a pause that served to fuel the anticipation, he came from around the table and placed his hands around the knight's own. Then he unsheathed his sword and gave a light tap to the knight's shoulder. The throng watched in silence until he raised the knight to his feet and with a sweep of his arm presented him to the assemblage.

A loud cheer erupted. Ian signaled to one of his armsmen and then bade the knight to partake of the feast with a promise that he would meet with him on the morrow.

For Anastasia, the knight's pledge was a welcome reprieve from Ian's throng of admirers. But then in the space of a breath, Miranda, the village leman, approached.

Anastasia had befriended Miranda when she had fallen ill. She was surprised now to find her within the manor walls for Anastasia had often tried to coax her friend to come within. But Miranda had kept her distance, insisting 'twas better for the wives of the men she served.

She stood before Ian now, with a jeweled cup in hand that she twirled with a lazy wrist. While her smile was warm, her eyes were amused. Her red hair flowed over her full lush body and her eyes twinkled with mischief as she gazed at him.

Anastasia suddenly felt like a girl beside the bold and sensual Miranda.

"Ian." She gave him a small smile. "I mean, your lordship." Her mouth twisted up at one corner.

His eyes brightened as he returned a warm smile of his own.

"I have brought you something," Miranda told him. "A gift of welcome for your return." She bowed and picked up the hem of her skirt and stepped up onto the dais. "It brings with it the hope that you will remain." The gentle folds of her gown flowed like water over rounded hips. The large amber stone she wore at her throat winked at him.

Anastasia felt her blood heat. Miranda kept her attention riveted on . . . the Lord of Pleasure. The intimate way she smiled at him left no doubt about what had passed between them.

Miranda touched Ian's sleeve. "When may I give you your gift, my lord?" she asked, her eyes holding a wealth of sensual promise. She lingered over a long sip of her wine, her gaze never breaking his.

Anastasia couldn't watch anymore. She turned her back on the sinful banter and turned to John. "After the minstrels finish their song," she said, "I am going to check on Margaret and make sure she is brought a plate of food."

John nodded. "That's fine, my dear, but don't be long." His warm smile fueled Anastasia's burdensome guilt. As soon as they turned back to the minstrels, a hand clamped onto her wrist.

She looked down at the long tapered fingers and the dusting of dark hair along the knuckles, and felt his warmth. She gave a tug but he held firm. She refused to look at him, but she could feel his lips close. He breathed into her ear. "Take care that you come back. This is not finished."

She swallowed and gave another tug but still he wouldn't let go. "Aye, your lordship."

He finally released her, but before Anastasia turned away, Miranda threw her an amused smile. Anastasia could not flee from them both fast enough.

Chapter Nine

Ian felt Anastasia's nearness before he saw her as one senses a soothing fire. Her heat drew him to where she knelt, deep in prayer. He slipped into the darkness behind her, not wishing to startle her. Such a fey creature deserved gentle wooing. He allowed himself the pleasure of watching her unobserved.

Bells chimed, signaling the late hour. She had disappeared from the hall soon after the tables were cleared and the minstrels struck a tune that signaled for the dancing to begin. This last place that he had come in search of her should have been his first.

He watched now as she bowed before the statue of the Holy Mother of God, palms flattened together and fingers pointed skyward. Two shivering candles lit the face of the virgin and the baby she swaddled. Ian's eyes dropped to the girdle of gold chains shaping Anastasia's hips and waist above the smooth curve of her bottom.

Savage need swept through him, threatening to break his tenuous control. He vowed that tonight would be the last time she would flee him. In the same way a warrior uses strategy to gain his objective, he would do the same tonight with Anastasia.

She crossed herself several times and then reached into a small pouch hidden in the folds of her skirt. She took out a string of shimmering beads. Holy beads, meant for the repeating rounds of prayer. Another ritual borrowed from the Saracens that the church claimed as its own.

Ian had a set of beads, a gift from a sultan while Ian was held captive in his tent and who, like him, decried the carnage of the crusades. Ian's beads were of solid gold and rubies.

The oil lamps that rested in corbels set into the walls flickered with each breath of wind. A hallowed glow surrounded Anastasia and a gentle mist enwrapped her.

She must have sensed him for she picked up her skirts and turned, standing abruptly.

Her eyes blinked wide. "What are you doing here?"

"I came for answers."

She glanced around as though searching for a protector. Despite her denial, he knew she feared him. When next he spoke, his voice was soft and low.

"Why did you come here? To de Ville?"

"I came here to be placed under Margaret's tutelage."

She wet her lips and swallowed. "I was not worthy to stay at the abbey after my grievous transgressions." She wrung her hands. "The holy mother guided me here."

He hid his surprise. She must mean the holy mother Mary had come to her in a dream. She couldn't be talking about the Abbess.

"You mean Mary?" He motioned towards the statue.

Her eyes followed his and then returned. "Nay. Abbess Anne, the holy mother at the abbey."

Now he *was* surprised. Did Anne think he would never return to his largest holding? It would seem not.

He thought a moment while the silence between them grew heavy. The moon rose and announced its presence by silvery threads that beamed through the high recessed windows, causing a halo of light to settle in the space between them. It beckoned them to enter the peaceful circle of light together. He had seen similar signs of God's presence—in an arrow that curved just short of spearing the child caught in battle, or the warrior who lived just long enough to send a message of love to his family and no longer.

He moved closer. "She sent you to me."

Anastasia blinked and then shook her head.

"Anne knew I would return someday and find you here. 'Twas her atonement for barring me that whole wretched year."

"I do not understand."

"She knew what passed between us," he said, his voice low. He motioned with his hand for her to come closer.

"'Tis impossible. I told her naught."

"I had come looking for you, begging to see you, but Anne wouldn't let me near you." He moved a fraction closer, but not enough for her to notice.

"You came to the abbey," she breathed. "For me?"

He gave her a half-smile. "I told myself that it mattered not that you'd left me alone in my bed, but my heart wouldn't listen."

"Nay." She backed up, clutching her skirts at her side. "I don't believe you. Abbess Anne would have told me."

"What *did* she tell you?" he asked, his voice whisper soft.

She looked at him, her eyes liquid with confusion, and swallowed lightly. "She told me to search my heart for what is right." Her fingers twisted her prayer beads. "And to ask guidance from God and believe I will receive it."

Ian forced himself not to reach for her. Instead he gave her a self-depreciating smile. "She said much the same to me, only I was to search my soul."

Anastasia's breath caught. "'Tis can't be true."

Ian reached for her then, brushing his fingers along her arms. "Anastasia, Anne knew more what was in our hearts than we did."

She shook her head. "'Tis the devil's tricks. I won't listen." She turned from him and covered her ears. Then she ran to the statue and dropped to her knees. Her fingers grasped for the beads now hanging from her gold girdle as she murmured the short repetitive chants he'd heard so often during the crusade while the blood and carnage mounted.

In a gesture meant to soothe, he dropped down beside her and caressed her shoulders.

She whirled on him. "Do not touch me." She jumped up and moved away from him, the look in her eyes unmistakable; she was terrified of him.

He stood, too, but moved no closer while she continued to back away. In a low voice made to reassure, he spoke to her. "Do you not see that we are meant to be together? Even Anne believed so."

"She could not." Anastasia began to pace before the moonlit window that bathed with light the raised altar behind. The silver chalice in its center gleamed with precious stones.

"Abbess Anne saw for herself God's awful retribution for what I had done. I cannot survive another," she sobbed.

"What retribution?" he asked, an unease stealing up his spine. Surely no torture was meted out to Anastasia for her indiscretion. But Anastasia was not listening to him. She was lost in her own pain, murmuring sounds he didn't understand.

He gripped her shoulders and turned her to face him. "What did they do to you when they found you had come to me?"

She wrenched away from him. "'Tis what *you* did," she choked. "The babe—" She covered her mouth.

He froze. "What babe?"

She doubled over, clutching her arms across her stomach, and cried. "God took it from me. 'Twas because I loved it and that was my punishment."

His heart slammed in his chest. He knelt down before her. "Anastasia?" He grabbed her arms and made her look at him. Tears spilled over finely honed cheekbones. He forced the words from his throat. "You were with child? Our child?"

The sob she rent shook her with a terrible trembling.

He held her fast. "Answer me."

"Aye." When she struggled to free herself, he let her go. The knowledge of a babe of theirs was like a hammer blow to his heart.

When next he spoke, it was a gentle whisper. "Where is the child now?"

Anastasia saw the raw pain in his eyes and her heart clenched. How could it be that he loved the babe, too, having had no knowledge of it until now? But she saw it was true. She knew how instantly love emerged. She had loved the babe with her whole heart and soul the moment she learned of it.

He looked at her as though memorizing her every feature. "I deserve to know, Anastasia," he said, his voice low.

She swallowed a sob. "With God." The memory was like a stab to her heart. Her arms still ached with emptiness for the babe she never held. "'Twas taken while still just a promise in my womb as punishment for my sin." She paused. "I am sorry," she choked, clenching her hands tight to her breast.

"Nay." He circled her wrists, gathering her hands in his. "'Tis not the work of God, but of nature. As a healer you know this." He cupped her chin and dried a tear with his thumb. "Surely Anne said as much."

The Abbess Anne had said many things during that awful time but little had penetrated through Anastasia's pain.

He tipped her chin. She looked into eyes as warm as a gentle sunrise. "I would have cared for you . . . if you had come to me." His fingers grew warm against her skin. "I wished for you to come to me."

The guilt over everything she had done revisited her, including the battle she had waged with herself over whether she would tell him. Over what she would have done had the babe not been taken from her.

"I am sorry for that, too." She gave a heavy sigh. "'Twas so frightening. And then I just wanted to forget. But 'twas not possible."

"Shh . . ." He drew her into the shelter of his arms. " 'Tis past," he murmured, his voice a soothing chant, his lips soft against her hair. She softened into his embrace and comforted herself with the feel of his strength surrounding her with its penetrating warmth.

His fingers glided along her throat and found the pulse that beat heavy. When his lips brushed along her forehead, she sighed. She had not remembered when she had felt so protected.

Then the memory of when she had felt thus came rushing back. She closed her heart against the feelings raised by the thought of that fateful night when he held her close in his bath and of her complete surrender to him. Her pulse quickened. She wrested away from his arms and backed up, refusing to let this one unguarded moment undo her.

She would not succumb to him again. Could not. She offered up a silent prayer of deliverance from the unspeakable temptation.

"You must go. Leave me to my prayer."

"For what do you pray this time?"

" 'Tis private." She felt the blush rise to her face.

His mouth pulled up at one corner as he took a half step toward her. "Perhaps you pray for me?" With the next step toward her she backed up and met the cold stone altar behind her. "And that"—he gave a small smile—"would be a task without end."

"Come no closer."

"What do you fear?" He reached out and ran a finger along her cheek.

She swatted his hand and slipped aside, backing around the altar. "You waste effort," she said, gathering her strength. "Only the devil could make me yield to you again."

He gave an unholy smile. "That can be arranged."

She stifled a cry as he made his way around the corner of the marbled stone. She clutched with fervor the silver cross at her breast.

His eyes dropped to her naked skin and a low chuckle rumbled up from his throat. "Think you a scrap of silver will save you from me?" He gave an artful smile. "Of course you do," he murmured softly, coming at her from around the altar with slow deliberate steps. "In the same way you placed your spoon down tonight to keep out the devil." A grin crooked his lips. "And yet, here I am."

"Leave me, please," she pleaded, even as she knew he would not. And she feared that she could not stop him. He would do what he willed with her, weaving his magic with his hands and his lips no matter how hard she fought.

Surely God could not hold her responsible against such a skilled sorcerer.

"Leave?" He gave her a hard look. "Why?" Another step closer and he had her backed against the arched windowsill. "You know you burn for me."

"Nay."

He lifted a brow. "Is it not a sin to lie, Anastasia?" He plucked her up and sat her on the sill. "Mayhap it is the worst of all sins, is it not?"

"I beg of you!"

"Aye," he murmured, bracing his hands on the sill alongside her and trapping her, " 'tis what I desire most."

Her heart leaped at the predatory look in his eyes. She glanced about. "Surely you won't take me in such a holy place?"

His eyes darkened. "It matters not," he said, his voice rough with desire. In a movement so tender it confused her, he cupped her face. " 'Tis no more holy than an open field or a thick forest after a cleansing rain." His eyes moved over her face. "Or a lovers' bed."

Her pulse quickened at his words and at the gentle way his fingers caressed her chin. "You cannot mean that," she breathed. " 'Tis a house of God."

He lifted a brow. " 'Tis a house built by the money of nobles in exchange for prayers on their behalf." With a casual hand, he unclasped his mantle and tossed it aside.

She felt a moment of fright. *Surely he was taunting her and aimed not to make good on his threat.* But when he stripped his tunic up over his head she let out a gasp.

Acres of golden skin just a touch away glowed in the candlelight and a light sweat glistened and clung to the dark silky hair that she remembered so well. His scent, dark and forbidden, teased her senses as he leaned in closer. She couldn't put out of her mind how that taut warm flesh felt over the muscle beneath. In a moment of weakness she almost reached out to run her fingers over the rough feel of it.

A shiver snaked over her skin. Then, to her mortification, her eyes dropped to his rigid arousal. Even the rough wool cloth couldn't contain the life that throbbed thick beneath.

"You see how much I desire you?" he said, amusement edging his voice.

Her eyes snapped to his. "Nay." She looked up into his warm gaze. He cupped her knees and with gentle pressure spread her legs.

She batted away his hands and hopped off the sill. "Did you not give your service to the church in the Crusades? I do not understand your disregard." She scurried around him.

He turned with calm assurance and followed her step for step as she discreetly backed toward the heavy door.

His eyes narrowed. "The Crusades were more about controlling the valuable trade route of the eastern Mediterranean than about the church."

Sensing that the open door was just a sword's length away, she watched him advance slowly. Despite his casual tone and the widened space between them, he was still aroused. She dragged her eyes away. Then she whirled around and made a run for the door. As she ran through it, his deep soft chuckle trailed behind her.

She soon discovered why. The outside door of the antechamber was bolted shut. As she struggled to lift the heavy support she heard the door to the chapel's inner sanctum close with a thump. Then he snatched her around the waist and hauled her up. Before she could catch her breath he flattened her back to his chest.

He pressed his lips to her ear. "You will not flee from me again," he growled. "Before God and all the saints tell me that you don't desire me," he whispered, his breath hot in her ear. "Do *not* compound your sins by lying, Anastasia."

"You are hateful—"

"Answer me." His hand slid up her neck and curved around her chin. He turned her mouth up to his. "Answer me, Anastasia." He caught her bottom lip between his teeth and nipped. Then he soothed the sting of it with hot little licks of his tongue.

She felt herself drowning. Her mind grew muddled with the press of his arousal against her bottom and at the feel of the traitorous flower of her sex opening shamelessly for him. She strangled a moan and finally managed to speak. "You trick me with your lips."

"Silly chit," he murmured, his voice like a soft embrace. He stroked her neck with gentle fingers and bared her throat to his teeth, scraping along the tender skin. "I need you now as you need me," he breathed. She felt him pull at his laces. A helpless sound that she couldn't stop escaped her.

Before she could protest, he whirled her around and trapped her against the carved wood panels. He pressed against her, covering her mouth with his, his lips moving over hers and drawing the breath from her. The feel of his tongue, sliding hot along hers and exploring the soft recesses of her mouth, sent her blood pumping everywhere.

She gave a useless push on his shoulders.

It was a mistake.

The moment her hands touched warm flesh, he groaned and lifted her.

At the feel of his thick arousal throbbing between them, memories of how he'd felt, warm and alive between her legs and filling her, consumed her as though no time had passed. A wicked throb of pleasure settled in her private center. And then he stripped her to the waist with an effortless tug.

"What do you do?" she choked, helplessly pulling at her tunic. But with the sleeves pinning her arms to her sides, she was powerless to cover herself.

Her breath caught at the feel of the cool night air settling on her naked skin and causing her nipples to tingle.

While his hands still encircled her waist, he stepped back, his eyes naked with need. "God's teeth," he muttered. The tip of his member peeked from his braies and the pearly drop that so fascinated her gleamed in the half-light.

She stifled a whimper and used the break in contact to gather her wits. She turned pleading eyes on him. "Do not do this."

But he wasn't listening. He pressed them hip to hip and then cupped one breast and rubbed a calloused thumb along her nipple. The pleasure that seared through her was punishing but she forced away the terrible need to succumb to him. "Please, 'tis unseemly," she choked.

He cupped the other breast, then with both hands idly twirled her erect nipples between his fingers. When he plucked the sensitive tips, she struggled against the desire to close her eyes and give herself over to the unbearable pleasure.

Then he was lifting her higher and anchoring her against the door, his shaft pressing her mons. His tongue traveled along her neck, wetting her skin and heating her beyond reason. He groaned aloud.

"Ian," she choked, twisting away from his lips. "'Tis . . . a sacrilege," she stammered, "to surrender to carnal lust in a holy place."

He muttered an unholy curse and then his lips stilled. Slowly he lowered her to her feet. His eyes were dark with arousal and his thick lashes were lowered to half-mast. With one long finger he stroked her bottom lip.

Ian stared at the lips that he had just kissed into submission and that now trembled under his touch. But they trembled not in arousal for as he gazed into the amethyst jewels that were her eyes, they filled with tears.

Still, 'twas neither that stopped him.

Nay, it was the sound of his name on her lips.

He could not take her. Not in this place that she considered sacred.

He allowed his eyes to linger on her ruby-tipped nipples, glimmering in the candlelight, and causing his blood to rush like a river after a storm. With a sigh of regret, he pulled the soft cloth over the swell of her breasts.

She simply watched him, her expression tentative.

He ran a hand down his face. "Bloody hell."

In one fluid movement, he swept her off her feet, flung open the door, and carried her out, down the long winding steps of the east tower.

"Where are you taking me?"

Without answering, he strode through the lower floor of the tower and out through the Watergate. The sentries on duty tipped their halberds. "Lord de Ville." They gave a quick glance at his bare chest and then at Anastasia and eyed each other.

Ian grunted in acknowledgement.

As he stepped out onto the grassy hillock the ocean thundered far below them. The salty mist cooled their skin and the full moon offered a shimmering light that enwrapped them. Ian set her down against the wall, tucked into the curve of the tower.

While the fields and forest sprawled just beyond the great wall, on this east side, before them spread only the vast sea that took ships to the ends of the earth and beyond. To the mysteries of other lands and cultures.

The wind swept Anastasia's hair off her face to tumble behind her and a light sheen of moisture covered her and plastered her gown to her body. Ian's eyes traced every swell and curve. Her nipples were erect and clearly outlined through the fine cloth, darkening the pale fabric to the rich color of wine.

She must have felt his eyes because she turned to him. Her gaze dropped to his chest and traveled over the dark mat of hair, wet now from the sea air.

His arousal came pounding back, full and urgent, straining his braies. He would have her now, slick with the salt of the sea and with the wind in her hair. He encircled her waist and drew her to him. When he rested his shaft between her thighs her lips parted and a small pleasured sound escaped. She closed her eyes and groaned.

"Let us not fight." He palmed her breast through cloth and pinched the hardened nipple between his thumb and forefinger. She let out a gasp but didn't push his hand away. He thrust once with his cock and then lifted her.

She gave a tiny cry of protest that he drowned with his lips against her mouth. "I need you," he groaned, licking the corners of her mouth and fighting with himself not to ravish her. "I've needed you for so long."

He gathered up the fabric of her skirt and bared her bottom to his hands. She was like silk. Exactly as he had remembered her. She gave a feeble attempt to push at his hand and then moaned in his mouth when he stroked her bottom and slid his fingers between the smooth mounds, spreading her legs wider and hooking them around his waist.

He stroked her netherlips, slipping his fingers around in her wetness.

"Ian!" She squirmed in his arms.

"I like it when you say my name," he growled, thrusting a finger and then two up into her wet heat. She shivered in his arms and he groaned at the feel of her silky lips opening for him. Her desire for him proved his undoing. Any attempt to restrain himself was lost in the feel of her sex softening and plumping up to receive him.

"You want me to ravish you, don't you?"

She gave a sound of distress but a new flush of wetness coated his fingers. "Don't you, Anastasia?" he taunted.

"Nay," she groaned at the same time her body writhed in response to his deliberate strokes.

"Don't lie, my sweet," he said, circling her little bud with two slippery fingers. It pebbled under his touch and then throbbed, so alive and sensitive. He pinched delicately.

"Ian," she screamed.

He moved another finger between her bottom and probed her tight little hole. When he pushed for entrance she gasped and beat his shoulders and then moaned when he slipped in deep.

" 'Tis *truly* unseemly," she breathed even as her body clamped down hard against his penetration and shuddered with pleasure.

"Aye." He smiled.

Her neck arched back in rapture. He nipped along the smooth column of her throat and licked the racing pulse that beat heavy beneath the delicate skin. Her wantonness pushed his own arousal to tormenting heights.

He set her on her feet and stripped her to the waist, trapping her as he had thus in the chapel, but this time she offered no protest. Instead, she stared at his cock head, peeking out of his braies, red and impatient. In a move so instinctual, she wet her lips.

He smiled to himself and laid her out along the grass. She looked up as he unlaced his braies. When his cock came bobbing out, she gave a tiny whimper, but her nipples were now as hard as cherry pits. He knelt between her legs and slipped his hands up her skirt.

The feel of his hands on her thighs brought her to life. He stopped at the look on her stricken face, the shifting look of arousal mingled with fear. Other than that steamy night, two years ago, she was a virgin. He schooled himself in patience even as his bullocks pulled up tight in anticipation.

Though her arms were trapped at her side, her hands could easily reach her mons. He took one hand and slipped it under her skirt. This time she gave no cry of protest.

"Feel how wet you are for me," he murmured, running her fingers along the slick wet lips. She groaned and pushed at his wrist, making him think she'd not touched herself since that night so long ago when he had taught her self-pleasuring. With his other hand, he lifted her skirt to her waist. The sight of her fingers slipping around her plump reddened lips was torture. He placed one small finger on the tiny organ that gave her so much pleasure and she jumped.

"Please . . ." She closed her eyes and moaned.

He increased the pressure and circled the bud with the smooth tip of her finger in the way that he longed to do with his tongue. And then he did, spreading her wide and settling his mouth between her legs. She let out a startled gasp and then moaned deep and low in her throat. He buried two fingers inside her, causing her breath to hitch in her throat as he stroked her with long sweeps of his tongue.

When he played with her little pebble, his teasing touch had her arching into his lips and fisting her hands into his hair to pull him closer. He nipped and suckled her and then dipped into her sweetness. She was delicious. Her scent filled him and her taste flooded his tongue. She cried out his name as he felt the little bud disappear under its silky hood.

But he stopped short of bringing her to pleasure. When he took her he wanted her burning for him, begging him. He wanted to feel her pleasure tighten around him as he pumped into her.

She looked up at him as he knelt above her, her eyes clouded in confusion and heavy with lust. Her flushed breasts heaved beneath him. He plucked the tender tips with his calloused fingers and watched her sex lips throb with each calculated pinch.

He looked at his own sex, slick and red, pulsing painfully. He shoved down his braies farther, freeing the heavy sac that ached for release. A dewy drop of his seed wept from the tip of his cock. Anastasia gasped and stared at him, mesmerized.

"Let me touch you," she said.

He chuckled deep in his throat. "God's bones, that would do me in." He slipped his hand between her legs and separated her pink lips. "It is time, Anastasia. I need you." He settled himself between her legs and lifted her bottom.

Her eyes glazed over as he took his cock in hand and slipped between her folds, stroking her with the blunt head. The hot wetness that pooled in her sex allowed him to slide along the plump lips and enter her. But still, she gloved him tight. Her silky depths swallowed him slowly. He groaned, warring with himself to go slow and fight his desire to take her with the brutal urgency he had naught the power to resist.

"Ian," she breathed against his skin as he trembled for control. She arched up against him, clutching him closer, her small hands slipping down his back and shyly covering his buttocks, urging him deeper. "Fill me, Ian."

It was all he needed. In one swift movement, he buried himself to the hilt, grunting with the effort. Despite her plea, she clamped down on him hard, making him groan with the tight hot feel of her. "By God and all the saints, if there is a heaven, this is it." He turned her face to his. When she looked at him it was with eyes liquid with wonder. He stroked her cheek. "You are mine, Anastasia. Make no mistake."

Chapter Ten

Anastasia drew up her knees and welcomed him into her body with a fervor that shook her to her very soul.

How could she have forgotten how completely he filled her? How complete they were when joined.

His heart pounded as she held him close, cradling his muscled body against her own. She wanted to keep him inside her forever. Wanted to blend their bodies into one.

The thought of it shocked her. Was it not what one pledged in the sacrament of marriage? The vow that two bodies were to become one? She realized at that moment she loved him. Realized she loved him with a purity she had failed to see before.

She gazed up at the stars above them and the heavenly mist that enwrapped them and felt at peace with herself and God in a way that she hadn't in a long time. And she was at peace with him—the infamous Lord of Pleasure. She smiled. Yes, he was that . . . and so much more.

You are mine, he had said.

"Yes," she answered him now.

"Anastasia?" He looked at her with those dark heart-melting eyes that could turn so wicked one moment and so tender in the next.

"Yes, Ian, I am yours."

"Oh, God," he groaned and hitched up higher. "I love you, Anastasia." He shuddered in her arms, then began to move.

She opened her legs wide and sighed, running her lips along his skin and licking the salty sweat from off his shoulder. She moaned at the familiar dark taste of him. He hooked her knees over his hips, allowing for the deepest penetration she could ever have imagined.

Her pleasure mounted quickly, sweeping her into a world of pure sensation. He licked her nipples and bit gently, sending stabs of pleasure straight to her lusty bud while he stroked her into a state of bliss, consuming her in this act of love.

She felt herself spinning beyond reason and temporal concerns, caught up in the rapture of communion with him. Awe filled her. An act so carnal could be spiritual as well.

"We belong thus. You're mine, Anastasia. And I'm yours," he growled.

Her breath caught at the sound of his words. When next she felt him probing her bottom, she moaned deep in her throat. *Spiritual indeed.* She knew the unspeakable act would undo her, but she was no longer ashamed by her wanton desires.

At the feel of his thumb sinking deep, her breath came out on a long pleasured sigh. Her sex throbbed thick and heavy. When he pumped gently, she could think no longer.

"Anastasia," he groaned, thrusting his cock furiously and grinding into her swollen lips. "I can't . . . Oh, God."

And then she burned everywhere and was pulled so tight he had her crying out her pleasure as her body surrendered to him. Surrendered to the delicious heat and bone-deep melting that had her convulsing in his arms.

He grunted and then let out a violent roar of release, his shaft pumping thick into her, his strong body tensing and then collapsing on top of her.

The joy that she felt and the utter completion of their act seemed to transcend this simple mortal world.

Chapter Eleven

Ian was in a state. He had not seen Anastasia since last eve.

When he sent a sentry to her cottage in the afternoon with a summons for her to come to his private solar that evening, she could not be found. He searched within the manor walls, every stall and garden, and questioned every shopkeeper's wife. The villagers were happy to see him about, and Ian forced himself to inquire after their well-being, although he was too distracted to listen for a response.

Before long, common sense led him back to the chapel.

On his way there, he was surprised to see Miranda coming down the tower steps.

"Ian?" She stopped abruptly before colliding with him on the landing. "Do not tell me that *you* are on your way to the chapel?" She gave an amused laugh.

He raised a brow. "Do not tell me that you have just left it."

"Perhaps I was with the spinners."

"T'would be almost as surprising."

Miranda frowned. "She's fled to the back gardens. She unburdens to no mortal. 'Tis only her statues that bring her comfort. Silly chit."

"Perhaps." He smiled. "Who are we to naysay her devotion?"

Miranda gave a husky chuckle. "True enough." She gave him a fond shove. "Go. Surely if anyone can reach her it is"—her lips quirked—"the infamous Lord of Pleasure." Her voice trailed off on a soft laugh as she scurried around him toward the barbican.

When Ian found Anastasia, she was indeed kneeling before a small grotto of the Blessed Mother built into one corner of the garden. He only hoped her prayers were in thanksgiving for the love they had found. But something in the bend of her slender neck told him differently.

He watched her rise slowly. This time when she turned and saw him, his heart warmed at the welcoming look in her eyes.

She ran to him. When she reached him, he scooped her up into his arms. The feel of her small body nestled against his brought him a joy he hadn't yet realized possible.

But his joy dimmed. She was troubled. He could feel it in the desperate way she clung to him.

He swept her into his arms and carried her over to the far corner of the rock walled garden. He set her down amidst a soft carpet of mossy groundcover tucked in a secluded crevice along the sea wall. A large sycamore tree shielded them from the entrance to the garden.

Before she could protest, he lifted her onto his lap and slipped his hand under her skirt and caressed her bottom.

She closed her eyes on a deep moan, her head falling back onto his shoulder.

"This time I will take your bottom if you do not want my seed just yet in your womb," he murmured, running his lips along her forehead.

"Take my . . ." Her eyes opened wide. "Do you mean— ohh . . ." She sucked in her breath and shuddered as he dipped one long finger into her sweetness. He dragged her wetness up between her tight little bottom and probed gently. He sighed with satisfaction at the deep guttural groan that rent from her throat.

"Ian," she breathed. "I cannot think when you touch me thus."

"Do not think," he murmured, pumping with shallow gentle thrusts. He laid her farther back and pushed her skirt to her waist. He looked at her spread legs and his finger imbedded deep in her bottom. Then he let his thumb play along her slickly aroused lips. The scent of her arousal filled his senses and pumped blood in heavy rushes to his groin. He watched as her satiny lips plumped and softened deliciously beneath his teasing touch.

She lifted her head and watched, too. "'Tis unseemly, Ian," she breathed. "Truly unseemly, but I like it so."

Her little bud pebbled so hard and tight that just one hard thrust up her bottom would have her exploding in his arms. But he wanted to draw out her pleasure.

He pulled his finger out of a sudden and left her wanting. She blinked up at him in surprise. "'Tis my turn now?"

"Your turn for what, my love?"

She slipped off his lap and knelt beside him. To his surprise, with shaking hands, she unlaced him and freed his aching cock. She let out a soft sigh when his swollen member sprang out, and then watched with fascination the pearly drop seep out of his slit.

When she grasped him, he groaned. Then she ran one finger over the tip of his cock and wiped off his seed. She brought it to her lips and licked.

"God's bones, you will un-man me."

Before he could protest, she brought him to her lips and licked delicately. He closed his eyes against the bone-melting pleasure she gave him, willing himself to control the driving need to give himself over to it, because he had intended to bring her to pleasure many times over tonight.

When she pushed the tip of her tongue into the tiny slit and licked up more of his weeping seed, he cupped her chin. "Nay, Anastasia. I'll come too soon, my love."

"Please, Ian." She looked up at him, with a mixture of lust and sadness that he didn't understand. "Let me take you in my mouth and feel you. Let me love you."

She stroked down his length as she spoke and cupped his sack. His hips rocked off the bed of moss. And then her lips were on him and covering the throbbing head. He fought for control as he allowed her to explore and fondle him, but he knew his control couldn't last. He felt like a young squire again. He fisted his hands in her silky hair and muttered a curse. When she began to suckle him like a babe at teat, he had had enough. He drew her lips off him.

The shimmer of his seed on her swollen mouth nearly did him in, drawing him to seek other lips that would be equally eager for him.

In one fluid move he laid her on her back and spread her legs wide. She opened eagerly but with a quiet desperation that disturbed him. "What is it, Anastasia?"

She shook her head and urged him to her. A tiny tear pooled at the corner of one eye. "Please, Ian. Love me."

She touched her sex lips with the tip of one finger and shyly opened her treasures to him. He nestled his head between her legs and licked her first delicately, the taste of her arousal sweet on his tongue, and then with a hunger he would never fully satisfy. The ragged sound of her breathing fueled his own desire so that his cock throbbed and ached. He could wait no more.

He turned her over onto her belly and lifted her hips. She startled and twisted her bottom. "Shh . . ." He smoothed his hands over the smooth globes. "I'll be gentle."

"Nay." She twisted back and opened her arms to him. "I want your seed deep inside me. I love you, Ian."

He muffled a groan and lowered himself between her thighs, covering her completely. He entered her wet heat in one long stroke that took her breath away. And then he thrust with a rhythm that sent them both spiraling together toward the desired abyss of pure pleasure.

"Ian," she screamed. He took her harder as she continued to scream and thrash beneath him, clinging to him with an almost unsettling agony.

Then she fell apart in his arms. His own release thundered through him like a raging fire consuming him and then soothing him as every muscle turned to liquid with the pleasure. He collapsed against her on one long shuddering sigh.

"I love you, Anastasia. I'll never stop loving you."

At his words she sobbed, with deep racking sobs that broke his heart.

"Anastasia," he crooned, slipping out of her and rolling to his side. He smoothed her skirt down over her hips and covered her. "Tell me what is in your heart."

She turned into his arms. "'Tis John. I cannot hurt him, Ian. I cannot hurt him with the knowledge that the two people he loves most have betrayed him."

"Nay. Not betrayed him. What you say is true. He loves us both. He has always loved me as a son, and now he loves you like a daughter." He tipped her chin up and ran his thumb along her cheeks to soak up the tears. "'Tis why he will be happy for us."

"I pledged a vow to him, Ian. I cannot break another vow. He is ill. He turned to me to soothe and comfort him in his final days and now I will cause him the greatest of pain if I do this. I am foresworn."

"We can both care for him and comfort him, my sweet." He brushed a tangle of hair from her forehead. "He would not want you to sacrifice your love—"

Ian stopped. At the word sacrifice, her eyes took on a wounded, haunted expression. "Anastasia," he murmured. "What is it?"

"Am I to sacrifice nothing then?" Her gaze drifted inward as she spoke as though asking the question of herself.

She slowly rose and turned her back to him. He stood and rested a tentative hand on her shoulder. She neither flinched nor relaxed into his touch but walked slowly away from him, her gaze lifted upward.

Then she turned back to him suddenly. "I must retreat, Ian. Only in prayer and meditation will I find the answers I seek."

"Anastasia, I shall go to my uncle—"

"Nay, Ian." She walked up close and took his hands in hers. She pressed them to her lips. "I love you. But I must first know what God intends for me."

"Anastasia—"

"Nay. While I willingly give you my heart and my body, only God may possess my soul. I must do this, Ian. I must know what He requires of me. Or I shall never truly find peace within myself."

Ian's heart ached for her. He wanted to shield her, protect her from all that she would find. The pain, the utter aloneness a soul first suffers when laid bare and vulnerable, open. But he knew he could not. Was certain he could not. As certain as he was that in the end she would come to him.

"Please, Ian." She looked up at him through lashes shimmering with tears. "I must do this."

"Aye." He drew her into his arms, cradling her to his chest. "I will let you go, my small falcon. I will set you free." *And when you are ready, you will fly back to me.*

Chapter Twelve

Three months later.

The two sentries that stood guard at Hawkwood Castle were surprised to see a finely covered wagon with a team of four stallions approach the drawbridge.

More to their surprise was the regal lady who emerged. While her cloak was of the heavy wool meant for travel, the clasp that held it closed at her throat was imbedded with jewels. An ornately beaded cap framed the fairest of skin, the hair beneath it like captured sunlight.

She greeted them with a warm smile. "Good day, sirs." Her driver stood guard at her back.

The sentries dropped down into a bow. "M'lady."

Anastasia wondered if they had recognized her, though it mattered not. "I've come to see the lord of the keep."

They gave a quick glance at one another. The older one gave a frown and spoke up. "You do know, m'lady, that this is Hawkwood, keep of Count Maxwell."

At the mention of his name, her heart turned over. The days of her journey had stretched into weeks and with each passing day that delayed her from seeing Ian, she felt she would expire.

"Aye." She smiled. "I've come to see Ian."

At the mention of his given name, the soldiers parted. The younger one, the same one who had escorted her to the infamous Count Maxwell that night, scurried to guide her through the gatehouse.

Visions of that tempestuous night came thundering back. The

fright she felt then as a young novice was replaced with the joy a woman feels who is about to be reunited with her fated love.

Anastasia's steps picked up in anticipation at seeing her wicked count once again.

As she was led around the barbican, deep male voices boomed from the tower above. Duncan flew down the stone steps, leaving a string of muttered curses in his wake. As he rounded the landing, he stopped when he saw Anastasia.

She smiled, wondering if he, too, would fail to recognize her. But he stepped up immediately, taking both her hands in his, and bowed. "Lady Bedovier." He kissed the back of her hands. "Thank God you are here." He gave her a subtle wink and then signaled for the guards to leave.

"Come." He took her arm and led her immediately up the tower stairs. "Perhaps now we might be spared the roar of the lion."

As if to underscore his hope, a young page came slipping and falling down the spiral stairs and would have crashed into them both had it not been for Duncan's restraining hands.

"Easy, lad," Duncan soothed. "Whatever Count Maxwell required of you, he no longer needs. Go about your duties and be sure you do not return." Duncan glanced at her and gave an amused smile.

"Aye, sir." The young boy looked more than eager to comply.

Duncan turned to her and motioned up the stairs. "He's been the devil himself since he returned."

"You mean more the devil than he already was?"

Duncan gave a laugh. "Aye. You go on. I'll see to it that you are not disturbed."

"Thank you." She smiled and placed her hand in his and then started up the steps, her heart pounding.

She turned the corner at the top but hesitated before walking through the large arch that supported the heavy wood doors.

He sat at his trestle table, writing with his long quill, his hair an inky thick mass that fell to remarkable shoulders. Damascus slumbered at his feet.

She took a deep breath. As soon as she stepped through the door, his covetous falcon fluttered on its perch and squawked her disapproval.

"Cleo," Ian growled, lifting his head to the petulant bird. "Be still or—"

He stopped mid-sentence when he saw her, his dark eyes flaming to life. The primal urge that always drew her to him returned with a force greater than life itself. Unable to utter a word, she simply ran into his arms.

"Anastasia." He held her with the fierce possessiveness of a warrior claiming his own. If she held him any closer, they would be as one.

"Tell me that you have flown back to me, my love."

"Aye, Ian, you'll not lose me again. If ever you did." She pressed her lips to his in a chaste kiss. "I have prayed and searched my soul." She ran her fingers through his hair. "I know now that for which I am destined and come to you with the greatest peace and joy in my heart." She sighed against his lips. "We *are* meant to be together. I believe with all my heart that God wishes it so. He sent me to you that night and he's brought me back to you again."

A ragged sigh of release vibrated through his strong body. "And John?" he whispered.

"Uncle John sends me here with a missive. Only under one condition will he give us his blessing."

Ian raised a skeptical brow. "And what is that?"

Anastasia gave him her most seductive smile. "That we give him the heirs to the Maxwell family that he would enjoy so much in his waning years."

Ian gave a bark of laughter. "With pleasure." He swept her up into his arms and marched over to the large sable pelt that graced the floor before the blazing hearth. "We shall start now."

"Nay, you will not." She gave him a stern frown.

He blinked his thick lashes but nonetheless stopped.

She stroked his rough cheek and watched him soften into her touch. "You will not do anything unseemly."

"I'll not?"

"Nay. Not until we are married."

The smile that broke across his handsome face brought the greatest joy to her heart.

He set her down and then stepped back and gave a little bow. "Aye, my lady. 'Tis most improper of me." His eyes glimmered in amusement.

She laughed and wrapped her arms around his neck. She stroked along the corded muscle. "Abbess Anne, Uncle John, and the visiting priest await us."

She pressed her lips to his with a kiss full of promise. "You would not want to wait too long, would you?"

He chuckled softly and then swept her up once again. "Nay, let us make haste."

"Aye, my Lord"—she gave him a teasing smile—"my Lord of Pleasure."

The soft laughter of their happiness echoed throughout the keep.

About the Author:

Kathryn Anne Dubois lives the demanding life of a mother of five, wife of 30+ years, and a public school art teacher. What better reason to escape into the delicious world of writing erotic romance. Kathryn invites you to visit her website at www.KathrynAnneDubois.com.